Collector's Library

PRIDE AND PREJUDICE

PRIDE AND PREJUDICE

Jane Austen

With Illustrations by
HUGH THOMSON
and an Afterword by
HENRY HITCHINGS

BARNES
&NOBLE
BOOKS
NEW YORK

© CRW 2003
Text and Afterword copyright ©
CRW Publishing Limited 2003

ISBN 0 7607 4868 3

Typeset in Great Britain by Antony Gray
Printed and bound in China by Imago

4 6 8 10 9 7 5 3

Illustrations

He came down in a chaise and four to see the place   10

Mr and Mrs Bennet   13

I hope Mr Bingley will like it   17

Though I am the youngest, I'm the tallest   18

When the party entered   21

He sat close to her for half an hour without once opening his lips   32

The entreaties of several that she would sing again   39

A note for Miss Bennet   45

Many cheerful prognostics of a bad day   47

They all paint tables, cover screens and net purses   57

Mrs Bennet, accompanied by her two youngest girls   61

No, no; stay where you are   74

The first half-hour was spent in piling up the fire   77

He started back, and begging pardon, protested that he never read novels   93

To examine their own indifferent imitations of china on the mantelpiece   101

The officers of the —shire were in general a very creditable, gentlemanlike set   103

The two ladies were delighted to see their dear friend again   115

Such very superior dancing is not often seen 123

To assure you in the most animated language 141

They entered the breakfast-room 148

Wickham and another officer walked back with them to Longbourn 153

So much love and eloquence 160

Protested he must be entirely mistaken 167

Whenever she spoke in a low voice to Mr Collins 171

Offended two or three young ladies 183

Will you come and see me? 189

On the stairs were a troop of little boys and girls 197

Mr Collins and Charlotte appeared at the door 201

'Lady Catherine,' said she, 'you have given me a treasure.' 213

He never failed coming to inform them 216

The gentlemen accompanied him 219

At church 221

Now and then accompanied by their aunt 231

She saw on looking up that Colonel Fitzwilliam was meeting her 235

Reading Jane's letters 241

In vain have I struggled 243

Meeting him accidentally in town 263

Dawson 269

They had hitherto forgotten to leave any message for the ladies of Rosings 276

How nicely we are crammed in! 281

I am determined never to speak of it again to anybody	289
When Colonel Millar's regiment went away	292
She saw herself seated beneath a tent, tenderly flirting	297
Mr and Mrs Gardiner, with their four children	305
The sound of a carriage drew them to the window	325
To make herself agreeable to all	327
I have not an instant to lose	343
The first pleasing earnest of their welcome	355
To whom I have related the affair	369
They saw the housekeeper coming towards them	373
But perhaps you would like to read it	375
The spiteful old ladies in Meryton	385
With an affectionate smile	391
I am sure she did not listen	403
She saw Mr Darcy with him	414
Jane happened to look round	421
Mrs Long and her nieces	425
Come here, my love, I want to speak to you	429
It was Lady Catherine de Bourgh	437
Pronouncing them, after a short survey, to be decent looking rooms	440
But now it comes out	451
The efforts of his aunt	457
Unable to utter a syllable	471
Obsequious civility of her husband	477

PRIDE AND PREJUDICE

He came down in a chaise and four to see the place

Chapter 1

It is a truth universally acknowledged, that a single man in possession of a good fortune, must be in want of a wife.

However little known the feelings or views of such a man may be on his first entering a neighbourhood, this truth is so well fixed in the minds of the surrounding families, that he is considered as the rightful property of someone or other of their daughters.

'My dear Mr Bennet,' said his lady to him one day, 'have you heard that Netherfield Park is let at last?'

Mr Bennet replied that he had not.

'But it is,' returned she; 'for Mrs Long has just been here, and she told me all about it.'

Mr Bennet made no answer.

'Do not you want to know who has taken it?' cried his wife impatiently.

'*You* want to tell me, and I have no objection to hearing it.'

This was invitation enough.

'Why, my dear, you must know, Mrs Long says that Netherfield is taken by a young man of large fortune from the north of England; that he came down on Monday in a chaise and four to see the place, and was so much delighted with it that he agreed with Mr Morris immediately; that he is to take possession before Michaelmas, and some of his servants are to be in the house by the end of next week.'

'What is his name?'

'Bingley.'

'Is he married or single?'

'Oh! single, my dear, to be sure! A single man of large fortune; four or five thousand a year. What a fine thing for our girls!'

'How so? how can it affect them?'

'My dear Mr Bennet,' replied his wife, 'how can you be so tiresome! You must know that I am thinking of his marrying one of them.'

'Is that his design in settling here?'

'Design! nonsense, how can you talk so! But it is very likely that he *may* fall in love with one of them, and therefore you must visit him as soon as he comes.'

'I see no occasion for that. You and the girls may go, or you may send them by themselves, which perhaps will be still better, for as you are as handsome as any of them, Mr Bingley might like you the best of the party.'

'My dear, you flatter me. I certainly *have* had my share of beauty, but I do not pretend to be anything extraordinary now. When a woman has five grown up daughters, she ought to give over thinking of her own beauty.'

'In such cases, a woman has not often much beauty to think of.'

'But, my dear, you must indeed go and see Mr Bingley when he comes into the neighbourhood.'

'It is more than I engage for, I assure you.'

'But consider your daughters. Only think what an establishment it would be for one of them. Sir William and Lady Lucas are determined to go, merely on that account, for in general you know they visit no new-comers. Indeed you must go, for it will be impossible for *us* to visit him, if you do not.'

'You are over scrupulous surely. I dare say Mr Bingley will be very glad to see you; and I will send a few lines by you to assure him of my hearty consent to

Mr and Mrs Bennet

his marrying which ever he chooses of the girls; though I must throw in a good word for my little Lizzy.'

'I desire you will do no such thing. Lizzy is not a bit better than the others; and I am sure she is not half so handsome as Jane, nor half so good humoured as Lydia. But you are always giving *her* the preference.'

'They have none of them much to recommend them,' replied he; 'they are all silly and ignorant like other girls; but Lizzy has something more of quickness than her sisters.'

'Mr Bennet, how can you abuse your own children in such a way? You take delight in vexing me. You have no compassion on my poor nerves.'

'You mistake me, my dear. I have a high respect for your nerves. They are my old friends. I have heard you mention them with consideration these twenty years at least.'

'Ah! you do not know what I suffer.'

'But I hope you will get over it, and live to see many young men of four thousand a year come into the neighbourhood.'

'It will be no use to us, if twenty such should come since you will not visit them.'

'Depend upon it, my dear, that when there are twenty, I will visit them all.'

Mr Bennet was so odd a mixture of quick parts, sarcastic humour, reserve, and caprice, that the experience of three and twenty years had been insufficient to make his wife understand his character. *Her* mind was less difficult to develop. She was a woman of mean understanding, little information, and uncertain temper. When she was discontented she fancied herself nervous. The business of her life was to get her daughters married; its solace was visiting and news.

Chapter 2

Mr Bennet was among the earliest of those who waited on Mr Bingley. He had always intended to visit him, though to the last always assuring his wife that he should not go; and till the evening after the visit was paid, she had no knowledge of it. It was then disclosed in the following manner. Observing his second daughter employed in trimming a hat, he suddenly addressed her with, 'I hope Mr Bingley will like it, Lizzy.'

'We are not in a way to know *what* Mr Bingley likes,' said her mother resentfully, 'since we are not to visit.'

'But you forget, mama,' said Elizabeth, 'that we shall meet him at the assemblies, and that Mrs Long has promised to introduce him.'

'I do not believe Mrs Long will do any such thing. She has two nieces of her own. She is a selfish, hypocritical woman, and I have no opinion of her.'

'No more have I,' said Mr Bennet; 'and I am glad to find that you do not depend on her serving you.'

Mrs Bennet deigned not to make any reply; but unable to contain herself, began scolding one of her daughters.

'Don't keep coughing so, Kitty, for heaven's sake! Have a little compassion on my nerves. You tear them to pieces.'

'Kitty has no discretion in her coughs,' said her father; 'she times them ill.'

'I do not cough for my own amusement,' replied Kitty fretfully.

'When is your next ball to be, Lizzy?'

'Tomorrow fortnight.'

'Aye, so it is,' cried her mother, 'and Mrs Long does not come back till the day before; so, it will be impossible for her to introduce him, for she will not know him herself.'

'Then, my dear, you may have the advantage of your friend, and introduce Mr Bingley to *her*.'

'Impossible, Mr Bennet, impossible, when I am not acquainted with him myself; how can you be so teasing?'

'I honour your circumspection. A fortnight's acquaintance is certainly very little. One cannot know what a man really is by the end of a fortnight. But if *we* do not venture, somebody else will; and after all, Mrs Long and her nieces must stand their chance; and therefore, as she will think it an act of kindness, if you decline the office, I will take it on myself.'

The girls stared at their father. Mrs Bennet said only, 'Nonsense, nonsense!'

'What can be the meaning of that emphatic exclamation?' cried he. 'Do you consider the forms of introduction, and the stress that is laid on them, as nonsense? I cannot quite agree with you *there*. What say you, Mary? for you are a young lady of deep reflection I know, and read great books, and make extracts.'

Mary wished to say something very sensible, but knew not how.

'While Mary is adjusting her ideas,' he continued, 'let us return to Mr Bingley.'

'I am sick of Mr Bingley,' cried his wife.

'I am sorry to hear *that*; but why did not you tell me so before? If I had known as much this morning, I certainly would not have called on him. It is very

I hope Mr Bingley will like it

unlucky; but as I have actually paid the visit, we cannot escape the acquaintance now.'

The astonishment of the ladies was just what he wished; that of Mrs Bennet perhaps surpassing the rest; though when the first tumult of joy was over, she began to declare that it was what she had expected all the while.

'How good it was in you, my dear Mr Bennet! But I knew I should persuade you at last. I was sure you loved your girls too well to neglect such an acquaintance. Well, how pleased I am! and it is such a good joke, too, that you should have gone this morning, and never said a word about it till now.'

'Now, Kitty, you may cough as much as you choose,' said Mr Bennet; and, as he spoke, he left the room, fatigued with the raptures of his wife.

PRIDE AND PREJUDICE

'What an excellent father you have, girls,' said she, when the door was shut. 'I do not know how you will ever make him amends for his kindness; or me either, for that matter. At our time of life, it is not so pleasant I can tell you, to be making new acquaintance every day; but for your sakes, we would do anything. Lydia, my love, though you *are* the youngest, I dare say Mr Bingley will dance with you at the next ball.'

'Oh!' said Lydia stoutly, 'I am not afraid; for though I *am* the youngest, I'm the tallest.'

The rest of the evening was spent in conjecturing how soon he would return Mr Bennet's visit, and determining when they should ask him to dinner.

Though I am the youngest, I'm the tallest

Chapter 3

Not all that Mrs Bennet, however, with the assistance of her five daughters, could ask on the subject was sufficient to draw from her husband any satisfactory description of Mr Bingley. They attacked him in various ways; with barefaced questions, ingenious suppositions, and distant surmises; but he eluded the skill of them all; and they were at last obliged to accept the second-hand intelligence of their neighbour Lady Lucas. Her report was highly favourable. Sir William had been delighted with him. He was quite young, wonderfully handsome, extremely agreeable, and to crown the whole, he meant to be at the next assembly with a large party. Nothing could be more delightful! To be fond of dancing was a certain step towards falling in love; and very lively hopes of Mr Bingley's heart were entertained.

'If I can but see one of my daughters happily settled at Netherfield,' said Mrs Bennet to her husband, 'and all the others equally well married, I shall have nothing to wish for.'

In a few days Mr Bingley returned Mr Bennet's visit, and sat about ten minutes with him in his library. He had entertained hopes of being admitted to a sight of the young ladies, of whose beauty he had heard much; but he saw only the father. The ladies were somewhat more fortunate, for they had the advantage of ascertaining from an upper window, that he wore a blue coat and rode a black horse.

An invitation to dinner was soon afterwards dispatched; and already had Mrs Bennet planned the courses that were to do credit to her housekeeping, when an answer arrived which deferred it all. Mr Bingley was obliged to be in town the following day, and consequently unable to accept the honour of their invitation, &c. Mrs Bennet was quite disconcerted. She could not imagine what business he could have in town so soon after his arrival in Hertfordshire; and she began to fear that he might be always flying about from one place to another, and never settled at Netherfield as he ought to be. Lady Lucas quieted her fears a little by starting the idea of his being gone to London only to get a large party for the ball; and a report soon followed that Mr Bingley was to bring twelve ladies and seven gentlemen with him to the assembly. The girls grieved over such a number of ladies; but were comforted the day before the ball by hearing, that instead of twelve, he had brought only six with him from London, his five sisters and a cousin. And when the party entered the assembly room, it consisted of only five altogether; Mr Bingley, his two sisters, the husband of the eldest, and another young man.

Mr Bingley was good looking and gentlemanlike; he had a pleasant countenance, and easy, unaffected manners. His sisters were fine women, with an air of decided fashion. His brother-in-law, Mr Hurst, merely looked the gentleman; but his friend Mr Darcy soon drew the attention of the room by his fine, tall person, handsome features, noble mien; and the report which was in general circulation within five minutes after his entrance, of his having ten thousand a year. The gentlemen pronounced him to be a fine figure of a man, the ladies declared he was much handsomer than Mr Bingley, and he was looked at with great

When the party entered

admiration for about half the evening, till his manners gave a disgust which turned the tide of his popularity; for he was discovered to be proud, to be above his company, and above being pleased; and not all his large estate in Derbyshire could then save him from having a most forbidding, disagreeable countenance, and being unworthy to be compared with his friend.

Mr Bingley had soon made himself acquainted with all the principal people in the room; he was lively and unreserved, danced every dance, was angry that the ball closed so early, and talked of giving one himself at Netherfield. Such amiable qualities must speak for themselves. What a contrast between him and his friend! Mr Darcy danced only once with Mrs Hurst and once with Miss Bingley, declined being introduced to any other lady, and spent the rest of the evening in walking about the room, speaking occasionally to one of his own party. His character was decided. He was the proudest, most disagreeable man in the world, and everybody hoped that he would never come there again. Amongst the most violent against him was Mrs Bennet, whose dislike of his general behaviour, was sharpened into particular resentment, by his having slighted one of her daughters.

Elizabeth Bennet had been obliged, by the scarcity of gentlemen, to sit down for two dances; and during part of that time, Mr Darcy had been standing near enough for her to overhear a conversation between him and Mr Bingley, who came from the dance for a few minutes, to press his friend to join it.

'Come, Darcy,' said he, 'I must have you dance. I hate to see you standing about by yourself in this stupid manner. You had much better dance.'

'I certainly shall not. You know how I detest it,

unless I am particularly acquainted with my partner. At such an assembly as this, it would be insupportable. Your sisters are engaged, and there is not another woman in the room, whom it would not be a punishment to me to stand up with.'

'I would not be so fastidious as you are,' cried Bingley, 'for a kingdom! Upon my honour, I never met with so many pleasant girls in my life, as I have this evening; and there are several of them you see uncommonly pretty.'

'*You* are dancing with the only handsome girl in the room,' said Mr Darcy, looking at the eldest Miss Bennet.

'Oh! she is the most beautiful creature I ever beheld! But there is one of her sisters sitting down just behind you, who is very pretty, and I dare say, very agreeable. Do let me ask my partner to introduce you.'

'Which do you mean?' and turning round, he looked for a moment at Elizabeth, till catching her eye, he withdrew his own and coldly said, 'She is tolerable; but not handsome enough to tempt *me*; and I am in no humour at present to give consequence to young ladies who are slighted by other men. You had better return to your partner and enjoy her smiles, for you are wasting your time with me.'

Mr Bingley followed his advice. Mr Darcy walked off; and Elizabeth remained with no very cordial feelings towards him. She told the story however with great spirit among her friends; for she had a lively, playful disposition, which delighted in anything ridiculous.

The evening altogether passed off pleasantly to the whole family. Mrs Bennet had seen her eldest daughter much admired by the Netherfield party. Mr Bingley had danced with her twice, and she had been distinguished by his sisters. Jane was as much gratified by this, as her mother could be, though in a quieter way. Elizabeth felt Jane's pleasure. Mary had heard herself mentioned to Miss Bingley as the most accomplished girl in the neighbourhood; and Catherine and Lydia had been fortunate enough to be never without partners, which was all that they had yet learnt to care for at a ball. They returned therefore in good spirits to Longbourn, the village where they lived, and of which they were the principal inhabitants. They found Mr Bennet still up. With a book he was regardless of time; and on the present occasion he had a good deal of curiosity as to the event of an evening which had raised such splendid expectations. He had rather hoped that all his wife's views on the stranger would be disappointed; but he soon found that he had a very different story to hear.

'Oh! my dear Mr Bennet,' as she entered the room, 'we have had a most delightful evening, a most excellent ball. I wish you had been there. Jane was so admired, nothing could be like it. Everybody said how well she looked; and Mr Bingley thought her quite beautiful, and danced with her twice. Only think of *that* my dear; he actually danced with her twice; and she was the only creature in the room that he asked a second time. First of all, he asked Miss Lucas. I was so vexed to see him stand up with her; but, however, he did not admire her at all: indeed, nobody can, you know; and he seemed quite struck with Jane as she was going down the dance. So, he enquired who she was, and got introduced, and asked her for the two next. Then, the two third he danced with Miss King, and the two fourth with Maria Lucas, and the two fifth with Jane again, and the two sixth with Lizzy, and the Boulanger – '

'If he had had any compassion for *me*,' cried her husband impatiently, 'he would not have danced half so much! For God's sake, say no more of his partners. Oh! that he had sprained his ankle in the first dance!'

'Oh! my dear,' continued Mrs Bennet, 'I am quite delighted with him. He is so excessively handsome! and his sisters are charming women. I never in my life saw anything more elegant than their dresses. I dare say the lace upon Mrs Hurst's gown – '

Here she was interrupted again. Mr Bennet protested against any description of finery. She was therefore obliged to seek another branch of the subject, and related, with much bitterness of spirit and some exaggeration, the shocking rudeness of Mr Darcy.

'But I can assure you,' she added, 'that Lizzy does not lose much by not suiting *his* fancy; for he is a most disagreeable, horrid man, not at all worth pleasing. So high and so conceited that there was no enduring him! He walked here, and he walked there, fancying himself so very great! Not handsome enough to dance with! I wish you had been there, my dear, to have given him one of your set downs. I quite detest the man.'

Chapter 4

When Jane and Elizabeth were alone, the former, who had been cautious in her praise of Mr Bingley before, expressed to her sister how very much she admired him.

'He is just what a young man ought to be,' said she,

'sensible, good humoured, lively; and I never saw such happy manners – so much ease, with such perfect good breeding!'

'He is also handsome,' replied Elizabeth, 'which a young man ought likewise to be, if he possibly can. His character is thereby complete.'

'I was very much flattered by his asking me to dance a second time. I did not expect such a compliment.'

'Did not you? *I* did for you. But that is one great difference between us. Compliments always take *you* by surprise, and *me* never. What could be more natural than his asking you again? He could not help seeing that you were about five times as pretty as every other woman in the room. No thanks to his gallantry for that. Well, he certainly is very agreeable, and I give you leave to like him. You have liked many a stupider person.'

'Dear Lizzy!'

'Oh! you are a great deal too apt you know, to like people in general. You never see a fault in anybody. All the world are good and agreeable in your eyes. I never heard you speak ill of a human being in my life.'

'I would wish not to be hasty in censuring anyone; but I always speak what I think.'

'I know you do; and it is *that* which makes the wonder. With *your* good sense, to be so honestly blind to the follies and nonsense of others! Affectation of candour is common enough – one meets it every where. But to be candid without ostentation or design – to take the good of everybody's character and make it still better, and say nothing of the bad – belongs to you alone. And so, you like this man's sisters too, do you? Their manners are not equal to his.'

'Certainly not; at first. But they are very pleasing

women when you converse with them. Miss Bingley is to live with her brother and keep his house; and I am much mistaken if we shall not find a very charming neighbour in her.'

Elizabeth listened in silence, but was not convinced; their behaviour at the assembly had not been calculated to please in general; and with more quickness of observation and less pliancy of temper than her sister, and with a judgement too unassailed by any attention to herself, she was very little disposed to approve them. They were in fact very fine ladies; not deficient in good humour when they were pleased, nor in the power of being agreeable where they chose it; but proud and conceited. They were rather handsome; had been educated in one of the first private seminaries in town, had a fortune of twenty thousand pounds, were in the habit of spending more than they ought, and of associating with people of rank; and were therefore in every respect entitled to think well of themselves, and meanly of others. They were of a respectable family in the north of England; a circumstance more deeply impressed on their memories than that their brother's fortune and their own had been acquired by trade.

Mr Bingley inherited property to the amount of nearly an hundred thousand pounds from his father, who had intended to purchase an estate, but did not live to do it. Mr Bingley intended it likewise, and sometimes made choice of his county; but as he was now provided with a good house and the liberty of a manor, it was doubtful to many of those who best knew the easiness of his temper, whether he might not spend the remainder of his days at Netherfield, and leave the next generation to purchase.

His sisters were very anxious for his having an estate of his own; but though he was now established only as a tenant, Miss Bingley was by no means unwilling to preside at his table, nor was Mrs Hurst, who had married a man of more fashion than fortune, less disposed to consider his house as her home when it suited her. Mr Bingley had not been of age two years, when he was tempted by an accidental recommendation to look at Netherfield House. He did look at it and into it for half an hour, was pleased with the situation and the principal rooms, satisfied with what the owner said in its praise, and took it immediately.

Between him and Darcy there was a very steady friendship, in spite of a great opposition of character. Bingley was endeared to Darcy by the easiness, openness, ductility of his temper, though no disposition could offer a greater contrast to his own, and though with his own he never appeared dissatisfied. On the strength of Darcy's regard Bingley had the firmest reliance, and of his judgement the highest opinion. In understanding Darcy was the superior. Bingley was by no means deficient, but Darcy was clever. He was at the same time haughty, reserved, and fastidious, and his manners, though well bred, were not inviting. In that respect his friend had greatly the advantage. Bingley was sure of being liked wherever he appeared, Darcy was continually giving offence.

The manner in which they spoke of the Meryton assembly was sufficiently characteristic. Bingley had never met with pleasanter people or prettier girls in his life; everybody had been most kind and attentive to him, there had been no formality, no stiffness, he had soon felt acquainted with all the room; and as to Miss

Bennet, he could not conceive an angel more beautiful.
Darcy, on the contrary, had seen a collection of people
in whom there was little beauty and no fashion, for
none of whom he had felt the smallest interest, and
from none received either attention or pleasure. Miss
Bennet he acknowledged to be pretty, but she smiled
too much.

Mrs Hurst and her sister allowed it to be so – but
still they admired her and liked her, and pronounced
her to be a sweet girl, and one whom they should not
object to know more of. Miss Bennet was therefore
established as a sweet girl, and their brother felt
authorised by such commendation to think of her as
he chose.

Chapter 5

Within a short walk of Longbourn lived a family with
whom the Bennets were particularly intimate. Sir
William Lucas had been formerly in trade in Meryton,
where he had made a tolerable fortune and risen to the
honour of knighthood by an address to the King,
during his mayoralty. The distinction had perhaps
been felt too strongly. It had given him a disgust to
his business and to his residence in a small market
town; and quitting them both, he had removed with
his family to a house about a mile from Meryton,
denominated from that period Lucas Lodge, where he
could think with pleasure of his own importance, and
unshackled by business, occupy himself solely in
being civil to all the world. For though elated by his
rank, it did not render him supercilious; on the
contrary, he was all attention to everybody. By nature

inoffensive, friendly and obliging, his presentation at St James's had made him courteous.

Lady Lucas was a very good kind of woman, not too clever to be a valuable neighbour to Mrs Bennet. They had several children. The eldest of them, a sensible, intelligent young woman, about twenty-seven, was Elizabeth's intimate friend.

That the Miss Lucases and the Miss Bennets should meet to talk over a ball was absolutely necessary; and the morning after the assembly brought the former to Longbourn to hear and to communicate.

'*You* began the evening well, Charlotte,' said Mrs Bennet with civil self-command to Miss Lucas. '*You* were Mr Bingley's first choice.'

'Yes – but he seemed to like his second better.'

'Oh! – you mean Jane, I suppose – because he danced with her twice. To be sure that *did* seem as if he admired her – indeed I rather believe he *did* – I heard something about it – but I hardly know what – something about Mr Robinson.'

'Perhaps you mean what I overheard between him and Mr Robinson; did not I mention it to you? Mr Robinson's asking him how he liked our Meryton assemblies, and whether he did not think there were a great many pretty women in the room, and *which* he thought the prettiest? and his answering immediately to the last question – Oh! the eldest Miss Bennet beyond a doubt, there cannot be two opinions on that point.'

'Upon my word! – Well, that was very decided indeed – that does seem as if – but however, it may all come to nothing you know.'

'*My* overhearings were more to the purpose than *yours*, Eliza,' said Charlotte. 'Mr Darcy is not so well worth listening to as his friend, is he? – Poor Eliza! – to be only just *tolerable*.'

'I beg you would not put it into Lizzy's head to be vexed by his ill-treatment; for he is such a disagreeable man that it would be quite a misfortune to be liked by him. Mrs Long told me last night that he sat close to her for half an hour without once opening his lips.'

'Are you quite sure, ma'am? – is not there a little mistake?' said Jane, 'I certainly saw Mr Darcy speaking to her.'

'Aye – because she asked him at last how he liked Netherfield, and he could not help answering her – but she said he seemed very angry at being spoke to.'

'Miss Bingley told me,' said Jane, 'that he never speaks much unless among his intimate acquaintance. With *them* he is remarkably agreeable.'

'I do not believe a word of it, my dear. If he had been so very agreeable he would have talked to Mrs Long. But I can guess how it was; everybody says that he is ate up with pride, and I dare say he had heard somehow that Mrs Long does not keep a carriage, and had come to the ball in a hack chaise.'

'I do not mind his not talking to Mrs Long,' said Miss Lucas, 'but I wish he had danced with Eliza.'

'Another time, Lizzy,' said her mother, 'I would not dance with *him*, if I were you.'

'I believe, ma'am, I may safely promise you *never* to dance with him.'

'His pride,' said Miss Lucas, 'does not offend *me* so much as pride often does, because there is an excuse for it One cannot wonder that so very fine a young man, with family, fortune, everything in his favour, should think highly of himself. If I may so express it, he has a *right* to be proud.'

*He sat close to her for half an hour without
once opening his lips*

'That is very true,' replied Elizabeth, 'and I could easily forgive *his* pride, if he had not mortified *mine*.'

'Pride,' observed Mary, who piqued herself upon the solidity of her reflections, 'is a very common failing I believe. By all that I have ever read, I am convinced that it is very common indeed, that human nature is particularly prone to it, and that there are very few of us who do not cherish a feeling of self-complacency on the score of some quality or other, real or imaginary. Vanity and pride are different things, though the words are often used synonymously. A person may be proud without being vain. Pride relates more to our opinion of ourselves, vanity to what we would have others think of us.'

'If I were as rich as Mr Darcy,' cried a young Lucas who came with his sisters, 'I should not care how proud I was. I would keep a pack of foxhounds, and drink a bottle of wine every day.'

'Then you would drink a great deal more than you ought,' said Mrs Bennet; 'and if I were to see you at it I should take away your bottle directly.'

The boy protested that she should not; she continued to declare that she would, and the argument ended only with the visit.

Chapter 6

The ladies of Longbourn soon waited on those of Netherfield. The visit was returned in due form. Miss Bennet's pleasing manners grew on the good will of Mrs Hurst and Miss Bingley; and though the mother was found to be intolerable and the younger sisters not worth speaking to, a wish of being better acquainted with *them*, was expressed towards the two eldest. By Jane this attention was received with the greatest pleasure; but Elizabeth still saw superciliousness in their treatment of everybody, hardly excepting even her sister, and could not like them; though their kindness to Jane, such as it was, had a value as arising in all probability from the influence of their brother's admiration. It was generally evident whenever they met, that he *did* admire her; and to *her* it was equally evident that Jane was yielding to the preference which she had begun to entertain for him from the first, and was in a way to be very much in love; but she considered with pleasure that it was not likely to be discovered by the world in general, since Jane united with great strength of feeling, a composure of temper and a uniform cheerfulness of manner, which would guard her from the suspicions of the impertinent. She mentioned this to her friend Miss Lucas.

'It may perhaps be pleasant,' replied Charlotte, 'to be able to impose on the public in such a case; but it is sometimes a disadvantage to be so very guarded. If a woman conceals her affection with the same skill from the object of it, she may lose the opportunity of fixing him; and it will then be but poor consolation to believe the world equally in the dark. There is so much of gratitude or vanity in almost every attachment, that it is not safe to leave any to itself. We can all *begin* freely – a slight preference is natural enough; but there are very few of us who have heart enough to be really in love without encouragement. In nine cases out of ten, a woman had better shew *more* affection than she feels. Bingley likes your sister undoubtedly; but he may never do more than like her, if she does not help him on.'

'But she does help him on, as much as her nature will allow. If *I* can perceive her regard for him, he must be a simpleton indeed not to discover it too.'

'Remember, Eliza, that he does not know Jane's disposition as you do.'

'But if a woman is partial to a man, and does not endeavour to conceal it, he must find it out.'

'Perhaps he must, if he sees enough of her. But though Bingley and Jane meet tolerably often, it is never for many hours together; and as they always see each other in large mixed parties, it is impossible that every moment should be employed in conversing together. Jane should therefore make the most of every half-hour in which she can command his attention. When she is secure of him, there will be leisure for falling in love as much as she chooses.'

'Your plan is a good one,' replied Elizabeth, 'where nothing is in question but the desire of being well married; and if I were determined to get a rich husband, or any husband, I dare say I should adopt it. But these are not Jane's feelings; she is not acting by design. As yet, she cannot even be certain of the degree of her own regard, nor of its reasonableness. She has known him only a fortnight. She danced four dances with him at Meryton; she saw him one morning at his own house, and has since dined in company with him four times. This is not quite enough to make her understand his character.'

'Not as you represent it. Had she merely *dined* with him, she might only have discovered whether he had a good appetite; but you must remember that four evenings have been also spent together – and four evenings may do a great deal.'

'Yes; these four evenings have enabled them to

ascertain that they both like *vingt-et-un* better than commerce; but with respect to any other leading characteristic, I do not imagine that much has been unfolded.'

'Well,' said Charlotte, 'I wish Jane success with all my heart; and if she were married to him tomorrow, I should think she had as good a chance of happiness, as if she were to be studying his character for a twelve-month. Happiness in marriage is entirely a matter of chance. If the dispositions of the parties are ever so well known to each other, or ever so similar before-hand, it does not advance their felicity in the least. They always continue to grow sufficiently unlike afterwards to have their share of vexation; and it is better to know as little as possible of the defects of the person with whom you are to pass your life.'

'You make me laugh, Charlotte; but it is not sound. You know it is not sound, and that you would never act in this way yourself.'

Occupied in observing Mr Bingley's attentions to her sister, Elizabeth was far from suspecting that she was herself becoming an object of some interest in the eyes of his friend. Mr Darcy had at first scarcely allowed her to be pretty; he had looked at her without admiration at the ball; and when they next met, he looked at her only to criticise. But no sooner had he made it clear to himself and his friends that she had hardly a good feature in her face, than he began to find it was rendered uncommonly intelligent by the beautiful expression of her dark eyes. To this discovery succeeded some others equally mortifying. Though he had detected with a critical eye more than one failure of perfect symmetry in her form, he was forced to acknowledge her figure to be light and pleasing; and in spite of his asserting that her manners were not those of the fashionable world, he was caught by their easy playfulness. Of this she was perfectly unaware – to her he was only the man who made himself agreeable no where, and who had not thought her handsome enough to dance with.

He began to wish to know more of her, and as a step towards conversing with her himself, attended to her conversation with others. His doing so drew her notice. It was at Sir William Lucas's, where a large party were assembled.

'What does Mr Darcy mean,' said she to Charlotte, 'by listening to my conversation with Colonel Forster?'

'That is a question which Mr Darcy only can answer.'

'But if he does it any more I shall certainly let him know that I see what he is about. He has a very satirical eye, and if I do not begin by being impertinent myself, I shall soon grow afraid of him.'

On his approaching them soon afterwards, though without seeming to have any intention of speaking, Miss Lucas defied her friend to mention such a subject to him, which immediately provoking Elizabeth to do it, she turned to him and said, 'Did not you think, Mr Darcy, that I expressed myself uncommonly well just now, when I was teasing Colonel Forster to give us a ball at Meryton?'

'With great energy – but it is a subject which always makes a lady energetic.'

'You are severe on us.'

'It will be *her* turn soon to be teased,' said Miss Lucas. 'I am going to open the instrument, Eliza, and you know what follows.'

'You are a very strange creature by way of a friend! – always wanting me to play and sing before anybody and everybody! – If my vanity had taken a musical turn, you would have been invaluable, but as it is, I would really rather not sit down before those who must be in the habit of hearing the very best performers.' On Miss Lucas's persevering, however, she added, 'Very well; if it must be so, it must.' And gravely glancing at Mr Darcy, 'There is a fine old saying, which everybody here is of course familiar with – "Keep your breath to cool your porridge," – and I shall keep mine to swell my song.'

Her performance was pleasing, though by no means capital. After a song or two, and before she could reply to the entreaties of several that she would sing again, she was eagerly succeeded at the instrument by her sister Mary, who having, in consequence of being the only plain one in the family, worked hard for knowledge and accomplishments, was always impatient for display.

Mary had neither genius nor taste; and though vanity had given her application, it had given her likewise a pedantic air and conceited manner, which would have injured a higher degree of excellence than she had reached. Elizabeth, easy and unaffected, had been listened to with much more pleasure, though not playing half so well; and Mary, at the end of a long concerto, was glad to purchase praise and gratitude by Scotch and Irish airs, at the request of her younger sisters, who with some of the Lucases and two or three officers joined eagerly in dancing at one end of the room.

Mr Darcy stood near them in silent indignation at such a mode of passing the evening, to the exclusion of

The entreaties of several that she would sing again

all conversation, and was too much engrossed by his own thoughts to perceive that Sir William Lucas was his neighbour, till Sir William thus began.

'What a charming amusement for young people this is, Mr Darcy! – There is nothing like dancing after all. I consider it as one of the first refinements of polished societies.'

'Certainly, sir – and it has the advantage also of being in vogue amongst the less polished societies of the world. Every savage can dance.'

Sir William only smiled. 'Your friend performs delightfully – ' he continued after a pause, on seeing Bingley join the group – 'and I doubt not that you are an adept in the science yourself, Mr Darcy.'

'You saw me dance at Meryton, I believe, sir.'

'Yes, indeed, and received no inconsiderable pleasure from the sight. Do you often dance at St James's?'

'Never, sir.'

'Do you not think it would be a proper compliment to the place?'

'It is a compliment which I never pay to any place if I can avoid it.'

'You have a house in town, I conclude?'

Mr Darcy bowed.

'I had once some thoughts of fixing in town myself – for I am fond of superior society; but I did not feel quite certain that the air of London would agree with Lady Lucas.'

He paused in hopes of an answer; but his companion was not disposed to make any; and Elizabeth at that instant moving towards them, he was struck with the notion of doing a very gallant thing, and called out to her, 'My dear Miss Eliza, why are not you dancing? – Mr Darcy, you must allow me to present this young lady to you as a very desirable partner. You cannot refuse to dance, I am sure, when so much beauty is before you.'

And taking her hand, he would have given it to Mr Darcy, who, though extremely surprised, was not unwilling to receive it, when she instantly drew back, and said with some discomposure to Sir William, 'Indeed, sir, I have not the least intention of dancing. I entreat you not to suppose that I moved this way in order to beg for a partner.'

Mr Darcy with grave propriety requested to be allowed the honour of her hand; but in vain. Elizabeth was determined; nor did Sir William at all shake her purpose by his attempt at persuasion.

'You excel so much in the dance, Miss Eliza, that it is cruel to deny me the happiness of seeing you; and though this gentleman dislikes the amusement in general, he can have no objection, I am sure, to oblige us for one half-hour.'

'Mr Darcy is all politeness,' said Elizabeth, smiling.

'He is indeed – but considering the inducement, my dear Miss Eliza, we cannot wonder at his complaisance; for who would object to such a partner?'

Elizabeth looked archly, and turned away. Her resistance had not injured her with the gentleman, and he was thinking of her with some complacency, when thus accosted by Miss Bingley, 'I can guess the subject of your reverie.'

'I should imagine not.'

'You are considering how insupportable it would be to pass many evenings in this manner – in such society; and indeed I am quite of your opinion. I was never more annoyed! The insipidity and yet the noise; the nothingness and yet the self-importance of all these people! – What would I give to hear your strictures on them!'

'Your conjecture is totally wrong, I assure you. My mind was more agreeably engaged. I have been meditating on the very great pleasure which a pair of fine eyes in the face of a pretty woman can bestow.'

Miss Bingley immediately fixed her eyes on his face, and desired he would tell her what lady had the credit of inspiring such reflections. Mr Darcy replied with great intrepidity, 'Miss Elizabeth Bennet.'

'Miss Elizabeth Bennet!' repeated Miss Bingley. 'I am all astonishment. How long has she been such a favourite? – and pray when am I to wish you joy?'

'That is exactly the question which I expected you to ask. A lady's imagination is very rapid; it jumps from admiration to love, from love to matrimony in a moment. I knew you would be wishing me joy.'

'Nay, if you are so serious about it, I shall consider the matter as absolutely settled. You will have a charming mother-in-law, indeed, and of course she will be always at Pemberley with you.'

He listened to her with perfect indifference, while she chose to entertain herself in this manner, and as his composure convinced her that all was safe, her wit flowed long.

Chapter 7

Mr Bennet's property consisted almost entirely in an estate of two thousand a year, which, unfortunately for his daughters, was entailed in default of heirs male, on a distant relation; and their mother's fortune, though ample for her situation in life, could but ill supply the deficiency of his. Her father had been an attorney in Meryton, and had left her four thousand pounds.

She had a sister married to a Mr Philips, who had been a clerk to their father, and succeeded him in the business, and a brother settled in London in a respectable line of trade.

The village of Longbourn was only one mile from Meryton; a most convenient distance for the young ladies, who were usually tempted thither three or four times a week, to pay their duty to their aunt and to a milliner's shop just over the way. The two youngest of the family, Catherine and Lydia, were particularly frequent in these attentions; their minds were more vacant than their sisters', and when nothing better offered, a walk to Meryton was necessary to amuse their morning hours and furnish conversation for the evening; and however bare of news the country in general might be, they always contrived to learn some from their aunt. At present, indeed, they were well supplied both with news and happiness by the recent arrival of a militia regiment in the neighbourhood; it was to remain the whole winter, and Meryton was the head quarters.

Their visits to Mrs Philips were now productive of the most interesting intelligence. Every day added something to their knowledge of the officers' names and connections. Their lodgings were not long a secret, and at length they began to know the officers themselves. Mr Philips visited them all, and this opened to his nieces a source of felicity unknown before. They could talk of nothing but officers; and Mr Bingley's large fortune, the mention of which gave animation to their mother, was worthless in their eyes when opposed to the regimentals of an ensign.

After listening one morning to their effusions on this subject, Mr Bennet coolly observed, 'From all that I can collect by your manner of talking, you must be two of the silliest girls in the country. I have suspected it some time, but I am now convinced.'

Catherine was disconcerted, and made no answer; but Lydia, with perfect indifference, continued to express her admiration of Captain Carter, and her hope of seeing him in the course of the day, as he was going the next morning to London.

'I am astonished, my dear,' said Mrs Bennet, 'that you should be so ready to think your own children silly. If I wished to think slightingly of anybody's children, it should not be of my own however.'

'If my children are silly I must hope to be always sensible of it.'

'Yes – but as it happens, they are all of them very clever.'

'This is the only point, I flatter myself, on which we do not agree. I had hoped that our sentiments coincided in every particular, but I must so far differ from you as to think our two youngest daughters uncommonly foolish.'

'My dear Mr Bennet, you must not expect such girls to have the sense of their father and mother. When they get to our age I dare say they will not think about officers any more than we do. I remember the time when I liked a red coat myself very well – and indeed so I do still at my heart; and if a smart young colonel, with five or six thousand a year, should want one of my girls, I shall not say nay to him; and I thought Colonel Forster looked very becoming the other night at Sir William's in his regimentals.'

'Mama,' cried Lydia, 'my aunt says that Colonel

A note for Miss Bennet

Forster and Captain Carter do not go so often to Miss Watson's as they did when they first came; she sees them now very often standing in Clarke's library.'

Mrs Bennet was prevented replying by the entrance of the footman with a note for Miss Bennet; it came from Netherfield, and the servant waited for an answer. Mrs Bennet's eyes sparkled with pleasure, and she was eagerly calling out, while her daughter read, 'Well, Jane, who is it from? what is it about? what does he say? Well, Jane, make haste and tell us; make haste, my love.'

'It is from Miss Bingley,' said Jane, and then read it aloud.

> MY DEAR FRIEND – If you are not so compassionate as to dine today with Louisa and me, we shall be in danger of hating each other for the rest of our lives, for a whole day's tête-à-tête between two women can never end without a quarrel. Come as soon as you can on the receipt of this. My brother and the gentlemen are to dine with the officers. Yours ever,
> CAROLINE BINGLEY

'With the officers!' cried Lydia. 'I wonder my aunt did not tell us of *that*.'

'Dining out,' said Mrs Bennet, 'that is very unlucky.'

'Can I have the carriage?' said Jane.

'No, my dear, you had better go on horseback, because it seems likely to rain; and then you must stay all night.'

'That would be a good scheme,' said Elizabeth, 'if you were sure that they would not offer to send her home.'

'Oh! but the gentlemen will have Mr Bingley's chaise to go to Meryton; and the Hursts have no horses to theirs.'

Many cheerful prognostics of a bad day

'I had much rather go in the coach.'

'But, my dear, your father cannot spare the horses, I am sure. They are wanted in the farm, Mr Bennet, are not they?'

'They are wanted in the farm much oftener than I can get them.'

'But if you have got them to day,' said Elizabeth, 'my mother's purpose will be answered.'

She did at last extort from her father an acknowledgment that the horses were engaged. Jane was therefore obliged to go on horseback, and her mother attended her to the door with many cheerful prognostics of a bad day. Her hopes were answered; Jane had not been gone long before it rained hard. Her sisters were uneasy for her, but her mother was delighted. The rain continued the whole evening without intermission; Jane certainly could not come back.

'This was a lucky idea of mine, indeed!' said Mrs Bennet, more than once, as if the credit of making it rain were all her own. Till the next morning, however, she was not aware of all the felicity of her contrivance. Breakfast was scarcely over when a servant from Netherfield brought the following note for Elizabeth:

MY DEAREST LIZZY – I find myself very unwell this morning, which, I suppose, is to be imputed to my getting wet through yesterday. My kind friends will not hear of my returning home till I am better. They insist also on my seeing Mr Jones – therefore do not be alarmed if you should hear of his having been to me – and excepting a sore throat and headache there is not much the matter with me.

'Yours, &c.'

'Well, my dear,' said Mr Bennet, when Elizabeth

had read the note aloud, 'if your daughter should have a dangerous fit of illness, if she should die, it would be a comfort to know that it was all in pursuit of Mr Bingley, and under your orders.'

'Oh! I am not at all afraid of her dying. People do not die of little trifling colds. She will be taken good care of. As long as she stays there, it is all very well. I would go and see her, if I could have the carriage.'

Elizabeth, feeling really anxious, was determined to go to her, though the carriage was not to be had; and as she was no horsewoman, walking was her only alternative. She declared her resolution.

'How can you be so silly,' cried her mother, 'as to think of such a thing, in all this dirt! You will not be fit to be seen when you get there.'

'I shall be very fit to see Jane – which is all I want.'

'Is this a hint to me, Lizzy,' said her father, 'to send for the horses?'

'No, indeed. I do not wish to avoid the walk. The distance is nothing, when one has a motive; only three miles. I shall be back by dinner.'

'I admire the activity of your benevolence,' observed Mary, 'but every impulse of feeling should be guided by reason; and, in my opinion, exertion should always be in proportion to what is required.'

'We will go as far as Meryton with you,' said Catherine and Lydia. Elizabeth accepted their company, and the three young ladies set off together.

'If we make haste,' said Lydia, as they walked along, 'perhaps we may see something of Captain Carter before he goes.'

In Meryton they parted; the two youngest repaired to the lodgings of one of the officers' wives, and Elizabeth continued her walk alone, crossing field after field at a quick pace, jumping over stiles and springing over puddles with impatient activity, and finding herself at last within view of the house, with weary ankles, dirty stockings, and a face glowing with the warmth of exercise.

She was shown into the breakfast parlour, where all but Jane were assembled, and where her appearance created a great deal of surprise. That she should have walked three miles so early in the day, in such dirty weather, and by herself, was almost incredible to Mrs Hurst and Miss Bingley; and Elizabeth was convinced that they held her in contempt for it. She was received, however, very politely by them; and in their brother's manners there was something better than politeness; there was good humour and kindness. Mr Darcy said very little, and Mr Hurst nothing at all. The former was divided between admiration of the brilliancy which exercise had given to her complexion, and doubt as to the occasion's justifying her coming so far alone. The latter was thinking only of his breakfast.

Her enquiries after her sister were not very favourably answered. Miss Bennet had slept ill, and though up, was very feverish and not well enough to leave her room. Elizabeth was glad to be taken to her immediately; and Jane, who had only been withheld by the fear of giving alarm or inconvenience, from expressing in her note how much she longed for such a visit, was delighted at her entrance. She was not equal, however, to much conversation, and when Miss Bingley left them together, could attempt little beside expressions of gratitude for the extraordinary kindness she was treated with. Elizabeth silently attended her.

When breakfast was over, they were joined by the sisters; and Elizabeth began to like them herself, when she saw how much affection and solicitude they showed for Jane. The apothecary came, and having examined his patient, said, as might be supposed, that she had caught a violent cold, and that they must endeavour to get the better of it; advised her to return to bed, and promised her some draughts. The advice was followed readily, for the feverish symptoms increased, and her head ached acutely. Elizabeth did not quit her room for a moment, nor were the other ladies often absent; the gentlemen being out, they had in fact nothing to do elsewhere.

When the clock struck three, Elizabeth felt that she must go; and very unwillingly said so. Miss Bingley offered her the carriage, and she only wanted a little pressing to accept it, when Jane testified such concern in parting with her, that Miss Bingley was obliged to convert the offer of the chaise into an invitation to remain at Netherfield for the present. Elizabeth most thankfully consented, and a servant was dispatched to Longbourn to acquaint the family with her stay, and bring back a supply of clothes.

Chapter 8

At five o'clock the two ladies retired to dress, and at half-past six Elizabeth was summoned to dinner. To the civil enquiries which then poured in, and amongst which she had the pleasure of distinguishing the much superior solicitude of Mr Bingley's, she could not make a very favourable answer. Jane was by no means better. The sisters, on hearing this, repeated three or four times how much they were grieved, how shocking it was to have a bad cold, and how excessively they disliked being ill themselves; and then thought no more of the matter: and their indifference towards Jane when not immediately before them, restored Elizabeth to the enjoyment of all her original dislike.

Their brother, indeed, was the only one of the party whom she could regard with any complacency. His anxiety for Jane was evident, and his attentions to herself most pleasing, and they prevented her feeling herself so much an intruder as she believed she was considered by the others. She had very little notice from any but him. Miss Bingley was engrossed by Mr Darcy, her sister scarcely less so; and as for Mr Hurst, by whom Elizabeth sat, he was an indolent man, who lived only to eat, drink, and play at cards, who when he found her prefer a plain dish to a ragout, had nothing to say to her.

When dinner was over, she returned directly to Jane, and Miss Bingley began abusing her as soon as she was out of the room. Her manners were pronounced to be very bad indeed, a mixture of pride and impertinence; she had no conversation, no stile, no taste, no beauty. Mrs Hurst thought the same, and added.

'She has nothing, in short, to recommend her, but being an excellent walker. I shall never forget her appearance this morning. She really looked almost wild.'

'She did indeed, Louisa. I could hardly keep my countenance. Very nonsensical to come at all! Why must *she* be scampering about the country, because her sister had a cold? Her hair so untidy, so blowsy!'

'Yes, and her petticoat; I hope you saw her petticoat, six inches deep in mud, I am absolutely certain; and the gown which had been let down to hide it, not doing its office.'

'Your picture may be very exact, Louisa,' said Bingley; 'but this was all lost upon me. I thought Miss Elizabeth Bennet looked remarkably well, when she came into the room this morning. Her dirty petticoat quite escaped my notice.'

'*You* observed it, Mr Darcy, I am sure,' said Miss Bingley; 'and I am inclined to think that you would not wish to see *your sister* make such an exhibition.'

'Certainly not.'

'To walk three miles, or four miles, or five miles, or whatever it is, above her ankles in dirt, and alone, quite alone! what could she mean by it? It seems to me to shew an abominable sort of conceited independence, a most country town indifference to decorum.'

'It shows an affection for her sister that is very pleasing,' said Bingley.

'I am afraid, Mr Darcy,' observed Miss Bingley, in a half whisper, 'that this adventure has rather affected your admiration of her fine eyes.'

'Not at all,' he replied; 'they were brightened by the exercise.' – A short pause followed this speech, and Mrs Hurst began again.

'I have an excessive regard for Jane Bennet, she is really a very sweet girl, and I wish with all my heart she were well settled. But with such a father and mother, and such low connections, I am afraid there is no chance of it.'

'I think I have heard you say, that their uncle is an attorney in Meryton.'

'Yes; and they have another, who lives somewhere near Cheapside.'

'That is capital,' added her sister, and they both laughed heartily.

'If they had uncles enough to fill *all* Cheapside,'

cried Bingley, 'it would not make them one jot less agreeable.'

'But it must very materially lessen their chance of marrying men of any consideration in the world,' replied Darcy.

To this speech Bingley made no answer; but his sisters gave it their hearty assent, and indulged their mirth for some time at the expense of their dear friend's vulgar relations.

With a renewal of tenderness, however, they repaired to her room on leaving the dining-parlour, and sat with her till summoned to coffee. She was still very poorly, and Elizabeth would not quit her at all, till late in the evening, when she had the comfort of seeing her asleep, and when it appeared to her rather right than pleasant that she should go downstairs herself. On entering the drawing-room she found the whole party at loo, and was immediately invited to join them; but suspecting them to be playing high she declined it, and making her sister the excuse, said she would amuse herself for the short time she could stay below with a book. Mr Hurst looked at her with astonishment.

'Do you prefer reading to cards?' said he; 'that is rather singular.'

'Miss Eliza Bennet,' said Miss Bingley, 'despises cards. She is a great reader and has no pleasure in anything else.'

'I deserve neither such praise nor such censure,' cried Elizabeth; 'I am *not* a great reader, and I have pleasure in many things.'

'In nursing your sister I am sure you have pleasure,' said Bingley; 'and I hope it will soon be increased by seeing her quite well.'

Elizabeth thanked him from her heart, and then

walked towards a table where a few books were lying. He immediately offered to fetch her others; all that his library afforded.

'And I wish my collection were larger for your benefit and my own credit; but I am an idle fellow, and though I have not many, I have more than I ever look into.'

Elizabeth assured him that she could suit herself perfectly with those in the room.

'I am astonished,' said Miss Bingley, 'that my father should have left so small a collection of books. What a delightful library you have at Pemberley, Mr Darcy!'

'It ought to be good,' he replied, 'it has been the work of many generations.'

'And then you have added so much to it yourself, you are always buying books.'

'I cannot comprehend the neglect of a family library in such days as these.'

'Neglect! I am sure you neglect nothing that can add to the beauties of that noble place. Charles, when you build *your* house, I wish it may be half as delightful as Pemberley.'

'I wish it may.'

'But I would really advise you to make your purchase in that neighbourhood, and take Pemberley for a kind of model. There is not a finer county in England than Derbyshire.'

'With all my heart; I will buy Pemberley itself if Darcy will sell it.'

'I am talking of possibilities, Charles.'

'Upon my word, Caroline, I should think it more possible to get Pemberley by purchase than by imitation.'

Elizabeth was so much caught by what passed, as to

leave her very little attention for her book; and soon laying it wholly aside, she drew near the card-table, and stationed herself between Mr Bingley and his eldest sister to observe the game.

'Is Miss Darcy much grown since the spring?' said Miss Bingley; 'will she be as tall as I am?'

'I think she will. She is now about Miss Elizabeth Bennet's height, or rather taller.'

'How I long to see her again! I never met with anybody who delighted me so much. Such a countenance, such manners! and so extremely accomplished for her age! Her performance on the pianoforte is exquisite.'

'It is amazing to me,' said Bingley, 'how young ladies can have patience to be so very accomplished, as they all are.'

'All young ladies accomplished! My dear Charles, what do you mean?'

'Yes, all of them, I think. They all paint tables, cover screens and net purses. I scarcely know anyone who cannot do all this, and I am sure I never heard a young lady spoken of for the first time, without being informed that she was very accomplished.'

'Your list of the common extent of accomplishments,' said Darcy, 'has too much truth. The word is applied to many a woman who deserves it no otherwise than by netting a purse, or covering a screen. But I am very far from agreeing with you in your estimation of ladies in general. I cannot boast of knowing more than half a dozen, in the whole range of my acquaintance, that are really accomplished.'

'Nor I, I am sure,' said Miss Bingley.

'Then,' observed Elizabeth, 'you must comprehend a great deal in your idea of an accomplished woman.'

They all paint tables, cover screens and net purses

'Yes; I do comprehend a great deal in it.'

'Oh! certainly,' cried his faithful assistant, 'no one can be really esteemed accomplished, who does not greatly surpass what is usually met with. A woman must have a thorough knowledge of music, singing, drawing, dancing, and the modern languages, to deserve the word; and besides all this, she must possess a certain something in her air and manner of walking, the tone of her voice, her address and expressions, or the word will be but half deserved.'

'All this she must possess,' added Darcy, 'and to all this she must yet add something more substantial, in the improvement of her mind by extensive reading.'

'I am no longer surprised at your knowing *only* six accomplished women. I rather wonder now at your knowing *any*.'

'Are you so severe upon your own sex, as to doubt the possibility of all this?'

'*I* never saw such a woman. *I* never saw such capacity, and taste, and application, and elegance, as you describe, united.'

Mrs Hurst and Miss Bingley both cried out against the injustice of her implied doubt, and were both protesting that they knew many women who answered this description, when Mr Hurst called them to order, with bitter complaints of their inattention to what was going forward. As all conversation was thereby at an end, Elizabeth soon afterwards left the room.

'Eliza Bennet,' said Miss Bingley, when the door was closed on her, 'is one of those young ladies who seek to recommend themselves to the other sex, by undervaluing their own; and with many men, I dare say, it succeeds. But, in my opinion, it is a paltry device, a very mean art.'

'Undoubtedly,' replied Darcy, to whom this remark was chiefly addressed, 'there is meanness in *all* the arts which ladies sometimes condescend to employ for captivation. Whatever bears affinity to cunning is despicable.'

Miss Bingley was not so entirely satisfied with this reply as to continue the subject.

Elizabeth joined them again only to say that her sister was worse, and that she could not leave her. Bingley urged Mr Jones's being sent for immediately; while his sisters, convinced that no country advice could be of any service, recommended an express to town for one of the most eminent physicians. This, she would not hear of; but she was not so unwilling to comply with their brother's proposal; and it was settled that Mr Jones should be sent for early in the morning, if Miss Bennet were not decidedly better. Bingley was quite uncomfortable; his sisters declared that they were miserable. They solaced their wretchedness, however, by duets after supper, while he could find no better relief to his feelings than by giving his housekeeper directions that every possible attention might be paid to the sick lady and her sister.

Chapter 9

Elizabeth passed the chief of the night in her sister's room, and in the morning had the pleasure of being able to send a tolerable answer to the enquiries which she very early received from Mr Bingley by a housemaid, and some time afterwards from the two elegant ladies who waited on his sisters. In spite of this amendment, however, she requested to have a note sent to Longbourn, desiring her mother to visit Jane, and form her own judgement of her situation. The note was immediately dispatched, and its contents as quickly complied with. Mrs Bennet, accompanied by her two youngest girls, reached Netherfield soon after the family breakfast.

Had she found Jane in any apparent danger, Mrs Bennet would have been very miserable; but being satisfied on seeing her that her illness was not alarming, she had no wish of her recovering immediately, as her restoration to health would probably remove her from Netherfield. She would not listen therefore to her daughter's proposal of being carried home; neither did the apothecary, who arrived about the same time, think it at all advisable. After sitting a little while with Jane, on Miss Bingley's appearance and invitation, the mother and three daughters all attended her into the breakfast parlour. Bingley met them with hopes that Mrs Bennet had not found Miss Bennet worse than she expected.

'Indeed I have, sir,' was her answer. 'She is a great deal too ill to be moved. Mr Jones says we must not think of moving her. We must trespass a little longer on your kindness.'

'Removed!' cried Bingley. 'It must not be thought of. My sister, I am sure, will not hear of her removal.'

'You may depend upon it, Madam,' said Miss Bingley, with cold civility, 'that Miss Bennet shall receive every possible attention while she remains with us.'

Mrs Bennet was profuse in her acknowledgments.

'I am sure,' she added, 'if it was not for such good friends I do not know what would become of her, for she is very ill indeed, and suffers a vast deal, though with the greatest patience in the world, which is always

Mrs Bennet, accompanied by her two youngest girls

the way with her, for she has, without exception, the sweetest temper I ever met with. I often tell my other girls they are nothing to *her*. You have a sweet room here, Mr Bingley, and a charming prospect over that gravel walk. I do not know a place in the country that is equal to Netherfield. You will not think of quitting it in a hurry I hope, though you have but a short lease.'

'Whatever I do is done in a hurry,' replied he; 'and therefore if I should resolve to quit Netherfield, I should probably be off in five minutes. At present, however, I consider myself as quite fixed here.'

'That is exactly what I should have supposed of you,' said Elizabeth.

'You begin to comprehend me, do you?' cried he, turning towards her.

'Oh! yes – I understand you perfectly.'

'I wish I might take this for a compliment; but to be so easily seen through I am afraid is pitiful.'

'That is as it happens. It does not necessarily follow that a deep, intricate character is more or less estimable than such a one as yours.'

'Lizzy,' cried her mother, 'remember where you are, and do not run on in the wild manner that you are suffered to do at home.'

'I did not know before,' continued Bingley immediately, 'that you were a studier of character. It must be an amusing study.'

'Yes; but intricate characters are the *most* amusing. They have at least that advantage.'

'The country,' said Darcy, 'can in general supply but few subjects for such a study. In a country neighbourhood you move in a very confined and unvarying society.'

'But people themselves alter so much, that there is something new to be observed in them for ever.'

'Yes, indeed,' cried Mrs Bennet, offended by his manner of mentioning a country neighbourhood. 'I assure you there is quite as much of *that* going on in the country as in town.'

Everybody was surprised; and Darcy, after looking at her for a moment, turned silently away. Mrs Bennet, who fancied she had gained a complete victory over him, continued her triumph.

'I cannot see that London has any great advantage over the country for my part, except the shops and public places. The country is a vast deal pleasanter, is not it, Mr Bingley?'

'When I am in the country,' he replied, 'I never wish to leave it; and when I am in town it is pretty much the same. They have each their advantages, and I can be equally happy in either.'

'Aye – that is because you have the right disposition. But that gentleman,' looking at Darcy, 'seemed to think the country was nothing at all.'

'Indeed, Mama, you are mistaken,' said Elizabeth, blushing for her mother. 'You quite mistook Mr Darcy. He only meant that there were not such a variety of people to be met with in the country as in town, which you must acknowledge to be true.'

'Certainly, my dear, nobody said there were; but as to not meeting with many people in this neighbour-hood, I believe there are few neighbourhoods larger. I know we dine with four and twenty families.'

Nothing but concern for Elizabeth could enable Bingley to keep his countenance. His sister was less delicate, and directed her eye towards Mr Darcy with a very expressive smile. Elizabeth, for the sake of saying something that might turn her mother's thoughts, now asked her if Charlotte Lucas had been at Longbourn since *her* coming away.

'Yes, she called yesterday with her father. What an agreeable man Sir William is, Mr Bingley – is not he? so much the man of fashion! so genteel and so easy! – He has always something to say to everybody. *That* is my idea of good breeding; and those persons who fancy themselves very important and never open their mouths, quite mistake the matter.'

'Did Charlotte dine with you?'

'No, she would go home. I fancy she was wanted

about the mince pies. For my part, Mr Bingley, *I* always keep servants that can do their own work; *my* daughters are brought up differently. But everybody is to judge for themselves, and the Lucases are very good sort of girls, I assure you. It is a pity they are not handsome! Not that *I* think Charlotte so *very* plain – but then she is our particular friend.'

'She seems a very pleasant young woman,' said Bingley.

'Oh! dear, yes – but you must own she is very plain. Lady Lucas herself has often said so, and envied me Jane's beauty. I do not like to boast of my own child, but to be sure, Jane – one does not often see anybody better looking. It is what everybody says. I do not trust my own partiality. When she was only fifteen, there was a gentleman at my brother Gardiner's in town, so much in love with her, that my sister-in-law was sure he would make her an offer before we came away. But however he did not. Perhaps he thought her too young. However, he wrote some verses on her, and very pretty they were.'

'And so ended his affection,' said Elizabeth impatiently. 'There has been many a one, I fancy, overcome in the same way. I wonder who first discovered the efficacy of poetry in driving away love!'

'I have been used to consider poetry as the *food* of love,' said Darcy.

'Of a fine, stout, healthy love it may. Everything nourishes what is strong already. But if it be only a slight, thin sort of inclination, I am convinced that one good sonnet will starve it entirely away.'

Darcy only smiled; and the general pause which ensued made Elizabeth tremble lest her mother should be exposing herself again. She longed to speak, but could think of nothing to say; and after a short silence Mrs Bennet began repeating her thanks to Mr Bingley for his kindness to Jane, with an apology for troubling him also with Lizzy. Mr Bingley was unaffectedly civil in his answer, and forced his younger sister to be civil also, and say what the occasion required. She performed her part indeed without much graciousness, but Mrs Bennet was satisfied, and soon afterwards ordered her carriage. Upon this signal, the youngest of her daughters put herself forward. The two girls had been whispering to each other during the whole visit, and the result of it was, that the youngest should tax Mr Bingley with having promised on his first coming into the country to give a ball at Netherfield.

Lydia was a stout, well-grown girl of fifteen, with a fine complexion and good-humoured countenance; a favourite with her mother, whose affection had brought her into public at an early age. She had high animal spirits, and a sort of natural self-consequence, which the attentions of the officers, to whom her uncle's good dinners and her own easy manners recommended her, had increased into assurance. She was very equal therefore to address Mr Bingley on the subject of the ball, and abruptly reminded him of his promise; adding, that it would be the most shameful thing in the world if he did not keep it. His answer to this sudden attack was delightful to their mother's ear.

'I am perfectly ready, I assure you, to keep my engagement; and when your sister is recovered, you shall if you please name the very day of the ball. But you would not wish to be dancing while she is ill.'

Lydia declared herself satisfied. 'Oh! yes – it would be much better to wait till Jane was well, and by that time most likely Captain Carter would be at Meryton again. And when you have given *your* ball,' she added, 'I shall insist on their giving one also. I shall tell Colonel Forster it will be quite a shame if he does not.'

Mrs Bennet and her daughters then departed, and Elizabeth returned instantly to Jane, leaving her own and her relations' behaviour to the remarks of the two ladies and Mr Darcy; the latter of whom, however, could not be prevailed on to join in their censure of *her*, in spite of all Miss Bingley's witticisms on *fine eyes*.

Chapter 10

The day passed much as the day before had done. Mrs Hurst and Miss Bingley had spent some hours of the morning with the invalid, who continued, though slowly, to mend; and in the evening Elizabeth joined their party in the drawing-room. The loo table, however, did not appear. Mr Darcy was writing, and Miss Bingley, seated near him, was watching the progress of his letter, and repeatedly calling off his attention by messages to his sister. Mr Hurst and Mr Bingley were at piquet, and Mrs Hurst was observing their game.

Elizabeth took up some needlework, and was sufficiently amused in attending to what passed between Darcy and his companion. The perpetual commendations of the lady either on his hand-writing, or on the evenness of his lines, or on the length of his letter, with the perfect unconcern with which her praises were received, formed a curious dialogue, and was exactly in unison with her opinion of each.

'How delighted Miss Darcy will be to receive such a letter!'

He made no answer.

'You write uncommonly fast.'

'You are mistaken. I write rather slowly.'

'How many letters you must have occasion to write in the course of the year! Letters of business too! How odious I should think them!'

'It is fortunate, then, that they fall to my lot instead of to yours.'

'Pray tell your sister that I long to see her.'

'I have already told her so once, by your desire.'

'I am afraid you do not like your pen. Let me mend it for you. I mend pens remarkably well.'

'Thank you – but I always mend my own.'

'How can you contrive to write so even?'

He was silent.

'Tell your sister I am delighted to hear of her improvement on the harp, and pray let her know that I am quite in raptures with her beautiful little design for a table, and I think it infinitely superior to Miss Grantley's.'

'Will you give me leave to defer your raptures till I write again? – At present I have not room to do them justice.'

'Oh! it is of no consequence. I shall see her in January. But do you always write such charming long letters to her, Mr Darcy?'

'They are generally long; but whether always charming, it is not for me to determine.'

'It is a rule with me, that a person who can write a long letter, with ease, cannot write ill.'

'That will not do for a compliment to Darcy, Caroline,' cried her brother – 'because he does *not* write with ease. He studies too much for words of four syllables. Do not you, Darcy?'

'My style of writing is very different from yours.'

'Oh!' cried Miss Bingley, 'Charles writes in the most careless way imaginable. He leaves out half his words, and blots the rest.'

'My ideas flow so rapidly that I have not time to express them – by which means my letters sometimes convey no ideas at all to my correspondents.'

'Your humility, Mr Bingley,' said Elizabeth, 'must disarm reproof.'

'Nothing is more deceitful,' said Darcy, 'than the appearance of humility. It is often only carelessness of opinion, and sometimes an indirect boast.'

'And which of the two do you call *my* little recent piece of modesty?'

'The indirect boast – for you are really proud of your defects in writing, because you consider them as proceeding from a rapidity of thought and carelessness of execution, which if not estimable, you think at least highly interesting. The power of doing anything with quickness is always much prized by the possessor, and often without any attention to the imperfection of the performance. When you told Mrs Bennet this morning that if you ever resolved on quitting Netherfield you should be gone in five minutes, you meant it to be a sort of panegyric, of compliment to yourself – and yet what is there so very laudable in a precipitance which must leave very necessary business undone, and can be of no real advantage to yourself or anyone else?'

'Nay,' cried Bingley, 'this is too much, to remember at night all the foolish things that were said in the morning. And yet, upon my honour, I believed what I said of myself to be true, and I believe it at this moment. At least, therefore, I did not assume the character of needless precipitance merely to shew off before the ladies.'

'I dare say you believed it; but I am by no means convinced that you would be gone with such celerity. Your conduct would be quite as dependant on chance as that of any man I know; and if, as you were mounting your horse, a friend were to say, "Bingley, you had better stay till next week", you would probably do it, you would probably not go – and, at another word, might stay a month.'

'You have only proved by this,' cried Elizabeth, 'that Mr Bingley did not do justice to his own disposition. You have shown him off now much more than he did himself.'

'I am exceedingly gratified,' said Bingley, 'by your converting what my friend says into a compliment on the sweetness of my temper. But I am afraid you are giving it a turn which that gentleman did by no means intend; for he would certainly think the better of me, if under such a circumstance I were to give a flat denial, and ride off as fast as I could.'

'Would Mr Darcy then consider the rashness of your original intention as atoned for by your obstinacy in adhering to it?'

'Upon my word I cannot exactly explain the matter, Darcy must speak for himself.'

'You expect me to account for opinions which you choose to call mine, but which I have never acknowledged. Allowing the case, however, to stand according to your representation, you must remember, Miss Bennet, that the friend who is supposed to desire his return to the house, and the delay of his plan, has merely desired it, asked it without offering one argument in favour of its propriety.'

'To yield readily – easily – to the *persuasion* of a friend is no merit with you.'

'To yield without conviction is no compliment to the understanding of either.'

'You appear to me, Mr Darcy, to allow nothing for the influence of friendship and affection. A regard for the requester would often make one readily yield to a request, without waiting for arguments to reason one into it. I am not particularly speaking of such a case as you have supposed about Mr Bingley. We may as well wait, perhaps, till the circumstance occurs, before we discuss the discretion of his behaviour thereupon. But in general and ordinary cases between friend and friend, where one of them is desired by the other to change a resolution of no very great moment, should you think ill of that person for complying with the desire, without waiting to be argued into it?'

'Will it not be advisable, before we proceed on this subject, to arrange with rather more precision the degree of importance which is to appertain to this request, as well as the degree of intimacy subsisting between the parties?'

'By all means,' cried Bingley; 'let us hear all the particulars, not forgetting their comparative height and size; for that will have more weight in the argument, Miss Bennet, than you may be aware of. I assure you that if Darcy were not such a great tall fellow, in comparison with myself, I should not pay him half so much deference. I declare I do not know a more awful object than Darcy, on particular occasions, and in particular places; at his own house especially, and of a Sunday evening when he has nothing to do.'

Mr Darcy smiled; but Elizabeth thought she could perceive that he was rather offended; and therefore checked her laugh. Miss Bingley warmly resented the indignity he had received, in an expostulation with her brother for talking such nonsense.

'I see your design, Bingley,' said his friend. 'You dislike an argument, and want to silence this.'

'Perhaps I do. Arguments are too much like disputes. If you and Miss Bennet will defer yours till I am out of the room, I shall be very thankful; and then you may say whatever you like of me.'

'What you ask,' said Elizabeth, 'is no sacrifice on my side; and Mr Darcy had much better finish his letter.'

Mr Darcy took her advice, and did finish his letter.

When that business was over, he applied to Miss Bingley and Elizabeth for the indulgence of some music. Miss Bingley moved with alacrity to the pianoforte, and after a polite request that Elizabeth would lead the way, which the other as politely and more earnestly negatived, she seated herself.

Mrs Hurst sang with her sister, and while they were thus employed Elizabeth could not help observing as she turned over some music books that lay on the instrument, how frequently Mr Darcy's eyes were fixed on her. She hardly knew how to suppose that she could be an object of admiration to so great a man; and yet that he should look at her because he disliked her, was still more strange. She could only imagine however at last, that she drew his notice because there was a something about her more wrong and reprehensible, according to his ideas of right, than in any other person present. The supposition did not pain her. She liked him too little to care for his approbation.

After playing some Italian songs, Miss Bingley

varied the charm by a lively Scotch air; and soon afterwards Mr Darcy, drawing near Elizabeth, said to her – 'Do not you feel a great inclination, Miss Bennet, to seize such an opportunity of dancing a reel?'

She smiled, but made no answer. He repeated the question, with some surprise at her silence.

'Oh!' said she, 'I heard you before; but I could not immediately determine what to say in reply. You wanted me, I know, to say "Yes," that you might have the pleasure of despising my taste; but I always delight in overthrowing those kind of schemes, and cheating a person of their premeditated contempt. I have therefore made up my mind to tell you, that I do not want to dance a reel at all – and now despise me if you dare.'

'Indeed I do not dare.'

Elizabeth, having rather expected to affront him, was amazed at his gallantry; but there was a mixture of sweetness and archness in her manner which made it difficult for her to affront anybody; and Darcy had never been so bewitched by any woman as he was by her. He really believed, that were it not for the inferiority of her connections, he should be in some danger.

Miss Bingley saw, or suspected enough to be jealous; and her great anxiety for the recovery of her dear friend Jane, received some assistance from her desire of getting rid of Elizabeth.

She often tried to provoke Darcy into disliking her guest, by talking of their supposed marriage, and planning his happiness in such an alliance.

'I hope,' said she, as they were walking together in the shrubbery the next day, 'you will give your mother-in-law a few hints, when this desirable event takes place, as to the advantage of holding her tongue; and if you can compass it, do cure the younger girls of running after the officers. And, if I may mention so delicate a subject, endeavour to check that little something, bordering on conceit and impertinence, which your lady possesses.'

'Have you anything else to propose for my domestic felicity?'

'Oh! yes. Do let the portraits of your uncle and aunt Philips be placed in the gallery at Pemberley. Put them next to your great uncle the judge. They are in the same profession, you know; only in different lines. As for your Elizabeth's picture, you must not attempt to have it taken, for what painter could do justice to those beautiful eyes?'

'It would not be easy, indeed, to catch their expression, but their colour and shape, and the eyelashes, so remarkably fine, might be copied.'

At that moment they were met from another walk, by Mrs Hurst and Elizabeth herself.

'I did not know that you intended to walk,' said Miss Bingley, in some confusion, lest they had been overheard.

'You used us abominably ill,' answered Mrs Hurst, 'in running away without telling us that you were coming out.'

Then taking the disengaged arm of Mr Darcy, she left Elizabeth to walk by herself. The path just admitted three. Mr Darcy felt their rudeness and immediately said, 'This walk is not wide enough for our party. We had better go into the avenue.'

But Elizabeth, who had not the least inclination to remain with them, laughingly answered, 'No, no; stay where you are. You are charmingly group'd, and

No, no; stay where you are

appear to uncommon advantage. The picturesque would be spoilt by admitting a fourth. Goodbye.'

She then ran gaily off, rejoicing as she rambled about, in the hope of being at home again in a day or two. Jane was already so much recovered as to intend leaving her room for a couple of hours that evening.

Chapter 11

When the ladies removed after dinner, Elizabeth ran up to her sister, and seeing her well guarded from cold, attended her into the drawing-room; where she was welcomed by her two friends with many professions of pleasure; and Elizabeth had never seen them so agreeable as they were during the hour which passed before the gentlemen appeared. Their powers of conversation were considerable. They could describe an entertainment with accuracy, relate an anecdote with humour, and laugh at their acquaintance with spirit.

But when the gentlemen entered, Jane was no longer the first object. Miss Bingley's eyes were instantly turned towards Darcy, and she had something to say to him before he had advanced many steps. He addressed himself directly to Miss Bennet, with a polite congratulation; Mr Hurst also made her a slight bow, and said he was 'very glad'; but diffuseness and warmth remained for Bingley's salutation. He was full of joy and attention. The first half-hour was spent in piling up the fire, lest she should suffer from the change of room; and she removed at his desire to the other side of the fireplace, that she might be farther from the door. He then sat down by her, and talked scarcely to anyone else. Elizabeth, at work in the opposite corner, saw it all with great delight.

When tea was over, Mr Hurst reminded his sister-in-law of the card-table – but in vain. She had obtained private intelligence that Mr Darcy did not wish for cards; and Mr Hurst soon found even his open petition rejected. She assured him that no one intended to play, and the silence of the whole party on the subject, seemed to justify her. Mr Hurst had therefore nothing to do, but to stretch himself on one of the sofas and go to sleep. Darcy took up a book; Miss Bingley did the same; and Mrs Hurst, principally occupied in playing with her bracelets and rings, joined now and then in her brother's conversation with Miss Bennet.

Miss Bingley's attention was quite as much engaged in watching Mr Darcy's progress through *his* book, as in reading her own; and she was perpetually either making some enquiry, or looking at his page. She could not win him, however, to any conversation; he merely answered her question, and read on. At length, quite exhausted by the attempt to be amused with her own book, which she had only chosen because it was the second volume of his, she gave a great yawn and said, 'How pleasant it is to spend an evening in this way! I declare after all there is no enjoyment like reading! How much sooner one tires of anything than of a book! – When I have a house of my own, I shall be miserable if I have not an excellent library.'

No one made any reply. She then yawned again, threw aside her book, and cast her eyes round the room in quest of some amusement; when hearing her brother mentioning a ball to Miss Bennet, she turned suddenly towards him and said, 'By the by, Charles,

The first half-hour was spent in piling up the fire

are you really serious in meditating a dance at Netherfield? – I would advise you, before you determine on it, to consult the wishes of the present party; I am much mistaken if there are not some among us to whom a ball would be rather a punishment than a pleasure.'

'If you mean Darcy,' cried her brother, 'he may go to bed, if he chooses, before it begins – but as for the ball, it is quite a settled thing; and as soon as Nicholls has made white soup enough I shall send round my cards.'

'I should like balls infinitely better,' she replied, 'if they were carried on in a different manner; but there is something insufferably tedious in the usual process of such a meeting. It would surely be much more rational if conversation instead of dancing made the order of the day.'

'Much more rational, my dear Caroline, I dare say, but it would not be near so much like a ball.'

Miss Bingley made no answer; and soon afterwards got up and walked about the room. Her figure was elegant, and she walked well – but Darcy, at whom it was all aimed, was still inflexibly studious. In the desperation of her feelings she resolved on one effort more; and, turning to Elizabeth, said, 'Miss Eliza Bennet, let me persuade you to follow my example, and take a turn about the room. I assure you it is very refreshing after sitting so long in one attitude.'

Elizabeth was surprised, but agreed to it immediately. Miss Bingley succeeded no less in the real object of her civility; Mr Darcy looked up. He was as much awake to the novelty of attention in that quarter as Elizabeth herself could be, and unconsciously closed his book. He was directly invited to join their party, but he declined it, observing, that he could imagine but two motives for their choosing to walk up and down the room together, with either of which motives his joining them would interfere. 'What could he mean? she was dying to know what could be his meaning' – and asked Elizabeth whether she could at all understand him?

'Not at all,' was her answer; 'but depend upon it, he means to be severe on us, and our surest way of disappointing him, will be to ask nothing about it.'

Miss Bingley, however, was incapable of disappointing Mr Darcy in anything, and persevered therefore in requiring an explanation of his two motives.

'I have not the smallest objection to explaining them,' said he, as soon as she allowed him to speak.

'You either choose this method of passing the evening because you are in each other's confidence and have secret affairs to discuss, or because you are conscious that your figures appear to the greatest advantage in walking – if the first, I should be completely in your way – and if the second, I can admire you much better as I sit by the fire.'

'Oh! shocking!' cried Miss Bingley. 'I never heard anything so abominable. How shall we punish him for such a speech?'

'Nothing so easy, if you have but the inclination,' said Elizabeth. 'We can all plague and punish one another. Tease him – laugh at him. Intimate as you are, you must know how it is to be done.'

'But upon my honour I do *not*. I do assure you that my intimacy has not yet taught me *that*. Tease calmness of temper and presence of mind! No, no – I feel he may defy us there. And as to laughter, we will not expose ourselves, if you please, by attempting to laugh without a subject. Mr Darcy may hug himself.'

'Mr Darcy is not to be laughed at!' cried Elizabeth. 'That is an uncommon advantage, and uncommon I hope it will continue, for it would be a great loss to *me* to have many such acquaintance. I dearly love a laugh.'

'Miss Bingley,' said he, 'has given me credit for more than can be. The wisest and the best of men, nay, the wisest and best of their actions, may be rendered ridiculous by a person whose first object in life is a joke.'

'Certainly,' replied Elizabeth – 'there are such people, but I hope I am not one of *them*. I hope I never ridicule what is wise or good. Follies and nonsense, whims and inconsistencies *do* divert me, I own, and I laugh at them whenever I can. But these, I suppose, are precisely what you are without.'

'Perhaps that is not possible for anyone. But it has been the study of my life to avoid those weaknesses which often expose a strong understanding to ridicule.'

'Such as vanity and pride.'

'Yes, vanity is a weakness indeed. But pride – where there is a real superiority of mind, pride will be always under good regulation.'

Elizabeth turned away to hide a smile.

'Your examination of Mr Darcy is over, I presume,' said Miss Bingley – 'and pray what is the result?'

'I am perfectly convinced by it that Mr Darcy has no defect. He owns it himself without disguise.'

'No' – said Darcy, 'I have made no such pretension. I have faults enough, but they are not, I hope, of understanding. My temper I dare not vouch for. It is I believe too little yielding – certainly too little for the convenience of the world. I cannot forget the follies and vices of others so soon as I ought, nor their offences against myself. My feelings are not puffed about with every attempt to move them. My temper would perhaps be called resentful. My good opinion once lost is lost for ever.'

'*That* is a failing indeed!' – cried Elizabeth. 'Implacable resentment *is* a shade in a character. But you have chosen your fault well. I really cannot *laugh* at it. You are safe from me.'

'There is, I believe, in every disposition a tendency to some particular evil, a natural defect, which not even the best education can overcome.'

'And *your* defect is a propensity to hate everybody.'

'And yours,' he replied with a smile, 'is wilfully to misunderstand them.'

'Do let us have a little music,' – cried Miss Bingley, tired of a conversation in which she had no share. 'Louisa, you will not mind my waking Mr Hurst.'

Her sister made not the smallest objection, and the pianoforte was opened, and Darcy, after a few moments recollection, was not sorry for it. He began to feel the danger of paying Elizabeth too much attention.

Chapter 12

In consequence of an agreement between the sisters, Elizabeth wrote the next morning to her mother, to beg that the carriage might be sent for them in the course of the day. But Mrs Bennet, who had calculated on her daughters remaining at Netherfield till the following Tuesday, which would exactly finish Jane's week, could not bring herself to receive them with pleasure before. Her answer, therefore, was not propitious, at least not to Elizabeth's wishes, for she was impatient to get home. Mrs Bennet sent them word that they could not possibly have the carriage before Tuesday; and in her postscript it was added, that if Mr Bingley and his sister pressed them to stay longer, she could spare them very well. Against staying longer, however, Elizabeth was positively resolved – nor did she much expect it would be asked; and fearful, on the contrary, as being considered as intruding themselves needlessly long, she urged Jane to borrow Mr Bingley's carriage immediately, and at length it was settled that their original design of leaving Netherfield that morning should be mentioned, and the request made.

The communication excited many professions of concern; and enough was said of wishing them to stay at least till the following day to work on Jane; and till the morrow, their going was deferred. Miss Bingley was then sorry that she had proposed the delay, for her jealousy and dislike of one sister much exceeded her affection for the other.

The master of the house heard with real sorrow that they were to go so soon, and repeatedly tried to persuade Miss Bennet that it would not be safe for her – that she was not enough recovered; but Jane was firm where she felt herself to be right.

To Mr Darcy it was welcome intelligence – Elizabeth had been at Netherfield long enough. She attracted him more than he liked – and Miss Bingley was uncivil to *her*, and more teasing than usual to himself. He wisely resolved to be particularly careful that no sign of admiration should *now* escape him, nothing that could elevate her with the hope of influencing his felicity; sensible that if such an idea had been suggested, his behaviour during the last day must have material weight in confirming or crushing it. Steady to his purpose, he scarcely spoke ten words to her through the whole of Saturday, and though they were at one time left by themselves for half an hour, he adhered most conscientiously to his book, and would not even look at her.

On Sunday, after morning service, the separation, so agreeable to almost all, took place. Miss Bingley's civility to Elizabeth increased at last very rapidly, as well as her affection for Jane; and when they parted, after assuring the latter of the pleasure it would always give her to see her either at Longbourn or Netherfield, and embracing her most tenderly, she even shook hands with the former. Elizabeth took leave of the whole party in the liveliest spirits.

They were not welcomed home very cordially by their mother. Mrs Bennet wondered at their coming, and thought them very wrong to give so much trouble, and was sure Jane would have caught cold again. But their father, though very laconic in his expressions of pleasure, was really glad to see them; he had felt their importance in the family circle. The evening conversation, when they were all assembled, had lost much of its animation, and almost all its sense, by the absence of Jane and Elizabeth.

They found Mary, as usual, deep in the study of thorough bass and human nature; and had some new extracts to admire, and some new observations of threadbare morality to listen to. Catherine and Lydia had information for them of a different sort. Much had been done, and much had been said in the regiment since the preceding Wednesday; several of the officers had dined lately with their uncle, a private had been flogged, and it had actually been hinted that Colonel Forster was going to be married.

Chapter 13

'I hope, my dear,' said Mr Bennet to his wife, as they were at breakfast the next morning, 'that you have ordered a good dinner today, because I have reason to expect an addition to our family party.'

'Who do you mean, my dear? I know of nobody that is coming I am sure, unless Charlotte Lucas should happen to call in, and I hope *my* dinners are good enough for her. I do not believe she often sees such at home.'

'The person of whom I speak, is a gentleman and a

stranger.' Mrs Bennet's eyes sparkled. 'A gentleman and a stranger! It is Mr Bingley I am sure. Why Jane – you never dropped a word of this; you sly thing! Well, I am sure I shall be extremely glad to see Mr Bingley. But – good lord! how unlucky! there is not a bit of fish to be got today. Lydia, my love, ring the bell. I must speak to Hill, this moment.'

'It is *not* Mr Bingley,' said her husband; 'it is a person whom I never saw in the whole course of my life.'

This roused a general astonishment; and he had the pleasure of being eagerly questioned by his wife and five daughters at once.

After amusing himself some time with their curiosity, he thus explained. 'About a month ago I received this letter, and about a fortnight ago I answered it, for I thought it a case of some delicacy, and requiring early attention. It is from my cousin, Mr Collins, who, when I am dead, may turn you all out of this house as soon as he pleases.'

'Oh! my dear,' cried his wife, 'I cannot bear to hear that mentioned. Pray do not talk of that odious man. I do think it is the hardest thing in the world, that your estate should be entailed away from your own children; and I am sure if I had been you, I should have tried long ago to do something or other about it.'

Jane and Elizabeth attempted to explain to her the nature of an entail. They had often attempted it before, but it was a subject on which Mrs Bennet was beyond the reach of reason; and she continued to rail bitterly against the cruelty of settling an estate away from a family of five daughters, in favour of a man whom nobody cared anything about.

'It certainly is a most iniquitous affair,' said Mr

Bennet, 'and nothing can clear Mr Collins from the guilt of inheriting Longbourn. But if you will listen to his letter, you may perhaps be a little softened by his manner of expressing himself.'

'No, that I am sure I shall not; and I think it was very impertinent of him to write to you at all, and very hypocritical. I hate such false friends. Why could not he keep on quarrelling with you, as his father did before him?'

'Why, indeed, he does seem to have had some filial scruples on that head, as you will hear.'

Hunsford, near Westerham, Kent, 15th October

DEAR SIR – The disagreement subsisting between yourself and my late honoured father, always gave me much uneasiness, and since I have had the misfortune to lose him, I have frequently wished to heal the breach; but for some time I was kept back by my own doubts, fearing lest it might seem disrespectful to his memory for me to be on good terms with anyone, with whom it had always pleased him to be at variance – 'There, Mrs Bennet.' – My mind however is now made up on the subject, for having received ordination at Easter, I have been so fortunate as to be distinguished by the patronage of the Right Honourable Lady Catherine de Bourgh, widow of Sir Lewis de Bourgh, whose bounty and beneficence has preferred me to the valuable rectory of this parish, where it shall be my earnest endeavour to demean myself with grateful respect towards her Ladyship, and be ever ready to perform those rites and ceremonies which are instituted by the Church of England. As a clergyman, moreover, I feel it my duty to promote and establish the blessing of peace in all families within the reach of my influence; and on these grounds I flatter myself that my present overtures of goodwill are highly commendable, and that the circumstance of my being next in the entail of Longbourn estate, will be kindly overlooked on your side, and not lead you to reject the offered olive branch. I cannot be otherwise than concerned at being the means of injuring your amiable daughters, and beg leave to apologise for it, as well as to assure you of my readiness to make them every possible amends – but of this hereafter. If you should have no objection to receive me into your house, I propose myself the satisfaction of waiting on you and your family, Monday, November 18th, by four o'clock, and shall probably trespass on your hospitality till the Saturday se'night following, which I can do without any inconvenience, as Lady Catherine is far from objecting to my occasional absence on a Sunday, provided that some other clergyman is engaged to do the duty of the day. I remain, dear sir, with respectful compliments to your lady and daughters, your well-wisher and friend,

WILLIAM COLLINS.

'At four o'clock, therefore, we may expect this peace-making gentleman,' said Mr Bennet, as he folded up the letter. 'He seems to be a most conscientious and polite young man, upon my word; and I doubt not will prove a valuable acquaintance, especially if Lady Catherine should be so indulgent as to let him come to us again.'

'There is some sense in what he says about the girls

however; and if he is disposed to make them any amends, I shall not be the person to discourage him.'

'Though it is difficult,' said Jane, 'to guess in what way he can mean to make us the atonement he thinks our due, the wish is certainly to his credit.'

Elizabeth was chiefly struck with his extraordinary deference for Lady Catherine, and his kind intention of christening, marrying, and burying his parishioners whenever it were required.

'He must be an oddity, I think,' said she. 'I cannot make him out. There is something very pompous in his style. And what can he mean by apologising for being next in the entail? – We cannot suppose he would help it, if he could. Can he be a sensible man, sir?'

'No, my dear; I think not. I have great hopes of finding him quite the reverse. There is a mixture of servility and self-importance in his letter, which promises well. I am impatient to see him.'

'In point of composition,' said Mary, 'his letter does not seem defective. The idea of the olive branch perhaps is not wholly new, yet I think it is well expressed.'

To Catherine and Lydia, neither the letter nor its writer were in any degree interesting. It was next to impossible that their cousin should come in a scarlet coat, and it was now some weeks since they had received pleasure from the society of a man in any other colour. As for their mother, Mr Collins's letter had done away much of her ill-will, and she was preparing to see him with a degree of composure, which astonished her husband and daughters.

Mr Collins was punctual to his time, and was received with great politeness by the whole family. Mr

Bennet indeed said little; but the ladies were ready enough to talk, and Mr Collins seemed neither in need of encouragement, nor inclined to be silent himself. He was a tall, heavy looking young man of five and twenty. His air was grave and stately, and his manners were very formal. He had not been long seated before he complimented Mrs Bennet on having so fine a family of daughters, said he had heard much of their beauty, but that, in this instance, fame had fallen short of the truth; and added, that he did not doubt her seeing them all in due time well disposed of in marriage.

This gallantry was not much to the taste of some of his hearers, but Mrs Bennet, who quarrelled with no compliments, answered most readily, 'You are very kind, sir, I am sure; and I wish with all my heart it may prove so; for else they will be destitute enough. Things are settled so oddly.'

'You allude perhaps to the entail of this estate.'

'Ah! sir, I do indeed. It is a grievous affair to my poor girls, you must confess. Not that I mean to find fault with *you*, for such things I know are all chance in this world. There is no knowing how estates will go when once they come to be entailed.'

'I am very sensible, madam, of the hardship to my fair cousins, and could say much on the subject, but that I am cautious of appearing forward and precipitate. But I can assure the young ladies that I come prepared to admire them. At present I will not say more, but perhaps when we are better acquainted – '

He was interrupted by a summons to dinner; and the girls smiled on each other. They were not the only objects of Mr Collins's admiration. The hall, the dining-room, and all its furniture were examined and praised; and his commendation of everything

would have touched Mrs Bennet's heart, but for the
mortifying supposition of his viewing it all as his own
future property. The dinner too in its turn was highly
admired; and he begged to know to which of his fair
cousins, the excellence of its cookery was owing. But
here he was set right by Mrs Bennet, who assured him
with some asperity that they were very well able to
keep a good cook, and that her daughters had nothing
to do in the kitchen. He begged pardon for having
displeased her. In a softened tone she declared herself
not at all offended; but he continued to apologise for
about a quarter of an hour.

Chapter 14

During dinner, Mr Bennet scarcely spoke at all; but
when the servants were withdrawn, he thought it time
to have some conversation with his guest, and therefore started a subject in which he expected him to
shine, by observing that he seemed very fortunate in
his patroness. Lady Catherine de Bourgh's attention
to his wishes, and consideration for his comfort,
appeared very remarkable. Mr Bennet could not have
chosen better. Mr Collins was eloquent in her praise.
The subject elevated him to more than usual solemnity
of manner, and with a most important aspect he
protested that he had never in his life witnessed such
behaviour in a person of rank – such affability and
condescension, as he had himself experienced from
Lady Catherine. She had been graciously pleased to
approve of both the discourses, which he had already
had the honour of preaching before her. She had
also asked him twice to dine at Rosings, and had sent

for him only the Saturday before, to make up her pool of quadrille in the evening. Lady Catherine was reckoned proud by many people he knew, but *he* had never seen anything but affability in her. She had always spoken to him as she would to any other gentleman; she made not the smallest objection to his joining in the society of the neighbourhood, nor to his leaving his parish occasionally for a week or two, to visit his relations. She had even condescended to advise him to marry as soon as he could, provided he chose with discretion; and had once paid him a visit in his humble parsonage; where she had perfectly approved all the alterations he had been making, and had even vouchsafed to suggest some herself – some shelves in the closets upstairs.'

'That is all very proper and civil, I am sure,' said Mrs Bennet, 'and I dare say she is a very agreeable woman. It is a pity that great ladies in general are not more like her. Does she live near you, sir?'

'The garden in which stands my humble abode, is separated only by a lane from Rosings Park, her ladyship's residence.'

'I think you said she was a widow, sir? has she any family?'

'She has one only daughter, the heiress of Rosings, and of very extensive property.'

'Ah!' cried Mrs Bennet, shaking her head, 'then she is better off than many girls. And what sort of young lady is she? Is she handsome?'

'She is a most charming young lady indeed. Lady Catherine herself says that in point of true beauty, Miss De Bourgh is far superior to the handsomest of her sex; because there is that in her features which marks the young woman of distinguished birth. She is unfortunately of a sickly constitution, which has prevented her making that progress in many accomplishments, which she could not otherwise have failed of; as I am informed by the lady who superintended her education, and who still resides with them. But she is perfectly amiable, and often condescends to drive by my humble abode in her little phaeton and ponies.'

'Has she been presented? I do not remember her name among the ladies at court.'

'Her indifferent state of health unhappily prevents her being in town; and by that means, as I told Lady Catherine myself one day, has deprived the British court of its brightest ornament. Her ladyship seemed pleased with the idea, and you may imagine that I am happy on every occasion to offer those little delicate compliments which are always acceptable to ladies. I have more than once observed to Lady Catherine, that her charming daughter seemed born to be a duchess, and that the most elevated rank, instead of giving her consequence, would be adorned by her. These are the kind of little things which please her ladyship, and it is a sort of attention which I conceive myself peculiarly bound to pay.'

'You judge very properly,' said Mr Bennet, 'and it is happy for you that you possess the talent of flattering with delicacy. May I ask whether these pleasing attentions proceed from the impulse of the moment, or are the result of previous study?'

'They arise chiefly from what is passing at the time, and though I sometimes amuse myself with suggesting and arranging such little elegant compliments as may be adapted to ordinary occasions, I always wish to give them as unstudied an air as possible.'

Mr Bennet's expectations were fully answered. His

cousin was as absurd as he had hoped, and he listened to him with the keenest enjoyment, maintaining at the same time the most resolute composure of countenance, and except in an occasional glance at Elizabeth, requiring no partner in his pleasure.

By teatime however the dose had been enough, and Mr Bennet was glad to take his guest into the drawing-room again, and when tea was over, glad to invite him to read aloud to the ladies. Mr Collins readily assented, and a book was produced; but on beholding it, (for everything announced it to be from a circulating library), he started back, and begging pardon, protested that he never read novels. Kitty stared at him, and Lydia exclaimed. Other books were produced, and after some deliberation he chose Fordyce's Sermons. Lydia gaped as he opened the volume, and before he had, with very monotonous solemnity, read three pages, she interrupted him with, 'Do you know, mama, that my uncle Philips talks of turning away Richard, and if he does, Colonel Forster will hire him. My aunt told me so herself on Saturday. I shall walk to Meryton tomorrow to hear more about it, and to ask when Mr Denny comes back from town.'

Lydia was bid by her two eldest sisters to hold her tongue; but Mr Collins, much offended, laid aside his book, and said, 'I have often observed how little young ladies are interested by books of a serious stamp, though written solely for their benefit. It amazes me, I confess – for certainly, there can be nothing so advantageous to them as instruction. But I will no longer importune my young cousin.'

Then turning to Mr Bennet, he offered himself as his antagonist at backgammon. Mr Bennet accepted the

He started back, and begging pardon, protested
that he never read novels

challenge, observing that he acted very wisely in leaving the girls to their own trifling amusements. Mrs Bennet and her daughters apologised most civilly for Lydia's interruption, and promised that it should not occur again, if he would resume his book; but Mr Collins, after assuring them that he bore his young cousin no ill will, and should never resent her behaviour as any affront, seated himself at another table with Mr Bennet, and prepared for backgammon.

Chapter 15

Mr Collins was not a sensible man, and the deficiency of nature had been but little assisted by education or society; the greatest part of his life having been spent under the guidance of an illiterate and miserly father; and though he belonged to one of the universities, he had merely kept the necessary terms, without forming at it any useful acquaintance. The subjection in which his father had brought him up, had given him originally great humility of manner, but it was now a good deal counteracted by the self-conceit of a weak head, living in retirement, and the consequential feelings of early and unexpected prosperity. A fortunate chance had recommended him to Lady Catherine de Bourgh when the living of Hunsford was vacant; and the respect which he felt for her high rank, and his veneration for her as his patroness, mingling with a very good opinion of himself, of his authority as a clergyman, and his rights as a rector, made him altogether a mixture of pride and obsequiousness, self-importance and humility.

Having now a good house and very sufficient income,

he intended to marry; and in seeking a reconciliation with the Longbourn family he had a wife in view, as he meant to choose one of the daughters, if he found them as handsome and amiable as they were represented by common report. This was his plan of amends – of atonement – for inheriting their father's estate; and he thought it an excellent one, full of eligibility and suitableness, and excessively generous and disinterested on his own part.

His plan did not vary on seeing them. Miss Bennet's lovely face confirmed his views, and established all his strictest notions of what was due to seniority; and for the first evening *she* was his settled choice. The next morning, however, made an alteration; for in a quarter of an hour's tête-à-tête with Mrs Bennet before breakfast, a conversation beginning with his parsonage-house, and leading naturally to the avowal of his hopes, that a mistress for it might be found at Longbourn, produced from her, amid very complaisant smiles and general encouragement, a caution against the very Jane he had fixed on. 'As to her *younger* daughters she could not take upon her to say – she could not positively answer – but she did not *know* of any prepossession – her *eldest* daughter, she must just mention – she felt it incumbent on her to hint, was likely to be very soon engaged.'

Mr Collins had only to change from Jane to Elizabeth – and it was soon done – done while Mrs Bennet was stirring the fire. Elizabeth, equally next to Jane in birth and beauty, succeeded her of course.

Mrs Bennet treasured up the hint, and trusted that she might soon have two daughters married; and the man whom she could not bear to speak of the day before, was now high in her good graces.

Lydia's intention of walking to Meryton was not forgotten; every sister except Mary agreed to go with her; and Mr Collins was to attend them, at the request of Mr Bennet, who was most anxious to get rid of him, and have his library to himself; for thither Mr Collins had followed him after breakfast, and there he would continue, nominally engaged with one of the largest folios in the collection, but really talking to Mr Bennet, with little cessation, of his house and garden at Hunsford. Such doings discomposed Mr Bennet exceedingly. In his library he had been always sure of leisure and tranquillity; and though prepared, as he told Elizabeth, to meet with folly and conceit in every other room in the house, he was used to be free from them there; his civility, therefore, was most prompt in inviting Mr Collins to join his daughters in their walk; and Mr Collins, being in fact much better fitted for a walker than a reader, was extremely well pleased to close his large book, and go.

In pompous nothings on his side, and civil assents on that of his cousins, their time passed till they entered Meryton. The attention of the younger ones was then no longer to be gained by *him*. Their eyes were immediately wandering up in the street in quest of the officers, and nothing less than a very smart bonnet indeed, or a really new muslin in a shop window, could recall them.

But the attention of every lady was soon caught by a young man, whom they had never seen before, of most gentlemanlike appearance, walking with an officer on the other side of the way. The officer was the very Mr Denny, concerning whose return from London Lydia came to enquire, and he bowed as they passed. All were struck with the stranger's air, all wondered who he could be, and Kitty and Lydia, determined if possible to find out, led the way across the street, under pretence of wanting something in an opposite shop, and fortunately had just gained the pavement when the two gentlemen turning back had reached the same spot. Mr Denny addressed them directly, and entreated permission to introduce his friend, Mr Wickham, who had returned with him the day before from town, and he was happy to say had accepted a commission in their corps. This was exactly as it should be; for the young man wanted only regimentals to make him completely charming. His appearance was greatly in his favour; he had all the best part of beauty, a fine countenance, a good figure, and very pleasing address. The introduction was followed up on his side by a happy readiness of conversation – a readiness at the same time perfectly correct and unassuming; and the whole party were still standing and talking together very agreeably, when the sound of horses drew their notice, and Darcy and Bingley were seen riding down the street. On distinguishing the ladies of the group, the two gentlemen came directly towards them, and began the usual civilities. Bingley was the principal spokesman, and Miss Bennet the principal object. He was then, he said, on his way to Longbourn on purpose to enquire after her. Mr Darcy corroborated it with a bow, and was beginning to determine not to fix his eyes on Elizabeth, when they were suddenly arrested by the sight of the stranger, and Elizabeth happening to see the countenance of both as they looked at each other, was all astonishment at the effect of the meeting. Both changed colour, one looked white, the other red. Mr Wickham, after a few moments, touched his hat – a salutation which Mr Darcy just deigned to return.

What could be the meaning of it? – It was impossible to imagine; it was impossible not to long to know.

In another minute Mr Bingley, but without seeming to have noticed what passed, took leave and rode on with his friend.

Mr Denny and Mr Wickham walked with the young ladies to the door of Mr Philips's house, and then made their bows, in spite of Miss Lydia's pressing entreaties that they would come in, and even in spite of Mrs Philips throwing up the parlour window, and loudly seconding the invitation.

Mrs Philips was always glad to see her nieces, and the two eldest, from their recent absence, were particularly welcome, and she was eagerly expressing her surprise at their sudden return home, which, as their own carriage had not fetched them, she should have known nothing about, if she had not happened to see Mr Jones's shop boy in the street, who had told her that they were not to send any more draughts to Netherfield because the Miss Bennets were come away, when her civility was claimed towards Mr Collins by Jane's introduction of him. She received him with her very best politeness, which he returned with as much more, apologising for his intrusion, without any previous acquaintance with her, which he could not help flattering himself however might be justified by his relationship to the young ladies who introduced him to her notice. Mrs Philips was quite awed by such an excess of good breeding; but her contemplation of one stranger was soon put an end to by exclamations and enquiries about the other, of whom, however, she could only tell her nieces what they already knew, that Mr Denny had brought him from London, and that he was to have a lieutenant's commission in the —shire.

She had been watching him the last hour, she said, as he walked up and down the street, and had Mr Wickham appeared Kitty and Lydia would certainly have continued the occupation, but unluckily no one passed the windows now except a few of the officers, who in comparison with the stranger, were become 'stupid, disagreeable fellows'. Some of them were to dine with the Philipses the next day, and their aunt promised to make her husband call on Mr Wickham, and give him an invitation also, if the family from Longbourn would come in the evening. This was agreed to, and Mrs Philips protested that they would have a nice comfortable noisy game of lottery tickets, and a little bit of hot supper afterwards. The prospect of such delights was very cheering, and they parted in mutual good spirits. Mr Collins repeated his apologies in quitting the room, and was assured with unwearying civility that they were perfectly needless.

As they walked home, Elizabeth related to Jane what she had seen pass between the two gentlemen; but though Jane would have defended either or both, had they appeared to be wrong, she could no more explain such behaviour than her sister.

Mr Collins on his return highly gratified Mrs Bennet by admiring Mrs Philips's manners and politeness. He protested that except Lady Catherine and her daughter, he had never seen a more elegant woman; for she had not only received him with the utmost civility, but had even pointedly included him in her invitation for the next evening, although utterly unknown to her before. Something he supposed might be attributed to his connection with them, but yet he had never met with so much attention in the whole course of his life.

Chapter 16

As no objection was made to the young people's engagement with their aunt, and all Mr Collins's scruples of leaving Mr and Mrs Bennet for a single evening during his visit were most steadily resisted, the coach conveyed him and his five cousins at a suitable hour to Meryton; and the girls had the pleasure of hearing, as they entered the drawing-room, that Mr Wickham had accepted their uncle's invitation, and was then in the house.

When this information was given, and they had all taken their seats, Mr Collins was at leisure to look around him and admire, and he was so much struck with the size and furniture of the apartment, that he declared he might almost have supposed himself in the small summer breakfast parlour at Rosings; a comparison that did not at first convey much gratification; but when Mrs Philips understood from him what Rosings was, and who was its proprietor, when she had listened to the description of only one of Lady Catherine's drawing-rooms, and found that the chimney-piece alone had cost eight hundred pounds, she felt all the force of the compliment, and would hardly have resented a comparison with the house-keeper's room.

In describing to her all the grandeur of Lady Catherine and her mansion, with occasional digressions in praise of his own humble abode, and the improvements it was receiving, he was happily employed until the gentlemen joined them; and he found in Mrs Philips a very attentive listener, whose opinion of his

To examine their own indifferent imitations of china on the mantelpiece

consequence increased with what she heard, and who was resolving to retail it all among her neighbours as soon as she could. To the girls, who could not listen to their cousin, and who had nothing to do but to wish for an instrument, and examine their own indifferent imitations of china on the mantelpiece, the interval of waiting appeared very long. It was over at last however. The gentlemen did approach; and when Mr Wickham walked into the room, Elizabeth felt that she had neither been seeing him before, nor thinking of him since, with the smallest degree of unreasonable admiration. The officers of the —shire were in general a very creditable, gentlemanlike set, and the best of them were of the present party; but Mr Wickham was as far beyond them all in person, countenance, air, and walk, as *they* were superior to the broad-faced stuffy uncle Philips, breathing port wine, who followed them into the room.

Mr Wickham was the happy man towards whom almost every female eye was turned, and Elizabeth was the happy woman by whom he finally seated himself; and the agreeable manner in which he immediately fell into conversation, though it was only on its being a wet night, and on the probability of a rainy season, made her feel that the commonest, dullest, most threadbare topic might be rendered interesting by the skill of the speaker.

With such rivals for the notice of the fair, as Mr Wickham and the officers, Mr Collins seemed likely to sink into insignificance; to the young ladies he certainly was nothing; but he had still at intervals a kind listener in Mrs Philips, and was, by her watchfulness, most abundantly supplied with coffee and muffin.

When the card-tables were placed, he had an

*The officers of the —shire were in general a very
creditable, gentlemanlike set*

opportunity of obliging her in return, by sitting down to whist.

'I know little of the game, at present,' said he, 'but I shall be glad to improve myself, for in my situation of life – ' Mrs Philips was very thankful for his compliance, but could not wait for his reason.

Mr Wickham did not play at whist, and with ready delight was he received at the other table between Elizabeth and Lydia. At first there seemed danger of Lydia's engrossing him entirely, for she was a most determined talker; but being likewise extremely fond of lottery tickets, she soon grew too much interested in the game, too eager in making bets and exclaiming after prizes, to have attention for anyone in particular. Allowing for the common demands of the game, Mr Wickham was therefore at leisure to talk to Elizabeth, and she was very willing to hear him, though what she chiefly wished to hear she could not hope to be told, the history of his acquaintance with Mr Darcy. She dared not even mention that gentleman. Her curiosity however was unexpectedly relieved. Mr Wickham began the subject himself. He enquired how far Netherfield was from Meryton; and, after receiving her answer, asked in an hesitating manner how long Mr Darcy had been staying there.

'About a month,' said Elizabeth; and then, unwilling to let the subject drop, added, 'He is a man of very large property in Derbyshire, I understand.'

'Yes,' replied Wickham – 'his estate there is a noble one. A clear ten thousand per annum. You could not have met with a person more capable of giving you certain information on that head than myself – for I have been connected with his family in a particular manner from my infancy.'

Elizabeth could not but look surprised.

'You may well be surprised, Miss Bennet, at such an assertion, after seeing, as you probably might, the very cold manner of our meeting yesterday. Are you much acquainted with Mr Darcy?'

'As much as I ever wish to be,' cried Elizabeth warmly, 'I have spent four days in the same house with him, and I think him very disagreeable.'

'I have no right to give *my* opinion,' said Wickham, 'as to his being agreeable or otherwise. I am not qualified to form one. I have known him too long and too well to be a fair judge. It is impossible for *me* to be impartial. But I believe your opinion of him would in general astonish – and perhaps you would not express it quite so strongly anywhere else. Here you are in your own family.'

'Upon my word I say no more *here* than I might say in any house in the neighbourhood, except Netherfield. He is not at all liked in Hertfordshire. Everybody is disgusted with his pride. You will not find him more favourably spoken of by anyone.'

'I cannot pretend to be sorry,' said Wickham, after a short interruption, 'that he or that any man should not be estimated beyond their deserts; but with *him* I believe it does not often happen. The world is blinded by his fortune and consequence, or frightened by his high and imposing manners, and sees him only as he chooses to be seen.'

'I should take him, even on *my* slight acquaintance, to be an ill-tempered man.' Wickham only shook his head.

'I wonder,' said he, at the next opportunity of speaking, 'whether he is likely to be in this country much longer.'

'I do not at all know; but I *heard* nothing of his going away when I was at Netherfield. I hope your plans in favour of the —shire will not be affected by his being in the neighbourhood.'

'Oh! no – it is not for *me* to be driven away by Mr Darcy. If *he* wishes to avoid seeing *me*, he must go. We are not on friendly terms, and it always gives me pain to meet him, but I have no reason for avoiding *him* but what I might proclaim to all the world; a sense of very great ill usage, and most painful regrets at his being what he is. His father, Miss Bennet, the late Mr Darcy, was one of the best men that ever breathed, and the truest friend I ever had; and I can never be in company with this Mr Darcy without being grieved to the soul by a thousand tender recollections. His behaviour to myself has been scandalous; but I verily believe I could forgive him anything and everything, rather than his disappointing the hopes and disgracing the memory of his father.'

Elizabeth found the interest of the subject increase, and listened with all her heart; but the delicacy of it prevented farther enquiry.

Mr Wickham began to speak on more general topics, Meryton, the neighbourhood, the society, appearing highly pleased with all that he had yet seen, and speaking of the latter especially, with gentle but very intelligible gallantry.

'It was the prospect of constant society, and good society,' he added, 'which was my chief inducement to enter the —shire. I knew it to be a most respectable, agreeable corps, and my friend Denny tempted me farther by his account of their present quarters, and the very great attentions and excellent acquaintance Meryton had procured them. Society, I own, is necessary to me. I have been a disappointed man, and my spirits will not bear solitude. I *must* have employment and society. A military life is not what I was intended for, but circumstances have now made it eligible. The church *ought* to have been my profession – I was brought up for the church, and I should at this time have been in possession of a most valuable living, had it pleased the gentleman we were speaking of just now.'

'Indeed!'

'Yes – the late Mr Darcy bequeathed me the next presentation of the best living in his gift. He was my godfather, and excessively attached to me. I cannot do justice to his kindness. He meant to provide for me amply, and thought he had done it; but when the living fell, it was given elsewhere.'

'Good heavens!' cried Elizabeth; 'but how could *that* be? – How could his will be disregarded? – Why did not you seek legal redress?'

'There was just such an informality in the terms of the bequest as to give me no hope from law. A man of honour could not have doubted the intention, but Mr Darcy chose to doubt it – or to treat it as a merely conditional recommendation, and to assert that I had forfeited all claim to it by extravagance, imprudence, in short anything or nothing. Certain it is, that the living became vacant two years ago, exactly as I was of an age to hold it, and that it was given to another man; and no less certain is it, that I cannot accuse myself of having really done anything to deserve to lose it. I have a warm, unguarded temper, and I may perhaps have sometimes spoken my opinion *of* him, and *to* him, too freely. I can recall nothing worse. But the fact is, that we are very different sort of men, and that he hates me.'

'This is quite shocking! – He deserves to be publicly disgraced.'

'Sometime or other he *will* be – but it shall not be by *me*. Till I can forget his father, I can never defy or expose *him*.'

Elizabeth honoured him for such feelings, and thought him handsomer than ever as he expressed them.

'But what,' said she, after a pause, 'can have been his motive? – what can have induced him to behave so cruelly?'

'A thorough, determined dislike of me – a dislike which I cannot but attribute in some measure to jealousy. Had the late Mr Darcy liked me less, his son might have borne with me better; but his father's uncommon attachment to me, irritated him I believe very early in life. He had not a temper to bear the sort of competition in which we stood – the sort of preference which was often given me.'

'I had not thought Mr Darcy so bad as this – though I have never liked him, I had not thought so very ill of him – I had supposed him to be despising his fellow-creatures in general, but did not suspect him of descending to such malicious revenge, such injustice, such inhumanity as this!'

After a few minutes reflection, however, she continued, 'I *do* remember his boasting one day, at Netherfield, of the implacability of his resentments, of his having an unforgiving temper. His disposition must be dreadful.'

'I will not trust myself on the subject,' replied Wickham, '*I* can hardly be just to him.'

Elizabeth was again deep in thought, and after a time exclaimed, 'To treat in such a manner, the godson, the friend, the favourite of his father!' – She could have added, 'A young man too, like *you*, whose very countenance may vouch for your being amiable' – but she contented herself with 'And one, too, who had probably been his own companion from childhood, connected together, as I think you said, in the closest manner!'

'We were born in the same parish, within the same park, the greatest part of our youth was passed together; inmates of the same house, sharing the same amusements, objects of the same parental care. *My* father began life in the profession which your uncle Mr Philips, appears to do so much credit to – but he gave up everything to be of use to the late Mr Darcy, and devoted all his time to the care of the Pemberley property. He was most highly esteemed by Mr Darcy, a most intimate, confidential friend. Mr Darcy often acknowledged himself to be under the greatest obligations to my father's active superintendence, and when immediately before my father's death, Mr Darcy gave him a voluntary promise of providing for me, I am convinced that he felt it to be as much a debt of gratitude to *him*, as of affection to myself.'

'How strange!' cried Elizabeth. 'How abominable! – I wonder that the very pride of this Mr Darcy has not made him just to you! – If from no better motive, that he should not have been too proud to be dishonest – for dishonesty I must call it.'

'It *is* wonderful – ,' replied Wickham, 'for almost all his actions may be traced to pride – and pride has often been his best friend. It has connected him nearer with virtue than any other feeling. But we are none of us consistent; and in his behaviour to me, there were stronger impulses even than pride.'

'Can such abominable pride as his, have ever done him good?'

'Yes. It has often led him to be liberal and generous – to give his money freely, to display hospitality, to assist his tenants, and relieve the poor. Family pride, and *filial* pride, for he is very proud of what his father was, have done this. Not to appear to disgrace his family, to degenerate from the popular qualities, or lose the influence of the Pemberley House, is a powerful motive. He has also *brotherly* pride, which with *some* brotherly affection, makes him a very kind and careful guardian of his sister; and you will hear him generally cried up as the most attentive and best of brothers.'

'What sort of a girl is Miss Darcy?'

He shook his head – 'I wish I could call her amiable. It gives me pain to speak ill of a Darcy. But she is too much like her brother – very, very proud. As a child, she was affectionate and pleasing, and extremely fond of me; and I have devoted hours and hours to her amusement. But she is nothing to me now. She is a handsome girl, about fifteen or sixteen, and I under-stand highly accomplished. Since her father's death, her home has been London, where a lady lives with her, and superintends her education.'

After many pauses and many trials of other subjects, Elizabeth could not help reverting once more to the first, and saying, 'I am astonished at his intimacy with Mr Bingley! How can Mr Bingley, who seems good humour itself, and is, I really believe, truly amiable, be in friendship with such a man? How can they suit each other? – Do you know Mr Bingley?'

'Not at all.'

'He is a sweet tempered, amiable, charming man. He cannot know what Mr Darcy is.'

'Probably not – but Mr Darcy can please where he chooses. He does not want abilities. He can be a conversable companion if he thinks it worth his while. Among those who are at all his equals in consequence, he is a very different man from what he is to the less prosperous. His pride never deserts him; but with the rich, he is liberal-minded, just, sincere, rational, honourable, and perhaps agreeable – allowing something for fortune and figure.'

The whist party soon afterwards breaking up, the players gathered round the other table, and Mr Collins took his station between his cousin Elizabeth and Mrs Philips. The usual enquiries as to his success were made by the latter. It had not been very great; he had lost every point; but when Mrs Philips began to express her concern thereupon, he assured her with much earnest gravity that it was not of the least importance, that he considered the money as a mere trifle, and begged she would not make herself uneasy.

'I know very well, madam,' said he, 'that when persons sit down to a card table, they must take their chance of these things – and happily I am not in such circumstances as to make five shillings any object. There are undoubtedly many who could not say the same, but thanks to Lady Catherine de Bourgh, I am removed far beyond the necessity of regarding little matters.'

Mr Wickham's attention was caught; and after observing Mr Collins for a few moments, he asked Elizabeth in a low voice whether her relation were very intimately acquainted with the family of de Bourgh.

'Lady Catherine de Bourgh,' she replied, 'has very lately given him a living. I hardly know how Mr Collins was first introduced to her notice, but he certainly has not known her long.'

'You know of course that Lady Catherine de Bourgh and Lady Anne Darcy were sisters; consequently that she is aunt to the present Mr Darcy.'

'No, indeed, I did not. I knew nothing at all of Lady Catherine's connections. I never heard of her existence till the day before yesterday.'

'Her daughter, Miss de Bourgh, will have a very large fortune, and it is believed that she and her cousin will unite the two estates.'

This information made Elizabeth smile, as she thought of poor Miss Bingley. Vain indeed must be all her attentions, vain and useless her affection for his sister and her praise of himself, if he were already self-destined to another.

'Mr Collins,' said she, 'speaks highly both of Lady Catherine and her daughter; but from some particulars that he has related of her ladyship, I suspect his gratitude misleads him, and that in spite of her being his patroness, she is an arrogant, conceited woman.'

'I believe her to be both in a great degree,' replied Wickham; 'I have not seen her for many years, but I very well remember that I never liked her, and that her manners were dictatorial and insolent. She has the reputation of being remarkably sensible and clever; but I rather believe she derives part of her abilities from her rank and fortune, part from her authoritative manner, and the rest from the pride of her nephew, who chooses that everyone connected with him should have an understanding of the first class.'

Elizabeth allowed that he had given a very rational account of it, and they continued talking together with mutual satisfaction till supper put an end to cards; and gave the rest of the ladies their share of Mr Wickham's attentions. There could be no conversation in the noise of Mrs Philips's supper party, but his manners recommended him to everybody. Whatever he said, was said well; and whatever he did, done gracefully. Elizabeth went away with her head full of him. She could think of nothing but of Mr Wickham, and of what he had told her, all the way home; but there was not time for her even to mention his name as they went, for neither Lydia nor Mr Collins were once silent. Lydia talked incessantly of lottery tickets, of the fish she had lost and the fish she had won, and Mr Collins, in describing the civility of Mr and Mrs Philips, protesting that he did not in the least regard his losses at whist, enumerating all the dishes at supper, and repeatedly fearing that he crowded his cousins, had more to say than he could well manage before the carriage stopped at Longbourn House.

Chapter 17

Elizabeth related to Jane the next day, what had passed between Mr Wickham and herself. Jane listened with astonishment and concern – she knew not how to believe that Mr Darcy could be so unworthy of Mr Bingley's regard; and yet, it was not in her nature to question the veracity of a young man of such amiable appearance as Wickham. The possibility of his having really endured such unkindness, was enough to interest all her tender feelings; and nothing therefore remained to be done, but to think well of them both, to defend the conduct of each, and throw into the account of accident or mistake, whatever could not be otherwise explained.

'They have both,' said she, 'been deceived, I dare

say, in some way or other, of which we can form no idea. Interested people have perhaps misrepresented each to the other. It is, in short, impossible for us to conjecture the causes or circumstances which may have alienated them, without actual blame on either side.'

'Very true, indeed – and now, my dear Jane, what have you got to say in behalf of the interested people who have probably been concerned in the business? – Do clear *them* too, or we shall be obliged to think ill of somebody.'

'Laugh as much as you choose, but you will not laugh me out of my opinion. My dearest Lizzy, do but consider in what a disgraceful light it places Mr Darcy, to be treating his father's favourite in such a manner – one, whom his father had promised to provide for. It is impossible. No man of common humanity, no man who had any value for his character, could be capable of it. Can his most intimate friends be so excessively deceived in him? oh! no.'

'I can much more easily believe Mr Bingley's being imposed on, than that Mr Wickham should invent such a history of himself as he gave me last night; names, facts, everything mentioned without ceremony. If it be not so, let Mr Darcy contradict it. Besides, there was truth in his looks.'

'It is difficult indeed – it is distressing. One does not know what to think.'

'I beg your pardon – one knows exactly what to think.'

But Jane could think with certainty on only one point – that Mr Bingley, if he *had been* imposed on, would have much to suffer when the affair became public.

The two young ladies were summoned from the shrubbery where this conversation passed, by the arrival of some of the very persons of whom they had been speaking; Mr Bingley and his sisters came to give their personal invitation for the long expected ball at Netherfield, which was fixed for the following Tuesday. The two ladies were delighted to see their dear friend again, called it an age since they had met, and repeatedly asked what she had been doing with herself since their separation. To the rest of the family they paid little attention; avoiding Mrs Bennet as much as possible, saying not much to Elizabeth, and nothing at all to the others. They were soon gone

The two ladies were delighted to see their dear friend again

again, rising from their seats with an activity which took their brother by surprise, and hurrying off as if eager to escape from Mrs Bennet's civilities.

The prospect of the Netherfield ball was extremely agreeable to every female of the family. Mrs Bennet chose to consider it as given in compliment to her eldest daughter, and was particularly flattered by receiving the invitation from Mr Bingley himself, instead of a ceremonious card. Jane pictured to herself a happy evening in the society of her two friends, and the attentions of their brother; and Elizabeth thought with pleasure of dancing a great deal with Mr Wickham, and of seeing a confirmation of everything in Mr Darcy's looks and behaviour. The happiness anticipated by Catherine and Lydia, depended less on any single event, or any particular person, for though they each, like Elizabeth, meant to dance half the evening with Mr Wickham, he was by no means the only partner who could satisfy them, and a ball was at any rate, a ball. And even Mary could assure her family that she had no disinclination for it.

'While I can have my mornings to myself,' said she, 'it is enough. I think it no sacrifice to join occasionally in evening engagements. Society has claims on us all; and I profess myself one of those who consider intervals of recreation and amusement as desirable for everybody.'

Elizabeth's spirits were so high on the occasion, that though she did not often speak unnecessarily to Mr Collins, she could not help asking him whether he intended to accept Mr Bingley's invitation, and if he did, whether he would think it proper to join in the evening's amusement; and she was rather surprised to find that he entertained no scruple whatever on that head, and was very far from dreading a rebuke either from the Archbishop, or Lady Catherine de Bourgh, by venturing to dance.

'I am by no means of opinion, I assure you,' said he, 'that a ball of this kind, given by a young man of character, to respectable people, can have any evil tendency; and I am so far from objecting to dancing myself that I shall hope to be honoured with the hands of all my fair cousins in the course of the evening, and I take this opportunity of soliciting yours, Miss Elizabeth, for the two first dances especially – a preference which I trust my cousin Jane will attribute to the right cause, and not to any disrespect for her.'

Elizabeth felt herself completely taken in. She had fully proposed being engaged by Wickham for those very dances – and to have Mr Collins instead! her liveliness had been never worse timed. There was no help for it however. Mr Wickham's happiness and her own was per force delayed a little longer, and Mr Collins's proposal accepted with as good a grace as she could. She was not the better pleased with his gallantry, from the idea it suggested of something more. It now first struck her, that *she* was selected from among her sisters as worthy of being the mistress of Hunsford Parsonage, and of assisting to form a quadrille table at Rosings, in the absence of more eligible visitors. The idea soon reached to conviction, as she observed his increasing civilities toward herself, and heard his frequent attempt at a compliment on her wit and vivacity; and though more astonished than gratified herself, by this effect of her charms, it was not long before her mother gave her to understand that the probability of their marriage was exceedingly agreeable to *her*. Elizabeth however did not choose to take the hint, being well aware that a serious dispute must be the consequence of any reply. Mr Collins might never make the offer, and till he did, it was useless to quarrel about him.

If there had not been a Netherfield ball to prepare for and talk of, the younger Miss Bennets would have been in a pitiable state at this time, for from the day of the invitation, to the day of the ball, there was such a succession of rain as prevented their walking to Meryton once. No aunt, no officers, no news could be sought after – the very shoe-roses for Netherfield were got by proxy. Even Elizabeth might have found some trial of her patience in weather, which totally suspended the improvement of her acquaintance with Mr Wickham; and nothing less than a dance on Tuesday, could have made such a Friday, Saturday, Sunday and Monday, endurable to Kitty and Lydia.

Chapter 18

Till Elizabeth entered the drawing-room at Nether-field and looked in vain for Mr Wickham among the cluster of red coats there assembled, a doubt of his being present had never occurred to her. The certainty of meeting him had not been checked by any of those recollections that might not unreasonably have alarmed her. She had dressed with more than usual care, and prepared in the highest spirits for the conquest of all that remained unsubdued of his heart, trusting that it was not more than might be won in the course of the evening. But in an instant arose the dreadful suspicion of his being purposely omitted for Mr Darcy's pleasure in the Bingleys' invitation to the officers; and though this was not exactly the case, the absolute fact of his absence was pronounced by his friend Mr Denny, to whom Lydia eagerly applied, and who told them that Wickham had been obliged to go to town on business the day before, and was not yet returned; adding, with a significant smile, 'I do not imagine his business would have called him away just now, if he had not wished to avoid a certain gentleman here.'

This part of his intelligence, though unheard by Lydia, was caught by Elizabeth, and as it assured her that Darcy was not less answerable for Wickham's absence than if her first surmise had been just, every feeling of displeasure against the former was so sharpened by immediate disappointment, that she could hardly reply with tolerable civility to the polite enquiries which he directly afterwards approached to make. Attention, forbearance, patience with Darcy, was injury to Wickham. She was resolved against any sort of conversation with him, and turned away with a degree of ill humour, which she could not wholly surmount even in speaking to Mr Bingley, whose blind partiality provoked her.

But Elizabeth was not formed for ill-humour; and though every prospect of her own was destroyed for the evening, it could not dwell long on her spirits; and having told all her griefs to Charlotte Lucas, whom she had not seen for a week, she was soon able to make a voluntary transition to the oddities of her cousin, and to point him out to her particular notice. The two first dances, however, brought a return of distress; they were dances of mortification. Mr Collins, awkward and solemn, apologising instead of attending, and often moving wrong without being aware of it, gave her all the shame and misery which a disagree-able partner for a couple of dances can give. The moment of her release from him was ecstasy.

She danced next with an officer, and had the refreshment of talking of Wickham, and of hearing that he was universally liked. When those dances were over she returned to Charlotte Lucas, and was in conversation with her, when she found herself suddenly addressed by Mr Darcy, who took her so much by surprise in his application for her hand, that, without knowing what she did, she accepted him. He walked away again immediately, and she was left to fret over her own want of presence of mind; Charlotte tried to console her.

'I dare say you will find him very agreeable.'

'Heaven forbid! – *That* would be the greatest misfortune of all! – To find a man agreeable whom one is determined to hate! – Do not wish me such an evil.'

When the dancing recommenced, however, and Darcy approached to claim her hand, Charlotte could not help cautioning her in a whisper not to be a simpleton and allow her fancy for Wickham to make her appear unpleasant in the eyes of a man of ten times his consequence. Elizabeth made no answer, and took her place in the set, amazed at the dignity to which she was arrived in being allowed to stand opposite to Mr Darcy, and reading in her neighbours' looks their equal amazement in beholding it. They stood for some time without speaking a word; and she began to imagine that their silence was to last through the two dances, and at first was resolved not to break it; till suddenly fancying that it would be the greater punishment to her partner to oblige him to talk, she made some slight observation on the dance. He replied, and was again silent. After a pause of some minutes she addressed him a second time with

'It is *your* turn to say something now, Mr Darcy – I talked about the dance, and *you* ought to make some kind of remark on the size of the room, or the number of couples.'

He smiled, and assured her that whatever she wished him to say should be said.

'Very well. That reply will do for the present. Perhaps by and by I may observe that private balls are much pleasanter than public ones. But *now* we may be silent.'

'Do you talk by rule then, while you are dancing?'

'Sometimes. One must speak a little, you know. It would look odd to be entirely silent for half an hour together, and yet for the advantage of *some*, conversation ought to be so arranged as that they may have the trouble of saying as little as possible.'

'Are you consulting your own feelings in the present case, or do you imagine that you are gratifying mine?'

'Both,' replied Elizabeth archly; 'for I have always seen a great similarity in the turn of our minds. We are each of an unsocial, taciturn disposition, unwilling to speak, unless we expect to say something that will amaze the whole room, and be handed down to posterity with all the éclat of a proverb.'

'This is no very striking resemblance of your own character, I am sure,' said he. 'How near it may be to *mine*, I cannot pretend to say. *You* think it a faithful portrait undoubtedly.'

'I must not decide on my own performance.'

He made no answer, and they were again silent till they had gone down the dance, when he asked her if she and her sisters did not very often walk to Meryton. She answered in the affirmative, and, unable to resist the temptation, added, 'When you met us there the other day, we had just been forming a new acquaintance.'

The effect was immediate. A deeper shade of hauteur overspread his features, but he said not a word, and Elizabeth, though blaming herself for her own weakness, could not go on. At length Darcy spoke, and in a constrained manner said, 'Mr Wickham is blessed with such happy manners as may ensure his *making* friends – whether he may be equally capable of *retaining* them, is less certain.'

'He has been so unlucky as to lose *your* friendship,' replied Elizabeth with emphasis, 'and in a manner which he is likely to suffer from all his life.'

Darcy made no answer, and seemed desirous of changing the subject. At that moment Sir William Lucas appeared close to them, meaning to pass through the set to the other side of the room; but on perceiving Mr Darcy he stopped with a bow of superior courtesy to compliment him on his dancing and his partner.

'I have been most highly gratified indeed, my dear sir. Such very superior dancing is not often seen. It is evident that you belong to the first circles. Allow me to say, however, that your fair partner does not disgrace you, and that I must hope to have this pleasure often repeated, especially when a certain desirable event, my dear Miss Eliza (glancing at her sister and Bingley), shall take place. What congratulations will then flow in! I appeal to Mr Darcy – but let me not interrupt you, sir. You will not thank me for detaining you from the bewitching converse of that young lady, whose bright eyes are also upbraiding me.'

Such very superior dancing is not often seen

The latter part of this address was scarcely heard by Darcy; but Sir William's allusion to his friend seemed to strike him forcibly, and his eyes were directed with a very serious expression towards Bingley and Jane, who were dancing together. Recovering himself, however, shortly, he turned to his partner, and said, 'Sir William's interruption has made me forget what we were talking of.'

'I do not think we were speaking at all. Sir William could not have interrupted any two people in the room who had less to say for themselves. We have tried two or three subjects already without success, and what we are to talk of next I cannot imagine.'

'What think you of books?' said he, smiling.

'Books – Oh! no. I am sure we never read the same, or not with the same feelings.'

'I am sorry you think so; but if that be the case, there can at least be no want of subject. We may compare our different opinions.'

'No – I cannot talk of books in a ballroom; my head is always full of something else.'

'The *present* always occupies you in such scenes – does it?' said he, with a look of doubt.

'Yes, always,' she replied, without knowing what she said, for her thoughts had wandered far from the subject, as soon afterwards appeared by her suddenly exclaiming, 'I remember hearing you once say, Mr Darcy, that you hardly ever forgave, that your resentment once created was unappeasable. You are very cautious, I suppose, as to its *being created*.'

'I am,' said he, with a firm voice.

'And never allow yourself to be blinded by prejudice?'

'I hope not.'

'It is particularly incumbent on those who never

change their opinion, to be secure of judging properly at first.'

'May I ask to what these questions tend?'

'Merely to the illustration of *your* character,' said she, endeavouring to shake off her gravity. 'I am trying to make it out.'

'And what is your success?'

She shook her head. 'I do not get on at all. I hear such different accounts of you as puzzle me exceedingly.'

'I can readily believe,' answered he gravely, 'that report may vary greatly with respect to me; and I could wish, Miss Bennet, that you were not to sketch my character at the present moment, as there is reason to fear that the performance would reflect no credit on either.'

'But if I do not take your likeness now, I may never have another opportunity.'

'I would by no means suspend any pleasure of yours,' he coldly replied. She said no more, and they went down the other dance and parted in silence; on each side dissatisfied, though not to an equal degree, for in Darcy's breast there was a tolerable powerful feeling towards her, which soon procured her pardon, and directed all his anger against another.

They had not long separated when Miss Bingley came towards her, and with an expression of civil disdain thus accosted her, 'So, Miss Eliza, I hear you are quite delighted with George Wickham! – Your sister has been talking to me about him, and asking me a thousand questions; and I find that the young man forgot to tell you, among his other communications, that he was the son of old Wickham, the late Mr Darcy's steward. Let me recommend you, however, as a friend, not to give implicit confidence to all his assertions; for as to Mr Darcy's using him ill, it is perfectly false; for, on the contrary, he has been always remarkably kind to him, though George Wickham has treated Mr Darcy in a most infamous manner. I do not know the particulars, but I know very well that Mr Darcy is not in the least to blame, that he cannot bear to hear George Wickham mentioned, and that though my brother thought he could not well avoid including him in his invitation to the officers, he was excessively glad to find that he had taken himself out of the way. His coming into the country at all, is a most insolent thing indeed, and I wonder how he could presume to do it. I pity you, Miss Eliza, for this discovery of your favourite's guilt; but really considering his descent, one could not expect much better.'

'His guilt and his descent appear by your account to be the same,' said Elizabeth angrily; 'for I have heard you accuse him of nothing worse than of being the son of Mr Darcy's steward, and of *that*, I can assure you, he informed me himself.'

'I beg your pardon,' replied Miss Bingley, turning away with a sneer. 'Excuse my interference. It was kindly meant.'

'Insolent girl!' said Elizabeth to herself – 'You are much mistaken if you expect to influence me by such a paltry attack as this. I see nothing in it but your own wilful ignorance and the malice of Mr Darcy.' She then sought her eldest sister, who had undertaken to make enquiries on the same subject of Bingley. Jane met her with a smile of such sweet complacency, a glow of such happy expression, as sufficiently marked how well she was satisfied with the occurrences of the evening. Elizabeth instantly read her feelings, and at that moment solicitude for Wickham, resentment against his enemies, and everything else gave way before the hope of Jane's being in the fairest way for happiness.

'I want to know,' said she, with a countenance no less smiling than her sister's, 'what you have learnt about Mr Wickham. But perhaps you have been too pleasantly engaged to think of any third person; in which case you may be sure of my pardon.'

'No,' replied Jane, 'I have not forgotten him; but I have nothing satisfactory to tell you. Mr Bingley does not know the whole of his history, and is quite ignorant of the circumstances which have principally offended Mr Darcy; but he will vouch for the good conduct, the probity and honour of his friend, and is perfectly convinced that Mr Wickham has deserved much less attention from Mr Darcy than he has received; and I am sorry to say that by his account as well as his sister's, Mr Wickham is by no means a respectable young man. I am afraid he has been very imprudent, and has deserved to lose Mr Darcy's regard.'

'Mr Bingley does not know Mr Wickham himself?'

'No; he never saw him till the other morning at Meryton.'

'This account then is what he has received from Mr Darcy. I am perfectly satisfied. But what does he say of the living?'

'He does not exactly recollect the circumstances, though he has heard them from Mr Darcy more than once, but he believes that it was left to him *conditionally* only.'

'I have not a doubt of Mr Bingley's sincerity,' said Elizabeth warmly; 'but you must excuse my not being convinced by assurances only. Mr Bingley's defence of his friend was a very able one I dare say, but since he is unacquainted with several parts of the story, and has learnt the rest from that friend himself, I shall venture still to think of both gentlemen as I did before.'

She then changed the discourse to one more gratifying to each, and on which there could be no difference of sentiment. Elizabeth listened with delight to the happy, though modest hopes which Jane entertained of Bingley's regard, and said all in her power to heighten her confidence in it. On their being joined by Mr Bingley himself, Elizabeth withdrew to Miss Lucas; to whose enquiry after the pleasantness of her last partner she had scarcely replied, before Mr Collins came up to them and told her with great exultation that he had just been so fortunate as to make a most important discovery.

'I have found out,' said he, 'by a singular accident, that there is now in the room a near relation of my patroness. I happened to overhear the gentleman himself mentioning to the young lady who does the honours of this house the names of his cousin Miss de Bourgh, and of her mother Lady Catherine. How wonderfully these sort of things occur! Who would have thought of my meeting with – perhaps – a nephew of Lady Catherine de Bourgh in this assembly! – I am most thankful that the discovery is made in time for me to pay my respects to him, which I am now going to do, and trust he will excuse my not having done it before. My total ignorance of the connection must plead my apology.'

'You are not going to introduce yourself to Mr Darcy?'

'Indeed I am. I shall entreat his pardon for not having done it earlier. I believe him to be Lady Catherine's *nephew*. It will be in my power to assure him that her ladyship was quite well yesterday se'nnight.'

Elizabeth tried hard to dissuade him from such a scheme; assuring him that Mr Darcy would consider his addressing him without introduction as an impertinent freedom, rather than a compliment to his aunt; that it was not in the least necessary there should be any notice on either side, and that if it were, it must belong to Mr Darcy, the superior in consequence, to begin the acquaintance.

Mr Collins listened to her with the determined air of following his own inclination, and when she ceased speaking, replied thus, 'My dear Miss Elizabeth, I have the highest opinion in the world of your excellent judgement in all matters within the scope of your understanding, but permit me to say that there must be a wide difference between the established forms of ceremony amongst the laity, and those which regulate the clergy; for give me leave to observe that I consider the clerical office as equal in point of dignity with the highest rank in the kingdom – provided that a proper humility of behaviour is at the same time maintained. You must therefore allow me to follow the dictates of my conscience on this occasion, which leads me to perform what I look on as a point of duty. Pardon me for neglecting to profit by your advice, which on every other subject shall be my constant guide, though in the case before us I consider myself more fitted by education and habitual study to decide on what is right than a young lady like yourself.' And with a low bow he left her to attack Mr Darcy, whose reception of his advances she eagerly watched, and whose astonishment at being so addressed was very evident. Her cousin prefaced his speech with a solemn bow, and though she could not hear a word of it, she felt as if hearing it all, and saw in the motion of his lips the words 'apology,' 'Hunsford,' and 'Lady Catherine de Bourgh.' – It vexed her to see him expose himself to such a man. Mr Darcy was eyeing him with unrestrained wonder, and when at last Mr Collins allowed him time to speak, replied with an air of distant civility. Mr Collins, however, was not discouraged from speaking again, and Mr Darcy's contempt seemed abundantly increasing with the length of his second speech, and at the end of it he only made him a slight bow, and moved another way. Mr Collins then returned to Elizabeth.

'I have no reason, I assure you,' said he, 'to be dissatisfied with my reception. Mr Darcy seemed much pleased with the attention. He answered me with the utmost civility, and even paid me the compliment of saying, that he was so well convinced of Lady Catherine's discernment as to be certain she could never bestow a favour unworthily. It was really a very handsome thought. Upon the whole, I am much pleased with him.'

As Elizabeth had no longer any interest of her own to pursue, she turned her attention almost entirely on her sister and Mr Bingley, and the train of agreeable reflections which her observations gave birth to, made her perhaps almost as happy as Jane. She saw her in idea settled in that very house in all the felicity which a marriage of true affection could bestow; and she felt capable under such circumstances, of endeavouring even to like Bingley's two sisters. Her mother's thoughts she plainly saw were bent the same way, and she determined not to venture near her, lest she might hear too much. When they sat down to supper, therefore, she considered it a most unlucky perverseness which placed them within one of each other; and deeply was she vexed to find that her mother was talking to that one person (Lady Lucas) freely, openly, and of nothing else but of her expectation that Jane would be soon married to Mr Bingley. It was an animating subject, and Mrs Bennet seemed incapable of fatigue while enumerating the advantages of the match. His being such a charming young man, and so rich, and living but three miles from them, were the first points of self-gratulation; and then it was such a comfort to think how fond the two sisters were of Jane, and to be certain that they must desire the connection as much as she could do. It was, moreover, such a promising thing for her younger daughters, as Jane's marrying so greatly must throw them in the way of other rich men; and lastly, it was so pleasant at her time of life to be able to consign her single daughters to the care of their sister, that she might not be obliged to go into company more than she liked. It was necessary to make this circumstance a matter of pleasure, because on such occasions it is the etiquette; but no one was less likely than Mrs Bennet to find comfort in staying at home at any period of her life. She concluded with many good wishes that Lady Lucas might soon be equally fortunate, though evidently and triumphantly believing there was no chance of it.

In vain did Elizabeth endeavour to check the rapidity of her mother's words, or persuade her to describe her felicity in a less audible whisper; for to her inexpressible vexation, she could perceive that the chief of it was overheard by Mr Darcy, who sat opposite to them. Her mother only scolded her for being nonsensical.

'What is Mr Darcy to me, pray, that I should be afraid of him? I am sure we owe him no such particular civility as to be obliged to say nothing *he* may not like to hear.'

'For heaven's sake, madam, speak lower. What advantage can it be to you to offend Mr Darcy? – You will never recommend yourself to his friend by so doing.'

Nothing that she could say, however, had any influence. Her mother would talk of her views in the same intelligible tone. Elizabeth blushed and blushed again with shame and vexation. She could not help frequently glancing her eye at Mr Darcy, though every glance convinced her of what she dreaded; for though he was not always looking at her mother, she was convinced that his attention was invariably fixed by her. The expression of his face changed gradually from indignant contempt to a composed and steady gravity.

At length however Mrs Bennet had no more to say; and Lady Lucas, who had been long yawning at the repetition of delights which she saw no likelihood of sharing, was left to the comforts of cold ham and chicken. Elizabeth now began to revive. But not long was the interval of tranquillity; for when supper was over, singing was talked of, and she had the mortification of seeing Mary, after very little entreaty, preparing to oblige the company. By many significant looks and silent entreaties, did she endeavour to prevent such a proof of complaisance – but in vain; Mary would not understand them; such an opportunity of exhibiting was delightful to her, and she began her song. Elizabeth's eyes were fixed on her with most painful sensations; and she watched her progress through the several stanzas with an impatience which was very ill rewarded at their close; for Mary, on receiving amongst the thanks of the table, the hint of a hope that she might be prevailed on to favour them again, after the pause of half a minute began another. Mary's powers were by no means fitted for such a display; her voice was weak, and her manner affected. Elizabeth was in agonies. She looked at Jane, to see how she bore it; but Jane was very composedly talking to Bingley. She looked at his two sisters, and saw them making signs of derision at each other, and at Darcy, who continued however impenetrably grave. She looked at her father to entreat his interference, lest Mary should be singing all night. He took the hint, and when Mary had finished her second song, said aloud, 'That will do extremely well, child. You have delighted us long enough. Let the other young ladies have time to exhibit.'

Mary, though pretending not to hear, was somewhat disconcerted; and Elizabeth sorry for her, and sorry for her father's speech, was afraid her anxiety had done no good. Others of the party were now applied to.

'If I,' said Mr Collins, 'were so fortunate as to be able to sing, I should have great pleasure, I am sure, in obliging the company with an air; for I consider music as a very innocent diversion, and perfectly compatible with the profession of a clergyman. I do not mean however to assert that we can be justified in devoting too much of our time to music, for there are certainly other things to be attended to. The rector of a parish has much to do. In the first place, he must make such an agreement for tithes as may be beneficial to himself and not offensive to his patron. He must write his own sermons; and the time that remains will not be too much for his parish duties, and the care and improvement of his dwelling, which he cannot be excused from making as comfortable as possible. And I do not think it of light importance that he should have attentive and conciliatory manners towards everybody, especially towards those to whom he owes his preferment. I cannot acquit him of that duty; nor could I think well of the man who should omit an occasion of testifying his respect towards anybody connected with the family.' And with a bow to Mr Darcy, he concluded his speech, which had been spoken so loud as to be heard by half the room. Many stared. Many smiled; but no one looked more amused than Mr Bennet himself, while his wife seriously commended Mr Collins for having spoken so sensibly, and observed in a half whisper to Lady Lucas, that he was a remarkably clever, good kind of young man.

To Elizabeth it appeared, that had her family made an agreement to expose themselves as much as they could during the evening, it would have been impossible for them to play their parts with more spirit, or finer success; and happy did she think it for Bingley and her sister that some of the exhibition had escaped his notice, and that his feelings were not of a sort to be much distressed by the folly which he must have witnessed. That his two sisters and Mr Darcy, however, should have such an opportunity of ridiculing her relations was bad enough, and she could not determine whether the silent contempt of the gentleman, or the insolent smiles of the ladies, were more intolerable.

The rest of the evening brought her little amusement. She was teased by Mr Collins, who continued most perseveringly by her side, and though he could not prevail with her to dance with him again, put it out of her power to dance with others. In vain did she entreat him to stand up with somebody else, and offer to introduce him to any young lady in the room. He assured her that as to dancing, he was perfectly indifferent to it; that his chief object was by delicate attentions to recommend himself to her, and that he should therefore make a point of remaining close to her the whole evening. There was no arguing upon such a project. She owed her greatest relief to her friend Miss Lucas, who often joined them, and good-naturedly engaged Mr Collins's conversation to herself.

She was at least free from the offence of Mr Darcy's farther notice; though often standing within a very short distance of her, quite disengaged, he never came near enough to speak. She felt it to be the probable consequence of her allusions to Mr Wickham, and rejoiced in it.

The Longbourn party were the last of all the company to depart; and by a manoeuvre of Mrs Bennet had to wait for their carriages a quarter of an hour after everybody else was gone, which gave them time to see how heartily they were wished away by some of the family. Mrs Hurst and her sister scarcely opened their mouths except to complain of fatigue, and were evidently impatient to have the house to themselves. They repulsed every attempt of Mrs Bennet at conversation, and by so doing, threw a languor over the whole party, which was very little relieved by the long speeches of Mr Collins, who was complimenting Mr Bingley and his sisters on the elegance of their entertainment, and the hospitality and politeness which had marked their behaviour to their guests. Darcy said nothing at all. Mr Bennet, in equal silence, was enjoying the scene. Mr Bingley and Jane were standing together, a little detached from the rest, and talked only to each other. Elizabeth preserved as steady a silence as either Mrs Hurst or Miss Bingley; and even Lydia was too much fatigued to utter more than the occasional exclamation of 'Lord, how tired I am!' accompanied by a violent yawn.

When at length they arose to take leave, Mrs Bennet was most pressingly civil in her hope of seeing the whole family soon at Longbourn; and addressed herself particularly to Mr Bingley, to assure him how happy he would make them, by eating a family dinner with them at any time, without the ceremony of a formal invitation. Bingley was all grateful pleasure, and he readily engaged for taking the earliest opportunity of waiting on her, after his return from London, whither he was obliged to go the next day for a short time.

Mrs Bennet was perfectly satisfied; and quitted the house under the delightful persuasion that, allowing for the necessary preparations of settlements, new carriages and wedding clothes, she should undoubtedly see her daughter settled at Netherfield, in the course of three or four months. Of having another daughter married to Mr Collins, she thought with equal certainty, and with considerable, though not equal, pleasure. Elizabeth was the least dear to her of all her children; and though the man and the match were quite good enough for *her*, the worth of each was eclipsed by Mr Bingley and Netherfield.

Chapter 19

The next day opened a new scene at Longbourn. Mr Collins made his declaration in form. Having resolved to do it without loss of time, as his leave of absence extended only to the following Saturday, and having no feelings of diffidence to make it distressing to himself even at the moment, he set about it in a very orderly manner, with all the observances which he supposed a regular part of the business. On finding Mrs Bennet, Elizabeth, and one of the younger girls together, soon after breakfast, he addressed the mother in these words, 'May I hope, Madam, for your interest with your fair daughter Elizabeth, when I solicit for the honour of a private audience with her in the course of this morning?'

Before Elizabeth had time for anything but a blush of surprise, Mrs Bennet instantly answered, 'Oh dear! – Yes – certainly. I am sure Lizzy will be very happy – I am sure she can have no objection. Come, Kitty, I want you upstairs.'

And gathering her work together, she was hastening away, when Elizabeth called out, 'Dear ma'am, do not go. I beg you will not go. Mr Collins must excuse me. He can have nothing to say to me that anybody need not hear. I am going away myself.'

'No, no, nonsense, Lizzy. I desire you will stay where you are.' – And upon Elizabeth's seeming really, with vexed and embarrassed looks, about to escape, she added, 'Lizzy, I *insist* upon your staying and hearing Mr Collins.'

Elizabeth would not oppose such an injunction – and

a moment's consideration making her also sensible that it would be wisest to get it over as soon and as quietly as possible, she sat down again, and tried to conceal by incessant employment the feelings which were divided between distress and diversion. Mrs Bennet and Kitty walked off, and as soon as they were gone Mr Collins began.

'Believe me, my dear Miss Elizabeth, that your modesty, so far from doing you any disservice, rather adds to your other perfections. You would have been less amiable in my eyes had there *not* been this little unwillingness; but allow me to assure you that I have your respected mother's permission for this address. You can hardly doubt the purport of my discourse, however your natural delicacy may lead you to dissemble; my attentions have been too marked to be mistaken. Almost as soon as I entered the house I singled you out as the companion of my future life. But before I am run away with by my feelings on this subject, perhaps it will be advisable for me to state my reasons for marrying – and moreover for coming into Hertfordshire with the design of selecting a wife, as I certainly did.'

The idea of Mr Collins, with all his solemn composure, being run away with by his feelings, made Elizabeth so near laughing that she could not use the short pause he allowed in any attempt to stop him further, and he continued.

'My reasons for marrying are, first, that I think it a right thing for every clergyman in easy circumstances (like myself) to set the example of matrimony in his parish. Secondly, that I am convinced it will add very greatly to my happiness; and thirdly – which perhaps I ought to have mentioned earlier, that it is the particular advice and recommendation of the very noble lady whom I have the honour of calling patroness. Twice has she condescended to give me her opinion (unasked too!) on this subject; and it was but the very Saturday night before I left Hunsford – between our pools at quadrille, while Mrs Jenkinson was arranging Miss de Bourgh's footstool, that she said, "Mr Collins, you must marry. A clergyman like you must marry. Choose properly, choose a gentlewoman for *my* sake; and for your *own*, let her be an active, useful sort of person, not brought up high, but able to make a small income go a good way. This is my advice. Find such a woman as soon as you can, bring her to Hunsford, and I will visit her." Allow me, by the way, to observe, my fair cousin, that I do not reckon the notice and kindness of Lady Catherine de Bourgh as among the least of the advantages in my power to offer. You will find her manners beyond anything I can describe; and your wit and vivacity I think must be acceptable to her, especially when tempered with the silence and respect which her rank will inevitably excite. Thus much for my general intention in favour of matrimony; it remains to be told why my views were directed to Longbourn instead of my own neighbourhood, where I assure you there are many amiable young women. But the fact is, that being, as I am, to inherit this estate after the death of your honoured father, (who, however, may live many years longer), I could not satisfy myself without resolving to choose a wife from among his daughters, that the loss to them might be as little as possible, when the melancholy event takes place – which, however, as I have already said, may not be for several years. This has been my motive, my fair cousin, and I flatter myself it will not sink me in your esteem.

And now nothing remains for me but to assure you in the most animated language of the violence of my affection. To fortune I am perfectly indifferent, and shall make no demand of that nature on your father, since I am well aware that it could not be complied with; and that one thousand pounds in the four per cents which will not be yours till after your mother's decease, is all that you may ever be entitled to. On that head, therefore, I shall be uniformly silent; and you may assure yourself that no ungenerous reproach shall ever pass my lips when we are married.'

It was absolutely necessary to interrupt him now.

'You are too hasty, sir,' she cried. 'You forget that I have made no answer. Let me do it without further loss of time. Accept my thanks for the compliment you are paying me. I am very sensible of the honour of your proposals, but it is impossible for me to do otherwise than decline them.'

'I am not now to learn,' replied Mr Collins, with a formal wave of the hand, 'that it is usual with young ladies to reject the addresses of the man whom they secretly mean to accept, when he first applies for their favour; and that sometimes the refusal is repeated a second or even a third time. I am therefore by no means discouraged by what you have just said, and shall hope to lead you to the altar ere long.'

'Upon my word, sir,' cried Elizabeth, 'your hope is rather an extraordinary one after my declaration. I do assure you that I am not one of those young ladies (if such young ladies there are) who are so daring as to risk their happiness on the chance of being asked a second time. I am perfectly serious in my refusal. You could not make *me* happy, and I am convinced that I am the last woman in the world who would make *you*

To assure you in the most animated language

so. Nay, were your friend Lady Catherine to know me, I am persuaded she would find me in every respect ill qualified for the situation.'

'Were it certain that Lady Catherine would think so,' said Mr Collins very gravely – 'but I cannot imagine that her ladyship would at all disapprove of you. And you may be certain that when I have the honour of seeing her again I shall speak in the highest terms of your modesty, economy, and other amiable qualifications.'

'Indeed, Mr Collins, all praise of me will be unnecessary. You must give me leave to judge for myself, and pay me the compliment of believing what I say. I wish you very happy and very rich, and by refusing your hand, do all in my power to prevent your being otherwise. In making me the offer, you must have satisfied the delicacy of your feelings with regard to my family, and may take possession of Longbourn estate whenever it falls, without any self-reproach. This matter may be considered, therefore, as finally settled.'

And rising as she thus spoke, she would have quitted the room, had not Mr Collins thus addressed her, 'When I do myself the honour of speaking to you next on this subject I shall hope to receive a more favourable answer than you have now given me; though I am far from accusing you of cruelty at present, because I know it to be the established custom of your sex to reject a man on the first application, and perhaps you have even now said as much to encourage my suit as would be consistent with the true delicacy of the female character.'

'Really, Mr Collins,' cried Elizabeth with some warmth, 'you puzzle me exceedingly. If what I have hitherto said can appear to you in the form of encouragement, I know not how to express my refusal in such a way as may convince you of its being one.'

'You must give me leave to flatter myself, my dear cousin, that your refusal of my addresses is merely words of course. My reasons for believing it are briefly these – It does not appear to me that my hand is unworthy your acceptance, or that the establishment I can offer would be any other than highly desirable. My situation in life, my connections with the family of De Bourgh, and my relationship to your own, are circumstances highly in my favour; and you should take it into farther consideration that in spite of your manifold attractions, it is by no means certain that another offer of marriage may ever be made you. Your portion is unhappily so small that it will in all likelihood undo the effects of your loveliness and amiable qualifications. As I must therefore conclude that you are not serious in your rejection of me, I shall choose to attribute it to your wish of increasing my love by suspense, according to the usual practice of elegant females.'

'I do assure you, sir, that I have no pretension whatever to that kind of elegance which consists in tormenting a respectable man. I would rather be paid the compliment of being believed sincere. I thank you again and again for the honour you have done me in your proposals, but to accept them is absolutely impossible. My feelings in every respect forbid it. Can I speak plainer? Do not consider me now as an elegant female intending to plague you, but as a rational creature speaking the truth from her heart.'

'You are uniformly charming!' cried he, with an air of awkward gallantry; 'and I am persuaded that when sanctioned by the express authority of both your excellent parents, my proposals will not fail of being acceptable.'

To such perseverance in wilful self-deception Elizabeth would make no reply, and immediately and in silence withdrew; determined, if he persisted in considering her repeated refusals as flattering encouragement, to apply to her father, whose negative might be uttered in such a manner as must be decisive, and whose behaviour at least could not be mistaken for the affectation and coquetry of an elegant female.

Chapter 20

Mr Collins was not left long to the silent contemplation of his successful love; for Mrs Bennet, having dawdled about in the vestibule to watch for the end of the conference, no sooner saw Elizabeth open the door and with quick step pass her towards the staircase, than she entered the breakfast-room, and congratulated both him and herself in warm terms on the happy prospect of their nearer connection. Mr Collins received and returned these felicitations with equal pleasure, and then proceeded to relate the particulars of their interview, with the result of which he trusted he had every reason to be satisfied, since the refusal which his cousin had steadfastly given him would naturally flow from her bashful modesty and the genuine delicacy of her character.

This information, however, startled Mrs Bennet – she would have been glad to be equally satisfied that her daughter had meant to encourage him by protesting against his proposals, but she dared not to believe it, and could not help saying so.

'But depend upon it, Mr Collins,' she added, 'that Lizzy shall be brought to reason. I will speak to her about it myself directly. She is a very headstrong foolish girl, and does not know her own interest; but I will *make* her know it.'

'Pardon me for interrupting you, Madam,' cried Mr Collins; 'but if she is really headstrong and foolish, I know not whether she would altogether be a very desirable wife to a man in my situation, who naturally looks for happiness in the marriage state. If therefore she actually persists in rejecting my suit, perhaps it were better not to force her into accepting me, because if liable to such defects of temper, she could not contribute much to my felicity.'

'Sir, you quite misunderstand me,' said Mrs Bennet, alarmed. 'Lizzy is only headstrong in such matters as these. In everything else she is as good natured a girl as ever lived. I will go directly to Mr Bennet, and we shall very soon settle it with her, I am sure.'

She would not give him time to reply, but hurrying instantly to her husband, called out as she entered the library, 'Oh! Mr Bennet, you are wanted immediately; we are all in an uproar. You must come and make Lizzy marry Mr Collins, for she vows she will not have him, and if you do not make haste he will change his mind and not have *her*.'

Mr Bennet raised his eyes from his book as she entered, and fixed them on her face with a calm unconcern which was not in the least altered by her communication.

'I have not the pleasure of understanding you,' said he, when she had finished her speech. 'Of what are you talking?'

'Of Mr Collins and Lizzy. Lizzy declares she will not have Mr Collins, and Mr Collins begins to say that he will not have Lizzy.'

'And what am I to do on the occasion? – It seems a hopeless business.'

'Speak to Lizzy about it yourself. Tell her that you insist upon her marrying him.'

'Let her be called down. She shall hear my opinion.'

Mrs Bennet rang the bell, and Miss Elizabeth was summoned to the library.

'Come here, child,' cried her father as she appeared. 'I have sent for you on an affair of importance. I understand that Mr Collins has made you an offer of marriage. Is it true?' Elizabeth replied that it was. 'Very well – and this offer of marriage you have refused?'

'I have, sir.'

'Very well. We now come to the point. Your mother insists upon your accepting it. Is not it so, Mrs Bennet?'

'Yes, or I will never see her again.'

'An unhappy alternative is before you, Elizabeth. From this day you must be a stranger to one of your parents. Your mother will never see you again if you do *not* marry Mr Collins, and I will never see you again if you *do*.'

Elizabeth could not but smile at such a conclusion of such a beginning; but Mrs Bennet, who had persuaded herself that her husband regarded the affair as she wished, was excessively disappointed.

'What do you mean, Mr Bennet, by talking in this way? You promised me to *insist* upon her marrying him.'

'My dear,' replied her husband, 'I have two small favours to request. First, that you will allow me the free use of my understanding on the present occasion; and secondly, of my room. I shall be glad to have the library to myself as soon as may be.'

Not yet, however, in spite of her disappointment in her husband, did Mrs Bennet give up the point. She talked to Elizabeth again and again; coaxed and threatened her by turns. She endeavoured to secure Jane in her interest, but Jane with all possible mildness declined interfering – and Elizabeth sometimes with real earnestness and sometimes with playful gaiety replied to her attacks. Though her manner varied however, her determination never did.

Mr Collins, meanwhile, was meditating in solitude on what had passed. He thought too well of himself to comprehend on what motive his cousin could refuse him; and though his pride was hurt, he suffered in no other way. His regard for her was quite imaginary; and the possibility of her deserving her mother's reproach prevented his feeling any regret.

While the family were in this confusion, Charlotte Lucas came to spend the day with them. She was met in the vestibule by Lydia, who, flying to her, cried in a half whisper, 'I am glad you are come, for there is such fun here! – What do you think has happened this morning? – Mr Collins has made an offer to Lizzy, and she will not have him.'

Charlotte had hardly time to answer, before they were joined by Kitty, who came to tell the same news, and no sooner had they entered the breakfast-room, where Mrs Bennet was alone, than she likewise began on the subject, calling on Miss Lucas for her compassion, and entreating her to persuade her friend Lizzy to comply with the wishes of all her family. 'Pray do, my dear Miss Lucas,' she added in a melancholy tone,

They entered the breakfast room

'for nobody is on my side, nobody takes part with me, I am cruelly used, nobody feels for my poor nerves.'

Charlotte's reply was spared by the entrance of Jane and Elizabeth.

'Aye, there she comes,' continued Mrs Bennet, 'looking as unconcerned as may be, and caring no more for us than if we were at York, provided she can have her own way. But I tell you what, Miss Lizzy, if you take it into your head to go on refusing every offer of marriage in this way, you will never get a husband at all – and I am sure I do not know who is to maintain you when your father is dead. *I* shall not be able to keep you – and so I warn you. I have done with you from this very day. I told you in the library, you know, that I should never speak to you again, and you will find me as good as my word. I have no pleasure in talking to undutiful children. Not that I have much pleasure indeed in talking to anybody. People who suffer as I do from nervous complaints can have no great inclination for talking. Nobody can tell what I suffer! – But it is always so. Those who do not complain are never pitied.'

Her daughters listened in silence to this effusion, sensible that any attempt to reason with or soothe her would only increase the irritation. She talked on, therefore, without interruption from any of them till they were joined by Mr Collins, who entered with an air more stately than usual, and on perceiving whom, she said to the girls, 'Now, I do insist upon it, that you, all of you, hold your tongues, and let Mr Collins and me have a little conversation together.'

Elizabeth passed quietly out of the room, Jane and Kitty followed, but Lydia stood her ground, determined to hear all she could; and Charlotte, detained first by the civility of Mr Collins, whose enquiries after herself and all her family were very minute, and then by a little curiosity, satisfied herself with walking to the window and pretending not to hear. In a doleful voice Mrs Bennet thus began the projected conversation. 'Oh! Mr Collins –'

'My dear Madam,' replied he, 'let us be for ever silent on this point. Far be it from me,' he presently continued in a voice that marked his displeasure, 'to resent the behaviour of your daughter. Resignation to inevitable evils is the duty of us all; the peculiar duty of a young man who has been so fortunate as I have been in early preferment; and I trust I am resigned. Perhaps not the less so from feeling a doubt of my positive happiness had my fair cousin honoured me with her hand; for I have often observed that resignation is never so perfect as when the blessing denied begins to lose somewhat of its value in our estimation. You will not, I hope, consider me as showing any disrespect to your family, my dear Madam, by thus withdrawing my pretensions to your daughter's favour, without having paid yourself and Mr Bennet the compliment of requesting you to interpose your authority in my behalf. My conduct may I fear be objectionable in having accepted my dismission from your daughter's lips instead of your own. But we are all liable to error. I have certainly meant well through the whole affair. My object has been to secure an amiable companion for myself, with due consideration for the advantage of all your family, and if my *manner* has been at all reprehensible, I here beg leave to apologise.'

Chapter 21

The discussion of Mr Collins's offer was now nearly at an end, and Elizabeth had only to suffer from the uncomfortable feelings necessarily attending it, and occasionally from some peevish allusion of her mother. As for the gentleman himself, *his* feelings were chiefly expressed, not by embarrassment or dejection, or by trying to avoid her, but by stiffness of manner and resentful silence. He scarcely ever spoke to her, and the assiduous attentions which he had been so sensible of himself, were transferred for the rest of the day to Miss Lucas, whose civility in listening to him, was a seasonable relief to them all, and especially to her friend.

The morrow produced no abatement of Mrs Bennet's ill humour or ill health. Mr Collins was also in the same state of angry pride. Elizabeth had hoped that his resentment might shorten his visit, but his plan did not appear in the least affected by it. He was always to have gone on Saturday, and to Saturday he still meant to stay.

After breakfast, the girls walked to Meryton to enquire if Mr Wickham were returned, and to lament over his absence from the Netherfield ball. He joined them on their entering the town and attended them to their aunt's, where his regret and vexation, and the concern of everybody was well talked over. To Elizabeth, however, he voluntarily acknowledged that the necessity of his absence *had* been self imposed.

'I found,' said he, 'as the time drew near, that I had better not meet Mr Darcy – that to be in the same room, the same party with him for so many hours together, might be more than I could bear, and that scenes might arise unpleasant to more than myself.'

She highly approved his forbearance, and they had leisure for a full discussion of it, and for all the commendation which they civilly bestowed on each other, as Wickham and another officer walked back with them to Longbourn, and during the walk, he particularly attended to her. His accompanying them was a double advantage; she felt all the compliment it offered to herself, and it was most acceptable as an occasion of introducing him to her father and mother.

Soon after their return, a letter was delivered to Miss Bennet; it came from Netherfield, and was opened immediately. The envelope contained a sheet of elegant, little, hot pressed paper, well covered with a lady's fair, flowing hand; and Elizabeth saw her

Wickham and another officer walked back with them to Longbourn

sister's countenance change as she read it, and saw her dwelling intently on some particular passages. Jane recollected herself soon, and putting the letter away, tried to join with her usual cheerfulness in the general conversation; but Elizabeth felt an anxiety on the subject which drew off her attention even from Wickham; and no sooner had he and his companion taken leave, than a glance from Jane invited her to follow her upstairs.

When they had gained their own room, Jane taking out the letter, said, 'This is from Caroline Bingley; what it contains, has surprised me a good deal. The whole party have left Netherfield by this time, and are on their way to town; and without any intention of coming back again. You shall hear what she says.'

She then read the first sentence aloud, which

comprised the information of their having just resolved to follow their brother to town directly, and of their meaning to dine that day in Grosvenor Street, where Mr Hurst had a house. The next was in these words. 'I do not pretend to regret anything I shall leave in Hertfordshire, except your society, my dearest friend; but we will hope at some future period, to enjoy many returns of the delightful intercourse we have known, and in the mean while may lessen the pain of separation by a very frequent and most unreserved correspondence. I depend on you for that.' To these high flown expressions, Elizabeth listened with all the insensibility of distrust; and though the suddenness of their removal surprised her, she saw nothing in it really to lament; it was not to be supposed that their absence from Netherfield would prevent Mr Bingley's being there; and as to the loss of their society, she was persuaded that Jane must soon cease to regard it, in the enjoyment of his.

'It is unlucky,' said she, after a short pause, 'that you should not be able to see your friends before they leave the country. But may we not hope that the period of future happiness to which Miss Bingley looks forward, may arrive earlier than she is aware, and that the delightful intercourse you have known as friends, will be renewed with yet greater satisfaction as sisters? – Mr Bingley will not be detained in London by them.'

'Caroline decidedly says that none of the party will return into Hertfordshire this winter. I will read it to you.

' "When my brother left us yesterday, he imagined that the business which took him to London, might be concluded in three or four days, but as we are certain it cannot be so, and at the same time convinced that when Charles gets to town, he will be in no hurry to leave it again, we have determined on following him thither, that he may not be obliged to spend his vacant hours in a comfortless hotel. Many of my acquaintance are already there for the winter; I wish I could hear that you, my dearest friend, had any intention of making one in the crowd, but of that I despair. I sincerely hope your Christmas in Hertfordshire may abound in the gaieties which that season generally brings, and that your beaux will be so numerous as to prevent your feeling the loss of the three, of whom we shall deprive you." '

'It is evident by this,' added Jane, 'that he comes back no more this winter.'

'It is only evident that Miss Bingley does not mean he *should*.'

'Why will you think so? It must be his own doing. He is his own master. But you do not know *all*. I *will* read you the passage which particularly hurts me. I will have no reserves from *you*. "Mr Darcy is impatient to see his sister, and to confess the truth, *we* are scarcely less eager to meet her again. I really do not think Georgiana Darcy has her equal for beauty, elegance, and accomplishments; and the affection she inspires in Louisa and myself, is heightened into something still more interesting, from the hope we dare to entertain of her being hereafter our sister. I do not know whether I ever before mentioned to you my feelings on this subject, but I will not leave the country without confiding them, and I trust you will not esteem them unreasonable. My brother admires her greatly already, he will have frequent opportunity now of seeing her on the most intimate footing, her relations all wish the connection as much as his own, and a sister's partiality is not misleading me, I think, when I call Charles most capable of engaging any woman's heart. With all these circumstances to favour an attachment and nothing to prevent it, am I wrong, my dearest Jane, in indulging the hope of an event which will secure the happiness of so many?" '

'What think you of *this* sentence, my dear Lizzy?' – said Jane as she finished it. 'Is it not clear enough? – Does it not expressly declare that Caroline neither expects nor wishes me to be her sister; that she is perfectly convinced of her brother's indifference, and that if she suspects the nature of my feelings for him, she means (most kindly!) to put me on my guard? Can there be any other opinion on the subject?'

'Yes, there can; for mine is totally different. Will you hear it?'

'Most willingly.'

' "You shall have it in few words. Miss Bingley sees that her brother is in love with you, and wants him to marry Miss Darcy. She follows him to town in the hope of keeping him there, and tries to persuade you that he does not care about you." '

Jane shook her head.

'Indeed, Jane, you ought to believe me. No one who has ever seen you together, can doubt his affection. Miss Bingley I am sure cannot. She is not such a simpleton. Could she have seen half as much love in Mr Darcy for herself, she would have ordered her wedding clothes. But the case is this. We are not rich enough, or grand enough for them; and she is the more anxious to get Miss Darcy for her brother, from the notion that when there has been *one* intermarriage, she may have less trouble in achieving a second; in which there is certainly some ingenuity, and I dare say it would succeed, if Miss de Bourgh were out of the way. But, my dearest Jane, you cannot seriously imagine that because Miss Bingley tells you her brother greatly admires Miss Darcy, he is in the smallest degree less sensible of *your* merit than when he took leave of you on Tuesday, or that it will be in her power to persuade him that instead of being in love with you, he is very much in love with her friend.'

'If we thought alike of Miss Bingley,' replied Jane, 'your representation of all this, might make me quite easy. But I know the foundation is unjust. Caroline is incapable of wilfully deceiving anyone; and all that I can hope in this case is, that she is deceived herself.'

'That is right. You could not have started a more happy idea, since you will not take comfort in mine. Believe her to be deceived by all means. You have now done your duty by her, and must fret no longer.'

'But, my dear sister, can I be happy, even supposing the best, in accepting a man whose sisters and friends are all wishing him to marry elsewhere?'

'You must decide for yourself,' said Elizabeth, 'and if upon mature deliberation, you find that the misery of disobliging his two sisters is more than equivalent to the happiness of being his wife, I advise you by all means to refuse him.'

'How can you talk so?' – said Jane faintly smiling, 'You must know that though I should be exceedingly grieved at their disapprobation, I could not hesitate.'

'I did not think you would – and that being the case, I cannot consider your situation with much compassion.'

'But if he returns no more this winter, my choice will never be required. A thousand things may arise in six months!'

The idea of his returning no more Elizabeth treated with the utmost contempt. It appeared to her merely the suggestion of Caroline's interested wishes, and she could not for a moment suppose that those wishes, however openly or artfully spoken, could influence a young man so totally independent of everyone.

She represented to her sister as forcibly as possible what she felt on the subject, and had soon the pleasure of seeing its happy effect. Jane's temper was not desponding, and she was gradually led to hope, though the diffidence of affection sometimes overcame the hope, that Bingley would return to Netherfield and answer every wish of her heart.

They agreed that Mrs Bennet should only hear of the departure of the family, without being alarmed on the score of the gentleman's conduct; but even this partial communication gave her a great deal of concern, and she bewailed it as exceedingly unlucky that the ladies should happen to go away, just as they were all getting so intimate together. After lamenting it however at some length, she had the consolation of thinking that Mr Bingley would be soon down again and soon dining at Longbourn, and the conclusion of all was the comfortable declaration that, though he had been invited only to a family dinner, she would take care to have two full courses.

Chapter 22

The Bennets were engaged to dine with the Lucases, and again during the chief of the day, was Miss Lucas so kind as to listen to Mr Collins. Elizabeth took an opportunity of thanking her. 'It keeps him in good humour,' said she, 'and I am more obliged to you than I can express.' Charlotte assured her friend of her satisfaction in being useful, and that it amply repaid her for the little sacrifice of her time. This was very amiable, but Charlotte's kindness extended farther than Elizabeth had any conception of – its object was nothing less, than to secure her from any return of Mr Collins's addresses, by engaging them towards herself. Such was Miss Lucas's scheme; and appearances were so favourable that when they parted at night, she would have felt almost sure of success if he had not been to leave Hertfordshire so very soon. But here, she did injustice to the fire and independence of his character, for it led him to escape out of Longbourn House the next morning with admirable slyness, and hasten to Lucas Lodge to throw himself at her feet. He was anxious to avoid the notice of his cousins, from a conviction that if they saw him depart, they could not fail to conjecture his design, and he was not willing to have the attempt known till its success could be known likewise; for though feeling almost secure, and with reason, for Charlotte had been tolerably encouraging, he was comparatively diffident since the adventure of Wednesday. His reception however was of the most flattering kind. Miss Lucas perceived him from an upper window as he walked towards the house, and instantly set out to meet him accidentally in the lane. But little had she dared to hope that so much love and eloquence awaited her there.

In as short a time as Mr Collins's long speeches would allow, everything was settled between them to the satisfaction of both; and as they entered the house, he earnestly entreated her to name the day that was to make him the happiest of men; and though

So much love and eloquence

such a solicitation must be waived for the present, the lady felt no inclination to trifle with his happiness. The stupidity with which he was favoured by nature, must guard his courtship from any charm that could make a woman wish for its continuance; and Miss Lucas, who accepted him solely from the pure and disinterested desire of an establishment, cared not how soon that establishment were gained.

Sir William and Lady Lucas were speedily applied to for their consent; and it was bestowed with a most joyful alacrity. Mr Collins's present circumstances made it a most eligible match for their daughter, to whom they could give little fortune; and his prospects of future wealth were exceedingly fair. Lady Lucas began directly to calculate with more interest than the matter had ever excited before, how many years longer Mr Bennet was likely to live; and Sir William gave it as his decided opinion, that whenever Mr Collins should be in possession of the Longbourn estate, it would be highly expedient that both he and his wife should make their appearance at St James's. The whole family in short were properly overjoyed on the occasion. The younger girls formed hopes of *coming out* a year or two sooner than they might otherwise have done; and the boys were relieved from their apprehension of Charlotte's dying an old maid. Charlotte herself was tolerably composed. She had gained her point, and had time to consider of it. Her reflections were in general satisfactory. Mr Collins to be sure was neither sensible nor agreeable; his society was irksome, and his attachment to her must be imaginary. But still he would be her husband. Without thinking highly either of men or of matrimony, marriage had always been her object; it was the only honourable provision for well-educated young women of small fortune, and however uncertain of giving happiness, must be their pleasantest preservative from want. This preservative she had now obtained; and at the age of twenty-seven, without having ever been handsome, she felt all the good luck of it. The least agreeable circumstance in the business, was the surprise it must occasion to Elizabeth Bennet, whose friendship she valued beyond that of any other person. Elizabeth would wonder, and probably would blame her; and though her resolution was not to be shaken, her feelings must be hurt by such disapprobation. She resolved to give her the information herself, and therefore charged Mr Collins when he returned to Longbourn to dinner, to drop no hint of what had passed before any of the family. A promise of secrecy was of course very dutifully given, but it could not be kept without difficulty; for the curiosity excited by his long absence, burst forth in such very direct questions on his return, as required some ingenuity to evade, and he was at the same time exercising great self-denial, for he was longing to publish his prosperous love.

As he was to begin his journey too early on the morrow to see any of the family, the ceremony of leave-taking was performed when the ladies moved for the night; and Mrs Bennet with great politeness and cordiality said how happy they should be to see him at Longbourn again, whenever his other engagements might allow him to visit them.

'My dear Madam,' he replied, 'this invitation is particularly gratifying, because it is what I have been hoping to receive; and you may be very certain that I shall avail myself of it as soon as possible.'

They were all astonished; and Mr Bennet, who

could by no means wish for so speedy a return, immediately said, 'But is there not danger of Lady Catherine's disapprobation here, my good sir? – You had better neglect your relations, than run the risk of offending your patroness.'

'My dear sir,' replied Mr Collins, 'I am particularly obliged to you for this friendly caution, and you may depend upon my not taking so material a step without her ladyship's concurrence.'

'You cannot be too much on your guard. Risk anything rather than her displeasure; and if you find it likely to be raised by your coming to us again, which I should think exceedingly probable, stay quietly at home, and be satisfied that *we* shall take no offence.'

'Believe me, my dear sir, my gratitude is warmly excited by such affectionate attention; and depend upon it, you will speedily receive from me a letter of thanks for this, as well as for every other mark of your regard during my stay in Hertfordshire. As for my fair cousins, though my absence may not be long enough to render it necessary, I shall now take the liberty of wishing them health and happiness, not excepting my cousin Elizabeth.'

With proper civilities the ladies then withdrew; all of them equally surprised to find that he meditated a quick return. Mrs Bennet wished to understand by it that he thought of paying his addresses to one of her younger girls, and Mary might have been prevailed on to accept him. She rated his abilities much higher than any of the others; there was a solidity in his reflections which often struck her, and though by no means so clever as herself, she thought that if encouraged to read and improve himself by such an example as hers, he might become a very agreeable companion. But on the following morning, every hope of this kind was done away. Miss Lucas called soon after breakfast, and in a private conference with Elizabeth related the event of the day before.

The possibility of Mr Collins's fancying himself in love with her friend had once occurred to Elizabeth within the last day or two; but that Charlotte could encourage him, seemed almost as far from possibility as that she could encourage him herself, and her astonishment was consequently so great as to overcome at first the bounds of decorum, and she could not help crying out, 'Engaged to Mr Collins! my dear Charlotte – impossible!'

The steady countenance which Miss Lucas had commanded in telling her story, gave way to a momentary confusion here on receiving so direct a reproach; though, as it was no more than she expected, she soon regained her composure, and calmly replied, 'Why should you be surprised, my dear Eliza? – Do you think it incredible that Mr Collins should be able to procure any woman's good opinion, because he was not so happy as to succeed with you?'

But Elizabeth had now recollected herself, and making a strong effort for it, was able to assure her with tolerable firmness that the prospect of their relationship was highly grateful to her, and that she wished her all imaginable happiness.

'I see what you are feeling,' replied Charlotte, 'you must be surprised, very much surprised – so lately as Mr Collins was wishing to marry you. But when you have had time to think it all over, I hope you will be satisfied with what I have done. I am not romantic you know. I never was. I ask only a comfortable home; and considering Mr Collins's character, connections, and situation in life, I am convinced that my chance of happiness with him is as fair, as most people can boast on entering the marriage state.'

Elizabeth quietly answered 'Undoubtedly.' – and after an awkward pause, they returned to the rest of the family. Charlotte did not stay much longer, and Elizabeth was then left to reflect on what she had heard. It was a long time before she became at all reconciled to the idea of so unsuitable a match. The strangeness of Mr Collins's making two offers of marriage within three days, was nothing in comparison of his being now accepted. She had always felt that Charlotte's opinion of matrimony was not exactly like her own, but she could not have supposed it possible that when called into action, she would have sacrificed every better feeling to worldly advantage. Charlotte the wife of Mr Collins, was a most humiliating picture! – And to the pang of a friend disgracing herself and sunk in her esteem, was added the distressing conviction that it was impossible for that friend to be tolerably happy in the lot she had chosen.

Chapter 23

Elizabeth was sitting with her mother and sisters, reflecting on what she had heard, and doubting whether she were authorised to mention it, when Sir William Lucas himself appeared, sent by his daughter to announce her engagement to the family. With many compliments to them, and much self-gratulation on the prospect of a connection between the houses, he unfolded the matter – to an audience not merely wondering, but incredulous; for Mrs Bennet, with more perseverance than politeness, protested he must be entirely mistaken, and Lydia, always unguarded and often uncivil, boisterously exclaimed, 'Good Lord! Sir William, how can you tell such a story? – Do not you know that Mr Collins wants to marry Lizzy?'

Nothing less than the complaisance of a courtier could have borne without anger such treatment; but Sir William's good breeding carried him through it all; and though he begged leave to be positive as to the truth of his information, he listened to all their impertinence with the most forbearing courtesy.

Elizabeth, feeling it incumbent on her to relieve him from so unpleasant a situation, now put herself forward to confirm his account, by mentioning her prior knowledge of it from Charlotte herself; and endeavoured to put a stop to the exclamations of her mother and sisters, by the earnestness of her congratulations to Sir William, in which she was readily joined by Jane, and by making a variety of remarks on the happiness that might be expected from the match, the excellent character of Mr Collins, and the convenient distance of Hunsford from London.

Mrs Bennet was in fact too much overpowered to say a great deal while Sir William remained; but no sooner had he left them than her feelings found a rapid vent. In the first place, she persisted in disbelieving the whole of the matter; secondly, she was very sure that Mr Collins had been taken in; thirdly, she trusted that they would never be happy together; and fourthly, that the match might be broken off. Two inferences, however, were plainly deduced from the whole; one, that Elizabeth was the real cause of all the mischief; and the other, that she herself had been barbarously

Protested he must be entirely mistaken

used by them all; and on these two points she principally dwelt during the rest of the day. Nothing could
console and nothing appease her. Nor did that day
wear out her resentment. A week elapsed before she
could see Elizabeth without scolding her, a month
passed away before she could speak to Sir William or
Lady Lucas without being rude, and many months
were gone before she could at all forgive their daughter.

Mr Bennet's emotions were much more tranquil
on the occasion, and such as he did experience he
pronounced to be of a most agreeable sort; for it

gratified him, he said, to discover that Charlotte Lucas, whom he had been used to think tolerably sensible, was as foolish as his wife, and more foolish than his daughter!

Jane confessed herself a little surprised at the match; but she said less of her astonishment than of her earnest desire for their happiness; nor could Elizabeth persuade her to consider it as improbable. Kitty and Lydia were far from envying Miss Lucas, for Mr Collins was only a clergyman; and it affected them in no other way than as a piece of news to spread at Meryton.

Lady Lucas could not be insensible of triumph on being able to retort on Mrs Bennet the comfort of having a daughter well married; and she called at Longbourn rather oftener than usual to say how happy she was, though Mrs Bennet's sour looks and ill-natured remarks might have been enough to drive happiness away.

Between Elizabeth and Charlotte there was a restraint which kept them mutually silent on the subject; and Elizabeth felt persuaded that no real confidence could ever subsist between them again. Her disappointment in Charlotte made her turn with fonder regard to her sister, of whose rectitude and delicacy she was sure her opinion could never be shaken, and for whose happiness she grew daily more anxious, as Bingley had now been gone a week, and nothing was heard of his return.

Jane had sent Caroline an early answer to her letter, and was counting the days till she might reasonably hope to hear again. The promised letter of thanks from Mr Collins arrived on Tuesday, addressed to their father, and written with all the solemnity of gratitude which a twelvemonth's abode in the family might have prompted. After discharging his conscience on that head, he proceeded to inform them, with many rapturous expressions, of his happiness in having obtained the affection of their amiable neighbour, Miss Lucas, and then explained that it was merely with the view of enjoying her society that he had been so ready to close with their kind wish of seeing him again at Longbourn, whither he hoped to be able to return on Monday fortnight; for Lady Catherine, he added, so heartily approved his marriage, that she wished it to take place as soon as possible, which he trusted would be an unanswerable argument with his amiable Charlotte to name an early day for making him the happiest of men.

Mr Collins's return into Hertfordshire was no longer a matter of pleasure to Mrs Bennet. On the contrary she was as much disposed to complain of it as her husband. It was very strange that he should come to Longbourn instead of to Lucas Lodge; it was also very inconvenient and exceedingly troublesome.

She hated having visitors in the house while her health was so indifferent, and lovers were of all people the most disagreeable. Such were the gentle murmurs of Mrs Bennet, and they gave way only to the greater distress of Mr Bingley's continued absence.

Neither Jane nor Elizabeth were comfortable on this subject. Day after day passed away without bringing any other tidings of him than the report which shortly prevailed in Meryton of his coming no more to Netherfield the whole winter; a report which highly incensed Mrs Bennet, and which she never failed to contradict as a most scandalous falsehood.

Even Elizabeth began to fear – not that Bingley was indifferent – but that his sisters would be successful in keeping him away. Unwilling as she was to admit an idea so destructive to Jane's happiness, and so dishonourable to the stability of her lover, she could not prevent its frequently recurring. The united efforts of his two unfeeling sisters and of his overpowering friend, assisted by the attractions of Miss Darcy and the amusements of London, might be too much, she feared, for the strength of his attachment.

As for Jane, *her* anxiety under this suspense was, of course, more painful than Elizabeth's; but whatever she felt she was desirous of concealing, and between herself and Elizabeth, therefore, the subject was never alluded to. But as no such delicacy restrained her mother, an hour seldom passed in which she did not talk of Bingley, express her impatience for his arrival, or even require Jane to confess that if he did not come back, she should think herself very ill used. It needed all Jane's steady mildness to bear these attacks with tolerable tranquillity.

Mr Collins returned most punctually on the Monday fortnight, but his reception at Longbourn was not quite so gracious as it had been on his first introduction. He was too happy, however, to need much attention; and luckily for the others, the business of love-making relieved them from a great deal of his company. The chief of every day was spent by him at Lucas Lodge, and he sometimes returned to Longbourn only in time to make an apology for his absence before the family went to bed.

Mrs Bennet was really in a most pitiable state. The very mention of anything concerning the match threw her into an agony of ill humour, and wherever she went she was sure of hearing it talked of. The sight of Miss Lucas was odious to her. As her successor in that

Whenever she spoke in a low voice to Mr Collins

house, she regarded her with jealous abhorrence. Whenever Charlotte came to see them she concluded her to be anticipating the hour of possession; and whenever she spoke in a low voice to Mr Collins, was convinced that they were talking of the Longbourn estate, and resolving to turn herself and her daughters out of the house, as soon as Mr Bennet were dead. She complained bitterly of all this to her husband.

'Indeed, Mr Bennet,' said she, 'it is very hard to think that Charlotte Lucas should ever be mistress of this house, that *I* should be forced to make way for *her*, and live to see her take my place in it!'

'My dear, do not give way to such gloomy thoughts. Let us hope for better things. Let us flatter ourselves that *I* may be the survivor.'

This was not very consoling to Mrs Bennet, and, therefore, instead of making any answer, she went on as before, 'I cannot bear to think that they should have all this estate. If it was not for the entail I should not mind it.'

'What should not you mind?'

'I should not mind anything at all.'

'Let us be thankful that you are preserved from a state of such insensibility.'

'I never can be thankful, Mr Bennet, for anything about the entail. How anyone could have the conscience to entail away an estate from one's own daughters I cannot understand; and all for the sake of Mr Collins too! – Why should *he* have it more than anybody else?'

'I leave it to yourself to determine,' said Mr Bennet.

Chapter 24

Miss Bingley's letter arrived, and put an end to doubt. The very first sentence conveyed the assurance of their being all settled in London for the winter, and concluded with her brother's regret at not having had time to pay his respects to his friends in Hertfordshire before he left the country.

Hope was over, entirely over; and when Jane could attend to the rest of the letter, she found little, except the professed affection of the writer, that could give her any comfort. Miss Darcy's praise occupied the chief of it. Her many attractions were again dwelt on, and Caroline boasted joyfully of their increasing intimacy, and ventured to predict the accomplishment of the wishes which had been unfolded in her former letter. She wrote also with great pleasure of her brother's being an inmate of Mr Darcy's house, and mentioned with raptures, some plans of the latter with regard to new furniture.

Elizabeth, to whom Jane very soon communicated the chief of all this, heard it in silent indignation. Her heart was divided between concern for her sister, and resentment against all the others. To Caroline's assertion of her brother's being partial to Miss Darcy she paid no credit. That he was really fond of Jane, she doubted no more than she had ever done; and much as she had always been disposed to like him, she could not think without anger, hardly without contempt, on that easiness of temper, that want of proper resolution which now made him the slave of his designing friends, and led him to sacrifice his own happiness to the caprice of their inclinations. Had his own happiness, however, been the only sacrifice, he might have been allowed to sport with it in what ever manner he thought best; but her sister's was involved in it, as she thought he must be sensible himself. It was a subject, in short, on which reflection would be long indulged, and must be unavailing. She could think of nothing else, and yet whether Bingley's regard had really died away, or were suppressed by his friends' interference; whether he had been aware of Jane's attachment, or whether it had escaped his observation; whichever were the case, though her opinion of him must be materially affected by the difference, her sister's situation remained the same, her peace equally wounded.

A day or two passed before Jane had courage to speak of her feelings to Elizabeth; but at last on Mrs Bennet's leaving them together, after a longer irritation than usual about Netherfield and its master, she could not help saying, 'Oh! that my dear mother had more command over herself; she can have no idea of the pain she gives me by her continual reflections on him. But I will not repine. It cannot last long. He will be forgot, and we shall all be as we were before.'

Elizabeth looked at her sister with incredulous solicitude, but said nothing.

'You doubt me,' cried Jane, slightly colouring; 'indeed you have no reason. He may live in my memory as the most amiable man of my acquaintance, but that is all. I have nothing either to hope or fear, and nothing to reproach him with. Thank God! I have not *that* pain. A little time therefore. I shall certainly try to get the better.'

With a stronger voice she soon added, 'I have this

comfort immediately, that it has not been more than an error of fancy on my side, and that it has done no harm to anyone but myself.'

'My dear Jane!' exclaimed Elizabeth, 'you are too good. Your sweetness and disinterestedness are really angelic; I do not know what to say to you. I feel as if I had never done you justice, or loved you as you deserve.'

Miss Bennet eagerly disclaimed all extraordinary merit, and threw back the praise on her sister's warm affection.

'Nay,' said Elizabeth, 'this is not fair. *You* wish to think all the world respectable, and are hurt if I speak ill of anybody. *I* only want to think *you* perfect, and you set yourself against it. Do not be afraid of my running into any excess, of my encroaching on your privilege of universal good will. You need not. There are few people whom I really love, and still fewer of whom I think well. The more I see of the world, the more am I dissatisfied with it; and every day confirms my belief of the inconsistency of all human characters, and of the little dependence that can be placed on the appearance of either merit or sense. I have met with two instances lately; one I will not mention; the other is Charlotte's marriage. It is unaccountable! in every view it is unaccountable!'

'My dear Lizzy, do not give way to such feelings as these. They will ruin your happiness. You do not make allowance enough for difference of situation and temper. Consider Mr Collins's respectability, and Charlotte's prudent, steady character. Remember that she is one of a large family; that as to fortune, it is a most eligible match; and be ready to believe, for everybody's sake, that she may feel something like regard and esteem for our cousin.'

'To oblige you, I would try to believe almost anything, but no one else could be benefited by such a
belief as this; for were I persuaded that Charlotte had
any regard for him, I should only think worse of her
understanding, than I now do of her heart. My dear
Jane, Mr Collins is a conceited, pompous, narrow-
minded, silly man; you know he is, as well as I do; and
you must feel, as well as I do, that the woman who
marries him, cannot have a proper way of thinking.
You shall not defend her, though it is Charlotte Lucas.
You shall not, for the sake of one individual, change the
meaning of principle and integrity, nor endeavour to
persuade yourself or me, that selfishness is prudence,
and insensibility of danger, security for happiness.'

'I must think your language too strong in speaking of
both,' replied Jane, 'and I hope you will be convinced
of it, by seeing them happy together. But enough of
this. You alluded to something else. You mentioned
two instances. I cannot misunderstand you, but I
entreat you, dear Lizzy, not to pain me by thinking *that
person* to blame, and saying your opinion of him is
sunk. We must not be so ready to fancy ourselves
intentionally injured. We must not expect a lively
young man to be always so guarded and circumspect.
It is very often nothing but our own vanity that
deceives us. Women fancy admiration means more
than it does.'

'And men take care that they should.'

'If it is designedly done, they cannot be justified; but
I have no idea of there being so much design in the
world as some persons imagine.'

'I am far from attributing any part of Mr Bingley's
conduct to design,' said Elizabeth; 'but without
scheming to do wrong, or to make others unhappy,

there may be error, and there may be misery. Thoughtlessness, want of attention to other people's feelings, and want of resolution, will do the business.'

'And do you impute it to either of those?'

'Yes; to the last. But if I go on, I shall displease you by saying what I think of persons you esteem. Stop me whilst you can.'

'You persist, then, in supposing his sisters influence him.'

'Yes, in conjunction with his friend.'

'I cannot believe it. Why should they try to influence him? They can only wish his happiness, and if he is attached to me, no other woman can secure it.'

'Your first position is false. They may wish many things besides his happiness; they may wish his increase of wealth and consequence; they may wish him to marry a girl who has all the importance of money, great connections, and pride.'

'Beyond a doubt, they *do* wish him to choose Miss Darcy,' replied Jane; 'but this may be from better feelings than you are supposing. They have known her much longer than they have known me; no wonder if they love her better. But, whatever may be their own wishes, it is very unlikely they should have opposed their brother's. What sister would think herself at liberty to do it, unless there were something very objectionable? If they believed him attached to me, they would not try to part us; if he were so, they could not succeed. By supposing such an affection, you make everybody acting unnaturally and wrong, and me most unhappy. Do not distress me by the idea. I am not ashamed of having been mistaken – or, at least, it is slight, it is nothing in comparison of what I should feel in thinking ill of him or his sisters. Let me take it in the best light, in the light in which it may be understood.'

Elizabeth could not oppose such a wish; and from this time Mr Bingley's name was scarcely ever mentioned between them.

Mrs Bennet still continued to wonder and repine at his returning no more, and though a day seldom passed in which Elizabeth did not account for it clearly, there seemed little chance of her ever considering it with less perplexity. Her daughter endeavoured to convince her of what she did not believe herself, that his attentions to Jane had been merely the effect of a common and transient liking, which ceased when he saw her no more; but though the probability of the statement was admitted at the time, she had the same story to repeat every day. Mrs Bennet's best comfort was, that Mr Bingley must be down again in the summer.

Mr Bennet treated the matter differently. 'So, Lizzy,' said he one day, 'your sister is crossed in love I find. I congratulate her. Next to being married, a girl likes to be crossed in love a little now and then. It is something to think of, and gives her a sort of distinction among her companions. When is your turn to come? You will hardly bear to be long outdone by Jane. Now is your time. Here are officers enough at Meryton to disappoint all the young ladies in the country. Let Wickham be *your* man. He is a pleasant fellow, and would jilt you creditably.'

'Thank you, sir, but a less agreeable man would satisfy me. We must not all expect Jane's good fortune.'

'True,' said Mr Bennet, 'but it is a comfort to think that, whatever of that kind may befall you, you have an affectionate mother who will always make the most of it.'

Mr Wickham's society was of material service in dispelling the gloom, which the late perverse occurrences had thrown on many of the Longbourn family. They saw him often, and to his other recommendations was now added that of general unreserve. The whole of what Elizabeth had already heard, his claims on Mr Darcy, and all that he had suffered from him, was now openly acknowledged and publicly canvassed; and everybody was pleased to think how much they had always disliked Mr Darcy before they had known anything of the matter.

Miss Bennet was the only creature who could suppose there might be any extenuating circumstances in the case, unknown to the society of Hertfordshire; her mild and steady candour always pleaded for allowances, and urged the possibility of mistakes – but by everybody else Mr Darcy was condemned as the worst of men.

Chapter 25

After a week spent in professions of love and schemes of felicity, Mr Collins was called from his amiable Charlotte by the arrival of Saturday. The pain of separation, however, might be alleviated on his side, by preparations for the reception of his bride, as he had reason to hope, that shortly after his next return into Hertfordshire, the day would be fixed that was to make him the happiest of men. He took leave of his relations at Longbourn with as much solemnity as before; wished his fair cousins health and happiness again, and promised their father another letter of thanks.

On the following Monday, Mrs Bennet had the pleasure of receiving her brother and his wife, who came as usual to spend the Christmas at Longbourn. Mr Gardiner was a sensible, gentlemanlike man, greatly superior to his sister as well by nature as education. The Netherfield ladies would have had difficulty in believing that a man who lived by trade, and within view of his own warehouses, could have been so well bred and agreeable. Mrs Gardiner, who was several years younger than Mrs Bennet and Mrs Philips, was an amiable, intelligent, elegant woman, and a great favourite with all her Longbourn nieces. Between the two eldest and herself especially, there subsisted a very particular regard. They had frequently been staying with her in town.

The first part of Mrs Gardiner's business on her arrival, was to distribute her presents and describe the newest fashions. When this was done, she had a less active part to play. It became her turn to listen. Mrs Bennet had many grievances to relate, and much to complain of. They had all been very ill-used since she last saw her sister. Two of her girls had been on the point of marriage, and after all there was nothing in it.

'I do not blame Jane,' she continued, 'for Jane would have got Mr Bingley, if she could. But, Lizzy! Oh, sister! it is very hard to think that she might have been Mr Collins's wife by this time, had not it been for her own perverseness. He made her an offer in this very room, and she refused him. The consequence of it is, that Lady Lucas will have a daughter married before I have, and that Longbourn estate is just as much entailed as ever. The Lucases are very artful people indeed, sister. They are all for what they can get. I am sorry to say it of them, but so it is. It makes me very nervous and poorly, to be thwarted so in my own family, and to have neighbours who think of themselves before anybody else. However, your coming just at this time is the greatest of comforts, and I am very glad to hear what you tell us, of long sleeves.'

Mrs Gardiner, to whom the chief of this news had been given before, in the course of Jane and Elizabeth's correspondence with her, made her sister a slight answer, and in compassion to her nieces turned the conversation.

When alone with Elizabeth afterwards, she spoke more on the subject. 'It seems likely to have been a desirable match for Jane,' said she. 'I am sorry it went off. But these things happen so often! A young man, such as you describe Mr Bingley, so easily falls in love with a pretty girl for a few weeks, and when accident separates them, so easily forgets her, that these sort of inconstancies are very frequent.'

'An excellent consolation in its way,' said Elizabeth, 'but it will not do for *us*. We do not suffer by *accident*. It does not often happen that the interference of friends will persuade a young man of independent fortune to think no more of a girl, whom he was violently in love with only a few days before.'

'But that expression of "violently in love" is so hackneyed, so doubtful, so indefinite, that it gives me very little idea. It is as often applied to feelings which arise from an half-hour's acquaintance, as to a real, strong attachment. Pray, how *violent was* Mr Bingley's love?'

'I never saw a more promising inclination. He was growing quite inattentive to other people, and wholly engrossed by her. Every time they met, it was more decided and remarkable. At his own ball he offended two or three young ladies, by not asking them to dance, and I spoke to him twice myself, without receiving an answer. Could there be finer symptoms? Is not general incivility the very essence of love?'

'Oh, yes! – of that kind of love which I suppose him to have felt. Poor Jane! I am sorry for her, because, with her disposition, she may not get over it immediately. It had better have happened to *you*, Lizzy; you would have laughed yourself out of it sooner. But do you think she would be prevailed on to go back with us? Change of scene might be of service – and perhaps a little relief from home, may be as useful as anything.'

Elizabeth was exceedingly pleased with this proposal, and felt persuaded of her sister's ready acquiescence.

'I hope,' added Mrs Gardiner, 'that no consideration with regard to this young man will influence her. We live in so different a part of town, all our connections are so different, and, as you well know, we go out so little, that it is very improbable they should meet at all, unless he really comes to see her.'

'And *that* is quite impossible; for he is now in the custody of his friend, and Mr Darcy would no more suffer him to call on Jane in such a part of London! My dear aunt, how could you think of it? Mr Darcy may perhaps have *heard* of such a place as Gracechurch Street, but he would hardly think a month's ablution enough to cleanse him from its impurities, were he once to enter it; and depend upon it, Mr Bingley never stirs without him.'

'So much the better. I hope they will not meet at all. But does not Jane correspond with the sister? *She* will not be able to help calling.'

'She will drop the acquaintance entirely.'

Offended two or three young ladies

But in spite of the certainty in which Elizabeth affected to place this point, as well as the still more interesting one of Bingley's being withheld from seeing Jane, she felt a solicitude on the subject which convinced her, on examination, that she did not consider it entirely hopeless. It was possible, and sometimes she thought it probable, that his affection might be re-animated, and the influence of his friends successfully combated by the more natural influence of Jane's attractions.

Miss Bennet accepted her aunt's invitation with pleasure; and the Bingleys were no otherwise in her thoughts at the time, than as she hoped that, by Caroline's not living in the same house with her brother, she might occasionally spend a morning with her, without any danger of seeing him.

The Gardiners staid a week at Longbourn; and what with the Philipses, the Lucases, and the officers, there was not a day without its engagement. Mrs Bennet had so carefully provided for the entertainment of her brother and sister, that they did not once sit down to a family dinner. When the engagement was for home, some of the officers always made part of it, of which officers Mr Wickham was sure to be one; and on these occasions, Mrs Gardiner, rendered suspicious by Elizabeth's warm commendation of him, narrowly observed them both. Without supposing them, from what she saw, to be very seriously in love, their preference of each other was plain enough to make her a little uneasy; and she resolved to speak to Elizabeth on the subject before she left Hertfordshire, and represent to her the imprudence of encouraging such an attachment.

To Mrs Gardiner, Wickham had one means of

affording pleasure, unconnected with his general powers. About ten or a dozen years ago, before her marriage, she had spent a considerable time in that very part of Derbyshire, to which he belonged. They had, therefore, many acquaintance in common; and, though Wickham had been little there since the death of Darcy's father, five years before, it was yet in his power to give her fresher intelligence of her former friends, than she had been in the way of procuring.

Mrs Gardiner had seen Pemberley, and known the late Mr Darcy by character perfectly well. Here consequently was an inexhaustible subject of discourse. In comparing her recollection of Pemberley, with the minute description which Wickham could give, and in bestowing her tribute of praise on the character of its late possessor, she was delighting both him and herself. On being made acquainted with the present Mr Darcy's treatment of him, she tried to remember something of that gentleman's reputed disposition when quite a lad, which might agree with it, and was confident at last, that she recollected having heard Mr Fitzwilliam Darcy formerly spoken of as a very proud, ill-natured boy.

Chapter 26

Mrs Gardiner's caution to Elizabeth was punctually and kindly given on the first favourable opportunity of speaking to her alone; after honestly telling her what she thought, she thus went on:

'You are too sensible a girl, Lizzy, to fall in love merely because you are warned against it; and, therefore, I am not afraid of speaking openly. Seriously, I would have you be on your guard. Do not involve yourself, or endeavour to involve him in an affection which the want of fortune would make so very imprudent. I have nothing to say against *him*; he is a most interesting young man; and if he had the fortune he ought to have, I should think you could not do better. But as it is – you must not let your fancy run away with you. You have sense, and we all expect you to use it. Your father would depend on *your* resolution and good conduct, I am sure. You must not disappoint your father.'

'My dear aunt, this is being serious indeed.'

'Yes, and I hope to engage you to be serious likewise.'

'Well, then, you need not be under any alarm. I will take care of myself, and of Mr Wickham too. He shall not be in love with me, if I can prevent it.'

'Elizabeth, you are not serious now.'

'I beg your pardon. I will try again. At present I am not in love with Mr Wickham; no, I certainly am not. But he is, beyond all comparison, the most agreeable man I ever saw – and if he becomes really attached to me – I believe it will be better that he should not. I see the imprudence of it. Oh! *that* abominable Mr Darcy! – My father's opinion of me does me the greatest honour; and I should be miserable to forfeit it. My father, however, is partial to Mr Wickham. In short, my dear aunt, I should be very sorry to be the means of making any of you unhappy; but since we see every day that where there is affection, young people are seldom withheld by immediate want of fortune, from entering into engagements with each other, how can I promise to be wiser than so many of my fellow creatures if I am tempted, or how am I even to know that it would be wisdom to resist? All that I can promise you, therefore, is not to be in a hurry. I will not be in a hurry to believe myself his first object. When I am in company with him, I will not be wishing. In short, I will do my best.'

'Perhaps it will be as well, if you discourage his coming here so very often. At least, you should not *remind* your Mother of inviting him.'

'As I did the other day,' said Elizabeth, with a conscious smile; 'very true, it will be wise in me to refrain from *that*. But do not imagine that he is always here so often. It is on your account that he has been so frequently invited this week. You know my mother's ideas as to the necessity of constant company for her friends. But really, and upon my honour, I will try to do what I think to be wisest; and now, I hope you are satisfied.'

Her aunt assured her that she was; and Elizabeth having thanked her for the kindness of her hints, they parted; a wonderful instance of advice being given on such a point, without being resented.

Mr Collins returned into Hertfordshire soon after it had been quitted by the Gardiners and Jane; but as he took up his abode with the Lucases, his arrival was no great inconvenience to Mrs Bennet. His marriage was now fast approaching, and she was at length so far resigned as to think it inevitable, and even repeatedly to say in an ill-natured tone that she '*wished* they might be happy.' Thursday was to be the wedding day, and on Wednesday Miss Lucas paid her farewell visit; and when she rose to take leave, Elizabeth, ashamed of her mother's ungracious and reluctant good wishes, and sincerely affected herself, accompanied her out of the room.

As they went downstairs together, Charlotte said, 'I shall depend on hearing from you very often, Eliza.'

'*That* you certainly shall.'

'And I have another favour to ask. Will you come and see me?'

'We shall often meet, I hope, in Hertfordshire.'

'I am not likely to leave Kent for some time. Promise me, therefore, to come to Hunsford.'

Elizabeth could not refuse, though she foresaw little pleasure in the visit.

'My father and Maria are to come to me in March,' added Charlotte, 'and I hope you will consent to be of the party. Indeed, Eliza, you will be as welcome to me as either of them.'

The wedding took place; the bride and bridegroom set off for Kent from the church door, and everybody had as much to say or to hear on the subject as usual. Elizabeth soon heard from her friend; and their correspondence was as regular and frequent as it had ever been; that it should be equally unreserved was impossible. Elizabeth could never address her without feeling that all the comfort of intimacy was over, and, though determined not to slacken as a correspondent, it was for the sake of what had been, rather than what was. Charlotte's first letters were received with a good deal of eagerness; there could not but be curiosity to know how she would speak of her new home, how she would like Lady Catherine, and how happy she would dare pronounce herself to be; though, when the letters were read, Elizabeth felt that Charlotte expressed herself on every point exactly as she might have foreseen. She wrote cheerfully, seemed surrounded with comforts, and mentioned nothing which she could not praise. The house,

Will you come and see me?

furniture, neighbourhood, and roads, were all to her taste, and Lady Catherine's behaviour was most friendly and obliging. It was Mr Collins's picture of Hunsford and Rosings rationally softened; and Elizabeth perceived that she must wait for her own visit there, to know the rest.

Jane had already written a few lines to her sister to announce their safe arrival in London; and when she wrote again, Elizabeth hoped it would be in her power to say something of the Bingleys.

Her impatience for this second letter was as well rewarded as impatience generally is. Jane had been a week in town, without either seeing or hearing from Caroline. She accounted for it, however, by supposing that her last letter to her friend from Longbourn, had by some accident been lost.

'My aunt,' she continued, 'is going tomorrow into that part of the town, and I shall take the opportunity of calling in Grosvenor Street.'

She wrote again when the visit was paid, and she had seen Miss Bingley. 'I did not think Caroline in spirits,' were her words, 'but she was very glad to see me, and reproached me for giving her no notice of my coming to London. I was right, therefore; my last letter had never reached her. I enquired after their brother, of course. He was well, but so much engaged with Mr Darcy, that they scarcely ever saw him. I found that Miss Darcy was expected to dinner. I wish I could see her. My visit was not long, as Caroline and Mrs Hurst were going out. I dare say I shall soon see them here.'

Elizabeth shook her head over this letter. It convinced her, that accident only could discover to Mr Bingley her sister's being in town.

PRIDE AND PREJUDICE

Four weeks passed away, and Jane saw nothing of him. She endeavoured to persuade herself that she did not regret it; but she could no longer be blind to Miss Bingley's inattention. After waiting at home every morning for a fortnight, and inventing every evening a fresh excuse for her, the visitor did at last appear; but the shortness of her stay, and yet more, the alteration of her manner, would allow Jane to deceive herself no longer. The letter which she wrote on this occasion to her sister, will prove what she felt.

My dearest Lizzy will, I am sure, be incapable of triumphing in her better judgement, at my expense, when I confess myself to have been entirely deceived in Miss Bingley's regard for me. But, my dear sister, though the event has proved you right, do not think me obstinate if I still assert, that, considering what her behaviour was, my confidence was as natural as your suspicion. I do not at all comprehend her reason for wishing to be intimate with me, but if the same circumstances were to happen again, I am sure I should be deceived again. Caroline did not return my visit till yesterday; and not a note, not a line, did I receive in the mean time. When she did come, it was very evident that she had no pleasure in it; she made a slight, formal, apology, for not calling before, said not a word of wishing to see me again, and was in every respect so altered a creature, that when she went away, I was perfectly resolved to continue the acquaintance no longer. I pity, though I cannot help blaming her. She was very wrong in singling me out as she did; I can safely say, that every advance to intimacy began on her side. But I pity her, because she must feel that she has been acting wrong, and because I am very sure that anxiety for her brother is the cause of it. I need not explain myself farther; and though *we* know this anxiety to be quite needless, yet if she feels it, it will easily account for her behaviour to me; and so deservedly dear as he is to his sister, whatever anxiety she may feel on his behalf, is natural and amiable. I cannot but wonder, however, at her having any such fears now, because, if he had at all cared about me, we must have met long, long ago. He knows of my being in town, I am certain, from something she said herself; and yet it should seem by her manner of talking, as if she wanted to persuade herself that he is really partial to Miss Darcy. I cannot understand it. If I were not afraid of judging harshly, I should be almost tempted to say, that there is a strong appearance of duplicity in all this. But I will endeavour to banish every painful thought, and think only of what will make me happy, your affection, and the invariable kindness of my dear uncle and aunt. Let me hear from you very soon. Miss Bingley said something of his never returning to Netherfield again, of giving up the house, but not with any certainty. We had better not mention it. I am extremely glad that you have such pleasant accounts from our friends at Hunsford. Pray go to see them, with Sir William and Maria. I am sure you will be very comfortable there.

Yours, &c.

This letter gave Elizabeth some pain; but her spirits returned as she considered that Jane would no longer be duped, by the sister at least. All expectation from the brother was now absolutely over. She would not even wish for any renewal of his attentions. His character sunk on every review of it; and as a punishment for him, as well as a possible advantage to Jane, she seriously hoped he might really soon marry Mr Darcy's sister, as, by Wickham's account, she would make him abundantly regret what he had thrown away.

Mrs Gardiner about this time reminded Elizabeth of her promise concerning that gentleman, and required information; and Elizabeth had such to send as might rather give contentment to her aunt than to herself. His apparent partiality had subsided, his attentions were over, he was the admirer of someone else. Elizabeth was watchful enough to see it all, but she could see it and write of it without material pain. Her heart had been but slightly touched, and her vanity was satisfied with believing that *she* would have been his only choice, had fortune permitted it. The sudden acquisition of ten thousand pounds was the most remarkable charm of the young lady, to whom he was now rendering himself agreeable; but Elizabeth, less clear-sighted perhaps in his case than in Charlotte's, did not quarrel with him for his wish of independence. Nothing, on the contrary, could be more natural; and while able to suppose that it cost him a few struggles to relinquish her, she was ready to allow it a wise and desirable measure for both, and could very sincerely wish him happy.

All this was acknowledged to Mrs Gardiner; and after relating the circumstances, she thus went on: 'I am now convinced, my dear aunt, that I have never been much in love; for had I really experienced that pure and elevating passion, I should at present detest his very name, and wish him all manner of evil. But my feelings are not only cordial towards *him*; they are even impartial towards Miss King. I cannot find out that I hate her at all, or that I am in the least unwilling to think her a very good sort of girl. There can be no love in all this. My watchfulness has been effectual; and though I should certainly be a more interesting object to all my acquaintance, were I distractedly in love with him, I cannot say that I regret my comparative insignificance. Importance may sometimes be purchased too dearly. Kitty and Lydia take his defection much more to heart than I do. They are young in the ways of the world, and not yet open to the mortifying conviction that handsome young men must have something to live on, as well as the plain.'

Chapter 27

With no greater events than these in the Longbourn family, and otherwise diversified by little beyond the walks to Meryton, sometimes dirty and sometimes cold, did January and February pass away. March was to take Elizabeth to Hunsford. She had not at first thought very seriously of going thither; but Charlotte, she soon found, was depending on the plan, and she gradually learned to consider it herself with greater pleasure as well as greater certainty. Absence had increased her desire of seeing Charlotte again, and weakened her disgust of Mr Collins. There was novelty in the scheme, and as, with such a mother and such uncompanionable sisters, home could not be faultless, a little change was not unwelcome for its own sake. The journey would moreover give her a peep at Jane; and, in short, as the time drew near, she would have been very sorry for any delay. Everything, however, went on smoothly, and was finally settled according to Charlotte's first sketch. She was to accompany Sir William and his second daughter. The improvement of spending a night in London was added in time, and the plan became perfect as plan could be.

The only pain was in leaving her father, who would certainly miss her, and who, when it came to the point, so little liked her going, that he told her to write to him, and almost promised to answer her letter.

The farewell between herself and Mr Wickham was perfectly friendly; on his side even more. His present pursuit could not make him forget that Elizabeth had been the first to excite and to deserve his attention, the first to listen and to pity, the first to be admired; and in his manner of bidding her adieu, wishing her every enjoyment, reminding her of what she was to expect in Lady Catherine de Bourgh, and trusting their opinion of her – their opinion of everybody – would always coincide, there was a solicitude, an interest which she felt must ever attach her to him with a most sincere regard; and she parted from him convinced, that whether married or single, he must always be her model of the amiable and pleasing.

Her fellow-travellers the next day, were not of a kind to make her think him less agreeable. Sir William Lucas, and his daughter Maria, a good-humoured girl, but as empty-headed as himself, had nothing to say that could be worth hearing, and were listened to with about as much delight as the rattle of the chaise. Elizabeth loved absurdities, but she had known Sir William's too long. He could tell her nothing new of the wonders of his presentation and knighthood; and his civilities were worn out like his information.

It was a journey of only twenty-four miles, and they began it so early as to be in Gracechurch Street by noon. As they drove to Mr Gardiner's door, Jane was at a drawing-room window watching their arrival; when they entered the passage she was there to welcome them, and Elizabeth, looking earnestly in her face, was pleased to see it healthful and lovely as ever. On the stairs were a troop of little boys and girls, whose eagerness for their cousin's appearance would not allow them to wait in the drawing-room, and whose shyness, as they had not seen her for a twelvemonth, prevented their coming lower. All was joy and kindness. The day passed most pleasantly away; the morning in bustle and shopping, and the evening at one of the theatres.

Elizabeth then contrived to sit by her aunt. Their first subject was her sister; and she was more grieved than astonished to hear, in reply to her minute enquiries, that though Jane always struggled to support her spirits, there were periods of dejection. It was reasonable, however, to hope, that they would not continue long. Mrs Gardiner gave her the particulars also of Miss Bingley's visit in Gracechurch Street, and repeated conversations occurring at different times between Jane and herself, which proved that the former had, from her heart, given up the acquaintance.

Mrs Gardiner than rallied her niece on Wickham's desertion, and complimented her on bearing it so well.

'But, my dear Elizabeth,' she added, 'what sort of girl is Miss King? I should be sorry to think our friend mercenary.'

'Pray, my dear aunt, what is the difference in matrimonial affairs, between the mercenary and the

On the stairs were a troop of little boys and girls

prudent motive? Where does discretion end, and avarice begin? Last Christmas you were afraid of his marrying me, because it would be imprudent; and now, because he is trying to get a girl with only ten thousand pounds, you want to find out that he is mercenary.'

'If you will only tell me what sort of girl Miss King is, I shall know what to think.'

'She is a very good kind of girl, I believe. I know no harm of her.'

'But he paid her not the smallest attention, till her grandfather's death made her mistress of this fortune.'

'No – why should he? If it was not allowable for him to gain *my* affections, because I had no money, what occasion could there be for making love to a girl whom he did not care about, and who was equally poor?'

'But there seems indelicacy in directing his attentions towards her, so soon after this event.'

'A man in distressed circumstances has not time for all those elegant decorums which other people may observe. If *she* does not object to it, why should *we*?'

'*Her* not objecting, does not justify *him*. It only shows her being deficient in something herself – sense or feeling.'

'Well,' cried Elizabeth, 'have it as you choose. *He* shall be mercenary, and *she* shall be foolish.'

'No, Lizzy, that is what I do *not* choose. I should be sorry, you know, to think ill of a young man who has lived so long in Derbyshire.'

'Oh! if that is all, I have a very poor opinion of young men who live in Derbyshire; and their intimate friends who live in Hertfordshire are not much better. I am sick of them all. Thank Heaven! I am going tomorrow where I shall find a man who has not one agreeable quality, who has neither manner nor sense to recommend him. Stupid men are the only ones worth knowing, after all.'

'Take care, Lizzy; that speech savours strongly of disappointment.'

Before they were separated by the conclusion of the play, she had the unexpected happiness of an invitation to accompany her uncle and aunt in a tour of pleasure which they proposed taking in the summer.

'We have not quite determined how far it shall carry us,' said Mrs Gardiner, 'but perhaps to the Lakes.'

No scheme could have been more agreeable to Elizabeth, and her acceptance of the invitation was most ready and grateful. 'My dear, dear aunt,' she rapturously cried, 'what delight! what felicity! You give me fresh life and vigour. Adieu to disappointment and spleen. What are men to rocks and mountains? Oh! what hours of transport we shall spend! And when we *do* return, it shall not be like other travellers, without being able to give one accurate idea of anything. We *will* know where we have gone – we *will* recollect what we have seen. Lakes, mountains, and rivers, shall not be jumbled together in our imaginations; nor, when we attempt to describe any particular scene, will we begin quarrelling about its relative situation. Let *our* first effusions be less insupportable than those of the generality of travellers.'

Chapter 28

Every object in the next day's journey was new and interesting to Elizabeth; and her spirits were in a state for enjoyment; for she had seen her sister looking so well as to banish all fear for her health, and the prospect of her northern tour was a constant source of delight.

When they left the high road for the lane to Hunsford, every eye was in search of the Parsonage, and every turning expected to bring it in view. The paling of Rosings Park was their boundary on one side. Elizabeth smiled at the recollection of all that she had heard of its inhabitants.

At length the Parsonage was discernible. The garden sloping to the road, the house standing in it, the green pales and the laurel hedge, everything declared they were arriving. Mr Collins and Charlotte appeared at the door, and the carriage stopped at the small gate, which led by a short gravel walk to the house, amidst the nods and smiles of the whole party. In a moment they were all out of the chaise, rejoicing at the sight of each other. Mrs Collins welcomed her friend with the liveliest pleasure, and Elizabeth was more and more satisfied with coming, when she found herself so affectionately received. She saw instantly that her cousin's manners were not altered by his marriage; his formal civility was just what it had been, and he detained her some minutes at the gate to hear and satisfy his enquiries after all her family. They were then, with no other delay than his pointing out the neatness of the entrance, taken into the house; and as

Mr Collins and Charlotte appeared at the door

soon as they were in the parlour, he welcomed them a
second time with ostentatious formality to his humble
abode, and punctually repeated all his wife's offers of
refreshment.

Elizabeth was prepared to see him in his glory; and
she could not help fancying that in displaying the
good proportion of the room, its aspect and its
furniture, he addressed himself particularly to her, as
if wishing to make her feel what she had lost in
refusing him. But though everything seemed neat and
comfortable, she was not able to gratify him by any
sigh of repentance; and rather looked with wonder at
her friend that she could have so cheerful an air, with
such a companion. When Mr Collins said anything of
which his wife might reasonably be ashamed, which
certainly was not unseldom, she involuntarily turned
her eye on Charlotte. Once or twice she could discern
a faint blush; but in general Charlotte wisely did not
hear. After sitting long enough to admire every article
of furniture in the room, from the sideboard to the
fender, to give an account of their journey and of all
that had happened in London, Mr Collins invited
them to take a stroll in the garden, which was large
and well laid out, and to the cultivation of which
he attended himself. To work in his garden was one
of his most respectable pleasures; and Elizabeth
admired the command of countenance with which
Charlotte talked of the healthfulness of the exercise,
and owned she encouraged it as much as possible.
Here, leading the way through every walk and cross
walk, and scarcely allowing them an interval to utter
the praises he asked for, every view was pointed out
with a minuteness which left beauty entirely behind.
He could number the fields in every direction, and

could tell how many trees there were in the most distant clump. But of all the views which his garden, or which the country, or the kingdom could boast, none were to be compared with the prospect of Rosings, afforded by an opening in the trees that bordered the park nearly opposite the front of his house. It was a handsome modern building, well situated on rising ground.

From his garden, Mr Collins would have led them round his two meadows, but the ladies not having shoes to encounter the remains of a white frost, turned back; and while Sir William accompanied him, Charlotte took her sister and friend over the house, extremely well pleased, probably, to have the opportunity of showing it without her husband's help. It was rather small, but well built and convenient; and everything was fitted up and arranged with a neatness and consistency of which Elizabeth gave Charlotte all the credit. When Mr Collins could be forgotten, there was really a great air of comfort throughout, and by Charlotte's evident enjoyment of it, Elizabeth supposed he must be often forgotten.

She had already learnt that Lady Catherine was still in the country. It was spoken of again while they were at dinner, when Mr Collins joining in, observed, 'Yes, Miss Elizabeth, you will have the honour of seeing Lady Catherine de Bourgh on the ensuing Sunday at church, and I need not say you will be delighted with her. She is all affability and condescension, and I doubt not but you will be honoured with some portion of her notice when service is over. I have scarcely any hesitation in saying that she will include you and my sister Maria in every invitation with which she honours us during your stay here. Her behaviour to my dear

Charlotte is charming. We dine at Rosings twice every week, and are never allowed to walk home. Her ladyship's carriage is regularly ordered for us. I *should* say, one of her ladyship's carriages, for she has several.'

'Lady Catherine is a very respectable, sensible woman indeed,' added Charlotte, 'and a most attentive neighbour.'

'Very true, my dear, that is exactly what I say. She is the sort of woman whom one cannot regard with too much deference.'

The evening was spent chiefly in talking over Hertfordshire news, and telling again what had been already written; and when it closed, Elizabeth in the solitude of her chamber had to meditate upon Charlotte's degree of contentment, to understand her address in guiding, and composure in bearing with her husband, and to acknowledge that it was all done very well. She had also to anticipate how her visit would pass, the quiet tenor of their usual employments, the vexatious interruptions of Mr Collins, and the gaieties of their intercourse with Rosings. A lively imagination soon settled it all.

About the middle of the next day, as she was in her room getting ready for a walk, a sudden noise below seemed to speak the whole house in confusion; and after listening a moment, she heard somebody running upstairs in a violent hurry, and calling loudly after her. She opened the door, and met Maria in the landing place, who, breathless with agitation, cried out, 'Oh, my dear Eliza! pray make haste and come into the dining-room, for there is such a sight to be seen! I will not tell you what it is. Make haste, and come down this moment.'

Elizabeth asked questions in vain; Maria would tell

her nothing more, and down they ran into the dining-room, which fronted the lane, in quest of this wonder; it was two ladies stopping in a low phaeton at the garden gate.

'And is this all?' cried Elizabeth. 'I expected at least that the pigs were got into the garden, and here is nothing but Lady Catherine and her daughter!'

'La! my dear,' said Maria quite shocked at the mistake, 'it is not Lady Catherine. The old lady is Mrs Jenkinson, who lives with them. The other is Miss De Bourgh. Only look at her. She is quite a little creature. Who would have thought she could be so thin and small!'

'She is abominably rude to keep Charlotte out of doors in all this wind. Why does she not come in?'

'Oh! Charlotte says, she hardly ever does. It is the greatest of favours when Miss De Bourgh comes in.'

'I like her appearance,' said Elizabeth, struck with other ideas. 'She looks sickly and cross. Yes, she will do for him very well. She will make him a very proper wife.'

Mr Collins and Charlotte were both standing at the gate in conversation with the ladies; and Sir William, to Elizabeth's high diversion, was stationed in the doorway, in earnest contemplation of the greatness before him, and constantly bowing whenever Miss De Bourgh looked that way.

At length there was nothing more to be said; the ladies drove on, and the others returned into the house. Mr Collins no sooner saw the two girls than he began to congratulate them on their good fortune, which Charlotte explained by letting them know that the whole party was asked to dine at Rosings the next day.

Chapter 29

Mr Collins's triumph in consequence of this invitation was complete. The power of displaying the grandeur of his patroness to his wondering visitors, and of letting them see her civility towards himself and his wife, was exactly what he had wished for; and that an opportunity of doing it should be given so soon, was such an instance of Lady Catherine's condescension as he knew not how to admire enough.

'I confess,' said he, 'that I should not have been at all surprised by her ladyship's asking us on Sunday to drink tea and spend the evening at Rosings. I rather expected, from my knowledge of her affability, that it would happen. But who could have foreseen such an attention as this? Who could have imagined that we should receive an invitation to dine there (an invitation moreover including the whole party) so immediately after your arrival!'

'I am the less surprised at what has happened,' replied Sir William, 'from that knowledge of what the manners of the great really are, which my situation in life has allowed me to acquire. About the Court, such instances of elegant breeding are not uncommon.'

Scarcely anything was talked of the whole day or next morning, but their visit to Rosings. Mr Collins was carefully instructing them in what they were to expect, that the sight of such rooms, so many servants, and so splendid a dinner might not wholly overpower them.

When the ladies were separating for the toilette, he said to Elizabeth, 'Do not make yourself uneasy, my dear cousin, about your apparel. Lady Catherine is far from requiring that elegance of dress in us, which becomes herself and daughter. I would advise you merely to put on whatever of your clothes is superior to the rest, there is no occasion for anything more. Lady Catherine will not think the worse of you for being simply dressed. She likes to have the distinction of rank preserved.'

While they were dressing, he came two or three times to their different doors, to recommend their being quick, as Lady Catherine very much objected to be kept waiting for her dinner. Such formidable accounts of her Ladyship, and her manner of living, quite frightened Maria Lucas, who had been little used to company, and she looked forward to her introduction at Rosings, with as much apprehension, as her father had done to his presentation at St James's.

As the weather was fine, they had a pleasant walk of about half a mile across the park. Every park has its beauty and its prospects; and Elizabeth saw much to be pleased with, though she could not be in such raptures as Mr Collins expected the scene to inspire, and was but slightly affected by his enumeration of the windows in front of the house, and his relation of what the glazing altogether had originally cost Sir Lewis De Bourgh.

When they ascended the steps to the hall, Maria's alarm was every moment increasing, and even Sir William did not look perfectly calm. Elizabeth's courage did not fail her. She had heard nothing of Lady Catherine that spoke her awful from any extraordinary talents or miraculous virtue, and the mere stateliness of money and rank, she thought she could witness without trepidation.

From the entrance hall, of which Mr Collins pointed out, with a rapturous air, the fine proportion and finished ornaments, they followed the servants through an ante-chamber, to the room where Lady Catherine, her daughter, and Mrs Jenkinson were sitting. Her ladyship, with great condescension, arose to receive them; and as Mrs Collins had settled it with her husband that the office of introduction should be her's, it was performed in a proper manner, without any of those apologies and thanks which he would have thought necessary.

In spite of having been at St James's, Sir William was so completely awed, by the grandeur surrounding him, that he had but just courage enough to make a very low bow, and take his seat without saying a word; and his daughter, frightened almost out of her senses, sat on the edge of her chair, not knowing which way to look. Elizabeth found herself quite equal to the scene, and could observe the three ladies before her composedly. Lady Catherine was a tall, large woman, with strongly-marked features, which might once have been handsome. Her air was not conciliating, nor was her manner of receiving them, such as to make her visitors forget their inferior rank. She was not rendered formidable by silence; but whatever she said, was spoken in so authoritative a tone, as marked her self-importance, and brought Mr Wickham immediately to Elizabeth's mind; and from the observation of the day altogether, she believed Lady Catherine to be exactly what he had represented.

When, after examining the mother, in whose countenance and deportment she soon found some resemblance of Mr Darcy, she turned her eyes on the daughter, she could almost have joined in Maria's astonishment, at her being so thin, and so small. There was neither in figure nor face, any likeness between the ladies. Miss De Bourgh was pale and sickly; her features, though not plain, were insignificant; and she spoke very little, except in a low voice, to Mrs Jenkinson, in whose appearance there was nothing remarkable, and who was entirely engaged in listening to what she said, and placing a screen in the proper direction before her eyes.

After sitting a few minutes, they were all sent to one of the windows, to admire the view, Mr Collins attending them to point out its beauties, and Lady Catherine kindly informing them that it was much better worth looking at in the summer.

The dinner was exceedingly handsome, and there were all the servants, and all the articles of plate which Mr Collins had promised; and, as he had likewise foretold, he took his seat at the bottom of the table, by her ladyship's desire, and looked as if he felt that life could furnish nothing greater. He carved, and ate, and praised with delighted alacrity; and every dish was commended, first by him, and then by Sir William, who was now enough recovered to echo whatever his son in law said, in a manner which Elizabeth wondered Lady Catherine could bear. But Lady Catherine seemed gratified by their excessive admiration, and gave most gracious smiles, especially when any dish on the table proved a novelty to them. The party did not supply much conversation. Elizabeth was ready to speak whenever there was an opening, but she was seated between Charlotte and Miss De Bourgh – the former of whom was engaged in listening to Lady Catherine, and the latter said not a word to her all dinner time. Mrs Jenkinson was chiefly employed in watching how little Miss De Bourgh ate, pressing her to try some other dish, and fearing she were indisposed. Maria thought speaking out of the question, and the gentlemen did nothing but eat and admire.

When the ladies returned to the drawing room, there was little to be done but to hear Lady Catherine talk, which she did without any intermission till coffee came in, delivering her opinion on every subject in so decisive a manner as proved that she was not used to have her judgement controverted. She enquired into Charlotte's domestic concerns familiarly and minutely, and gave her a great deal of advice, as to the management of them all; told her how everything ought to be regulated in so small a family as hers, and instructed her as to the care of her cows and her poultry. Elizabeth found that nothing was beneath this great lady's attention, which could furnish her with an occasion of dictating to others. In the intervals of her discourse with Mrs Collins, she addressed a variety of questions to Maria and Elizabeth, but especially to the latter, of whose connections she knew the least, and who she observed to Mrs Collins, was a very genteel, pretty kind of girl. She asked her at different times, how many sisters she had, whether they were older or younger than herself, whether any of them were likely to be married, whether they were handsome, where they had been educated, what carriage her father kept, and what had been her mother's maiden name? Elizabeth felt all the impertinence of her questions, but answered them very composedly. Lady Catherine then observed, 'Your father's estate is entailed on Mr Collins, I think. For your sake,' turning to Charlotte, 'I am glad of it; but otherwise I see no occasion for entailing estates from the female line. It was not thought necessary in Sir Lewis de Bourgh's family. Do you play and sing, Miss Bennet?'

'A little.'

'Oh! then – sometime or other we shall be happy to hear you. Our instrument is a capital one, probably superior to – . You shall try it someday. Do your sisters play and sing?'

'One of them does.'

'Why did not you all learn? – You ought all to have learned. The Miss Webbs all play, and their father has not so good an income as yours. Do you draw?'

'No, not at all.'

'What, none of you?'

'Not one.'

'That is very strange. But I suppose you had no opportunity. Your mother should have taken you to town every spring for the benefit of masters.'

'My mother would have had no objection, but my father hates London.'

'Has your governess left you?'

'We never had any governess.'

'No governess! How was that possible? Five daughters brought up at home without a governess! – I never heard of such a thing. Your mother must have been quite a slave to your education.'

Elizabeth could hardly help smiling, as she assured her that had not been the case.

'Then, who taught you? who attended to you? Without a governess you must have been neglected.'

'Compared with some families, I believe we were; but such of us as wished to learn, never wanted the means. We were always encouraged to read, and had all the masters that were necessary. Those who chose to be idle, certainly might.'

'Aye, no doubt; but that is what a governess will prevent, and if I had known your mother, I should have advised her most strenuously to engage one. I always say that nothing is to be done in education without steady and regular instruction, and nobody but a governess can give it. It is wonderful how many families I have been the means of supplying in that way. I am always glad to get a young person well placed out. Four nieces of Mrs Jenkinson are most delightfully situated through my means; and it was but the other day, that I recommended another young person, who was merely accidentally mentioned to me, and the family are quite delighted with her. Mrs Collins, did I tell you of Lady Metcalfe's calling yesterday to thank me? She finds Miss Pope a treasure. "Lady Catherine," said she, "you have given me a treasure." Are any of your younger sisters out, Miss Bennet?'

'Yes, ma'am, all.'

'All! – What, all five out at once? Very odd! – And you only the second. The younger ones out before the elder are married! – Your younger sisters must be very young?'

'Yes, my youngest is not sixteen. Perhaps *she* is full young to be much in company. But really, ma'am, I think it would be very hard upon younger sisters, that they should not have their share of society and amusement because the elder may not have the means or inclination to marry early. The last born has as good a right to the pleasures of youth, as the first. And to be kept back on *such* a motive! – I think it would be not very likely to promote sisterly affection or delicacy of mind.'

'Upon my word,' said her Ladyship, 'you give your

'Lady Catherine,' said she, 'you have given me a treasure.'

opinion very decidedly for so young a person. Pray, what is your age?'

'With three younger sisters grown up,' replied Elizabeth smiling, 'your Ladyship can hardly expect me to own it.'

Lady Catherine seemed quite astonished at not receiving a direct answer; and Elizabeth suspected herself to be the first creature who had ever dared to trifle with so much dignified impertinence.

'You cannot be more than twenty, I am sure – therefore you need not conceal your age.'

'I am not one and twenty.'

When the gentlemen had joined them, and tea was over, the card-tables were placed. Lady Catherine,

Sir William, and Mr and Mrs Collins sat down to quadrille; and as Miss De Bourgh chose to play at casino, the two girls had the honour of assisting Mrs Jenkinson to make up her party. Their table was superlatively stupid. Scarcely a syllable was uttered that did not relate to the game, except when Mrs Jenkinson expressed her fears of Miss De Bourgh's being too hot or too cold, or having too much or too little light. A great deal more passed at the other table. Lady Catherine was generally speaking – stating the mistakes of the three others, or relating some anecdote of herself. Mr Collins was employed in agreeing to everything her Ladyship said, thanking her for every fish he won, and apologising if he thought he won too many. Sir William did not say much. He was storing his memory with anecdotes and noble names.

When Lady Catherine and her daughter had played as long as they chose, the tables were broke up, the carriage was offered to Mrs Collins, gratefully accepted, and immediately ordered. The party then gathered round the fire to hear Lady Catherine determine what weather they were to have on the morrow. From these instructions they were summoned by the arrival of the coach, and with many speeches of thankfulness on Mr Collins's side, and as many bows on Sir William's, they departed. As soon as they had driven from the door, Elizabeth was called on by her cousin, to give her opinion of all that she had seen at Rosings, which, for Charlotte's sake, she made more favourable than it really was. But her commendation, though costing her some trouble, could by no means satisfy Mr Collins, and he was very soon obliged to take her Ladyship's praise into his own hands.

Chapter 30

Sir William stayed only a week at Hunsford; but his visit was long enough to convince him of his daughter's being most comfortably settled, and of her possessing such a husband and such a neighbour as were not often met with. While Sir William was with them, Mr Collins devoted his mornings to driving him out in his gig, and showing him the country; but when he went away, the whole family returned to their usual employments, and Elizabeth was thankful to find that they did not see more of her cousin by the alteration, for the chief of the time between breakfast and dinner was now passed by him either at work in the garden, or in reading and writing, and looking out of window in his own book room, which fronted the road. The room in which the ladies sat was backwards. Elizabeth at first had rather wondered that Charlotte should not prefer the dining-parlour for common use; it was a better sized room, and had a pleasanter aspect; but she soon saw that her friend had an excellent reason for what she did, for Mr Collins would undoubtedly have been much less in his own apartment, had they sat in one equally lively; and she gave Charlotte credit for the arrangement.

From the drawing-room they could distinguish nothing in the lane, and were indebted to Mr Collins for the knowledge of what carriages went along, and how often especially Miss De Bourgh drove by in her phaeton, which he never failed coming to inform them of, though it happened almost every day. She not unfrequently stopped at the Parsonage, and had a few

He never failed coming to inform them

minutes' conversation with Charlotte, but was scarcely ever prevailed on to get out.

Very few days passed in which Mr Collins did not walk to Rosings, and not many in which his wife did not think it necessary to go likewise; and till Elizabeth recollected that there might be other family livings to be disposed of, she could not understand the sacrifice of so many hours. Now and then, they were honoured with a call from her Ladyship, and nothing escaped her observation that was passing in the room during these visits. She examined into their employments, looked at their work, and advised them to do it differently; found fault with the arrangement of the furniture, or detected the housemaid in negligence; and if she accepted any refreshment, seemed to do it only for the sake of finding out that Mrs Collins's joints of meat were too large for her family.

Elizabeth soon perceived that though this great lady was not in the commission of the peace for the county, she was a most active magistrate in her own parish, the minutest concerns of which were carried to her by Mr Collins; and whenever any of the cottagers were disposed to be quarrelsome, discontented or too poor, she sallied forth into the village to settle their differences, silence their complaints, and scold them into harmony and plenty.

The entertainment of dining at Rosings was repeated about twice a week; and, allowing for the loss of Sir William, and there being only one card table in the evening, every such entertainment was the counterpart of the first. Their other engagements were few; as the style of living of the neighbourhood in general, was beyond the Collinses' reach. This however was no evil to Elizabeth, and upon the whole she spent her time comfortably enough; there were half-hours of pleasant conversation with Charlotte, and the weather was so fine for the time of year, that she had often great enjoyment out of doors. Her favourite walk, and where she frequently went while the others were calling on Lady Catherine, was along the open grove which edged that side of the park, where there was a nice sheltered path, which no one seemed to value but herself, and where she felt beyond the reach of Lady Catherine's curiosity.

In this quiet way, the first fortnight of her visit soon passed away. Easter was approaching, and the week preceding it, was to bring an addition to the family at Rosings, which in so small a circle must be important. Elizabeth had heard soon after her arrival, that Mr Darcy was expected there in the course of a few weeks, and though there were not many of her acquaintance whom she did not prefer, his coming would furnish one comparatively new to look at in their Rosings parties, and she might be amused in seeing how hopeless Miss Bingley's designs on him were, by his behaviour to his cousin, for whom he was evidently destined by Lady Catherine; who talked of his coming with the greatest satisfaction, spoke of him in terms of the highest admiration, and seemed almost angry to find that he had already been frequently seen by Miss Lucas and herself.

His arrival was soon known at the Parsonage, for Mr Collins was walking the whole morning within view of the lodges opening into Hunsford Lane, in order to have the earliest assurance of it; and after making his bow as the carriage turned into the Park, hurried home with the great intelligence. On the following morning he hastened to Rosings to pay his respects. There were two nephews of Lady Catherine to require them, for Mr Darcy had brought with him a Colonel Fitzwilliam, the younger son of his uncle, Lord — and to the great surprise of all the party, when Mr Collins returned the gentlemen accompanied him.

Charlotte had seen them from her husband's room, crossing the road, and immediately running into the other, told the girls what an honour they might expect, adding, 'I may thank you, Eliza, for this piece of civility. Mr Darcy would never have come so soon to wait upon me.'

Elizabeth had scarcely time to disclaim all right to the compliment, before their approach was announced by the doorbell, and shortly afterwards the three gentlemen entered the room. Colonel Fitzwilliam, who led the way, was about thirty, not handsome, but in person

The gentlemen accompanied him

and address most truly the gentleman. Mr Darcy looked just as he had been used to look in Hertford-shire, paid his compliments, with his usual reserve, to Mrs Collins; and whatever might be his feelings towards her friend, met her with every appearance of composure. Elizabeth merely curtseyed to him, without saying a word.

Colonel Fitzwilliam entered into conversation directly with the readiness and ease of a well-bred man, and talked very pleasantly; but his cousin, after having addressed a slight observation on the house and garden to Mrs Collins, sat for some time without speaking to anybody. At length, however, his civility was so far awakened as to enquire of Elizabeth after the health of her family.

She answered him in the usual way, and after a moment's pause, added, 'My eldest sister has been in town these three months. Have you never happened to see her there?'

She was perfectly sensible that he never had; but she wished to see whether he would betray any conscious-ness of what had passed between the Bingleys and Jane; and she thought he looked a little confused as he answered that he had never been so fortunate as to meet Miss Bennet. The subject was pursued no farther, and the gentlemen soon afterwards went away.

Chapter 31

Colonel Fitzwilliam's manners were very much admired at the parsonage, and the ladies all felt that he must add considerably to the pleasure of their engagements at Rosings. It was some days, however,

At church

before they received any invitation thither, for while
there were visitors in the house, they could not be
necessary; and it was not till Easter Day, almost a
week after the gentlemen's arrival, that they were
honoured by such an attention, and then they were
merely asked on leaving church to come there in the
evening. For the last week they had seen very little of
either Lady Catherine or her daughter. Colonel
Fitzwilliam had called at the parsonage more than
once during the time, but Mr Darcy they had only
seen at church.

The invitation was accepted of course, and at a proper hour they joined the party in Lady Catherine's drawing-room. Her ladyship received them civilly, but it was plain that their company was by no means so acceptable as when she could get nobody else; and she was, in fact, almost engrossed by her nephews, speaking to them, especially to Darcy, much more than to any other person in the room.

Colonel Fitzwilliam seemed really glad to see them; anything was a welcome relief to him at Rosings; and Mrs Collins's pretty friend had moreover caught his fancy very much. He now seated himself by her, and talked so agreeably of Kent and Hertfordshire, of travelling and staying at home, of new books and music, that Elizabeth had never been half so well entertained in that room before; and they conversed with so much spirit and flow, as to draw the attention of Lady Catherine herself, as well as of Mr Darcy. *His* eyes had been soon and repeatedly turned towards them with a look of curiosity; and that her ladyship after a while shared the feeling, was more openly acknowledged, for she did not scruple to call out, 'What is that you are saying, Fitzwilliam? What is it you are talking of? What are you telling Miss Bennet? Let me hear what it is.'

'We are speaking of music, Madam,' said he, when no longer able to avoid a reply.

'Of music! Then pray speak aloud. It is of all subjects my delight. I must have my share in the conversation, if you are speaking of music. There are few people in England, I suppose, who have more true enjoyment of music than myself, or a better natural taste. If I had ever learnt, I should have been a great proficient. And so would Anne, if her health had allowed her to apply. I am confident that she would have performed delightfully. How does Georgiana get on, Darcy?'

Mr Darcy spoke with affectionate praise of his sister's proficiency.

'I am very glad to hear such a good account of her,' said Lady Catherine; 'and pray tell her from me, that she cannot expect to excel, if she does not practise a great deal.'

'I assure you, Madam,' he replied, 'that she does not need such advice. She practises very constantly.'

'So much the better. It cannot be done too much; and when I next write to her, I shall charge her not to neglect it on any account. I often tell young ladies, that no excellence in music is to be acquired, without constant practice. I have told Miss Bennet several times, that she will never play really well, unless she practises more; and though Mrs Collins has no instrument, she is very welcome, as I have often told her, to come to Rosings every day, and play on the pianoforte in Mrs Jenkinson's room. She would be in nobody's way, you know, in that part of the house.'

Mr Darcy looked a little ashamed of his aunt's ill breeding, and made no answer.

When coffee was over, Colonel Fitzwilliam reminded Elizabeth of having promised to play to him; and she sat down directly to the instrument. He drew a chair near her. Lady Catherine listened to half a song, and then talked, as before, to her other nephew; till the latter walked away from her, and moving with his usual deliberation towards the pianoforte, stationed himself so as to command a full view of the fair performer's countenance.

Elizabeth saw what he was doing, and at the first

convenient pause, turned to him with an arch smile, and said, 'You mean to frighten me, Mr Darcy, by coming in all this state to hear me? But I will not be alarmed though your sister *does* play so well. There is a stubbornness about me that never can bear to be frightened at the will of others. My courage always rises with every attempt to intimidate me.'

'I shall not say that you are mistaken,' he replied, 'because you could not really believe me to entertain any design of alarming you; and I have had the pleasure of your acquaintance long enough to know, that you find great enjoyment in occasionally professing opinions which in fact are not your own.'

Elizabeth laughed heartily at this picture of herself, and said to Colonel Fitzwilliam, 'Your cousin will give you a very pretty notion of me, and teach you not to believe a word I say. I am particularly unlucky in meeting with a person so well able to expose my real character, in a part of the world, where I had hoped to pass myself off with some degree of credit. Indeed, Mr Darcy, it is very ungenerous in you to mention all that you knew to my disadvantage in Hertfordshire – and, give me leave to say, very impolitic too – for it is provoking me to retaliate, and such things may come out, as will shock your relations to hear.'

'I am not afraid of you,' said he, smilingly.

'Pray let me hear what you have to accuse him of,' cried Colonel Fitzwilliam. 'I should like to know how he behaves among strangers.'

'You shall hear then – but prepare yourself for something very dreadful. The first time of my ever seeing him in Hertfordshire, you must know, was at a ball – and at this ball, what do you think he did? He danced only four dances! I am sorry to pain you – but so it was. He danced only four dances, though gentlemen were scarce; and, to my certain knowledge, more than one young lady was sitting down in want of a partner. Mr Darcy, you cannot deny the fact.'

'I had not at that time the honour of knowing any lady in the assembly beyond my own party.'

'True; and nobody can ever be introduced in a ball room. Well, Colonel Fitzwilliam, what do I play next? My fingers wait your orders.'

'Perhaps,' said Darcy, 'I should have judged better, had I sought an introduction, but I am ill qualified to recommend myself to strangers.'

'Shall we ask your cousin the reason of this?' said Elizabeth, still addressing Colonel Fitzwilliam. 'Shall we ask him why a man of sense and education, and who has lived in the world, is ill qualified to recommend himself to strangers?'

'I can answer your question,' said Fitzwilliam, 'without applying to him. It is because he will not give himself the trouble.'

'I certainly have not the talent which some people possess,' said Darcy, 'of conversing easily with those I have never seen before. I cannot catch their tone of conversation, or appear interested in their concerns, as I often see done.'

'My fingers,' said Elizabeth, 'do not move over this instrument in the masterly manner which I see so many women's do. They have not the same force or rapidity, and do not produce the same expression. But then I have always supposed it to be my own fault – because I would not take the trouble of practising. It is not that I do not believe *my* fingers as capable as any other woman's of superior execution.'

Darcy smiled and said, 'You are perfectly right.

You have employed your time much better. No one admitted to the privilege of hearing you, can think anything wanting. We neither of us perform to strangers.'

Here they were interrupted by Lady Catherine, who called out to know what they were talking of. Elizabeth immediately began playing again. Lady Catherine approached, and, after listening for a few minutes, said to Darcy, 'Miss Bennet would not play at all amiss, if she practised more, and could have the advantage of a London master. She has a very good notion of fingering, though her taste is not equal to Anne's. Anne would have been a delightful performer, had her health allowed her to learn.'

Elizabeth looked at Darcy to see how cordially he assented to his cousin's praise; but neither at that moment nor at any other could she discern any symptom of love; and from the whole of his behaviour to Miss De Bourgh she derived this comfort for Miss Bingley, that he might have been just as likely to marry *her*, had she been his relation.

Lady Catherine continued her remarks on Elizabeth's performance, mixing with them many instructions on execution and taste. Elizabeth received them with all the forbearance of civility; and at the request of the gentlemen remained at the instrument till her ladyship's carriage was ready to take them all home.

Chapter 32

Elizabeth was sitting by herself the next morning, and writing to Jane, while Mrs Collins and Maria were gone on business into the village, when she was startled by a ring at the door, the certain signal of a visitor. As she had heard no carriage, she thought it not unlikely to be Lady Catherine, and under that apprehension was putting away her half-finished letter that she might escape all impertinent questions, when the door opened, and to her very great surprise, Mr Darcy, and Mr Darcy only, entered the room.

He seemed astonished too on finding her alone, and apologised for his intrusion, by letting her know that he had understood all the ladies to be within.

They then sat down, and when her enquiries after Rosings were made, seemed in danger of sinking into total silence. It was absolutely necessary, therefore, to think of something, and in this emergence recollecting *when* she had seen him last in Hertfordshire, and feeling curious to know what he would say on the subject of their hasty departure, she observed, 'How very suddenly you all quitted Netherfield last November, Mr Darcy! It must have been a most agreeable surprise to Mr Bingley to see you all after him so soon; for, if I recollect right, he went but the day before. He and his sisters were well, I hope, when you left London.'

'Perfectly so – I thank you.'

She found that she was to receive no other answer – and, after a short pause, added, 'I think I have understood that Mr Bingley has not much idea of ever returning to Netherfield again?'

'I have never heard him say so; but it is probable that he may spend very little of his time there in future. He has many friends, and he is at a time of life when friends and engagements are continually increasing.'

'If he means to be but little at Netherfield, it would be better for the neighbourhood that he should give up the place entirely, for then we might possibly get a settled family there. But perhaps Mr Bingley did not take the house so much for the convenience of the neighbourhood as for his own, and we must expect him to keep or quit it on the same principle.'

'I should not be surprised,' said Darcy, 'if he were to give it up, as soon as any eligible purchase offers.'

Elizabeth made no answer. She was afraid of talking longer of his friend; and, having nothing else to say, was now determined to leave the trouble of finding a subject to him.

He took the hint, and soon began with, 'This seems a very comfortable house. Lady Catherine, I believe, did a great deal to it when Mr Collins first came to Hunsford.'

'I believe she did – and I am sure she could not have bestowed her kindness on a more grateful object.'

'Mr Collins appears very fortunate in his choice of a wife.'

'Yes, indeed; his friends may well rejoice in his having met with one of the very few sensible women who would have accepted him, or have made him happy if they had. My friend has an excellent under-standing – though I am not certain that I consider her marrying Mr Collins as the wisest thing she ever did. She seems perfectly happy, however, and in a prudential light, it is certainly a very good match for her.'

'It must be very agreeable to her to be settled within so easy a distance of her own family and friends.'

'An easy distance do you call it? It is nearly fifty miles.'

'And what is fifty miles of good road? Little more than half a day's journey. Yes, I call it a *very* easy distance.'

'I should never have considered the distance as one of the *advantages* of the match,' cried Elizabeth. 'I should never have said Mrs Collins was settled *near* her family.'

'It is a proof of your own attachment to Hertfordshire. Anything beyond the very neighbourhood of Longbourn, I suppose, would appear far.'

As he spoke there was a sort of smile, which Elizabeth fancied she understood; he must be supposing her to be thinking of Jane and Netherfield, and she blushed as she answered, 'I do not mean to say that a woman may not be settled too near her family. The far and the near must be relative, and depend on many varying circumstances. Where there is fortune to make the expense of travelling unimportant, distance becomes no evil. But that is not the case *here*. Mr and Mrs Collins have a comfortable income, but not such a one as will allow of frequent journeys – and I am persuaded my friend would not call herself *near* her family under less than *half* the present distance.'

Mr Darcy drew his chair a little towards her, and said, '*You* cannot have a right to such very strong local attachment. *You* cannot have been always at Longbourn.'

Elizabeth looked surprised. The gentleman experienced some change of feeling; he drew back his chair, took a newspaper from the table, and, glancing over it, said, in a colder voice, 'Are you pleased with Kent?'

A short dialogue on the subject of the country ensued, on either side calm and concise – and soon put an end to by the entrance of Charlotte and her sister, just returned from their walk. The tête à tête surprised them. Mr Darcy related the mistake which had occasioned his intruding on Miss Bennet, and after sitting a few minutes longer without saying much to anybody, went away.

'What can be the meaning of this!' said Charlotte, as soon as he was gone. 'My dear Eliza he must be in love with you, or he would never have called on us in this familiar way.'

But when Elizabeth told of his silence, it did not seem very likely, even to Charlotte's wishes, to be the case; and after various conjectures, they could at last only suppose his visit to proceed from the difficulty of finding anything to do, which was the more probable from the time of year. All field sports were over. Within doors there was Lady Catherine, books, and a billiard table, but gentlemen cannot be always within doors; and in the nearness of the Parsonage, or the pleasantness of the walk to it, or of the people who lived in it, the two cousins found a temptation from this period of walking thither almost every day. They called at various times of the morning, sometimes separately, sometimes together, and now and then accompanied by their aunt. It was plain to them all that Colonel Fitzwilliam came because he had pleasure in their society, a persuasion which of course recommended him still more; and Elizabeth was reminded by her own satisfaction in being with him,

Now and then accompanied by their aunt

as well as by his evident admiration of her, of her former favourite George Wickham; and though, in comparing them, she saw there was less captivating softness in Colonel Fitzwilliam's manners, she believed he might have the best informed mind.

But why Mr Darcy came so often to the Parsonage, it was more difficult to understand. It could not be for society, as he frequently sat there ten minutes together without opening his lips; and when he did speak, it seemed the effect of necessity rather than of choice – a sacrifice to propriety, not a pleasure to himself. He seldom appeared really animated. Mrs Collins knew not what to make of him. Colonel Fitzwilliam's occasionally laughing at his stupidity, proved that he was generally different, which her own knowledge of him could not have told her; and as she would have liked to believe this change the effect of love, and the object of that love, her friend Eliza, she sat herself seriously to work to find it out. She watched him whenever they were at Rosings, and whenever he came to Hunsford; but without much success. He certainly looked at her friend a great deal, but the expression of that look was disputable. It was an earnest, steadfast gaze, but she often doubted whether there were much admiration in it, and sometimes it seemed nothing but absence of mind.

She had once or twice suggested to Elizabeth the possibility of his being partial to her, but Elizabeth always laughed at the idea; and Mrs Collins did not think it right to press the subject, from the danger of raising expectations which might only end in disappointment; for in her opinion it admitted not of a doubt, that all her friend's dislike would vanish, if she could suppose him to be in her power.

In her kind schemes for Elizabeth, she sometimes planned her marrying Colonel Fitzwilliam. He was beyond comparison the pleasantest man; he certainly admired her, and his situation in life was most eligible; but, to counterbalance these advantages, Mr Darcy had considerable patronage in the church, and his cousin could have none at all.

Chapter 33

More than once did Elizabeth in her ramble within the Park unexpectedly meet Mr Darcy. She felt all the perverseness of the mischance that should bring him where no one else was brought; and to prevent its ever happening again, took care to inform him at first, that it was a favourite haunt of hers. How it could occur a second time therefore was very odd! – Yet it did, and even a third. It seemed like wilful ill-nature, or a voluntary penance, for on these occasions it was not merely a few formal enquiries and an awkward pause and then away, but he actually thought it necessary to turn back and walk with her. He never said a great deal, nor did she give herself the trouble of talking or of listening much; but it struck her in the course of their third rencontre that he was asking some odd unconnected questions – about her pleasure in being at Hunsford, her love of solitary walks, and her opinion of Mr and Mrs Collins's happiness; and that in speaking of Rosings and her not perfectly under-standing the house, he seemed to expect that whenever she came into Kent again she would be staying *there* too. His words seemed to imply it. Could he have Colonel Fitzwilliam in his thoughts? She supposed, if he meant anything, he must mean an allusion to what might arise in that quarter. It distressed her a little, and she was quite glad to find herself at the gate in the pales opposite the Parsonage.

She was engaged one day as she walked, in re-perusing Jane's last letter, and dwelling on some passages which proved that Jane had not written in spirits, when, instead of being again surprised by Mr Darcy, she saw on looking up that Colonel Fitzwilliam was meeting her. Putting away the letter immediately and forcing a smile, she said, 'I did not know before that you ever walked this way.'

'I have been making the tour of the Park,' he replied, 'as I generally do every year, and intend to close it with a call at the Parsonage. Are you going much farther?'

'No, I should have turned in a moment.'

And accordingly she did turn, and they walked towards the Parsonage together.

'Do you certainly leave Kent on Saturday?' said she.

'Yes – if Darcy does not put it off again. But I am at his disposal. He arranges the business just as he pleases.'

'And if not able to please himself in the arrangement, he has at least great pleasure in the power of choice. I do not know anybody who seems more to enjoy the power of doing what he likes than Mr Darcy.'

'He likes to have his own way very well,' replied Colonel Fitzwilliam. 'But so we all do. It is only that he has better means of having it than many others, because he is rich, and many others are poor. I speak feelingly. A younger son, you know, must be inured to self-denial and dependence.'

234

She saw on looking up that Colonel Fitzwilliam
was meeting her

'In my opinion, the younger son of an Earl can know very little of either. Now, seriously, what have you ever known of self-denial and dependence? When have you been prevented by want of money from going wherever you chose, or procuring anything you had a fancy for?'

'These are home questions – and perhaps I cannot say that I have experienced many hardships of that nature. But in matters of greater weight, I may suffer from the want of money. Younger sons cannot marry where they like.'

'Unless where they like women of fortune, which I think they very often do.'

'Our habits of expense make us too dependent, and there are not many in my rank of life who can afford to marry without some attention to money.'

'Is this,' thought Elizabeth, 'meant for me?' and she coloured at the idea; but, recovering herself, said in a lively tone, 'And pray, what is the usual price of an Earl's younger son? Unless the elder brother is very sickly, I suppose you would not ask above fifty thousand pounds.'

He answered her in the same style, and the subject dropped. To interrupt a silence which might make him fancy her affected with what had passed, she soon afterwards said, 'I imagine your cousin brought you down with him chiefly for the sake of having some-body at his disposal. I wonder he does not marry, to secure a lasting convenience of that kind. But, perhaps his sister does as well for the present, and, as she is under his sole care, he may do what he likes with her.'

'No,' said Colonel Fitzwilliam, 'that is an advantage which he must divide with me. I am joined with him in the guardianship of Miss Darcy.'

'Are you, indeed? And pray what sort of guardians do you make? Does your charge give you much trouble? Young ladies of her age, are sometimes a little difficult to manage, and if she has the true Darcy spirit, she may like to have her own way.'

As she spoke, she observed him looking at her earnestly, and the manner in which he immediately asked her why she supposed Miss Darcy likely to give them any uneasiness, convinced her that she had somehow or other got pretty near the truth. She directly replied, 'You need not be frightened. I never heard any harm of her; and I dare say she is one of the most tractable creatures in the world. She is a very great favourite with some ladies of my acquaintance, Mrs Hurst and Miss Bingley. I think I have heard you say that you know them.'

'I know them a little. Their brother is a pleasant gentlemanlike man – he is a great friend of Darcy's.'

'Oh! yes,' said Elizabeth drily – 'Mr Darcy is uncommonly kind to Mr Bingley, and takes a prodigious deal of care of him.'

'Care of him! – Yes, I really believe Darcy *does* take care of him in those points where he most wants care. From something that he told me in our journey hither, I have reason to think Bingley very much indebted to him. But I ought to beg his pardon, for I have no right to suppose that Bingley was the person meant. It was all conjecture.'

'What is it you mean?'

'It is a circumstance which Darcy of course would not wish to be generally known, because if it were to get round to the lady's family, it would be an unpleasant thing.'

'You may depend upon my not mentioning it.'

'And remember that I have not much reason for supposing it to be Bingley. What he told me was merely this; that he congratulated himself on having lately saved a friend from the inconveniences of a most imprudent marriage, but without mentioning names or any other particulars, and I only suspected it to be Bingley from believing him the kind of young man to get into a scrape of that sort, and from knowing them to have been together the whole of last summer.'

'Did Mr Darcy give you his reasons for this interference?'

'I understood that there were some very strong objections against the lady.'

'And what arts did he use to separate them?'

'He did not talk to me of his own arts,' said Fitzwilliam smiling. 'He only told me, what I have now told you.'

Elizabeth made no answer, and walked on, her heart swelling with indignation. After watching her a little, Fitzwilliam asked her why she was so thoughtful.

'I am thinking of what you have been telling me,' said she. 'Your cousin's conduct does not suit my feelings. Why was he to be the judge?'

'You are rather disposed to call his interference officious?'

'I do not see what right Mr Darcy had to decide on the propriety of his friend's inclination, or why, upon his own judgement alone, he was to determine and direct in what manner that friend was to be happy.'

'But,' she continued, recollecting herself, 'as we know none of the particulars, it is not fair to condemn him. It is not to be supposed that there was much affection in the case.'

'That is not an unnatural surmise,' said Fitzwilliam,

'but it is lessening the honour of my cousin's triumph very sadly.'

This was spoken jestingly, but it appeared to her so just a picture of Mr Darcy, that she would not trust herself with an answer; and, therefore, abruptly changing the conversation, talked on indifferent matters till they reached the parsonage. There, shut into her own room, as soon as their visitor left them, she could think without interruption of all that she had heard. It was not to be supposed that any other people could be meant than those with whom she was connected. There could not exist in the world *two* men, over whom Mr Darcy could have such boundless influence. That he had been concerned in the measures taken to separate Mr Bingley and Jane, she had never doubted; but she had always attributed to Miss Bingley the principal design and arrangement of them. If his own vanity, however, did not mislead him, *he* was the cause, his pride and caprice were the cause of all that Jane had suffered, and still continued to suffer. He had ruined for a while every hope of happiness for the most affectionate, generous heart in the world; and no one could say how lasting an evil he might have inflicted.

'There were some very strong objections against the lady,' were Colonel Fitzwilliam's words, and these strong objections probably were, her having one uncle who was a country attorney, and another who was in business in London.

'To Jane herself,' she exclaimed, 'there could be no possibility of objection. All loveliness and goodness as she is! Her understanding excellent, her mind improved, and her manners captivating. Neither could anything be urged against my father, who, though with some peculiarities, has abilities which Mr Darcy himself need not disdain, and respectability which he will probably never reach.' When she thought of her mother indeed, her confidence gave way a little, but she would not allow that any objections *there* had material weight with Mr Darcy, whose pride, she was convinced, would receive a deeper wound from the want of importance in his friend's connections, than from their want of sense; and she was quite decided at last, that he had been partly governed by this worst kind of pride, and partly by the wish of retaining Mr Bingley for his sister.

The agitation and tears which the subject occasioned, brought on a headache; and it grew so much worse towards the evening that, added to her unwillingness to see Mr Darcy, it determined her not to attend her cousins to Rosings, where they were engaged to drink tea. Mrs Collins, seeing that she was really unwell, did not press her to go, and as much as possible prevented her husband from pressing her, but Mr Collins could not conceal his apprehension of Lady Catherine's being rather displeased by her staying at home.

Chapter 34

When they were gone, Elizabeth, as if intending to exasperate herself as much as possible against Mr Darcy, chose for her employment the examination of all the letters which Jane had written to her since her being in Kent. They contained no actual complaint, nor was there any revival of past occurrences, or any communication of present suffering. But in all, and in

Reading Jane's letters

almost every line of each, there was a want of that cheerfulness which had been used to characterise her style, and which, proceeding from the serenity of a mind at ease with itself, and kindly disposed towards everyone, had been scarcely ever clouded. Elizabeth noticed every sentence conveying the idea of uneasiness, with an attention which it had hardly received on the first perusal. Mr Darcy's shameful boast of what misery he had been able to inflict, gave her a keener sense of her sister's sufferings. It was some consolation to think that his visit to Rosings was to end on the day after the next, and a still greater, that in less than a fortnight she should herself be with Jane again, and enabled to contribute to the recovery of her spirits, by all that affection could do.

She could not think of Darcy's leaving Kent, without remembering that his cousin was to go with him; but Colonel Fitzwilliam had made it clear that he had no intentions at all, and agreeable as he was, she did not mean to be unhappy about him.

While settling this point, she was suddenly roused by the sound of the door bell, and her spirits were a little fluttered by the idea of its being Colonel Fitzwilliam himself, who had once before called late in the evening, and might now come to enquire particularly after her. But this idea was soon banished, and her spirits were very differently affected, when, to her utter amazement, she saw Mr Darcy walk into the room. In an hurried manner he immediately began an enquiry after her health, imputing his visit to a wish of hearing that she were better. She answered him with cold civility. He sat down for a few moments, and then getting up walked about the room. Elizabeth was surprised, but said not a word.

In vain have I struggled

After a silence of several minutes he came towards her in an agitated manner, and thus began, 'In vain have I struggled. It will not do. My feelings will not be repressed. You must allow me to tell you how ardently I admire and love you.'

Elizabeth's astonishment was beyond expression. She stared, coloured, doubted, and was silent. This he considered sufficient encouragement, and the avowal of all that he felt and had long felt for her, immediately followed. He spoke well, but there were feelings besides those of the heart to be detailed, and he was not more eloquent on the subject of tenderness than of pride. His sense of her inferiority – of its being a degradation – of the family obstacles which judgement had always opposed to inclination, were dwelt on with a warmth which seemed due to the consequence he was wounding, but was very unlikely to recommend his suit.

In spite of her deeply-rooted dislike, she could not be insensible to the compliment of such a man's affection, and though her intentions did not vary for an instant, she was at first sorry for the pain he was to receive; till, roused to resentment by his subsequent language, she lost all compassion in anger. She tried, however, to compose herself to answer him with patience, when he should have done. He concluded with representing to her the strength of that attachment which, in spite of all his endeavours, he had found impossible to conquer; and with expressing his hope that it would now be rewarded by her acceptance of his hand. As he said this, she could easily see that he had no doubt of a favourable answer. He *spoke* of apprehension and anxiety, but his countenance expressed real security.

Such a circumstance could only exasperate farther, and when he ceased, the colour rose into her cheeks, and she said, 'In such cases as this, it is, I believe, the established mode to express a sense of obligation for the sentiments avowed, however unequally they may be returned. It is natural that obligation should be felt, and if I could *feel* gratitude, I would now thank you. But I cannot – I have never desired your good opinion, and you have certainly bestowed it most unwillingly. I am sorry to have occasioned pain to anyone. It has been most unconsciously done, however, and I hope will be of short duration. The feelings which, you tell me, have long prevented the acknowledgment of your regard, can have little difficulty in overcoming it after this explanation.'

Mr Darcy, who was leaning against the mantlepiece with his eyes fixed on her face, seemed to catch her words with no less resentment than surprise. His complexion became pale with anger, and the disturbance of his mind was visible in every feature. He was struggling for the appearance of composure, and would not open his lips, till he believed himself to have attained it. The pause was to Elizabeth's feelings dreadful.

At length, in a voice of forced calmness, he said, 'And this is all the reply which I am to have the honour of expecting! I might, perhaps, wish to be informed why, with so little *endeavour* at civility, I am thus rejected. But it is of small importance.'

'I might as well enquire,' replied she, 'why with so evident a design of offending and insulting me, you chose to tell me that you liked me against your will, against your reason, and even against your character? Was not this some excuse for incivility, if I *was* uncivil? But I have other provocations. You know I have. Had not my own feelings decided against you, had they been indifferent, or had they even been favourable, do you think that any consideration would tempt me to accept the man, who has been the means of ruining, perhaps for ever, the happiness of a most beloved sister?'

As she pronounced these words, Mr Darcy changed colour; but the emotion was short, and he listened without attempting to interrupt her while she continued.

'I have every reason in the world to think ill of you. No motive can excuse the unjust and ungenerous part you acted *there*. You dare not, you cannot deny that you have been the principal, if not the only means of dividing them from each other, of exposing one to the censure of the world for caprice and instability, the other to its derision for disappointed hopes, and involving them both in misery of the acutest kind.'

She paused, and saw with no slight indignation that he was listening with an air which proved him wholly unmoved by any feeling of remorse. He even looked at her with a smile of affected incredulity.

'Can you deny that you have done it?' she repeated.

With assumed tranquillity he then replied, 'I have no wish of denying that I did everything in my power to separate my friend from your sister, or that I rejoice in my success. Towards *him* I have been kinder than towards myself.'

Elizabeth disdained the appearance of noticing this civil reflection, but its meaning did not escape, nor was it likely to conciliate her.

'But it is not merely this affair,' she continued, 'on which my dislike is founded. Long before it had taken place, my opinion of you was decided. Your character was unfolded in the recital which I received many months ago from Mr Wickham. On this subject, what can you have to say? In what imaginary act of friendship can you here defend yourself? or under what misrepresentation, can you here impose upon others?'

'You take an eager interest in that gentleman's concerns,' said Darcy in a less tranquil tone, and with a heightened colour.

'Who that knows what his misfortunes have been, can help feeling an interest in him?'

'His misfortunes!' repeated Darcy contemptuously; 'yes, his misfortunes have been great indeed.'

'And of your infliction,' cried Elizabeth with energy. 'You have reduced him to his present state of poverty, comparative poverty. You have withheld the advantages, which you must know to have been designed for him. You have deprived the best years of his life, of that independence which was no less his due than his desert. You have done all this! and yet you can treat the mention of his misfortunes with contempt and ridicule.'

'And this,' cried Darcy, as he walked with quick steps across the room, 'is your opinion of me! This is the estimation in which you hold me! I thank you for explaining it so fully. My faults, according to this calculation, are heavy indeed! But perhaps,' added he, stopping in his walk, and turning towards her, 'these offences might have been overlooked, had not your pride been hurt by my honest confession of the scruples that had long prevented my forming any serious design. These bitter accusations might have been suppressed, had I with greater policy concealed my struggles, and flattered you into the belief of my being impelled by unqualified, unalloyed inclination; by reason, by reflection, by everything. But disguise of every sort is my abhorrence. Nor am I ashamed of the feelings I related. They were natural and just. Could you expect me to rejoice in the inferiority of your connections? To congratulate myself on the hope of relations, whose condition in life is so decidedly beneath my own?'

Elizabeth felt herself growing more angry every

moment; yet she tried to the utmost to speak with composure when she said, 'You are mistaken, Mr Darcy, if you suppose that the mode of your declaration affected me in any other way, than as it spared me the concern which I might have felt in refusing you, had you behaved in a more gentlemanlike manner.'

She saw him start at this, but he said nothing, and she continued, 'You could not have made me the offer of your hand in any possible way that would have tempted me to accept it.'

Again his astonishment was obvious; and he looked at her with an expression of mingled incredulity and mortification. She went on.

'From the very beginning, from the first moment I may almost say, of my acquaintance with you, your manners impressing me with the fullest belief of your arrogance, your conceit, and your selfish disdain of the feelings of others, were such as to form that groundwork of disapprobation, on which succeeding events have built so immoveable a dislike; and I had not known you a month before I felt that you were the last man in the world whom I could ever be prevailed on to marry.'

'You have said quite enough, madam. I perfectly comprehend your feelings, and have now only to be ashamed of what my own have been. Forgive me for having taken up so much of your time, and accept my best wishes for your health and happiness.'

And with these words he hastily left the room, and Elizabeth heard him the next moment open the front door and quit the house.

The tumult of her mind was now painfully great. She knew not how to support herself, and from actual weakness sat down and cried for half an hour. Her astonishment, as she reflected on what had passed, was increased by every review of it. That she should receive an offer of marriage from Mr Darcy! that he should have been in love with her for so many months! so much in love as to wish to marry her in spite of all the objections which had made him prevent his friend's marrying her sister, and which must appear at least with equal force in his own case, was almost incredible! it was gratifying to have inspired unconsciously so strong an affection. But his pride, his abominable pride, his shameless avowal of what he had done with respect to Jane, his unpardonable assurance in acknowledging, though he could not justify it, and the unfeeling manner in which he had mentioned Mr Wickham, his cruelty towards whom he had not attempted to deny, soon overcame the pity which the consideration of his attachment had for a moment excited.

She continued in very agitating reflections till the sound of Lady Catherine's carriage made her feel how unequal she was to encounter Charlotte's observation, and hurried her away to her room.

Chapter 35

Elizabeth awoke the next morning to the same thoughts and meditations which had at length closed her eyes. She could not yet recover from the surprise of what had happened; it was impossible to think of anything else, and totally indisposed for employment, she resolved soon after breakfast to indulge herself in air and exercise. She was proceeding directly to her favourite walk, when the recollection of Mr Darcy's sometimes coming there stopped her, and instead of entering the park, she turned up the lane, which led her farther from the turnpike road. The park paling was still the boundary on one side, and she soon passed one of the gates into the ground.

After walking two or three times along that part of the lane, she was tempted, by the pleasantness of the morning, to stop at the gates and look into the park. The five weeks which she had now passed in Kent, had made a great difference in the country, and every day was adding to the verdure of the early trees. She was on the point of continuing her walk, when she caught a glimpse of a gentleman within the sort of grove which edged the park; he was moving that way; and fearful of its being Mr Darcy, she was directly retreating. But the person who advanced, was now near enough to see her, and stepping forward with eagerness, pronounced her name. She had turned away, but on hearing herself called, though in a voice which proved it to be Mr Darcy, she moved again towards the gate. He had by that time reached it also, and holding out a letter, which she instinctively took, said with a look of haughty composure, 'I have been walking in the grove some time in the hope of meeting you. Will you do me the honour of reading that letter?' – And then, with a slight bow, turned again into the plantation, and was soon out of sight.

With no expectation of pleasure, but with the strongest curiosity, Elizabeth opened the letter, and to her still increasing wonder, perceived an envelope containing two sheets of letter paper, written quite through, in a very close hand. The envelope itself was likewise full. Pursuing her way along the lane, she then began it. It was dated from Rosings, at eight o'clock in the morning, and was as follows:

Be not alarmed, Madam, on receiving this letter, by the apprehension of its containing any repetition of those sentiments, or renewal of those offers, which were last night so disgusting to you. I write without any intention of paining you, or humbling myself, by dwelling on wishes, which, for the happiness of both, cannot be too soon forgotten; and the effort which the formation, and the perusal of this letter must occasion, should have been spared, had not my character required it to be written and read. You must, therefore, pardon the freedom with which I demand your attention ; your feelings, I know, will bestow it unwillingly, but I demand it of your justice.

Two offences of a very different nature, and by no means of equal magnitude, you last night laid to my charge. The first mentioned was, that, regardless of the sentiments of either, I had detached Mr Bingley from your sister – and the other, that I had, in defiance of various claims, in defiance of honour and humanity, ruined the immediate prosperity, and blasted the prospects of Mr Wickham. Wilfully and wantonly to have thrown off the companion of my youth, the acknowledged favourite of my father, a young man who had scarcely any other dependence than on our patronage, and who had been brought up to expect its exertion, would be a depravity, to which the separation of two young persons, whose affection could be the growth of only a few weeks, could bear no comparison. But from the severity of that blame which was last night so liberally bestowed, respecting each circumstance, I shall hope to be in future secured, when the following account of my actions and their motives has been read. If, in the explanation of them which is due to myself, I am under the necessity of relating feelings which may be offensive to your's, I can only say that I am sorry. The necessity must be obeyed – and farther apology would be absurd. I had not been long in Hertford-shire, before I saw, in common with others, that Bingley preferred your eldest sister, to any other young woman in the country. But it was not till the evening of the dance at Netherfield that I had any apprehension of his feeling a serious attachment. I had often seen him in love before. At that ball, while I had the honour of dancing with you, I was first made acquainted, by Sir William Lucas's accidental information, that Bingley's attentions to your sister had given rise to a general expectation of their marriage. He spoke of it as a certain event, of which the time alone could be undecided. From that moment I observed my friend's behaviour attentively; and I could then perceive that his partiality for Miss Bennet was beyond what I had ever witnessed in him. Your sister I also watched. Her look and manners were open, cheerful and engaging as ever, but without any symptom of peculiar regard, and I remained convinced from the evening's scrutiny, that though she received his attentions with pleasure, she did not invite them by any participation of sentiment. If *you* have not been mistaken here, *I* must have been in an error. Your superior knowledge of your sister must make the latter probable. If it be so, if I have been misled by such error, to inflict pain on her, your resentment has not been unreasonable. But I shall not scruple to assert, that the serenity of your sister's counte-nance and air was such, as might have given the most acute observer, a conviction that, however amiable her temper, her heart was not likely to be easily touched. That I was desirous of believing her indifferent is certain – but I will venture to say that my investigations and decisions are not usually influenced by my hopes or fears. I did not believe her to be indifferent because I wished it – I believed it on impartial conviction, as truly as I wished it in reason. My objections to the marriage were not merely those, which I last night acknowledged to have required the utmost force of passion to put aside, in my own case; the want of connection could not be so great an evil to my friend as to me. But there were other causes of repugnance – causes which, though still existing, and existing to an equal degree in both instances, I had myself endeavoured to forget, because they were not immediately before me. These causes must be stated, though briefly. The situation of your mother's family, though objectionable, was nothing in comparison of that total want of propriety so frequently, so almost uniformly betrayed by herself, by your three younger sisters, and occasionally even by your father. Pardon me. It pains me to offend you. But amidst your concern for the defects of your nearest relations, and your displeasure at this representation of them, let it give you consolation to consider that, to have conducted yourselves so as to avoid any share of the like censure, is praise no less generally bestowed on you and your eldest sister, than it is honourable to the sense and disposition of both. I will only say further, that from what passed that evening, my opinion of all parties was confirmed, and every inducement heightened, which could have led me before, to preserve my friend from what I esteemed a most unhappy connection. He left Netherfield for London, on the day following, as you, I am certain, remember, with the design of soon returning. The part which I acted, is now to be explained. His sisters' uneasiness had been equally excited with my own; our coincidence of feeling was soon discovered; and, alike sensible that no time was to be lost in detaching their brother, we shortly resolved on joining him directly in London. We accordingly went – and there I readily engaged in the office of pointing out to my friend, the certain evils of such a choice. I described, and enforced them earnestly. But, however this remonstrance might have staggered or delayed his determination, I do not suppose that it would ultimately have prevented the marriage, had it not been seconded by the assurance which I hesitated not in giving, of your sister's indifference. He had before believed her to return his affection with sincere, if not with equal regard. But Bingley has great natural modesty, with a stronger dependence on my judgement than on his own. To convince him, therefore, that he had deceived himself, was no very difficult point. To persuade him against returning into Hertfordshire, when that conviction had been given, was scarcely the work of a moment. I cannot blame myself for having done thus much. There is but one part of my conduct in the whole affair, on which I do not reflect with satisfaction; it is that I condescended to adopt the measures of art so far as to conceal from him your sister's being in town. I knew it myself, as it was known to Miss Bingley, but her brother is even yet ignorant of it. That they might have met without ill consequence,

is perhaps probable – but hi...
to me enough extinguish...
without some danger. P...cealment,
this disguise, was benea... ...ie, however,
and it was done for ... ...this subject I
have nothing more to s... ...pology to offer.
If I have wounded you... ...feelings, it was
unknowingly done; and though the motives which
governed me may to you very naturally appear
insufficient, I have not yet learnt to condemn them.
With respect to that other, more weighty accusa-
tion, of having injured Mr Wickham, I can only
refute it by laying before you the whole of his
connection with my family. Of what he has *particularly* accused me I am ignorant; but of the truth of
what I shall relate, I can summon more than one
witness of undoubted veracity. Mr Wickham is the
son of a very respectable man, who had for many
years the management of all the Pemberley estates;
and whose good conduct in the discharge of his
trust, naturally inclined my father to be of service to
him, and on George Wickham, who was his godson, his kindness was therefore liberally bestowed.
My father supported him at school, and afterwards
at Cambridge – most important assistance, as his
own father, always poor from the extravagance of
his wife, would have been unable to give him a
gentleman's education. My father was not only
fond of this young man's society, whose manners
were always engaging; he had also the highest
opinion of him, and hoping the church would be
his profession, intended to provide him in it. As for
myself, it is many, many years since I first began to
think of him in a very different manner. The vicious

es – the want of principle which he was
to guard from the knowledge of his best
friend, could not escape the observation of a young
man of nearly the same age with himself, and who
had opportunities of seeing him in unguarded moments, which Mr Darcy could not have. Here again
I shall give you pain – to what degree you only can
tell. But whatever may be the sentiments which Mr
Wickham has created, a suspicion of their nature
shall not prevent me from unfolding his real character. It adds even another motive. My excellent father
died about five years ago; and his attachment to Mr
Wickham was to the last so steady, that in his will he
particularly recommended it to me, to promote his
advancement in the best manner that his profession
might allow, and if he took orders, desired that a
valuable family living might be his as soon as it
became vacant. There was also a legacy of one
thousand pounds. His own father did not long
survive mine, and within half a year from these
events, Mr Wickham wrote to inform me that,
having finally resolved against taking orders, he
hoped I should not think it unreasonable for him to
expect some more immediate pecuniary advantage,
in lieu of the preferment, by which he could not be
benefited. He had some intention, he added, of
studying the law, and I must be aware that the
interest of one thousand pounds would be a very
insufficient support therein. I rather wished, than
believed him to be sincere; but at any rate, was
perfectly ready to accede to his proposal. I knew
that Mr Wickham ought not to be a clergyman. The
business was therefore soon settled. He resigned all
claim to assistance in the church, were it possible

that he could ever be in a situation to receive it, and accepted in return three thousand pounds. All connection between us seemed now dissolved. I thought too ill of him, to invite him to Pemberley, or admit his society in town. In town I believe he chiefly lived, but his studying the law was a mere pretence, and being now free from all restraint, his life was a life of idleness and dissipation. For about three years I heard little of him; but on the decease of the incumbent of the living which had been, designed for him, he applied to me again by letter for the presentation. His circumstances, he assured me, and I had no difficulty in believing it, were exceedingly bad. He had found the law a most unprofitable study, and was now absolutely resolved on being ordained, if I would present him to the living in question – of which he trusted there could be little doubt, as he was well assured that I had no other person to provide for, and I could not have forgotten my revered father's intentions. You will hardly blame me for refusing to comply with this entreaty, or for resisting every repetition of it. His resentment was in proportion to the distress of his circumstances – and he was doubtless as violent in his abuse of me to others, as in his reproaches to myself. After this period, every appearance of acquaintance was dropped. How he lived I know not. But last summer he was again most painfully obtruded on my notice. I must now mention a circumstance which I would wish to forget myself, and which no obligation less than the present should induce me to unfold to any human being. Having said thus much, I feel no doubt of your secrecy. My sister, who is more than ten years my junior, was left to the guardianship of my mother's nephew, Colonel Fitzwilliam, and myself. About a year ago, she was taken from school, and an establishment formed for her in London; and last summer she went with the lady who presided over it, to Ramsgate; and thither also went Mr Wickham, undoubtedly by design; for there proved to have been a prior acquaintance between him and Mrs Younge, in whose character we were most unhappily deceived; and by her connivance and aid, he so far recommended himself to Georgiana, whose affectionate heart retained a strong impression of his kindness to her as a child, that she was persuaded to believe herself in love, and to consent to an elopement. She was then but fifteen, which must be her excuse; and after stating her imprudence, I am happy to add, that I owed the knowledge of it to herself. I joined them unexpectedly a day or two before the intended elopement, and then Georgiana, unable to support the idea of grieving and offending a brother whom she almost looked up to as a father, acknowledged the whole to me. You may imagine what I felt and how I acted. Regard for my sister's credit and feelings prevented any public exposure, but I wrote to Mr Wickham, who left the place immediately, and Mrs Younge was of course removed from her charge. Mr Wickham's chief object was unquestionably my sister's fortune, which is thirty thousand pounds; but I cannot help supposing that the hope of revenging himself on me, was a strong inducement. His revenge would have been complete indeed. This, madam, is a faithful narrative of every event in which we have been concerned together; and if you do not absolutely reject it as false, you will, I hope, acquit me henceforth of cruelty towards Mr Wickham. I know not in what manner, under what form of falsehood he has imposed on you; but his success is not perhaps to be wondered at. Ignorant as you previously were of everything concerning either, detection could not be in your power, and suspicion certainly not in your inclination. You may possibly wonder why all this was not told you last night. But I was not then master enough of myself to know what could or ought to be revealed. For the truth of everything here related, I can appeal more particularly to the testimony of Colonel Fitzwilliam, who from our near relationship and constant intimacy, and still more as one of the executors of my father's will, has been unavoidably acquainted with every particular of these transactions. If your abhorrence of *me* should make *my* assertions valueless, you cannot be prevented by the same cause from confiding in my cousin; and that there may be the possibility of consulting him, I shall endeavour to find some opportunity of putting this letter in your hands in the course of the morning. I will only add, God bless you.

FITZWILLIAM DARCY

Chapter 36

If Elizabeth, when Mr Darcy gave her the letter, did not expect it to contain a renewal of his offers, she had formed no expectation at all of its contents. But such as they were, it may be well supposed how eagerly she went through them, and what a contrariety of emotion they excited. Her feelings as she read were scarcely to be defined. With amazement did she first understand that he believed any apology to be in his power; and steadfastly was she persuaded that he could have no explanation to give, which a just sense of shame would not conceal. With a strong prejudice against everything he might say, she began his account of what had happened at Netherfield. She read, with an eagerness which hardly left her power of comprehension, and from impatience of knowing what the next sentence might bring, was incapable of attending to the sense of the one before her eyes. His belief of her sister's insensibility, she instantly resolved to be false, and his account of the real, the worst objections to the match, made her too angry to have any wish of doing him justice. He expressed no regret for what he had done which satisfied her; his style was not penitent, but haughty. It was all pride and insolence.

But when this subject was succeeded by his account of Mr Wickham, when she read with somewhat clearer attention, a relation of events, which, if true, must overthrow every cherished opinion of his worth, and which bore so alarming an affinity to his own history of himself, her feelings were yet more acutely painful and more difficult of definition. Astonishment, apprehension, and even horror, oppressed her. She wished to discredit it entirely, repeatedly exclaiming, 'This must be false! This cannot be! This must be the grossest falsehood!' – and when she had gone through the whole letter, though scarcely knowing anything of the last page or two, put it hastily away, protesting that she would not regard it, that she would never look in it again.

In this perturbed state of mind, with thoughts that could rest on nothing, she walked on; but it would not do; in half a minute the letter was unfolded again, and collecting herself as well as she could, she again began the mortifying perusal of all that related to Wickham, and commanded herself so far as to examine the meaning of every sentence. The account of his connection with the Pemberley family, was exactly what he had related himself; and the kindness of the late Mr Darcy, though she had not before known its extent, agreed equally well with his own words. So far each recital confirmed the other: but when she came to the will, the difference was great. What Wickham had said of the living was fresh in her memory, and as she recalled his very words, it was impossible not to feel that there was gross duplicity on one side or the other; and, for a few moments, she flattered herself that her wishes did not err. But when she read, and re-read with the closest attention, the particulars immediately following of Wickham's resigning all pretensions to the living, of his receiving in lieu, so considerable a sum as three thousand pounds, again was she forced to hesitate. She put down the letter, weighed every circumstance with what she meant to be impartiality – deliberated on the probability of each statement – but with little success. On both sides it was only assertion. Again she read on. But every line proved more clearly that the affair, which she had believed it impossible that any contrivance could so represent, as to render Mr Darcy's conduct in it less than infamous, was capable of a turn which must make him entirely blameless throughout the whole.

The extravagance and general profligacy which he scrupled not to lay to Mr Wickham's charge, exceedingly shocked her; the more so, as she could bring no proof of its injustice. She had never heard of him before his entrance into the —shire Militia, in which he had engaged at the persuasion of the young man, who, on meeting him accidentally in town, had there renewed a slight acquaintance. Of his former way of life, nothing had been known in Hertfordshire but what he told himself. As to his real character, had information been in her power, she had never felt a wish of enquiring. His countenance, voice, and manner, had established him at once in the possession of every virtue. She tried to recollect some instance of goodness, some distinguished trait of integrity or benevolence, that might rescue him from the attacks of Mr Darcy; or at least, by the predominance of virtue, atone for those casual errors, under which she would endeavour to class, what Mr Darcy had described as the idleness and vice of many years continuance. But no such recollection befriended her. She could see him instantly before her, in every charm of air and address; but she could remember no more substantial good than the general approbation of the neighbourhood, and the regard which his social powers had gained him in the mess. After pausing on this point a considerable while, she once more continued to read. But, alas! the story which followed

Meeting him accidentally in town

of his designs on Miss Darcy, received some confirmation from what had passed between Colonel Fitzwilliam and herself only the morning before; and at last she was referred for the truth of every particular to Colonel Fitzwilliam himself – from whom she had previously received the information of his near concern in all his cousin's affairs, and whose character she had no reason to question. At one time she had almost resolved on applying to him, but the idea was checked by the awkwardness of the application, and at length wholly banished by the conviction that Mr Darcy would never have hazarded such a proposal, if he had not been well assured of his cousin's corroboration.

She perfectly remembered everything that had passed in conversation between Wickham and herself, in their first evening at Mr Philips's. Many of his expressions were still fresh in her memory. She was *now* struck with the impropriety of such communications to a stranger, and wondered it had escaped her before. She saw the indelicacy of putting himself forward as he had done, and the inconsistency of his professions with his conduct. She remembered that he had boasted of having no fear of seeing Mr Darcy – that Mr Darcy might leave the country, but that *he* should stand his ground; yet he had avoided the Netherfield ball the very next week. She remembered also, that till the Netherfield family had quitted the country, he had told his story to no one but herself; but that after their removal, it had been every where discussed; that he had then no reserves, no scruples in sinking Mr Darcy's character, though he had assured her that respect for the father, would always prevent his exposing the son.

How differently did everything now appear in which he was concerned! His attentions to Miss King were now the consequence of views solely and hatefully mercenary; and the mediocrity of her fortune proved no longer the moderation of his wishes, but his eagerness to grasp at anything. His behaviour to herself could now have had no tolerable motive; he had either been deceived with regard to her fortune, or had been gratifying his vanity by encouraging the preference which she believed she had most incautiously shown. Every lingering struggle in his favour grew fainter and fainter; and in farther justification of Mr Darcy, she could not but allow that Mr Bingley, when questioned by Jane, had long ago asserted his blamelessness in the affair; that proud and repulsive as were his manners, she had never, in the whole course of their acquaintance, an acquaintance which had latterly brought them much together, and given her a sort of intimacy with his ways, seen anything that betrayed him to be unprincipled or unjust – anything that spoke him of irreligious or immoral habits. That among his own connections he was esteemed and valued – that even Wickham had allowed him merit as a brother, and that she had often heard him speak so affectionately of his sister as to prove him capable of *some* amiable feeling. That had his actions been what Wickham represented them, so gross a violation of everything right could hardly have been concealed from the world; and that friendship between a person capable of it, and such an amiable man as Mr Bingley, was incomprehensible.

She grew absolutely ashamed of herself. Of neither Darcy nor Wickham could she think, without feeling that she had been blind, partial, prejudiced, absurd.

'How despicably have I acted!' she cried. 'I, who have prided myself on my discernment! – I, who have valued myself on my abilities! who have often disdained the generous candour of my sister, and gratified my vanity, in useless or blameable distrust. How humiliating is this discovery! – Yet, how just a humiliation! – Had I been in love, I could not have been more wretchedly blind. But vanity, not love, has been my folly. Pleased with the preference of one, and offended by the neglect of the other, on the very beginning of our acquaintance, I have courted prepossession and ignorance, and driven reason away, where either were concerned. Till this moment, I never knew myself.'

From herself to Jane – from Jane to Bingley, her thoughts were in a line which soon brought to her recollection that Mr Darcy's explanation *there*, had appeared very insufficient; and she read it again. Widely different was the effect of a second perusal. How could she deny that credit to his assertions, in one instance, which she had been obliged to give in the other? – He declared himself to have been totally unsuspicious of her sister's attachment – and she could not help remembering what Charlotte's opinion had always been. Neither could she deny the justice of his description of Jane. She felt that Jane's feelings, though fervent, were little displayed, and that there was a constant complacency in her air and manner, not often united with great sensibility.

When she came to that part of the letter in which her family were mentioned, in terms of such mortifying, yet merited reproach, her sense of shame was severe. The justice of the charge struck her too forcibly for denial, and the circumstances to which he particularly alluded, as having passed at the Netherfield ball, and as confirming all his first disapprobation, could not have made a stronger impression on his mind than on hers.

The compliment to herself and her sister, was not unfelt. It soothed, but it could not console her for the contempt which had been thus self-attracted by the rest of her family – and as she considered that Jane's disappointment had in fact been the work of her nearest relations, and reflected how materially the credit of both must be hurt by such impropriety of conduct, she felt depressed beyond anything she had ever known before.

After wandering along the lane for two hours, giving way to every variety of thought; re-considering events, determining probabilities, and reconciling herself as well as she could, to a change so sudden and so important, fatigue, and a recollection of her long absence, made her at length return home; and she entered the house with the wish of appearing cheerful as usual, and the resolution of repressing such reflections as must make her unfit for conversation.

She was immediately told, that the two gentlemen from Rosings had each called during her absence; Mr Darcy, only for a few minutes to take leave, but that Colonel Fitzwilliam had been sitting with them at least an hour, hoping for her return, and almost resolving to walk after her till she could be found. Elizabeth could but just *affect* concern in missing him; she really rejoiced at it. Colonel Fitzwilliam was no longer an object. She could think only of her letter.

Chapter 37

The two gentlemen left Rosings the next morning; and Mr Collins having been in waiting near the lodges, to make them his parting obeisance, was able to bring home the pleasing intelligence, of their appearing in very good health, and in as tolerable spirits as could be expected, after the melancholy scene so lately gone through at Rosings. To Rosings he then hastened to console Lady Catherine, and her daughter; and on his return, brought back, with great satisfaction, a message from her Ladyship, importing that she felt herself so

dull as to make her very desirous of having them all to
dine with her.

Elizabeth could not see Lady Catherine without
recollecting, that had she chosen it, she might by this
time have been presented to her, as her future niece;
nor could she think, without a smile, of what her
ladyship's indignation would have been. 'What would
she have said? – how would she have behaved?' were
questions with which she amused herself.

Their first subject was the diminution of the
Rosings party. 'I assure you, I feel it exceedingly,' said
Lady Catherine; 'I believe nobody feels the loss of
friends so much as I do. But I am particularly attached
to these young men; and know them to be so much
attached to me! – They were excessively sorry to go!
But so they always are. The dear colonel rallied his
spirits tolerably till just at last; but Darcy seemed to
feel it most acutely, more I think than last year. His
attachment to Rosings, certainly increases.'

Mr Collins had a compliment, and an allusion to
throw in here, which were kindly smiled on by the
mother and daughter.

Lady Catherine observed, after dinner, that
Miss Bennet seemed out of spirits, and immediately
accounting for it herself, by supposing that she did not
like to go home again so soon, she added, 'But if that
is the case, you must write to your mother to beg that
you may stay a little longer. Mrs Collins will be very
glad of your company, I am sure.'

'I am much obliged to your ladyship for your kind
invitation,' replied Elizabeth, 'but it is not in my
power to accept it. I must be in town next Saturday.'

'Why, at that rate, you will have been here only six
weeks. I expected you to stay two months. I told Mrs

Collins so before you came. There can be no occasion for your going so soon. Mrs Bennet could certainly spare you for another fortnight.'

'But my father cannot. He wrote last week to hurry my return.'

'Oh! your father of course may spare you, if your mother can. Daughters are never of so much consequence to a father. And if you will stay another *month* complete, it will be in my power to take one of you as far as London, for I am going there early in June, for a week; and as Dawson does not object to the barouche box, there will be very good room for one of you – and indeed, if the weather should happen to be cool, I should not object to taking you both, as you are neither of you large.'

Dawson

'You are all kindness, Madam; but I believe we must abide by our original plan.'

Lady Catherine seemed resigned.

'Mrs Collins, you must send a servant with them. You know I always speak my mind, and I cannot bear the idea of two young women travelling post by themselves. It is highly improper. You must contrive to send somebody. I have the greatest dislike in the world to that sort of thing. Young women should always be properly guarded and attended, according to their situation in life. When my niece Georgiana went to Ramsgate last summer, I made a point of her having two men servants go with her. Miss Darcy, the daughter of Mr Darcy, of Pemberley, and Lady Anne, could not have appeared with propriety in a different manner. I am excessively attentive to all those things. You must send John with the young ladies, Mrs Collins. I am glad it occurred to me to mention it; for it would really be discreditable to *you* to let them go alone.'

'My uncle is to send a servant for us.'

'Oh! – Your uncle! – He keeps a manservant, does he? – I am very glad you have somebody who thinks of those things. Where shall you change horses? – Oh! Bromley, of course. If you mention my name at the Bell, you will be attended to.'

Lady Catherine had many other questions to ask respecting their journey, and as she did not answer them all herself, attention was necessary, which Elizabeth believed to be lucky for her; or, with a mind so occupied, she might have forgotten where she was. Reflection must be reserved for solitary hours; whenever she was alone, she gave way to it as the greatest relief; and not a day went by without a solitary walk, in which she might indulge in all the delight of unpleasant recollections.

Mr Darcy's letter, she was in a fair way of soon knowing by heart. She studied every sentence: and her feelings towards its writer were at times widely different. When she remembered the style of his address, she was still full of indignation; but when she considered how unjustly she had condemned and upbraided him, her anger was turned against herself; and his disappointed feelings became the object of compassion. His attachment excited gratitude, his general character respect; but she could not approve him; nor could she for a moment repent her refusal, or feel the slightest inclination ever to see him again. In her own past behaviour, there was a constant source of vexation and regret; and in the unhappy defects of her family a subject of yet heavier chagrin. They were hopeless of remedy. Her father, contented with laughing at them, would never exert himself to restrain the wild giddiness of his youngest daughters; and her mother, with manners so far from right herself, was entirely insensible of the evil. Elizabeth had frequently united with Jane in an endeavour to check the imprudence of Catherine and Lydia; but while they were supported by their mother's indulgence, what chance could there be of improvement? Catherine, weak-spirited, irritable, and completely under Lydia's guidance, had been always affronted by their advice; and Lydia, self-willed and careless, would scarcely give them a hearing. They were ignorant, idle, and vain. While there was an officer in Meryton, they would flirt with him; and while Meryton was within a walk of Longbourn, they would be going there for ever.

Anxiety on Jane's behalf, was another prevailing concern, and Mr Darcy's explanation, by restoring Bingley to all her former good opinion, heightened the sense of what Jane had lost. His affection was proved to have been sincere, and his conduct cleared of all blame, unless any could attach to the implicitness of his confidence in his friend. How grievous then was the thought that, of a situation so desirable in every respect, so replete with advantage, so promising for happiness, Jane had been deprived, by the folly and indecorum of her own family!

When to these recollections was added the development of Wickham's character, it may be easily believed that the happy spirits which had seldom been depressed before, were now so much affected as to make it almost impossible for her to appear tolerably cheerful.

Their engagements at Rosings were as frequent during the last week of her stay, as they had been at first. The very last evening was spent there; and her Ladyship again enquired minutely into the particulars of their journey, gave them directions as to the best method of packing, and was so urgent on the necessity of placing gowns in the only right way, that Maria thought herself obliged, on her return, to undo all the work of the morning, and pack her trunk afresh.

When they parted, Lady Catherine, with great condescension, wished them a good journey, and invited them to come to Hunsford again next year; and Miss De Bourgh exerted herself so far as to curtsey and hold out her hand to both.

Chapter 38

On Saturday morning Elizabeth and Mr Collins met for breakfast a few minutes before the others appeared; and he took the opportunity of paying the parting civilities which he deemed indispensably necessary.

'I know not, Miss Elizabeth,' said he, 'whether Mrs Collins has yet expressed her sense of your kindness in coming to us, but I am very certain you will not leave the house without receiving her thanks for it. The favour of your company has been much felt, I assure you. We know how little there is to tempt anyone to our humble abode. Our plain manner of living, our small rooms, and few domestics, and the little we see of the world, must make Hunsford extremely dull to a young lady like yourself; but I hope you will believe us grateful for the condescension, and that we have done everything in our power to prevent your spending your time unpleasantly.'

Elizabeth was eager with her thanks and assurances of happiness. She had spent six weeks with great enjoyment; and the pleasure of being with Charlotte, and the kind attentions she had received, must make *her* feel the obliged.

Mr Collins was gratified; and with a more smiling solemnity replied, 'It gives me the greatest pleasure to hear that you have passed your time not disagreeably. We have certainly done our best; and most fortunately having it in our power to introduce you to very superior society, and from our connection with Rosings, the frequent means of varying the humble home scene, I think we may flatter ourselves that your

Hunsford visit cannot have been entirely irksome. Our situation with regard to Lady Catherine's family is indeed the sort of extraordinary advantage and blessing which few can boast. You see on what a footing we are. You see how continually we are engaged there. In truth I must acknowledge that, with all the disadvantages of this humble parsonage, I should not think anyone abiding in it an object of compassion, while they are sharers of our intimacy at Rosings.'

Words were insufficient for the elevation of his feelings; and he was obliged to walk about the room, while Elizabeth tried to unite civility and truth in a few short sentences.

'You may, in fact, carry a very favourable report of us into Hertfordshire, my dear cousin. I flatter myself at least that you will be able to do so. Lady Catherine's great attentions to Mrs Collins you have been a daily witness of; and altogether I trust it does not appear that your friend has drawn an unfortunate – but on this point it will be as well to be silent. Only let me assure you, my dear Miss Elizabeth, that I can from my heart most cordially wish you equal felicity in marriage. My dear Charlotte and I have but one mind and one way of thinking. There is in everything a most remarkable resemblance of character and ideas between us. We seem to have been designed for each other.'

Elizabeth could safely say that it was a great happiness where that was the case, and with equal sincerity could add that she firmly believed and rejoiced in his domestic comforts. She was not sorry, however, to have the recital of them interrupted by the entrance of the lady from whom they sprung. Poor Charlotte! – it was melancholy to leave her to such society! – But she had chosen it with her eyes open; and though evidently regretting that her visitors were to go, she did not seem to ask for compassion. Her home and her housekeeping, her parish and her poultry, and all their dependent concerns, had not yet lost their charms.

At length the chaise arrived, the trunks were fastened on, the parcels placed within, and it was pronounced to be ready. After an affectionate parting between the friends, Elizabeth was attended to the carriage by Mr Collins, and as they walked down the garden, he was commissioning her with his best respects to all her family, not forgetting his thanks for the kindness he had received at Longbourn in the winter, and his compliments to Mr and Mrs Gardiner, though unknown. He then handed her in, Maria followed, and the door was on the point of being closed, when he suddenly reminded them, with some consternation, that they had hitherto forgotten to leave any message for the ladies of Rosings.

'But,' he added, 'you will of course wish to have your humble respects delivered to them, with your grateful thanks for their kindness to you while you have been here.'

Elizabeth made no objection – the door was then allowed to be shut, and the carriage drove off.

'Good gracious!' cried Maria, after a few minutes silence, 'it seems but a day or two since we first came! – and yet how many things have happened!'

'A great many indeed,' said her companion with a sigh.

'We have dined nine times at Rosings, besides drinking tea there twice! – How much I shall have to tell!'

*They had hitherto forgotten to leave any message
for the ladies of Rosings*

Elizabeth privately added, 'And how much I shall have to conceal.'

Their journey was performed without much conversation, or any alarm; and within four hours of their leaving Hunsford, they reached Mr Gardiner's house, where they were to remain a few days.

Jane looked well, and Elizabeth had little opportunity of studying her spirits, amidst the various engagements which the kindness of her aunt had reserved for them. But Jane was to go home with her, and at Longbourn there would be leisure enough for observation.

It was not without an effort meanwhile that she could wait even for Longbourn, before she told her sister of Mr Darcy's proposals. To know that she had the power of revealing what would so exceedingly astonish Jane, and must, at the same time, so highly gratify whatever of her own vanity she had not yet been able to reason away, was such a temptation to openness as nothing could have conquered, but the state of indecision in which she remained, as to the extent of what she should communicate; and her fear, if she once entered on the subject, of being hurried into repeating something of Bingley, which might only grieve her sister farther.

Chapter 39

It was the second week in May, in which the three young ladies set out together from Gracechurch Street, for the town of — in Hertfordshire; and, as they drew near the appointed inn where Mr Bennet's carriage was to meet them, they quickly perceived, in token of the coachman's punctuality, both Kitty and

Lydia looking out of a dining-room upstairs. These two girls had been above an hour in the place, happily employed in visiting an opposite milliner, watching the sentinel on guard, and dressing a salad and cucumber.

After welcoming their sisters, they triumphantly displayed a table set out with such cold meat as an inn larder usually affords, exclaiming, 'Is not this nice? is not this an agreeable surprise?'

'And we mean to treat you all,' added Lydia; 'but you must lend us the money, for we have just spent ours at the shop out there.' Then showing her purchases: 'Look here, I have bought this bonnet. I do not think it is very pretty; but I thought I might as well buy it as not. I shall pull it to pieces as soon as I get home, and see if I can make it up any better.'

And when her sisters abused it as ugly, she added, with perfect unconcern, 'Oh! but there were two or three much uglier in the shop; and when I have bought some prettier-coloured satin to trim it with fresh, I think it will be very tolerable. Besides, it will not much signify what one wears this summer, after the —shire have left Meryton, and they are going in a fortnight.'

'Are they indeed?' cried Elizabeth, with the greatest satisfaction.

'They are going to be encamped near Brighton; and I do so want papa to take us all there for the summer! It would be such a delicious scheme, and I dare say would hardly cost anything at all. Mamma would like to go too of all things! Only think what a miserable summer else we shall have!'

'Yes,' thought Elizabeth, '*that* would be a delightful scheme, indeed, and completely do for us at once. Good Heaven! Brighton, and a whole camp full of soldiers, to us, who have been overset already by one poor regiment of militia, and the monthly balls of Meryton.'

'Now I have got some news for you,' said Lydia, as they sat down to table. 'What do you think? It is excellent news, capital news, and about a certain person that we all like.'

Jane and Elizabeth looked at each other, and the waiter was told that he need not stay. Lydia laughed, and said, 'Aye, that is just like your formality and discretion. You thought the waiter must not hear, as if he cared! I dare say he often hears worse things said than I am going to say. But he is an ugly fellow! I am glad he is gone. I never saw such a long chin in my life. Well, but now for my news: it is about dear Wickham; too good for the waiter, is not it? There is no danger of Wickham's marrying Mary King. There's for you! She is gone down to her uncle at Liverpool; gone to stay. Wickham is safe.'

'And Mary King is safe!' added Elizabeth; 'safe from a connection imprudent as to fortune.'

'She is a great fool for going away, if she liked him.'

'But I hope there is no strong attachment on either side,' said Jane.

'I am sure there is not on *his*. I will answer for it he never cared three straws about her. Who *could* about such a nasty little freckled thing?'

Elizabeth was shocked to think that, however incapable of such coarseness of *expression* herself, the coarseness of the *sentiment* was little other than her own breast had formerly harboured and fancied liberal!

As soon as all had ate, and the elder ones paid, the carriage was ordered; and after some contrivance, the whole party, with all their boxes, workbags, and parcels, and the unwelcome addition of Kitty's and Lydia's purchases, were seated in it.

'How nicely we are crammed in!' cried Lydia. 'I am glad I bought my bonnet, if it is only for the fun of having another bandbox! Well, now let us be quite comfortable and snug, and talk and laugh all the way home. And in the first place, let us hear what has happened to you all, since you went away. Have you seen any pleasant men? Have you had any flirting? I was in great hopes that one of you would have got a husband before you came back. Jane will be quite an old maid soon, I declare. She is almost three and twenty! Lord, how ashamed I should be of not being married before three and twenty! My aunt Philips wants you so to get husbands, you can't think. She says Lizzy had better have taken Mr Collins; but *I* do not think there would have been any fun in it. Lord! how I should like to be married before any of you; and then I would chaperon you about to all the balls. Dear me! we had such a good piece of fun the other day at Colonel Forster's. Kitty and me were to spend the day there, and Mrs Forster promised to have a little dance in the evening; (by the by, Mrs Forster and me are *such* friends!) and so she asked the two Harringtons to come, but Harriet was ill, and so Pen was forced to come by herself; and then, what do you think we did? We dressed up Chamberlayne in woman's clothes, on purpose to pass for a lady – only think what fun! Not a soul knew of it, but Colonel and Mrs Forster, and Kitty and me, except my aunt, for we were forced to borrow one of her gowns; and you cannot imagine how well he looked! When Denny, and Wickham, and Pratt, and two or three more of the men came in, they

How nicely we are crammed in!

PRIDE AND PREJUDICE

did not know him in the least. Lord! how I laughed!
and so did Mrs Forster. I thought I should have died.
And *that* made the men suspect something, and then
they soon found out what was the matter.'

With such kind of histories of their parties and good
jokes, did Lydia, assisted by Kitty's hints and addi-
tions, endeavour to amuse her companions all the way
to Longbourn. Elizabeth listened as little as she could,
but there was no escaping the frequent mention of
Wickham's name.

Their reception at home was most kind. Mrs
Bennet rejoiced to see Jane in undiminished beauty;
and more than once during dinner did Mr Bennet say
voluntarily to Elizabeth, 'I am glad you are come back,
Lizzy.'

Their party in the dining-room was large, for
almost all the Lucases came to meet Maria and
hear the news: and various were the subjects which
occupied them; lady Lucas was enquiring of Maria
across the table, after the welfare and poultry of
her eldest daughter; Mrs Bennet was doubly engaged,
on one hand collecting an account of the present
fashions from Jane, who sat some way below her,
and on the other, retailing them all to the younger
Miss Lucases; and Lydia, in a voice rather louder
than any other person's, was enumerating the various
pleasures of the morning to anybody who would
hear her.

'Oh! Mary,' said she, 'I wish you had gone with us,
for we had such fun! as we went along, Kitty and me
drew up all the blinds, and pretended there was
nobody in the coach; and I should have gone so all the
way, if Kitty had not been sick; and when we got to the
George, I do think we behaved very handsomely, for

we treated the other three with the nicest cold lunch-
eon in the world, and if you would have gone, we
would have treated you too. And then when we came
away it was such fun! I thought we never should have
got into the coach. I was ready to die of laughter. And
then we were so merry all the way home! we talked
and laughed so loud, that anybody might have heard
us ten miles off!'

To this, Mary very gravely replied, 'Far be it from
me, my dear sister, to depreciate such pleasures. They
would doubtless be congenial with the generality of
female minds. But I confess they would have no
charms for *me*. I should infinitely prefer a book.'

But of this answer Lydia heard not a word. She
seldom listened to anybody for more than half a
minute, and never attended to Mary at all.

In the afternoon Lydia was urgent with the rest of
the girls to walk to Meryton and see how everybody
went on; but Elizabeth steadily opposed the scheme. It
should not be said, that the Miss Bennets could not be
at home half a day before they were in pursuit of
the officers. There was another reason too for her
opposition. She dreaded seeing Wickham again, and
was resolved to avoid it as long as possible. The
comfort to *her*, of the regiment's approaching removal,
was indeed beyond expression. In a fortnight they
were to go, and once gone, she hoped there could be
nothing more to plague her on his account.

She had not been many hours at home, before she
found that the Brighton scheme, of which Lydia had
given them a hint at the inn, was under frequent
discussion between her parents. Elizabeth saw directly
that her father had not the smallest intention of
yielding; but his answers were at the same time so

vague and equivocal, that her mother, though often disheartened, had never yet despaired of succeeding at last.

Chapter 40

Elizabeth's impatience to acquaint Jane with what had happened could no longer be overcome; and at length resolving to suppress every particular in which her sister was concerned, and preparing her to be surprised, she related to her the next morning the chief of the scene between Mr Darcy and herself.

Miss Bennet's astonishment was soon lessened by the strong sisterly partiality which made any admiration of Elizabeth appear perfectly natural; and all surprise was shortly lost in other feelings. She was sorry that Mr Darcy should have delivered his sentiments in a manner so little suited to recommend them; but still more was she grieved for the unhappiness which her sister's refusal must have given him.

'His being so sure of succeeding, was wrong,' said she; 'and certainly ought not to have appeared; but consider how much it must increase his disappointment.'

'Indeed,' replied Elizabeth, 'I am heartily sorry for him; but he has other feelings which will probably soon drive away his regard for me. You do not blame me, however, for refusing him?'

'Blame you! Oh, no.'

'But you blame me for having spoken so warmly of Wickham.'

'No – I do not know that you were wrong in saying what you did.'

'But you *will* know it, when I have told you what happened the very next day.'

She then spoke of the letter, repeating the whole of its contents as far as they concerned George Wickham. What a stroke was this for poor Jane! who would willingly have gone through the world without believing that so much wickedness existed in the whole race of mankind, as was here collected in one individual. Nor was Darcy's vindication, though grateful to her feelings, capable of consoling her for such discovery. Most earnestly did she labour to prove the probability of error, and seek to clear one, without involving the other.

'This will not do,' said Elizabeth. 'You never will be able to make both of them good for anything. Take your choice, but you must be satisfied with only one. There is but such a quantity of merit between them; just enough to make one good sort of man; and of late it has been shifting about pretty much. For my part, I am inclined to believe it all Mr Darcy's, but you shall do as you choose.'

It was some time, however, before a smile could be extorted from Jane.

'I do not know when I have been more shocked,' said she. 'Wickham so very bad! It is almost past belief. And poor Mr Darcy! dear Lizzy, only consider what he must have suffered. Such a disappointment! and with the knowledge of your ill opinion too! and having to relate such a thing of his sister! It is really too distressing. I am sure you must feel it so.'

'Oh! no, my regret and compassion are all done away by seeing you so full of both. I know you will do him such ample justice, that I am growing every moment more unconcerned and indifferent. Your profusion makes me saving; and if you lament over him much longer, my heart will be as light as a feather.'

'Poor Wickham; there is such an expression of goodness in his countenance! such an openness and gentleness in his manner.'

'There certainly was some great mismanagement in the education of those two young men. One has got all the goodness, and the other all the appearance of it.'

'I never thought Mr Darcy so deficient in the *appearance* of it as you used to do.'

'And yet I meant to be uncommonly clever in taking so decided a dislike to him, without any reason. It is such a spur to one's genius, such an opening for wit to have a dislike of that kind. One may be continually abusive without saying anything just; but one cannot be always laughing at a man without now and then stumbling on something witty.'

'Lizzy, when you first read that letter, I am sure you could not treat the matter as you do now.'

'Indeed I could not. I was uncomfortable enough. I was very uncomfortable, I may say unhappy. And with no one to speak to, of what I felt, no Jane to comfort me and say that I had not been so very weak and vain and nonsensical as I knew I had! Oh! how I wanted you!'

'How unfortunate that you should have used such very strong expressions in speaking of Wickham to Mr Darcy, for now they *do* appear wholly undeserved.'

'Certainly. But the misfortune of speaking with bitterness, is a most natural consequence of the prejudices I had been encouraging. There is one point, on which I want your advice. I want to be told whether I ought, or ought not to make our acquaintance in general understand Wickham's character.'

Miss Bennet paused a little and then replied, 'Surely there can be no occasion for exposing him so dreadfully. What is your own opinion?'

'That it ought not to be attempted. Mr Darcy has not authorised me to make his communication public. On the contrary every particular relative to his sister, was meant to be kept as much as possible to myself; and if I endeavour to undeceive people as to the rest of his conduct, who will believe me? The general prejudice against Mr Darcy is so violent, that it would be the death of half the good people in Meryton, to attempt to place him in an amiable light. I am not equal to it. Wickham will soon be gone; and therefore it will not signify to anybody here, what he really is. Sometime hence it will be all found out, and then we may laugh at their stupidity in not knowing it before. At present I will say nothing about it.'

'You are quite right. To have his errors made public might ruin him for ever. He is now perhaps sorry for what he has done, and anxious to re-establish a character. We must not make him desperate.'

The tumult of Elizabeth's mind was allayed by this conversation. She had got rid of two of the secrets which had weighed on her for a fortnight, and was certain of a willing listener in Jane, whenever she might wish to talk again of either. But there was still something lurking behind, of which prudence forbad the disclosure. She dared not relate the other half of Mr Darcy's letter, nor explain to her sister how sincerely she had been valued by his friend. Here was knowledge in which no one could partake; and she was sensible that nothing less than a perfect understanding between the parties could justify her in throwing off this last encumbrance of mystery. 'And then,' said she, 'if that very improbable event should ever take place, I shall merely be able to tell what Bingley may tell in a much more agreeable manner himself. The liberty of communication cannot be mine till it has lost all its value!'

She was now, on being settled at home, at leisure to observe the real state of her sister's spirits. Jane was not happy. She still cherished a very tender affection for Bingley. Having never even fancied herself in love before, her regard had all the warmth of first attachment, and from her age and disposition, greater steadiness than first attachments often boast; and so fervently did she value his remembrance, and prefer him to every other man, that all her good sense, and all her attention to the feelings of her friends, were requisite to check the indulgence of those regrets, which must have been injurious to her own health and their tranquillity.

'Well, Lizzy,' said Mrs Bennet one day, 'what is your opinion *now* of this sad business of Jane's? For my part, I am determined never to speak of it again to anybody. I told my sister Philips so the other day. But I cannot find out that Jane saw anything of him in London. Well, he is a very undeserving young man – and I do not suppose there is the least chance in the world of her ever getting him now. There is no talk of his coming to Netherfield again in the summer; and I have enquired of everybody too, who is likely to know.'

'I do not believe that he will ever live at Netherfield any more.'

'Oh, well! it is just as he chooses. Nobody wants him to come. Though I shall always say that he used my daughter extremely ill; and if I was her, I would not

I am determined never to speak of it again to anybody

have put up with it. Well, my comfort is, I am sure Jane will die of a broken heart, and then he will be sorry for what he has done.'

But as Elizabeth could not receive comfort from any such expectation, she made no answer.

'Well, Lizzy,' continued her mother soon afterwards, 'and so the Collinses live very comfortable, do they? Well, well, I only hope it will last. And what sort of table do they keep? Charlotte is an excellent manager, I dare say. If she is half as sharp as her mother, she is saving enough. There is nothing extravagant in *their* housekeeping, I dare say.'

'No, nothing at all.'

'A great deal of good management, depend upon it. Yes, yes. *They* will take care not to outrun their income. *They* will never be distressed for money. Well, much good may it do them! And so, I suppose, they often talk of having Longbourn when your father is dead. They look upon it quite as their own, I dare say, whenever that happens.'

'It was a subject which they could not mention before me.'

'No. It would have been strange if they had. But I make no doubt, they often talk of it between them-selves. Well, if they can be easy with an estate that is not lawfully their own, so much the better. *I* should be ashamed of having one that was only entailed on me.'

Chapter 41

The first week of their return was soon gone. The second began. It was the last of the regiment's stay in Meryton, and all the young ladies in the neighbourhood were drooping apace. The dejection was almost universal. The elder Miss Bennets alone were still able to eat, drink, and sleep, and pursue the usual course of their employments. Very frequently were they reproached for this insensibility by Kitty and Lydia, whose own misery was extreme, and who could not comprehend such hard heartedness in any of the family.

'Good Heaven! What is to become of us! What are we to do!' would they often exclaim in the bitterness of woe. 'How can you be smiling so, Lizzy?'

Their affectionate mother shared all their grief; she remembered what she had herself endured on a similar occasion, five and twenty years ago.

'I am sure,' said she, 'I cried for two days together when Colonel Millar's regiment went away. I thought I should have broke my heart.'

'I am sure I shall break *mine*,' said Lydia.

'If one could but go to Brighton!' observed Mrs Bennet.

'Oh, yes! – if one could but go to Brighton! But papa is so disagreeable.'

'A little sea-bathing would set me up for ever.'

'And my aunt Philips is sure it would do *me* a great deal of good,' added Kitty.

Such were the kind of lamentations resounding perpetually through Longbourn House. Elizabeth tried

When Colonel Millar's regiment went away

to be diverted by them; but all sense of pleasure was lost in shame. She felt anew the justice of Mr Darcy's objections; and never had she before been so much disposed to pardon his interference in the views of his friend.

But the gloom of Lydia's prospect was shortly cleared away; for she received an invitation from Mrs Forster, the wife of the Colonel of the regiment, to accompany her to Brighton. This invaluable friend was a very young woman, and very lately married. A resemblance in good humour and good spirits had recommended her and Lydia to each other, and out of their *three* months' acquaintance they had been intimate *two*.

The rapture of Lydia on this occasion, her adoration of Mrs Forster, the delight of Mrs Bennet, and the mortification of Kitty, are scarcely to be described. Wholly inattentive to her sister's feelings, Lydia flew about the house in restless ecstacy, calling for everyone's congratulations, and laughing and talking with more violence than ever; whilst the luckless Kitty continued in the parlour repining at her fate in terms as unreasonable as her accent was peevish.

'I cannot see why Mrs Forster should not ask *me* as well as Lydia,' said she, 'though I am *not* her particular friend. I have just as much right to be asked as she has, and more too, for I am two years older.'

In vain did Elizabeth attempt to make her reasonable, and Jane to make her resigned. As for Elizabeth herself, this invitation was so far from exciting in her the same feelings as in her mother and Lydia, that she considered it as the death-warrant of all possibility of common sense for the latter; and detestable as such a step must make her were it known, she could not help secretly advising her father not to let her go. She represented to him all the improprieties of Lydia's general behaviour, the little advantage she could derive from the friendship of such a woman as Mrs Forster, and the probability of her being yet more imprudent with such a companion at Brighton, where the temptations must be greater than at home. He heard her attentively, and then said, 'Lydia will never be easy till she has exposed herself in some public place or other, and we can never expect her to do it with so little expense or inconvenience to her family as under the present circumstances.'

'If you were aware,' said Elizabeth, 'of the very great disadvantage to us all, which must arise from the public notice of Lydia's unguarded and imprudent manner; nay, which has already arisen from it, I am sure you would judge differently in the affair.'

'Already arisen!' repeated Mr Bennet. 'What, has she frightened away some of your lovers? Poor little Lizzy! But do not be cast down. Such squeamish youths as cannot bear to be connected with a little absurdity, are not worth a regret. Come, let me see the list of the pitiful fellows who have been kept aloof by Lydia's folly.'

'Indeed you are mistaken. I have no such injuries to resent. It is not of peculiar, but of general evils, which I am now complaining. Our importance, our respect-ability in the world, must be affected by the wild volatility, the assurance and disdain of all restraint which mark Lydia's character. Excuse me – for I must speak plainly. If you, my dear father, will not take the trouble of checking her exuberant spirits, and of teaching her that her present pursuits are not to be the business of her life, she will soon be beyond the reach of amendment. Her character will be fixed, and she will, at sixteen, be the most determined flirt that ever made herself and her family ridiculous. A flirt too, in the worst and meanest degree of flirtation; without any attraction beyond youth and a tolerable person; and from the ignorance and emptiness of her mind, wholly unable to ward off any portion of that universal contempt which her rage for admiration will excite. In this danger Kitty is also comprehended. She will follow wherever Lydia leads. Vain, ignorant, idle, and absolutely uncontrolled! Oh! my dear father, can you suppose it possible that they will not be censured and despised wherever they are known, and that their sisters will not be often involved in the disgrace?'

Mr Bennet saw that her whole heart was in the subject; and affectionately taking her hand, said in reply, 'Do not make yourself uneasy, my love. Wherever you and Jane are known, you must be respected and valued; and you will not appear to less advantage for having a couple of – or I may say, three very silly sisters. We shall have no peace at Longbourn if Lydia does not go to Brighton. Let her go then. Colonel Forster is a sensible man, and will keep her out of any real mischief; and she is luckily too poor to be an object of prey to anybody. At Brighton she will be of less importance even as a common flirt than she has been here. The officers will find women better worth their notice. Let us hope, therefore, that her being there may teach her her own insignificance. At any rate, she cannot grow many degrees worse, without authorising us to lock her up for the rest of her life.'

With this answer Elizabeth was forced to be content; but her own opinion continued the same, and she left him disappointed and sorry. It was not in her nature, however, to increase her vexations, by dwelling on them. She was confident of having performed her duty, and to fret over unavoidable evils, or augment them by anxiety, was no part of her disposition.

Had Lydia and her mother known the substance of her conference with her father, their indignation would hardly have found expression in their united volubility. In Lydia's imagination, a visit to Brighton comprised every possibility of earthly happiness. She saw with the creative eye of fancy, the streets of that gay bathing place covered with officers. She saw herself the object of attention, to tens and to scores of them at present unknown. She saw all the glories of the camp; its tents stretched forth in beauteous uniformity of lines, crowded with the young and the gay, and dazzling with scarlet; and to complete the view, she saw herself seated beneath a tent, tenderly flirting with at least six officers at once.

Had she known that her sister sought to tear her from such prospects and such realities as these, what would have been her sensations? They could have been understood only by her mother, who might have felt nearly the same. Lydia's going to Brighton was all that consoled her for the melancholy conviction of her husband's never intending to go there himself.

But they were entirely ignorant of what had passed; and their raptures continued with little intermission to the very day of Lydia's leaving home.

Elizabeth was now to see Mr Wickham for the last time. Having been frequently in company with him since her return, agitation was pretty well over; the agitations of former partiality entirely so. She had even learnt to detect, in the very gentleness which had first delighted her, an affectation and a sameness to disgust and weary. In his present behaviour to herself, moreover, she had a fresh source of displeasure, for the inclination he soon testified of renewing those attentions which had marked the early part of their acquaintance, could only serve, after what had since passed, to provoke her. She lost all concern for him in finding herself thus selected as the object of such idle and frivolous gallantry; and while she steadily repressed it, could not but feel the reproof contained in his believing, that however long, and for whatever cause, his attentions had been withdrawn, her vanity would be gratified and her preference secured at any time by their renewal.

On the very last day of the regiment's remaining in

She saw herself seated beneath a tent, tenderly flirting

Meryton, he dined with others of the officers at
Longbourn; and so little was Elizabeth disposed to
part from him in good humour, that on his making
some enquiry as to the manner in which her time had
passed at Hunsford, she mentioned Colonel Fitzwilliam's and Mr Darcy's having both spent three
weeks at Rosings, and asked him if he were acquainted
with the former.

He looked surprised, displeased, alarmed; but
with a moment's recollection and a returning smile,
replied, that he had formerly seen him often; and after
observing that he was a very gentlemanlike man, asked
her how she had liked him. Her answer was warmly

in his favour. With an air of indifference he soon afterwards added, 'How long did you say that he was at Rosings?'

'Nearly three weeks.'

'And you saw him frequently?'

'Yes, almost every day.'

'His manners are very different from his cousin's.'

'Yes, very different. But I think Mr Darcy improves on acquaintance.'

'Indeed!' cried Wickham with a look which did not escape her. 'And pray may I ask?' but checking himself, he added in a gayer tone, 'Is it in address that he improves? Has he deigned to add ought of civility to his ordinary style? for I dare not hope,' he continued in a lower and more serious tone, 'that he is improved in essentials.'

'Oh, no!' said Elizabeth. 'In essentials, I believe, he is very much what he ever was.'

While she spoke, Wickham looked as if scarcely knowing whether to rejoice over her words, or to distrust their meaning. There was a something in her countenance which made him listen with an apprehensive and anxious attention, while she added, 'When I said that he improved on acquaintance, I did not mean that either his mind or manners were in a state of improvement, but that from knowing him better, his disposition was better understood.'

Wickham's alarm now appeared in a heightened complexion and agitated look; for a few minutes he was silent; till, shaking off his embarrassment, he turned to her again, and said in the gentlest of accents, 'You, who so well know my feelings towards Mr Darcy, will readily comprehend how sincerely I must rejoice that he is wise enough to assume even the *appearance* of what is right. His pride, in that direction, may be of service, if not to himself, to many others, for it must deter him from such foul misconduct as I have suffered by. I only fear that the sort of cautiousness, to which you, I imagine, have been alluding, is merely adopted on his visits to his aunt, of whose good opinion and judgement he stands much in awe. His fear of her, has always operated, I know, when they were together; and a good deal is to be imputed to his wish of forwarding the match with Miss De Bourgh, which I am certain he has very much at heart.'

Elizabeth could not repress a smile at this, but she answered only by a slight inclination of the head. She saw that he wanted to engage her on the old subject of his grievances, and she was in no humour to indulge him. The rest of the evening passed with the *appearance*, on his side, of usual cheerfulness, but with no farther attempt to distinguish Elizabeth; and they parted at last with mutual civility, and possibly a mutual desire of never meeting again.

When the party broke up, Lydia returned with Mrs Forster to Meryton, from whence they were to set out early the next morning. The separation between her and her family was rather noisy than pathetic. Kitty was the only one who shed tears; but she did weep from vexation and envy. Mrs Bennet was diffuse in her good wishes for the felicity of her daughter, and impressive in her injunctions that she would not miss the opportunity of enjoying herself as much as possible; advice, which there was every reason to believe would be attended to; and in the clamorous happiness of Lydia herself in bidding farewell, the more gentle adieus of her sisters were uttered without being heard.

Chapter 42

Had Elizabeth's opinion been all drawn from her own family, she could not have formed a very pleasing picture of conjugal felicity or domestic comfort. Her father captivated by youth and beauty, and that appearance of good humour, which youth and beauty generally give, had married a woman whose weak understanding and illiberal mind, had very early in their marriage put an end to all real affection for her. Respect, esteem, and confidence, had vanished for ever; and all his views of domestic happiness were overthrown. But Mr Bennet was not of a disposition to seek comfort for the disappointment which his own imprudence had brought on, in any of those pleasures which too often console the unfortunate for their folly or their vice. He was fond of the country and of books; and from these tastes had arisen his principal enjoyments. To his wife he was very little otherwise indebted, than as her ignorance and folly had contributed to his amusement. This is not the sort of happiness which a man would in general wish to owe to his wife; but where other powers of entertainment are wanting, the true philosopher will derive benefit from such as are given.

Elizabeth, however, had never been blind to the impropriety of her father's behaviour as a husband. She had always seen it with pain; but respecting his abilities, and grateful for his affectionate treatment of herself, she endeavoured to forget what she could not overlook, and to banish from her thoughts that continual breach of conjugal obligation and decorum which, in exposing his wife to the contempt of her own children, was so highly reprehensible. But she had never felt so strongly as now, the disadvantages which must attend the children of so unsuitable a marriage, nor ever been so fully aware of the evils arising from so ill-judged a direction of talents; talents which rightly used, might at least have preserved the respectability of his daughters, even if incapable of enlarging the mind of his wife.

When Elizabeth had rejoiced over Wickham's departure, she found little other cause for satisfaction in the loss of the regiment. Their parties abroad were less varied than before; and at home she had a mother and sister whose constant repinings at the dullness of everything around them, threw a real gloom over their domestic circle; and, though Kitty might in time regain her natural degree of sense, since the disturbers of her brain were removed, her other sister, from whose disposition greater evil might be apprehended, was likely to be hardened in all her folly and assurance, by a situation of such double danger as a watering place and a camp. Upon the whole, therefore, she found, what has been sometimes found before, that an event to which she had looked forward with impatient desire, did not in taking place, bring all the satisfaction she had promised herself. It was consequently necessary to name some other period for the commencement of actual felicity; to have some other point on which her wishes and hopes might be fixed, and by again enjoying the pleasure of anticipation, console herself for the present, and prepare for another disappointment. Her tour to the Lakes was now the object of her happiest thoughts; it was her best consolation for all the uncomfortable hours, which the discontentedness of her mother and

Kitty made inevitable; and could she have included Jane in the scheme, every part of it would have been perfect.

'But it is fortunate,' thought she, 'that I have something to wish for. Were the whole arrangement complete, my disappointment would be certain. But here, by carrying with me one ceaseless source of regret in my sister's absence, I may reasonably hope to have all my expectations of pleasure realised. A scheme of which every part promises delight, can never be successful; and general disappointment is only warded off by the defence of some little peculiar vexation.'

When Lydia went away, she promised to write very often and very minutely to her mother and Kitty; but her letters were always long expected, and always very short. Those to her mother, contained little else, than that they were just returned from the library, where such and such officers had attended them, and where she had seen such beautiful ornaments as made her quite wild; that she had a new gown, or a new parasol, which she would have described more fully, but was obliged to leave off in a violent hurry, as Mrs Forster called her, and they were going to the camp – and from her correspondence with her sister, there was still less to be learnt – for her letters to Kitty, though rather longer, were much too full of lines under the words to be made public.

After the first fortnight or three weeks of her absence, health, good humour and cheerfulness began to reappear at Longbourn. Everything wore a happier aspect. The families who had been in town for the winter came back again, and summer finery and summer engagements arose. Mrs Bennet was restored to her usual querulous serenity, and by the middle of June Kitty was so much recovered as to be able to enter Meryton without tears; an event of such happy promise as to make Elizabeth hope, that by the following Christmas, she might be so tolerably reasonable as not to mention an officer above once a day, unless by some cruel and malicious arrangement at the War Office, another regiment should be quartered in Meryton.

The time fixed for the beginning of their Northern tour was now fast approaching; and a fortnight only was wanting of it, when a letter arrived from Mrs Gardiner, which at once delayed its commencement and curtailed its extent. Mr Gardiner would be prevented by business from setting put till a fortnight later in July, and must be in London again within a month; and as that left too short a period for them to go so far, and see so much as they had proposed, or at least to see it with the leisure and comfort they had built on, they were obliged to give up the Lakes, and substitute a more contracted tour; and, according to the present plan, were to go no farther northward than Derbyshire. In that county, there was enough to be seen, to occupy the chief of their three weeks; and to Mrs Gardiner it had a peculiarly strong attraction. The town where she had formerly passed some years of her life, and where they were now to spend a few days, was probably as great an object of her curiosity, as all the celebrated beauties of Matlock, Chatsworth, Dovedale, or the Peak.

Elizabeth was excessively disappointed; she had set her heart on seeing the Lakes; and still thought there might have been time enough. But it was her business to be satisfied – and certainly her temper to be happy; and all was soon right again.

With the mention of Derbyshire, there were many ideas connected. It was impossible for her to see the word without thinking of Pemberley and its owner. 'But surely,' said she, 'I may enter his county with impunity, and rob it of a few petrified spars without his perceiving me.'

The period of expectation was now doubled. Four weeks were to pass away before her uncle and aunt's arrival. But they did pass away, and Mr and Mrs Gardiner, with their four children, did at length appear at Longbourn. The children, two girls of six and eight years old, and two younger boys, were to be left under the particular care of their cousin Jane, who was the general favourite, and whose steady sense and sweetness of temper exactly adapted her for attending to them in every way – teaching them, playing with them, and loving them.

The Gardiners staid only one night at Longbourn, and set off the next morning with Elizabeth in pursuit – that of suitableness as companions; a suitableness which comprehended health and temper to bear inconveniences – cheerfulness to enhance every pleasure – and affection and intelligence, which might supply it among themselves if there were disappointments abroad.

It is not the object of this work to give a description of Derbyshire, nor of any of the remarkable places through which their route thither lay; Oxford, Blenheim, Warwick, Kenilworth, Birmingham, &c. are sufficiently known. A small part of Derbyshire is all the present concern. To the little town of Lambton, the scene of Mrs Gardiner's former residence, and where she had lately learned that some acquaintance still remained, they bent their steps, after having seen

Mr and Mrs Gardiner, with their four children

all the principal wonders of the country; and within five miles of Lambton, Elizabeth found from her aunt, that Pemberley was situated. It was not in their direct road, nor more than a mile or two out of it. In talking over their route the evening before, Mrs Gardiner expressed an inclination to see the place again. Mr Gardiner declared his willingness, and Elizabeth was applied to for her approbation.

'My love, should not you like to see a place of which you have heard so much?' said her aunt. 'A place too, with which so many of your acquaintance are connected. Wickham passed all his youth there, you know.'

Elizabeth was distressed. She felt that she had no business at Pemberley, and was obliged to assume a disinclination for seeing it. She must own that she was tired of great houses; after going over so many, she really had no pleasure in fine carpets or satin curtains.

Mrs Gardiner abused her stupidity. 'If it were merely a fine house richly furnished,' said she, 'I should not care about it myself; but the grounds are delightful. They have some of the finest woods in the country.'

Elizabeth said no more – but her mind could not acquiesce. The possibility of meeting Mr Darcy, while viewing the place, instantly occurred. It would be dreadful! She blushed at the very idea; and thought it would be better to speak openly to her aunt, than to run such a risk. But against this, there were objections; and she finally resolved that it could be the last resource, if her private enquiries as to the absence of the family, were unfavourably answered.

Accordingly, when she retired at night, she asked the chambermaid whether Pemberley were not a very fine place, what was the name of its proprietor, and with no little alarm, whether the family were down for the summer. A most welcome negative followed the last question – and her alarms being now removed, she was at leisure to feel a great deal of curiosity to see the house herself; and when the subject was revived the next morning, and she was again applied to, could readily answer, and with a proper air of indifference, that she had not really any dislike to the scheme.

To Pemberley, therefore, they were to go.

Chapter 43

Elizabeth, as they drove along, watched for the first appearance of Pemberley Woods with some perturbation; and when at length they turned in at the lodge, her spirits were in a high flutter.

The park was very large, and contained great variety of ground. They entered it in one of its lowest points, and drove for some time through a beautiful wood, stretching over a wide extent.

Elizabeth's mind was too full for conversation, but she saw and admired every remarkable spot and point of view. They gradually ascended for half a mile, and then found themselves at the top of a considerable eminence, where the wood ceased, and the eye was instantly caught by Pemberley House, situated on the opposite side of a valley, into which the road with some abruptness wound. It was a large, handsome, stone building, standing well on rising ground, and backed by a ridge of high woody hills – and in front, a stream of some natural importance was swelled into greater, but without any artificial appearance. Its banks were neither formal, nor falsely adorned. Elizabeth was delighted. She had never seen a place for which nature had done more, or where natural beauty had been so little counteracted by an awkward taste. They were all of them warm in their admiration; and at that moment she felt, that to be mistress of Pemberley might be something!

They descended the hill, crossed the bridge, and drove to the door; and, while examining the nearer aspect of the house, all her apprehensions of meeting its owner returned. She dreaded lest the chambermaid had been mistaken. On applying to see the place, they were admitted into the hall; and Elizabeth, as they waited for the housekeeper, had leisure to wonder at her being where she was.

The housekeeper came; a respectable-looking, elderly woman, much less fine, and more civil, than she had any notion of finding her. They followed her into the dining-parlour. It was a large, well-proportioned room, handsomely fitted up. Elizabeth, after slightly surveying it, went to a window to enjoy its prospect. The hill, crowned with wood, from which they had descended, receiving increased abruptness from the distance, was a beautiful object. Every disposition of the ground was good; and she looked on the whole scene, the river, the trees scattered on its banks, and the winding of the valley, as far as she could trace it, with delight. As they passed into other rooms, these objects were taking different positions; but from every window there were beauties to be seen. The rooms were lofty and handsome, and their furniture suitable to the fortune of their proprietor; but Elizabeth saw, with admiration of his taste, that it was neither gaudy nor uselessly fine; with less of splendour, and more real elegance, than the furniture of Rosings.

'And of this place,' thought she, 'I might have been mistress! With these rooms I might now have been familiarly acquainted! Instead of viewing them as a stranger, I might have rejoiced in them as my own, and welcomed to them as visitors my uncle and aunt. But no,' – recollecting herself – 'that could never be: my uncle and aunt would have been lost to me: I should not have been allowed to invite them.'

This was a lucky recollection – it saved her from something like regret.

She longed to enquire of the housekeeper, whether her master were really absent, but had not courage for it. At length, however, the question was asked by her uncle; and she turned away with alarm, while Mrs Reynolds replied, that he was, adding, 'but we expect him tomorrow, with a large party of friends.' How rejoiced was Elizabeth that their own journey had not by any circumstance been delayed a day!

Her aunt now called her to look at a picture. She approached, and saw the likeness of Mr Wickham suspended, amongst several other miniatures, over the mantelpiece. Her aunt asked her, smilingly, how she liked it. The housekeeper came forward, and told them it was the picture of a young gentleman, the son of her late master's steward, who had been brought up by him at his own expense. 'He is now gone into the army,' she added, 'but I am afraid he has turned out very wild.'

Mrs Gardiner looked at her niece with a smile, but Elizabeth could not return it.

'And that,' said Mrs Reynolds, pointing to another of the miniatures, 'is my master – and very like him. It was drawn at the same time as the other – about eight years ago.'

'I have heard much of your master's fine person,' said Mrs Gardiner, looking at the picture; 'it is a handsome face. But, Lizzy, you can tell us whether it is like or not.'

Mrs Reynolds's respect for Elizabeth seemed to increase on this intimation of her knowing her master.

'Does that young lady know Mr Darcy?'

Elizabeth coloured, and said – 'A little.'

'And do not you think him a very handsome gentleman, ma'am?'

'Yes, very handsome.'

'I am sure *I* know none so handsome; but in the
gallery upstairs you will see a finer, larger picture of
him than this. This room was my late master's
favourite room, and these miniatures are just as they
used to be then. He was very fond of them.'

This accounted to Elizabeth for Mr Wickham's
being among them.

Mrs Reynolds then directed their attention to one
of Miss Darcy, drawn when she was only eight years
old.

'And is Miss Darcy as handsome as her brother?'
said Mr Gardiner.

'Oh! yes – the handsomest young lady that ever was
seen; and so accomplished! – She plays and sings all
day long. In the next room is a new instrument just
come down for her – a present from my master; she
comes here tomorrow with him.'

Mr Gardiner, whose manners were easy and
pleasant, encouraged her communicativeness by his
questions and remarks; Mrs Reynolds, either from
pride or attachment, had evidently great pleasure in
talking of her master and his sister.

'Is your master much at Pemberley in the course of
the year?'

'Not so much as I could wish, sir; but I dare say he
may spend half his time here; and Miss Darcy is
always down for the summer months.'

'Except,' thought Elizabeth, 'when she goes to
Ramsgate.'

'If your master would marry, you might see more of
him.'

'Yes, sir; but I do not know when *that* will be. I do not know who is good enough for him.'

Mr and Mrs Gardiner smiled. Elizabeth could not help saying, 'It is very much to his credit, I am sure, that you should think so.'

'I say no more than the truth, and what everybody will say that knows him,' replied the other. Elizabeth thought this was going pretty far; and she listened with increasing astonishment as the housekeeper added, 'I have never had a cross word from him in my life, and I have known him ever since he was four years old.'

This was praise, of all others most extraordinary, most opposite to her ideas. That he was not a good-tempered man, had been her firmest opinion. Her keenest attention was awakened; she longed to hear more, and was grateful to her uncle for saying, 'There are very few people of whom so much can be said. You are lucky in having such a master.'

'Yes, sir, I know I am. If I was to go through the world, I could not meet with a better. But I have always observed, that they who are good-natured when children, are good-natured when they grow up; and he was always the sweetest-tempered, most generous-hearted, boy in the world.'

Elizabeth almost stared at her. 'Can this be Mr Darcy!' thought she.

'His father was an excellent man,' said Mrs Gardiner.

'Yes, ma'am, that he was indeed; and his son will be just like him – just as affable to the poor.'

Elizabeth listened, wondered, doubted, and was impatient for more. Mrs Reynolds could interest her on no other point. She related the subject of the pictures, the dimensions of the rooms, and the price of the furniture, in vain. Mr Gardiner, highly amused by the kind of family prejudice, to which he attributed her excessive commendation of her master, soon led again to the subject; and she dwelt with energy on his many merits, as they proceeded together up the great staircase.

'He is the best landlord, and the best master,' said she, 'that ever lived. Not like the wild young men nowadays, who think of nothing but themselves. There is not one of his tenants or servants but what will give him a good name. Some people call him proud; but I am sure I never saw anything of it. To my fancy, it is only because he does not rattle away like other young men.'

'In what an amiable light does this place him!' thought Elizabeth.

'This fine account of him,' whispered her aunt, as they walked, 'is not quite consistent with his behaviour to our poor friend.'

'Perhaps we might be deceived.'

'That is not very likely; our authority was too good.'

On reaching the spacious lobby above, they were shown into a very pretty sitting-room, lately fitted up with greater elegance and lightness than the apartments below; and were informed that it was but just done, to give pleasure to Miss Darcy, who had taken a liking to the room, when last at Pemberley.

'He is certainly a good brother,' said Elizabeth, as she walked towards one of the windows.

Mrs Reynolds anticipated Miss Darcy's delight, when she should enter the room. 'And this is always the way with him,' she added, 'Whatever can give his sister any pleasure, is sure to be done in a moment. There is nothing he would not do for her.'

The picture gallery, and two or three of the principal

bedrooms, were all that remained to be shown. In the former were many good paintings; but Elizabeth knew nothing of the art; and from such as had been already visible below, she had willingly turned to look at some drawings of Miss Darcy's, in crayons, whose subjects were usually more interesting, and also more intelligible.

In the gallery there were many family portraits, but they could have little to fix the attention of a stranger. Elizabeth walked on in quest of the only face whose features would be known to her. At last it arrested her – and she beheld a striking resemblance of Mr Darcy, with such a smile over the face, as she remembered to have sometimes seen, when he looked at her. She stood several minutes before the picture in earnest contemplation, and returned to it again before they quitted the gallery. Mrs Reynolds informed them, that it had been taken in his father's life time.

There was certainly at this moment, in Elizabeth's mind, a more gentle sensation towards the original, than she had ever felt in the height of their acquaintance. The commendation bestowed on him by Mrs Reynolds was of no trifling nature. What praise is more valuable than the praise of an intelligent servant? As a brother, a landlord, a master, she considered how many people's happiness were in his guardianship! – How much of pleasure or pain it was in his power to bestow! – How much of good or evil must be done by him! Every idea that had been brought forward by the housekeeper was favourable to his character, and as she stood before the canvas, on which he was represented, and fixed his eyes upon herself, she thought of his regard with a deeper sentiment of gratitude than it had ever raised before;

she remembered its warmth, and softened its impropriety of expression.

When all of the house that was open to general inspection had been seen, they returned downstairs, and taking leave of the housekeeper, were consigned over to the gardener, who met them at the hall door.

As they walked across the lawn towards the river, Elizabeth turned back to look again; her uncle and aunt stopped also, and while the former was conjecturing as to the date of the building, the owner of it himself suddenly came forward from the road, which led behind it to the stables.

They were within twenty yards of each other, and so abrupt was his appearance, that it was impossible to avoid his sight. Their eyes instantly met, and the cheeks of each were overspread with the deepest blush. He absolutely started, and for a moment seemed immoveable from surprise; but shortly recovering himself, advanced towards the party, and spoke to Elizabeth, if not in terms of perfect composure, at least of perfect civility.

She had instinctively turned away; but, stopping on his approach, received his compliments with an embarrassment impossible to be overcome. Had his first appearance, or his resemblance to the picture they had just been examining, been insufficient to assure the other two that they now saw Mr Darcy, the gardener's expression of surprise, on beholding his master, must immediately have told it. They stood a little aloof while he was talking to their niece, who, astonished and confused, scarcely dared lift her eyes to his face, and knew not what answer she returned to his civil enquiries after her family. Amazed at the alteration in his manner since they last parted, every sentence that he uttered was increasing her embarrassment; and every idea of the impropriety of her being found there, recurring to her mind, the few minutes in which they continued together, were some of the most uncomfortable of her life. Nor did he seem much more at ease; when he spoke, his accent had none of its usual sedateness; and he repeated his enquiries as to the time of her having left Longbourn, and of her stay in Derbyshire, so often, and in so hurried a way, as plainly spoke the distraction of his thoughts.

At length, every idea seemed to fail him; and, after standing a few moments without saying a word, he suddenly recollected himself, and took leave.

The others then joined her, and expressed their admiration of his figure; but Elizabeth heard not a word, and, wholly engrossed by her own feelings, followed them in silence. She was overpowered by shame and vexation. Her coming there was the most unfortunate, the most ill-judged thing in the world! How strange must it appear to him! In what a disgraceful light might it not strike so vain a man! It might seem as if she had purposely thrown herself in his way again! Oh! why did she come? or, why did he thus come a day before he was expected? Had they been only ten minutes sooner, they should have been beyond the reach of his discrimination, for it was plain that he was that moment arrived, that moment alighted from his horse or his carriage. She blushed again and again over the perverseness of the meeting. And his behaviour, so strikingly altered – what could it mean? That he should even speak to her was amazing! – but to speak with such civility, to enquire after her family! Never in her life had she seen his manners so little dignified, never had he spoken with such gentleness as on this unexpected meeting. What a contrast did it offer to his last address in Rosings Park, when he put his letter into her hand! She knew not what to think, nor how to account for it.

They had now entered a beautiful walk by the side of the water, and every step was bringing forward a nobler fall of ground, or a finer reach of the woods to which they were approaching; but it was some time before Elizabeth was sensible of any of it; and, though she answered mechanically to the repeated appeals of her uncle and aunt, and seemed to direct her eyes to such objects as they pointed out, she distinguished no part of the scene. Her thoughts were all fixed on that one spot of Pemberley House, whichever it might be, where Mr Darcy then was. She longed to know what at that moment was passing in his mind; in what manner he thought of her, and whether, in defiance of everything, she was still dear to him. Perhaps he had been civil, only because he felt himself at ease; yet there had been *that* in his voice, which was not like ease. Whether he had felt more of pain or of pleasure in seeing her, she could not tell, but he certainly had not seen her with composure.

At length, however, the remarks of her companions on her absence of mind roused her, and she felt the necessity of appearing more like herself.

They entered the woods, and bidding adieu to the river for a while, ascended some of the higher grounds; whence, in spots where the opening of the trees gave the eye power to wander, were many charming views of the valley, the opposite hills, with the long range of woods overspreading many, and occasionally part of the stream. Mr Gardiner expressed a wish of going round the whole Park, but feared it might be beyond a walk. With a triumphant smile, they were told, that it was ten miles round. It settled the matter; and they pursued the accustomed circuit; which brought them again, after some time, in a descent among hanging woods, to the edge of the water, in one of its narrowest parts. They crossed it by a simple bridge, in character with the general air of the scene; it was a spot less adorned than any they had yet visited; and the valley, here contracted into a glen, allowed room only for the stream, and a narrow walk amidst the rough coppice wood which bordered it. Elizabeth longed to explore its windings; but when they had crossed the bridge, and perceived their distance from the house, Mrs Gardiner, who was not a great walker, could go no farther, and thought only of returning to the carriage as quickly as possible. Her niece was, therefore, obliged to submit, and they took their way towards the house on the opposite side of the river, in the nearest direction; but their progress was slow, for Mr Gardiner, though seldom able to indulge the taste, was very fond of fishing, and was so much engaged in watching the occasional appearance of some trout in the water, and talking to the man about them, that he advanced but little. Whilst wandering on in this slow manner, they were again surprised, and Elizabeth's astonishment was quite equal to what it had been at first, by the sight of Mr Darcy approaching them, and at no great distance. The walk being here less sheltered than on the other side, allowed them to see him before they met. Elizabeth, however astonished, was at least more prepared for an interview than before, and resolved to appear and to speak with calmness, if he really intended to meet them. For a few moments, indeed, she felt that he would probably strike into some other path. This idea lasted while a turning in the walk concealed him from their view; the turning past, he was immediately before them. With a glance she saw, that he had lost none of his recent civility; and, to imitate his politeness, she began, as they met, to admire the beauty of the place; but she had not got beyond the words 'delightful', and 'charming', when some unlucky recollections obtruded, and she fancied that praise of Pemberley from her, might be mischievously construed. Her colour changed, and she said no more.

Mrs Gardiner was standing a little behind; and on her pausing, he asked her, if she would do him the honour of introducing him to her friends. This was a stroke of civility for which she was quite unprepared; and she could hardly suppress a smile, at his being now seeking the acquaintance of some of those very people, against whom his pride had revolted, in his offer to herself. 'What will be his surprise,' thought she, 'when he knows who they are! He takes them now for people of fashion.'

The introduction, however, was immediately made; and as she named their relationship to herself, she stole a sly look at him, to see how he bore it; and was not without the expectation of his decamping as fast as he could from such disgraceful companions. That he was *surprised* by the connection was evident; he sustained it however with fortitude, and so far from going away, turned back with them, and entered into conversation with Mr Gardiner. Elizabeth could not but be pleased, could not but triumph. It was consoling, that he should know she had some relations for whom there was no need to blush. She listened most attentively to all that passed between them, and gloried in every expression, every sentence of her uncle, which marked his intelligence, his taste, or his good manners.

The conversation soon turned upon fishing, and she heard Mr Darcy invite him, with the greatest civility, to fish there as often as he chose, while he continued in the neighbourhood, offering at the same time to supply him with fishing tackle, and pointing out those parts of the stream where there was usually most sport. Mrs Gardiner, who was walking arm in arm with Elizabeth, gave her a look expressive of her wonder. Elizabeth said nothing, but it gratified her exceedingly; the compliment must be all for herself. Her astonishment, however, was extreme; and continually was she repeating, 'Why is he so altered? From what can it proceed? It cannot be for *me*, it cannot be for *my* sake that his manners are thus softened. My reproofs at Hunsford could not work such a change as this. It is impossible that he should still love me.'

After walking some time in this way, the two ladies in front, the two gentlemen behind, on resuming their places, after descending to the brink of the river for the better inspection of some curious water-plant, there chanced to be a little alteration. It originated in Mrs Gardiner, who, fatigued by the exercise of the morning, found Elizabeth's arm inadequate to her support, and consequently preferred her husband's. Mr Darcy took her place by her niece, and they walked on together. After a short silence, the lady first spoke. She wished him to know that she had been assured of his absence before she came to the place, and accordingly began by observing, that his arrival had been very unexpected –

'for your housekeeper,' she added, 'informed us that you would certainly not be here till tomorrow; and indeed, before we left Bakewell, we understood that you were not immediately expected in the country.' He acknowledged the truth of it all; and said that business with his steward had occasioned his coming forward a few hours before the rest of the party with whom he had been travelling. 'They will join me early tomorrow,' he continued, 'and among them are some who will claim an acquaintance with you – Mr Bingley and his sisters.'

Elizabeth answered only by a slight bow. Her thoughts were instantly driven back to the time when Mr Bingley's name had been last mentioned between them; and if she might judge from his complexion, *his* mind was not very differently engaged.

'There is also one other person in the party,' he continued after a pause, 'who more particularly wishes to be known to you – Will you allow me, or do I ask too much, to introduce my sister to your acquaintance during your stay at Lambton?'

The surprise of such an application was great indeed; it was too great for her to know in what manner she acceded to it. She immediately felt that whatever desire Miss Darcy might have of being acquainted with her, must be the work of her brother, and without looking farther, it was satisfactory; it was gratifying to know that his resentment had not made him think really ill of her.

They now walked on in silence; each of them deep in thought. Elizabeth was not comfortable; that was impossible; but she was flattered and pleased. His wish of introducing his sister to her, was a compliment of the highest kind. They soon outstripped the others, and when they had reached the carriage, Mr and Mrs Gardiner were half a quarter of a mile behind.

He then asked her to walk into the house – but she declared herself not tired, and they stood together on the lawn. At such a time, much might have been said, and silence was very awkward. She wanted to talk, but there seemed an embargo on every subject. At last she recollected that she had been travelling, and they talked of Matlock and Dove Dale with great perseverance. Yet time and her aunt moved slowly – and her patience and her ideas were nearly worn out before the tête-à-tête was over. On Mr and Mrs Gardiner's coming up, they were all pressed to go into the house and take some refreshment; but this was declined, and they parted on each side with the utmost politeness. Mr Darcy handed the ladies into the carriage, and when it drove off, Elizabeth saw him walking slowly towards the house.

The observations of her uncle and aunt now began; and each of them pronounced him to be infinitely superior to anything they had expected. 'He is perfectly well behaved, polite, and unassuming,' said her uncle.

'There *is* something a little stately in him to be sure,' replied her aunt, 'but it is confined to his air, and is not unbecoming. I can now say with the housekeeper, that though some people may call him proud, *I* have seen nothing of it.'

'I was never more surprised than by his behaviour to us. It was more than civil; it was really attentive; and there was no necessity for such attention. His acquaintance with Elizabeth was very trifling.'

'To be sure, Lizzy,' said her aunt, 'he is not so handsome as Wickham; or rather he has not Wickham's countenance, for his features are perfectly good. But how came you to tell us that he was so disagreeable?'

Elizabeth excused herself as well as she could; said that she had liked him better when they met in Kent than before, and that she had never seen him so pleasant as this morning.

'But perhaps he may be a little whimsical in his civilities,' replied her uncle. 'Your great men often are; and therefore I shall not take him at his word about fishing, as he might change his mind another day, and warn me off his grounds.'

Elizabeth felt that they had entirely mistaken his character, but said nothing.

'From what we have seen of him,' continued Mrs Gardiner, 'I really should not have thought that he could have behaved in so cruel a way by anybody, as he has done by poor Wickham. He has not an ill-natured look. On the contrary, there is something pleasing about his mouth when he speaks. And there is something of dignity in his countenance, that would not give one an unfavourable idea of his heart. But to be sure, the good lady who showed us the house, did give him a most flaming character! I could hardly help laughing aloud sometimes. But he is a liberal master, I suppose, and *that* in the eye of a servant comprehends every virtue.'

Elizabeth here felt herself called on to say something in vindication of his behaviour to Wickham; and therefore gave them to understand, in as guarded a manner as she could, that by what she had heard from his relations in Kent, his actions were capable of a very different construction; and that his character was by no means so faulty, nor Wickham's so amiable, as they had been considered in Hertfordshire. In confirmation of this, she related the particulars of all the pecuniary transactions in which they had been connected, without actually naming her authority, but stating it to be such as might be relied on.

Mrs Gardiner was surprised and concerned; but as they were now approaching the scene of her former pleasures, every idea gave way to the charm of recollection; and she was too much engaged in pointing out to her husband all the interesting spots in its environs, to think of anything else. Fatigued as she had been by the morning's walk, they had no sooner dined than she set off again in quest of her former acquaintance, and the evening was spent in the satisfactions of an intercourse renewed after many years discontinuance.

The occurrences of the day were too full of interest to leave Elizabeth much attention for any of these new friends; and she could do nothing but think, and think with wonder, of Mr Darcy's civility, and above all, of his wishing her to be acquainted with his sister.

Chapter 44

Elizabeth had settled it that Mr Darcy would bring his sister to visit her, the very day after her reaching Pemberley; and was consequently resolved not to be out of sight of the inn the whole of that morning. But her conclusion was false; for on the very morning after their own arrival at Lambton, these visitors came. They had been walking about the place with some of their new friends, and were just returned to the inn to dress themselves for dining with the same family, when the sound of a carriage drew them to the window, and they saw a gentleman and lady in a curricle, driving up the street. Elizabeth immediately recognising the livery, guessed what it meant, and imparted no small degree of surprise to her relations, by acquainting them with the honour which she expected. Her uncle and aunt were all amazement; and the embarrassment of her manner as she spoke, joined to the circumstance itself, and many of the circumstances of the preceding day, opened to them a new idea on the business. Nothing had ever suggested it before, but they now felt that there was no other way of accounting for such attentions from such a quarter, than by supposing a partiality for their niece. While these newly-born notions were passing in their heads, the perturbation of Elizabeth's feelings was every moment increasing. She was quite amazed at her own discomposure; but amongst other causes of disquiet, she dreaded lest the partiality of the brother should have said too much in her favour; and more than commonly anxious to please, she naturally suspected that every power of pleasing would fail her.

She retreated from the window, fearful of being seen; and as she walked up and down the room, endeavouring to compose herself, saw such looks of enquiring surprise in her uncle and aunt, as made everything worse.

Miss Darcy and her brother appeared, and this formidable introduction took place. With astonishment did Elizabeth see, that her new acquaintance was at least as much embarrassed as herself. Since her being at Lambton, she had heard that Miss Darcy was exceedingly proud; but the observation of a very few minutes convinced her, that she was only exceedingly

The sound of a carriage drew them to the window

shy. She found it difficult to obtain even a word from her beyond a monosyllable.

Miss Darcy was tall, and on a larger scale than Elizabeth; and, though little more than sixteen, her figure was formed, and her appearance womanly and graceful. She was less handsome than her brother, but there was sense and good humour in her face, and her manners were perfectly unassuming and gentle. Elizabeth, who had expected to find in her as acute and unembarrassed an observer as ever Mr Darcy had been, was much relieved by discerning such different feelings.

They had not been long together, before Darcy told her that Bingley was also coming to wait on her; and she had barely time to express her satisfaction, and prepare for such a visitor, when Bingley's quick step was heard on the stairs, and in a moment he entered the room. All Elizabeth's anger against him had been long done away; but, had she still felt any, it could hardly have stood its ground against the unaffected cordiality with which he expressed himself, on seeing her again. He enquired in a friendly, though general way, after her family, and looked and spoke with the same good-humoured ease that he had ever done.

To Mr and Mrs Gardiner he was scarcely a less interesting personage than to herself. They had long wished to see him. The whole party before them, indeed, excited a lively attention. The suspicions which had just arisen of Mr Darcy and their niece, directed their observation towards each with an earnest, though guarded, enquiry; and they soon drew from those enquiries the full conviction that one of them at least knew what it was to love. Of the lady's sensations they remained a little in doubt; but that the gentleman was overflowing with admiration was evident enough.

Elizabeth, on her side, had much to do. She wanted to ascertain the feelings of each of her visitors, she wanted to compose her own, and to make herself agreeable to all; and in the latter object, where she feared most to fail, she was most sure of success, for those to whom she endeavoured to give pleasure were prepossessed in her favour. Bingley was ready, Georgiana was eager, and Darcy determined, to be pleased.

In seeing Bingley, her thoughts naturally flew to her

To make herself agreeable to all

sister; and oh! how ardently did she long to know, whether any of his were directed in a like manner. Sometimes she could fancy, that he talked less than on former occasions, and once or twice pleased herself with the notion that as he looked at her, he was trying to trace a resemblance. But, though this might be imaginary, she could not be deceived as to his behaviour to Miss Darcy, who had been set up as a rival of Jane. No look appeared on either side that spoke particular regard. Nothing occurred between them that could justify the hopes of his sister. On this point she was soon satisfied; and two or three little circumstances occurred ere they parted, which, in her anxious interpretation, denoted a recollection of Jane, not untinctured by tenderness, and a wish of saying more that might lead to the mention of her, had he dared. He observed to her, at a moment when the others were talking together, and in a tone which had something of real regret, that it 'was a very long time since he had had the pleasure of seeing her;' and, before she could reply, he added, 'It is above eight months. We have not met since the 26th of November, when we were all dancing together at Netherfield.'

Elizabeth was pleased to find his memory so exact; and he afterwards took occasion to ask her, when unattended to by any of the rest, whether *all* her sisters were at Longbourn. There was not much in the question, nor in the preceding remark, but there was a look and a manner which gave them meaning.

It was not often that she could turn her eyes on Mr Darcy himself; but, whenever she did catch a glimpse, she saw an expression of general complaisance, and in all that he said, she heard an accent so far removed from hauteur or disdain of his companions, as convinced her that the improvement of manners which she had yesterday witnessed, however temporary its existence might prove, had at least outlived one day. When she saw him thus seeking the acquaintance, and courting the good opinion of people, with whom any intercourse a few months ago would have been a disgrace; when she saw him thus civil, not only to herself, but to the very relations whom he had openly disdained, and recollected their last lively scene in Hunsford Parsonage, the difference, the change was so great, and struck so forcibly on her mind, that she could hardly restrain her astonishment from being visible. Never, even in the company of his dear friends at Netherfield, or his dignified relations at Rosings, had she seen him so desirous to please, so free from self-consequence, or unbending reserve as now, when no importance could result from the success of his endeavours, and when even the acquaintance of those to whom his attentions were addressed, would draw down the ridicule and censure of the ladies both of Netherfield and Rosings.

Their visitors staid with them above half an hour, and when they arose to depart, Mr Darcy called on his sister to join him in expressing their wish of seeing Mr and Mrs Gardiner, and Miss Bennet, to dinner at Pemberley, before they left the country. Miss Darcy, though with a diffidence which marked her little in the habit of giving invitations, readily obeyed. Mrs Gardiner looked at her niece, desirous of knowing how *she*, whom the invitation most concerned, felt disposed as to its acceptance, but Elizabeth had turned away her head. Presuming, however, that this studied avoidance spoke rather a momentary embarrassment, than any dislike of the proposal, and seeing in her husband, who was fond of society, a perfect willingness to accept it, she ventured to engage for her attendance, and the day after the next was fixed on.

Bingley expressed great pleasure in the certainty of seeing Elizabeth again, having still a great deal to say to her, and many enquiries to make after all their Hertfordshire friends. Elizabeth, construing all this into a wish of hearing her speak of her sister, was pleased; and on this account, as well as some others, found herself, when their visitors left them, capable of considering the last half-hour with some satisfaction, though while it was passing, the enjoyment of it had been little. Eager to be alone, and fearful of enquiries or hints from her uncle and aunt, she staid with them only long enough to hear their favourable opinion of Bingley, and then hurried away to dress.

But she had no reason to fear Mr and Mrs Gardiner's curiosity; it was not their wish to force her communication. It was evident that she was much better acquainted with Mr Darcy than they had before any idea of; it was evident that he was very much in love with her. They saw much to interest, but nothing to justify enquiry.

Of Mr Darcy it was now a matter of anxiety to think well; and, as far as their acquaintance reached, there was no fault to find. They could not be untouched by his politeness, and had they drawn his character from their own feelings, and his servant's report, without any reference to any other account, the circle in Hertfordshire to which he was known, would not have recognised it for Mr Darcy. There was now an interest, however, in believing the housekeeper; and they soon became sensible, that the authority of a servant who had known him since he was four years old, and whose own manners indicated respectability, was not to be hastily rejected. Neither had anything occurred in the intelligence of their Lambton friends, that could materially lessen its weight. They had nothing to accuse him of but pride; pride he probably had, and if not, it would certainly be imputed by the inhabitants of a small market town, where the family did not visit.

It was acknowledged, however, that he was a liberal man, and did much good among the poor.

With respect to Wickham, the travellers soon found that he was not held there in much estimation; for though the chief of his concerns, with the son of his patron, were imperfectly understood, it was yet a well known fact that, on his quitting Derbyshire, he had left many debts behind him, which Mr Darcy afterwards discharged.

As for Elizabeth, her thoughts were at Pemberley this evening more than the last; and the evening, though as it passed it seemed long, was not long enough to determine her feelings towards *one* in that mansion; and she lay awake two whole hours, endeavouring to make them out. She certainly did not hate him. No; hatred had vanished long ago, and she had almost as long been ashamed of ever feeling a dislike against him, that could be so called. The respect created by the conviction of his valuable qualities, though at first unwillingly admitted, had for some time ceased to be repugnant to her feelings; and it was now heightened into somewhat of a friendlier nature, by the testimony so highly in his favour, and bringing forward his disposition in so amiable a light, which yesterday had produced. But above all, above respect and esteem, there was a motive within her of good will which could not be overlooked. It was gratitude. Gratitude, not merely for having once loved her, but for loving her still well enough, to forgive all the petulance and acrimony of her manner in rejecting him, and all the unjust accusations accompanying her rejection. He who, she had been persuaded, would avoid her as his greatest enemy, seemed, on this accidental meeting, most eager to preserve the acquaintance, and without any indelicate display of regard, or any peculiarity of manner, where their two selves only were concerned, was soliciting the good opinion of her friends, and bent on making her known to his sister. Such a change in a man of so much pride, excited not only astonishment but gratitude – for to love, ardent love, it must be attributed; and as such its impression on her was of a sort to be encouraged, as by no means unpleasing, though it could not be exactly defined. She respected, she esteemed, she was grateful to him, she felt a real interest in his welfare; and she only wanted to know how far she wished that welfare to depend upon herself, and how far it would be for the happiness of both that she should employ the power, which her fancy told her she still possessed, of bringing on the renewal of his addresses.

It had been settled in the evening, between the aunt and niece, that such a striking civility as Miss Darcy's, in coming to them on the very day of her arrival at Pemberley, for she had reached it only to a late breakfast, ought to be imitated, though it could not be equalled, by some exertion of politeness on their side; and, consequently, that it would be highly expedient to wait on her at Pemberley the following morning. They were, therefore, to go. Elizabeth was pleased, though, when she asked herself the reason, she had very little to say in reply.

Mr Gardiner left them soon after breakfast. The fishing scheme had been renewed the day before, and a positive engagement made of his meeting some of the gentlemen at Pemberley by noon.

Chapter 45

Convinced as Elizabeth now was that Miss Bingley's dislike of her had originated in jealousy, she could not help feeling how very unwelcome her appearance at Pemberley must be to her, and was curious to know with how much civility on that lady's side, the acquaintance would now be renewed.

On reaching the house, they were shown through the hall into the saloon, whose northern aspect rendered it delightful for summer. Its windows opening to the ground, admitted a most refreshing view of the high woody hills behind the house, and of the beautiful oaks and Spanish chestnuts which were scattered over the intermediate lawn.

In this room they were received by Miss Darcy, who was sitting there with Mrs Hurst and Miss Bingley, and the lady with whom she lived in London. Georgiana's reception of them was very civil; but attended with all that embarrassment which, though proceeding from shyness and the fear of doing wrong, would easily give to those who felt themselves inferior, the belief of her being proud and reserved. Mrs Gardiner and her niece, however, did her justice, and pitied her.

By Mrs Hurst and Miss Bingley, they were noticed only by a curtsey; and on their being seated, a pause, awkward as such pauses must always be, succeeded for a few moments. It was first broken by Mrs Annesley, a genteel, agreeable-looking woman, whose endeavour to introduce some kind of discourse, proved her to be more truly well bred than either of the others; and between her and Mrs Gardiner, with occasional help from Elizabeth, the conversation was carried on. Miss Darcy looked as if she wished for courage enough to join in it; and sometimes did venture a short sentence, when there was least danger of its being heard.

Elizabeth soon saw that she was herself closely watched by Miss Bingley, and that she could not speak a word, especially to Miss Darcy, without calling her attention. This observation would not have prevented her from trying to talk to the latter, had they not been seated at an inconvenient distance; but she was not sorry to be spared the necessity of saying much. Her own thoughts were employing her. She expected every moment that some of the gentlemen would enter the room. She wished, she feared that the master of the house might be amongst them; and whether she wished or feared it most, she could scarcely determine. After sitting in this manner a quarter of an hour, without hearing Miss Bingley's voice, Elizabeth was roused by receiving from her a cold enquiry after the health of her family. She answered with equal indifference and brevity, and the other said no more.

The next variation which their visit afforded was produced by the entrance of servants with cold meat, cake, and a variety of all the finest fruits in season; but this did not take place till after many a significant look and smile from Mrs Annesley to Miss Darcy had been given, to remind her of her post. There was now employment for the whole party; for though they could not all talk, they could all eat; and the beautiful pyramids of grapes, nectarines, and peaches, soon collected them round the table.

While thus engaged, Elizabeth had a fair opportunity of deciding whether she most feared or wished for the appearance of Mr Darcy, by the feelings which prevailed on his entering the room; and then, though but a moment before she had believed her wishes to predominate, she began to regret that he came.

He had been some time with Mr Gardiner, who, with two or three other gentlemen from the house, was engaged by the river, and had left him only on learning that the ladies of the family intended a visit to Georgiana that morning. No sooner did he appear, than Elizabeth wisely resolved to be perfectly easy and unembarrassed – a resolution the more necessary to be made, but perhaps not the more easily kept, because she saw that the suspicions of the whole party were awakened against them, and that there was scarcely an eye which did not watch his behaviour when he first came into the room. In no countenance was attentive curiosity so strongly marked as in Miss Bingley's, in spite of the smiles which overspread her face whenever she spoke to one of its objects; for jealousy had not yet made her desperate, and her attentions to Mr Darcy were by no means over. Miss Darcy, on her brother's entrance, exerted herself much more to talk; and Elizabeth saw that he was anxious for his sister and herself to get acquainted, and forwarded, as much as possible, every attempt at conversation on either side. Miss Bingley saw all this likewise; and, in the imprudence of anger, took the first opportunity of saying, with sneering civility, 'Pray, Miss Eliza, are not the —shire militia removed from Meryton? They must be a great loss to *your* family.'

In Darcy's presence she dared not mention Wickham's name; but Elizabeth instantly comprehended that he was uppermost in her thoughts; and the various recollections connected with him gave her a moment's distress; but, exerting herself vigorously to repel the ill-natured attack, she presently answered the question in a tolerably disengaged tone. While she spoke, an involuntary glance showed her Darcy with an heightened complexion, earnestly looking at her, and his sister overcome with confusion, and unable to lift up her eyes. Had Miss Bingley known what pain she was then giving her beloved friend, she undoubtedly would have refrained from the hint; but she had merely intended to discompose Elizabeth, by bringing forward the idea of a man to whom she believed her partial, to make her betray a sensibility which might injure her in Darcy's opinion, and perhaps to remind the latter of all the follies and absurdities, by which some part of her family were connected with that corps. Not a syllable had ever reached her of Miss Darcy's meditated elopement. To no creature had it been revealed, where secrecy was possible, except to Elizabeth; and from all Bingley's connections her brother was particularly anxious to conceal it, from that very wish which Elizabeth had long ago attributed to him, of their becoming hereafter her own. He had certainly formed such a plan, and without meaning that it should affect his endeavour to separate him from Miss Bennet, it is probable that it might add something to his lively concern for the welfare of his friend.

Elizabeth's collected behaviour, however, soon quieted his emotion; and as Miss Bingley, vexed and disappointed, dared not approach nearer to Wickham, Georgiana also recovered in time, though not enough to be able to speak any more. Her brother, whose eye she feared to meet, scarcely recollected her interest in the affair, and the very circumstance which had been designed to turn his thoughts from Elizabeth, seemed to have fixed them on her more, and more cheerfully.

Their visit did not continue long after the question and answer above-mentioned; and while Mr Darcy was attending them to their carriage, Miss Bingley was venting her feelings in criticisms on Elizabeth's person, behaviour, and dress. But Georgiana would not join her. Her brother's recommendation was enough to ensure her favour: his judgement could not err, and he had spoken in such terms of Elizabeth, as to leave Georgiana without the power of finding her otherwise than lovely and amiable. When Darcy returned to the saloon, Miss Bingley could not help repeating to him some part of what she had been saying to his sister.

'How very ill Eliza Bennet looks this morning, Mr Darcy,' she cried; 'I never in my life saw anyone so much altered as she is since the winter. She is grown so brown and coarse! Louisa and I were agreeing that we should not have known her again.'

However little Mr Darcy might have liked such an address, he contented himself with coolly replying, that he perceived no other alteration than her being rather tanned – no miraculous consequence of travelling in the summer.

'For my own part,' she rejoined, 'I must confess that I never could see any beauty in her. Her face is too thin; her complexion has no brilliancy; and her features are not at all handsome. Her nose wants character; there is nothing marked in its lines. Her teeth are tolerable, but not out of the common way; and as for her eyes, which have sometimes been called so fine, I never could perceive anything extraordinary in them. They have a sharp, shrewish look, which I do not like at all; and in her air altogether, there is a self-sufficiency without fashion, which is intolerable.'

Persuaded as Miss Bingley was that Darcy admired Elizabeth, this was not the best method of recommending herself; but angry people are not always wise; and in seeing him at last look somewhat nettled, she had all the success she expected. He was resolutely silent however; and, from a determination of making him speak, she continued, 'I remember, when we first knew her in Hertfordshire, how amazed we all were to find that she was a reputed beauty; and I particularly recollect your saying one night, after they had been dining at Netherfield, "*She* a beauty! – I should as soon call her mother a wit." But afterwards she seemed to improve on you, and I believe you thought her rather pretty at one time.'

'Yes,' replied Darcy, who could contain himself no longer, 'but *that* was only when I first knew her, for it is many months since I have considered her as one of the handsomest women of my acquaintance.'

He then went away, and Miss Bingley was left to all the satisfaction of having forced him to say what gave no one any pain but herself.

Mrs Gardiner and Elizabeth talked of all that had occurred, during their visit, as they returned, except what had particularly interested them both. The looks and behaviour of everybody they had seen were discussed, except of the person who had mostly engaged their attention. They talked of his sister, his friends, his house, his fruit, of everything but himself; yet Elizabeth was longing to know what

Mrs Gardiner thought of him, and Mrs Gardiner would have been highly gratified by her niece's beginning the subject.

Chapter 46

Elizabeth had been a good deal disappointed in not finding a letter from Jane, on their first arrival at Lambton; and this disappointment had been renewed on each of the mornings that had now been spent there; but on the third, her repining was over, and her sister justified by the receipt of two letters from her at once, on one of which was marked that it had been mis-sent elsewhere. Elizabeth was not surprised at it, as Jane had written the direction remarkably ill.

They had just been preparing to walk as the letters came in; and her uncle and aunt, leaving her to enjoy them in quiet, set off by themselves. The one mis-sent must be first attended to; it had been written five days ago. The beginning contained an account of all their little parties and engagements, with such news as the country afforded; but the latter half, which was dated a day later, and written in evident agitation, gave more important intelligence. It was to this effect:

'Since writing the above, dearest Lizzy, something has occurred of a most unexpected and serious nature; but I am afraid of alarming you – be assured that we are all well. What I have to say relates to poor Lydia. An express came at twelve last night, just as we were all gone to bed, from Colonel Forster, to inform us that she was gone off to Scotland with one of his officers; to own the truth, with Wickham! – Imagine our surprise. To Kitty, however, it does not seem so wholly unexpected. I am very, very sorry. So imprudent a match on both sides! – But I am willing to hope the best, and that his character has been misunderstood. Thoughtless and indiscreet I can easily believe him, but this step (and let us rejoice over it) marks nothing bad at heart. His choice is disinterested at least, for he must know my father can give her nothing. Our poor mother is sadly grieved. My father bears it better. How thankful am I, that we never let them know what has been said against him; we must forget it ourselves. They were off Saturday night about twelve, as is conjectured, but were not missed till yesterday morning at eight. The express was sent off directly. My dear Lizzy, they must have passed within ten miles of us. Colonel Forster gives us reason to expect him here soon. Lydia left a few lines for his wife, informing her of their intention. I must conclude, for I cannot be long from my poor mother. I am afraid you will not be able to make it out, but I hardly know what I have written.'

Without allowing herself time for consideration, and scarcely knowing what she felt, Elizabeth on finishing this letter, instantly seized the other, and opening it with the utmost impatience, read as follows: it had been written a day later than the conclusion of the first.

'By this time, my dearest sister, you have received my hurried letter; I wish this may be more intelligible, but though not confined for time, my head is so bewildered that I cannot answer for being coherent. Dearest Lizzy, I hardly know what I would write, but I have bad news for you, and it cannot be delayed. Imprudent as a marriage between Mr Wickham and our poor Lydia would be, we are now anxious to be assured it has taken place, for there is but too much reason to fear they are not gone to Scotland. Colonel Forster came yesterday, having left Brighton the day before, not many hours after the express. Though Lydia's short letter to Mrs F. gave them to understand that they were going to Gretna Green, something was dropped by Denny expressing his belief that W. never intended to go there, or to marry Lydia at all, which was repeated to Colonel F. who instantly taking the alarm, set off from B. intending to trace their route. He did trace them easily to Clapham, but no farther; for on entering that place they removed into a hackney-coach and dismissed the chaise that brought them from Epsom. All that is known after this is, that they were seen to continue the London road. I know not what to think. After making every possible enquiry on that side London, Colonel F. came on into Hertford-shire, anxiously renewing them at all the turnpikes, and at the inns in Barnet and Hatfield, but without any success, no such people had been seen to pass through. With the kindest concern he came on to Longbourn, and broke his apprehensions to us in a manner most creditable to his heart. I am sincerely grieved for him and Mrs F. but no one can throw any blame on them. Our distress, my dear Lizzy, is very great. My father and mother believe the worst, but I cannot think so ill of him. Many circumstances might make it more eligible for them to be married privately in town than to pursue their first plan; and even if *he* could form such a design against a young woman of Lydia's connections, which is not likely, can I suppose her so lost to everything? – Impossible. I grieve to find, however, that Colonel F. is not disposed to depend upon their marriage; he shook his head when I expressed my hopes, and said he feared W. was not a man to be trusted. My poor mother is really ill and keeps her room. Could she exert herself it would be better, but this is not to be expected; and as to my father, I never in my life saw him so affected. Poor Kitty has anger for having concealed their attachment; but as it was a matter of confidence one cannot wonder. I am truly glad, dearest Lizzy, that you have been spared something of these distressing scenes; but now as the first shock is over, shall I own that I long for your return? I am not so selfish, however, as to press for it, if inconvenient. Adieu. I take up my pen again to do, what I have just told you I would not, but circumstances are such, that I cannot help earnestly begging you all to come here, as soon as possible. I know my dear uncle and aunt so well, that I am not afraid of requesting it, though I have still something more to ask of the former. My father is going to London with Colonel Forster instantly, to try to discover her. What he means to do, I am sure I know not; but his excessive distress will not allow him to pursue any measure in the best and safest way, and Colonel Forster is obliged to be at Brighton again tomorrow evening. In such an exigence my uncle's advice and assistance would be everything in the world; he will immediately comprehend what I must feel, and I rely upon his goodness.'

'Oh! where, where is my uncle?' cried Elizabeth, darting from her seat as she finished the letter, in eagerness to follow him, without losing a moment of the time so precious; but as she reached the door, it was opened by a servant, and Mr Darcy appeared. Her pale face and impetuous manner made him start, and before he could recover himself enough to speak, she, in whose mind every idea was superseded by Lydia's

I have not an instant to lose

situation, hastily exclaimed, 'I beg your pardon, but I must leave you. I must find Mr Gardiner this moment, on business that cannot be delayed; I have not an instant to lose.'

'Good God! what is the matter?' cried he, with more feeling than politeness; then recollecting himself, 'I will not detain you a minute, but let me, or let the servant, go after Mr and Mrs Gardiner. You are not well enough – you cannot go yourself.'

Elizabeth hesitated, but her knees trembled under her, and she felt how little would be gained by her attempting to pursue them. Calling back the servant, therefore, she commissioned him, though in so breathless an accent as made her almost unintelligible, to fetch his master and mistress home, instantly.

On his quitting the room, she sat down, unable to support herself, and looking so miserably ill, that it was impossible for Darcy to leave her, or to refrain from saying, in a tone of gentleness and commiseration, 'Let me call your maid. Is there nothing you could take, to give you present relief? – A glass of wine – shall I get you one? – You are very ill.'

'No, I thank you,' she replied, endeavouring to recover herself. 'There is nothing the matter with me. I am quite well. I am only distressed by some dreadful news which I have just received from Longbourn.'

She burst into tears as she alluded to it, and for a few minutes could not speak another word. Darcy, in wretched suspense, could only say something indistinctly of his concern, and observe her in compassionate silence. At length, she spoke again. 'I have just had a letter from Jane, with such dreadful news. It cannot be concealed from anyone. My youngest sister has left all her friends – has eloped – has thrown herself into the power of – of Mr Wickham. They are gone off together from Brighton. *You* know him too well to doubt the rest. She has no money, no connections, nothing that can tempt him to – she is lost for ever.'

Darcy was fixed in astonishment. 'When I consider,' she added, in a yet more agitated voice, 'that *I* might have prevented it! – *I* who knew what he was. Had I but explained some part of it only – some part of what I learnt, to my own family! Had his character been known, this could not have happened. But it is all, all too late now.'

'I am grieved, indeed,' cried Darcy; 'grieved – shocked. But is it certain, absolutely certain?'

'Oh yes! – They left Brighton together on Sunday night, and were traced almost to London, but not beyond; they are certainly not gone to Scotland.'

'And what has been done, what has been attempted, to recover her?'

'My father is gone to London, and Jane has written to beg my uncle's immediate assistance, and we shall be off, I hope, in half an hour. But nothing can be done; I know very well that nothing can be done. How is such a man to be worked on? How are they even to be discovered? I have not the smallest hope. It is every way horrible!'

Darcy shook his head in silent acquiescence.

'When *my* eyes were opened to his real character. Oh! had I known what I ought, what I dared, to do! But I knew not – I was afraid of doing too much. Wretched, wretched, mistake!'

Darcy made no answer. He seemed scarcely to hear her, and was walking up and down the room in earnest meditation; his brow contracted, his air gloomy.

Elizabeth soon observed, and instantly understood it. Her power was sinking; everything *must* sink under such a proof of family weakness, such an assurance of the deepest disgrace. She could neither wonder nor condemn, but the belief of his self-conquest brought nothing consolatory to her bosom, afforded no palliation of her distress. It was, on the contrary, exactly calculated to make her understand her own wishes; and never had she so honestly felt that she could have loved him, as now, when all love must be vain.

But self, though it would intrude, could not engross her. Lydia – the humiliation, the misery, she was bringing on them all, soon swallowed up every private care; and covering her face with her handkerchief, Elizabeth was soon lost to everything else; and, after a pause of several minutes, was only recalled to a sense of her situation by the voice of her companion, who, in a manner, which though it spoke compassion, spoke likewise restraint, said, 'I am afraid you have been long desiring my absence, nor have I anything to plead in excuse of my stay, but real, though unavailing, concern. Would to heaven that anything could be either said or done on my part, that might offer consolation to such distress. But I will not torment you with vain wishes, which may seem purposely to ask for your thanks. This unfortunate affair will, I fear, prevent my sister's having the pleasure of seeing you at Pemberley to day.'

'Oh, yes. Be so kind as to apologise for us to Miss Darcy. Say that urgent business calls us home immediately. Conceal the unhappy truth as long as it is possible. I know it cannot be long.'

He readily assured her of his secrecy – again expressed his sorrow for her distress, wished it a happier conclusion than there was at present reason to hope, and leaving his compliments for her relations, with only one serious, parting, look, went away.

As he quitted the room, Elizabeth felt how improbable it was that they should ever see each other again on such terms of cordiality as had marked their several meetings in Derbyshire; and as she threw a retrospective glance over the whole of their acquaintance, so full of contradictions and varieties, sighed at the perverseness of those feelings which would now have promoted its continuance, and would formerly have rejoiced in its termination.

If gratitude and esteem are good foundations of affection, Elizabeth's change of sentiment will be neither improbable nor faulty. But if otherwise, if the regard springing from such sources is unreasonable or unnatural, in comparison of what is so often described as arising on a first interview with its object, and even before two words have been exchanged, nothing can be said in her defence, except that she had given somewhat of a trial to the latter method, in her partiality for Wickham, and that its ill-success might perhaps authorise her to seek the other less interesting mode of attachment. Be that as it may, she saw him go with regret; and in this early example of what Lydia's infamy must produce, found additional anguish as she reflected on that wretched business. Never, since reading Jane's second letter, had she entertained a hope of Wickham's meaning to marry her. No one but Jane, she thought, could flatter herself with such an expectation. Surprise was the least of her feelings on this development. While the contents of the first letter remained on her mind, she was all surprise – all astonishment that Wickham should marry a girl, whom it was impossible he could marry for money; and how Lydia could ever have attached him, had appeared incomprehensible. But now it was all too natural. For such an attachment as this, she might have sufficient charms; and though she did not suppose Lydia to be deliberately engaging in an elopement, without the intention of marriage, she had no difficulty in believing that neither her virtue nor her understanding would preserve her from falling an easy prey.

She had never perceived, while the regiment was in Hertfordshire, that Lydia had any partiality for him, but she was convinced that Lydia had wanted only encouragement to attach herself to anybody. Sometimes one officer, sometimes another had been her favourite, as their attentions raised them in her opinion. Her affections had been continually fluctuating, but never without an object. The mischief of neglect and mistaken indulgence towards such a girl. Oh! how acutely did she now feel it.

She was wild to be at home – to hear, to see, to be upon the spot, to share with Jane in the cares that must now fall wholly upon her, in a family so deranged; a father absent, a mother incapable of exertion, and requiring constant attendance; and though almost persuaded that nothing could be done for Lydia, her uncle's interference seemed of the utmost importance, and till he entered the room, the misery of her impatience was severe. Mr and Mrs Gardiner had hurried back in alarm, supposing, by the servant's account, that their niece was taken suddenly ill – but satisfying them instantly on that head, she eagerly communicated the cause of their summons, reading the two letters aloud, and dwelling on the postscript of the last, with trembling energy. Though Lydia had never been a favourite with them, Mr and Mrs Gardiner could not but be deeply affected. Not Lydia only, but all were concerned in it; and after the first exclamations of surprise and horror, Mr Gardiner readily promised every assistance in his power. Elizabeth, though expecting no less, thanked him with tears of gratitude; and all three being actuated by one spirit, everything relating to their journey was speedily settled. They were to be off as soon as possible. 'But what is to be done about Pemberley?' cried Mrs Gardiner. 'John told us Mr Darcy was here when you sent for us – was it so?'

'Yes; and I told him we should not be able to keep our engagement. *That* is all settled.'

'That is all settled,' repeated the other, as she ran into her room to prepare. 'And are they upon such terms as for her to disclose the real truth! Oh, that I knew how it was!'

But wishes were vain; or at best could serve only to amuse her in the hurry and confusion of the following hour. Had Elizabeth been at leisure to be idle, she would have remained certain that all employment was impossible to one so wretched as herself; but she had her share of business as well as her aunt, and amongst the rest there were notes to be written to all their friends in Lambton, with false excuses for their sudden departure. An hour, however, saw the whole completed; and Mr Gardiner meanwhile having settled his account at the inn, nothing remained to be done but to go; and Elizabeth, after all the misery of the morning, found herself, in a shorter space of time than she could have supposed, seated in the carriage, and on the road to Longbourn.

Chapter 47

'I have been thinking it over again, Elizabeth,' said her uncle, as they drove from the town; 'and really, upon serious consideration, I am much more inclined than I was to judge as your eldest sister does of the matter. It appears to me so very unlikely, that any young man should form such a design against a girl who is by no means unprotected or friendless, and who was actually staying in his colonel's family, that I am strongly inclined to hope the best. Could he expect that her friends would not step forward? Could he expect to be noticed again by the regiment, after such an affront to Colonel Forster? His temptation is not adequate to the risk.'

'Do you really think so?' cried Elizabeth, brightening up for a moment.

'Upon my word,' said Mrs Gardiner, 'I begin to be of your uncle's opinion. It is really too great a violation of decency, honour, and interest, for him to be guilty of it. I cannot think so very ill of Wickham. Can you, yourself, Lizzy, so wholly give him up, as to believe him capable of it?'

'Not perhaps of neglecting his own interest. But of every other neglect I can believe him capable. If, indeed, it should be so! But I dare not hope it. Why should they not go on to Scotland, if that had been the case?'

'In the first place,' replied Mr Gardiner, 'there is no absolute proof that they are not gone to Scotland.'

'Oh! but their removing from the chaise into an hackney coach is such a presumption! And, besides, no traces of them were to be found on the Barnet road.'

'Well, then – supposing them to be in London. They may be there, though for the purpose of concealment, for no more exceptionable purpose. It is not likely that money should be very abundant on either side; and it might strike them that they could be more economically, though less expeditiously, married in London, than in Scotland.'

'But why all this secrecy? Why any fear of detection? Why must their marriage be private? Oh! no, no, this is not likely. His most particular friend, you see by Jane's account, was persuaded of his never intending to marry her. Wickham will never marry a woman without some money. He cannot afford it. And what claims has Lydia, what attractions has she beyond youth, health, and good humour, that could make him for her sake, forgo every chance of benefiting himself by marrying well? As to what restraint the apprehension of disgrace in the corps might throw on a dishonourable elopement with her, I am not able to judge; for I know nothing of the effects that such a step might produce. But as to your other objection, I am afraid it will hardly hold good. Lydia has no brothers to step forward; and he might imagine, from my father's behaviour, from his indolence and the little attention he has ever seemed to give to what was going forward in his family, that *he* would do as little, and think as little about it, as any father could do, in such a matter.'

'But can you think that Lydia is so lost to everything but love of him, as to consent to live with him on any other terms than marriage?'

'It does seem, and it is most shocking indeed,' replied Elizabeth, with tears in her eyes, 'that a sister's sense of decency and virtue in such a point should admit of doubt. But, really, I know not what to say. Perhaps I am not doing her justice. But she is very young; she has never been taught to think on serious subjects; and for the last half-year, nay, for a twelvemonth, she has been given up to nothing but amusement and vanity. She has been allowed to dispose of her time in the most idle and frivolous manner, and to adopt any opinions that came in her way. Since the ——shire were first quartered in Meryton, nothing but love, flirtation, and officers, have been in her head. She has been doing everything in her power by thinking and talking on the subject, to give greater – what shall I call it? susceptibility to her feelings; which are naturally lively enough. And we all know that Wickham has every charm of person and address that can captivate a woman.'

'But you see that Jane,' said her aunt, 'does not think so ill of Wickham, as to believe him capable of the attempt.'

'Of whom does Jane ever think ill? And who is there, whatever might be their former conduct, that she would believe capable of such an attempt, till it were proved against them? But Jane knows, as well as I do, what Wickham really is. We both know that he has been profligate in every sense of the word. That he has neither integrity nor honour. That he is as false and deceitful, as he is insinuating.'

'And do you really know all this?' cried Mrs Gardiner, whose curiosity as to the mode of her intelligence was all alive.

'I do, indeed,' replied Elizabeth, colouring. 'I told you the other day, of his infamous behaviour to Mr Darcy; and you, yourself, when last at Longbourn, heard in what manner he spoke of the man, who had behaved with such forbearance and liberality towards him. And there are other circumstances which I am not at liberty – which it is not worth while to relate; but his lies about the whole Pemberley family are endless. From what he said of Miss Darcy, I was thoroughly prepared to see a proud, reserved, disagreeable girl. Yet he knew to the contrary himself. He must know that she was as amiable and unpretending as we have found her.'

'But does Lydia know nothing of this? Can she be ignorant of what you and Jane seem so well to understand?'

'Oh, yes! – that, that is the worst of all. Till I was in Kent, and saw so much both of Mr Darcy and his relation, Colonel Fitzwilliam, I was ignorant of the truth myself. And when I returned home, the —shire was to leave Meryton in a week or fortnight's time. As that was the case, neither Jane, to whom I related the whole, nor I, thought it necessary to make our knowledge public; for of what use could it apparently be to anyone, that the good opinion which all the neighbourhood had of him, should then be over-thrown? And even when it was settled that Lydia should go with Mrs Forster, the necessity of opening her eyes to his character never occurred to me. That *she* could be in any danger from the deception never entered my head. That such a consequence as *this* should ensue, you may easily believe was far enough from my thoughts.'

'When they all removed to Brighton, therefore, you had no reason, I suppose, to believe them fond of each other.'

'Not the slightest. I can remember no symptom of

affection on either side; and had anything of the kind been perceptible, you must be aware that ours is not a family, on which it could be thrown away. When first he entered the corps, she was ready enough to admire him; but so we all were. Every girl in, or near Mery– ton, was out of her senses about him for the first two months; but he never distinguished *her* by any particular attention, and, consequently, after a moderate period of extravagant and wild admiration, her fancy for him gave way, and others of the regiment, who treated her with more distinction, again became her favourites.'

It may be easily believed, that however little of novelty could be added to their fears, hopes, and conjectures, on this interesting subject, by its repeated discussion, no other could detain them from it long, during the whole of the journey. From Elizabeth's thoughts it was never absent. Fixed there by the keenest of all anguish, self reproach, she could find no interval of ease or forgetfulness.

They travelled as expeditiously as possible; and sleeping one night on the road, reached Longbourn by dinner-time the next day. It was a comfort to Elizabeth to consider that Jane could not have been wearied by long expectations.

The little Gardiners, attracted by the sight of a chaise, were standing on the steps of the house, as they entered the paddock; and when the carriage drove up to the door, the joyful surprise that lighted up their faces, and displayed itself over their whole bodies, in a variety of capers and frisks, was the first pleasing earnest of their welcome.

Elizabeth jumped out; and, after giving each of them

The first pleasing earnest of their welcome

an hasty kiss, hurried into the vestibule, where Jane, who came running downstairs from her mother's apartment, immediately met her.

Elizabeth, as she affectionately embraced her, whilst tears filled the eyes of both, lost not a moment in asking whether anything had been heard of the fugitives.

'Not yet,' replied Jane. 'But now that my dear uncle is come, I hope everything will be well.'

'Is my father in town?'

'Yes, he went on Tuesday as I wrote you word.'

'And have you heard from him often?'

'We have heard only once. He wrote me a few lines on Wednesday, to say that he had arrived in safety, and to give me his directions, which I particularly begged him to do. He merely added, that he should not write again, till he had something of importance to mention.'

'And my mother – How is she? How are you all?'

'My mother is tolerably well, I trust; though her spirits are greatly shaken. She is upstairs, and will have great satisfaction in seeing you all. She does not yet leave her dressing-room. Mary and Kitty, thank Heaven! are quite well.'

'But you – How are you?' cried Elizabeth. 'You look pale. How much you must have gone through!'

Her sister, however, assured her, of her being perfectly well; and their conversation, which had been passing while Mr and Mrs Gardiner were engaged with their children, was now put an end to, by the approach of the whole party. Jane ran to her uncle and aunt, and welcomed and thanked them both, with alternate smiles and tears.

When they were all in the drawing-room, the questions which Elizabeth had already asked, were of course repeated by the others, and they soon found that Jane had no intelligence to give. The sanguine hope of good, however, which the benevolence of her heart suggested, had not yet deserted her; she still expected that it would all end well, and that every morning would bring some letter, either from Lydia or her father, to explain their proceedings, and perhaps announce the marriage.

Mrs Bennet, to whose apartment they all repaired, after a few minutes conversation together, received them exactly as might be expected; with tears and lamentations of regret, invectives against the villainous conduct of Wickham, and complaints of her own sufferings and ill usage; blaming everybody but the person to whose ill judging indulgence the errors of her daughter must be principally owing.

'If I had been able,' said she, 'to carry my point of going to Brighton, with all my family, *this* would not have happened; but poor dear Lydia had nobody to take care of her. Why did the Forsters ever let her go out of their sight? I am sure there was some great neglect or other on their side, for she is not the kind of girl to do such a thing, if she had been well looked after. I always thought they were very unfit to have the charge of her; but I was overruled, as I always am. Poor dear child! And now here's Mr Bennet gone away, and I know he will fight Wickham, wherever he meets him, and then he will be killed, and what is to become of us all? The Collinses will turn us out, before he is cold in his grave; and if you are not kind to us, brother, I do not know what we shall do.'

They all exclaimed against such terrific ideas; and Mr Gardiner, after general assurances of his affection for her and all her family, told her that he meant to be in London the very next day, and would assist Mr Bennet in every endeavour for recovering Lydia.

'Do not give way to useless alarm,' added he, 'though it is right to be prepared for the worst, there is no occasion to look on it as certain. It is not quite a week since they left Brighton. In a few days more, we may gain some news of them, and till we know that they are not married, and have no design of marrying, do not let us give the matter over as lost. As soon as I get to town, I shall go to my brother, and make him come home with me to Gracechurch Street, and then we may consult together as to what is to be done.'

'Oh! my dear brother,' replied Mrs Bennet, 'that is exactly what I could most wish for. And now do, when you get to town, find them out, wherever they may be; and if they are not married already, *make* them marry. And as for wedding clothes, do not let them wait for that, but tell Lydia she shall have as much money as she chooses, to buy them, after they are married. And, above all things, keep Mr Bennet from fighting. Tell him what a dreadful state I am in – that I am frightened out of my wits; and have such tremblings, such flutterings, all over me, such spasms in my side, and pains in my head, and such beatings at heart, that I can get no rest by night nor by day. And tell my dear Lydia, not to give any directions about her clothes, till she has seen me, for she does not know which are the best warehouses. Oh, brother, how kind you are! I know you will contrive it all.'

But Mr Gardiner, though he assured her again of his earnest endeavours in the cause, could not avoid recommending moderation to her, as well in her hopes as her fears; and, after talking with her in this manner till dinner was on table, they left her to vent all her feelings on the housekeeper, who attended, in the absence of her daughters.

Though her brother and sister were persuaded that there was no real occasion for such a seclusion from the family, they did not attempt to oppose it, for they knew that she had not prudence enough to hold her tongue before the servants, while they waited at table, and judged it better that *one* only of the household, and the one whom they could most trust, should comprehend all her fears and solicitude on the subject.

In the dining-room they were soon joined by Mary and Kitty, who had been too busily engaged in their separate apartments, to make their appearance before. One came from her books, and the other from her toilette. The faces of both, however, were tolerably calm; and no change was visible in either, except that the loss of her favourite sister, or the anger which she had herself incurred in the business, had given something more of fretfulness than usual, to the accents of Kitty. As for Mary, she was mistress enough of herself to whisper to Elizabeth with a countenance of grave reflection, soon after they were seated at table.

'This is a most unfortunate affair; and will probably be much talked of. But we must stem the tide of malice, and pour into the wounded bosoms of each other, the balm of sisterly consolation.'

Then, perceiving in Elizabeth no inclination of replying, she added, 'Unhappy as the event must be for Lydia, we may draw from it this useful lesson; that loss of virtue in a female is irretrievable – that one false step involves her in endless ruin – that her reputation is no less brittle than it is beautiful – and that she cannot be too much guarded in her behaviour towards the undeserving of the other sex.'

Elizabeth lifted up her eyes in amazement, but was too much oppressed to make any reply. Mary, however, continued to console herself with such kind of moral extractions from the evil before them.

In the afternoon, the two elder Miss Bennets were able to be for half an hour by themselves; and Elizabeth instantly availed herself of the opportunity of making any enquiries, which Jane was equally eager to satisfy. After joining in general lamentations over the dreadful sequel of this event, which Elizabeth considered as all but certain, and Miss Bennet could not assert to be wholly impossible; the former continued the subject, by saying, 'But tell me all and everything about it, which I have not already heard. Give me farther particulars. What did Colonel Forster say? Had they no apprehension of anything before the elopement took place? They must have seen them together for ever.'

'Colonel Forster did own that he had often suspected some partiality, especially on Lydia's side, but nothing to give him any alarm. I am so grieved for him. His behaviour was attentive and kind to the utmost. He *was* coming to us, in order to assure us of his concern, before he had any idea of their not being gone to Scotland: when that apprehension first got abroad, it hastened his journey.'

'And was Denny convinced that Wickham would not marry? Did he know of their intending to go off? Had Colonel Forster seen Denny himself?'

'Yes; but when questioned by *him* Denny denied knowing anything of their plan, and would not give his real opinion about it. He did not repeat his persuasion of their not marrying – and from *that*, I am inclined to hope, he might have been misunderstood before.'

'And till Colonel Forster came himself, not one of you entertained a doubt, I suppose, of their being really married?'

'How was it possible that such an idea should enter our brains! I felt a little uneasy – a little fearful of my sister's happiness with him in marriage, because I knew that his conduct had not been always quite right. My father and mother knew nothing of that, they only felt how imprudent a match it must be. Kitty then owned, with a very natural triumph on knowing more than the rest of us, that in Lydia's last letter, she had prepared her for such a step. She had known, it seems, of their being in love with each other, many weeks.'

'But not before they went to Brighton?'

'No, I believe not.'

'And did Colonel Forster appear to think ill of Wickham himself? Does he know his real character?'

'I must confess that he did not speak so well of Wickham as he formerly did. He believed him to be imprudent and extravagant. And since this sad affair has taken place, it is said, that he left Meryton greatly in debt; but I hope this may be false.'

'Oh, Jane, had we been less secret, had we told what we knew of him, this could not have happened!'

'Perhaps it would have been better;' replied her sister. 'But to expose the former faults of any person, without knowing what their present feelings were, seemed unjustifiable. We acted with the best intentions.'

'Could Colonel Forster repeat the particulars of Lydia's note to his wife?'

'He brought it with him for us to see.'

Jane then took it from her pocketbook, and gave it to Elizabeth. These were the contents:

MY DEAR HARRIET – You will laugh when you know where I am gone, and I cannot help laughing myself at your surprise tomorrow morning, as soon as I am missed. I am going to Gretna Green, and if you cannot guess with who, I shall think you a simpleton, for there is but one man in the world I

361

love, and he is an angel. I should never be happy without him, so think it no harm to be off. You need not send them word at Longbourn of my going, if you do not like it, for it will make the surprise the greater, when I write to them, and sign my name Lydia Wickham. What a good joke it will be! I can hardly write for laughing. Pray make my excuses to Pratt, for not keeping my engagement, and dancing with him to night. Tell him I hope he will excuse me when he knows all, and tell him I will dance with him at the next ball we meet, with great pleasure. I shall send for my clothes when I get to Longbourn; but I wish you would tell Sally to mend a great slit in my worked muslin gown, before they are packed up. Goodbye. Give my love to Colonel Forster, I hope you will drink to our good journey.

Your affectionate friend,

LYDIA BENNET

'Oh! thoughtless, thoughtless Lydia!' cried Elizabeth when she had finished it. 'What a letter is this, to be written as such a moment. But at least it shows, that *she* was serious in the object of her journey. Whatever he might afterwards persuade her to, it was not on her side a *scheme* of infamy. My poor father! how he must have felt it!'

'I never saw anyone so shocked. He could not speak a word for full ten minutes. My mother was taken ill immediately, and the whole house in such confusion!'

'Oh! Jane,' cried Elizabeth, 'was there a servant belonging to it, who did not know the whole story before the end of the day?'

'I do not know. I hope there was. But to be guarded at such a time, is very difficult. My mother was in hysterics, and though I endeavoured to give her every assistance in my power, I am afraid I did not do so much as I might have done! But the horror of what might possibly happen, almost took from me my faculties.'

'Your attendance upon her, has been too much for you. You do not look well. Oh! that I had been with you, you have had every care and anxiety upon yourself alone.'

'Mary and Kitty have been very kind, and would have shared in every fatigue, I am sure, but I did not think it right for either of them. Kitty is slight and delicate, and Mary studies so much, that her hours of repose should not be broken in on. My aunt Philips came to Longbourn on Tuesday, after my father went away; and was so good as to stay till Thursday with me. She was of great use and comfort to us all, and lady Lucas has been very kind; she walked here on Wednesday morning to condole with us, and offered her services, or any of her daughters, if they could be of use to us.'

'She had better have stayed at home,' cried Elizabeth; 'perhaps she *meant* well, but, under such a misfortune as this, one cannot see too little of one's neighbours. Assistance is impossible; condolence, insufferable. Let them triumph over us at a distance, and be satisfied.'

She then proceeded to enquire into the measures which her father had intended to pursue, while in town, for the recovery of his daughter.

'He meant, I believe,' replied Jane, 'to go to Epsom, the place where they last changed horses, see the postilions, and try if anything could be made out from them. His principal object must be, to discover the number of the hackney coach which took them from Clapham. It had come with a fare from London; and as he thought the circumstance of a gentleman and lady's removing from one carriage into another, might be remarked, he meant to make enquiries at Clapham. If he could anyhow discover at what house the coachman had before set down his fare, he determined to make enquiries there, and hoped it might not be impossible to find out the stand and number of the coach. I do not know of any other designs that he had formed: but he was in such a hurry to be gone, and his spirits so greatly discomposed, that I had difficulty in finding out even so much as this.'

Chapter 48

The whole party were in hopes of a letter from Mr Bennet the next morning, but the post came in without bringing a single line from him. His family knew him to be on all common occasions, a most negligent and dilatory correspondent, but at such a time, they had hoped for exertion. They were forced to conclude, that he had no pleasing intelligence to send, but even of *that* they would have been glad to be certain. Mr Gardiner had waited only for the letters before he set off.

When he was gone, they were certain at least of receiving constant information of what was going on, and their uncle promised, at parting, to prevail on Mr Bennet to return to Longbourn, as soon as he could, to the great consolation of his sister, who considered it as the only security for her husband's not being killed in a duel.

Mrs Gardiner and the children were to remain in Hertfordshire a few days longer, as the former thought her presence might be serviceable to her nieces. She shared in their attendance on Mrs Bennet, and was a great comfort to them, in their hours of freedom. Their other aunt also visited them frequently, and always, as she said, with the design of cheering and heartening them up, though as she never came without reporting some fresh instance of Wickham's extravagance or irregularity, she seldom went away without leaving them more dispirited than she found them.

All Meryton seemed striving to blacken the man, who, but three months before, had been almost an angel of light. He was declared to be in debt to every tradesman in the place, and his intrigues, all honoured with the title of seduction, had been extended into every tradesman's family. Everybody declared that he was the wickedest young man in the world; and everybody began to find out, that they had always distrusted the appearance of his goodness. Elizabeth, though she did not credit above half of what was said, believed enough to make her former assurance of her sister's ruin still more certain; and even Jane, who believed still less of it, became almost hopeless, more especially as the time was now come, when if they had gone to Scotland, which she had never before entirely despaired of, they must in all probability have gained some news of them.

Mr Gardiner left Longbourn on Sunday; on Tuesday, his wife received a letter from him; it told them, that on his arrival, he had immediately found out his brother, and persuaded him to come to Gracechurch Street. That Mr Bennet had been to Epsom and Clapham, before his arrival, but without gaining any satisfactory information; and that he was now determined to enquire at all the principal hotels in town, as Mr Bennet thought it possible they might have gone to one of them, on their first coming to London, before they procured lodgings. Mr Gardiner himself did not expect any success from this measure, but as his brother was eager in it, he meant to assist him in pursuing it. He added, that Mr Bennet seemed wholly disinclined at present, to leave London, and promised to write again very soon. There was also a postscript to this effect.

'I have written to Colonel Forster to desire him to find out, if possible, from some of the young man's intimates in the regiment, whether Wickham has any relations or connections, who would be likely to know in what part of the town he has now concealed himself. If there were anyone, that one could apply to, with a probability of gaining such a clue as that, it might be of essential consequence. At present we have nothing to guide us. Colonel Forster will, I dare say, do everything in his power to satisfy us on this head. But, on second thoughts, perhaps Lizzy could tell us, what relations he has now living, better than any other person.'

Elizabeth was at no loss to understand from whence this deference for her authority proceeded; but it was not in her power to give any information of so satisfactory a nature, as the compliment deserved.

She had never heard of his having had any relations, except a father and mother, both of whom had been dead many years. It was possible, however, that some of his companions in the —shire, might be able to give more information; and, though she was not very sanguine in expecting it, the application was a something to look forward to.

Every day at Longbourn was now a day of anxiety; but the most anxious part of each was when the post was expected. The arrival of letters was the first grand object of every morning's impatience. Through letters, whatever of good or bad was to be told, would be communicated, and every succeeding day was expected to bring some news of importance.

But before they heard again from Mr Gardiner, a letter arrived for their father, from a different quarter, from Mr Collins; which, as Jane had received directions to open all that came for him in his absence, she accordingly read; and Elizabeth, who knew what curiosities his letters always were, looked over her, and read it likewise. It was as follows:

MY DEAR SIR – I feel myself called upon, by our relationship, and my situation in life, to condole with you on the grievous affliction you are now suffering under, of which we were yesterday informed by a letter from Hertfordshire. Be assured, my dear sir, that Mrs Collins and myself sincerely sympathise with you, and all your respectable family, in your present distress, which must be of the bitterest kind, because proceeding from a cause which no time can remove. No arguments shall be wanting on my part, that can alleviate so severe a misfortune; or that may comfort you, under a circumstance that must be of all others most afflicting to a parent's mind. The death of your daughter would have been a blessing in comparison of this. And it is the more to be lamented, because there is reason to suppose, as my dear Charlotte informs me, that this licentiousness of behaviour in your daughter, has proceeded from a faulty degree of indulgence, though, at the same time, for the consolation of yourself and Mrs Bennet, I am inclined to think that her own disposition must be naturally bad, or she could not be guilty of such an enormity, at so early an age. Howsoever that may be, you are grievously to be pitied, in which opinion I am not only joined by Mrs Collins, but likewise by Lady Catherine and her daughter, to whom I have related the affair. They agree with me in apprehending that this false step in one daughter, will be injurious to the fortunes of all the others, for who, as lady Catherine herself condescendingly says, will connect themselves with such a family. And this consideration leads me moreover to reflect with augmented satisfaction on a certain event of last November, for had it been otherwise, I must have been involved in all your sorrow and disgrace. Let me advise you then, my dear Sir, to console yourself as much as possible, to throw off your unworthy child from your affection for ever, and leave her to reap the fruits of her own heinous offence.

I am, dear Sir, &c. &c.

Mr Gardiner did not write again, till he had received an answer from Colonel Forster; and then he had nothing of a pleasant nature to send. It was not known that Wickham had a single relation, with whom he kept up any connection, and it was certain that he had no near one living. His former acquaintance had been numerous; but since he had been in the militia, it did not appear that he was on terms of particular friendship with any of them. There was no one therefore who could be pointed out, as likely to give any news of him. And in the wretched state of his own finances, there was a very powerful motive for secrecy, in addition to

To whom I have related the affair

his fear of discovery by Lydia's relations, for it had just transpired that he had left gaming debts behind him, to a very considerable amount. Colonel Forster believed that more than a thousand pounds would be necessary to clear his expenses at Brighton. He owed a good deal in the town, but his debts of honour were still more formidable. Mr Gardiner did not attempt to conceal these particulars from the Longbourn family; Jane heard them with horror. 'A gamester!' she cried. 'This is wholly unexpected. I had not an idea of it.'

Mr Gardiner added in his letter, that they might expect to see their father at home on the following day, which was Saturday. Rendered spiritless by the ill-success of all their endeavours, he had yielded to his brother-in-law's entreaty that he would return to his family, and leave it to him to do, whatever occasion might suggest to be advisable for continuing their pursuit. When Mrs Bennet was told of this, she did not express so much satisfaction as her children expected, considering what her anxiety for his life had been before.

'What, is he coming home, and without poor Lydia!' she cried. 'Sure he will not leave London before he has found them. Who is to fight Wickham, and make him marry her, if he comes away?'

As Mrs Gardiner began to wish to be at home, it was settled that she and her children should go to London, at the same time that Mr Bennet came from it. The coach, therefore, took them the first stage of their journey, and brought its master back to Longbourn.

Mrs Gardiner went away in all the perplexity about Elizabeth and her Derbyshire friend, that had attended her from that part of the world. His name had never been voluntarily mentioned before them by her niece; and the kind of half-expectation which Mrs Gardiner had formed, of their being followed by a letter from him, had ended in nothing. Elizabeth had received none since her return, that could come from Pemberley.

The present unhappy state of the family, rendered

any other excuse for the lowness of her spirits unnecessary; nothing, therefore, could be fairly conjectured from *that*, though Elizabeth, who was by this time tolerably well acquainted with her own feelings, was perfectly aware, that, had she known nothing of Darcy, she could have borne the dread of Lydia's infamy somewhat better. It would have spared her, she thought, one sleepless night out of two.

When Mr Bennet arrived, he had all the appearance of his usual philosophic composure. He said as little as he had ever been in the habit of saying; made no mention of the business that had taken him away, and it was some time before his daughters had courage to speak of it.

It was not till the afternoon, when he joined them at tea, that Elizabeth ventured to introduce the subject; and then, on her briefly expressing her sorrow for what he must have endured, he replied, 'Say nothing of that. Who should suffer but myself? It has been my own doing, and I ought to feel it.'

'You must not be too severe upon yourself,' replied Elizabeth.

'You may well warn me against such an evil. Human nature is so prone to fall into it! No, Lizzy, let me once in my life feel how much I have been to blame. I am not afraid of being overpowered by the impression. It will pass away soon enough.'

'Do you suppose them to be in London?'

'Yes; where else can they be so well concealed?'

'And Lydia used to want to go to London,' added Kitty.

'She is happy, then,' said her father, drily; 'and her residence there will probably be of some duration.'

Then, after a short silence, he continued, 'Lizzy, I

bear you no ill-will for being justified in your advice to me last May, which, considering the event, shows some greatness of mind.'

They were interrupted by Miss Bennet, who came to fetch her mother's tea.

'This is a parade,' cried he, 'which does one good; it gives such an elegance to misfortune! Another day I will do the same; I will sit in my library, in my night cap and powdering gown, and give as much trouble as I can – or, perhaps, I may defer it, till Kitty runs away.'

'I am not going to run away, Papa,' said Kitty, fretfully; 'if *I* should ever go to Brighton, I would behave better than Lydia.'

'*You* go to Brighton! – I would not trust you so near it as Eastbourne, for fifty pounds! No, Kitty, I have at last learnt to be cautious, and you will feel the effects of it. No officer is ever to enter my house again, nor even to pass through the village. Balls will be absolutely prohibited, unless you stand up with one of your sisters. And you are never to stir out of doors, till you can prove, that you have spent ten minutes of every day in a rational manner.'

Kitty, who took all these threats in a serious light, began to cry.

'Well, well,' said he, 'do not make yourself unhappy. If you are a good girl for the next ten years, I will take you to a review at the end of them.'

Chapter 49

Two days after Mr Bennet's return, as Jane and Elizabeth were walking together in the shrubbery behind the house, they saw the housekeeper coming towards them, and, concluding that she came to call them to their mother, went forward to meet her; but, instead of the expected summons, when they approached her, she said to Miss Bennet, 'I beg your pardon, madam, for interrupting you, but I was in hopes you might have got some good news from town, so I took the liberty of coming to ask.'

They saw the housekeeper coming towards them

'What do you mean, Hill? We have heard nothing from town.'

'Dear madam,' cried Mrs Hill, in great astonishment, 'don't you know there is an express come for master from Mr Gardiner? He has been here this half-hour, and master has had a letter.'

Away ran the girls, too eager to get in to have time for speech. They ran through the vestibule into the breakfast room; from thence to the library – their father was in neither; and they were on the point of seeking him upstairs with their mother, when they were met by the butler, who said, 'If you are looking for my master, ma'am, he is walking towards the little copse.'

Upon this information, they instantly passed through the hall once more, and ran across the lawn after their father, who was deliberately pursuing his way towards a small wood on one side of the paddock.

Jane, who was not so light, nor so much in the habit of running as Elizabeth, soon lagged behind, while her sister, panting for breath, came up with him, and eagerly cried out, 'Oh, Papa, what news? what news? have you heard from my uncle?'

'Yes, I have had a letter from him by express.'

'Well, and what news does it bring? good or bad?'

'What is there of good to be expected?' said he, taking the letter from his pocket; 'but perhaps you would like to read it.'

Elizabeth impatiently caught it from his hand. Jane now came up.

'Read it aloud,' said their father, 'for I hardly know myself what it is about.'

Gracechurch Street, Monday
August 2

MY DEAR BROTHER – At last I am able to send you some tidings of my niece, and such as, upon the whole, I hope will give you satisfaction. Soon after you left me on Saturday, I was fortunate enough to find out in what part of London they were. The particulars, I reserve till we meet. It is enough to know they are discovered, I have seen them both – '

But perhaps you would like to read it

'Then it is, as I always hoped,' cried Jane; 'they are married!'

Elizabeth read on:

I have seen them both. They are not married, nor can I find there was any intention of being so; but if you are willing to perform the engagements which I have ventured to make on your side, I hope it will not be long before they are. All that is required of you is, to assure to your daughter, by settlement, her equal share of the five thousand pounds, secured among your children after the decease of yourself and my sister; and, moreover, to enter into an engagement of allowing her, during your life, one hundred pounds per annum. These are conditions, which, considering everything, I had no hesitation in complying with, as far as I thought myself privileged, for you. I shall send this by express, that no time may be lost in bringing me your answer. You will easily comprehend, from these particulars, that Mr Wickham's circumstances are not so hopeless as they are generally believed to be. The world has been deceived in that respect; and I am happy to say, there will be some little money, even when all his debts are discharged, to settle on my niece, in addition to her own fortune. If, as I conclude will be the case, you send me your full powers to act in your name, throughout the whole of this business, I will immediately give directions to Haggerston for preparing a proper settlement. There will not be the smallest occasion for your coming to town again; therefore, stay quietly at Longbourn, and depend on my diligence and care. Send back your answer as soon as you can, and be careful to write explicitly. We have judged it best, that my niece should be married from this house, of which I hope you will approve. She comes to us today. I shall write again as soon as anything more is determined on.

Your's, &c.

EDW. GARDINER

'Is it possible!' cried Elizabeth, when she had finished. 'Can it be possible that he will marry her?'

'Wickham is not so undeserving, then, as we have thought him,' said her sister. 'My dear father, I congratulate you.'

'And have you answered the letter?' said Elizabeth.

'No; but it must be done soon.'

Most earnestly did she then entreat him to lose no more time before he wrote.

'Oh! my dear father,' she cried, 'come back, and write immediately. Consider how important every moment is, in such a case.'

'Let me write for you,' said Jane, 'if you dislike the trouble yourself.'

'I dislike it very much,' he replied; 'but it must be done.'

And so saying, he turned back with them, and walked towards the house.

'And may I ask?' said Elizabeth, 'but the terms, I suppose, must be complied with.'

'Complied with! I am only ashamed of his asking so little.'

'And they *must* marry! Yet he is *such* a man!'

'Yes, yes, they must marry. There is nothing else to be done. But there are two things that I want very much to know: one is, how much money your uncle has laid down, to bring it about; and the other, how I am ever to pay him.'

'Money! my uncle!' cried Jane, 'what do you mean, sir?'

'I mean, that no man in his senses, would marry Lydia on so slight a temptation as one hundred a year during my life, and fifty after I am gone.'

'That is very true,' said Elizabeth; 'though it had not occurred to me before. His debts to be discharged, and something still to remain! Oh! it must be my uncle's doings! Generous, good man, I am afraid he has distressed himself. A small sum could not do all this.'

'No,' said her father, 'Wickham's a fool, if he takes her with a farthing less than ten thousand pounds. I should be sorry to think so ill of him, in the very beginning of our relationship.'

'Ten thousand pounds! Heaven forbid! How is half such a sum to be repaid?'

Mr Bennet made no answer, and each of them, deep in thought, continued silent till they reached the house. Their father then went to the library to write, and the girls walked into the breakfast-room.

'And they are really to be married!' cried Elizabeth, as soon as they were by themselves. 'How strange this is! And for *this* we are to be thankful. That they should marry, small as is their chance of happiness, and wretched as is his character, we are forced to rejoice! Oh, Lydia!'

'I comfort myself with thinking,' replied Jane, 'that he certainly would not marry Lydia, if he had not a real regard for her. Though our kind uncle has done something towards clearing him, I cannot believe that ten thousand pounds, or anything like it, has been advanced. He has children of his own, and may have more. How could he spare half ten thousand pounds?'

'If we are ever able to learn what Wickham's debts have been,' said Elizabeth, 'and how much is settled on his side on our sister, we shall exactly know what Mr Gardiner has done for them, because Wickham has not sixpence of his own. The kindness of my uncle and aunt can never be requited. Their taking her home, and affording her their personal protection and countenance, is such a sacrifice to her advantage, as years of gratitude cannot enough acknowledge. By this time she is actually with them! If such goodness does not make her miserable now, she will never deserve to be happy! What a meeting for her, when she first sees my aunt!'

'We must endeavour to forget all that has passed on either side,' said Jane: 'I hope and trust they will yet be happy. His consenting to marry her is a proof, I will believe, that he is come to a right way of thinking. Their mutual affection will steady them; and I flatter myself they will settle so quietly, and live in so rational a manner, as may in time make their past imprudence forgotten.'

'Their conduct has been such,' replied Elizabeth, 'as neither you, nor I, nor anybody, can ever forget. It is useless to talk of it.'

It now occurred to the girls that their mother was in all likelihood perfectly ignorant of what had happened. They went to the library, therefore, and asked their father, whether he would not wish them to make it known to her. He was writing, and, without raising his head, coolly replied, 'Just as you please.'

'May we take my uncle's letter to read to her?'

'Take whatever you like, and get away.'

Elizabeth took the letter from his writing-table, and

they went upstairs together. Mary and Kitty were both with Mrs Bennet: one communication would, therefore, do for all. After a slight preparation for good news, the letter was read aloud. Mrs Bennet could hardly contain herself. As soon as Jane had read Mr Gardiner's hope of Lydia's being soon married, her joy burst forth, and every following sentence added to its exuberance. She was now in an irritation as violent from delight, as she had ever been fidgety from alarm and vexation. To know that her daughter would be married was enough. She was disturbed by no fear for her felicity, nor humbled by any remembrance of her misconduct.

'My dear, dear Lydia!' she cried: 'This is delightful indeed! – She will be married! – I shall see her again! – She will be married at sixteen! – My good, kind brother! – I knew how it would be – I knew he would manage everything. How I long to see her! and to see dear Wickham too! But the clothes, the wedding clothes! I will write to my sister Gardiner about them directly. Lizzy, my dear, run down to your father, and ask him how much he will give her. Stay, stay, I will go myself. Ring the bell, Kitty, for Hill. I will put on my things in a moment. My dear, dear Lydia! – How merry we shall be together when we meet!'

Her eldest daughter endeavoured to give some relief to the violence of these transports, by leading her thoughts to the obligations which Mr Gardiner's behaviour laid them all under.

'For we must attribute this happy conclusion,' she added, 'in a great measure, to his kindness. We are persuaded that he has pledged himself to assist Mr Wickham with money.'

'Well,' cried her mother, 'it is all very right; who

should do it but her own uncle? If he had not had a family of his own, I and my children must have had all his money you know, and it is the first time we have ever had anything from him, except a few presents. Well! I am so happy. In a short time, I shall have a daughter married. Mrs Wickham! How well it sounds. And she was only sixteen last June. My dear Jane, I am in such a flutter, that I am sure I can't write; so I will dictate, and you write for me. We will settle with your father about the money afterwards; but the things should be ordered immediately.'

She was then proceeding to all the particulars of calico, muslin, and cambric, and would shortly have dictated some very plentiful orders, had not Jane, though with some difficulty, persuaded her to wait, till her father was at leisure to be consulted. One day's delay she observed, would be of small importance; and her mother was too happy, to be quite so obstinate as usual. Other schemes too came into her head.

'I will go to Meryton,' said she, 'as soon as I am dressed, and tell the good, good news to my sister Philips. And as I come back, I can call on Lady Lucas and Mrs Long. Kitty, run down and order the carriage. An airing would do me a great deal of good, I am sure. Girls, can I do anything for you in Meryton? Oh! here comes Hill. My dear Hill, have you heard the good news? Miss Lydia is going to be married; and you shall all have a bowl of punch, to make merry at her wedding.'

Mrs Hill began instantly to express her joy. Elizabeth received her congratulations amongst the rest, and then, sick of this folly, took refuge in her own room, that she might think with freedom.

Poor Lydia's situation must, at best, be bad enough;

but that it was no worse, she had need to be thankful. She felt it so; and though, in looking forward, neither rational happiness nor worldly prosperity, could be justly expected for her sister; in looking back to what they had feared, only two hours ago, she felt all the advantages of what they had gained.

Chapter 50

Mr Bennet had very often wished, before this period of his life, that, instead of spending his whole income, he had laid by an annual sum, for the better provision of his children, and of his wife, if she survived him. He now wished it more than ever. Had he done his duty in that respect, Lydia need not have been indebted to her uncle, for whatever of honour or credit could now be purchased for her. The satisfaction of prevailing on one of the most worthless young men in Great Britain to be her husband, might then have rested in its proper place.

He was seriously concerned, that a cause of so little advantage to anyone, should be forwarded at the sole expense of his brother-in-law, and he was determined, if possible, to find out the extent of his assistance, and to discharge the obligation as soon as he could.

When first Mr Bennet had married, economy was held to be perfectly useless; for, of course, they were to have a son. This son was to join in cutting off the entail, as soon as he should be of age, and the widow and younger children would by that means be provided for. Five daughters successively entered the world, but yet the son was to come; and Mrs Bennet, for many years after Lydia's birth, had been certain that he would.

This event had at last been despaired of, but it was then too late to be saving. Mrs Bennet had no turn for economy, and her husband's love of independence had alone prevented their exceeding their income.

Five thousand pounds was settled by marriage articles on Mrs Bennet and the children. But in what proportions it should be divided amongst the latter, depended on the will of the parents. This was one point, with regard to Lydia at least, which was now to be settled, and Mr Bennet could have no hesitation in acceding to the proposal before him. In terms of grateful acknowledgment for the kindness of his brother, though expressed most concisely, he then delivered on paper his perfect approbation of all that was done, and his willingness to fulfil the engagements that had been made for him. He had never before supposed that, could Wickham be prevailed on to marry his daughter, it would be done with so little inconvenience to himself, as by the present arrangement. He would scarcely be ten pounds a year the loser, by the hundred that was to be paid them; for, what with her board and pocket allowance, and the continual presents in money, which passed to her, through her mother's hands, Lydia's expenses had been very little within that sum.

That it would be done with such trifling exertion on his side, too, was another very welcome surprise; for his chief wish at present, was to have as little trouble in the business as possible. When the first transports of rage which had produced his activity in seeking her were over, he naturally returned to all his former indolence. His letter was soon dispatched; for though dilatory in undertaking business, he was quick in its execution. He begged to know farther particulars of what he was indebted to his brother; but was too angry with Lydia, to send any message to her.

The good news quickly spread through the house; and with proportionate speed through the neighbourhood. It was borne in the latter with decent philosophy. To be sure it would have been more for the advantage of conversation, had Miss Lydia Bennet come upon the town; or, as the happiest alternative, been secluded from the world, in some distant farm house. But there was much to be talked of, in marrying her; and the good-natured wishes for her well-doing, which had proceeded before, from all the spiteful old ladies in Meryton, lost but little of their spirit in this change of circumstances, because with such an husband, her misery was considered certain.

It was a fortnight since Mrs Bennet had been downstairs, but on this happy day, she again took her seat at the head of her table, and in spirits oppressively high. No sentiment of shame gave a damp to her triumph. The marriage of a daughter, which had been the first object of her wishes, since Jane was sixteen, was now on the point of accomplishment, and her thoughts and her words ran wholly on those attendants of elegant nuptials, fine muslins, new carriages, and servants. She was busily searching through the neighbourhood for a proper situation for her daughter, and, without knowing or considering what their income might be, rejected many as deficient in size and importance.

'Haye Park might do,' said she, 'if the Gouldings would quit it, or the great house at Stoke, if the drawing-room were larger; but Ashworth is too far off! I could not bear to have her ten miles from me; and as for Purvis Lodge, the attics are dreadful.'

The spiteful old ladies in Meryton

Her husband allowed her to talk on without interruption, while the servants remained. But when they
had withdrawn, he said to her, 'Mrs Bennet, before
you take any, or all of these houses, for your son and
daughter, let us come to a right understanding. Into
one house in this neighbourhood, they shall never have
admittance. I will not encourage the impudence of
either, by receiving them at Longbourn.'

385

A long dispute followed this declaration; but Mr Bennet was firm: it soon led to another; and Mrs Bennet found, with amazement and horror, that her husband would not advance a guinea to buy clothes for his daughter. He protested that she should receive from him no mark of affection whatever, on the occasion. Mrs Bennet could hardly comprehend it. That his anger could be carried to such a point of inconceivable resentment, as to refuse his daughter a privilege, without which her marriage would scarcely seem valid, exceeded all that she could believe possible. She was more alive to the disgrace, which the want of new clothes must reflect on her daughter's nuptials, than to any sense of shame at her eloping and living with Wickham, a fortnight before they took place.

Elizabeth was now most heartily sorry that she had, from the distress of the moment, been led to make Mr Darcy acquainted with their fears for her sister; for since her marriage would so shortly give the proper termination to the elopement, they might hope to conceal its unfavourable beginning, from all those who were not immediately on the spot.

She had no fear of its spreading farther, through his means. There were few people on whose secrecy she would have more confidently depended; but at the same time, there was no one, whose knowledge of a sister's frailty would have mortified her so much. Not, however, from any fear of disadvantage from it, individually to herself; for at any rate, there seemed a gulf impassable between them. Had Lydia's marriage been concluded on the most honourable terms, it was not to be supposed that Mr Darcy would connect himself with a family, where to every other objection would now be added, an alliance and relationship of the nearest kind with the man whom he so justly scorned.

From such a connection she could not wonder that he should shrink. The wish of procuring her regard, which she had assured herself of his feeling in Derbyshire, could not in rational expectation survive such a blow as this. She was humbled, she was grieved; she repented, though she hardly knew of what. She became jealous of his esteem, when she could no longer hope to be benefited by it. She wanted to hear of him, when there seemed the least chance of gaining intelligence. She was convinced that she could have been happy with him; when it was no longer likely they should meet.

What a triumph for him, as she often thought, could he know that the proposals which she had proudly spurned only four months ago, would now have been gladly and gratefully received! He was as generous, she doubted not, as the most generous of his sex. But while he was mortal, there must be a triumph.

She began now to comprehend that he was exactly the man, who, in disposition and talents, would most suit her. His understanding and temper, though unlike her own, would have answered all her wishes. It was an union that must have been to the advantage of both; by her ease and liveliness, his mind might have been softened, his manners improved, and from his judgement, information, and knowledge of the world, she must have received benefit of greater importance.

But no such happy marriage could now teach the admiring multitude what connubial felicity really was. An union of a different tendency, and precluding the possibility of the other, was soon to be formed in their family.

How Wickham and Lydia were to be supported in tolerable independence, she could not imagine. But how little of permanent happiness could belong to a couple who were only brought together because their passions were stronger than their virtue, she could easily conjecture.

Mr Gardiner soon wrote again to his brother. To Mr Bennet's acknowledgments he briefly replied, with assurances of his eagerness to promote the welfare of any of his family; and concluded with entreaties that the subject might never be mentioned to him again. The principal purport of his letter was to inform them, that Mr Wickham had resolved on quitting the Militia.

It was greatly my wish that he should do so [he added], as soon as his marriage was fixed on. And I think you will agree with me, in considering a removal from that corps as highly advisable, both on his account and my niece's. It is Mr Wickham's intention to go into the regulars; and, among his former friends, there are still some who are able and willing to assist him in the army. He has the promise of an ensigncy in General —'s regiment, now quartered in the North. It is an advantage to have it so far from this part of the kingdom. He promises fairly, and I hope among different people, where they may each have a character to preserve, they will both be more prudent. I have written to Colonel Forster, to inform him of our present arrangements, and to request that he will satisfy the various creditors of Mr Wickham in and near Brighton, with assurances of speedy payment, for which I have pledged myself. And will you give yourself the trouble of carrying similar assurances to his creditors in Meryton, of whom I shall subjoin a list, according to his information. He has given in all his debts; I hope at least he has not deceived us. Haggerston has our directions, and all will be completed in a week. They will then join his regiment, unless they are first invited to Longbourn; and I understand from Mrs Gardiner, that my niece is very desirous of seeing you all, before she leaves the South. She is well, and begs to be dutifully remembered to you and her mother. – Yours, &c.

E. GARDINER

Mr Bennet and his daughters saw all the advantages of Wickham's removal from the —shire, as clearly as Mr Gardiner could do. But Mrs Bennet, was not so well pleased with it. Lydia's being settled in the North, just when she had expected most pleasure and pride in her company, for she had by no means given up her plan of their residing in Hertfordshire, was a severe disappointment; and besides, it was such a pity that Lydia should be taken from a regiment where she was acquainted with everybody, and had so many favourites.

'She is so fond of Mrs Forster,' said she, 'it will be quite shocking to send her away! And there are several of the young men, too, that she likes very much. The officers may not be so pleasant in General —'s regiment.'

His daughter's request, for such it might be considered, of being admitted into her family again, before she set off for the North, received at first an absolute negative. But Jane and Elizabeth, who agreed in wishing, for the sake of their sister's feelings and consequence, that she should be noticed on her marriage by her parents, urged him so earnestly, yet so rationally and so mildly, to receive her and her husband at Longbourn, as soon as they were married, that he was prevailed on to think as they thought, and act as they wished. And their mother had the satisfaction of knowing, that she should be able to shew her married daughter in the neighbourhood, before she was banished to the North. When Mr Bennet wrote again to his brother, therefore, he sent his permission for them to come; and it was settled, that as soon as the ceremony was over, they should proceed to Longbourn. Elizabeth was surprised, however, that Wickham should consent to such a scheme, and, had she consulted only her own inclination, any meeting with him would have been the last object of her wishes.

Chapter 51

Their sister's wedding day arrived; and Jane and Elizabeth felt for her probably more than she felt for herself. The carriage was sent to meet them at —, and they were to return in it, by dinner-time. Their arrival was dreaded by the elder Miss Bennets; and Jane more especially, who gave Lydia the feelings which would have attended herself, had *she* been the culprit, was wretched in the thought of what her sister must endure.

They came. The family were assembled in the breakfast room, to receive them. Smiles decked the face of Mrs Bennet, as the carriage drove up to the door; her husband looked impenetrably grave; her daughters, alarmed, anxious, uneasy.

Lydia's voice was heard in the vestibule; the door was

With an affectionate smile

thrown open, and she ran into the room. Her mother stepped forwards, embraced her, and welcomed her with rapture; gave her hand with an affectionate smile to Wickham, who followed his lady, and wished them both joy, with an alacrity which showed no doubt of their happiness.

Their reception from Mr Bennet, to whom they then turned, was not quite so cordial. His countenance rather gained in austerity; and he scarcely opened his lips. The easy assurance of the young couple, indeed, was enough to provoke him. Elizabeth was disgusted, and even Miss Bennet was shocked. Lydia was Lydia still; untamed, unabashed, wild, noisy, and fearless. She turned from sister to sister, demanding their congratulations, and when at length they all sat down, looked eagerly round the room, took notice of some little alteration in it, and observed, with a laugh, that it was a great while since she had been there.

Wickham was not at all more distressed then herself, but his manners were always so pleasing, that had his character and his marriage been exactly what they ought, his smiles and his easy address, while he claimed their relationship, would have delighted them all. Elizabeth had not before believed him quite equal to such assurance; but she sat down, resolving within herself, to draw no limits in future to the impudence of an impudent man. *She* blushed, and Jane blushed; but the cheeks of the two who caused their confusion, suffered no variation of colour.

There was no want of discourse. The bride and her mother could neither of them talk fast enough; and Wickham, who happened to sit near Elizabeth, began enquiring after his acquaintance in that neighbourhood, with a good humoured ease, which she felt very unable to equal in her replies. They seemed each of them to have the happiest memories in the world. Nothing of the past was recollected with pain; and Lydia led voluntarily to subjects, which her sisters would not have alluded to for the world.

'Only think of its being three months,' she cried,

'since I went away; it seems but a fortnight I declare; and yet there have been things enough happened in the time. Good gracious! when I went away, I am sure I had no more idea of being married till I came back again! though I thought it would be very good fun if I was.'

Her father lifted up his eyes. Jane was distressed. Elizabeth looked expressively at Lydia; but she, who never heard or saw anything of which she chose to be insensible, gaily continued, 'Oh! mamma, do the people here abouts know I am married today? I was afraid they might not; and we overtook William Goulding in his curricle, so I was determined he should know it, and so I let down the side glass next to him, and took off my glove, and let my hand just rest upon the window frame, so that he might see the ring, and then I bowed and smiled like anything.'

Elizabeth could bear it no longer. She got up, and ran out of the room; and returned no more, till she heard them passing through the hall to the dining-parlour. She then joined them soon enough to see Lydia, with anxious parade, walk up to her mother's right hand, and heard her say to her eldest sister, 'Ah! Jane, I take your place now, and you must go lower, because I am a married woman.'

It was not to be supposed that time would give Lydia that embarrassment, from which she had been so wholly free at first. Her ease and good spirits increased. She longed to see Mrs Philips, the Lucasses, and all their other neighbours, and to hear herself called 'Mrs Wickham,' by each of them; and in the mean time, she went after dinner to shew her ring and boast of being married, to Mrs Hill and the two housemaids.

'Well, mamma,' said she, when they were all

returned to the breakfast room, 'and what do you think of my husband? Is not he a charming man? I am sure my sisters must all envy me. I only hope they may have half my good luck. They must all go to Brighton. That is the place to get husbands. What a pity it is, mamma, we did not all go.'

'Very true; and if I had my will, we should. But my dear Lydia, I don't at all like your going such a way off. Must it be so?'

'Oh, lord! yes – there is nothing in that. I shall like it of all things. You and papa, and my sisters, must come down and see us. We shall be at Newcastle all the winter, and I dare say there will be some balls, and I will take care to get good partners for them all.'

'I should like it beyond anything!' said her mother.

'And then when you go away, you may leave one or two of my sisters behind you; and I dare say I shall get husbands for them before the winter is over.'

'I thank you for my share of the favour,' said Elizabeth; 'but I do not particularly like your way of getting husbands.'

Their visitors were not to remain above ten days with them. Mr Wickham had received his commission before he left London, and he was to join his regiment at the end of a fortnight.

No one but Mrs Bennet, regretted that their stay would be so short; and she made the most of the time, by visiting about with her daughter, and having very frequent parties at home. These parties were acceptable to all; to avoid a family circle was even more desirable to such as did think, than such as did not.

Wickham's affection for Lydia, was just what Elizabeth had expected to find it; not equal to Lydia's for him. She had scarcely needed her present observation to be satisfied, from the reason of things, that their elopement had been brought on by the strength of her love, rather than by his; and she would have wondered why, without violently caring for her, he chose to elope with her at all, had she not felt certain that his flight was rendered necessary by distress of circumstances; and if that were the case, he was not the young man to resist an opportunity of having a companion.

Lydia was exceedingly fond of him. He was her dear Wickham on every occasion; no one was to be put in competition with him. He did everything best in the world; and she was sure he would kill more birds on the first of September, than anybody else in the country.

One morning, soon after their arrival, as she was sitting with her two elder sisters, she said to Elizabeth, 'Lizzy, I never gave *you* an account of my wedding, I believe. You were not by, when I told mamma, and the others, all about it. Are not you curious to hear how it was managed?'

'No really,' replied Elizabeth; 'I think there cannot be too little said on the subject.'

'La! You are so strange! But I must tell you how it went off. We were married, you know, at St Clement's, because Wickham's lodgings were in that parish. And it was settled that we should all be there by eleven o'clock. My uncle and aunt and I were to go together; and the others were to meet us at the church. Well, Monday morning came, and I was in such a fuss! I was so afraid you know that something would happen to put it off, and then I should have gone quite distracted. And there was my aunt, all the time I was dressing, preaching and talking away just as if she was reading a sermon. However, I did not hear above one word in ten, for I was thinking, you may suppose, of my dear

Wickham. I longed to know whether he would be married in his blue coat.

'Well, and so we breakfasted at ten as usual; I thought it would never be over; for, by the by, you are to understand, that my uncle and aunt were horrid unpleasant all the time I was with them. If you'll believe me, I did not once put my foot out of doors, though I was there a fortnight. Not one party, or scheme, or anything. To be sure London was rather thin, but however the little Theatre was open. Well, and so just as the carriage came to the door, my uncle was called away upon business to that horrid man Mr Stone. And then, you know, when once they get together, there is no end of it. Well, I was so frightened I did not know what to do, for my uncle was to give me away; and if we were beyond the hour, we could not be married all day. But, luckily, he came back again in ten minutes' time, and then we all set out. However, I recollected afterwards, that if he *had* been prevented going, the wedding need not be put off, for Mr Darcy might have done as well.'

'Mr Darcy!' repeated Elizabeth, in utter amazement.

'Oh, yes! – he was to come there with Wickham, you know. But gracious me! I quite forgot! I ought not to have said a word about it. I promised them so faithfully! What will Wickham say? It was to be such a secret!'

'If it was to be secret,' said Jane, 'say not another word on the subject. You may depend upon my seeking no further.'

'Oh! certainly,' said Elizabeth, though burning with curiosity; 'we will ask you no questions.'

'Thank you,' said Lydia, 'for if you did, I should certainly tell you all, and then Wickham would be angry.'

On such encouragement to ask, Elizabeth was forced to put it out of her power, by running away.

But to live in ignorance on such a point was impossible; or at least it was impossible not to try for information. Mr Darcy had been at her sister's wedding. It was exactly a scene, and exactly among people, where he had apparently least to do, and least temptation to go. Conjectures as to the meaning of it, rapid and wild, hurried into her brain; but she was satisfied with none. Those that best pleased her, as placing his conduct in the noblest light, seemed most improbable. She could not bear such suspense; and hastily seizing a sheet of paper, wrote a short letter to her aunt, to request an explanation of what Lydia had dropped, if it were compatible with the secrecy which had been intended.

'You may readily comprehend,' she added, 'what my curiosity must be to know how a person unconnected with any of us, and (comparatively speaking) a stranger to our family, should have been amongst you at such a time. Pray write instantly, and let me understand it – unless it is, for very cogent reasons, to remain in the secrecy which Lydia seems to think necessary; and then I must endeavour to be satisfied with ignorance.'

'Not that I *shall* though,' she added to herself, as she finished the letter; 'and my dear aunt, if you do not tell me in an honourable manner, I shall certainly be reduced to tricks and stratagems to find it out.'

Jane's delicate sense of honour would not allow her to speak to Elizabeth privately of what Lydia had let fall; Elizabeth was glad of it – till it appeared whether her enquiries would receive any satisfaction, she had rather be without a confidante.

Chapter 52

Elizabeth had the satisfaction of receiving an answer to her letter, as soon as she possibly could. She was no sooner in possession of it, than hurrying into the little copse, where she was least likely to be interrupted, she sat down on one of the benches, and prepared to be happy; for the length of the letter convinced her that it did not contain a denial.

Gracechurch Street, September 6

MY DEAR NIECE – I have just received your letter, and shall devote this whole morning to answering it, as I foresee that a *little* writing will not comprise what I have to tell you. I must confess myself surprised by your application; I did not expect it from *you*. Don't think me angry, however, for I only mean to let you know, that I had not imagined such enquiries to be necessary on *your* side. If you do not choose to understand me, forgive my impertinence. Your uncle is as much surprised as I am – and nothing but the belief of your being a party concerned, would have allowed him to act as he has done. But if you are really innocent and ignorant, I must be more explicit. On the very day of my coming home from Longbourn, your uncle had a most unexpected visitor. Mr Darcy called, and was shut up with him several hours. It was all over before I arrived; so my curiosity was not so dreadfully racked as *yours* seems to have been. He came to tell Mr Gardiner that he had found out where your sister and Mr Wickham were, and that he had seen and talked with them both, Wickham repeatedly, Lydia once. From what I can collect, he left Derbyshire only one day after ourselves, and came to town with the resolution of hunting for them. The motive professed, was his conviction of its being owing to himself that Wickham's worthlessness had not been so well known, as to make it impossible for any young woman of character, to love or confide in him. He generously imputed the whole to his mistaken pride, and confessed that he had before thought it beneath him, to lay his private actions open to the world. His character was to speak for itself. He called it, therefore, his duty to step forward, and endeavour to remedy an evil, which had been brought on by himself. If he *had another* motive, I am sure it would never disgrace him. He had been some days in town, before he was able to discover them; but he had something to direct his search, which was more than *we* had; and the consciousness of this, was another reason for his resolving to follow us. There is a lady, it seems, a Mrs Younge, who was some time ago governess to Miss Darcy, and was dismissed from her charge on some cause of disapprobation, though he did not say what. She then took a large house in Edward Street, and has since maintained herself by letting lodgings. This Mrs Younge was, he knew, intimately acquainted with Wickham; and he went to her for intelligence of him, as soon as he got to town. But it was two or three days before he could get from her what he wanted. She would not betray her trust, I suppose, without bribery and corruption, for she really did know where her friend was to be found. Wickham indeed had gone to her, on their first arrival in

London, and had she been able to receive them into her house, they would have taken up their abode with her. At length, however, our kind friend procured the wished-for direction. They were in — Street. He saw Wickham, and afterwards insisted on seeing Lydia. His first object with her, he acknowledged, had been to persuade her to quit her present disgraceful situation, and return to her friends as soon as they could be prevailed on to receive her, offering his assistance, as far as it would go. But he found Lydia absolutely resolved on remaining where she was. She cared for none of her friends, she wanted no help of his, she would not hear of leaving Wickham. She was sure they should be married sometime or other, and it did not much signify when. Since such were her feelings, it only remained, he thought, to secure and expedite a marriage, which, in his very first conversation with Wickham, he easily learnt, had never been *his* design. He confessed himself obliged to leave the regiment, on account of some debts of honour, which were very pressing; and scrupled not to lay all the ill-consequences of Lydia's flight, on her own folly alone. He meant to resign his commission immediately; and as to his future situation, he could conjecture very little about it. He must go somewhere, but he did not know where, and he knew he should have nothing to live on. Mr Darcy asked him why he had not married your sister at once. Though Mr Bennet was not imagined to be very rich, he would have been able to do something for him, and his situation must have been benefited by marriage. But he found, in reply to this question, that Wickham still cherished the hope of more effectually making his fortune by marriage, in some other country. Under such circumstances, however, he was not likely to be proof against the temptation of immediate relief. They met several times, for there was much to be discussed. Wickham of course wanted more than he could get; but at length was reduced to be reasonable. Everything being settled between *them*, Mr Darcy's next step was to make your uncle acquainted with it, and he first called in Gracechurch Street the evening before I came home. But Mr Gardiner could not be seen, and Mr Darcy found, on further enquiry, that your father was still with him, but would quit town the next morning. He did not judge your father to be a person whom he could so properly consult as your uncle, and therefore readily postponed seeing him, till after the departure of the former. He did not leave his name, and till the next day, it was only known that a gentleman had called on business. On Saturday he came again. Your father was gone, your uncle at home, and, as I said before, they had a great deal of talk together. They met again on Sunday, and then *I* saw him too. It was not all settled before Monday: as soon as it was, the express was sent off to Longbourn. But our visitor was very obstinate. I fancy, Lizzy, that obstinacy is the real defect of his character after all. He has been accused of many faults at different times; but *this* is the true one. Nothing was to be done that he did not do himself; though I am sure (and I do not speak it to be thanked, therefore say nothing about it), your uncle would most readily have settled the whole. They battled it together for a long time, which was more than either the gentleman or lady concerned in it deserved. But at last your uncle was forced to yield, and instead of being allowed to be of use to his niece, was forced to put up with only having the probable credit of it, which went sorely against the grain; and I really believe your letter this morning gave him great pleasure, because it required an explanation that would rob him of his borrowed feathers, and give the praise where it was due. But, Lizzy, this must go no farther than yourself, or Jane at most. You know pretty well, I suppose, what has been done for the young people. His debts are to be paid, amounting, I believe, to considerably more than a thousand pounds, another thousand in addition to her own settled upon *her*, and his commission purchased. The reason why all this was to be done by him alone, was such as I have given above. It was owing to him, to his reserve, and want of proper consideration, that Wickham's character had been so misunderstood, and consequently that he had been received and noticed as he was. Perhaps there was some truth in *this*; though I doubt whether *his* reserve, or *anybody's* reserve, can be answerable for the event. But in spite of all this fine talking, my dear Lizzy, you may rest perfectly assured, that your uncle would never have yielded, if we had not given him credit for *another interest* in the affair. When all this was resolved on, he returned again to his friends, who were still staying at Pemberley; but it was agreed that he should be in London once more when the wedding took place, and all money matters were then to receive the last finish. I believe I have now told you everything. It is a relation which you tell me is to give you great surprise; I hope at least it will not afford you any

I am sure she did not listen

displeasure. Lydia came to us; and Wickham had constant admission to the house. *He* was exactly what he had been, when I knew him in Hertfordshire; but I would not tell you how little I was satisfied with *her* behaviour while she staid with us, if I had not perceived, by Jane's letter last Wednesday, that her conduct on coming home was exactly of a piece with it, and therefore what I now tell you, can give you no fresh pain. I talked to her repeatedly in the most serious manner, representing to her all the wickedness of what she had done, and all the unhappiness she had brought on her family. If she heard me, it was by good luck, for I am sure she did not listen. I was sometimes quite provoked, but then I recollected my dear Elizabeth and Jane, and for their sakes had patience with her. Mr Darcy was punctual in his return, and as Lydia informed you, attended the wedding. He dined with us the next day, and was to leave town again on Wednesday or Thursday. Will you be very angry with me, my dear Lizzy, if I take this opportunity of saying (what I was never bold enough to say before) how much I like him? His behaviour to us has, in every respect, been as pleasing as when we were in Derbyshire. His understanding and opinions all please me; he wants nothing but a little more liveliness, and *that*, if he marry *prudently*, his wife may teach him. I thought him very sly – he hardly ever mentioned your name. But slyness seems the fashion. Pray forgive me, if I have been very presuming, or at least do not punish me so far, as to exclude me from P. I shall never be quite happy till I have been all round the park. A low phaeton, with a nice little pair of ponies, would be the very thing. But I must write no more. The children have been wanting me this half-hour.

Yours, very sincerely,

M. GARDINER

The contents of this letter threw Elizabeth into a flutter of spirits, in which it was difficult to determine whether pleasure or pain bore the greatest share. The vague and unsettled suspicions which uncertainty had produced of what Mr Darcy might have been doing to forward her sister's match, which she had feared to encourage, as an exertion of goodness too great to be probable, and at the same time dreaded to be just, from the pain of obligation, were proved beyond their greatest extent to be true! He had followed them purposely to town, he had taken on himself all the trouble and mortification attendant on such a research; in which supplication had been necessary to a woman whom he must abominate and despise, and where he was reduced to meet, frequently meet, reason with, persuade, and finally bribe, the man whom he always most wished to avoid, and whose very name it was punishment to him to pronounce. He had done all this for a girl whom he could neither regard nor esteem. Her heart did whisper, that he had done it for her. But it was a hope shortly checked by other considerations, and she soon felt that even her vanity was insufficient, when required to depend on his affection for her, for a woman who had already refused him, as able to overcome a sentiment so natural as abhorrence against relationship with Wickham. Brother-in-law of Wickham! Every kind of pride must revolt from the connection. He had to be sure done much. She was ashamed to think how much. But he had given a reason for his interference, which asked no extra-ordinary stretch of belief. It was reasonable that he should feel he had been wrong; he had liberality, and he had the means of exercising it; and though she would not place herself as his principal inducement, she could, perhaps, believe, that remaining partiality for her, might assist his endeavours in a cause where her peace of mind must be materially concerned. It was painful, exceedingly painful, to know that they were under obligations to a person who could never receive a return. They owed the restoration of Lydia, her character, everything to him. Oh! how heartily did she grieve over every ungracious sensation she had ever encouraged, every saucy speech she had ever directed towards him. For herself she was humbled; but she was proud of him. Proud that in a cause of compassion and honour, he had been able to get the better of himself. She read over her aunt's commendation of him again and again. It was hardly enough; but it pleased her. She was even sensible of some pleasure, though mixed with regret, on finding how steadfastly both she and her uncle had been persuaded that affection and confidence subsisted between Mr Darcy and herself.

She was roused from her seat, and her reflections, by someone's approach; and before she could strike into another path, she was overtaken by Wickham.

'I am afraid I interrupt your solitary ramble, my dear sister?' said he, as he joined her.

'You certainly do,' she replied with a smile; 'but it does not follow that the interruption must be unwelcome.'

'I should be sorry indeed, if it were. *We* were always good friends; and now we are better.'

'True. Are the others coming out?'

'I do not know. Mrs Bennet and Lydia are going in the carriage to Meryton. And so, my dear sister, I find from our uncle and aunt, that you have actually seen Pemberley.'

She replied in the affirmative.

'I almost envy you the pleasure, and yet I believe it would be too much for me, or else I could take it in my way to Newcastle. And you saw the old housekeeper, I suppose? Poor Reynolds, she was always very fond of me. But of course she did not mention my name to you.'

'Yes, she did.'

'And what did she say?'

'That you were gone into the army, and she was afraid had – not turned out well. At such a distance as *that*, you know, things are strangely misrepresented.'

'Certainly,' he replied, biting his lips. Elizabeth hoped she had silenced him; but he soon afterwards said, 'I was surprised to see Darcy in town last month. We passed each other several times. I wonder what he can be doing there.'

'Perhaps preparing for his marriage with Miss de Bourgh,' said Elizabeth. 'It must be something particular, to take him there at this time of year.'

'Undoubtedly. Did you see him while you were at Lambton? I thought I understood from the Gardiners that you had.'

'Yes; he introduced us to his sister.'

'And do you like her?'

'Very much.'

'I have heard, indeed, that she is uncommonly improved within this year or two. When I last saw her, she was not very promising. I am very glad you liked her. I hope she will turn out well.'

'I dare say she will; she has got over the most trying age.'

'Did you go by the village of Kympton?'

'I do not recollect that we did.'

'I mention it, because it is the living which I ought to have had. A most delightful place! – Excellent Parsonage House! It would have suited me in every respect.'

'How should you have liked making sermons?'

'Exceedingly well. I should have considered it as part of my duty, and the exertion would soon have been nothing. One ought not to repine – but, to be sure, it would have been such a thing for me! The quiet, the retirement of such a life, would have answered all my ideas of happiness! But it was not to be. Did you ever hear Darcy mention the circumstance, when you were in Kent?'

'I *have* heard from authority, which I thought *as good*, that it was left you conditionally only, and at the will of the present patron.'

'You have. Yes, there was something in *that*; I told you so from the first, you may remember.'

'I *did* hear, too, that there was a time, when sermon-making was not so palatable to you as it seems to be at present; that you actually declared your resolution of never taking orders, and that the business had been compromised accordingly.'

'You did! and it was not wholly without foundation. You may remember what I told you on that point, when first we talked of it.'

They were now almost at the door of the house, for she had walked fast to get rid of him; and unwilling for her sister's sake, to provoke him, she only said in reply, with a good-humoured smile, 'Come, Mr Wickham, we are brother and sister, you know. Do not let us quarrel about the past. In future, I hope we shall be always of one mind.'

She held out her hand; he kissed it with affectionate gallantry, though he hardly knew how to look, and they entered the house.

Chapter 53

Mr Wickham was so perfectly satisfied with this conversation, that he never again distressed himself, or provoked his dear sister Elizabeth, by introducing the subject of it; and she was pleased to find that she had said enough to keep him quiet.

The day of his and Lydia's departure soon came, and Mrs Bennet was forced to submit to a separation, which, as her husband by no means entered into her scheme of their all going to Newcastle, was likely to continue at least a twelvemonth.

'Oh! my dear Lydia,' she cried, 'when shall we meet again?'

'Oh, lord! I don't know. Not these two or three years perhaps.'

'Write to me very often, my dear.'

'As often as I can. But you know married women have never much time for writing. My sisters may write to *me*. They will have nothing else to do.'

Mr Wickham's adieus were much more affectionate than his wife's. He smiled, looked handsome, and said many pretty things.

'He is as fine a fellow,' said Mr Bennet, as soon as they were out of the house, 'as ever I saw. He simpers, and smirks, and makes love to us all. I am prodigiously proud of him. I defy even Sir William Lucas himself, to produce a more valuable son-in-law.'

The loss of her daughter made Mrs Bennet very dull for several days.

'I often think,' said she, 'that there is nothing so bad

as parting with one's friends. One seems so forlorn without them.'

'This is the consequence you see, Madam, of marrying a daughter,' said Elizabeth. 'It must make you better satisfied that your other four are single.'

'It is no such thing. Lydia does not leave me because she is married; but only because her husband's regiment happens to be so far off. If that had been nearer, she would not have gone so soon.'

But the spiritless condition which this event threw her into, was shortly relieved, and her mind opened again to the agitation of hope, by an article of news, which then began to be in circulation. The housekeeper at Netherfield had received orders to prepare for the arrival of her master, who was coming down in a day or two, to shoot there for several weeks. Mrs Bennet was quite in the fidgets. She looked at Jane, and smiled, and shook her head by turns.

'Well, well, and so Mr Bingley is coming down, sister' (for Mrs Philips first brought her the news). 'Well, so much the better. Not that I care about it, though. He is nothing to us, you know, and I am sure *I* never want to see him again. But, however, he is very welcome to come to Netherfield, if he likes it. And who knows what *may* happen? But that is nothing to us. You know, sister, we agreed long ago never to mention a word about it. And so, is it quite certain he is coming?'

'You may depend on it,' replied the other, 'for Mrs Nicholls was in Meryton last night; I saw her passing by, and went out myself on purpose to know the truth of it; and she told me that it was certain true. He comes down on Thursday at the latest, very likely on Wednesday. She was going to the butcher's, she told me, on purpose to order in some meat on Wednesday, and she has got three couple of ducks, just fit to be killed.'

Miss Bennet had not been able to hear of his coming, without changing colour. It was many months since she had mentioned his name to Elizabeth; but now, as soon as they were alone together, she said, 'I saw you look at me to day, Lizzy, when my aunt told us of the present report; and I know I appeared distressed. But don't imagine it was from any silly cause. I was only confused for the moment, because I felt that I *should* be looked at. I do assure you, that the news does not affect me either with pleasure or pain. I am glad of one thing, that he comes alone; because we shall see the less of him. Not that I am afraid of *myself*, but I dread other people's remarks.'

Elizabeth did not know what to make of it. Had she not seen him in Derbyshire, she might have supposed him capable of coming there, with no other view than what was acknowledged; but she still thought him partial to Jane, and she wavered as to the greater probability of his coming there *with* his friend's permission, or being bold enough to come without it.

'Yet it is hard,' she sometimes thought 'that this poor man cannot come to a house, which he has legally hired, without raising all this speculation! I *will* leave him to himself.'

In spite of what her sister declared, and really believed to be her feelings, in the expectation of his arrival, Elizabeth could easily perceive that her spirits were affected by it. They were more disturbed, more unequal, than she had often seen them.

The subject which had been so warmly canvassed between their parents, about a twelvemonth ago, was now brought forward again.

'As soon as ever Mr Bingley comes, my dear,' said Mrs Bennet, 'you will wait on him of course.'

'No, no. You forced me into visiting him last year, and promised if I went to see him, he should marry one of my daughters. But it ended in nothing, and I will not be sent on a fool's errand again.'

His wife represented to him how absolutely necessary such an attention would be from all the neighbouring gentlemen, on his returning to Netherfield.

' 'Tis an etiquette I despise,' said he. 'If he wants our society, let him seek it. He knows where we live. I will not spend *my* hours in running after my neighbours every time they go away, and come back again.'

'Well, all I know is, that it will be abominably rude if you do not wait on him. But, however, that shan't prevent my asking him to dine here, I am determined. We must have Mrs Long and the Gouldings soon. That will make thirteen with ourselves, so there will be just room at table for him.'

Consoled by this resolution, she was the better able to bear her husband's incivility; though it was very mortifying to know that her neighbours might all see Mr Bingley in consequence of it, before *they* did.

As the day of his arrival drew near, 'I begin to be sorry that he comes at all,' said Jane to her sister. 'It would be nothing; I could see him with perfect indifference, but I can hardly bear to hear it thus perpetually talked of. My mother means well; but she does not know, no one can know how much I suffer from what she says. Happy shall I be, when his stay at Netherfield is over!'

'I wish I could say anything to comfort you,' replied Elizabeth; 'but it is wholly out of my power. You must feel it; and the usual satisfaction of preaching patience to a sufferer is denied me, because you have always so much.'

Mr Bingley arrived. Mrs Bennet, through the assistance of servants, contrived to have the earliest tidings of it, that the period of anxiety and fretfulness on her side, might be as long as it could. She counted the days that must intervene before their invitation could be sent; hopeless of seeing him before. But on the third morning after his arrival in Hertfordshire, she saw him from her dressing-room window, enter the paddock, and ride towards the house.

Her daughters were eagerly called to partake of her joy. Jane resolutely kept her place at the table; but Elizabeth, to satisfy her mother, went to the window – she looked – she saw Mr Darcy with him, and sat down again by her sister.

'There is a gentleman with him, mamma,' said Kitty; 'who can it be?'

'Some acquaintance or other, my dear, I suppose; I am sure I do not know.'

'La!' replied Kitty, 'it looks just like that man that used to be with him before. Mr what's-his-name. That tall, proud man.'

'Good gracious! Mr Darcy! – and so it does I vow. Well, any friend of Mr Bingley's will always be welcome here to be sure; but else I must say that I hate the very sight of him.'

Jane looked at Elizabeth with surprise and concern. She knew but little of their meeting in Derbyshire, and therefore felt for the awkwardness which must attend her sister, in seeing him almost for the first time after receiving his explanatory letter. Both sisters were uncomfortable enough. Each felt for the other, and of course for themselves; and their mother talked on, of

She saw Mr Darcy with him

her dislike of Mr Darcy, and her resolution to be civil to him only as Mr Bingley's friend, without being heard by either of them. But Elizabeth had sources of uneasiness which could not be suspected by Jane, to whom she had never yet had courage to shew Mrs Gardiner's letter, or to relate her own change of sentiment towards him. To Jane, he could be only a man whose proposals she had refused, and whose merit she had undervalued; but to her own more extensive information, he was the person, to whom the whole family were indebted for the first of benefits, and whom she regarded herself with an interest, if not quite so tender, at least as reasonable and just, as what Jane felt for Bingley. Her astonishment at his coming – at his coming to Netherfield, to Longbourn, and voluntarily seeking her again, was almost equal to what she had known on first witnessing his altered behaviour in Derbyshire.

The colour which had been driven from her face, returned for half a minute with an additional glow, and a smile of delight added lustre to her eyes, as she thought for that space of time, that his affection and wishes must still be unshaken. But she would not be secure.

'Let me first see how he behaves,' said she; 'it will then be early enough for expectation.'

She sat intently at work, striving to be composed, and without daring to lift up her eyes, till anxious curiosity carried them to the face of her sister, as the servant was approaching the door. Jane looked a little paler than usual, but more sedate than Elizabeth had expected. On the gentlemen's appearing, her colour increased; yet she received them with tolerable ease, and with a propriety of behaviour equally free from any symptom of resentment, or any unnecessary complaisance.

Elizabeth said as little to either as civility would allow, and sat down again to her work, with an eagerness which it did not often command. She had ventured only one glance at Darcy. He looked serious as usual; and she thought, more as he had been used to look in Hertfordshire, than as she had seen him at Pemberley. But, perhaps he could not in her mother's presence be what he was before her uncle and aunt. It was a painful, but not an improbable, conjecture.

Bingley, she had likewise seen for an instant, and in that short period saw him looking both pleased and embarrassed. He was received by Mrs Bennet with a degree of civility, which made her two daughters ashamed, especially when contrasted with the cold and ceremonious politeness of her curtsey and address to his friend.

Elizabeth particularly, who knew that her mother owed to the latter the preservation of her favourite daughter from irremediable infamy, was hurt and distressed to a most painful degree by a distinction so ill applied.

Darcy, after enquiring of her how Mr and Mrs Gardiner did, a question which she could not answer without confusion, said scarcely anything. He was not seated by her; perhaps that was the reason of his silence; but it had not been so in Derbyshire. There he had talked to her friends, when he could not to herself. But now several minutes elapsed, without bringing the sound of his voice; and when occasionally, unable to resist the impulse of curiosity, she raised her eyes to his face, she as often found him looking at Jane, as at herself, and frequently on no object but the ground. More thoughtfulness, and less anxiety to please than when they last met, were plainly expressed. She was disappointed, and angry with herself for being so.

'Could I expect it to be otherwise!' said she. 'Yet why did he come?'

She was in no humour for conversation with anyone

but himself; and to him she had hardly courage to speak.

She enquired after his sister, but could do no more.

'It is a long time, Mr Bingley, since you went away,' said Mrs Bennet.

He readily agreed to it.

'I began to be afraid you would never come back again. People *did* say, you meant to quit the place entirely at Michaelmas; but, however, I hope it is not true. A great many changes have happened in the neighbourhood, since you went away. Miss Lucas is married and settled. And one of my own daughters. I suppose you have heard of it; indeed, you must have seen it in the papers. It was in *The Times* and the *Courier*, I know; though it was not put in as it ought to be. It was only said, "Lately, George Wickham, Esq. to Miss Lydia Bennet", without there being a syllable said of her father, or the place where she lived, or anything. It was my brother Gardiner's drawing up too, and I wonder how he came to make such an awkward business of it. Did you see it?'

Bingley replied that he did, and made his congratulations. Elizabeth dared not lift up her eyes. How Mr Darcy looked, therefore, she could not tell.

'It is a delightful thing, to be sure, to have a daughter well married,' continued her mother, 'but at the same time, Mr Bingley, it is very hard to have her taken such a way from me. They are gone down to Newcastle, a place quite northward, it seems, and there they are to stay, I do not know how long. His regiment is there; for I suppose you have heard of his leaving the —shire, and of his being gone into the regulars. Thank Heaven! he has *some* friends, though perhaps not so many as he deserves.'

Elizabeth, who knew this to be levelled at Mr Darcy, was in such misery of shame, that she could hardly keep her seat. It drew from her, however, the exertion of speaking, which nothing else had so effectually done before; and she asked Bingley, whether he meant to make any stay in the country at present. A few weeks, he believed.

'When you have killed all your own birds, Mr Bingley,' said her mother, 'I beg you will come here, and shoot as many as you please, on Mr Bennet's manor. I am sure he will be vastly happy to oblige you, and will save all the best of the covies for you.'

Elizabeth's misery increased, at such unnecessary, such officious attention! Were the same fair prospect to arise at present, as had flattered them a year ago, everything, she was persuaded, would be hastening to the same vexatious conclusion. At that instant she felt, that years of happiness could not make Jane or herself amends, for moments of such painful confusion.

'The first wish of my heart,' said she to herself, 'is never more to be in company with either of them. Their society can afford no pleasure, that will atone for such wretchedness as this! Let me never see either one or the other again!'

Yet the misery, for which years of happiness were to offer no compensation, received soon afterwards material relief, from observing how much the beauty of her sister re-kindled the admiration of her former lover. When first he came in, he had spoken to her but little; but every five minutes seemed to be giving her more of his attention. He found her as handsome as she had been last year; as good natured, and as unaffected, though not quite so chatty. Jane was anxious that no difference should be perceived in her at all, and was really persuaded that she talked as much as ever. But her mind was so busily engaged, that she did not always know when she was silent.

When the gentlemen rose to go away, Mrs Bennet was mindful of her intended civility, and they were invited and engaged to dine at Longbourn in a few days time.

'You are quite a visit in my debt, Mr Bingley,' she added, 'for when you went to town last winter, you promised to take a family dinner with us, as soon as you returned. I have not forgot, you see; and I assure you, I was very much disappointed that you did not come back and keep your engagement.'

Bingley looked a little silly at this reflection, and said something of his concern, at having been prevented by business. They then went away.

Mrs Bennet had been strongly inclined to ask them to stay and dine there, that day; but, though she always kept a very good table, she did not think anything less than two courses, could be good enough for a man, on whom she had such anxious designs, or satisfy the appetite and pride of one who had ten thousand a year.

Chapter 54

As soon as they were gone, Elizabeth walked out to recover her spirits; or in other words, to dwell without interruption on those subjects that must deaden them more. Mr Darcy's behaviour astonished and vexed her.

'Why, if he came only to be silent, grave, and indifferent,' said she, 'did he come at all?'

She could settle it in no way that gave her pleasure.

'He could be still amiable, still pleasing, to my uncle and aunt, when he was in town; and why not to me? If he fears me, why come hither? If he no longer cares for me, why silent? Teasing, teasing, man! I will think no more about him.'

Her resolution was for a short time involuntarily kept by the approach of her sister, who joined her with a cheerful look, which showed her better satisfied with their visitors, than Elizabeth.

'Now,' said she, 'that this first meeting is over, I feel perfectly easy. I know my own strength, and I shall never be embarrassed again by his coming. I am glad he dines here on Tuesday. It will then be publicly seen, that on both sides, we meet only as common and indifferent acquaintance.'

'Yes, very indifferent indeed,' said Elizabeth, laughingly. 'Oh, Jane, take care.'

'My dear Lizzy, you cannot think me so weak, as to be in danger now.'

'I think you are in very great danger of making him as much in love with you as ever.'

They did not see the gentlemen again till Tuesday; and Mrs Bennet, in the meanwhile, was giving way to all the happy schemes, which the good humour, and common politeness of Bingley, in half an hour's visit, had revived.

On Tuesday there was a large party assembled at Longbourn; and the two, who were most anxiously expected, to the credit of their punctuality as sportsmen, were in very good time. When they repaired to the dining-room, Elizabeth eagerly watched to see whether Bingley would take the place, which, in all

Jane happened to look round

their former parties, had belonged to him, by her sister. Her prudent mother, occupied by the same ideas, forbore to invite him to sit by herself. On entering the room, he seemed to hesitate; but Jane happened to look round, and happened to smile: it was decided. He placed himself by her.

Elizabeth, with a triumphant sensation, looked towards his friend. He bore it with noble indifference, and she would have imagined that Bingley had received his sanction to be happy, had she not seen his eyes likewise turned towards Mr Darcy, with an expression of half-laughing alarm.

His behaviour to her sister was such, during dinner time, as showed an admiration of her, which, though more guarded than formerly, persuaded Elizabeth, that if left wholly to himself, Jane's happiness, and his own, would be speedily secured. Though she dared not depend upon the consequence, she yet received pleasure from observing his behaviour. It gave her all the animation that her spirits could boast; for she was in no cheerful humour. Mr Darcy was almost as far from her, as the table could divide them. He was on one side of her mother. She knew how little such a situation would give pleasure to either, or make either appear to advantage. She was not near enough to hear any of their discourse, but she could see how seldom they spoke to each other, and how formal and cold was their manner, whenever they did. Her mother's ungraciousness, made the sense of what they owed him more painful to Elizabeth's mind; and she would, at times, have given anything to be privileged to tell him, that his kindness was neither unknown nor unfelt by the whole of the family.

She was in hopes that the evening would afford some opportunity of bringing them together; that the whole of the visit would not pass away without enabling them to enter into something more of conversation, than the mere ceremonious salutation attending his entrance. Anxious and uneasy, the period which passed in the drawing-room, before the gentlemen came, was wearisome and dull to a degree, that almost made her uncivil. She looked forward to their entrance, as the point on which all her chance of pleasure for the evening must depend.

'If he does not come to me, *then*,' said she, 'I shall give him up for ever.'

The gentlemen came; and she thought he looked as if he would have answered her hopes; but, alas! the ladies had crowded round the table, where Miss Bennet was making tea, and Elizabeth pouring out the coffee, in so close a confederacy, that there was not a single vacancy near her, which would admit of a chair.

And on the gentlemen's approaching, one of the girls moved closer to her than ever, and said, in a whisper, 'The men shan't come and part us, I am determined. We want none of them; do we?'

Darcy had walked away to another part of the room. She followed him with her eyes, envied everyone to whom he spoke, had scarcely patience enough to help anybody to coffee; and then was enraged against herself for being so silly!

'A man who has once been refused! How could I ever be foolish enough to expect a renewal of his love? Is there one among the sex, who would not protest against such a weakness as a second proposal to the same woman? There is no indignity so abhorrent to their feelings!'

She was a little revived, however, by his bringing back his coffee cup himself; and she seized the opportunity of saying, 'Is your sister at Pemberley still?'

'Yes, she will remain there till Christmas.'

'And quite alone? Have all her friends left her?'

'Mrs Annesley is with her. The others have been gone on to Scarborough, these three weeks.'

She could think of nothing more to say; but if he wished to converse with her, he might have better success. He stood by her, however, for some minutes, in silence; and, at last, on the young lady's whispering to Elizabeth again, he walked away.

When the tea-things were removed, and the card tables placed, the ladies all rose, and Elizabeth was then hoping to be soon joined by him, when all her views were overthrown, by seeing him fall a victim to her mother's rapacity for whist players, and in a few moments after seated with the rest of the party. She now lost every expectation of pleasure. They were confined for the evening at different tables, and she had nothing to hope, but that his eyes were so often turned towards her side of the room, as to make him play as unsuccessfully as herself.

Mrs Bennet had designed to keep the two Netherfield gentlemen to supper; but their carriage was unluckily ordered before any of the others, and she had no opportunity of detaining them.

'Well girls,' said she, as soon as they were left to themselves, 'What say you to the day? I think everything has passed off uncommonly well, I assure you. The dinner was as well dressed as any I ever saw. The venison was roasted to a turn – and everybody said, they never saw so fat a haunch. The soup was fifty times better than what we had at the Lucases' last week; and even Mr Darcy acknowledged, that the partridges were remarkably well done; and I suppose he has two or three French cooks at least. And, my dear Jane, I never saw you look in greater beauty. Mrs Long said so too, for I asked her whether you did not. And what do you think she said besides? "Ah! Mrs Bennet, we shall have her at Netherfield at last." She did

Mrs Long and her nieces

indeed. I do think Mrs Long is as good a creature as ever lived – and her nieces are very pretty-behaved girls, and not at all handsome: I like them prodigiously.'

Mrs Bennet, in short, was in very great spirits; she had seen enough of Bingley's behaviour to Jane, to be convinced that she would get him at last; and her expectations of advantage to her family, when in a happy humour, were so far beyond reason, that she was quite disappointed at not seeing him there again the next day, to make his proposals.

'It has been a very agreeable day,' said Miss Bennet to Elizabeth. 'The party seemed so well selected, so suitable one with the other. I hope we may often meet again.'

Elizabeth smiled.

'Lizzy, you must not do so. You must not suspect me. It mortifies me. I assure you that I have now learnt to enjoy his conversation as an agreeable and sensible young man, without having a wish beyond it. I am perfectly satisfied from what his manners now are, that he never had any design of engaging my affection. It is only that he is blessed with greater sweetness of address, and a stronger desire of generally pleasing than any other man.'

'You are very cruel,' said her sister, 'you will not let me smile, and are provoking me to it every moment.'

'How hard it is in some cases to be believed!'

'And how impossible in others!'

'But why should you wish to persuade me that I feel more than I acknowledge?'

'That is a question which I hardly know how to answer. We all love to instruct, though we can teach only what is not worth knowing. Forgive me; and if you persist in indifference, do not make *me* your confidante.'

Chapter 55

A few days after this visit, Mr Bingley called again, and alone. His friend had left him that morning for London, but was to return home in ten days time. He sat with them above an hour, and was in remarkably good spirits. Mrs Bennet invited him to dine with them; but, with many expressions of concern, he confessed himself engaged elsewhere.

'Next time you call,' said she, 'I hope we shall be more lucky.'

He should be particularly happy at any time, &c. &c.; and if she would give him leave, would take an early opportunity of waiting on them.

'Can you come tomorrow?'

Yes, he had no engagement at all for tomorrow; and her invitation was accepted with alacrity.

He came, and in such very good time, that the ladies were none of them dressed. In ran Mrs Bennet to her daughter's room, in her dressing gown, and with her hair half finished, crying out, 'My dear Jane, make haste and hurry down. He is come – Mr Bingley is come. He is, indeed. Make haste, make haste. Here, Sarah, come to Miss Bennet this moment, and help her on with her gown. Never mind Miss Lizzy's hair.'

'We will be down as soon as we can,' said Jane; 'but I dare say Kitty is forwarder than either of us, for she went upstairs half an hour ago.'

'Oh! hang Kitty! what has she to do with it? Come be quick, be quick! where is your sash my dear?'

But when her mother was gone, Jane would not be prevailed on to go down without one of her sisters.

The same anxiety to get them by themselves, was visible again in the evening. After tea, Mr Bennet retired to the library, as was his custom, and Mary went upstairs to her instrument. Two obstacles of the five being thus removed, Mrs Bennet sat looking and winking at Elizabeth and Catherine for a considerable time, without making any impression on them. Elizabeth would not observe her; and when at last Kitty did, she very innocently said, 'What is the matter mamma? What do you keep winking at me for? What am I to do?'

'Nothing child, nothing. I did not wink at you.' She then sat still five minutes longer; but unable to waste such a precious occasion, she suddenly got up, and saying to Kitty, 'Come here, my love, I want to speak to you,' took her out of the room. Jane instantly gave a look at Elizabeth, which spoke her distress at such premeditation, and her entreaty that *she* would not give into it. In a few minutes, Mrs Bennet half opened the door and called out, 'Lizzy, my dear, I want to speak with you.'

Elizabeth was forced to go.

'We may as well leave them by themselves you know,' said her mother as soon as she was in the hall. 'Kitty and I are going upstairs to sit in my dressing room.'

Elizabeth made no attempt to reason with her mother, but remained quietly in the hall, till she and Kitty were out of sight, then returned into the drawing room.

Mrs Bennet's schemes for this day were ineffectual. Bingley was everything that was charming, except the professed lover of her daughter. His ease and cheerfulness rendered him a most agreeable addition to their evening party; and he bore with the ill-judged

Come here, my love, I want to speak to you

officiousness of the mother, and heard all her silly remarks with a forbearance and command of countenance, particularly grateful to the daughter.

He scarcely needed an invitation to stay supper; and before he went away, an engagement was formed, chiefly through his own and Mrs Bennet's means, for his coming next morning to shoot with her husband.

After this day, Jane said no more of her indifference. Not a word passed between the sisters concerning Bingley; but Elizabeth went to bed in the happy belief that all must speedily be concluded, unless Mr Darcy returned within the stated time. Seriously, however, she felt tolerably persuaded that all this must have taken place with that gentleman's concurrence.

Bingley was punctual to his appointment; and he and Mr Bennet spent the morning together, as had been agreed on. The latter was much more agreeable than his companion expected. There was nothing of presumption or folly in Bingley, that could provoke his ridicule, or disgust him into silence; and he was more communicative, and less eccentric than the other had ever seen him. Bingley of course returned with him to dinner; and in the evening Mrs Bennet's invention was again at work to get everybody away from him and her daughter. Elizabeth, who had a letter to write, went into the breakfast room for that purpose soon after tea; for as the others were all going to sit down to cards, she could not be wanted to counteract her mother's schemes.

But on returning to the drawing-room, when her letter was finished, she saw, to her infinite surprise, there was reason to fear that her mother had been too ingenious for her. On opening the door, she perceived her sister and Bingley standing together over the hearth, as if engaged in earnest conversation; and had this led to no suspicion, the faces of both as they hastily turned round, and moved away from each other, would have told it all. *Their* situation was awkward enough; but *her's* she thought was still worse. Not a syllable was uttered by either; and Elizabeth was on the point of going away again, when Bingley, who as well as the other had sat down, suddenly rose, and whispering a few words to her sister, ran out of the room.

Jane could have no reserves from Elizabeth, where confidence would give pleasure; and instantly embracing her, acknowledged, with the liveliest emotion, that she was the happiest creature in the world.

''Tis too much!' she added, 'by far too much. I do not deserve it. Oh! why is not everybody as happy?'

Elizabeth's congratulations were given with a sincerity, a warmth, a delight, which words could but poorly express. Every sentence of kindness was a fresh source of happiness to Jane. But she would not allow herself to stay with her sister, or say half that remained to be said, for the present.

'I must go instantly to my mother;' she cried. 'I would not on any account trifle with her affectionate solicitude; or allow her to hear it from anyone but myself. He is gone to my father already. Oh! Lizzy, to know that what I have to relate will give such pleasure to all my dear family! how shall I bear so much happiness!'

She then hastened away to her mother, who had purposely broken up the card party, and was sitting upstairs with Kitty.

Elizabeth, who was left by herself, now smiled at the

rapidity and ease with which an affair was finally settled, that had given them so many previous months of suspense and vexation.

'And this,' said she, 'is the end of all his friend's anxious circumspection! of all his sister's falsehood and contrivance! the happiest, wisest, most reasonable end!'

In a few minutes she was joined by Bingley, whose conference with her father had been short and to the purpose.

'Where is your sister?' said he hastily, as he opened the door.

'With my mother upstairs. She will be down in a moment I dare say.'

He then shut the door, and coming up to her, claimed the good wishes and affection of a sister. Elizabeth honestly and heartily expressed her delight in the prospect of their relationship. They shook hands with great cordiality; and then till her sister came down, she had to listen to all he had to say, of his own happiness, and of Jane's perfections; and in spite of his being a lover, Elizabeth really believed all his expectations of felicity, to be rationally founded, because they had for basis the excellent under-standing, and super-excellent disposition of Jane, and a general similarity of feeling and taste between her and himself.

It was an evening of no common delight to them all; the satisfaction of Miss Bennet's mind gave a glow of such sweet animation to her face, as made her look handsomer than ever. Kitty simpered and smiled, and hoped her turn was coming soon. Mrs Bennet could not give her consent, or speak her approbation in terms warm enough to satisfy her feelings, though she talked to Bingley of nothing else, for half an hour; and when Mr Bennet joined them at supper, his voice and manner plainly showed how really happy he was.

Not a word, however, passed his lips in allusion to it, till their visitor took his leave for the night; but as soon as he was gone, he turned to his daughter and said, 'Jane, I congratulate you. You will be a very happy woman.'

Jane went to him instantly, kissed him, and thanked him for his goodness.

'You are a good girl,' he replied, 'and I have great pleasure in thinking you will be so happily settled. I have not a doubt of your doing very well together. Your tempers are by no means unlike. You are each of you so complying, that nothing will ever be resolved on; so easy, that every servant will cheat you; and so generous, that you will always exceed your income.'

'I hope not so. Imprudence or thoughtlessness in money matters, would be unpardonable in *me*.'

'Exceed their income! My dear Mr Bennet,' cried his wife, 'what are you talking of? Why, he has four or five thousand a year, and very likely more.' Then addressing her daughter, 'Oh! my dear, dear Jane, I am so happy! I am sure I shan't get a wink of sleep all night. I knew how it would be. I always said it must be so, at last. I was sure you could not be so beautiful for nothing! I remember, as soon as ever I saw him, when he first came into Hertfordshire last year, I thought how likely it was that you should come together. Oh! he is the handsomest young man that ever was seen!'

Wickham, Lydia, were all forgotten. Jane was beyond competition her favourite child. At that moment, she cared for no other. Her younger sisters soon began to make interest with her for objects of happiness which she might in future be able to dispense.

Mary petitioned for the use of the library at Netherfield; and Kitty begged very hard for a few balls there every winter.

Bingley, from this time, was of course a daily visitor at Longbourn; coming frequently before breakfast, and always remaining till after supper; unless when some barbarous neighbour, who could not be enough detested, had given him an invitation to dinner, which he thought himself obliged to accept.

Elizabeth had now but little time for conversation with her sister; for while he was present, Jane had no attention to bestow on anyone else; but she found herself considerably useful to both of them, in those hours of separation that must sometimes occur. In the absence of Jane, he always attached himself to Elizabeth, for the pleasure of talking to her; and when Bingley was gone, Jane constantly sought the same means of relief.

'He has made me so happy,' said she, one evening, 'by telling me, that he was totally ignorant of my being in town last spring! I had not believed it possible.'

'I suspected as much,' replied Elizabeth. 'But how did he account for it?'

'It must have been his sister's doing. They were certainly no friends to his acquaintance with me, which I cannot wonder at, since he might have chosen so much more advantageously in many respects. But when they see, as I trust they will, that their brother is happy with me, they will learn to be contented, and we shall be on good terms again; though we can never be what we once were to each other.'

'That is the most unforgiving speech,' said Elizabeth, 'that I ever heard you utter. Good girl! It would vex me, indeed, to see you again the dupe of Miss

Bingley's pretended regard.'

'Would you believe it, Lizzy, that when he went to town last November, he really loved me, and nothing but a persuasion of *my* being indifferent, would have prevented his coming down again!'

'He made a little mistake to be sure; but it is to the credit of his modesty.'

This naturally introduced a panegyric from Jane on his diffidence, and the little value he put on his own good qualities.

Elizabeth was pleased to find, that he had not betrayed the interference of his friend, for, though Jane had the most generous and forgiving heart in the world, she knew it was a circumstance which must prejudice her against him.

'I am certainly the most fortunate creature that ever existed!' cried Jane. 'Oh! Lizzy, why am I thus singled from my family, and blessed above them all! If I could but see *you* as happy! If there *were* but such another man for you!'

'If you were to give me forty such men, I never could be so happy as you. Till I have your disposition, your goodness, I never can have your happiness. No, no, let me shift for myself; and, perhaps, if I have very good luck, I may meet with another Mr Collins in time.'

The situation of affairs in the Longbourn family could not be long a secret. Mrs Bennet was privileged to whisper it to Mrs Philips, and *she* ventured, without any permission, to do the same by all her neighbours in Meryton.

The Bennets were speedily pronounced to be the luckiest family in the world, though only a few weeks before, when Lydia had first run away, they had been generally proved to be marked out for misfortune.

Chapter 56

One morning, about a week after Bingley's engagement with Jane had been formed, as he and the females of the family were sitting together in the dining room, their attention was suddenly drawn to the window, by the sound of a carriage; and they perceived a chaise and four driving up the lawn. It was too early in the morning for visitors, and besides, the equipage did not answer to that of any of their neighbours. The horses were post; and neither the carriage, nor the livery of the servant who preceded it, were familiar to them. As it was certain, however, that somebody was coming, Bingley instantly prevailed on Miss Bennet to avoid the confinement of such an intrusion, and walk away with him into the shrubbery. They both set off, and the conjectures of the remaining three continued, though with little satisfaction, till the door was thrown open, and their visitor entered. It was Lady Catherine de Bourgh.

They were of course all intending to be surprised; but their astonishment was beyond their expectation; and on the part of Mrs Bennet and Kitty, though she was perfectly unknown to them, even inferior to what Elizabeth felt.

She entered the room with an air more than usually ungracious, made no other reply to Elizabeth's salutation, than a slight inclination of the head, and sat down without saying a word. Elizabeth had mentioned her name to her mother, on her ladyship's entrance, though no request of introduction had been made.

It was Lady Catherine de Bourgh

Mrs Bennet all amazement, though flattered by having a guest of such high importance, received her with the utmost politeness. After sitting for a moment in silence, she said very stiffly to Elizabeth, 'I hope you are well, Miss Bennet. That lady I suppose is your mother.'

Elizabeth replied very concisely that she was.

'And *that* I suppose is one of your sisters.'

'Yes, madam,' said Mrs Bennet, delighted to speak

437

to a Lady Catherine. 'She is my youngest girl but one. My youngest of all, is lately married, and my eldest is somewhere about the grounds, walking with a young man, who I believe will soon become a part of the family.'

'You have a very small park here,' returned Lady Catherine after a short silence.

'It is nothing in comparison of Rosings, my lady, I dare say; but I assure you it is much larger than Sir William Lucas's.'

'This must be a most inconvenient sitting room for the evening, in summer; the windows are full west.'

Mrs Bennet assured her that they never sat there after dinner; and then added, 'May I take the liberty of asking your ladyship whether you left Mr and Mrs Collins well.'

'Yes, very well. I saw them the night before last.'

Elizabeth now expected that she would produce a letter for her from Charlotte, as it seemed the only probable motive for her calling. But no letter appeared, and she was completely puzzled.

Mrs Bennet, with great civility, begged her ladyship to take some refreshment; but Lady Catherine very resolutely, and not very politely, declined eating anything; and then rising up, said to Elizabeth,

'Miss Bennet, there seemed to be a prettyish kind of a little wilderness on one side of your lawn. I should be glad to take a turn in it, if you will favour me with your company.'

'Go, my dear,' cried her mother, 'and shew her ladyship about the different walks. I think she will be pleased with the hermitage.'

Elizabeth obeyed, and running into her own room for her parasol, attended her noble guest downstairs.

As they passed through the hall, Lady Catherine opened the doors into the dining-parlour and drawing-room, and pronouncing them, after a short survey, to be decent-looking rooms, walked on.

Her carriage remained at the door, and Elizabeth saw that her waiting-woman was in it. They proceeded in silence along the gravel walk that led to the copse; Elizabeth was determined to make no effort for conversation with a woman, who was now more than usually insolent and disagreeable.

'How could I ever think her like her nephew?' said she, as she looked in her face.

As soon as they entered the copse, Lady Catherine began in the following manner: 'You can be at no loss, Miss Bennet, to understand the reason of my journey hither. Your own heart, your own conscience, must tell you why I come.'

Elizabeth looked with unaffected astonishment.

'Indeed, you are mistaken, Madam. I have not been at all able to account for the honour of seeing you here.'

'Miss Bennet,' replied her ladyship, in an angry tone, 'you ought to know, that I am not to be trifled with. But however insincere *you* may choose to be, you shall not find *me* so. My character has ever been celebrated for its sincerity and frankness, and in a cause of such moment as this, I shall certainly not depart from it. A report of a most alarming nature, reached me two days ago. I was told, that not only your sister was on the point of being most advantageously married, but that *you*, that Miss Elizabeth Bennet, would, in all likelihood, be soon afterwards united to my nephew, my own nephew, Mr Darcy. Though I *know* it must be a scandalous falsehood; though I would not injure him so much as to suppose the truth

*Pronouncing them, after a short survey, to be
decent-looking rooms*

of it possible, I instantly resolved on setting off for this place, that I might make my sentiments known to you.'

'If you believed it impossible to be true,' said Elizabeth, colouring with astonishment and disdain, 'I wonder you took the trouble of coming so far. What could your ladyship propose by it?'

'At once to insist upon having such a report universally contradicted.'

'Your coming to Longbourn, to see me and my family,' said Elizabeth, coolly, 'will be rather a confirmation of it; if, indeed, such a report is in existence.'

'If! do you then pretend to be ignorant of it? Has it not been industriously circulated by yourselves? Do you not know that such a report is spread abroad?'

'I never heard that it was.'

'And can you likewise declare, that there is no *foundation* for it?'

'I do not pretend to possess equal frankness with your ladyship. *You* may ask questions, which *I* shall not choose to answer.'

'This is not to be borne. Miss Bennet, I insist on being satisfied. Has he, has my nephew, made you an offer of marriage?'

'Your ladyship has declared it to be impossible.'

'It ought to be so; it must be so, while he retains the use of his reason. But *your* arts and allurements may, in a moment of infatuation, have made him forget what he owes to himself and to all his family. You may have drawn him in.'

'If I have, I shall be the last person to confess it.'

'Miss Bennet, do you know who I am? I have not been accustomed to such language as this. I am almost the nearest relation he has in the world, and am entitled to know all his dearest concerns.'

'But you are not entitled to know *mine*; nor will such behaviour as this, ever induce me to be explicit.'

'Let me be rightly understood. This match, to which you have the presumption to aspire, can never take place. No, never. Mr Darcy is engaged to *my daughter*. Now what have you to say?'

'Only this; that if he is so, you can have no reason to suppose he will make an offer to me.'

Lady Catherine hesitated for a moment, and then replied, 'The engagement between them is of a peculiar kind. From their infancy, they have been intended for each other. It was the favourite wish of *his* mother, as well as of her's. While in their cradles, we planned the union: and now, at the moment when the wishes of both sisters would be accomplished, in their marriage, to be prevented by a young woman of inferior birth, of no importance in the world, and wholly unallied to the family! Do you pay no regard to the wishes of his friends? To his tacit engagement with Miss de Bourgh? Are you lost to every feeling of propriety and delicacy? Have you not heard me say, that from his earliest hours he was destined for his cousin?'

'Yes, and I had heard it before. But what is that to me? If there is no other objection to my marrying your nephew, I shall certainly not be kept from it, by knowing that his mother and aunt wished him to marry Miss de Bourgh. You both did as much as you could, in planning the marriage. Its completion depended on others. If Mr Darcy is neither by honour nor inclination confined to his cousin, why is not he to make another choice? And if I am that choice, why may not I accept him?'

'Because honour, decorum, prudence, nay, interest, forbid it. Yes, Miss Bennet, interest; for do not expect to be noticed by his family or friends, if you wilfully act against the inclinations of all. You will be censured, slighted, and despised, by everyone connected with him. Your alliance will be a disgrace; your name will never even be mentioned by any of us.'

'These are heavy misfortunes,' replied Elizabeth. 'But the wife of Mr Darcy must have such extra ordinary sources of happiness necessarily attached to her situation, that she could, upon the whole, have no cause to repine.'

'Obstinate, headstrong girl! I am ashamed of you! Is this your gratitude for my attentions to you last spring? Is nothing due to me on that score?

'Let us sit down. You are to understand, Miss Bennet, that I came here with the determined resolution of carrying my purpose; nor will I be dissuaded from it. I have not been used to submit to any person's whims. I have not been in the habit of brooking disappointment.'

'*That* will make your ladyship's situation at present more pitiable; but it will have no effect on *me*.'

'I will not be interrupted. Hear me in silence. My daughter and my nephew are formed for each other. They are descended on the maternal side, from the same noble line; and, on the father's, from respectable, honourable, and ancient, though untitled families. Their fortune on both sides is splendid. They are destined for each other by the voice of every member of their respective houses; and what is to divide them? The upstart pretensions of a young woman without family, connections, or fortune. Is this to be endured! But it must not, shall not be. If you were sensible of your own good, you would not wish to quit the sphere, in which you have been brought up.'

443

'In marrying your nephew, I should not consider myself as quitting that sphere. He is a gentleman; I am a gentleman's daughter; so far we are equal.'

'True. You *are* a gentleman's daughter. But who was your mother? Who are your uncles and aunts? Do not imagine me ignorant of their condition.'

'Whatever my connections may be,' said Elizabeth, 'if your nephew does not object to them, they can be nothing to *you*.'

'Tell me once for all, are you engaged to him?'

Though Elizabeth would not, for the mere purpose of obliging Lady Catherine, have answered this question; she could not but say, after a moment's deliberation, 'I am not.'

Lady Catherine seemed pleased.

'And will you promise me, never to enter into such an engagement?'

'I will make no promise of the kind.'

'Miss Bennet, I am shocked and astonished. I expected to find a more reasonable young woman. But do not deceive yourself into a belief that I will ever recede. I shall not go away, till you have given me the assurance I require.'

'And I certainly *never* shall give it. I am not to be intimidated into anything so wholly unreasonable. Your ladyship wants Mr Darcy to marry your daughter; but would my giving you the wished-for promise, make *their* marriage at all more probable? Supposing him to be attached to me, would *my* refusing to accept his hand, make him wish to bestow it on his cousin? Allow me to say, Lady Catherine, that the arguments with which you have supported this extraordinary application, have been as frivolous as the application was ill-judged. You have widely mistaken my character, if you think I can be worked on by such persuasions as these. How far your nephew might approve of your interference in *his* affairs, I cannot tell; but you have certainly no right to concern yourself in mine. I must beg, therefore, to be importuned no farther on the subject.'

'Not so hasty, if you please. I have by no means done. To all the objections I have already urged, I have still another to add. I am no stranger to the particulars of your youngest sister's infamous elopement. I know it all; that the young man's marrying her, was a patched-up business, at the expense of your father and uncles. And is *such* a girl to be my nephew's sister? Is *her* husband, is the son of his late father's steward, to be his brother? Heaven and earth! – of what are you thinking? Are the shades of Pemberley to be thus polluted?'

'You can *now* have nothing farther to say,' she resentfully answered. 'You have insulted me, in every possible method. I must beg to return to the house.'

And she rose as she spoke. Lady Catherine rose also, and they turned back. Her ladyship was highly incensed.

'You have no regard, then, for the honour and credit of my nephew! Unfeeling, selfish girl! Do you not consider that a connection with you, must disgrace him in the eyes of everybody?'

'Lady Catherine, I have nothing farther to say. You know my sentiments.'

'You are then resolved to have him?'

'I have said no such thing. I am only resolved to act in that manner, which will, in my own opinion, constitute my happiness, without reference to *you*, or to any person so wholly unconnected with me.'

'It is well. You refuse, then, to oblige me. You refuse to obey the claims of duty, honour, and gratitude. You are determined to ruin him in the opinion of all his friends, and make him the contempt of the world.'

'Neither duty, nor honour, nor gratitude,' replied Elizabeth, 'have any possible claim on me, in the present instance. No principle of either, would be violated by my marriage with Mr Darcy. And with regard to the resentment of his family, or the indignation of the world, if the former *were* excited by his marrying me, it would not give me one moment's concern – and the world in general would have too much sense to join in the scorn.'

'And this is your real opinion! This is your final resolve! Very well. I shall now know how to act. Do not imagine, Miss Bennet, that your ambition will ever be gratified. I came to try you. I hoped to find you reasonable; but depend upon it I will carry my point.'

In this manner Lady Catherine talked on, till they were at the door of the carriage, when turning hastily round, she added, 'I take no leave of you, Miss Bennet. I send no compliments to your mother. You deserve no such attention. I am most seriously displeased.'

Elizabeth made no answer; and without attempting to persuade her ladyship to return into the house, walked quietly into it herself. She heard the carriage drive away as she proceeded upstairs. Her mother impatiently met her at the door of the dressing-room, to ask why Lady Catherine would not come in again and rest herself.

'She did not choose it,' said her daughter, 'she would go.'

'She is a very fine-looking woman! and her calling here was prodigiously civil! for she only came, I suppose, to tell us the Collinses were well. She is on her road somewhere, I dare say, and so passing through Meryton, thought she might as well call on you. I suppose she had nothing particular to say to you, Lizzy?'

Elizabeth was forced to give into a little falsehood here; for to acknowledge the substance of their conversation was impossible.

Chapter 57

The discomposure of spirits, which this extraordinary visit threw Elizabeth into, could not be easily overcome; nor could she for many hours, learn to think of it less than incessantly. Lady Catherine it appeared, had actually taken the trouble of this journey from Rosings, for the sole purpose of breaking off her supposed engagement with Mr Darcy. It was a rational scheme to be sure! but from what the report of their engagement could originate, Elizabeth was at a loss to imagine; till she recollected that *his* being the intimate friend of Bingley, and *her* being the sister of Jane, was enough, at a time when the expectation of one wedding, made everybody eager for another, to supply the idea. She had not herself forgotten to feel that the marriage of her sister must bring them more frequently together. And her neighbours at Lucas lodge, therefore, (for through their communication with the Collinses, the report she concluded had reached Lady Catherine) had only set *that* down, as almost certain and immediate, which *she* had looked forward to as possible, at some future time.

In revolving Lady Catherine's expressions, however,

she could not help feeling some uneasiness as to the possible consequence of her persisting in this interference. From what she had said of her resolution to prevent their marriage, it occurred to Elizabeth that she must meditate an application to her nephew; and how *he* might take a similar representation of the evils attached to a connection with her, she dared not pronounce. She knew not the exact degree of his affection for his aunt, or his dependence on her judgement, but it was natural to suppose that he thought much higher of her ladyship than *she* could do; and it was certain, that in enumerating the miseries of a marriage with *one*, whose immediate connections were so unequal to his own, his aunt would address him on his weakest side. With his notions of dignity, he would probably feel that the arguments, which to Elizabeth had appeared weak and ridiculous, contained much good sense and solid reasoning.

If he had been wavering before, as to what he should do, which had often seemed likely, the advice and entreaty of so near a relation might settle every doubt, and determine him at once to be as happy, as dignity unblemished could make him. In that case he would return no more. Lady Catherine might see him in her way through town; and his engagement to Bingley of coming again to Netherfield must give way.

'If, therefore, an excuse for not keeping his promise, should come to his friend within a few days,' she added, 'I shall know how to understand it. I shall then give over every expectation, every wish of his constancy. If he is satisfied with only regretting me, when he might have obtained my affections and hand, I shall soon cease to regret him at all.'

The surprise of the rest of the family, on hearing who their visitor had been, was very great; but they obligingly satisfied it, with the same kind of supposition, which had appeased Mrs Bennet's curiosity; and Elizabeth was spared from much teasing on the subject.

The next morning, as she was going downstairs, she was met by her father, who came out of his library with a letter in his hand.

'Lizzy,' said he, 'I was going to look for you; come into my room.'

She followed him hither; and her curiosity to know what he had to tell her, was heightened by the supposition of its being in some manner connected with the letter he held. It suddenly struck her that it might be from Lady Catherine; and she anticipated with dismay all the consequent explanations.

She followed her father to the fire place, and they both sat down. He then said, 'I have received a letter this morning that has astonished me exceedingly. As it principally concerns yourself, you ought to know its contents. I did not know before, that I had *two* daughters on the brink of matrimony. Let me congratulate you, on a very important conquest.'

The colour now rushed into Elizabeth's cheeks in the instantaneous conviction of its being a letter from the nephew, instead of the aunt; and she was undetermined whether most to be pleased that he explained himself at all, or offended that his letter was not rather addressed to herself; when her father continued, 'You look conscious. Young ladies have great penetration in such matters as these; but I think I may defy even *your* sagacity, to discover the name of your admirer. This letter is from Mr Collins.'

'From Mr Collins! and what can *he* have to say?'

'Something very much to the purpose of course. He begins with congratulations on the approaching nuptials of my eldest daughter, of which it seems he has been told, by some of the good-natured, gossiping Lucases. I shall not sport with your impatience, by reading what he says on that point. What relates to yourself, is as follows. "Having thus offered you the sincere congratulations of Mrs Collins and myself on this happy event, let me now add a short hint on the subject of another; of which we have been advertised by the same authority. Your daughter Elizabeth, it is presumed, will not long bear the name of Bennet, after her elder sister has resigned it, and the chosen partner of her fate, may be reasonably looked up to, as one of the most illustrious personages in this land."

'Can you possibly guess, Lizzy, who is meant by this? "This young gentleman is blessed in a peculiar way, with everything the heart of mortal can most desire – splendid property, noble kindred, and extensive patronage. Yet in spite of all these temptations, let me warn my cousin Elizabeth, and yourself, of what evils you may incur, by a precipitate closure with this gentleman's proposals, which, of course, you will be inclined to take immediate advantage of."

'Have you any idea, Lizzy, who this gentleman is? But now it comes out.

' "My motive for cautioning you, is as follows. We have reason to imagine that his aunt, Lady Catherine de Bourgh, does not look on the match with a friendly eye."

'*Mr Darcy*, you see, is the man! Now, Lizzy, I think I *have* surprised you. Could he, or the Lucases, have pitched on any man, within the circle of our

But now it comes out

acquaintance, whose name would have given the lie
more effectually to what they related? Mr Darcy, who
never looks at any woman but to see a blemish, and
who probably never looked at *you* in his life! It is
admirable!'

Elizabeth tried to join in her father's pleasantry, but
could only force one most reluctant smile. Never had
his wit been directed in a manner so little agreeable
to her.

'Are you not diverted?'

'Oh! yes. Pray read on.'

' "After mentioning the likelihood of this marriage
to her ladyship last night, she immediately, with her
usual condescension, expressed what she felt on the

occasion; when it became apparent, that on the score of some family objections on the part of my cousin, she would never give her consent to what she termed so disgraceful a match. I thought it my duty to give the speediest intelligence of this to my cousin, that she and her noble admirer may be aware of what they are about, and not run hastily into a marriage which has not been properly sanctioned." Mr Collins moreover adds, "I am truly rejoiced that my cousin Lydia's sad business has been so well hushed up, and am only concerned that their living together before the marriage took place, should be so generally known. I must not, however, neglect the duties of my station, or refrain from declaring my amazement, at hearing that you received the young couple into your house as soon as they were married. It was an encouragement of vice; and had I been the rector of Longbourn, I should very strenuously have opposed it. You ought certainly to forgive them as a Christian, but never to admit them in your sight, or allow their names to be mentioned in your hearing." *That* is his notion of Christian forgiveness! The rest of his letter is only about his dear Charlotte's situation, and his expectation of a young olive branch. But, Lizzy, you look as if you did not enjoy it. You are not going to be *Missish*, I hope, and pretend to be affronted at an idle report. For what do we live, but to make sport for our neighbours, and laugh at them in our turn?'

'Oh!' cried Elizabeth, 'I am excessively diverted. But it is so strange!'

'Yes – *that* is what makes it amusing. Had they fixed on any other man it would have been nothing; but *his* perfect indifference, and *your* pointed dislike, make it so delightfully absurd! Much as I abominate writing, I would not give up Mr Collins's correspondence for any consideration. Nay, when I read a letter of his, I cannot help giving him the preference even over Wickham, much as I value the impudence and hypocrisy of my son-in-law. And pray, Lizzy, what said Lady Catherine about this report? Did she call to refuse her consent?'

To this question his daughter replied only with a laugh; and as it had been asked without the least suspicion, she was not distressed by his repeating it. Elizabeth had never been more at a loss to make her feelings appear what they were not. It was necessary to laugh, when she would rather have cried. Her father had most cruelly mortified her, by what he said of Mr Darcy's indifference, and she could do nothing but wonder at such a want of penetration, or fear that perhaps, instead of his seeing too *little*, she might have fancied too *much*.

Chapter 58

Instead of receiving any such letter of excuse from his friend, as Elizabeth half expected Mr Bingley to do, he was able to bring Darcy with him to Longbourn before many days had passed after Lady Catherine's visit. The gentlemen arrived early; and, before Mrs Bennet had time to tell him of their having seen his aunt, of which her daughter sat in momentary dread, Bingley, who wanted to be alone with Jane, proposed their all walking out. It was agreed to. Mrs Bennet was not in the habit of walking, Mary could never spare time, but the remaining five set off together. Bingley and Jane, however, soon allowed the others to outstrip them. They lagged behind, while Elizabeth, Kitty, and Darcy, were to entertain each other. Very little was said by either; Kitty was too much afraid of him to talk; Elizabeth was secretly forming a desperate resolution; and perhaps he might be doing the same.

They walked towards the Lucases, because Kitty wished to call upon Maria; and as Elizabeth saw no occasion for making it a general concern, when Kitty left them, she went boldly on with him alone.

Now was the moment for her resolution to be executed, and, while her courage was high, she immediately said, 'Mr Darcy, I am a very selfish creature; and, for the sake of giving relief to my own feelings, care not how much I may be wounding your's. I can no longer help thanking you for your unexampled kindness to my poor sister. Ever since I have known it, I have been most anxious to acknowledge to you how gratefully I feel it. Were it known to the rest of my family, I should not have merely my own gratitude to express.'

'I am sorry, exceedingly sorry,' replied Darcy, in a tone of surprise and emotion, 'that you have ever been informed of what may, in a mistaken light, have given you uneasiness. I did not think Mrs Gardiner was so little to be trusted.'

'You must not blame my aunt. Lydia's thoughtlessness first betrayed to me that you had been concerned in the matter; and, of course, I could not rest till I knew the particulars. Let me thank you again and again, in the name of all my family, for that generous compassion which induced you to take so much trouble, and bear so many mortifications, for the sake of discovering them.'

'If you *will* thank me,' he replied, 'let it be for yourself alone. That the wish of giving happiness to you, might add force to the other inducements which led me on, I shall not attempt to deny. But your *family* owe me nothing. Much as I respect them, I believe, I thought only of *you*.'

Elizabeth was too much embarrassed to say a word. After a short pause, her companion added, 'You are too generous to trifle with me. If your feelings are still what they were last April, tell me so at once. *My* affections and wishes are unchanged, but one word from you will silence me on this subject for ever.'

Elizabeth feeling all the more than common awkwardness and anxiety of his situation, now forced herself to speak; and immediately, though not very fluently, gave him to understand, that her sentiments had undergone so material a change, since the period to which he alluded, as to make her receive with gratitude and pleasure, his present assurances. The happiness which this reply produced, was such as he had probably never felt before; and he expressed himself on the occasion as sensibly and as warmly as a man violently in love can be supposed to do. Had Elizabeth been able to encounter his eye, she might have seen how well the expression of heartfelt delight, diffused over his face, became him; but, though she could not look, she could listen, and he told her of feelings, which, in proving of what importance she was to him, made his affection every moment more valuable.

They walked on, without knowing in what direction. There was too much to be thought, and felt, and said, for attention to any other objects. She soon learnt that they were indebted for their present good understanding to the efforts of his aunt, who *did* call on him in her return through London, and there relate her journey to Longbourn, its motive, and the substance of her conversation with Elizabeth; dwelling emphatically on every expression of the latter, which, in her ladyship's apprehension, peculiarly denoted her perverseness and assurance, in the belief that such a relation must assist her endeavours to obtain that promise from her nephew, which *she* had refused to give. But, unluckily for her ladyship, its effect had been exactly contrariwise. 'It taught me to hope,' said he, 'as I had scarcely ever allowed myself to hope before. I knew enough of your disposition to be certain, that, had you been absolutely, irrevocably decided against me, you would have acknowledged it to Lady Catherine, frankly and openly.'

Elizabeth coloured and laughed as she replied, 'Yes, you know enough of my *frankness* to believe me capable of *that*. After abusing you so abominably to

The efforts of his aunt

your face, I could have no scruple in abusing you to all your relations.'

'What did you say of me, that I did not deserve? For, though your accusations were ill-founded, formed on mistaken premises, my behaviour to you at the time, had merited the severest reproof. It was unpardonable. I cannot think of it without abhorrence.'

'We will not quarrel for the greater share of blame annexed to that evening,' said Elizabeth. 'The conduct of neither, if strictly examined, will be irreproachable; but since then, we have both, I hope, improved in civility.'

'I cannot be so easily reconciled to myself. The recollection of what I then said, of my conduct, my manners, my expressions during the whole of it, is now, and has been many months, inexpressibly painful to me. Your reproof, so well applied, I shall never forget: "had you behaved in a more gentleman-like manner." Those were your words. You know not, you can scarcely conceive, how they have tortured me – though it was some time, I confess, before I was reasonable enough to allow their justice.'

'I was certainly very far from expecting them to make so strong an impression. I had not the smallest idea of their being ever felt in such a way.'

'I can easily believe it. You thought me then devoid of every proper feeling, I am sure you did. The turn of your countenance I shall never forget, as you said that I could not have addressed you in any possible way, that would induce you to accept me.'

'Oh! do not repeat what I then said. These recollections will not do at all. I assure you, that I have long been most heartily ashamed of it.'

Darcy mentioned his letter. 'Did it,' said he, 'did it *soon* make you think better of me? Did you, on reading it, give any credit to its contents?'

She explained what its effect on her had been, and how gradually all her former prejudices had been removed.

'I knew,' said he, 'that what I wrote must give you pain, but it was necessary. I hope you have destroyed the letter. There was one part especially, the opening of it, which I should dread your having the power of reading again. I can remember some expressions which might justly make you hate me.'

'The letter shall certainly be burnt, if you believe it essential to the preservation of my regard; but, though we have both reason to think my opinions not entirely unalterable, they are not, I hope, quite so easily changed as that implies.'

'When I wrote that letter,' replied Darcy, 'I believed myself perfectly calm and cool, but I am since convinced that it was written in a dreadful bitterness of spirit.'

'The letter, perhaps, began in bitterness, but it did not end so. The adieu is charity itself. But think no more of the letter. The feelings of the person who wrote, and the person who received it, are now so widely different from what they were then, that every unpleasant circumstance attending it, ought to be forgotten. You must learn some of my philosophy. Think only of the past as its remembrance gives you pleasure.'

'I cannot give you credit for any philosophy of the kind. *Your* retrospections must be so totally void of reproach, that the contentment arising from them, is not of philosophy, but what is much better, of ignorance. But with *me*, it is not so. Painful recollections will intrude, which cannot, which ought not to be repelled. I have been a selfish being all my life, in practice, though not in principle. As a child I was taught what was *right*, but I was not taught to correct my temper. I was given good principles, but left to follow them in pride and conceit. Unfortunately an only son (for many years an only *child*), I was spoilt by my parents, who though good themselves, (my father particularly, all that was benevolent and amiable), allowed, encouraged, almost taught me to be selfish and overbearing, to care for none beyond my own family circle, to think meanly of all the rest of the world, to *wish* at least to think meanly of their sense and worth compared with my own. Such I was, from eight to eight and twenty; and such I might still have been but for you, dearest, loveliest Elizabeth! What do I not owe you! You taught me a lesson, hard indeed at first, but most advantageous. By you, I was properly humbled. I came to you without a doubt of my reception. You showed me how insufficient were all my pretensions to please a woman worthy of being pleased.'

'Had you then persuaded yourself that I should?'

'Indeed I had. What will you think of my vanity? I believed you to be wishing, expecting my addresses.'

'My manners must have been in fault, but not intentionally I assure you. I never meant to deceive you, but my spirits might often lead me wrong. How you must have hated me after *that* evening?'

'Hate you! I was angry perhaps at first, but my anger soon began to take a proper direction.'

'I am almost afraid of asking what you thought of me; when we met at Pemberley. You blamed me for coming?'

'No indeed; I felt nothing but surprise.'

'Your surprise could not be greater than *mine* in being noticed by you. My conscience told me that I deserved no extraordinary politeness, and I confess that I did not expect to receive *more* than my due.'

'My object *then*,' replied Darcy, 'was to shew you, by every civility in my power, that I was not so mean as to resent the past; and I hoped to obtain your forgiveness, to lessen your ill opinion, by letting you see that your reproofs had been attended to. How soon any other wishes introduced themselves I can hardly tell, but I believe in about half an hour after I had seen you.'

He then told her of Georgiana's delight in her acquaintance, and of her disappointment at its sudden interruption; which naturally leading to the cause of that interruption, she soon learnt that his resolution of following her from Derbyshire in quest of her sister, had been formed before he quitted the inn, and that his gravity and thoughtfulness there, had arisen from no other struggles than what such a purpose must comprehend.

She expressed her gratitude again, but it was too painful a subject to each, to be dwelt on farther.

After walking several miles in a leisurely manner, and too busy to know anything about it, they found at last, on examining their watches, that it was time to be at home.

'What could become of Mr Bingley and Jane!' was a wonder which introduced the discussion of *their* affairs. Darcy was delighted with their engagement; his friend had given him the earliest information of it.

'I must ask whether you were surprised?' said Elizabeth.

'Not at all. When I went away, I felt that it would soon happen.'

'That is to say, you had given your permission. I guessed as much.' And though he exclaimed at the term, she found that it had been pretty much the case.

'On the evening before my going to London,' said he 'I made a confession to him, which I believe I ought to have made long ago. I told him of all that had occurred to make my former interference in his affairs, absurd and impertinent. His surprise was great. He had never had the slightest suspicion. I told him, moreover, that I believed myself mistaken in supposing, as I had done, that your sister was indifferent to him; and as I could easily perceive that his attachment to her was unabated, I felt no doubt of their happiness together.'

Elizabeth could not help smiling at his easy manner of directing his friend.

'Did you speak from your own observation,' said she, 'when you told him that my sister loved him, or merely from my information last spring?'

'From the former. I had narrowly observed her during the two visits which I had lately made her here; and I was convinced of her affection.'

'And your assurance of it, I suppose, carried immediate conviction to him.'

'It did. Bingley is most unaffectedly modest. His diffidence had prevented his depending on his own judgement in so anxious a case, but his reliance on mine, made everything easy. I was obliged to confess one thing, which for a time, and not unjustly, offended him. I could not allow myself to conceal that your sister had been in town three months last winter, that I had known it, and purposely kept it from him. He was angry. But his anger, I am persuaded, lasted no longer than he remained in any doubt of your sister's sentiments. He has heartily forgiven me now.'

Elizabeth longed to observe that Mr Bingley had been a most delightful friend; so easily guided that his worth was invaluable; but she checked herself. She remembered that he had yet to learn to be laughed at, and it was rather too early to begin. In anticipating the happiness of Bingley, which of course was to be inferior only to his own, he continued the conversation till they reached the house. In the hall they parted.

Chapter 59

'My dear Lizzy, where can you have been walking to?' was a question which Elizabeth received from Jane as soon as she entered the room, and from all the others when they sat down to table. She had only to say in reply, that they had wandered about, till she was beyond her own knowledge. She coloured as she spoke; but neither that, nor anything else, awakened a suspicion of the truth.

The evening passed quietly, unmarked by anything extraordinary. The acknowledged lovers talked and laughed, the unacknowledged were silent. Darcy was not of a disposition in which happiness overflows in mirth; and Elizabeth, agitated and confused, rather *knew* that she was happy, than *felt* herself to be so; for, besides the immediate embarrassment, there were other evils before her. She anticipated what would be felt in the family when her situation became known; she was aware that no one liked him but Jane; and even feared that with the others it was a *dislike* which not all his fortune and consequence might do away.

At night she opened her heart to Jane. Though suspicion was very far from Miss Bennet's general habits, she was absolutely incredulous here.

'You are joking, Lizzy. This cannot be! – engaged to Mr Darcy! No no, you shall not deceive me. I know it to be impossible.'

'This is a wretched beginning indeed! My sole dependence was on you; and I am sure nobody else will believe me, if you do not. Yet, indeed, I am in earnest. I speak nothing but the truth. He still loves me, and we are engaged.'

Jane looked at her doubtingly. 'Oh, Lizzy! it cannot be. I know how much you dislike him.'

'You know nothing of the matter. *That* is all to be forgot. Perhaps I did not always love him so well as I do now. But in such cases as these, a good memory is unpardonable. This is the last time I shall ever remember it myself.'

Miss Bennet still looked all amazement. Elizabeth again, and more seriously assured her of its truth.

'Good Heaven! can it be really so! Yet now I must believe you,' cried Jane. 'My dear, dear Lizzy, I would – I do congratulate you – but are you certain? forgive the question – are you quite certain that you can be happy with him?'

'There can be no doubt of that. It is settled between us already, that we are to be the happiest couple in the world. But are you pleased, Jane? Shall you like to have such a brother?'

'Very, very much. Nothing could give either Bingley or myself more delight. But we considered it, we talked of it as impossible. And do you really love him quite well enough? Oh, Lizzy! do anything rather than marry without affection. Are you quite sure that you feel what you ought to do?'

'Oh, yes! You will only think I feel *more* than I ought to do, when I tell you all.'

'What do you mean?'

'Why, I must confess, that I love him better than I do Bingley. I am afraid you will be angry.'

'My dearest sister, now *be* serious. I want to talk very seriously. Let me know everything that I am to know, without delay. Will you tell me how long you have loved him?'

'It has been coming on so gradually, that I hardly know when it began. But I believe I must date it from my first seeing his beautiful grounds at Pemberley.'

Another entreaty that she would be serious, however, produced the desired effect; and she soon satisfied Jane by her solemn assurances of attachment. When convinced on that article, Miss Bennet had nothing farther to wish.

'Now I am quite happy,' said she, 'for you will be as happy as myself. I always had a value for him. Were it for nothing but his love of you, I must always have esteemed him; but now, as Bingley's friend and your husband, there can be only Bingley and yourself more dear to me. But Lizzy, you have been very sly, very reserved with me. How little did you tell me of what passed at Pemberley and Lambton! I owe all that I know of it, to another, not to you.'

Elizabeth told her the motives of her secrecy. She had been unwilling to mention Bingley; and the unsettled state of her own feelings had made her equally avoid the name of his friend. But now she would no longer conceal from her, his share in Lydia's marriage. All was acknowledged, and half the night spent in conversation.

'Good gracious!' cried Mrs Bennet, as she stood at a window the next morning, 'if that disagreeable Mr Darcy is not coming here again with our dear Bingley! What can he mean by being so tiresome as to be always coming here? I had no notion but he would go a shooting, or something or other, and not disturb us with his company. What shall we do with him? Lizzy, you must walk out with him again, that he may not be in Bingley's way.'

Elizabeth could hardly help laughing at so convenient a proposal; yet was really vexed that her mother should be always giving him such an epithet.

As soon as they entered, Bingley looked at her so expressively, and shook hands with such warmth, as left no doubt of his good information; and he soon afterwards said aloud, 'Mr Bennet, have you no more lanes hereabouts in which Lizzy may lose her way again today?'

'I advise Mr Darcy, and Lizzy, and Kitty,' said Mrs Bennet, 'to walk to Oakham Mount this morning. It is a nice long walk, and Mr Darcy has never seen the view.'

'It may do very well for the others,' replied Mr Bingley; 'but I am sure it will be too much for Kitty. Won't it, Kitty?'

Kitty owned that she had rather stay at home. Darcy professed a great curiosity to see the view from the Mount, and Elizabeth silently consented. As she went upstairs to get ready, Mrs Bennet followed her, saying, 'I am quite sorry, Lizzy, that you should be forced to have that disagreeable man all to yourself. But I hope you will not mind it: it is all for Jane's sake, you know; and there is no occasion for talking to him, except just now and then. So, do not put yourself to inconvenience.'

During their walk, it was resolved that Mr Bennet's consent should be asked in the course of the evening. Elizabeth reserved to herself the application for her mother's. She could not determine how her mother would take it; sometimes doubting whether all his wealth and grandeur would be enough to overcome her abhorrence of the man. But whether she were violently set against the match, or violently delighted with it, it was certain that her manner would be

466

equally ill adapted to do credit to her sense; and she could no more bear that Mr Darcy should hear the first raptures of her joy, than the first vehemence of her disapprobation.

In the evening, soon after Mr Bennet withdrew to the library, she saw Mr Darcy rise also and follow him, and her agitation on seeing it was extreme. She did not fear her father's opposition, but he was going to be made unhappy, and that it should be through her means, that *she*, his favourite child, should be distressing him by her choice, should be filling him with fears and regrets in disposing of her, was a wretched reflection, and she sat in misery till Mr Darcy appeared again, when, looking at him, she was a little relieved by his smile. In a few minutes he approached the table where she was sitting with Kitty; and, while pretending to admire her work, said in a whisper, 'Go to your father, he wants you in the library.' She was gone directly.

Her father was walking about the room, looking grave and anxious. 'Lizzy,' said he, 'what are you doing? Are you out of your senses, to be accepting this man? Have not you always hated him?'

How earnestly did she then wish that her former opinions had been more reasonable, her expressions more moderate! It would have spared her from explanations and professions which it was exceedingly awkward to give; but they were now necessary, and she assured him with some confusion, of her attachment to Mr Darcy.

'Or in other words, you are determined to have him. He is rich, to be sure, and you may have more fine clothes and fine carriages than Jane. But will they make you happy?'

'Have you any other objection,' said Elizabeth, 'than your belief of my indifference?'

'None at all. We all know him to be a proud, unpleasant sort of man; but this would be nothing if you really liked him.'

'I do, I do like him,' she replied, with tears in her eyes, 'I love him. Indeed he has no improper pride. He is perfectly amiable. You do not know what he really is; then pray do not pain me by speaking of him in such terms.'

'Lizzy,' said her father, 'I have given him my consent. He is the kind of man, indeed, to whom I should never dare refuse anything, which he condescended to ask. I now give it to *you*, if you are resolved on having him. But let me advise you to think better of it. I know your disposition, Lizzy. I know that you could be neither happy nor respectable, unless you truly esteemed your husband; unless you looked up to him as a superior. Your lively talents would place you in the greatest danger in an unequal marriage. You could scarcely escape discredit and misery. My child, let me not have the grief of seeing *you* unable to respect your partner in life. You know not what you are about.'

Elizabeth, still more affected, was earnest and solemn in her reply; and at length, by repeated assurances that Mr Darcy was really the object of her choice, by explaining the gradual change which her estimation of him had undergone, relating her absolute certainty that his affection was not the work of a day, but had stood the test of many months suspense, and enumerating with energy all his good qualities, she did conquer her father's incredulity, and reconcile him to the match.

'Well, my dear,' said he, when she ceased speaking, 'I have no more to say. If this be the case, he deserves you. I could not have parted with you, my Lizzy, to anyone less worthy.'

To complete the favourable impression, she then told him what Mr Darcy had voluntarily done for Lydia. He heard her with astonishment.

'This is an evening of wonders, indeed! And so, Darcy did everything; made up the match, gave the money, paid the fellow's debts, and got him his commission! So much the better. It will save me a world of trouble and economy. Had it been your uncle's doing, I must and *would* have paid him; but these violent young lovers carry everything their own way. I shall offer to pay him tomorrow; he will rant and storm about his love for you, and there will be an end of the matter.'

He then recollected her embarrassment a few days before, on his reading Mr Collins's letter; and after laughing at her some time, allowed her at last to go – saying, as she quitted the room, 'If any young men come for Mary or Kitty, send them in, for I am quite at leisure.'

Elizabeth's mind was now relieved from a very heavy weight; and, after half an hour's quiet reflection in her own room, she was able to join the others with tolerable composure. Everything was too recent for gaiety, but the evening passed tranquilly away; there was no longer anything material to be dreaded, and the comfort of ease and familiarity would come in time.

When her mother went up to her dressing-room at night, she followed her, and made the important communication. Its effect was most extraordinary; for on first hearing it, Mrs Bennet sat quite still, and unable to utter a syllable. Nor was it under many,

many minutes, that she could comprehend what she heard; though not in general backward to credit what was for the advantage of her family, or that came in the shape of a lover to any of them. She began at length to recover, to fidget about in her chair, get up, sit down again, wonder, and bless herself.

'Good gracious! Lord bless me! only think! dear me! Mr Darcy! Who would have thought it! And is it really true? Oh! my sweetest Lizzy! how rich and how great you will be! What pin-money, what jewels, what carriages you will have! Jane's is nothing to it – nothing at all. I am so pleased – so happy. Such a charming man! – so handsome! so tall! – Oh, my dear Lizzy! pray apologise for my having disliked him so much before. I hope he will overlook it. Dear, dear Lizzy. A house in town! Everything that is charming! Three daughters married! Ten thousand a year! Oh, Lord! What will become of me. I shall go distracted.'

This was enough to prove that her approbation need not be doubted: and Elizabeth, rejoicing that such an effusion was heard only by herself, soon went away. But before she had been three minutes in her own room, her mother followed her.

'My dearest child,' she cried, 'I can think of nothing else! Ten thousand a year, and very likely more! 'Tis as good as a Lord! And a special licence. You must and shall be married by a special licence. But my dearest love, tell me what dish Mr Darcy is particularly fond of, that I may have it tomorrow.'

This was a sad omen of what her mother's behaviour to the gentleman himself might be; and Elizabeth found, that though in the certain possession of his warmest affection, and secure of her relations' consent, there was still something to be wished for. But the

Unable to utter a syllable

morrow passed off much better than she expected; for Mrs Bennet luckily stood in such awe of her intended son-in-law, that she ventured not to speak to him, unless it was in her power to offer him any attention, or mark her deference for his opinion.

Elizabeth had the satisfaction of seeing her father taking pains to get acquainted with him; and Mr Bennet soon assured her that he was rising every hour in his esteem.

'I admire all my three sons-in-law highly,' said he. 'Wickham, perhaps, is my favourite; but I think I shall like *your* husband quite as well as Jane's.'

Chapter 60

Elizabeth's spirits soon rising to playfulness again, she wanted Mr Darcy to account for his having ever fallen in love with her. 'How could you begin?' said she. 'I can comprehend your going on charmingly, when you had once made a beginning; but what could set you off in the first place?'

'I cannot fix on the hour, or the spot, or the look, or the words, which laid the foundation. It is too long ago. I was in the middle before I knew that I *had* begun.'

'My beauty you had early withstood, and as for my manners – my behaviour to *you* was at least always bordering on the uncivil, and I never spoke to you without rather wishing to give you pain than not. Now be sincere; did you admire me for my impertinence?'

'For the liveliness of your mind, I did.'

'You may as well call it impertinence at once. It was very little less. The fact is, that you were sick of civility, of deference, of officious attention. You were disgusted with the women who were always speaking and looking, and thinking for *your* approbation alone. I roused, and interested you, because I was so unlike *them*. Had you not been really amiable you would have hated me for it; but in spite of the pains you took to disguise yourself, your feelings were always noble and just; and in your heart, you thoroughly despised the persons who so assiduously courted you. There – I have saved you the trouble of accounting for it; and really, all things considered, I begin to think it perfectly reasonable. To be sure, you knew no actual good of me – but nobody thinks of *that* when they fall in love.'

'Was there no good in your affectionate behaviour to Jane, while she was ill at Netherfield?'

'Dearest Jane! who could have done less for her? But make a virtue of it by all means. My good qualities are under your protection, and you are to exaggerate them as much as possible; and, in return, it belongs to me to find occasions for teasing and quarrelling with you as often as may be; and I shall begin directly by asking you what made you so unwilling to come to the point at last. What made you so shy of me, when you first called, and afterwards dined here? Why, especially, when you called, did you look as if you did not care about me?'

'Because you were grave and silent, and gave me no encouragement.'

'But I was embarrassed.'

'And so was I.'

'You might have talked to me more when you came to dinner.'

'A man who had felt less, might.'

'How unlucky that you should have a reasonable answer to give, and that I should be so reasonable as to admit it! But I wonder how long you *would* have gone on, if you had been left to yourself. I wonder when you *would* have spoken, if I had not asked you! My resolution of thanking you for your kindness to Lydia had certainly great effect. *Too much*, I am afraid; for what becomes of the moral, if our comfort springs from a breach of promise, for I ought not to have mentioned the subject? This will never do.'

'You need not distress yourself. The moral will be perfectly fair. Lady Catherine's unjustifiable endeavours to separate us, were the means of removing all my doubts. I am not indebted for my present happiness

473

to your eager desire of expressing your gratitude. I was not in a humour to wait for any opening of your's. My aunt's intelligence had given me hope, and I was determined at once to know everything.'

'Lady Catherine has been of infinite use, which ought to make her happy, for she loves to be of use. But tell me, what did you come down to Netherfield for? Was it merely to ride to Longbourn and be embarrassed? or had you intended any more serious consequence?'

'My real purpose was to see *you*, and to judge, if I could, whether I might ever hope to make you love me. My avowed one, or what I avowed to myself, was to see whether your sister were still partial to Bingley, and if she were, to make the confession to him which I have since made.'

'Shall you ever have courage to announce to Lady Catherine, what is to befall her?'

'I am more likely to want time than courage, Elizabeth. But it ought to be done, and if you will give me a sheet of paper, it shall be done directly.'

'And if I had not a letter to write myself, I might sit by you, and admire the evenness of your writing, as another young lady once did. But I have an aunt, too, who must not be longer neglected.'

From an unwillingness to confess how much her intimacy with Mr Darcy had been overrated, Elizabeth had never yet answered Mrs Gardiner's long letter, but now, having *that* to communicate which she knew would be most welcome, she was almost ashamed to find, that her uncle and aunt had already lost three days of happiness, and immediately wrote as follows:

I would have thanked you before, my dear aunt, as I

ought to have done, for your long, kind, satisfactory, detail of particulars; but to say the truth, I was too cross to write. You supposed more than really existed. But *now* suppose as much as you choose; give a loose to your fancy, indulge your imagination in every possible flight which the subject will afford, and unless you believe me actually married, you cannot greatly err. You must write again very soon, and praise him a great deal more than you did in your last. I thank you, again and again, for not going to the Lakes. How could I be so silly as to wish it! Your idea of the ponies is delightful. We will go round the Park every day. I am the happiest creature in the world. Perhaps other people have said so before, but not one with such justice. I am happier even than Jane; she only smiles, I laugh. Mr Darcy sends you all the love in the world, that he can spare from me. You are all to come to Pemberley at Christmas. Your's, &c.

Mr Darcy's letter to Lady Catherine, was in a different style; and still different from either, was what Mr Bennet sent to Mr Collins, in reply to his last.

DEAR SIR – I must trouble you once more for congratulations. Elizabeth will soon be the wife of Mr Darcy. Console Lady Catherine as well as you can. But, if I were you, I would stand by the nephew. He has more to give.

Your's sincerely, &c.

Miss Bingley's congratulations to her brother, on his approaching marriage, were all that was affectionate and insincere. She wrote even to Jane on the occasion, to express her delight, and repeat all her former professions of regard. Jane was not deceived, but she was affected; and though feeling no reliance on her, could not help writing her a much kinder answer than she knew was deserved.

The joy which Miss Darcy expressed on receiving similar information, was as sincere as her brother's in sending it. Four sides of paper were insufficient to contain all her delight, and all her earnest desire of being loved by her sister.

Before any answer could arrive from Mr Collins, or any congratulations to Elizabeth, from his wife, the Longbourn family heard that the Collinses were come themselves to Lucas lodge. The reason of this sudden removal was soon evident. Lady Catherine had been rendered so exceedingly angry by the contents of her nephew's letter, that Charlotte, really rejoicing in the match, was anxious to get away till the storm was blown over. At such a moment, the arrival of her friend was a sincere pleasure to Elizabeth, though in the course of their meetings she must sometimes think the pleasure dearly bought, when she saw Mr Darcy exposed to all the parading and obsequious civility of her husband. He bore it however with admirable calmness. He could even listen to Sir William Lucas, when he complimented him on carrying away the brightest jewel of the country, and expressed his hopes of their all meeting frequently at St James's, with very decent composure. If he did shrug his shoulders, it was not till Sir William was out of sight.

Mrs Philips's vulgarity was another, and perhaps a greater tax on his forbearance; and though Mrs Philips, as well as her sister, stood in too much awe of him to speak with the familiarity which Bingley's good humour encouraged, yet, whenever she *did* speak, she

Obsequious civility of her husband

must be vulgar. Nor was her respect for him, though it made her more quiet, at all likely to make her more elegant. Elizabeth did all she could, to shield him from the frequent notice of either, and was ever anxious to keep him to herself, and to those of her family with whom he might converse without mortification; and though the uncomfortable feelings arising from all this took from the season of courtship much of its pleasure, it added to the hope of the future; and she looked forward with delight to the time when they should be removed from society so little pleasing to either, to all the comfort and elegance of their family party at Pemberley.

Chapter 61

Happy for all her maternal feelings was the day on which Mrs Bennet got rid of her two most deserving daughters. With what delighted pride she afterwards visited Mrs Bingley and talked of Mrs Darcy may be guessed. I wish I could say, for the sake of her family, that the accomplishment of her earnest desire in the establishment of so many of her children, produced so happy an effect as to make her a sensible, amiable, well-informed woman for the rest of her life; though perhaps it was lucky for her husband, who might not have relished domestic felicity in so unusual a form, that she still was occasionally nervous and invariably silly.

Mr Bennet missed his second daughter exceedingly; his affection for her drew him oftener from home than anything else could do. He delighted in going to Pemberley, especially when he was least expected.

Mr Bingley and Jane remained at Netherfield only a twelvemonth. So near a vicinity to her mother and Meryton relations was not desirable even to *his* easy temper, or *her* affectionate heart. The darling wish of his sisters was then gratified; he bought an estate in a neighbouring county to Derbyshire, and Jane and Elizabeth, in addition to every other source of happiness, were within thirty miles of each other.

Kitty, to her very material advantage, spent the chief of her time with her two elder sisters. In society so superior to what she had generally known, her improvement was great. She was not of so ungovernable a temper as Lydia, and, removed from the influence of

Lydia's example, she became, by proper attention and management, less irritable, less ignorant, and less insipid. From the farther disadvantage of Lydia's society she was of course carefully kept, and though Mrs Wickham frequently invited her to come and stay with her, with the promise of balls and young men, her father would never consent to her going.

Mary was the only daughter who remained at home; and she was necessarily drawn from the pursuit of accomplishments by Mrs Bennet's being quite unable to sit alone. Mary was obliged to mix more with the world, but she could still moralise over every morning visit; and as she was no longer mortified by comparisons between her sisters' beauty and her own, it was suspected by her father that she submitted to the change without much reluctance.

As for Wickham and Lydia, their characters suffered no revolution from the marriage of her sisters. He bore with philosophy the conviction that Elizabeth must now become acquainted with whatever of his ingratitude and falsehood had before been unknown to her; and in spite of everything, was not wholly without hope that Darcy might yet be prevailed on to make his fortune. The congratulatory letter which Elizabeth received from Lydia on her marriage, explained to her that, by his wife at least, if not by himself, such a hope was cherished. The letter was to this effect:

My dear Lizzy – I wish you joy. If you love Mr Darcy half as well as I do my dear Wickham, you must be very happy. It is a great comfort to have you so rich, and when you have nothing else to do, I hope you will think of us. I am sure Wickham would like a place at court very much, and I do not think we shall have quite money enough to live upon without some help. Any place would do, of about three or four hundred a year; but, however, do not speak to Mr Darcy about it, if you had rather not.

Yours, &c.

As it happened that Elizabeth had much rather not, she endeavoured in her answer to put an end to every entreaty and expectation of the kind. Such relief, however, as it was in her power to afford, by the practice of what might be called economy in her own private expenses, she frequently sent them. It had always been evident to her that such an income as theirs, under the direction of two persons so extravagant in their wants, and heedless of the future, must be very insufficient to their support; and whenever they changed their quarters, either Jane or herself were sure of being applied to, for some little assistance towards discharging their bills. Their manner of living, even when the restoration of peace dismissed them to a home, was unsettled in the extreme. They were always moving from place to place in quest of a cheap situation, and always spending more than they ought. His affection for her soon sunk into indifference; hers lasted a little longer; and in spite of her youth and her manners, she retained all the claims to reputation which her marriage had given her.

Though Darcy could never receive *him* at Pemberley, yet, for Elizabeth's sake, he assisted him farther in his profession. Lydia was occasionally a visitor there, when her husband was gone to enjoy himself in London or Bath; and with the Bingleys they both of them frequently staid so long, that even

Bingley's good humour was overcome, and he proceeded so far as to *talk* of giving them a hint to be gone.

Miss Bingley was very deeply mortified by Darcy's marriage; but as she thought it advisable to retain the right of visiting at Pemberley, she dropped all her resentment; was fonder than ever of Georgiana, almost as attentive to Darcy as heretofore, and paid off every arrear of civility to Elizabeth.

Pemberley was now Georgiana's home; and the attachment of the sisters was exactly what Darcy had hoped to see. They were able to love each other, even as well as they intended. Georgiana had the highest opinion in the world of Elizabeth; though at first she often listened with an astonishment bordering on alarm, at her lively, sportive, manner of talking to her brother. He, who had always inspired in herself a respect which almost overcame her affection, she now saw the object of open pleasantry. Her mind received knowledge which had never before fallen in her way. By Elizabeth's instructions she began to comprehend that a woman may take liberties with her husband, which a brother will not always allow in a sister more than ten years younger than himself.

Lady Catherine was extremely indignant on the marriage of her nephew; and as she gave way to all the genuine frankness of her character, in her reply to the letter which announced its arrangement, she sent him language so very abusive, especially of Elizabeth, that for some time all intercourse was at an end. But at length, by Elizabeth's persuasion, he was prevailed on to overlook the offence, and seek a reconciliation; and, after a little farther resistance on the part of his aunt, her resentment gave way, either to her affection for him, or her curiosity to see how his wife conducted herself; and she condescended to wait on them at Pemberley, in spite of that pollution which its woods had received, not merely from the presence of such a mistress, but the visits of her uncle and aunt from the city.

With the Gardiners, they were always on the most intimate terms. Darcy, as well as Elizabeth, really loved them; and they were both ever sensible of the warmest gratitude towards the persons who, by bringing her into Derbyshire, had been the means of uniting them.

Afterword

Pride and Prejudice is one of the most enduringly popular of English novels. It offers both a rich comedy of manners and a lively, affecting love story. Its principal character, Elizabeth Bennet, is among literature's most charming heroines, while the name of Mr Darcy has become a synonym for brooding male sex appeal. The novel's popularity was instant; its early readers found it realistic, poised and entertaining, and Sir Walter Scott, an important champion of Austen's work, pronounced her creation 'a very pretty thing.' With characteristic modesty, Austen herself was less sure of its qualities; she worried that it might prove 'too light, and bright, and sparkling.' It is, of course, the lightness and brightness of *Pride and Prejudice* that make it so enjoyable, but Austen's concern reminds us that she had more serious intentions too.

Given the novel's undeniable allure, we are not surprised that it has inspired several screen adaptations, as well as a clutch of literary imitations and even some fanciful sequels. When the MGM Company released their big screen version in 1940, they billed it as the story of 'Five charming sisters on the gayest, merriest manhunt that ever snared a bewildered bachelor.' 'Girls!' the advertisement blared, 'Take a lesson from these husband hunters!' The strident language is pure Hollywood, but this kind of view of the novel has been common. Regrettably, it fails to recognize *Pride and Prejudice* as a sharp critique of the conventions of romance, which perfectly exhibits Austen's skills as both a satirist and an observant chronicler of her age.

The novel's opening sentence is one of the most celebrated in English literature. It alerts us, quite subtly, to Austen's powers of irony. 'It is a truth universally acknowledged,' she writes, 'that a single man in possession of a good fortune, must be in want of a wife.' This seems straightforward, but ought to prompt at least two questions: is this alleged 'truth' really acknowledged 'universally,' and 'must' an affluent man always be 'in want of a wife'? Austen is not endorsing the view that all affluent men should marry; instead she gently mocks the notion that there can be universal truths, and at the same time she mocks the shallowness of her contemporaries. She is keenly aware that social success depends on adherence to certain rules, many of them unspoken. These rules assume common values – a particular understanding, for instance, of what kind of behavior is appropriate in a young lady. But the truth about these values is that anyone who thinks as an individual is unlikely to espouse them. Throughout *Pride and Prejudice*, and indeed throughout all her work, Austen shows the tension between conformism and the individual's will, between truths universally acknowledged and authentic human feelings.

This tension is lost on some readers. Traditionally, many of Austen's admirers esteem her work because they feel it promotes romantic ideals. Demure, attractive young women marry handsome, slightly older men; there is no violence, and everyone sports immaculate clothes and impeccable manners. E. M. Forster suggested that Austen's most loyal fans prove to be her most blinkered and 'like all regular churchgoers . . . scarcely notice what is being said.' In fact, if her work has an abiding message, it is that it is easy to skate along on the surface of things, enjoying their immediate appeal, but that beneath the veneer there is always a more complex truth.

It is significant that Austen originally planned to call *Pride and Prejudice* 'First Impressions.' The novel is concerned with the initial impact characters make on one another – and with the reversal of the feelings that result. Austen's working title lacks the punch of the one she eventually selected, and she abandoned it when another contemporary writer, a Mrs Holford, published a novel by this name. The revised title appears to have been taken from a passage near the end of Fanny Burney's novel *Cecilia* (1782), a classic romance of the kind Austen quietly parodies. But the resonance of the original title remains; the novel shows quite beautifully how fallible our first impressions can be.

When Elizabeth and Darcy meet they experience what we quickly recognize to be mutual dislike. She suspects he has 'a propensity to hate everybody' and is 'above being pleased.' Her misgivings appear justified; Darcy's attitude is certainly disagreeable. He complains, for instance, that Elizabeth's sister Jane smiles too much. Elsewhere he pronounces Elizabeth herself merely 'tolerable.' She is openly suspicious of him; at the Netherfield ball, she tells him he is of 'unsocial taciturn disposition.' Again, Darcy provides little evidence to the contrary. We are supposed to agree with Elizabeth, yet we are also meant to understand that, for all her perceptiveness, she is capable of misjudgment. Her youth (she is only twenty) means that she can be naïve. It takes time for her to become aware of the moral strength that resides behind Darcy's somewhat forbidding exterior. Equally, it takes time for Darcy to become sensitive to Elizabeth's true qualities. Initially he thinks she tends 'wilfully to misunderstand' people.

What Elizabeth and Darcy do not realise at first is that they share both a logical cast of mind and a tendency to find fault with other people's moral standards. Elizabeth, we learn, has a disposition 'which delighted in anything ridiculous.' For his part Darcy is considered to have 'a very satirical eye.' This symmetry goes unrecognised because it is not immediately obvious, and this is important: the novel ridicules the notion of love at first sight, and Austen shows that satisfying relationships can develop only gradually. Darcy may be 'bewitched' by Elizabeth, but the magic is necessarily slow.

In part this is because Elizabeth is so disarmingly natural. Caroline Bingley says to Darcy that Elizabeth 'is one of those young ladies who seek to recommend themselves to the other sex by undervaluing their own.' She continues: 'and with many men, I dare say, it succeeds. But, in my opinion, it is a paltry device, a very mean art.' In fact it is Caroline who undervalues Elizabeth, and Darcy sees this. In Caroline's eyes, Elizabeth's conduct is at odds with received notions of femininity. For instance, she plays the piano in a pleasantly unaffected way, which is contrasted with her sister Mary's mannered technique. Elizabeth's style may be more agreeable, but it is not the norm.

One of the most important episodes in defining our response to Elizabeth occurs when the loathsome Mr Collins proposes to her. Mr Collins is a thoroughly unsuitable match. It is easy to lose track of the fact that he is twenty-five; he seems twice as old. Elizabeth sensibly rejects him. Mr Collins assumes the rejection is an act of coquetry of the sort common among 'elegant females.' He cannot countenance the possibility that she might not want to marry him. After all, as he explains, she has little money and 'it is by no means certain that another offer of marriage may ever be made.' Yet she is brave enough to rebuff him – and to explain her decision to do so. She refutes his charge that she is trying to behave in a fashionably dismissive way: 'Do not consider me now as an elegant female intending to plague you, but as a rational creature speaking the truth from her heart.' Elizabeth's description of herself as 'rational' is telling. The word, to Austen's contemporary audience, would have called to mind the philosophical arguments of David Hume, who stressed the relationship between reason and intuition. Equally, it would have seemed a vigorous assertion, on Elizabeth's part, of her rights and capabilities as a woman. Mr Collins seeks to belittle these, but his own lack of rational powers is suggested by his decision – just one day later – to propose to Charlotte Lucas. As we know, Charlotte, whom Elizabeth deems to have 'sacrificed every better feeling to worldly advantage,' accepts.

The irony of this is that it is Elizabeth who in the end secures the greater worldly advantage, marrying a man whose annual income is £10,000. However, she imagines her marriage in spiritual and intellectual terms; she anticipates benefiting from Darcy's 'knowledge of the world' and powers of judgement, and expects in turn to 'soften' his mind. Her marriage is pronounced the 'happiest, wisest, most reasonable end.' As before, the word 'reasonable' is key, implying not only good judgement, but also emancipation.

For all this, the conduct of Austen's characters can to a modern audience seem maddeningly coy. Yet the rituals of courtship are – in structure, if not in substance – broadly similar to those of today. Display is crucial. This is why public gatherings, like the ball at Netherfield, are so important; they are opportunities to perform. 'Performance' is a keyword in Austen's works; her characters have an animal desire to outdo each other. Card games and after-noon walks give them a chance to inspect each other at close quarters; nuances of behaviour, dress and conversation are scrutinized as if they are sexual characteristics – which indeed they almost are. Darcy accounts for his initial difficulties with Elizabeth when he reflects that 'We neither of us perform to strangers.' The performances expected of characters are not liberating acts of self-expression, but empty charades of a kind neither Elizabeth nor Darcy can quite tolerate.

In the light of all this public display, it is significant that a vast amount of letter-writing takes place in *Pride and Prejudice*. More than forty letters are quoted or referred to in the course of the novel. The significance of letters is that they allow what public communication does not – a full account of their authors' feelings, carefully composed rather than hastily blurted out. Darcy's famous letter in Chapter 35 is the best example of this; he exposes his emotions as he would never risk doing in public. Yet Elizabeth cannot respond: to do so would be to imply they were engaged.

The emphasis on letter-writing, along with the

protocols surrounding it, increases the novel's claustrophobic atmosphere. Austen was the first to acknowledge the narrowness of her fictional world. 'Three or four families in a country village is the very thing to work on,' she wrote to her niece, while in a letter to her brother Edward she likened her art to painting with a fine brush on a 'little bit (two inches wide) of ivory.' It is worth remembering that the period in which *Pride and Prejudice* is set witnessed the rise of Napoleon Bonaparte; this was a time of political upheaval right across Europe. Austen is not oblivious to this; there are tremors of war, and her male characters are preoccupied with military matters. But in choosing not to write at length about contemporary events, she was rebelling against the norms of her genre. One of the reasons for the enduring popularity of her work is that it contains very little that is overtly political. We know, for instance, that she read Mary Wollstonecraft's *Vindication of the Rights of Woman* (1792), but the polemical mood of Wollstonecraft's manifesto could not be farther from the mood of Austen's works. There are feminist and revolutionary notes in Austen's writing, but they are discreet: her first duty is always to her story.

Jane Austen's skills are easily underestimated. 'Of all great writers,' claimed Virginia Woolf, 'she is the most difficult to catch in the act of greatness.' She is not, it is true, a flashily brilliant artist – it seems bizarre that she should ever have been likened to Mozart. However, her knowledge of human nature is remarkable, and her awareness of the importance of class, money and appearances makes her a peculiarly modern author. Perhaps the most striking thing about *Pride and Prejudice* is that, despite being almost two hundred years old, it addresses the politics of dating, courtship and mating with an incisive intelligence that both fore-shadows and outstrips those narratives of romance that might be considered its modern counterparts: *Bridget Jones*, *The Girls' Guide to Hunting and Fishing*, and *Sex and the City*.

Further Reading

Chapman, Robert W, *Letters of Jane Austen* (Oxford University Press, 1969)

Bradbrook, Frank W, *Jane Austen and her Predecessors* (Cambridge University Press, 1966)

Johnson, Claudia L, *Jane Austen: Women, Politics, and the Novel* (University of Chicago Press, 1988)

Biography

Jane Austen was born in 1775 in rural Hampshire, the daughter of an affluent village rector who encouraged her in her artistic pursuits. Jane remained in the vicinity of her childhood home for much of her life. As such it was through family and friends that she learned most of her considerable understanding of manners and relationships. In novels such as *Pride and Prejudice*, *Mansfield Park* and *Emma* she developed her subtle analysis of contemporary life through depictions of the middle-classes in small towns. Her sharp wit and incisive portraits of ordinary people have given her novels enduring popularity. She died in 1817.

The New York Coffee Guide.

2018

Edited by
Jeffrey Young

Author: Allegra Strategies
Reviewers: Richard Ehrlich, Jeremy Hersh
and Marisa Kanter
Project Co-ordinator: Samantha Hughes
Researcher: Sabrina Jen
Photography: Dan Carter, Jael Marschner,
Sam & Melissa Ortiz and provided by venues
Design: John Osborne
Cover illustration: John Osborne, inspired by a
photograph by Jael Marschner
Website: Tim Spring
Publisher: Allegra Publications Ltd

Allegra
PUBLICATIONS

Visit our website:
www.newyorkcoffeeguide.com

🐦 **@NYCoffeeGuide**

f **NYCoffeeGuide**

📷 **newyorkcoffeeguide**

All information was accurate at time of going to press.

Published by *Allegra* PUBLICATIONS Ltd © 2017

Walkden House, 10 Melton Street, London, NW1 2EB, UK

Foreword

by **Howard Schultz**, Executive Chairman, Starbucks Coffee Company

I have always celebrated my New York City origins.

I was born in Brooklyn, in the housing projects of Canarsie. As a kid I played ball on concrete playgrounds, cheered for the Yankees and at 16 worked at a factory in Manhattan's garment district.

The New York City I grew up in was not sophisticated - and neither was its coffee. Then, coffee was freeze-dried, dispensed from vending machines, or a tasteless staple at all-night diners. It was a drink consumed more for its caffeine than savored for its flavors. Habit, not ritual.

Ever since I left the city to attend college, I have returned often. Perhaps my most memorable visit was in 1994, when Starbucks first opened in New York City at 87th Street and Broadway on the Upper West Side. The morning the store opened, a line of curious customers snaked around the block; not many people then had tasted espresso drinks. Coffee as craft was just emerging in America.

More than 20 years later, I still marvel at how this city, coffee, and coffee culture continue to transform. Where West Coast cities once led coffee innovation, the New York City of today has established its own artisanal voice. Aging techniques, flavor infusions, cold coffee combinations and handcrafting have turned neighborhoods throughout the five boroughs into vibrant coffee destinations.

On these streets, New Yorkers and visitors enjoy an eclectic yet accessible variety of coffee experiences. Taste profiles range from simple to complex, and beans are sourced from all over the world, many roasted locally, some right before your eyes.

Most exciting, New Yorkers are more engaged than ever in the beverage's story from farm to cup. They know the origin of their favorite coffees and they know the names of their favorite baristas - in part because the baristas of today are expert, artist, host and friend. Whether working for an independent proprietor or a large purveyor, the men and women who bring coffee to life for their customers are the soul of the city they serve.

For me, New York City will always be a place that honors its past while embracing the present. Coffee's story is no different - a beverage rich with history and always ripe for innovation. I am so proud to be part of coffee's journey, especially as it continues to unfold in what truly is one of the greatest cities in the world.

Contents

Coffee passport   Inside front cover
Foreword   iii
Introduction   v
About the guide   vi
A brief history of New York coffee shops   viii

Venue profiles:
Manhattan map   1
Lower Manhattan   4
East Village & Lower East Side   18
Soho & Neighboring   44
West Village & Neighboring   64
Chelsea   80
Midtown & Gramercy   92
Upper Manhattan   122
Park Slope & Surrounding   142
Downtown Brooklyn   162
Bushwick & Surrounding   172
Williamsburg map   181
Williamsburg   182
Greenpoint & Queens   196

Coffee Knowledge   **218**
Coffee at origin   219
Small batch roasting   221
Coffee grinding   223
Water – The Enigma   225
Brewing coffee at home   227
Latte art   231
What does 'local' coffee mean?   233
Espresso   235
Coffee History in New York City   237
Coffee glossary   241

A-Z list of coffee venues   246
The New York coffee map   Fold-out at back

Introduction

Welcome to The New York Coffee Guide 2018 – the definitive guide to New York's best craft coffee venues.

The New York Coffee Guide was born in 2012 out of a quest to discover the best coffee venues in New York. This great city has a long, rich coffee house tradition and is now home to a thriving craft coffee scene. The past year has seen a multitude of wonderful coffee venues emerging across the city, providing the good people of New York with a cornucopia of coffee destinations. The 2018 edition features 195 of the very best venues.

The New York Coffee Guide has been written to lead coffee lovers around the city on the hunt for a great coffee experience. The main attraction might be the coffee itself or, perhaps, the excitement of visiting a new and unique coffee shop. Overall, our aim is to encourage fellow coffee lovers to try something different and discover places they otherwise may never have known existed.

In this edition, we have expanded the venue content, added 51 new venues, and included a New & Noteworthy feature for venues that are new to this edition of the guide and which we feel merit a special mention. We would like to thank all who have contributed.

Allegra Strategies is an established leader in research and business intelligence for the coffee industry. We have drawn on this research as well as a variety of other sources to compile The New York Coffee Guide. We hope you enjoy it.

City of Saints

About the Guide

Ratings

Every venue featured in The New York Coffee Guide 2018 has been visited and rated by our expert team. The ratings fall into two distinct categories: Coffee Rating and Overall Rating on a score of 1-5, with 5 being the highest possible score. Customer feedback received via The New York Coffee Guide website and app also informs the venue shortlist and the final scores.

Coffee Rating

The Coffee Rating is about much more than just taste in the cup. An excellent coffee experience depends on a host of factors including: barista skills, coffee supplier, equipment, consistency, working processes and coffee presentation. The venue's coffee philosophy and commitment to excellence are also taken into consideration.

Overall Rating

In combination with the Coffee Rating, the Overall Rating reflects the total coffee shop experience for the customer. Factors taken into account include: service, café ambience, venue scale and impact, design and food quality. Feedback from the industry is also taken into consideration.

Key to symbols

Roaster		Disabled access	
Alternative brew methods available		Credit cards accepted	
Decaffeinated coffee available		WiFi available	
Coffee beans sold on site		Alcohol served	
Gluten-free products available		Coffee courses available	
Venue has a loyalty card		Outdoor seating	
Milk alternatives available		Brunch available at weekends	
Restrooms		Cold brew available	
Parent & baby friendly		Computer friendly	

Venues marked as are new to this edition of the Guide.

Venues marked as are venues added to this edition of the guide that we feel are worthy of special mention.

A Brief History of New York Coffee Shops

THE EARLY YEARS

800 AD The coffee plant (Coffea) attracts human interest and consumption as early as 800 AD in the Kaffe region of Ethiopia. According to legend, it was an Ethiopian goat herder named Kaldi who first discovered how animated his herd of goats became after chewing on the red berries.

13TH - 16TH CENTURIES

Coffee berries are brought to the Arabian Peninsula and the first known cultivation of coffee is established in the area known today as Yemen. A crude version of coffee - roasted beans crushed and boiled in water - is developed and by 1475 coffee houses are established in Constantinople, Cairo and throughout Persia.

17TH AND 18TH CENTURIES

Travelers to the Arabian Peninsula bring coffee to Europe and Britain. Coffee houses are established as centers for the exchange of ideas and information, as well as forums for debate.

1650 The first English coffee house is established in Oxford by a Jewish gentleman named Jacob at the Angel in the parish of St Peter.

1668 Coffee is brought to New Amsterdam (Old New York) by Dutch settlers.

1696 Built in the style of the coffee houses of Europe, The King's Arms is the first coffee house established in New York.

1732 The Exchange Coffee House is opened on Broadway and establishes itself as a center for commerce.

1750 The Exchange Coffee House loses favor and is replaced by The Merchants Coffee House (on what is now known as Wall Street), which grows to be the foremost gathering place in the city for trade and political debate.

1765 A warning to the citizens of New York to end their rioting against the Stamp Act is read at The Merchants Coffee House.

1773 The Boston Tea Party, a revolt against the high taxation levied by King George III on tea imported to the New World, sees coffee replace tea as the drink of choice in the colonies.

1784 The Bank of New York, the oldest bank in the country, is founded at The Merchants Coffee House.

1792 The New York Stock Exchange is established at the Tontine Coffee House on Wall Street, where the first public stocks are sold.

19TH AND 20TH CENTURIES

With the rise of industrialization and technological advances, coffee drinking becomes accessible to everyone, not just the elite. People begin drinking it more in their homes and the demand for the beans rises, leading to rapid growth in coffee production.

1840 The Gillies Coffee Company is founded in New York, a company that survives as the oldest coffee merchant in the city.

1850 Folgers Coffee is founded in San Francisco.

1864 The first commercial coffee roasting machine, New York's Jabez Burns' #1 Coffee Roaster, receives a US patent.

1882 The Coffee Exchange of New York begins regulating the coffee trade, setting standards for the traffic of the commodity as well as the quality of the product.

1892 Maxwell House Coffee is founded.

1907 Porto Rico Importing Company opens on Bleecker Street.

1911 The National Coffee Association of the USA is established, the first trade association for the US coffee industry.

1920s As Prohibition takes effect, national coffee sales flourish.

1923 Green Coffee Association of New York founded.

1927 Caffe Reggio opens in Greenwich Village with the first espresso machine in New York.

1946 Coffee consumption in the US hits an all-time high, reaching 19.8 pounds per person per annum, twice what it was in 1900.

1950s / 1960s After WWII, the importation of coffee is impeded. The Pan American Coffee Bureau is established to promote the drinking of coffee and assist its production in Central America. One such promotion is the popularization of the "coffee break".

Italian-style cafés serving espresso and pastries begin to pop up in Greenwich Village and Little Italy. These coffee shops become creative and intellectual centers for artists, writers, musicians, and intellectuals.

1953 Howard Schultz is born in Brooklyn.

1971 Starbucks opens its first store at Pike Place Market in Seattle, Washington.

1982 The Specialty Coffee Association of America (SCAA) is founded.

Late 1980s

After an inspiring visit to Italy, Howard Schultz buys Starbucks and revamps the brand.

1994 Manhattan's first Starbucks store opens on the Upper West Side at 86th Street and Broadway.

1995 Intelligentsia Coffee & Tea opens in Chicago and grows to become one of the major names in the American coffee industry.

1999 Stumptown Coffee Roasters opens in Portland, Oregon.

The Cup of Excellence is established.

LAST DECADE

The 2000s see specialty coffee and the third-wave coffee movement emerge in the US, starting in Portland and Seattle and spreading to California, New York and beyond. This movement focuses on ethical trading, coffee freshness and new roasting techniques.

2000 The first World Barista Championship takes place in Monte Carlo.

2001 Ninth Street Espresso opens in Alphabet City.

2003 Gorilla Coffee opens in Park Slope, Brooklyn.

The first Joe location opened.

2005 Café Grumpy established.

2007 La Colombe Torrefaction opens its first New York outpost in Tribeca.

2009 Stumptown Coffee opens its first New York location at The Ace Hotel in Brooklyn.

2010 The Blue Bottle Coffee Company opens its roastery in a converted warehouse in Williamsburg, Brooklyn.

American Michael Phillips wins the World Barista Championship.

2012 The US Barista champion is Katie Carguilo.

Australian-owned Toby's Estate opens in Williamsburg, Brooklyn.

The New York Coffee Guide first published.

2013 The US Barista Champion is Pete Licata.

Key openings in the New York coffee scene include Devoción, Rex and Stumptown on West 8th Street.

2014 The US Barista Champion is Laila Ghambari.

Starbucks opens it first reserve store in Williamsburg. Bluestone Lane on Greenwich Avenue and FIKA Tower & Bakery are other notable openings.

2015 New York Coffee Festival launched.

The US Barista Champion is Charles Babinski.

Bluestone Lane on East 90th Street open their first store inside a church.

2016 The US Barista Champion is Lemuel Butler.

Taylor St. Baristas open their first New York store after their huge success in London.

New York Coffee Guide publishes its second edition.

2017 The US Barista Champion is Kyle Ramage.

New York Coffee Festival returns for its third year.

Variety open their first Manhattan outpost in Chelsea.

Extraction Lab by Alpha Dominche launched in Industry City.

COFFEE VENUES KEY

Lower Manhattan

1 Black Fox Coffee Co. p5 ◊
2 Bluestone Lane (Financial District) p6 *
3 Café Grumpy (Financial District) p6 *
4 Gotan p7
5 Irving Farm Coffee Roasters (Lower Manhattan) p8
6 Joe Coffee (World Trade Center) p9 *
7 Kaffe 1668 p10
8 La Colombe (Financial District) p11
9 Laughing Man p12
10 Nobletree p13 * ◊
11 R & R Coffee p15
12 Two Hands (Tribeca) p15
13 Voyager Espresso p16 ◊
14 The Wooly Daily p16 *

East Village & Lower East Side

15 Abraço p19 ◊
16 Blue Bottle (Clinton Street) p20 * ◊
17 Bluestone Lane (Astor Place) p21 *
18 Café Grumpy (Lower East Side) p23
19 Café Henrie p23
20 Caffe Vita (Lower East Side) p24
21 City of Saints (East Village) p24 ◊
22 El Rey p25
23 Everyman Espresso (East Village) p26 ◊
24 Gasoline Alley Coffee (Noho) p27 ◊
25 Hi-Collar p28
26 La Colombe Torrefaction p29 ◊
27 The Lazy Llama p30
28 Little Canal p31 *
29 Ludlow Coffee Supply p33
30 Ninth Street Espresso (East Village) p33 ◊
31 Ost Cafe p34
32 River Coyote p35 *
33 The Roost p36
34 Round K p37 *
35 Spreadhouse p38
36 Three Seat Espresso & Barber p39 *
37 Whynot p41

Soho & Neighboring

38 Birch Coffee (Soho) p45 * ◊
39 Café Grumpy (Nolita) p47 *
40 Café Integral p48
41 Chalait (Hudson Square) p49 *
42 Gasoline Alley Coffee (Nolita) p49
43 Gimme! Coffee (Nolita) p50
44 Greecologies p51
45 Ground Support Cafe p52
46 Happy Bones p53 ◊
47 Housing Works Bookstore Cafe p54
48 Joe & The Juice (Soho) p55
49 McNally Jackson Café p55
50 Ruby's Café (Soho) p56 *
51 Saturdays Surf NYC p57
52 Seven Grams Caffé (Soho) p58 *
53 TOMS Roasting Co. p59 *
54 Two Hands (Soho) p61 ◊

West Village & Neighboring

55 Banter p65 * ◊
56 Bluestone Lane (Greenwich Village) p67
57 Bluestone Lane (West Village) p68
58 Fair Folks & a Goat p68
59 Jack's Stir Brew Coffee p69
60 Kava Cafe p69
61 Kobrick Coffee Co. p70
62 Merriweather p71 * ◊
63 Oren's Daily Roast (Greenwich Village) p73 *
64 Porto Rico Importing Company p73
65 Prodigy Coffee p74
66 Rebel Coffee p74 *
67 Stumptown (Greenwich Village) p75 ◊
68 Third Rail Coffee p76 ◊
69 Toby's Estate (West Village) p77

Chelsea

70 Blue Bottle (Chelsea) p81
71 The Commons Chelsea p82
72 Intelligentsia Coffee p83
73 Joe Coffee Pro Shop + HQ p84
74 La Colombe (Chelsea) p84 * ◊
75 MatchaBar (Chelsea) p85
76 Seven Grams Caffé (Chelsea) p86 ◊
77 Think Coffee (Chelsea) p87
78 Underline Coffee p88
79 Variety Coffee Roasters (Chelsea) p89 * ◊

Midtown & Gramercy

80 Birch Coffee (Flatiron District) p93
81 Brooklyn Roasting Company (Flatiron District) p94
82 Café Grumpy (Grand Central Terminal) p94
83 Chalait (Nomad) p95
84 Culture 36 p96
85 Culture Espresso p96 ◊
86 Dr Smood p97 *
87 FIKA Tower & Bakery p99
88 Frisson Espresso p100
89 Gasoline Alley (Flatiron District) p101 *
90 Gregorys Coffee (Gramercy) p102 *
91 Ground Central Coffee Co. (2nd Avenue) p102
92 Ground Central Coffee Co. (52nd Street) p103
93 Hole in the Wall p104
94 Irving Farm Coffee Roasters (Gramercy) p105
95 Irving Farm Coffee Roasters (Midtown East) p106
96 Joe & The Juice (Midtown East) p106 *
97 Kahve p107
98 Le Café Coffee p108
99 Little Collins p109 *
100 Ninth Street Espresso (Midtown East) p110
101 Oren's Daily Roast (Midtown West) p110
102 Perk Kafé p111
103 Pushcart Coffee p112
104 Ramini Espresso Bar and Café p113
105 REX p114
106 Ruby's Café (Murray Hill) p115 *
107 Simon Sips p115
108 Stumptown (Ace Hotel) p116 ◊
109 Taylor St. Baristas p117 ◊
110 Think Coffee (Gramercy) p118 *
111 Trademark p118
112 Zibetto Espresso Bar p119

* NEW
◊ TOP 40

Lower Manhattan is a diverse and exciting area with a variety of identities. The business-savvy Financial District has the hustle and bustle of Wall Street at its heart, while trendy Tribeca is a hip, fashionable neighborhood that overlooks the Hudson River. By night, the Meatpacking District is immensely fashionable, with great shopping, chic restaurants and popular bars and clubs. Most importantly it is home to The World Trade Center.

Lower Manhattan

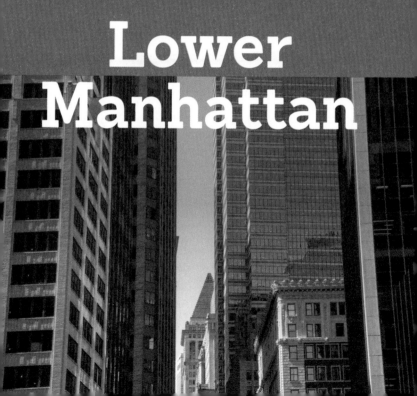

Black Fox Coffee Co.

70 Pine Street, Manhattan, NY 10005 | **Financial District**

Black Fox is a beautiful downtown venue, located just around the corner from the South Street Seaport. The space is large and open, designed purposely to emphasize service and make everyone feel at one with the space. Manager Kris Wood makes it clear that he does not want to dictate taste, instead offering a small selection of high quality roasters to provide an element of choice. The menu is Australian inspired, with fresh ingredients prepared by a chef straight from Melbourne. Be sure to try the Australian take on the PB&J, you won't regret it.

www.blackfoxcoffee.com
Subway 2, 3 (Wall St)

MON–FRI.	6:30am – 5:30pm
SAT.	8:00am – 3:00pm
SUN.	Fall – Spring: 8:00am – 3:00pm (closed during Summer)

First opened 2016
Roaster Heart Coffee, Small Batch, 49th Parallel, Ritual
Machine Kees Van Der Westen Spirit, 3 groups
Grinder Nuova Simonelli Mythos Clima Pro x2, Mahlkönig EK 43

Espresso	$3.50
Cappuccino	$4.50
Latte	$5.00

MAP REF. ❶

COFFEE 4.50 / 5

OVERALL 4.50 / 5 ★★★★⯪

Bluestone Lane Financial District

90 Water Street, Manhattan, NY 10005 | **Financial District**

Situated blocks away from South Street Seaport, Bluestone Lane's downtown venue might just be its cutest spot yet. It is not the largest of locations. However, what it lacks in square footage, it certainly makes up for in beauty - exposed brick and quartz counter tops add a premium touch to this venue. Bluestone Lane beans always hit the spot, and the full brunch menu is offered. Seating is limited, but it is also a perfect place to drop in for a flat white on your way to work.

(212) 747-9082
www.bluestonelaneny.com
Subway 2, 3 (Wall St)

Sister locations Multiple locations

MON-SUN.	7:00am - 6:00pm

First opened 2016
Roaster Bluestone Lane Coffee
Machine La Marzocco Linea PB3
Grinder Mazzer Robur

Espresso	$3.00
Cappuccino	$4.00
Latte	$4.00

MAP REF. **2**

COFFEE 4.50 / 5	OVERALL 4.50 / 5 ★★★★½

Café Grumpy Financial District

20 Stone Street, Manhattan, NY 10004 | **Financial District**

Upon entering this Café Grumpy location, the visual experience is stunning. With beautiful artwork that adorns every wall, this café is reminiscent of a museum. As always, do not let the venue's name fool you, Café Grumpy baristas are among the most friendly and attentive in the city. As for the coffee, the Synesso pulls excellent shots from their specialty beans. Newly inserting itself in the ever-busy financial district, Café Grumpy is the perfect spot to take a break, slow down, and relax in the midst of your chaotic work day.

(646) 838-9306
www.cafegrumpy.com
Subway 4, 5 (Bowling Green)

Sister locations Multiple locations

MON-FRI.	6:00am - 8:00pm
SAT-SUN.	8:00am - 6:00pm

First opened 2017
Roaster Café Grumpy
Machine Synesso Hydra MVP, 3 groups
Grinder Nuova Simonelli Mythos,
Mahlkönig Guatemala

Espresso	$3.25
Cappuccino	$4.00
Latte	$4.50

MAP REF. **3**

COFFEE 4.50 / 5	OVERALL 4.50 / 5 ★★★★½

Gotan

130 Franklin Street, Manhattan, NY 10013 | **Tribeca**

A spacious café full of blonde wood and huge windows letting in light, Gotan is a favorite among the well-dressed residents of Tribeca, and those who work in the area (If you need a primer on Tribeca, four words: Taylor Swift lives here). The uniformed and bow-tied baristas are serious about their coffee, made on the fairly unique and handsome ModBar espresso machine, built right into the bar. Drop in for an expertly made latte, it is worth the trip.

(212) 431-5200
www.gotannyc.com
Subway 1, 2 (Franklin St)

Sister locations Midtown / Williamsburg

MON-FRI.   7:00am - 5:00pm
SAT-SUN.   9:00am - 5:00pm

First opened 2014
Roaster Counter Culture Coffee
Machine ModBar
Grinder Mazzer Luigi

Espresso $3.50
Cappuccino $4.25
Latte $4.75

MAP REF. **4**

COFFEE 4.25 / 5

OVERALL 4.25 / 5   ★ ★ ★ ★ ⯪

Irving Farm Coffee Roasters

Lower Manhattan Fulton Center, Manhattan, NY 10038 | Financial District

While most of Irving Farm's early venues are very much 'Old New York', this location is all about new, new, new. Plunked down in the heart of the Fulton Center transit hub, it is inevitably a place where commuters abound. But it's also a good place to sit and watch the world go by, and to marvel at the shifting patterns of light cast down by the "sky-reflector net" in the building's skylight. Irving's coffee is outstanding, whether pour-over or espresso-based, and the latte art is a thing of true beauty.

(646) 918-7761
www.irvingfarm.com
Subway 4, 5, A, C, J, Z (Fulton St)

Sister locations Multiple locations

MON–FRI.	7:00am – 7:00pm
SAT–SUN.	8:00am – 6:00pm

First opened 2016
Roaster Irving Farm Coffee Roasters
Machine La Marzocco Linea PB, 3 groups
Grinder Nuova Simonelli Mythos Clima Pro

Espresso	$3.25
Cappuccino	$4.25
Latte	$4.75

MAP REF. **5**

Joe Coffee World Trade Center

185 Greenwich Street, Manhattan, NY 10007 | **Financial District**

On a first visit to the newest branch of Joe, in the Westfield World Trade Center (also known as the Oculus), you may find yourself getting lost and asking for directions. Stick with it: this is a calm haven of good coffee in a shopping/transportation hub that's pretty much always packed. The look is bright and slightly space-age modern, and if you're not rushing off for work or taking a PATH train home, the seating is comfortable. Milky drinks are well presented, but drip brews (including decaf) are an equally big draw. As for the service, it couldn't be more friendly or efficient. Great job Joe!

(212) 924-7400
www.joenewyork.com
Subway N, R, W (Cortlandt St) or
E (Chambers St)

Sister locations Multiple locations

| MON-FRI. | 6:00am – 9:00pm |
| SAT-SUN. | 8:00am – 8:00pm |

First opened 2017
Roaster Joe Coffee Roasters
Machine La Marzocco Linea PB, 3 groups,
La Marzocco Linea PB, 2 groups
Grinder Nuova Simonelli Mythos One,
Mahlkönig EK 43

Espresso	$3.30
Cappuccino	$4.40
Latte	$4.40

MAP REF. **6**

| COFFEE 4.25 / 5 | OVERALL 4.25 / 5 ★★★★⯪ |

Kaffe 1668

401 Greenwich Street, Manhattan, NY 10013 | **Tribeca**

After a leisurely walk in Hudson River Park, there are few better places to relax and refuel than Kaffe 1668 - as long as you can find a seat. At lunchtime especially, this place is crazy-busy. The big, low-lit room is a pleasure to be in, with zany décor dominated by dozens of cute little fluffy sheep. But it isn't the sheep that get people flocking here. The coffee is made to exacting standards even when crowds are huge, and sandwiches, salads and fresh-squeezed juices provide non-caffeinated sustenance of superior quality.

(646) 559-2637
www.kaffe1668.com
Subway A, C, E (Canal St)

Sister locations Lower Manhattan / Midtown

MON-FRI.	6:30am - 8:00pm
SAT-SUN.	7:00am - 7:00pm

First opened 2012
Roaster Landskap Coffee
Machine Synesso, 3 groups
Grinder Mahlkönig EK 43, Mazzer Luigi Robur E

Espresso	$3.25
Cappuccino	$4.50
Latte	$4.75

MAP REF.

COFFEE 4.25 / 5	OVERALL 4.25 / 5
🫘🫘🫘🫘🫘	★★★★★

La Colombe Financial District

67 Wall Street, Manhattan, NY 10005 | **Financial District**

Photo: La Colombe

La Colombe's Wall Street location is a small place that does a lot of takeout business, which increases your chance of finding a free table. And it's a temptation that's easy to give in to; this attractive place, dominated by pale wood, provides a quiet haven on the Financial District's main drag. Latte art is exceptional, as at their other locations, and they serve both cold brew and latte "on tap." A combination of the two, called Black and Tan, is a wonderfully zingy and invigorating drink.

(212) 220-0415
www.lacolombe.com
Subway 2, 3 (Wall St)

Sister locations Multiple locations

| MON-FRI. | 6:00am - 6:30pm |
| SAT-SUN. | 7:00am - 6.30pm |

First opened 2015
Roaster La Colombe Coffee Roasters
Machine La Marzocco GB5, 3 groups
Grinder Nuova Simonelli Mythos

Espresso	$2.50
Cappuccino	$4.00
Latte	$4.00

MAP REF. **8**

| COFFEE 4.50 / 5 | OVERALL 4.25 / 5 |

11

Laughing Man

184 Duane Street, Manhattan, NY 10014 | **Tribeca**

This tiny Tribeca café serves up an excellent cup of coffee for a great cause. Inspired by a trip to Ethiopia, Hugh Jackman opened The Laughing Man Café in order to provide a market for coffee farmers in developing countries. The café is quite crowded during peak hours, but it serves only as a testament to the quality of their roasts, and the wait is always worth it. The best part - one hundred percent of Hugh Jackman's proceeds are donated to the Laughing Man Foundation, supporting social entrepreneurs around the world.

(212) 680-1111
www.laughingmanfoundation.org/cafe
Subway 1, 2, 3 (Chambers St)

MON–FRI.	6:30am – 7:00pm
SAT–SUN.	7:00am – 7:00pm

First opened 2009
Roaster Laughing Man Coffee
Machine Nuova Simonelli, 2 groups
Grinder Nuova Simonelli Mythos

Espresso	$2.75
Cappuccino	$3.65
Latte	$4.10

MAP REF. ❾

Nobletree World Trade Center

185 Greenwich Street, Manhattan, NY 10006 | **Financial District**

Known for beans grown on their award-winning farms in Brazil, Nobletree Coffee opened their first retail shop in Manhattan in May 2017. Located in the heart of the Financial District at the 4 World Trade Center building, the shop is designed for orders to-go. Nobletree is unique in that it is a roastery first, with beans being roasted fresh in the café, right in front of customers. Coffee offerings appear on a rotating menu of single-origins, along with coffee from Nobletree's farms, of course. Whether you are in the mood for a refreshing cold brew or a skillfully pulled espresso, you can never go wrong with a delicious Nobletree brew. What this location lacks in size it more than makes up for in style and coffee quality. Be sure to try one of their specialty pour overs!

MAP REF.

13

COFFEE
4.50 / 5

OVERALL
4.25 / 5

★ ★ ★ ★ ⯪

MON–FRI.	7:00am – 9:00pm
SAT.	9:00am – 9:00pm
SUN.	9:00am – 7:00pm

Sister locations Red Hook

First opened 2017
Roaster Nobletree
Machine ModBar
Grinder Mahlkönig Peak

Espresso	$3.00
Cappuccino	$4.00
Latte	$4.50

(718) 643-6080
Subway E (Chambers St) or N, R, W
(Cortlandt St)

R & R Coffee

76 Fulton Street, Manhattan, NY 10038 | **Financial District**

Wall Street is on its doorstep, but in spirit and atmosphere R&R is more akin to the Fulton Street Market, also just a step away. Far from being a slick, money-talks kind of Financial District operation, this is a laid-back neighborhood place - more Main Street than Wall Street. Coffee comes from a changing selection of roasters, such as Brooklyn Roasting Company and Parlor Coffee Roasters. It's crafted with care and includes stunning latte art. There's also an extensive list of cold drinks. Bought-in baked goods are rich enough to make love handles at first sight.

(646) 449-8908
Subway 2, 3 (Fulton St)

| **MON-FRI.** | 7:00am – 7:00pm |
| **SAT-SUN.** | 8:00am – 7:00pm |

First opened 2013
Roaster Multiple roasters
Machine La Marzocco, 3 groups
Grinder Mahlkönig EK 43,
Mazzer Luigi Super Jolly

Espresso	$2.75
Cappuccino	$3.90
Latte	$3.90

MAP REF. **11**

COFFEE 4.25 / 5   **OVERALL** 4.00 / 5 ★★★★☆

Two Hands Tribeca

251 Church Street, Manhattan, NY 10013 | **Tribeca**

Two Hands deserves a loud clap for looks, variety, and vibe. This big Tribeca room looks great and hums with activity from a crowd that seems mostly locals rather than workers. The owners are Australian, and the menu does the whole Oz thing - make it healthy, but make it look and taste great - very well. Grab a table if you're eating. But if you just crave a well-made coffee and some quality time with your smartphone, settle in at the bar in the back of the room.

www.twohandsnyc.com
Subway A, C, E (Canal St)

Sister locations Soho

| **MON-SUN.** | 8:00am – 10:00pm |

First opened 2016
Roaster Café Integral
Machine La Marzocco Strada, 2 groups
Grinder Compak F8

Espresso	$3.50
Cappuccino	$4.00
Latte	$5.00

MAP REF. **12**

COFFEE 4.25 / 5   **OVERALL** 4.25 / 5 ★★★★☆

Voyager Espresso

110 William Street, Manhattan, NY 10038 | **Financial District**

Ignore the address: the easiest way to find Voyager is through the John Street subway exit. However you get here, it's well worth the voyage. This unlikely location houses one of the most distinctively elegant-looking coffee spots in town - the silver-painted chipboard is particularly unique. More importantly, it houses seriously terrific espresso drinks. They use beans from an assortment of roasters, including Portland stars Heart and Roseline, and get fabulous results through expert handling. If you love coffee (and talking about coffee with friendly baristas), Voyager is a genius subterranean heaven.

(646) 885-6792
www.voyagerespresso.com
Subway 2, 3 (Fulton St)

MON-FRI.	7:30am - 5:00pm
SAT-SUN.	Closed

First opened 2015
Roaster La Cabra Coffee Roasters
Machine Synesso Hydra, 3 groups
Grinder Mahlkönig K30, Mahlkönig EK 43

Espresso	$3.50
Cappuccino	$4.25
Latte	$4.75

MAP REF. **13**

COFFEE 4.50 / 5		OVERALL 4.50 / 5	★★★★✦

The Wooly Daily

NEW

11 Barclay Street, Manhattan, NY 10007 | **Financial District**

If you weren't smiling before you walked into The Wooly Daily, you certainly will be inside. This place is a hoot to look at, with more decorative features in its box-size space than you'd have thought possible. The food offering is not large, just a few sandwiches and some serious in-house-baked sweetness, but the coffee offering - beans from Sightglass in San Francisco - is excellent. Like the whole operation, it will make you smile - well, it should make you smile. If you're wondering about the name, look up: the café is on the ground floor of the Woolworth Building, formerly the tallest building in the world.

(646) 807-9665
www.thewoolydaily.com
Subway 2, 3 (Park Pl)

MON-THU.	7:30am - 6:30pm
FRI.	7:30am - 6:00pm
SAT.	8:30am - 3:00pm
SUN.	Closed

First opened 2015
Roaster Sight Glass
Machine La Marzocco Linea, 2 groups
Grinder Mazzer Luigi Super Jolly, Mazzer Luigi Major E

Espresso	$3.00
Cappuccino	$4.00
Latte	$4.50

MAP REF. **14**

COFFEE 4.25 / 5	OVERALL 4.25 / 5	★★★★✦

Lower Manhattan

TOP 40

16

ROCKET ESPRESSO AT HOME

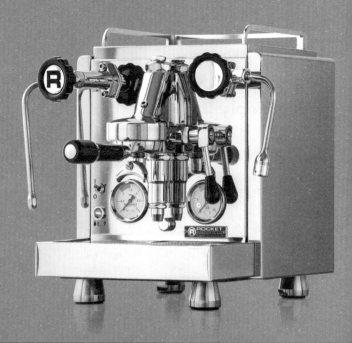

The East Village and surrounding areas all have a laidback, colourful vibe. Tompkins Square Park in Alphabet City and the range of vibrant off-Broadway theaters in the East Village are worth a visit, while the Lower East Side is packed with trendy shops, vintage stores, contemporary art galleries, rich local history and vibrant nightlife. The neighborhood still retains much of its Jewish heritage in the buildings, restaurants and synagogues that were established by immigrant communities during the 20th century.

East Village & Lower East Side

Abraço

81 East 7th Street, Manhattan, NY 10003 | **East Village**

TOP 40

When Abraço moved to its current location from a closet-sized space just down the street, it became one of the most serious coffee destinations in downtown Manhattan. Not that it wasn't serious before: a lively local community packed in for expertly crafted drinks from the company's own roaster. The new space is big, airy, and attractive - terrific for anything from solo sipping to coffee conversation in a big group. Coffee tourists from as far afield as Japan and Australia come here to get that very special Abraço taste. Get something sweet with your drip or espresso, and hang out for a while. Did you know Abraço means hug in Portuguese? The name says a lot.

www.abraconyc.com
Subway 4, 6 (Astor Pl)

MON. Closed
TUE-SAT. 8:00am - 6:00pm
SUN. 9:00am - 6:00pm

First opened 2007
Roaster Abraço
Machine La Marzocco Linea, 2 groups
Grinder Mazzer Robur E

Espresso $2.00
Cappuccino $3.50
Latte $4.00

MAP REF.

COFFEE 4.50 / 5 | OVERALL 4.50 / 5 ★★★★⯪

Blue Bottle Clinton Street

71 Clinton Street, Manhattan, NY 10002 | **Lower East Side**

Photo: Brandon Lowder

Blue Bottle continues its relentless expansion, and this Lower East Side incarnation shows how adaptable it is to each venue. The place isn't huge, but it's made to seem spacious by huge windows on two sides. Happily, it isn't just a pick-up-and-leave place but a true neighborhood hangout, with friends and young parents parking themselves for some conversation and R&R. Milky drinks are always fabulous at Blue Bottle, and the pour-overs highlight the quality of the roasting. A beautiful, new and untraditional find in the Lower East Side.

(510) 653-3394
www.bluebottlecoffee.com
Subway F (Delancey St)

MON-SUN. 7:00am - 7:00pm

First opened 2017
Roaster Blue Bottle Coffee
Machine La Marzocco Linea, 2 groups
Grinder Mazzer Robur E x2, Mazzer Kony E

Espresso	$3.25
Cappuccino	$4.25
Latte	$4.75

Sister locations Multiple locations

MAP REF. **16**

COFFEE 4.75 / 5

OVERALL 4.50 / 5 ★★★★⯪

20

Bluestone Lane Astor Place

51 Astor Place, Manhattan, NY 10003 | **East Village**

Forming part of the major rejuvenation of Astor Place, this Bluestone Lane venue with plenty of seating inside is a lovely spot to meet for brunch and enjoy watching the traffic pass by. Designed with the brand in mind, the glass storefront affords beautiful natural light, creating a bright and inviting space. While Bluestone coffee never disappoints, this particular café boasts to have the "most powerful espresso bar setup," with two La Marzocco Linea PB machines to ensure both quality and authenticity of their famous flat whites. Whether you are grabbing a fresh baked pastry on the go, or settling in to a relaxed avo smash brunch, Bluestone Lane Astor Place hits the spot with their simple yet absolutely delicious menu.

MAP REF.

COFFEE
4.50 / 5

OVERALL
4.50 / 5
★★★★⯪

MON-SUN. 7:00am - 7:00pm

Sister locations Multiple locations

First opened 2015
Roaster Bluestone Lane Coffee
Machine La Marzocco Linea PB3
Grinder Mazzer Robur

Espresso	$3.00
Cappuccino	$4.00
Latte	$4.00

(646) 863-3197
www.bluestonelaneny.com
Subway 4, 6 (Astor Pl)

Café Grumpy Lower East Side

13 Essex Street, Manhattan, NY 10002 | **Lower East Side**

We're not sure how many visits it takes before you get greeted by name in this tiny place, but we do know that most customers seem to have met the minimum. The very un-grumpy welcome is at its warmest here, from the big smile to always-remembered regular orders to advice about which baked goods to order. ('Do you want healthy or sweet?') All this comes with expertly pulled shots, great latte art and fabulous brewed coffees. 'We want to add to the community,' says the staff here. And they certainly do.

(212) 777-7515
www.cafegrumpy.com
Subway F (East Broadway Rutgers St)

Sister locations Multiple locations

| MON-FRI. | 7:00am - 7:00pm |
| SAT-SUN. | 7:30am - 7:00pm |

First opened 2011
Roaster Café Grumpy Coffee
Machine Synesso, 2 groups
Grinder Nuova Simonelli Mythos,
Mazzer Luigi Robur E, Ditting

Espresso	$3.25
Cappuccino	$4.00
Latte	$4.50

MAP REF. **18**

| COFFEE 4.50 / 5 | OVERALL 4.25 / 5 |

Café Henrie

116 Forsyth Street, Manhattan, NY 10002 | **Chinatown**

Café Henrie may have a French name, but it pays homage to a concept of hipness that's 100 percent downtown Manhattan. Owner Andre Saraiva is an artist, and the visuals here are full of treats and surprises, from the artwork hung on a pegboard, to the one-of-a-kind espresso cups. The young clientele pile in for beautifully made coffee and for fashionably healthy 'Dragon Bowl' salads. Venues that set out to be hip are sometimes too much like someone else's formula. The only formula here is Henrie's own, and it's executed with flair - and a smile.

(212) 966-0571
www.cafehenrie.com
Subway J, Z (Bowery) or B, D (Grand St)

| MON-TUE. | 8:30am - 6:00pm |
| WED-SUN. | 8:30am - 10:30pm |

First opened 2015
Roaster Counter Culture Coffee
Machine La Marzocco Linea, 2 groups
Grinder Nuova Simonelli Mythos

Espresso	$3.00
Cappuccino	$4.00
Latte	$4.00

MAP REF. **19**

| COFFEE 4.00 / 5 | OVERALL 4.00 / 5 |

Caffe Vita Lower East Side

124 Ludlow Street, Manhattan, NY 10002 | **Lower East Side**

Caffe Vita's Lower East Side operation is a tiny but trendy hole in the wall, with seating for three people. If you're lucky enough to sit, you'll enjoy watching an exemplary operation at work. The baristas make cup after cup for thirsty locals, many of them regulars, while talking, filling growlers and tending lovingly to the gleaming Kees machine. Vita has its origins on the West Coast, and the pedigree shows in the effortless combination of hip, friendly, casual, and ultra-professional. Make sure to check out the artisan roaster at the back of the room.

(212) 260-8482
www.caffevita.com
Subway F (Delancy St)

MON-FRI.	7:00am – 9:00pm
SAT-SUN.	8:00am – 9:00pm

First opened 2012
Roaster Caffe Vita
Machine Kees van der Westen, 3 groups
Grinder Mazzer Luigi Robur E

Espresso	$3.25
Cappuccino	$4.65
Latte	$4.65 / $4.95 / $5.25

Sister locations Bushwick

MAP REF. **20**

 COFFEE 4.25 / 5  **OVERALL** 4.00 / 5 ★★★★☆

City of Saints East Village

TOP 40

79 East 10th Street, Manhattan, NY 10003 | **East Village**

With its extremely friendly service and thoughtful but effortless design (lots of wood and epiphytes), City of Saints is remarkably welcoming and relaxed for the often sharp-edged, fast-paced East Village neighborhood. Go for a single-origin cold brew - they roast their own beans in Bushwick - and skip the milk to fully taste its light, floral, black-tea-esque complexity. If you're in the mood for something sweet, try the lavender agave latte (available hot or iced), which has a nice rosemary flavor peeking out behind the agave.

(646) 590-1624
www.cityofsaintscoffee.com
Subway 4, 6 (Astor Pl) or N, Q, R, W (8th St - NYU)

MON-FRI.	7:00am – 7:00pm
SAT.	8:00am – 6:00pm
SUN.	9:00am – 5:00pm

First opened 2014
Roaster City of Saints Coffee Roasters
Machine ModBar
Grinder Mazzer Luigi Robur E

Espresso	$3.00
Cappuccino	$4.00
Latte	$4.50

Sister locations Bushwick   MAP REF. **21**

COFFEE 4.50 / 5  **OVERALL** 4.50 / 5 ★★★★½

El Rey

100 Stanton Street, Manhattan, NY 10018 | **Lower East Side**

This unique shop stands out with superior coffee and a deliciously inventive menu. The kitchen is small but mighty, with food focused on fresh vegetables and unique baked goods. They use locally roasted Parlor Coffee and have cold brew on tap. This compact shop is bright and lively, accented with greenery and warm light which bounces off mirrors adorning the walls. Relax and enjoy this bustling trendy eatery and café.

(212) 260-3950
www.elreynyc.com
Subway F (Delancy St)

MON-FRI.   7:00am - 10:00pm
SAT-SUN.   8:00am - 10:00pm

First opened 2013
Roaster Parlor Coffee
Machine La Marzocco Strada
Grinder Mazzer Luigi Robur

Espresso $3.00
Cappuccino $3.75
Latte $4.25

MAP REF. 22

COFFEE 4.25 / 5

OVERALL 4.50 / 5 ★★★★⯨

Everyman Espresso East Village

136 East 13th Street, Manhattan, NY 10003 | **East Village**

Everyman shares its space with the lobby of the Classic Stage Company theater, but to say that it's the best theater-lobby coffee you've ever had would not do this place justice. This is a serious coffee shop in its own right; the fact that Meryl Streep might brush past your table on her way into the theater is merely a pleasant side effect. Everyman baristas are fanatical, expert and approachable, while the Counter Culture espresso is smooth and reliable. Everyman is a must visit.

(212) 533-0524
www.everymanespresso.com
Subway L (3rd Ave)

Sister locations Soho / Park Slope

MON.	7:00am – 7:00pm
TUE–FRI.	7:00am – 8:00pm
SAT.	8:00am – 8:00pm
SUN.	8:00am – 7:00pm

First opened 2007
Roaster Counter Culture Coffee
Machine La Marzocco Linea, 2 groups
Grinder Nuova Simonelli Mythos

Espresso	$3.50
Cappuccino	$4.25
Latte	$5.00

MAP REF. 23

COFFEE 4.25 / 5		OVERALL 4.50 / 5		26

Gasoline Alley Coffee Noho

325 Lafayette Street, Manhattan, NY 10012 | **Noho**

Gasoline Alley's Lafayette Street location is the perfect place to pop in and refuel during a long day of shopping. The warehouse aesthetic is made chic - fitting in effortlessly with the Noho vibe. Customers flow in and out of this busy shop, whose stripped down seasonal menu prides quality above all else. Those with a sweet tooth ought to pair their beverage with a delicious chocolate chip cookie. During the summer heat, this shop serves a small selection of refreshing organic iced teas

www.gasolinealleycoffee.com
Subway 6 (Bleecker St) or B, D, F, M (Broadway - Lafayette St)

Sister locations Nolita / Flatiron District

MON-FRI.	7:00am - 7:00pm
SAT-SUN.	8:00am - 7:00pm

First opened 2011
Roaster Intelligentsia Coffee
Machine La Marzocco GB5, 3 groups
Grinder Mazzer Luigi Robur E

Espresso	$2.75
Cappuccino	$4.00
Latte	$4.25

MAP REF. 24

COFFEE 4.50 / 5

OVERALL 4.50 / 5  ★★★★⯪

Hi-Collar

214 East 10th Street, Manhattan, NY 10003 | **East Village**

This wondrous concept shop specializes in variety of both taste and form. At night, this elegantly designed shop transforms into a sake bar but during the day, it focuses on coffee with lots of choice. You're handed a beautifully bound menu when you sit at the sleek 13-seat bar, lit by stained glass lamps above. Flip through and you'll find a special house blend and multiple single origin coffees from Counter Culture. Hi-Collar offers six different manual brewing options, so you can adventure through processes and tastes.

(212) 777-7018
www.hi-collar.com
Subway 4, 6 (Astor Pl) or L (1st Ave)

MON-SUN. 11:00am – 5:00pm
(for coffee)

First opened 2013
Roaster Counter Culture Coffee, Madcap, George Howell, Ceremony Coffee Roasters
Grinder Ditting KF804

MAP REF.

COFFEE
4.25 / 5

OVERALL
4.25 / 5 ★★★★☆

La Colombe Torrefaction

400 Lafayette Street, Manhattan, NY 10003 | **Noho**

TOP 40

La Colombe's big Noho location always seems to be packed, day or evening. The lines get particularly enormous in the spacious, and very beautiful corner room during the lunch rush, but ample staffing levels and good systems keep them moving through at a reasonable pace. Grabbing a table is a different matter, not that customers ordering to go will care about that. What draws them in is really fine coffee, with single-origin espresso, drip and pour-over given special prominence. Despite plenty of competition, La Colombe remains a high flyer.

(212) 677-5834
www.lacolombe.com
Subway 4, 6 (Astor Pl) or N, Q, R, W (8th St - NYU)

Sister locations Multiple locations

MON-SUN.   7:30am - 6:30pm

Roaster La Colombe Coffee Roasters
Machine La Marzocco GB5, 4 groups
Grinder Nuova Simonelli Mythos

Espresso	$3.00
Cappuccino	$4.00
Latte	$4.00

MAP REF. **26**

COFFEE 4.50 / 5

OVERALL 4.50 / 5

The Lazy Llama

72 East 1st Street, Manhattan, NY 10002 | **East Village**

East Village & Lower East Side

This offshoot of Hell's Kitchen's The Jolly Goat has a name that fits its leisurely vibe. In the warm months, the tiny shop's front windows swing open and the whole place feels like it's outdoors. Serving Stumptown roasted espresso and a lovely drip by Sweetleaf, the delicious coffee goes hand in hand with its stripped back decor of reclaimed wood and copper tables.
A handy, user-friendly drawing on the chalk board above the bar explains the difference between a latte, flat white, macchiato, etc. Order a silky, rich cold brew (sometimes single-origin) and watch the East village rush by.

(646) 509-8957
Subway F (2nd Ave)

MON–SAT.	7:00am – 7:00pm
SUN.	8:00am – 7:00pm

First opened 2016
Roaster Stumptown Coffee Roasters, Sweetleaf Coffee
Machine La Marzocco
Grinder Mazzer Luigi Major

Espresso	$3.25
Cappuccino	$4.00
Latte	$4.50

MAP REF.

COFFEE 4.25 / 5   OVERALL 4.25 / 5 ★★★★★

30

Little Canal

26 Canal Street, Manhattan, NY 10002 | **Lower East Side**

At the corner of Essex and Canal, steps away from the F train, sits Little Canal. Large windows on two sides create a sort of fishbowl effect, offering patrons a lovely view of bustling Canal Street. Prepare to be greeted by friendly staff as they pull perfect espresso and craft each cup of coffee with care. Breakfast, lunch, and dinner are served daily, the menu being largely vegetarian with unique options such as "The Hangover Sandwich". At night, the venue transforms into a full-service coffee and wine bar that stays open to serve the bustling Soho streets well into the evening - and even in the next morning some nights! Compact Little Canal is the sort of café that strikes a perfect balance with its ambiance - lively without ever feeling overcrowded.

MAP REF. 28

COFFEE
4.25 / 5

OVERALL
4.00 / 5 ★★★★☆

MON–WED.	7:00am – 12:00am
THU–FRI.	7:00am – 1:00am
SAT.	7.30am – 1:00am
SUN.	7:30am – 12:00am

First opened 2015
Roaster Madcap Coffee
Machine La Marzocco Linea, 3 groups
Grinder Mazzer Luigi

Espresso	$3.00
Cappuccino	$3.75
Latte	$4.00 / $4.50

(917) 472-7479
Subway F (East Broadway Rutgers St) or
B, D (Grand St)

Ludlow Coffee Supply

176 Ludlow Street, Manhattan, NY 10002 | **Lower East Side**

Ludlow Coffee Supply roasts its own beans in Red Hook, and the excellent espresso is so strong that their latte (made with Battenkill milk) taste like some of the best cortados you might have had. But the real standout is the bourbon vanilla latte-made with real vanilla and bourbon, and almost no added sugar, which once and for all dispels the notion that a vanilla latte shouldn't be a drink of choice. With great background music and free WiFi, this is a great place to sit with your laptop and get some work done, or relax into their comfortable sofas out the back with a delicious latte and a good book.

(212) 777-7465
www.ludlowcoffeesupply.com
Subway F (Delancy St)

MON-SUN.   8:00am - 8:00pm

First opened 2016
Roaster Ludlow Coffee Supply
Machine La Marzocco GB5, 2 groups
Grinder Mazzer Luigi Kony E

Espresso	$3.25
Cappuccino	$3.75
Latte	$4.00

MAP REF. **29**

COFFEE 4.25 / 5	🫘🫘🫘🫘◖	OVERALL 4.25 / 5	★★★★⯪

Ninth Street Espresso East Village   TOP 40

341 East 10th Street, Manhattan, NY 10009 | **East Village**

Ninth Street Espresso is featured regularly in lists of New York's best espresso, and there's good reason for this reputation: the coffee is awesome. Ninth Street has been doing its own roasting since 2013, and total control from green beans to pulled shots yields beautiful results. There are tables at the front of this small location, but sitting at the bar gives you the chance to talk to the friendly - and exceptionally skilled - baristas.

(212) 777-3508
www.ninthstreetespresso.com
Subway L (1st Ave)

Sister locations Alphabet City / Chelsea / Downtown Brooklyn / Midtown East

MON-SUN.   7:00am - 8:00pm

First opened 2008
Roaster Ninth Street Espresso
Machine La Marzocco GB5, 2 groups
Grinder Mazzer Luigi Robur E, Mahlkönig EK 43

Espresso	$3.00
Cappuccino	$4.00
Latte	$4.00

MAP REF. **30**

COFFEE 4.50 / 5	🫘🫘🫘🫘◖	OVERALL 4.25 / 5	★★★★⯪

Ost Cafe

511 Grand Street, Manhattan, NY 10002 | **Lower East Side**

Recently relocated from the East Village, you feel at home the instant you walk through the door of Ost. Set in the first floor of an old Lower East Side building, the space preserves the spirit of the early 20th century while the coffee brewing is right up to date - beans from PT's in Topeka, Kansas, and gorgeous latte art. With grand windows providing a view of the street outside, you can spend a very restful interlude with your coffee, a piece of cake, and a good book. (Or your phone, if you insist.) An absolute pleasure, and much needed in this area.

(516) 808-4764
www.ostcafenyc.com
Subway M (Essex St) or
F (East Broadway)

MON-FRI.	7:30am - 7:00pm
SAT-SUN.	8:00am - 7:00pm

First opened 2013
Roaster PT's Coffee Roasting Company
Machine La Marzocco Linea, 2 groups
Grinder Mazzer Luigi Robur E

Espresso	$2.50
Cappuccino	$4.00
Latte	$4.25

MAP REF. **31**

COFFEE 4.50 / 5

OVERALL 4.50 / 5 ★★★★✬

River Coyote

121 Ludlow Street, Manhattan, NY 10002 | **Lower East Side**

River Coyote is perhaps the coolest spot for coffee nerds in the city. Aesthetically, the brick and wood lined space is low-lit, creating a wonderful ambiance. The space also doubles as a wine bar, serving sixteen varieties of wine on tap. As for the coffee, Nobletree beans are brewed to perfection, and espressos are weighted and drawn to order. Drip coffee and nitro brew are also great options. We recommend stopping by for their weekend brunch, in which guests have the opportunity to sample a delicious variety of pour-over methods.

(212) 477-0100
www.rivercoyoteles.com
Subway F (Delancey St)

SUN-MON.	8:00am - 8:00pm
TUE-THU.	8:00am - 12:00am
FRI-SAT.	8:00am - 2:00am

First opened 2017
Roaster Nobletree Coffee
Machine ModBar, 2 groups
Grinder Mahlkönig EK 43, Nuova Simonelli Mythos Clima Pro

Espresso	$3.00
Cappuccino	$4.00
Latte	$4.00

MAP REF. 32

COFFEE 4.50 / 5
OVERALL 4.25 / 5 ★★★★⯪

The Roost

222 Avenue B, Manhattan, NY 10009 | **East Village**

The Roost ticks so many Lower East Side boxes you'd think they had an algorithm for peak hipsterdom. Bare brick, distressed wood, gleaming tiles, craft beers, cool cocktails, Balthazar pastries - it's all here. But if it sounds calculating, it comes across as friendly and sincere. Service is sweet, and rather than pushing customers in the direction of milky espresso-based drinks, they make a big feature of their single-origin Brooklyn Roasting Company coffees brewed or made in the French press. At night the Roost is a bar, and - understandably - it gets crowded.

(646) 918-6700
www.theroostnyc.com
Subway L (1st Ave)

MON-SUN. 7:00am - 2:00am

First opened 2013
Roaster Brooklyn Roasting Co.
Machine La Marzocco Linea, 2 groups
Grinder Mazzer Luigi

Espresso	$2.50
Cappuccino	$4.00
Latte	$4.00

MAP REF. **33**

COFFEE	OVERALL
4.25 / 5	4.25 / 5 ★★★★⯪

Round K

99 Allen Street, Manhattan, NY 10002 | **Lower East Side**

There are so many lovable quirks about Round K, it seems unfair to highlight one above the others. The décor is nonstop fun, even in the restroom, and the little roaster in the window makes an instant talking point. But the sight of owner, Ockhy Eon, making scrambled eggs using the steam wand of his gleaming Arduino wins our deepest devotion for off-the-wall eccentricity. It's used in various all-day breakfast dishes, bundled into set menus with a house brew and a small yogurt. The espresso blend is brisk, punchy, and best with milk. And even if you don't have any espresso machine eggs, it's nice to know they're there.

(917) 475-1423
www.roundk.com
Subway F (Delancey St) or B, D (Grand St)

MON-WED.	8:00am - 10:00pm
THU-FRI.	8:00am - 12:00am
SAT.	9:00am - 12:00am
SUN.	9:00am - 10:00pm

First opened 2015
Roaster Round K Coffee
Machine Victoria Arduino
Grinder Mazzer Luigi Mini

Espresso	$3.00
Cappuccino	$3.75
Latte	$4.00

MAP REF.

 COFFEE 4.00 / 5

OVERALL 4.25 / 5 ★★★★⯪

Spreadhouse

116 Suffolk Street, Manhattan, NY 10002 | **Lower East Side**

Walk in to Spreadhouse once and you might not want to leave ever again. That's partly because of the look and feel of the place, with oriental carpets a major decorative element in the high-ceilinged ex-industrial space. Customers lounge on the kaftan-lined seats (and sometimes on the floor) as if they were at home. Many treat the place as their office, and friends meet up for more sociable activities. Coffee is well made, with or without milk, by ultra-friendly baristas. During the day, light rolls in through the big windows. At night, the atmosphere becomes moody and seductive, and caffeine gives way to alcohol.

(646) 524-6353
www.spreadhousecoffee.com
Subway J, M (Essex St)

MON-FRI.	7:30am - 12:00am
SAT-SUN.	8:00am - 12:00am

First opened 2015
Roaster Joe
Machine La Marzocco Linea, 2 groups
Grinder Nuova Simonelli Mythos One Clima Pro, Mahlkönig EK 43

Espresso	$3.00
Cappuccino	$4.50
Latte	$5.00

MAP REF. **35**

 COFFEE 4.50 / 5

 OVERALL 4.50 / 5 ★★★★⯨

38

Three Seat Espresso & Barber

137 Avenue A, Manhattan, NY 10009 | **East Village**

Salon-bar-cafés are the latest trend in the city's coffee scene, and Three Seat Espresso & Barber has quickly proven itself as an Alphabet City hotspot. The "Barber" aspect of the shop is unassuming-it appears to be a regular coffee shop at first glance. However, there really is a barber in the back (book your appointment online!). In addition to serving up new hairstyles, the venue also produces an excellent cup of joe. Friendly baristas prepare the espresso-based beverages with care. Their food menu is limited but delicious, including local favorites such as avocado toast and summer crumpets. The interior is spacious, featuring large windows that let in natural light, and plenty of seating. Inside, feel free to chill with friends at their laptop-free seating areas, unplug, and enjoy an excellent brew. Three Seat is a cut above the rest.

MAP REF. **36**

COFFEE 4.25 / 5	OVERALL 4.50 / 5

MON-FRI.	7:00am - 8:00pm	
SAT-SUN.	8:00am - 7:00pm	

First opened 2016
Roaster Ceremony Coffee Roasters
Machine La Marzocco, 2 groups
Grinder Mazzer Luigi

Espresso	$2.75
Cappuccino	$3.50
Latte	$3.50

(917) 388-2769
www.threeseatespresso.com
Subway L (1st Ave)

Whynot

175 Orchard Street, Manhattan, NY 10002 | **Lower East Side**

Whynot packs in customers despite the Lower East Side competition, especially those seeking to combine caffeine-time with keyboard-time: you're just as likely to hear click-click as talk-talk in this office-away-from home. Those looking up from their devices get a good view of bare brick and big windows with a high ceiling. The coffee comes from Toby's Estate, and it's well made; big jugs of self-service water complete the picture. A table by the window, or a bench outside, is the best place to perch.

(646) 682-9065
Subway F (2nd Ave)

MON-FRI.	8:30am – 8:30pm
SAT-SUN.	9:30am – 9:00pm

First opened 2013
Roaster Toby's Estate Coffee
Machine La Marzocco, 4 groups
Grinder Mazzer Luigi Robur E

Espresso	$3.27
Cappuccino	$4.36
Latte	$4.36

MAP REF. **37**

COFFEE 4.25 / 5	OVERALL 4.25 / 5
🫘🫘🫘🫘🫘	★★★★☆

Soho refers to South of Houston Street and is home to some of New York's best shopping with a variety of stores from trendy boutiques and upscale designers to highstreet favorites and chains. Originally an artist's haven before making way for the shopping district, Soho is a firm favorite for residential loft living. Neighboring Nolita, deriving from North of Little Italy, extends the shopping district and includes some of the best kept secrets.

Soho & Neighboring

Birch Coffee Soho

71 West Houston Street, Manhattan, NY 10012 | **Soho**

The founders of Birch believe that coffee should bring people together. Their latest venue, located on bustling West Houston Street, is designed to facilitate this culture of togetherness (which they call The Ignition Initiative). Inside, there are no individual tables - just one long bench, a communal space to be shared by all. The WiFi-free space encourages conversations with friends and strangers alike, they even have helpful little cards to place on the table beside you to get you started, such as: "Tell me about a life changing book I should read" or "ask me about my first date". Pop into Birch for their satisfying own-blend coffees served on a rotating menu, delicious pastries, and baristas who are as exuberant as they are knowledgeable. The Kyoto slow drip is particularly good, you can never really go wrong with a Birch coffee. Try out the Birch style; drink great coffee and say hello to a stranger while you're there!

MAP REF. **38**

COFFEE 4.50 / 5	OVERALL 4.50 / 5

MON-SUN.   7:00am - 8:00pm

First opened 2017
Roaster Birch Coffee
Machine La Marzocco Strada
Grinder Mazzer Luigi

Espresso $3.00
Cappuccino $4.00
Latte $4.50

(212) 686-1444
www.birchcoffee.com
Subway B, D, F, M (Broadway-Lafayette St)

Sister locations Multiple locations

Café Grumpy Nolita

177 Mott Street, Manhattan, NY 10012 | **Nolita**

Situated moments away from Little Italy, this Café Grumpy location is the perfect spot to grab your daily dose of caffeine amidst this bustling area on the edge of Chinatown. A bit smaller than other Grumpy locations, this shop facilitates the sort of grab-and-go environment that comes with its busy location. But have no fear, the quality service is never compromised - and neither is the exquisite coffee. And the location couldn't be more perfect. Pop in for a quality caffeine hit whilst exploring the attractions of Downtown Manhattan.

(212) 226-6810
www.cafegrumpy.com
Subway 4, 6 (Spring St)

Sister locations Multiple locations

MON-FRI.	7:00am - 7:30pm
SAT-SUN.	7:30am - 7:30pm

First opened 2016
Roaster Café Grumpy Coffee
Machine Synesso Hydra MVP, 2 groups
Grinder Nuova Simonelli Mythos x3, Mahlkönig Guatemala

Espresso	$3.25
Cappuccino	$4.00
Latte	$4.50

MAP REF. **39**

COFFEE 4.50 / 5	OVERALL 4.25 / 5

Café Integral

149 Elizabeth Street, Manhattan, NY 10012 | **Nolita**

With its clean, minimalist aesthetic, Café Integral exudes calm amidst its crowded Nolita location. The smart design maximizes seating, making the shop a comfortable spot to meet with friends. Shop owner César Martin Vega is committed to serving beautiful Nicaraguan coffees, a promise that is evident as soon as you taste his pour-overs. In addition to the Nicaraguan offerings, the café has crafted a unique selection of specialty beverages, including the delicious Matcha Fizz and Horchata Latte. One not to be missed!

(305) 773-3066
www.cafeintegral.com
Subway 6 (Spring St) or B, D (Grand St)

MON-FRI. 7:00am - 5:00pm
SAT-SUN. 8:00am - 5:00pm

First opened 2016
Roaster Café Integral Coffee
Machine La Marzocco Strada MP
Grinder Compak F10

Espresso $3.00
Cappuccino $4.00
Latte $4.50

MAP REF. **40**

COFFEE 4.50 / 5	OVERALL 4.25 / 5

48

Chalait Hudson Square

299 West Houston Street, Manhattan, NY 10014 | **West Village**

The setting of Chalait's newest branch couldn't be more corporate - it's part of the Saatchi & Saatchi HQ - but the feeling inside this big room is anything but soulless. The serving counters sit in the middle of the room, leaving plenty of space to sit and sip in blissful, WiFi-free solitude. Chalait emphasizes its teas and healthy eating options as much as its skilfully brewed coffees. Beans are from Counter Culture and they perform well both in drip and from the La Marzocco Linea PB. While there is loads of coffee and casual dining competition in the area, Chalait outshines them all.

(212) 929-0266
www.chalait.com
Subway 1, 2 (Houston St)

| MON-FRI. | 7:00am - 7:00pm |
| SAT-SUN. | 8:00am - 5:00pm |

First opened 2017
Roaster Counter Culture Coffee
Machine La Marzocco Linea PB, 2 groups
Grinder Nuova Simonelli Mythos Pro

Espresso $3.00
Cappuccino $4.00
Latte $4.50

Sister locations Nomad / Chelsea

MAP REF. **41**

| COFFEE 4.50 / 5 | | OVERALL 4.50 / 5 | ★★★★✦ |

Gasoline Alley Coffee Nolita

154 Grand Street, Manhattan, NY 10013 | **Nolita**

At Gasoline Alley's Nolita location, the group-heads on the espresso machine outnumber the seats. Three of one, two of the other. However the irresistible baked goods (dive for a donut if you see one) will certainly sweeten your stay. They need three groups because people pile in for cups to go, everything is made well using Intelligentsia beans. Gasoline Alley provides the fuel for local workers and residents with cheerful efficiency, which they guzzle down eagerly.

www.gasolinealleycoffee.com
Subway 4, 6 (Canal St)

Sister locations Noho / Flatiron District

| MON-FRI. | 7:00am - 7:00pm |
| SAT-SUN. | 8:00am - 7:00pm |

First opened 2011
Roaster Intelligentsia Coffee
Machine La Marzocco GB5, 3 groups
Grinder Mazzer Luigi Robur E

Espresso $2.75
Cappuccino $4.00
Latte $4.25

MAP REF. **42**

| COFFEE 4.50 / 5 | OVERALL 4.25 / 5 | ★★★★✦ |

Gimme! Coffee Nolita

228 Mott Street, Manhattan, NY 10012 | **Nolita**

Photo courtesy of the venue

This Nolita outpost of the Ithaca-based roastery is an unassuming gem. It's nothing flashy, just the model of a local café where lots of regulars come through, and everyone gets a warm welcome. Most people come in for drinks to go, but those who drink on the premises get the full benefit of exquisite latte art on the well-made latte and cappuccino. Sit on the bench outside if weather permits and watch the world go by.

(212) 226-4011
buy.gimmecoffee.com
Subway F (2nd Ave)

Sister locations Williamsburg (Roebling St) / Williamsburg (Lorimer St)

MON-FRI.	7:00am - 7:00pm
SAT-SUN.	8:00am - 7:00pm

First opened 2008
Roaster Gimme! Coffee
Machine La Marzocco Strada, 2 groups
Grinder Mazzer Luigi

Espresso	$3.00
Cappuccino	$3.75
Latte	$4.00

MAP REF. **43**

COFFEE 4.25 / 5

OVERALL 4.25 / 5 ★★★★✩

50

Greecologies

379 Broome Street, Manhattan, NY 10013 | **Soho**

Situated in the heart of Soho, Greecologies is a must-visit venue. Authentic Greek Yogurt from grass-fed cows is made on site; you can watch it being produced through the large viewing window in the back. The food offering is largely Greek inspired yogurts and salads, and their coffee is equally unique. Choose from typical espresso-based beverages, a variety of matcha, or try their grass-fed butter coffee. On a lovely day, take advantage of their private outdoor seating, with greenery and a sense of serenity that will truly make you forget that you're in the middle of Manhattan.

(212) 941-0100
www.greecologies.com
Subway J, Z (Bowery)

MON-FRI.	8:00am - 8:00pm
SAT-SUN.	9:00am - 8:00pm

First opened 2014
Roaster Intelligentsia Coffee
Machine La Marzocco, 2 groups
Grinder Mazzer Luigi

Espresso	$3.25
Cappuccino	$4.00 / $4.50
Latte	$4.00 / $4.50

MAP REF. **44**

 COFFEE 4.25 / 5    **OVERALL** 4.50 / 5 ★★★★⯪

Ground Support Cafe

399 West Broadway, Manhattan, NY 10012 | **Soho**

Photo courtesy of the venue

Shoppers and local creatives comprise a constant stream of devotees to this oasis of great coffee in bustling Soho. If you can't get a seat at one of the rustic picnic tables, don't worry, the bench outside is even more pleasant. You can't go wrong with an espresso drink, but the delicate, nuanced pour-over here is truly a must.

(212) 219-8722
www.groundsupportcafe.com
Subway C, E (Spring St) or 4, 6 (Spring St)

MON-FRI.	7:00am – 8:00pm
SAT-SUN.	8:00am – 8:00pm

First opened 2009
Roaster Ground Support Coffee
Machine La Marzocco Linea, 3 groups
Grinder Mahlkönig EK 43, Mazzer Luigi Robur E

Espresso	$3.25
Cappuccino	$4.25
Latte	$4.25

MAP REF. **45**

COFFEE 4.25 / 5

OVERALL 4.25 / 5 ★★★★☆

Happy Bones

394 Broome Street, Manhattan, NY 10013 | **Nolita**

This shop used to be a walk-in refrigerator, if you can believe it, and before that, an alleyway. But with some imaginative design, it's become a fashionable café instead. Happy Bones is a neighborhood favorite, popular for flat whites and long blacks, drinks made popular since jumping over from Australia and New Zealand. The definite space is both industrial and elegant in feel, the white palette creates an excellent space for clearing your thoughts. Happy Bones sports only a few tables, but it's a beautiful spot to grab a drink before exploring the neighborhood.

(212) 673-3754
www.happybonesnyc.com
Subway 4, 6 (Spring St)

MON-FRI.	7:30am - 7:00pm
SAT-SUN.	8:00am - 7:00pm

First opened 2013
Roaster Counter Culture Coffee
Machine La Marzocco FB80
Grinder Mazzer Luigi

Espresso	$3.00
Cappuccino	$4.00
Latte	$4.50

MAP REF. 46

COFFEE 4.50 / 5	OVERALL 4.50 / 5
🫘🫘🫘🫘🫘	★★★★⯪

Housing Works Bookstore Cafe

126 Crosby Street, Manhattan, NY 10012 | **Soho**

Photo courtesy of the venue

This Soho bookstore café serves up great coffee for a great cause. The Housing Works Organization is a non-profit that works to combat AIDs and homelessness through advocacy, services, and its businesses. As it is run by volunteers, one hundred percent of the proceeds from the bookstore and the café go toward Housing Works' mission. The café serves well-prepared Intelligentsia beans alongside baked goods and freshly made sandwiches. With spacious and comfortable seating, it's the perfect spot to curl up with great read or meet with friends for lunch, all for an amazing cause.

(212) 334-3324
www.housingworks.org/social-enterprise/
bookstore-cafe

Subway B, D, F, M (Broadway - Lafayette St)
or 4, 6 (Bleecker St)

MON-FRI.   9:00am - 9:00pm
SAT-SUN.   9:00am - 5:00pm

First opened 1996
Roaster Intelligentsia Coffee
Machine La Marzocco Linea, 2 groups
Grinder Mazzer Luigi Major

Espresso $2.50
Cappuccino $4.00
Latte $4.00

MAP REF. **47**

COFFEE
4.00 / 5

OVERALL
4.00 / 5 ★ ★ ★ ★ ☆

54

Joe & The Juice Soho

161 Prince Street, Manhattan, NY 10036 | **Soho**

With its dim lighting and loud dance music, this spacious New York outpost of the popular Danish coffee-and-juice bar feels more night club than café at times. However, that doesn't affect Joe & The Juice's regulars from stopping by to do some work. Alongside your caffeine kick, make sure to try one of their many delicious smoothies for a burst of healthy flavor.

(917) 565-4016
www.joejuice.com
Subway C, E (Spring St)

Sister locations Multiple locations

MON-FRI.	6:00am - 8:00pm
SAT-SUN.	8:00am - 8:00pm

First opened 2016
Roaster Bewleys
Machine La Marzocco GB5, 3 groups
Grinder Nuova Simonelli Mythos

Espresso	$2.75
Cappuccino	$3.50
Latte	$2.75 / $3.75

MAP REF. **48**

COFFEE 4.00 / 5		OVERALL 4.25 / 5	★★★★☆

McNally Jackson Café

52 Prince Street, Manhattan, NY 10012 | **Soho**

Literary lovers will fall head over heels for this charming café on the ground floor of McNally Jackson, one of the city's most popular independent bookstores. This cozy space effortlessly blends coffee and culture. Stumptown coffee is proudly served, along with a selection of fair trade teas and light dishes. It's the perfect spot to start that new book you've been dying to read, and an inspiring location for writers and other creatives to do some work.

(212) 274-1160
www.mcnallyjackson.com/cafe
Subway 4, 6 (Spring St) or N, R (Prince St) or B, D, F, M (Broadway - Lafayette St)

MON-SAT.	10:00am - 10:00pm
SUN.	10:00am - 9:00pm

First opened 2004
Roaster Stumptown Coffee Roasters
Machine La Marzocco Linea, 2 groups
Grinder Mazzer Luigi

Espresso	$2.75
Cappuccino	$3.50
Latte	$3.75 / $4.00

MAP REF. **49**

COFFEE 4.00 / 5	OVERALL 4.00 / 5	★★★★☆

Ruby's Café Soho

219 Mulberry Street, Manhattan, NY 10012 | **Soho**

If Ruby's Mulberry Street restaurant ever has a quiet day, it's never happened when we've been passing by - or trying to get a seat. There's always a bunch of people waiting outside for a taste of Ruby's Aussie-inspired breakfast, brunch, burgers, pasta or salads. Their coffee is carefully brewed from Counter Culture beans in filter as well as espresso, though not many people go there for coffee alone (the food is just too good). If it's a nice day, however, and there are a few seats outside, a perfect place to sit and sip.

(212) 925-5755
www.rubyscafe.com
Subway N, Q, R, W (Prince St)

MON-SUN.   9:00am - 10:30pm

First opened 2003
Roaster Counter Culture Coffee
Machine La Marzocco GB5, 2 groups
Grinder Mazzer Luigi Kony E

Espresso	$3.00
Cappuccino	$4.00
Latte	$4.00

Sister locations Murray Hill

MAP REF.

 **COFFEE** 4.25 / 5   **OVERALL** 4.25 / 5 ★★★★

Saturdays Surf NYC

31 Crosby Street, Manhattan, NY 10013 | **Soho**

Many stores in Manhattan now happen to serve nice coffee, but Saturdays Surf feels like a genuine coffee shop which happens to also be a surf apparel store. This is mostly thanks to a gobsmackingly beautiful, spacious reclaimed-wood backyard, full of tulips, and the fact that it's staffed by folks who truly seem about to go for a surf.

La Colombe makes a special blend for their drip, delicious and complex. And on a hot summers day when you might prefer to go for a surf, order a hot black coffee and lounge in the backyard, one of the most pleasant outdoor areas in Manhattan.

(212) 966-7875
www.saturdaysnyc.com
Subway 4, 6 (Canal St)

Sister locations West Village

MON-FRI.	8:00am - 7:00pm
SAT-SUN.	10:00am - 7:00pm

First opened 2009
Roaster La Colombe Torrefaction Coffee Roasters
Machine La Marzocco Linea, 3 groups
Grinder Mazzer Luigi

Espresso	$3.00
Cappuccino	$4.00
Latte	$4.00

MAP REF. 51

  COFFEE 4.00 / 5   **OVERALL** 4.25 / 5 ★★★★

Seven Grams Caffé Soho

175 Varick Street, Manhattan, NY 10014 | **Soho**

NEW

After winning over the Chelsea neighbourhood three years ago, Seven Grams Caffe decided to launch a second venue - a 1,500 square foot West Soho flagship. This new location features an in-house bakery offering up a delicious array of freshly baked artisanal treats daily, including their famous EV Olive Oil Loaf Cake and Banana Chocolate Bread. And of course, it wouldn't be a true Seven Grams location without the meticulously sourced and independently roasted Seven Grams coffee. This beautiful location is a must visit; with generous seating and free WiFi, creating an inviting and thoughtful ambiance.

(212) 727-1777
www.sevengramscaffe.com
Subway 1 (Houston St)

Sister locations Chelsea

MON-FRI.	7:00am - 7:00pm
SAT-SUN.	8:00am - 3:00pm

First opened 2017
Roaster Seven Grams Coffee Roasters
Machine La Marzocco GB5, 3 groups
Grinder Nuova Simonelli Clima Pro

Espresso	$3.00
Cappuccino	$4.25
Latte	$4.25

MAP REF.

COFFEE P E N D I N G   OVERALL P E N D I N G

TOMS Roasting Co.

264 Elizabeth Street, Manhattan, NY 10012 | **Nolita**

Serving TOMS Roasting Co. blends, TOMS Café is your ethical one stop shop for all your coffee and footwear needs. Beans are sourced from around the globe at Fairtrade prices, and are roasted to highlight their unique flavor profiles. Roasts are rotated seasonally, so there is always something new to try. Additionally, the café offers a small selection of baked goods, including delicious donuts by Dough. With plenty of comfy seating out back, TOMS is the perfect place to sit and sip with friends, or to grab one of their delicious milky espressos to go. After ordering your cup of joe, follow the signs to the shoes, as this venue has a fully-stocked TOMS store in the back. Whether you're looking to pop in for a great espresso and study session, or to add a stop to your Soho shopping trip, TOMS has your size. And the best part about TOMS Café? Their One for One policy. For each TOMS Roasting Co product purchased, the company will provide safe water to a person in need – do good, and feel good doing it!

MAP REF.

COFFEE 4.25 / 5	OVERALL 4.25 / 5

MON–SAT.	7:00am – 7:00pm
SUN.	8:00am – 6:00pm

First opened 2015
Roaster TOMS Roasting Co.
Machine La Marzocco Linea, 3 groups
Grinder BUNN G3A HD

Espresso	$2.75
Cappuccino	$3.75
Latte	$4.00

(212) 219-8392
www.toms.com/toms-roasting-co
Subway F, M (2nd Ave)

Soho & Neighboring

Two Hands Soho

164 Mott Street, Manhattan, NY 10013 | **Soho**

TOP **40**

The laidback attitude at this Aussie-run shop is more than welcome in this busy neighborhood. They've got a full menu of food with favorites like avocado toast and acai bowls, and though the flat white reigns here, all their coffee drinks are good and strong, made with delicious Café Integral coffee. The space is bright and airy with its pristinely white interior and accents of greenery. This is a neighborhood favorite that gets packed on the weekends and weekdays, so hang with other coffee lovers and ride the wave over to this buzzing spot.

www.twohandsnyc.com
Subway B, D (Grand St)

Sister locations Tribeca

MON-SUN.   8:00am - 5:00pm

First opened 2014
Roaster Café Integral
Machine La Marzocco Strada, 2 groups
Grinder Compak F8

Espresso	$3.50
Cappuccino	$4.00
Latte	$5.00

MAP REF. 54

COFFEE 4.50 / 5

OVERALL 4.50 / 5 ★★★★✦

The hottest thing in coffee right now is also the coolest.

Detpak Ripple-Wrap™ cups — the cooler way to serve coffee.™

Air pocket insulation keeps the hot stuff hot!

Air cushioning to protect your fingers from heat.

All-in-one corrugated cup means just one product to store.

Distinctive, quality design will impress your customers.

Can be custom printed, with runs from 25,000 cups.

Available in 4oz, 8oz, 12oz, 16oz and 20oz sizes.

WWW.DETPAK.COM
CUPS@DETPAK.COM
+1-253-380-5091

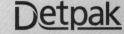

Known as 'The Village' to locals, Greenwich village houses some of the most expensive homes in Manhattan. With the area a landmark for bohemian culture, the desirable location is very sought after. Washington Square park is at the center of the neighborhood and provides much needed green space amongst the packed residential quarters. Nestled in the unique streets of the West Village lie many trendy food and coffee spots which offer a local vibe.

West Village & Neighboring

Banter

169 Sullivan Street, Manhattan, NY 10012 | **West Village**

Founded by former Two Hands baristas and Australian natives, Nick Duckworth and Josh Evans, Banter is a new and exciting Australian café just off Houston. It brings together a delicious restaurant menu with a casual sit-down aesthetic, creating a perfect balance between formal dining and café casual. Banter features a health-conscious menu with items popular in both Australia and the US. The light wood interior and airy aesthetic, along with the beautiful prints lining the walls, gives the whole room a friendly, inviting feel, and the beautifully prepared dishes are not to be missed. From tempting chia pudding bowls to skillfully poured golden lattes or flat whites, there really is something for every discerning New Yorker. Added bonus? Their lovely patio offering airy outdoor seating during the warmer months.

MAP REF. **55**

COFFEE	OVERALL
4.50 / 5	4.50 / 5 ★★★★⯪

West Village & Neighboring

MON–SUN.   8:00am – 6:00pm

First opened 2017
Roaster Café Integral
Machine La Marzocco Strada EE, 2 groups
Grinder Compak E10

Espresso	$3.00
Cappuccino	$4.00
Latte	$4.50

www.banternyc.com
Subway C, E (Spring St)

Bluestone Lane Greenwich Village

55 Greenwich Avenue, Manhattan, NY 10014 | **Greenwich Village**

Bluestone Lane does not do unattractive: all its locations are a treat for the eye. But the Collective Café is particularly pretty, especially on a sunny day. The white picket fence might make you think you're in Melbourne or Sydney. The menu will do the same trick, with its Antipodean views of clean and healthy living (including a totally delectable brunch menu). Coffee at Bluestone is never anything less than outstanding: it's just a question of whether you're in the mood for a well-pulled espresso shot or a famous flat white.

(646) 368-1988
www.bluestonelaneny.com
Subway 1, 2 (Christopher St - Sheridan Sq) or 1, 2, 3 (14th St)

MON–SUN. 8:00am - 6:00pm

First opened 2014
Roaster Bluestone Lane, Niccolo Coffee
Machine La Marzocco Linea PB, 3 groups
Grinder Nuova Simonelli Mythos

Espresso	$2.75
Cappuccino	$4.00
Latte	$4.00

Sister locations Multiple locations

MAP REF. 56

COFFEE 4.50 / 5

OVERALL 4.50 / 5 ★★★★⯪

Bluestone Lane West Village

30 Carmine Street, Manhattan, NY 10014 | **West Village**

The table service at this West Village branch of Bluestone couldn't be sweeter. And the café itself is gleaming with white walls, pale wood flooring and large windows letting in lots of light. The menu features delicious Aussie brunch items, including eggs, avocados and sourdough, with several gluten-free options available. It's easy to linger with friends - having no WiFi means that people actually talk to each other. For something different in your cup, try the "Magic": a double ristretto in a 4.5-ounce cup with steamed and micro-foamed milk.

(212) 627-2763
www.bluestonelaneny.com
Subway A, C, E, B, D, F, M (West 4th St)

MON-SUN.   8:00am - 6:00pm

First opened 2016
Roaster Bluestone Lane, Niccolo
Machine La Marzocco Linea, 3 groups
Grinder Nuova Simonelli Mythos

Espresso $2.75
Cappuccino $4.00
Latte $4.00

Sister locations Multiple locations

MAP REF. **57**

| COFFEE 4.50 / 5 |  | OVERALL 4.25 / 5 | ★★★★⭒ |

Fair Folks & a Goat

96 West Houston Street, Manhattan, NY 10012 | **Greenwich Village**

Fair Folks is a retailer of clothes, jewelry and accessories. But you'd be foolish not to turn left and address yourself to the barista. The coffees look as good as the clothes, with fine latte art adorning well-pulled shots using beans from the venerable Porto Rico roasters in the Village. A diverse set of local coffee drinkers and apparel shoppers puts the surprisingly light-filled room to good use, with some drawn by the membership deal: $35 a month buys you free drinks and discounts on other items. Doesn't that seem fair, folks?

(212) 420-7900
www.fairfolksandagoat.com
Subway B, D, F, M (Broadway - Lafayette St)

Sister locations East Village

MON-THU.   7:00am - 8:00pm
FRI.   7:00am - 9:00pm
SAT-SUN.   8:00am - 9:00pm

First opened 2012
Roaster Porto Rico Coffee Roasters
Machine Rancilio
Grinder Mazzer Luigi

Espresso $2.50
Cappuccino $3.50
Latte $4.00

MAP REF. **58**

| COFFEE 4.00 / 5 | | OVERALL 4.00 / 5 | ★★★★☆ |

Jack's Stir Brew Coffee

138 West 10th Street, Manhattan, NY 10014 | **West Village**

Established in 2003, Jack's is an old school favorite amongst the NYC coffee scene. Photographs cover the walls of their 10th Street café, giving it a homey atmosphere. It is quiet and serene, the perfect spot to do work or just relax with a great cup of coffee. Community is emphasized at Jack's, baristas know a regular's order as soon as they step up to the counter. Pair your coffee with one of their delicious vegan baked goods, or take a bar of chocolate to-go.

(212) 929-0821
www.jacksstirbrew.com
Subway 1, 2 (Christopher St - Sheridan Sq)

| MON-FRI. | 6:30am - 7:00pm |
| SAT-SUN. | 7:00am - 7:00pm |

First opened 2003
Roaster Jack's Stir Brew Roast
Machine La Marzocco GB5, 2 groups
Grinder Mazzer Luigi

Espresso	$2.96
Cappuccino	$2.96
Latte	$2.96

Sister locations Financial District / West Village / Chelsea / Tribeca MAP REF. 59

COFFEE 4.25 / 5 OVERALL 4.25 / 5 ★★★★⯪

Kava Cafe

803 Washington Street, Manhattan, NY 10014 | **West Village**

This polished coffee bar pulls excellent shots on their sleek La Marzocco Strada, and the filter coffee is notable. Its classical Italian-inspired interior and coffee to match make this Washington Street café truly authentic. If you are after something other than coffee then give the beer a try.

(212) 255-7495
www.kavanyc.com
Subway L (8th Ave) or A, C, E (14th St)

MON-WED.	7:00am - 7:00pm
THU-FRI.	7:00am - 9:00pm
SAT.	8:00am - 9:00pm
SUN.	8:00am - 7:00pm

First opened 2011
Roaster Ceremony
Machine La Marzocco Strada
Grinder Mazzer Luigi

Espresso	$3.50
Cappuccino	$4.50
Latte	$5.00

MAP REF. 60

COFFEE 4.25 / 5 OVERALL 4.25 / 5 ★★★★⯪

Kobrick Coffee Co.

24 9th Avenue, Manhattan, NY 10014 | **Meatpacking District**

After roasting beans for nearly a century, Kobrick decided to open a café in the trendy Meatpacking District in 2015. Yet it feels as if it might have been there forever, with its tasteful and timeless dark wood décor (look up at the ceiling) and deeply comfortable gentleman's-club-type seating in the small back room. Kobrick makes incredibly good coffee, whether espresso or drip. Food is simple, like the room: eggs, sandwiches, boards of charcuterie and cheeses are served here. The place is open late, with coffee joined by cocktails as the drinks of choice. Kobrick is a little piece of Old Manhattan on Ninth Avenue - more 1920 than 20-whatever.

(212) 255-5588
www.kobricks.com
Subway A, C, E (14th St)

MON-FRI.	7:00am - 4:00am
SAT-SUN.	8:00am - 4:00am

First opened 2015
Roaster Kobrick Coffee Co.
Machine La Marzocco GB5, 3 groups
Grinder Mahlkönig K30 Espresso, Mahlkönig Guatemala

Espresso	$3.25
Cappuccino	$4.00
Latte	$4.00

MAP REF. **61**

Merriweather

428 Hudson Street, Manhattan, NY 10014 | **West Village**

Inspired by the trendy beach cafés of Australia, Merriweather Coffee + Kitchen is a new standout spot in the picturesque West Village. Large windows paired with the light wood and mint green aesthetic generate a vibrant, welcoming space. Merriweather is always busy during lunch rush, and for good reason. Counter Culture beans are expertly brewed, and the food menu is as delicious as it is unique, with lots of healthy options across the board, including their popular Merriweather Morning Sandwiches and turmeric ginger oatmeal. There is also a wonderful outdoor bench to perch on if the weather is good, and watch the world go by with a refreshing cold brew. Whether meeting friends for lunch or just in need of a delicious drink to-go, Merriweather is your perfect ray of sunshine.

MAP REF.

COFFEE 4.50 / 5	🫘🫘🫘🫘🫘	OVERALL 4.50 / 5	★★★★✦

West Village & Neighboring

MON-FRI.	7:00am - 6:00pm
SAT-SUN.	8:00am - 6:00pm

First opened 2016
Roaster Counter Culture, rotating roasters
Machine La Marzocco Linea PB, 2 groups
Grinder Mahlkönig Peak x2,
Mahlkönig EK 43

Espresso	$3.25
Cappuccino	$4.00
Latte	$4.50

(646) 678-5678
www.merriweathernyc.com
Subway 1, 2 (Houston St)

Oren's Daily Roast Greenwich Village

29 Waverly Place, Manhattan, NY 10003 | **Greenwich Village**

This branch of legendary Oren's Daily Roast could hardly have a better location, with thousands of people at NYU's main campus right on the doorstep. But it's not only caffeine-craving students and professors who benefit here. This is the heart of the Village, and Washington Square Park is one minute away. Grab your brew and go out to watch the passing parade, or grab a seat in the small but attractive café. Drip coffee is always good at Oren's, and the least expensive drink in the place if you buy the small (but still generous) serving.

(212) 420-5958
Subway N, Q, R, W (8th Street - NYU)

Sister locations Multiple locations

MON.-FRI.	7:00am - 7:00pm
SAT.-SUN.	8:00am - 6:00pm

First opened 2013
Roaster Oren's Daily Roast
Machine La Marzocco GB, 3 groups
Grinder Mazzer Luigi Super Jolly, Mazzer Luigi Robur E

Espresso	$2.75
Cappuccino	$3.60
Latte	$3.60

MAP REF. **63**

COFFEE 4.25 / 5   **OVERALL** 4.25 / 5 ★★★★

Porto Rico Importing Co.

201 Bleecker Street, Manhattan, NY 10012 | **Greenwich Village**

Porto Rico is truly a coffee emporium, offering a comprehensive selection of direct-trade beans imported from around the world. Established in 1907, this family-owned coffee store has been passed down through the generations, gathering a loyal following throughout the years. Though not a café, head to the coffee bar in the back, where a friendly barista will gladly pour a brew for you. No matter your taste, Porto Rico offers a blend for everyone, as well as selling quality machinery to get the most out of their flavor-filled beans.

(212) 477-5421
www.portorico.com
Subway 1, 2 (Houston St) or A, C, E (Spring St)

MON.-FRI.	8:00am - 9:00pm
SAT.	9:00am - 9:00pm
SUN.	12:00pm - 7:00pm

First opened 1907
Roaster Porto Rico Coffee Roasters
Machine Astoria SEP Perla, 2 groups
Grinder Mahlkönig

Espresso	$1.60
Cappuccino	$3.25
Latte	$3.25

Sister location East Village / Lower East Side / Williamsburg

MAP REF. **64**

COFFEE 4.00 / 5   **OVERALL** 4.25 / 5 ★★★★

Prodigy Coffee

33 Carmine Street, Manhattan, NY 10014 | **Greenwich Village**

Prodigy Coffee uses its own roaster to prepare exceptional traditional coffees and their own specially concocted drinks too. When it's hot try the Frostbite, cold brew over shaved ice, or maybe the Snakebite, melted dark chocolate with a shot of espresso, when the weather cools down. With these potions, and their family of seasonal single origins and blends, it's easy to have fun experimenting with your taste of coffee here. The six table shop is handsome, with gilded frames and chandeliers composing the space with a polished flare.

(212) 414-4142
www.prodigycoffee.com
Subway A, C, E, B, D, F, M (West 4th St)

| MON–FRI. | 7:00am – 7:00pm |
| SAT–SUN. | 8:00am – 7:00pm |

First opened 2012
Roaster Gotham Coffee Roasters
Machine La Marzocco Linea, 2 groups
Grinder Mazzer Luigi Robur, Kony

Espresso $3.25
Cappuccino $4.00
Latte $4.25

MAP REF. **65**

COFFEE 4.25 / 5 🫘🫘🫘🫘🫘   OVERALL 4.25 / 5 ★★★★✫

Rebel Coffee

19 8th Avenue, Manhattan, NY 10014 | **West Village**

NEW

If you're looking for a place with great coffee and a quiet relaxing atmosphere, Rebel Coffee is the place for you. Situated in a quiet corner of the West Village, it is the perfect spot to get work done while sipping on a latte. Stumptown beans are brewed perfectly on the La Marzocco, pulling espresso that is rich, strong, and full of flavor. Also available are delicious artisan donuts by Underwest Donuts, a New York City delicacy. Homey yet upscale, Rebel Coffee is a great place to unwind.

(917) 261-4299
www.rebelcoffeenyc.com
Subway A, C, E, L (14th St)

| MON–SUN. | 7:00am – 7:00pm |

First opened 2016
Roaster Stumptown Coffee Roasters
Machine La Marzocco Strada, 2 groups
Grinder Mazzer Luigi Kony E

Espresso $3.25
Cappuccino $4.00
Latte $4.25

MAP REF. **66**

COFFEE 4.25 / 5 🫘🫘🫘🫘🫘   OVERALL 4.25 / 5 ★★★★✫

Stumptown Greenwich Village

30 West 8th Street, Manhattan, NY 10011 | **Greenwich Village**

TOP **40**

Stumptown found a new home here in 2013, bringing its signature Portland style and meticulously prepared coffees downtown. This former village bookshop now houses Stumptown's library of perfectly prepared coffees. The delicious Nitro cold brew is served on tap, with a strong dark and creamy taste reminiscent of a nice Guinness. There's an adjoining brew bar where you can get any coffee made any way you like, and they play kind hosts with regular tastings there too.

(855) 711-3385
www.stumptowncoffee.com
Subway N, Q, R, W (8th St - NYU)

Sister locations Midtown West

MON-SUN. 7:00am - 8:00pm

First opened 2013
Roaster Stumptown Coffee Roasters
Machine La Marzocco Strada
Grinder Mazzer Luigi Robur E

Espresso	$3.25
Cappuccino	$4.00
Latte	$4.00 / $4.50 / $5.00

MAP REF.

West Village & Neighboring

COFFEE 4.75 / 5	OVERALL 4.50 / 5

Third Rail Coffee

240 Sullivan Street, Manhattan, NY 10012 | **Greenwich Village**

Despite being tiny, Third Rail is a comfortable place to sip your coffee, thanks to the genuine, relaxed warmth of the baristas. They always serve ethics-focused, consistently great Counter Culture Coffee beans, complete with exquisite latte art on milky brews, but also rotate a second roaster for pour-overs (at the time of writing, Sweetbloom from Denver). The lattes are excellent, but if you have time, stay for a pour-over.

(646) 580-1240
www.thirdrailcoffee.com
Subway A, C, E, B, D, F, M (West 4th St)

Sister locations East Village

MON-FRI.	7:00am - 8:00pm
SAT-SUN.	8:00am - 8:00pm

First opened 2009
Roaster Counter Culture Coffee and guests
Machine La Marzocco GB5, 2 groups
Grinder Mazzer Luigi Robur E

Espresso	$3.50
Cappuccino	$4.25
Latte	$4.25 / $4.75

MAP REF. **68**

Toby's Estate West Village

44 Charles Street, Manhattan, NY 10014 | **West Village**

Toby's West Village location began life as an artist's studio almost a century ago, and there are huge windows on two sides of the V-shaped room. Combined with high ceilings, this creates an airy and spacious feel - and a great setting for digging in to their excellent baked goods from highest quality suppliers, including Ovenly, or relaxing over breakfast of eggs or granola. The pour-over coffees are outstanding, and showcase the roasting skill at Toby's Brooklyn base. If you crave caffeine enlightenment, go to one of their classes in the training lab downstairs.

(646) 590-1924
www.tobysestate.com
Subway 1 (Christopher St - Sheridan Sq)

Sister locations Williamsburg / Flatiron District / Long Island City / Midtown East

MON-SUN. 7:00am - 7:00pm

First opened 2014
Roaster Toby's Estate Coffee
Machine La Marzocco Strada, 2 groups
Grinder Nuova Simonelli Mythos One

Espresso	$3.00
Cappuccino	$3.75
Latte	$4.50

MAP REF. 69

COFFEE 4.50 / 5		OVERALL 4.50 / 5	

INSPIRING BEAUTIFUL
COFFEE MOMENTS
SINCE 1933

For three generations, the Ill
family has spent eight decade
refining a singular blend o
coffee, sustainably source
from the top 1% of Arabic
beans grown worldwide.

Perfected for Italian espress
and enjoyed in your favorit
coffee beverage, delight in th
beautiful taste of illy.

**Discover illy at 2Beans Café
throughout Manhattan.**

live
happilly

100 Park Ave. • 254 Park Ave. S. • 461 Amsterdam Ave.
817 Avenue of America's • 1000 8th Ave. – Turnstyle

Running along the Hudson River, Chelsea is home to the popular green oasis of the High Line, the historic Chelsea Piers, bustling Chelsea Market and busy Hudson Yards. With these fantastic areas offering residents a variety of local charms it's easy to see why Chelsea is one of Manhattan's hotspots. Featuring some of the best dinning, nightlife and art galleries in Manhattan, Chelsea is a definite neighborhood to visit.

Chelsea

Blue Bottle Chelsea

450 West 15th Street, Manhattan, NY 10014 | **Chelsea**

Photo courtesy of the venue

This pocket-size branch of the San Francisco-based chain is perfectly situated for visits to Chelsea Market or the High Line. The space, originally a loading dock, is cleverly used: the café is at street level, while the rear mezzanine accommodates Saturday classes (free of charge) in cupping and home brewing. Blue Bottle roasts at its Bushwick site, and the beans include both blends and single origins. Whether pulled through the three-group Strada or lovingly hand-poured, the coffee is treated like royalty. Blue Bottle is blue chip all the way, right down to its delectable in-house baking.

(510) 653-3394
bluebottlecoffee.com
Subway A, C, E (14th St)

MON-FRI.	7:00am - 6:00pm
SAT-SUN.	8:00am - 6:00pm

First opened 2012
Roaster Blue Bottle Coffee
Machine La Marzocco Strada, 3 groups
Grinder Mazzer Luigi, Baratza Forte

Espresso	$3.00
Cappuccino	$4.00
Latte	$4.50

Sister locations Multiple locations

MAP REF.

COFFEE 4.50 / 5

OVERALL 4.25 / 5 ★★★★⯪

The Commons Chelsea

128th 7th Avenue, Manhattan, NY 10014 | **Chelsea**

Photo courtesy of the venue

The terrific beans from La Colombe get excellent care in this small, very calm Chelsea local. It places strong emphasis on food, served from breakfast onward through dinner, when you can relax with beer or wine as well as coffee. The owners were the first people selling on the High Line, so they're West Side veterans. Tables outside are a great place to perch in fine weather; and latte art can reach some pretty impressive heights. A remarkable venue.

(212) 929-9333
www.thecommonschelsea.com
Subway A, C, E (14th St)

MON.	7:00am - 6:00pm
TUE.-FRI.	7:00am - 11:00pm
SAT.	8:00am - 6:00pm
SUN.	9:00am - 6:00pm

First opened 2011
Roaster La Colombe Coffee Roasters
Machine La Marzocco Linea, 2 groups
Grinder Mazzer Luigi Super Jolly

Espresso	$3.00 / $3.50
Cappuccino	$4.00 / $4.75
Latte	$4.00 / $4.75

MAP REF. **71**

COFFEE 4.00 / 5		OVERALL 4.25 / 5	

Intelligentsia Coffee

180 10th Avenue, Manhattan, NY 10011 | **Chelsea**

This Chicago behemoth has made a home inside the elegant lobby of the High Line Hotel. 'Twas the night before Christmas' was written in an apple orchard that once grew upon these historic grounds, and now you too can wax poetic here with an exceptional coffee in hand. The menu changes often with seasonal offerings and they feature a slow bar in lieu of filter coffee where single origins are brewed with care. We suggest drinking al fresco, as the hotel offers beautiful outdoor spaces where coffee patrons can relax in style.

(212) 933-9736
www.intelligentsiacoffee.com
Subway C, E (23rd St)

SUN-THU.	7:00am - 6:00pm
FRI-SAT.	7:00am - 7:00pm

First opened 2013
Roaster Intelligentsia Coffee
Machine La Marzocco Strada, 2 groups
Grinder Mazzer Luigi Robur

Espresso	$3.25
Cappuccino	$4.25
Latte	$4.50

MAP REF.

COFFEE 4.50 / 5	OVERALL 4.50 / 5
🫘🫘🫘🫘🫘	★★★★⯪

Joe Coffee Pro Shop + HQ

131 West 21st Street, Manhattan, NY 10011 | **Chelsea**

There isn't much seating at Joe Pro's Flatiron shop, but it's probably not needed as most people seem to come in for something to drink on the go. In spite of its size, it's worth coming in to drink on the premises. This is where Joe does his roasting, an operation you can watch behind the glass panels. And while you're watching, you can talk to your heart's content with baristas who are as eager and as knowledgeable as any in the city. While you're there, stock up on beans.

(212) 924-7400
www.joenewyork.com
Subway F, M (23rd St)

Sister locations Multiple locations

MON–FRI.	8:00am – 7:00pm
SAT–SUN.	9:00am – 4:00pm

First opened 2012
Roaster Joe Coffee and guests
Machine La Marzocco Strada, 2 groups
Grinder Mazzer Luigi Robur E, Mahlkönig EK 43

Espresso	$3.00
Cappuccino	$4.00
Latte	$4.50

MAP REF. **73**

COFFEE 4.25 / 5   🫘🫘🫘🫘🫘   **OVERALL** 4.25 / 5   ★★★★⯨

La Colombe Chelsea

601 West 27th Street, Manhattan, NY 10001 | **Chelsea**

La Colombe's spacious Chelsea outpost provides a coffee oasis in an area that doesn't have a great deal of choice. That alone would make it a hit, even without the signature Colombe highlights: a large choice of drinks both hot and cold, efficient service, and simple yet tempting baked goodies. This inspired, minimalist, well designed interior is a great place to stop off at when you're going for a walk along the High Line, just a few minutes away, and definitely worth a trip if you're in the area.

(646) 885-0677
www.lacolombe.com
Subway 1 (28th St)

Sister locations Multiple locations

MON–FRI.	7:00am – 7:00pm
SAT–SUN.	8:00am – 7:00pm

First opened 2015
Roaster La Colombe Coffee Roasters
Machine La Marzocco GB5, 3 groups
Grinder Nuova Simonelli Mythos One

Espresso	$3.00
Cappuccino	$4.00
Latte	$4.00

MAP REF. **74**

COFFEE 4.50 / 5   🫘🫘🫘🫘🫘   **OVERALL** 4.50 / 5   ★★★★⯨

MatchaBar Chelsea

256 West 15th Street, Manhattan, NY 10011 | **Chelsea**

This Chelsea outpost of MatchaBar proves the proposition that good things come in small packages. The place is so pint-sized it needs just a one-group machine, a real rarity. Set in a quiet residential block just east of 8th Avenue, MatchaBar Chelsea has space for just a handful of drinkers, with a large proportion of business coming from those on the go. Like the Williamsburg original, the espresso machine, a Simonelli, is operated with skill, making the bracing Toby's Estate espresso blend, in addition to the matcha, a lively base for skilled latte art. And here too, goods are the star turn on the food counter.

(212) 627-1058
www.matchabarnyc.com
Subway A, C, E, L (14th St)

Sister locations Williamsburg

MON–FRI.	8:00am – 7:00pm
SAT-SUN.	10:00am – 7:00pm

First opened 2015
Roaster Toby's Estate Coffee
Machine Nuova Simonelli, 1 group
Grinder Cuisinart

Espresso	$3.00
Cappuccino	$4.50
Latte	$4.85

MAP REF.

 COFFEE 4.00 / 5

 OVERALL 4.00 / 5 ★★★★☆

Seven Grams Caffé Chelsea

275 7th Avenue, Manhattan, NY 10001 | **Chelsea**

Photo courtesy of the venue

Seven Grams punches way above its weight through an enviable combination of great looks (including white walls hung with interesting art), eager service, and delicious baked goods all made in-house. It would be worth coming here even if the place didn't sell such good coffee - but the coffee is great, small doses of ground Fairtrade beans crowned with latte art that's inventive and highly skilled. Chelsea may have lots of other coffee spots to visit, but you should consider tipping the scales in favor of a visit to this one.

(212) 229-2163
www.sevengramscaffe.com
Subway 1, 2, F, M, A, C, E (23rd St)

Sister locations Soho

MON-FRI.	7:00am - 7:00pm
SAT-SUN.	8:00am - 7:00pm

First opened 2014
Roaster Seven Grams Coffee Roasters
Machine La Marzocco GB5, 3 groups
Grinder Nuova Simonelli Clima Pro

Espresso	$3.00
Cappuccino	$4.25
Latte	$4.25

MAP REF. **76**

COFFEE 4.25 / 5

OVERALL 4.50 / 5 ★★★★⯪

Think Coffee Chelsea

500 West 30th Street, Manhattan, NY 10001 | **Chelsea**

Think's consistent high quality continues in this Chelsea outpost, but the setting is unusual. It's on the edge of the Hudson Yards development. The entrance to the Holland Tunnel isn't far away. But Think makes its own charm with a smallish, colourful interior with nice glass panelling, a friendly crew, and excellent coffee; check out their killer drip and multitude of well-crafted espresso-based drinks. With the Abington Towers apartment building having recently opened, and The High Line just a few minutes away, Think Coffee Chelsea is proving to be a popular spot.

(646) 649-4053
www.thinkcoffeenyc.com
Subway 7 (34th St - Hudson Yards)

Sister locations Multiple locations

MON-FRI.	6:30am - 8:00pm
SAT-SUN.	7:30am - 8:00pm

First opened 2015
Roaster Red House
Machine Synesso Hydra, 3 groups
Grinder Mahlkönig Guatemala, Mazzer Luigi Robur E

Espresso	$2.75
Cappuccino	$3.85
Latte	$3.85

MAP REF. **77**

COFFEE 4.25 / 5		OVERALL 4.25 / 5	★★★★✫

Underline Coffee

511 West 20th Street, Manhattan, NY 10011 | **Chelsea**

Photo courtesy of the venue

The "line" they refer to in the title of this cool, artisan shop is of course the High Line, the beautiful elevated park that runs over this great little café. Classic tunes play throughout this chilled, but serious coffee shop, as their handsome menus dutifully describe and explain the plenitude of offers they have on the bar. They use Apes & Peacocks for house-made speciality drinks and keep a slow bar going with single origins made to order, with both a blend and seasonal option available for espresso too.

(917) 447-9476
underlinecoffee.com
Subway C, E (23rd St)

MON-SAT.	7:00am - 7:00pm
SUN.	9:00am - 6:00pm

First opened 2014
Roaster Apes & Peacocks
Machine Kees Van Der Westen Mirage Idrocompresso, 2 groups
Grinder Compak K10, Mahlkönig EK 43

Espresso	$3.00
Cappuccino	$3.75
Latte	$4.25

MAP REF. 78

COFFEE 4.25 / 5

OVERALL 4.25 / 5 ★★★★☆

88

Variety Coffee Roasters Chelsea

261 7th Avenue, Manhattan, NY 10001 | **Chelsea**

Beloved Brooklyn based Variety has made its Manhattan debut with a gorgeous corner spot in Chelsea. A large neon sign provides a great welcome, and the interior is truly superb with beautifully designed tile floors, seating along the walls, and on-trend lighting. Whether meeting up with friends or using the space as your new favorite study stop, its versatile interior makes this new location the perfect spot for everyone. Enjoy a delicious cup of single-origin, ethically sourced coffee, which is roasted locally. These Bushwick roasts are on-sale in store, so you can certainly take your beans to-go and brew at home! The food menu is also worth noting, particularly for its variety of vegan options. From its origins in laid-back Bushwick, Variety Coffee is a truly welcome addition to the fast-paced Manhattan coffee scene.

MAP REF.

COFFEE 4.50 / 5

OVERALL 4.75 / 5 ★★★★★

MON–SUN. 7:00am – 9:00pm

First opened 2017
Roaster Variety Coffee Roasters
Machine La Marzocco Linea PB, 3 groups
Grinder Mahlkönig Peak

Espresso $3.00
Cappuccino $4.00
Latte $4.50

(917) 409-0106
www.varietycoffeeroasters.com
Subway 1 (23rd St)

Sister locations Williamsburg / Greenpoint
/ Bushwick

Midtown is fast-paced, bustling and one of the greatest commercial centers in the world. The Empire State Building, The New York Public Library, MoMA and the core of New York's theater district - including the bright lights of Times Square - can all be found in Midtown. This area is also home to the small and elegant Gramercy, a quiet neighborhood with the private, preserved Gramercy Park at its center: a lovely reminder of New York's Victorian history.

Midtown & Gramercy

Birch Coffee Flatiron District

21 East 27th Street, Manhattan, NY 10016 | **Flatiron District**

Birch Coffee has made a cozy home at this end of 27th Street, with its assertively charming belief that coffee can and should bring people together. The shop has an "Ignition Initiative" with its collection of conversation starters that they suggest people enjoy with a neighbor. Their deeply satisfying own blend coffees make for lovely treats to share with old and new friends alike.

(212) 686-1444
www.birchcoffee.com
Subway N, Q, R, W (28th St)

Sister locations Multiple locations

MON-SUN. 7:00am - 8:00pm

First opened 2009
Roaster Birch Coffee Roasters
Machine La Marzocco Strada
Grinder Mazzer Luigi Robur

Espresso	$3.00
Cappuccino	$4.00
Latte	$4.00

MAP REF.

COFFEE 4.50 / 5   OVERALL 4.50 / 5 ★★★★⯪

Brooklyn Roasting Company
Flatiron District 50 West 23rd Street, Manhattan, NY 10010 | **Flatiron District**

While Brooklyn's flagship Navy Yard roastery/café embraces its industrial origins, this Flatiron space is much more Manhattan-slick, with checked floor tiles and soothing cream paint on the walls and ceiling. It's a big place, and needs to be: Brooklyn's well-deserved reputation for great coffee (single-origin drip is always sensational) and good food draws in crowds so big they need a rope barrier to keep them orderly. There's a nice mix of office workers and hipster aficionados here.

(718) 412-0080
www.brooklynroasting.com
Subway F, M (23rd St)

Sister locations Multiple locations

MON-SUN. 7:00am - 7:00pm

First opened 2015
Roaster Brooklyn Roasting Company
Machine La Marzocco Linea, 2 groups
Grinder Nuova Simonelli Mythos One

Espresso	$2.50
Cappuccino	$3.75
Latte	$4.50

MAP REF. **81**

COFFEE 4.25 / 5	OVERALL 4.00 / 5 ★★★★☆

Café Grumpy Grand Central Terminal
89 East 42nd Street, Manhattan, NY 10017 | **Midtown East**

Café Grumpy's Grand Central outlet has loads of competitors for your brew-time buck, but it offers something special: a small, attractive space with a window onto Lexington Avenue. It feels like a real café rather than a mass-transit pit stop. Despite the size you may have luck getting a seat, because so much of the trade is takeout. Carry your beautifully crafted latte to a table and sit down to read The New Yorker, or just look out the window. GCT is all hustle and bustle, but Grumpy is all sip and chill.

(212) 661-2198
www.cafegrumpy.com
Subway S, 4, 5, 6, 7 (Grand Central - 42nd St)

Sister locations Multiple locations

MON-FRI. 6:00am - 8:00pm
SAT-SUN. 7:00am - 8:00pm

First opened 2014
Roaster Café Grumpy Coffee
Machine Synesso Hydra, 2 groups
Grinder Nuova Simonelli Mythos, Mazzer Luigi Robur E, Ditting

Espresso	$3.25
Cappuccino	$4.00
Latte	$4.50

MAP REF. **82**

COFFEE 4.25 / 5	OVERALL 4.00 / 5 ★★★★☆

Chalait Nomad

1216 Broadway, Manhattan, NY 10001 | **Midtown West**

A compact but beautiful venue in the heart of Midtown, Chalait is the spot in New York City for a delicious and extensive matcha menu. However, do not be deterred if you are not a fan of matcha - the Counter Culture coffee here is expertly crafted on the La Marzocco Linea. The tasty food menu includes healthy and delicious favorites such as avocado and salmon sandwiches. Seating is limited and the shop also serves as the entrance to residents above, making it an ideal grab-and-go location for your matcha and macchiato!

(212) 929-0266
www.chalait.com
Subway N, Q, R, W (28th St)

Sister locations Hudson / Chelsea

MON-FRI.	7.30am - 6:00pm
SAT-SUN.	9:00am - 4:00pm

First opened 2017
Roaster Counter Culture Coffee
Machine La Marzocco Linea, 2 groups
Grinder Mazzer Luigi

Espresso	$3.25
Cappuccino	$4.00
Latte	$4.50

MAP REF. 83

COFFEE 4.25 / 5   **OVERALL** 4.25 / 5 ★★★★☆

Culture 36

247 West 36th Street, Manhattan, NY 10018 | **Garment District**

The second Garment District outpost of Culture Espresso is true to its name: only espresso and its milky offspring are served. You won't be disappointed, because the baristas know what they're doing with their gleaming Synesso. The Heart blend is bright and bracing, easily good enough to drink without sugar. There's an original ceiling high overhead and one big table offering the bulk of the seating in the spacious room. They bake their own delicious chocolate chip cookies, and once you've had one, you'll keep coming back for more.

www.cultureespresso.com
Subway A, C, E (34th St - Penn Station)

Sister locations Garment District (W 38th St) / Midtown West

MON-FRI.	7:00am - 7:00pm
SAT-SUN.	8:00am - 7:00pm

First opened 2015
Roaster Heart Coffee Roasters
Machine Synesso Hydra, 3 groups
Grinder Mazzer Luigi Robur E, Mahlkönig

Espresso	$3.00
Cappuccino	$4.00
Latte	$4.50

MAP REF. 84

COFFEE 4.50 / 5	🫘🫘🫘🫘🫘	OVERALL 4.25 / 5	★★★★⯪

Culture Espresso

72 West 38th Street, Manhattan, NY 10018 | **Midtown West**

TOP 40

Years ago, Culture was pretty much the only place to get great coffee near 42nd Street. Even though that's no longer the case, Culture's relaxed California-tinged atmosphere - despite constant foot-traffic - makes it stand out. Besides Stumptown's impossibly creamy, must-try nitro cold-brew on draught, the beans are from the excellent Heart Roasters of Portland. The baristas know what they're doing here, and you can't go wrong, whether you order an espresso, macchiato, or flat white. There's just enough space to sit down and relax, as you watch Midtown race by.

(212) 302-0200
www.cultureespresso.com
Subway B, D, F, M (42nd St - Bryant Park)

MON-FRI.	7:00am - 7:00pm
SAT-SUN.	8:00am - 7:00pm

First opened 2009
Roaster Heart Coffee Roasters
Machine La Marzocco Strada, 3 groups
Grinder Mazzer Luigi Robur E

Espresso	$3.00
Cappuccino	$4.50
Latte	$4.50

Sister locations Garment District (W 36th St) / Garment District (W 38th St)

MAP REF. 85

COFFEE 4.50 / 5	🫘🫘🫘🫘🫘	OVERALL 4.25 / 5	★★★★⯪

Dr Smood

1151 Broadway, Manhattan, NY 10001 | **Midtown West**

"Smart food for a good mood." That is the slogan for Dr. Smood, a stylish new venue situated near Madison Square Park. The Miami-based brand's NYC venture has only just begun, and already it is a hit among locals and tourists alike. With its sleek interior aesthetic that includes an exposed brick wall, comfortable seating, WiFi, and charging ports a plenty, Dr. Smood is the latest popular hub for health conscious millennials on a lunchbreak. In terms of their beverage servings, the brew never disappoints - and if you're in the mood for something a little fruity, their extensive own brand juice catalogue has you covered too. With two more locations already open in New York, and a further two coming soon, Dr Smood is making healthy waves in the New York coffee scene, and we are loving it!

MAP REF.

COFFEE 4.25 / 5	OVERALL 4.50 / 5

MON–FRI.   8:00am - 9:00pm
SAT–SUN.   9:00am - 7:00pm

First opened 2015
Roaster Joe Van Gogh
Machine La Marzocco Linea PB, 3 groups
Grinder La Marzocco Swift

Espresso	$2.75
Cappuccino	$4.75
Latte	$4.75

(305) 409-4830
www.drsmood.com
Subway N, Q, R, W (28th St)

Sister locations Midtown / Soho /
Midtown East / Lower East Side

FIKA Tower & Bakery

824 10th Avenue, Manhattan, NY 10019 | **Hell's Kitchen**

FIKA's 10th Avenue space is one of its best, with tall ceilings, white walls, copious light from the front windows and skylight, and discreet but distinctive decorative touches. This is a place to come and eat gorgeous Swedish-inspired food, with large platters a specialty. Of course, being Swedish, it does not neglect the sweet stuff either. There is a touch of berry sweetness in their well-made espresso, made with care and served with a smile. A great place to come after exploring the pier, just two blocks away.

(646) 490-7650
www.fikanyc.com
Subway 1, A, B, C, D (59th St - Columbus Circle)

Sister locations Multiple locations

MON-FRI.	7:00am – 7:00pm
SAT-SUN.	9:00am – 7:00pm

First opened 2014
Roaster FIKA
Machine Synesso Cyncra, 3 groups
Grinder BUNN

Espresso	$2.30
Cappuccino	$4.13
Latte	$4.36

MAP REF. **87**

COFFEE 4.00 / 5	OVERALL 4.50 / 5

Frisson Espresso

326 West 47th Street, Manhattan, NY 10036 | **Midtown West**

Owners Tulian Sanchez and Robert Melo have been friends since they were five, so it's not surprising that they work together well in running this peachy Theater District espresso spot. The place which sits around sixteen people, can be jumping any time of day, with a clientele they describe as "a little bit of everything,". Coffee is well made using beans from Dallis Bros. in Long Island City, and latte art is beautiful. Try to bag a table if you can and just sit back and enjoy the show.

(646) 850-3928
Subway 1, 2, A, C, E (50th St) or N, Q, R, W (49th St)

MON-TUE.	7:00am - 7:00pm
WED-FRI.	7:00am - 7:30pm
SAT.	8:00am - 8:00pm
SUN.	8:00am - 6:30pm

First opened 2014
Roaster Dallis Bros. Coffee
Machine Synesso Cyncra, 3 groups
Grinder Compak E10

Espresso	$3.00
Cappuccino	$4.00
Latte	$4.50

COFFEE 4.00 / 5		OVERALL 4.00 / 5	

Gasoline Alley Flatiron District

24 East 23rd Street, Manhattan, NY 10010 | **Flatiron District**

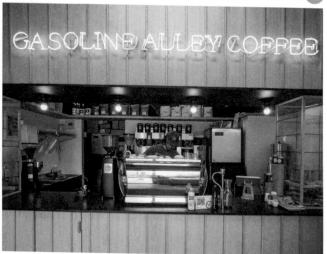

Gasoline Alley always wins with its memorable coffee, and this snug Flatiron venue is no different. Conveniently placed for those needing to power up on their way to work, the service is as friendly and efficient as you'd expect from the guys at Gasoline Alley. Beans are from Intelligentsia and brewed with skill across the board. There's a bit of seating too, with a good view across 23rd Street of Madison Square Park.

(212) 933-0113
www.gasolinealleycoffee.com
Subway N, Q, R, W (23 St) or 4, 6 (23 St)

Sister locations Noho / Nolita

MON-FRI.	7:00am – 7:00pm
SAT.	8:00am – 6:00pm
SUN.	8:00am – 5:00pm

First opened 2016
Roaster Intelligentsia Coffee
Machine La Marzocco GB5, 3 groups
Grinder Mazzer Luigi Robur E

Espresso	$2.75
Cappuccino	$4.00
Latte	$4.25

MAP REF. **89**

COFFEE 4.25 / 5

OVERALL 4.25 / 5 ★★★★⯪

101

Gregorys Coffee Gramercy

327 Park Avenue South, Manhattan, NY 10010 | **Gramercy**

This branch of Gregory's is one of the most popular places in the area among office workers who want conviviality with their coffee: the tables lining the long, narrow room are often full, and it's not just with those tapping on a keyboard. It's a very welcoming space, nicely decorated with a combination of dark colors and bright lighting, and the customary Gregory's offerings of both food and drink keep up the company's high standards. Gregory's own in-house baked goods are exceptional, and a wide range of non-espresso brews makes coffee selection a challenging pleasure.

(917) 388-3850
www.gregoryscoffee.com
Subway 4, 6 (23 St)

Sister locations Multiple locations

MON-FRI.	6:00am - 8:00pm
SAT-SUN.	7:00am - 7:00pm

First opened 2006
Roaster Gregorys Coffee
Machine La Marzocco GB5
Grinder Mazzer Luigi

Espresso	$3.00
Cappuccino	$4.00
Latte	$4.00

MAP REF. **90**

COFFEE 4.25 / 5	●●●●◐	OVERALL 4.25 / 5	★★★★☆

Ground Central Coffee Co. 2nd Avenue

800 2nd Avenue, Manhattan, NY 10013 | **Midtown East**

This small branch of Ground Central, the company's second, maintains a steady buzz thanks to two huge nearby suppliers of thirsty workers: Grand Central Station and the UN. It's not surprising that customers choose Ground Central, with coffee this good pouring steadily out of their machines. Single-origin drip and pour-over are outstanding, from a changing range. The espresso-based drinks feature latte art that could easily win professional competitions. No wonder Ground Central is almost as busy as Grand Central.

(646) 484-5697
www.ground-central.com
Subway S, 4, 5, 6, 7 (Grand Central - 42nd St)

MON-FRI.	6:30am - 7:00pm
SAT-SUN.	7:00am - 5:00pm

First opened 2015
Roaster La Colombe Coffee Roasters
Machine La Marzocco Custom
Grinder Mazzer Luigi Super Jolly

Espresso	$3.10
Cappuccino	$4.10
Latte	$4.25 / $4.75

Sister locations Theater District / Lower Manhattan

MAP REF. **91**

COFFEE 4.25 / 5	●●●●◐	OVERALL 4.00 / 5	★★★★☆

Ground Central Coffee Co. 52nd Street

155 East 52nd Street, Manhattan, NY 10017 | **Midtown East**

This original branch of Ground Central feels more like a European-style café than a contemporary-style coffee place. It's sleek and elegant, and the prominence given to their serious sandwiches and enticing baked goods makes it clear that food plays a major role. Swap your coffee for a cocktail later in the day. A collection of vinyl discs lines a front wall, and the soundtrack favors timeless rock 'n' roll classics. The baristas rock their three-group Faema, too, but don't neglect the single-origin drip brews.

(646) 964-4438
www.ground-central.com
Subway E, M (Lexington Ave / 53rd St)

Sister locations Midtown East / Lower Manhattan

MON-FRI.	6:30am - 9:00pm
SAT-SUN.	9:00am - 6:00pm

First opened 2014
Roaster La Colombe Coffee Roasters
Machine Faema E61, 3 groups
Grinder Mazzer Luigi Robur E

Espresso	$3.10
Cappuccino	$4.10
Latte	$4.25 / $4.75

MAP REF. **92**

COFFEE 4.25 / 5

OVERALL 4.00 / 5 ★★★★☆

Hole in the Wall

420 5th Avenue, Manhattan, NY 10018 | **Murray Hill**

Photo courtesy of the venue

The name does not do this coffee bar justice, wriggled into the corner of a busy office building. It streamlines the morning dash, bringing fine coffee as close to the office as possible. But this smart shop's open to the public too! Enter around either corner of the building and grab a coffee to enjoy while you pound the streets. They also offer sandwiches (including the ever popular avocado toast) as well as fresh, locally baked goods like big, glorious doughnuts.

(212) 602-9991
www.holeinthewallnyc.com
Subway N, Q, R, B, D, F, M (34th St - Herald Sq)

MON-SUN. 7:00am - 10:00pm

First opened 2014
Roaster Novo Coffee
Machine Synesso, 2 groups
Grinder Mazzer Luigi Robur E

Espresso	$3.25
Cappuccino	$4.00
Latte	$4.50

MAP REF. **93**

 COFFEE 4.00 / 5   OVERALL 4.00 / 5

Irving Farm Coffee Roasters

Gramercy 71 Irving Place, Manhattan, NY 10003 | **Gramercy**

Settled at the bottom of a brownstone on quiet Irving Place, Irving Farm is a New York City institution. The street may be serene, but step inside to find a café bustling with energy. There is a constant stream of people moving in and out of this cozy café, which can be a bit snug in terms of seating, but that is part of its charming atmosphere. The lights are low, the baristas are pros, and their coffee, which is roasted at their Hudson Valley roastery, is expertly brewed.

(212) 995-5252
www.irvingfarm.com
Subway N, R, W, 4, 5, 6, L (14th St - Union Sq)

Sister locations Multiple locations

| MON-FRI. | 7:00am – 10:00pm |
| SAT-SUN. | 8:00am – 10:00pm |

First opened 1996
Roaster Irving Farm Coffee Roasters
Machine La Marzocco Linea, 2 groups
Grinder Nuova Simonelli Mythos Clima Pro

Espresso	$3.25
Cappuccino	$4.25
Latte	$4.75

MAP REF. **94**

COFFEE 4.50 / 5

OVERALL 4.50 / 5 ★★★★⯨

Irving Farm Coffee Roasters
Midtown East 135 East 50th Street, Manhattan, NY 10022 | **Midtown East**

Irving Farm's latest spot in Midtown East truly outdoes itself in all areas; quality, aesthetic, and customer service. Friendly baristas execute their craft with knowledge and care, pulling consistently great espressos and delicious cappuccinos. With its black concrete floors and burnished brass details, the shop's design is heavily influenced by the surrounding neighborhood. Additionally, the spot boasts a brand-new menu by Danielle Dillon, serving up modern comfort food. It's a place for anyone really: Mom's wheeling strollers, co-workers on their lunch break, or diligent students studying for midterms.

(646) 649-3263
www.irvingfarm.com
Subway 4, 6 (51st St)

MON-FRI.	7:00am - 8:00pm
SAT-SUN.	8:00am - 7:00pm

First opened 2017
Roaster Irving Farm Coffee Roasters
Machine La Marzocco Linea, 3 groups
Grinder Nuova Simonelli Mythos

Espresso	$3.50
Cappuccino	$4.50
Latte	$5.00

Sister locations Multiple locations

MAP REF. 95

COFFEE 4.50 / 5 **OVERALL** 4.50 / 5 ★★★★½

Joe & The Juice Midtown East

286 Madison Avenue, Manhattan, NY 10017 | **Midtown East**

The east 40s don't suffer from a shortage of places to eat and drink, but this branch of Joe & The Juice is an extremely welcome addition to the scene. Yes, you can come and get your latte and your avocado sandwich to go and eat them at your desk. But if you want a break from the office, this is an unexpectedly pleasant place to sit and talk - well spaced tables in an attractive corner site, not to forget the upbeat Danish vibes. Espresso-based drinks are always well made, and a big cup of filter is also a great option. And then there are famous juices, for those who want fruit with their beans.

(917) 565-4016
www.joejuice.com
Subway 7 (5th Ave)

MON-FRI.	6:00am - 9:00pm
SAT-SUN.	8:00am - 9:00pm

First opened 2016
Roaster Bewleys
Machine La Marzocco
Grinder Nuova Simonelli Mythos

Espresso	$2.75
Cappuccino	$3.50
Latte	$2.75 / $3.75

Sister locations Multiple locations

MAP REF. 96

COFFEE 4.00 / 5  **OVERALL** 4.25 / 5 ★★★★½

Kahve

667 10th Avenue, Manhattan, NY 10019 | **Hell's Kitchen**

The second incarnation of Kahve is brightly modern in décor and has much more seating space than the nearby original. It's a very good place to settle in for working, though the seats in the window make a good place for people-watching. In addition to the signature Kahve offerings of brewed coffee, espresso-based drinks, and indulgent latte tweaks, this branch serves nitro-brew from a tap on the counter. The baristas know their business, and they know how to smile, a winning combination from this rising star of New York's coffee scene.

(646) 649-4503
www.kahvenyc.com
Subway A, C, E (50th St)

Sister locations Hell's Kitchen

MON-FRI.	7:00am – 8:00pm
SAT.	7:30am – 8:00pm
SUN.	8:30am – 8:00pm

First opened 2016
Roaster Secret
Machine Nuova Simonelli Aurelia, 2 groups
Grinder Nuova Simonelli MDX

Espresso	$2.00
Cappuccino	$3.25
Latte	$3.25

MAP REF.

COFFEE 4.00 / 5

OVERALL 4.00 / 5 ★★★★☆

Le Café Coffee

7 East 14th Street, Manhattan, NY 10003 | **Gramercy**

Photo courtesy of the venue

Situated in the middle of the always hectic 14th Street, Le Café Coffee is an oasis from the Manhattan mayhem. It's small, but never too crowded, making it the perfect spot to take a seat and relax amidst the outside chaos. The service is refreshingly friendly, the conversation personalized as they prepare your order. They serve espresso-based beverages as well as drip alongside a small menu of fresh sandwiches. Additionally, there is a seasonal menu of specialty beverages, and their matcha latte is especially of note.

(212) 365-1060
www.lecafecoffee.com
Subway 4, 5,6, N, Q, R, W, L (14th St - Union Sq)

MON-THU.	7:00am - 8:30pm	
FRI.	7:00am - 9:00pm	
SAT.	8:00am - 9:00pm	
SUN.	8:00am - 8:00pm	

First opened 2013
Roaster La Colombe Coffee Roasters
Machine La Marzocco, 2 groups
Grinder Mazzer Luigi

Espresso	$2.75
Cappuccino	$3.75
Latte	$4.00

MAP REF.

COFFEE 4.25 / 5

OVERALL 4.00 / 5 ★★★★☆

108

Little Collins

667 Lexington Avenue, Manhattan, NY 10022 | **Midtown East**

Australian-influenced Little Collins is the civilized coffee shop Midtown East has always needed but didn't have until 2013. Focused, friendly baristas in old-fashioned uniforms work diligently and quickly to serve a constant stream of business people and yogis. If you're able to snag a stool, the staff make you feel at home, pouring you tap water without being asked to do so. The espresso, strong and delicious, comes with a tiny almond cookie, a nice touch. Single-origin pour-overs are made with a ModBar contraption which heats and pours the water - it's like having a robot hand-pour your coffee.

(212) 308-1969
www.littlecollinsnyc.com
Subway E, M (Lexington Ave / 53rd St)

MON-FRI.	7:00am - 5:00pm
SAT-SUN.	8:00am - 4:00pm

First opened 2013
Roaster Counter Culture Coffee
Machine ModBar
Grinder Mazzer Luigi Robur, Nuova Simonelli Mythos

Espresso	$3.25
Cappuccino	$4.00
Latte	$4.25

MAP REF.

 COFFEE 4.50 / 5  OVERALL 4.50 / 5 ★★★★½

Ninth Street Espresso Midtown East

109 East 56th Street, Manhattan, NY 10022 | **Midtown East**

The Ninth Street Espresso menu boasts just 4 options, none of which are "cappuccino" or latte" - instead, simply "espresso with milk". This minimalist touch is one of several ways it conveys it's serious about espresso, and their strong, viscous shots back that up. The timeless, black-and-white-tiled space, inside the swanky Lombardy hotel, has a few stools, but is more suited to the droves of businesspeople who line up to throw back a shot. If you can avoid feeling like a philistine in comparison, order the smooth, sweet cold-brew; it's the best in the city.

(646) 559-4793
www.ninthstreetespresso.com
Subway E, M (Lexington Ave / 53rd St)

| MON-FRI. | 7:00am - 7:00pm |
| SAT-SUN. | 8:00am - 5:00pm |

First opened 2013
Roaster Ninth Street Espresso
Machine La Marzocco Linea, 2 groups
Grinder Mazzer Luigi Robur E, Mahlkönig EK 43

Espresso	$3.00
Cappuccino	$4.00
Latte	$4.00

Sister locations Alphabet City / Chelsea / Downtown Brooklyn / East Village

MAP REF. **100**

| COFFEE 4.50 / 5 |  | OVERALL 4.25 / 5 | ★★★★☆ |

Oren's Daily Roast Midtown West

1440 Broadway, Manhattan, NY 10018 | **Midtown West**

Oren's does a brisk business for good reasons: the coffee is solid and the store's well run. At this branch, nearly everyone seems to come in for something to go. Single-origin brews, using beans bought directly from the producers, are the obvious choice for drinking on the move. This branch, one of Oren's nine locations in New York is right on the doorstep of the tourist-and-traffic magnet that is Times Square and 42nd Street, a welcome addition to this busy area.

(646) 291-2090
www.orensdailyroast.com
Subway S, 4, 5, 6, 7 (Grand Central - 42nd St)

Sister locations Multiple locations

MON-FRI.	7:00am - 7:00pm
SAT.	8:00am - 2:00pm
SUN.	Closed

First opened 2011
Roaster Oren's Daily Roast
Machine La Marzocco GB, 2 groups
Grinder Mazzer Luigi Robur E, Mahlkönig Guatemala Lab

Espresso	$2.75
Cappuccino	$3.60 / $4.15 / $4.60
Latte	$3.60 / $4.15 / $4.60

MAP REF. **101**

| COFFEE 4.00 / 5 |  | OVERALL 4.00 / 5 | ★★★★☆ |

Perk Kafé

162 East 37th Street, Manhattan, NY 10016 | **Murray Hill**

Photo courtesy of the venue

The sedate precincts of Murray Hill are probably not the first place you'd think of as the location for a seriously distinguished, extremely laid-back coffee destination. But that's what you get in Perk Kafé. It's not a big place, and can get crowded, but it's worth a visit for the quality of the coffee alone. Beans from Stumptown get the royal treatment, including various non-espresso alternatives if you're a single-origin lover. Latte art is exemplary, and the welcome is friendly. A great place in an unexpected area.

(212) 686-7375
perkkafe.com
Subway 4, 6 (33rd St)

Sister locations East Harlem

MON–SAT.	7:00am – 7:00pm
SUN.	8:00am – 7:00pm

First opened 2013
Roaster Stumptown Coffee Roasters and guests
Machine La Marzocco, 2 groups
Grinder Mazzer Luigi Super Jolly, Mazzer Luigi Kony

Espresso	$2.95
Cappuccino	$3.95
Latte	$4.25

MAP REF. **102**

COFFEE 4.25 / 5

OVERALL 4.25 / 5 ★★★★

Pushcart Coffee

362 2nd Avenue, Manhattan, NY 10010 | **Gramercy**

This branch of Pushcart likes to think that it places itself at the heart of its local community. While claims like this are common enough, Pushcart pursues the idea with singular devotion. Pictures from the local elementary school are commonplace, and there's a "community board" for flyers and a well-scribbled whiteboard. The airy corner room is equally welcoming to solitary workers and groups of all ages and sizes, and the coffee - bought directly from origin - is expertly made, with great latte art included. A wonderful place indeed.

(917) 224-0761
www.pushcartcoffee.com
Subway L (3rd Ave)

Sister locations Chelsea / Williamsburg

MON-SUN. 7:00am - 7:00pm

First opened 2012
Roaster Pushcart Coffee
Machine La Marzocco, 2 groups
Grinder Mazzer Luigi

Espresso	$3.25
Cappuccino	$4.00
Latte	$4.00 /$4.50 / $5.00

MAP REF.

COFFEE 4.25 / 5	OVERALL 4.25 / 5

Ramini Espresso Bar and Café

265 West 37th Street, Manhattan, NY 10018 | **Midtown West**

Photo courtesy of the venue

Ramini is a key player in major-league coffee. Its pretty interior has some quirky features and you can always expect an exceptionally warm welcome from coffee-obsessed baristas. The tasty baked goods, are mostly made on the premises and they also offer a superior selection of teas and fresh-squeezed juices. Liquids from the two-group La Marzocco are common, but if you want a real change, go for a cup from the towering 'Kyoto' drip apparatus, the world's slowest drip machine. An unexpected and really delightful find in Midtown.

(347) 907-0343
www.ramininyc.com
Subway A, C, E (34th St - Penn Station)

MON-FRI.	7:00am - 5:30pm
SAT.	9:00am - 1:00pm
SUN.	Closed

First opened 2012
Roaster 49th Parallel Roasters, Vassilaros & Sons
Machine La Marzocco GB5, 2 groups
Grinder Mazzer Luigi Robur

Espresso	$2.75
Cappuccino	$4.00 / $5.75
Latte	$4.00 / $5.75

MAP REF. **104**

COFFEE 4.25 / 5 **OVERALL** 4.00 / 5 ★★★★☆

REX

864 10th Avenue, Manhattan, NY 10039 | **Hell's Kitchen**

REX does its name proud, as this shop is one of the kings. It's got wonderfully prepared coffees from Counter Culture and features a slow bar with seasonal single origins that the staff will happily discuss with you. They also run an astonishingly impressive kitchen, preparing surprises such as house-cured gravlax for fresh sandwiches and impossibly delicious baked goods; the flourless chocolate brownies are one to try. It's a welcome coffee oasis in Hell's Kitchen and though small, it's got two comfy, communal tables and enough charm to make it a cozy, inviting space to visit for a refuel.

(212) 757-0580
www.rexcoffeenyc.com
Subway 1, A, B, C, D (59th St - Columbus Circle)

MON-FRI. 7:00am - 7:00pm
SAT-SUN. 7:00am - 6:00pm

First opened 2013
Roaster Counter Culture Coffee
Machine La Marzocco Linea, 2 groups
Grinder Mazzer Luigi Robur, Mahlkönig EK 43

Espresso	$3.00
Cappuccino	$3.75
Latte	$4.00

MAP REF. **105**

COFFEE 4.25 / 5	OVERALL 4.25 / 5
	★★★★⯪

114

Ruby's Café Murray Hill

442 3rd Avenue, Manhattan, NY 10016 | **Murray Hill**

You'll spot the Murray Hill branch of Ruby's from some distance, because there's almost certain to be a crowd standing outside waiting for a table. This Midtown spot duplicates the wildly successful model of the Aussie-inspired Soho original, but in a somewhat smaller package. If you're looking for just a quick coffee, we'd recommend arriving outside mealtimes to avoid the food rush. Though even that's no guarantee of instant entry; a true testament to its popularity. If the weather is right, the iced coffee at Ruby's is a particularly tasty option.

(212) 300-4245
www.rubyscafe.com
Subway 4, 6 (28th St)

MON.-SUN. 9:00am - 10:30pm

First opened 2016
Roaster Counter Culture Coffee
Machine La Marzocco GB5, 2 groups
Grinder Nuova Simonelli Mythos One

Espresso	$3.00
Cappuccino	$4.00
Latte	$4.00

Sister locations Soho

MAP REF. 106

| COFFEE 4.25 / 5 |  | OVERALL 4.25 / 5 | ★★★★☆ |

Simon Sips

1185 Avenue of the Americas, Manhattan, NY 10036 | **Midtown West**

Simon Sips is in the business of making good coffee, plain and simple. It embraces a no-nonsense approach to providing exceptional coffee to those who are lucky enough to have found this unexpected shop, settled behind the lobby of a large office building. Head down to this industrious shop from the plaza entrance, open to the public from one of the side streets. The space has a simple, clean interior while their espressos are carefully pulled by attentive baristas. Simon Sips is a welcoming little resting place in the bustle of Midtown.

(212) 354-2100
www.simonsips.com
Subway 1, 2, 3 (42nd St) or 1 (50th St) or B, D, F, M (47 - 50th St)

MON.-FRI. 7:00am - 5:30pm
SAT.-SUN. Closed

First opened 2012
Roaster Parlor Coffee Roasters
Machine La Marzocco Linea, 2 groups
Grinder Nuova Simonelli Mythos, Mahlkönig EK 43

Espresso	$2.20
Cappuccino	$3.00
Latte	$3.40

MAP REF. 102

| COFFEE 4.00 / 5 | | OVERALL 4.00 / 5 | ★★★★☆ |

Stumptown Ace Hotel

Ace Hotel, 18 West 29th Street, Manhattan, NY 10001 | **Nomad**

Stumptown has expanded considerably in the decade since opening their first New York outpost, but the consistency of the quality here hasn't changed a bit. They offer several types of cold brew including "Nitro". Grab a can to-go, and order a single origin Chemex pour over. Don't be fooled by the fact that these are not listed on the chalkboard menu; the baristas are verifiable wizards at extracting maximum flavor from the many single-origin bean offerings available.

(855) 711-3385
www.stumptowncoffee.com
Subway N, Q, R, W (28th St) or 4, 6 (28th St)

MON-FRI.	6:00am - 8:00pm
SAT-SUN.	7:00am - 8:00pm

First opened 2008
Roaster Stumptown Coffee Roasters
Machine La Marzocco Linea, 3 groups
Grinder Mazzer Luigi Robur E

Espresso	$3.25
Cappuccino	$4.00
Latte	$4.00 / $4.50 / $5.00

Sister locations Greenwich Village

MAP REF.

COFFEE
4.50 / 5

OVERALL
4.50 / 5
★★★★⯪

116

Taylor St. Baristas

33 East 40th Street, Manhattan, NY 10016 | **Midtown East**

TOP 40

Aussie inspired Taylor Street Baristas is an extra ordinary place to spend an afternoon. It's immediately welcoming and upstairs is an inspiring sight for midtowners: tons of space. The constantly-rotating menu features several types of Counter Culture Coffee drip: Classic, Delicate and Wild, each so nuanced. Nothing here feels pretentious thanks to infectiously high-spirited baristas who gladly offer a free taste of each. They're as skilled as they are friendly. The espresso is excellent, as is their flat white made on the gleaming Victoria Arduino Black Eagle.

www.taylor-st.com
Subway S, 4, 5, 6, 7 (Grand Central - 42nd St)

MON-FRI.	7:00am - 6:00pm
SAT-SUN.	Closed

First opened 2016
Roaster Counter Culture Coffee
Machine Victoria Arduino Black Eagle, 3 groups x2, Victoria Arduino Black Eagle, 2 groups, Marco SP9, 2 groups x2
Grinder Nuova Simonelli Mythos x6, Mahlkönig EK 43 x2

Espresso	$3.50
Cappuccino	$4.25 / $5.00
Latte	$4.25 / $5.00

MAP REF. 109

COFFEE 4.50 / 5

OVERALL 4.50 / 5 ★★★★⯪

Think Coffee Gramercy

280 3rd Avenue, Manhattan, NY 10010 | **Gramercy**

This branch of Think just looks great. It has high ceilings and big windows on two sides of its L-shaped space, letting in lots of light and giving an airy feeling. The seating arrangement was designed with comfort in mind. Add a no-WiFi policy and you've got a formula for old-fashioned coffee conviviality in a very contemporary setting. Lots of people come for coffee to go, but sitting down with a perfectly made macchiato or single-country pour-over blend is by far the better option. Think Gramercy is a top choice in an area that provides plenty of it.

(212) 255-6452
www.thinkcoffee.com
Subway 6 (23rd St)

MON-FRI.	6:30am - 9:00pm
SAT-SUN.	7:00am - 9:00pm

First opened 2016
Roaster Red House Roasters
Machine La Marzocco
Grinder Mahlkönig Peak

Espresso $2.75
Cappuccino $4.00
Latte $4.50

Sister locations Multiple locations

MAP REF. **110**

 COFFEE 4.25 / 5   **OVERALL** 4.50 / 5 ★★★★⯨

Trademark

38 West 36th Street, Manhattan, NY 10018 | **Midtown West**

Midtown Manhattan is full of all kinds of coffee-drinkers, and Trademark seems intent on subtly customizing the experience for each customer. If you're in a hurry and like vanilla lattes, they've got you covered. If you feel like staying a while, they'll make you an excellent, floral single-origin Phoenix pour-over and serve it to you in a beautiful carafe. But you don't want to miss the espresso, extracted on a Mavam matte red espresso machine built into the bar - straight out of the production design of the movie "Her," it's probably the most beautiful espresso machine you've ever seen. Plus there are only about 20 in the world.

(646) 858-2320
www.ingoodcompanyhg.com
Subway B,D,F,M,N,Q,R, W (34th St - Herald Sq)

MON-FRI.	7:00am - 6:00pm
SAT.	8:00am - 5:00pm
SUN.	11:00am - 3:00pm

First opened 2016
Roaster 4 J's Roaster
Machine Custom Mavam
Grinder Mazzer Luigi Kold, Mahlkönig EK 43

Espresso $3.25
Cappuccino $4.00
Latte $4.50

MAP REF. **111**

COFFEE 4.25 / 5  **OVERALL** 4.25 / 5 ★★★★⯨

Zibetto Espresso Bar

501 5th Avenue, Manhattan, NY 10017 | **Midtown East**

Step inside Zibetto and you're not in Manhattan, you're in Milan. This sleek little number, gleaming with marble and tiling, is as authentically Italian as Sophia Loren's smile. The classic Italian short shot of espresso is bracing stuff. There's little seating, in tribute to the Italian view of espresso as something drunk quickly before dashing off. But they don't push you to dash. Though the service is polished and brisk, it's very friendly in a very Italian way. Note: the entrance is around the corner on 42nd Street.

(646) 838-6314
www.zibettoespresso.com
Subway 7 (5th Ave)

Sister locations Midtown (W 56th St) /
Midtown (W 49th St)

MON-FRI.	7:00am - 8:00pm	
SAT.	9:00am - 6:00pm	
SUN.	10:00am - 5:00pm	

First opened 2014
Roaster Zibetto Coffee
Machine La Cimbali M100, 3 groups
Grinder Sanremo

Espresso	$3.00
Cappuccino	$4.50
Latte	$5.00

MAP REF.

COFFEE
4.50 / 5

OVERALL
4.25 / 5

★★★★⯪

From the Apollo Theatre in Harlem to the world-famous Metropolitan Museum of Art, upper northern Manhattan has a rich and varied cultural heritage. The Upper East Side boasts Museum Row, home to some of the greatest art and history museums in the country, as well as some of the best and most exclusive shopping in New York on Madison Avenue. The Upper West Side has a calmer feel, with the Lincoln Center for the performing Arts and The Museum of Natural History. In between sits the vast Central Park, New York's beloved urban oasis.

Upper Manhattan

Bluestone Lane Upper East Side

2 East 90th Street, Manhattan, NY 10128 | **Upper East Side**

Photo: Ben Hider

Aussie inspired Bluestone Lane has bagged a site that many cafés would kill for: a superb space in a Gothic-style church just across Fifth Avenue from Central Park. Sit in the sandstone interior or grab a table on the sidewalk. The food has a focus on virtue that doesn't sacrifice good flavour, while outstanding house-roasted beans get careful treatment on the La Marzocco. There's a notably warm welcome, and the barista skills extend to outstanding latte art: appropriate when the Guggenheim and the Met are a short walk away and Cooper Hewitt is right across the street.

(646) 869-7812
www.bluestonelaneny.com
Subway 4, 5, 6 (86th St)

Sister locations Multiple locations

MON–SUN.   7:30am – 6:00pm

First opened 2015
Roaster Bluestone Lane & Niccolo
Machine La Marzocco Linea, 3 groups
Grinder Nuova Simonelli

Espresso	$2.75
Cappuccino	$4.00
Latte	$4.00

MAP REF.

COFFEE 4.50 / 5	OVERALL 4.50 / 5 ★★★★⯨

Box Kite Upper West Side

128 West 72nd Street, Manhattan, NY 10023 | **Upper West Side**

Photo courtesy of the venue

The lower end of the Upper West Side does not exactly overflow with places for a superior cup, which makes it all the more thrilling that Box Kite chose to open a branch here in 2015. The place is small, with seating for just six people, so the emphasis is inevitably on coffee to take away rather than drink on the premises. But it's an attractive place to sit, and being a WiFi-free zone, it's something of a refuge from the busy world outside.

(212) 574-8203
www.boxkitenyc.com
Subway 1, 2, 3 (72nd St)

Sister locations East Village

MON-SUN. 7:00am - 7:00pm

First opened 2015
Roaster Rotating roasters
Machine Synesso, 2 groups
Grinder Mahlkönig Peak, Mahlkönig EK 40

Espresso	$3.50
Cappuccino	$4.50
Latte	$4.75

MAP REF.

COFFEE 4.25 / 5	🫘 🫘 🫘 🫘 🫘	OVERALL 4.25 / 5	★★★★⭒

Café Jax

318 East 84th Street, Manhattan, NY 10028 | **Upper East Side**

Café Jax is a dream of a neighborhood coffee spot. It's a place where all drinks are taken seriously - even as the sense of childhood is preserved in pours such as cold brew ice cream float and lavender lemonade. Stumptown beans make up the house blend, enjoyable in numerous hot and cold forms as you eat a salad, sandwich or baked good. The long front room is lovely, but the large downstairs seating space and especially the garden, are to be admired.

(212) 510-7084
www.cafejaxnyc.com
Subway Q (86th St)

MON-FRI.	7:00am - 9:00pm
SAT-SUN.	8:00am - 9:00am

First opened 2014
Roaster Stumptown Coffee Roasters
Machine La Marzocco Linea, 2 groups
Grinder Mazzer Luigi Major E

Espresso	$3.00
Cappuccino	$4.00
Latte	$4.25

MAP REF. 115

COFFEE 4.25 / 5   **OVERALL** 4.00 / 5 ★★★★☆

The Chipped Cup

3610 Broadway, Manhattan, NY 10031 | **Harlem**

This Harlem anchor offers great coffee in a comforting environment. It boasts fresh pastries from Balthazar and toasted bagel sandwiches if you're really peckish to go along with well-drawn shots of Counter Culture espresso. The space is fitted out with lots of tables for all the computer-clacking workers, and there's also a sweet backyard if you're feeling like a breath of fresh air instead.

(212) 368-8881
www.chippedcupcoffee.com
Subway 1 (145 St)

| MON–FRI. | 7:00am – 8:00pm |
| SAT–SUN. | 8:00am – 8:00pm |

First opened 2012
Roaster Counter Culture Coffee
Machine La Marzocco GB5
Grinder Mazzer Luigi Robur E

Espresso	$2.75
Cappuccino	$3.75
Latte	$4.25

MAP REF. 116

| COFFEE 4.00 / 5 | | OVERALL 4.00 / 5 | ★★★★☆ |

Darling Coffee

TOP 40

NEW

4961 Broadway, Manhattan, NY 10034 | **Inwood**

Darling Coffee checks every box you could want - and probably others that you're not even aware of. It's a happy place, with a diverse crowd of Inwood locals. The food is all made in-house, even pickles and preserves. There's a laptop-free zone at the back, for people who understand that the first purpose of a coffee shop is to get people talking. The beans come from Plowshares, a small Brooklyn roaster. The staff smile, even as they work hard. Come here for a meal, or just an expertly made macchiato, and relax. Locals say that Darling "feels like home." You'll see exactly what they mean when you pay a visit.

www.darlingcoffeenyc.com
Subway A (207th St)

| MON–FRI. | 7:00am – 7:00pm |
| SAT–SUN. | 8:00am – 7:00pm |

First opened 2012
Roaster Plowshares Coffee
Machine La Marzocco Linea, 2 groups
Grinder Mazzer Luigi Robur E

Espresso	$2.75
Cappuccino	$3.75
Latte	$4.00

MAP REF. 117

| COFFEE 4.50 / 5 |  | OVERALL 4.50 / 5 | ★★★★⯪ |

Dear Mama

308 East 109th Street, Manhattan, NY 10029 | **Harlem**

Dear Mama was the first specialty coffee venue to open in this area of East Harlem, and being the first in a neighborhood still relatively un-gentrified by Manhattan standards would have to be regarded as bold verging on risky. But the bold move turned out to be a shrewd one: they started out strong and have only become "busier and busier." Beans come from Nobletree's roastery in Red Hook, with milky versions the top choice for espresso-based drinks. But many of the regulars who walk through the door go there for food, and the kitchen in back never disappoints. The menu is simple yet serious from breakfast through dinner. You can go light with a salad or a soup of the day (very good), or eat substantially with steak and eggs.

And vegans are particularly well catered for too. The owner started out in the bar business, so it's not surprising that alcohol is chosen with care. Dear Mama set out to be a "neighborhood hub," and there's definitely a great local feel here, right down to the pictures by local artists hanging on the walls. Your mama would love it, and so will you.

MAP REF. **118**

COFFEE	OVERALL
4.50 / 5	4.25 / 5 ★★★★⯪

MON.	7:00am - 9:00pm
TUE-SUN.	7:00am - 10:00pm

First opened 2016
Roaster Nobletree Coffee
Machine Synesso Hydra, 2 groups
Grinder Nuova Simonelli Mythos Clima Pro,
Mahlkönig EK 43

Espresso	$3.00
Cappuccino	$4.00
Latte	$4.00

(929) 279-2225
www.dearmamacoffee.com
Subway 4, 6 (110th St)

Double Dutch Espresso

2194 Frederick Douglass Boulevard, Manhattan, NY 10026 | **Harlem**

This busy Harlem shop offers a delightful atmosphere for an afternoon coffee respite. Double Dutch serves locally baked treats, make fresh home-made sandwiches and prepare great coffee to charge you through the last few pages of that book you're just aching to finish. There is plenty of seating in a winsome atmosphere, with antique accents that make it feel warm and inviting. They keep two espressos on bar at a time, a blend and a rotating single origin, so be sure to ask for what's available.

(646) 429-8834
www.doubledutchespresso.com
Subway B, C (116th St)

MON-FRI.	7:00am - 8:00pm
SAT-SUN.	8:00am - 8:00pm

First opened 2013
Roaster Counter Culture Coffee
Machine La Marzocco GB5
Grinder Mazzer Luigi

Espresso	$2.50
Cappuccino	$3.50
Latte	$4.25 / $4.75

MAP REF. 119

COFFEE 4.25 / 5
OVERALL 4.25 / 5 ★★★★

Filtered Coffee

1616 Amsterdam Avenue, Manhattan, NY 10031 | **Harlem**

With the huge CCNY campus just outside, Filtered could probably do good business even if it sold diner coffee. But this tiny, chilled Hamilton Heights venue shows a deep commitment to getting high quality from its Counter Culture beans — and it's a very nice place to sit, as well. All espresso-based drinks are available on ice if you don't like it hot, and the simple food offering majors on bagels and highly tempting baked goods. In an area that isn't rich in specialty coffee, Filtered is a real find.

(917) 475-1120
www.filtered.nyc
Subway 137th St - City College

Sister locations Washington Heights

MON-FRI.	7:00am - 7:00pm
SAT-SUN.	8:00am - 5:00pm

First opened 2015
Roaster Counter Culture Coffee
Machine La Marzocco, 2 groups
Grinder Mazzer Luigi Robur E

Espresso	$2.75
Cappuccino	$3.75
Latte	$4.75

MAP REF. **120**

COFFEE 4.25 / 5 ●●●●◐ **OVERALL** 4.25 / 5 ★★★★☆

Gregorys Coffee Upper East Side

878 Lexington Avenue, Manhattan, NY 10065 | **Upper East Side**

Gregorys must be doing something right. At the time of writing it has 26 branches and all do a steady-to-roaring trade. This one has an enviable location, with Hunter College nearby, and while the college supplied most business in the early days, now it's much more broadly based. WiFi all week is one draw, but the big room (especially in the back), relaxed vibe, and great brewing from the well-trained team is surely more important. Milky drinks are excellent, and so are single-origin coffees from the drip brewers.

(917) 388-3850
www.gregoryscoffee.com
Subway F, Q (Lexington Ave - 63rd St)

Sister locations Multiple locations

MON-FRI.	6:00am - 8:00pm
SAT.	7:00am - 7:00pm
SUN.	9:00am - 5:00pm

First opened 2015
Roaster Gregorys Coffee
Machine La Marzocco Linea, 3 groups
Grinder Mazzer Luigi Major E,
Mazzer Luigi Kold

Espresso	$3.00
Cappuccino	$4.00
Latte	$4.00

MAP REF. **121**

COFFEE 4.25 / 5 ●●●●◐ **OVERALL** 4.25 / 5 ★★★★☆

Irving Farm Coffee Roasters
Upper East Side 1424 3rd Avenue, Manhattan, NY 10028 | **Upper East Side**

Coffee connoisseurs cannot miss Irving Farm's grand Upper East Side location. This 1,700 square foot space boasts Irving Farm's largest, both in terms of the seating area and the kitchen. It is a space that affords customers the luxury of choice: either sit in the front bar and absorb the bustling energy, or relax in the mezzanine area, where there is plenty of seating spread throughout. Music in the background gives a comfortable atmosphere without being intrusive or distracting, striking a perfect balance. A delicious array of donuts from Underwest Donuts is the perfect accompaniment to any Irving Farm coffee. As always, Irving Farm is all about delivering a quality brew, and this location features espresso, filter, and by-the-cup Kalita pour-overs. What's not to like about this beautiful venue?

MAP REF. **122**

COFFEE
4.50 / 5

OVERALL
4.50 / 5 ★★★★⯪

Upper Manhattan

MON–FRI.	7:00am – 8:00pm
SAT–SUN.	8:00am – 7:00pm

First opened 2016
Roaster Irving Farm Coffee Roasters
Machine La Marzocco Linea, 3 groups
Grinder Nuova Simonelli Mythos

Espresso	$3.50
Cappuccino	$4.75
Latte	$5.00

(646) 861-2949
www.irvingfarm.com
Subway 4, 5, 6 (86th St)

Sister locations Multiple locations

Joe Coffee Upper East Side

1045 Lexington Avenue, Manhattan, NY 10021 | **Upper East Side**

TOP
40

Joe has seen new competition arrive since it landed on the Upper East Side in 2011, but it remains a hot favorite with locals. The look is more downtown than uptown, with bare brick and some out-there lampshades. And you'll be lucky to find a seat: there are just a few, in the window and at a communal table. All the hallmark Joe qualities are here in the cup, from great beans (blends or single-origin) through to expert brewing and dazzling latte art.

(212) 988-2500
www.joenewyork.com
Subway 4, 5, 6 (77th St)

Sister locations Multiple locations

MON–SAT.	7:00am – 8:00pm
SUN.	8:00am – 8:00pm

First opened 2011
Roaster Joe Coffee Roasting
Machine La Marzocco GB5, 2 groups
Grinder Nuova Simonelli Mythos

Espresso	$3.00
Cappuccino	$4.00 / $4.50
Latte	$4.00 / $4.50

MAP REF. **123**

COFFEE
4.50 / 5

OVERALL
4.25 / 5 ★★★★⯪

Kuro Kuma Espresso & Coffee

121 La Salle Street, Manhattan, NY 10027 | **Harlem**

Part of Kuro Kuma's success arises from location: this part of Morningside Heights isn't packed with good coffee purveyors. But Kuro Kuma would be smashing it anywhere, however stiff the competition, because this tiny place (seating for six or so) is sensationally good. The coffee is made from Counter Culture beans by highly skilled baristas who take equal care with every type of drink. Even iced coffee, so often a pallid potion, turns to magic here. No wonder Columbia students (and just about everyone else) line up to buy.

MON-SAT.	7:00am - 7:30pm
SUN.	8:00am - 7:30pm

First opened 2012
Roaster Counter Culture Coffee
Machine La Marzocco GB5
Grinder Mazzer Luigi

Espresso	$2.75
Cappuccino	$4.00
Latte	$4.00

(347) 577-3177
Subway 1 (125th St)

MAP REF. **124**

COFFEE 4.25 / 5	OVERALL 4.25 / 5 ★★★★⯪

The Monkey Cup

1730 Amsterdam Avenue, Manhattan, NY 10031 | **Upper Manhattan**

Laura Leonardi, the Argentinian-born owner of Monkey Cup, trained as a dentist but has now drilled deep into the essence of coffee culture. Her diminutive drop is one of the best places in Harlem for superior cups, either espresso-based or brewed - including the slow-drip cold-brew Kyoto method. The espresso beans change every three months ("We like the variables") and pour-overs are single-origin. This is a warm, friendly place where people love to talk to each other. If you want to guarantee a smile on your face, order a "Monkeyccino."

MON-FRI.	7:00am - 8:00pm
SAT.	8:00am - 8:00pm
SUN.	8:00am - 6:00pm

First opened 2015
Roaster Irving Farm Coffee Roasters
Machine La Marzocco Linea, 3 groups
Grinder Mahlkönig K 30

Espresso	$2.50
Cappuccino	$3.25
Latte	$3.25

(646) 665-3906
Subway A, B, C, D (145th St)

MAP REF. **125**

COFFEE 4.25 / 5	OVERALL 4.25 / 5 ★★★★⯪

Moss Café

3260 Johnson Avenue, Bronx, NY 10463 | **Kingsbridge**

 Photo courtesy of the venue

They're all about things local and fresh at Moss Café, as the shop bustles with neighbors and families who come in to enjoy the healthy food and charming environment. One of the first third wave coffee shops to come to the Bronx, Moss Café shares Stumptown beans with the neighbors, alongside house made baked goods and a seasonal menu that all happens to be Kosher too. You'll even find gluten free and dairy-free items, so it's pretty easy to find something delicious and wholesome to go along with your lovely latte.

(347) 275-5000
www.mosscafeny.com
Subway 1 (238th St)

MON-THU.	7:00am – 9:00pm
FRI.	7:00am – 4:00pm
SAT.	Closed
SUN.	8:00am – 9:00pm

First opened 2015
Roaster Stumptown Coffee Roasters
Machine La Marzocco GB5, 2 groups
Grinder Mazzer Luigi Kony E, Mazzer Luigi Super Jolly E

Espresso	$2.50
Cappuccino	$3.75
Latte	$4.00

MAP REF. **126**

 COFFEE 4.00 / 5  **OVERALL** 4.00 / 5 ★★★★☆

Oslo Coffee Roasters Upper East Side

422 East 75th Street, Manhattan, NY 10021 | **Upper East Side**

Oslo's Yorkville location is a tiny neighborhood caffeinery with a big heart. The baristas welcome local customers as if they were old friends - which many of them appear to be. The real star here is the old, lovingly maintained authentic San Marco espresso machine - a manual job complete with gleaming levers. Baristas pull great shots of Oslo's creamy espresso blend using those levers, and watching them at work is an all-too-rare pleasure.

(718) 782-0332
www.oslocoffee.com
Subway Q (72nd St)

Sister locations Williamsburg (Bedford Ave) / Williamsburg (Roebling St)

MON-FRI.	7:00am - 7:00pm
SAT-SUN.	8:00am - 7:00pm
	(6:00pm in winter)

First opened 2011
Roaster Oslo Coffee Roasters
Machine San Marco, 3 groups
Grinder Mazzer Luigi Robur

Espresso	$3.00
Cappuccino	$3.75
Latte	$3.75

MAP REF. **127**

COFFEE 4.25 / 5

OVERALL 4.25 / 5 ★★★★

Petite Shell

1269 Lexington Avenue, Manhattan, NY 10028 | **Upper East Side**

Petite Shell marries serious coffee with a perfect companion - freshly baked rugelach. They offer a variety of inventive flavors, like pear blue cheese and chocolate Nutella cream, that pair perfectly with their coffees. They offer three different kinds of iced coffee (Kyoto, ice-brewed and cold brewed) as well as a pour-over bar. The space is bright and gleaming, with sunlight that soaks the space in a warm, inviting glow.

(212) 828-2233
Subway 4, 5, 6 (86th St)

MON–FRI.	7:00am – 8:00pm
SAT.	7:00am – 10:00pm
SUN.	7:00am – 8:00pm

First opened 2015
Roaster 40 Weight Coffee Roasters
Machine La Marzocco Strada
Grinder Nuova Simonelli

Espresso	$2.50
Cappuccino	$3.50
Latte	$4.00

MAP REF. 128

 COFFEE 4.25 / 5

OVERALL 4.25 / 5 ★★★★

Plowshares

2730 Broadway, Manhattan, NY 10025 | **Upper West Side**

Plowshares opened this spot quietly, but word of mouth travels quickly in this town, and their wonderfully prepared coffees are making waves among the caffeinated elite. They roast their own coffees and serve them with care at this 11-seat shop. They only have one blend here, while all the others are single origin varieties from across the coffee-producing world. They offer at least two batch-brewed coffees at a time, a pour-over bar, and both a regular and nitrogen-infused cold brew that's extra rich and caffeinated.

(212) 222-0285
www.plowsharescoffee.com
Subway 1 (103rd St)

| MON-FRI. | 7:00am - 7:00pm |
| SAT-SUN. | 8:00am - 7:00pm |

First opened 2014
Roaster Plowshares Coffee Roasters
Machine Slayer, 2 groups
Grinder Mahlkönig K30, Mahlkönig EK 43

Espresso	$2.75
Cappuccino	$4.00
Latte	$4.50

MAP REF. 129

COFFEE 4.25 / 5  OVERALL 4.25 / 5 ★★★★½

Uptown Roasters

135 East 110th Street, Manhattan, NY 10029 | **East Harlem**

East Harlem has relatively few independent artisanal coffee places, so the arrival of Uptown was a blessing for locals. And both long-time residents and newer 'yuppie' arrivals have taken to the place. It's small and quiet, with simple brick-and-wood décor that provides a perfect hangout and a showcase for beans from the roastery in the South Bronx. The owners have a Peruvian background, so there's an emphasis on South American beans. Pour-over is the best way to appreciate single-origin, but espresso-based drinks are made carefully.

(646) 918-6600
www.uptownroasters.com
Subway 4, 6 (110th St)

| MON-FRI. | 6:30am - 2:00pm |
| SAT-SUN. | 7:00am - 2:00pm |

First opened 2015
Roaster Uptown Roasters
Machine Sanremo Zoe, 2 groups
Grinder Mahlkönig Vario

Espresso	$2.50
Cappuccino	$3.50
Latte	$4.00

Sister locations Park Slope / East Harlem

MAP REF. 130

COFFEE 4.25 / 5  OVERALL 4.25 / 5 ★★★★½

The largely residential neighborhoods of Park Slope, Kensington, Ditmas Park, Crown Heights and Prospect Gardens make up this area of Brooklyn. Kensington and Ditmas Park still retain many examples of beautiful Victorian architecture, while Prospect Heights is known for its rich cultural history. The Brooklyn Botanical Gardens, The Brooklyn Museum and The Pratt Institute all be found there. Park Slope itself, with its picturesque tree-lined streets, historic brownstones, popular restaurants and shops, is a great neighborhood to explore.

Park Slope & Surrounding

Blue Bottle Park Slope

203 7th Avenue, Brooklyn, NY 11215 | **Park Slope**

Blue Bottle continues its NYC takeover with this new spot in Park Slope. Situated in a more residential area of the neighborhood, just a short walk from Prospect Park, the café is exceptionally accommodating to its patrons - offering stroller parking outside, highchairs inside, and a wonderful array of trendy wooden toys for their youngest clientele. Of course, there is beautiful seating for adults too, and delicious well-catered coffee to boot! With its bright, airy layout and quiet environment, it's the sort of place one can turn to for refuge, inspiration, or both. You can also learn the art of creating a perfect brew yourself at their weekly coffee making classes. With relaxing off-sidewalk outdoor seating and no WiFi, it is the perfect spot to kick back in the sun and socialize with friends.

MAP REF.

COFFEE
4.75 / 5

OVERALL
4.50 / 5 ★★★★½

| **MON-FRI.** | 6:30am - 7:00pm |
| **SAT-SUN.** | 8:00am - 7:00pm |

First opened 2016
Roaster Blue Bottle Coffee
Machine Kees van der Westen, 2 groups
Grinder Baratza

Espresso	$3.25
Cappuccino	$4.25
Latte	$4.75

(510) 653-3394
www.bluebottlecoffee.com
Subway F, G (7th Ave)

Sister locations Multiple locations

Breukelen Coffee House

764a Franklin Avenue, Brooklyn, NY 11238 | **Crown Heights**

Photo courtesy of the venue

Breukelen Coffee House has been a staple venue in Crown Heights since it first opened in 2009, and after spending some time inside, it's easy to see why. The relaxed atmosphere is the perfect spot for everyone, from Crown Heights hipsters to white collar Wall Street. The espresso is strong, the pastries are sweet, and the baristas treat every customer as if they are a regular. Expertly brewed Stumptown beans are served with enthusiasm. For food, pastries are sold alongside a seasonal menu of light fare prepared with locally sourced ingredients.

(718) 789-7070
www.breukelencoffeehouse.com
Subway 2, 3, 4, 5 (Franklin Ave)

MON-FRI.	7:00am - 8:00pm
SAT-SUN.	8:00am - 8:00pm

First opened 2009
Roaster Stumptown Coffee Roasters
Machine La Marzocco, 2 groups
Grinder Mazzer Luigi Major

Espresso	$2.30
Cappuccino	$3.75
Latte	$4.25

MAP REF. 132

COFFEE 4.00 / 5

OVERALL 4.00 / 5 ★★★★☆

Café Regular du Nord

158a Berkeley Place, Brooklyn, NY 11217 | **Park Slope**

Photo courtesy of the venue

Good things come in small packages. Café Regular du Nord is a beautiful café with vintage vibes, from the funky painting on the wall to the crystal chandelier. The espresso-based beverages are great, but the best quality of this café is its versatile menu, where there is something for adults and kids alike. Not a coffee drinker, or bringing the kids with you? No need to worry, delicious Jacques Torres hot chocolate is served here. Teachers and students, be sure to take advantage of the discounts offered.

(718) 768-4170
www.caferegular.com
Subway B, Q (7th Ave) or 2, 3, 4 (Grand Army Plaza)

Sister locations Park Slope

MON–SUN. 7:00am – 7:00pm

First opened 2009
Roaster La Colombe Torrefaction Coffee Roasters
Machine La Marzocco FB80, 2 groups
Grinder Mazzer Luigi Super Jolly E

Espresso	$3.00
Cappuccino	$4.00
Latte	$4.00

MAP REF.

COFFEE
4.00 / 5

OVERALL
4.00 / 5
★★★★☆

Clever Blend

97 5th Avenue, Brooklyn, NY 11217 | **Park Slope**

Clever Blend truly lives up to its name - it is a haven for coffee enthusiasts who are also lovers of literature. With a counter that doubles as a bookshelf, there is never a shortage of literary works to indulge in while sipping your delicious cold brew. The staff are friendly, and the rotating menu of single-origin coffee never disappoints. Featuring plenty of seating and great music, Clever Blend is the perfect spot to meet with friends in the latest hip, intellectual environment nestled in Park Slope.

Subway 2, 3 (Bergen St)

MON-SAT.	6:30am - 6:30pm
SUN.	7:30am - 6:30pm

First opened 2016
Roaster Clever Blend
Machine Elektra, 2 groups
Grinder Mazzer Luigi

Espresso	$2.50 / $3.25
Cappuccino	$3.50 / $4.00
Latte	$3.50 / $4.00

MAP REF. 134

COFFEE 4.25 / 5   **OVERALL** 4.25 / 5 ★★★★⯪

Coffee Mob

1514 Newkirk Avenue, Brooklyn, NY 11226 | **Ditmas Park**

If you're looking for quality (both of the roast and musical variety) look no further than Coffee Mob. Situated in a lovely corner spot in the Flatbush neighborhood, this venue promises expertly brewed, single-origin espresso. The beans are roasted in house on a rotating basis, sourced from fair-trade plantations around the world. In addition to its roast, the venue offers a variety of sandwiches and pastries, making it the perfect lunch spot. Vinyl turntables sit next to the La Marzocco GB5, allowing the baristas to double as DJs and offer some sweet tunes.

(917) 545-5857
www.coffeemob.space
Subway B, Q (Newkirk Plaza)

| MON-FRI. | 7:00am - 7:00pm |
| SAT-SUN. | 8:00am - 7:00pm |

First opened 2013
Roaster Coffee Mob
Machine La Marzocco
Grinder Mazzer Luigi

Espresso	$2.75
Cappuccino	$3.50
Latte	$4.00

MAP REF. **135**

 COFFEE 4.25 / 5   OVERALL 4.25 / 5 ★★★★☆

Dean Street Café

87 Utica Avenue, Brooklyn, NY 11213 | **Crown Heights**

Dean Street Café is a spot you cannot miss - literally! The signage outside proclaims "This is a coffee shop!", just in case. Situated in a lovely spot on the corner of Utica and Dean Street, this new café has made its mark as a hot spot in Crown Heights. With modern decor, including trendy flower-filled mason jar centrepieces, it serves as a nice place to relax with a cup of joe. Additionally, the food is made to order, served fresh and is absolutely delicious. We recommend the kale salad or avocado toast.

(718) 578-2757
www.deanstreetbrooklyn.com
Subway A, C (Utica Ave)

SUN-THU.	7:00am - 4:00pm
FRI.	7:00am - 12:00pm
SAT.	Closed

First opened 2017
Roaster Crown Heights Roasting Company
Machine La Marzocco, 3 groups
Grinder Mazzer Luigi

Espresso	$3.00
Cappuccino	$4.00
Latte	$4.50 / $5.00

MAP REF. **136**

 COFFEE 4.00 / 5  OVERALL 4.25 / 5 ★★★★☆

Everyman Espresso Park Slope

162 5th Avenue, Brooklyn, NY 11217 | **Park Slope**

Everyman Espresso, welcome to Brooklyn. Situated in quaint Park Slope, the "Damn Fine Coffee", as proclaimed in neon lettering, is a satisfying addition to Brooklyn's bustling coffee scene, because it is damn fine coffee. Counter culture beans are brewed to perfection on the La Marzocco Strada, and the matcha latte might just be the best in the borough. In addition to the top-notch brew, the shop itself is a visual delight with its colorful tiled walls and well-designed lighting. Seating at the bar makes it a great place to watch the highly skilled baristas create exquisite brews. People come in with family, friends, and their devices - a nice mix that creates a genuinely friendly neighborhood café. Home to the "4th best barista in the USA", you know you're in for a treat!

MAP REF. **137**

COFFEE 4.25 / 5	OVERALL 4.25 / 5

MON-FRI. 7:00am - 7:00pm
SAT-SUN. 8:00am - 7:00pm

  decaf

First opened 2017
Roaster Counter Culture Coffee
Machine La Marzocco Strada, 2 groups
Grinder Mazzer Luigi Robur E

Espresso $3.50
Cappuccino $4.50
Latte $5.00

(212) 533-0524
www.everymanespresso.com
Subway D, N, R, W (Union St)

Sister locations Soho / East Village

Park Slope & Surrounding

Gorilla Coffee

472 Bergen Street, Brooklyn, NY 11217 | **Park Slope**

Gorilla's Park Slope branch, its second in Brooklyn, is a big, modern, functionally decorated place with very fifties-looking tables. Somehow none of that makes it feel institutional, because this is a comfortable place to sit and hang out. Gorilla has been roasting in Brooklyn since 2002 and their full variety is shown best in the Chemex or pour-over, but espresso-based drinks are made to the same high standards. Baked goods are very popular; but don't be surprised if the selection's shrunk if you get there later in the day.

(347) 987-3766
www.gorillacoffee.com
Subway 2, 3 (Bergen St)

| MON–SAT. | 7:00am – 9:00pm |
| SUN. | 8:00am – 9:00pm |

First opened 2014
Roaster Gorilla Coffee
Machine La Marzocco Strada, 3 groups
Grinder Mazzer Luigi Robur

Espresso	$2.50
Cappuccino	$3.50
Latte	$3.50

MAP REF. 138

COFFEE 4.25 / 5

OVERALL 4.25 / 5 ★★★★½

Hungry Ghost

253 Flatbush Avenue, Brooklyn, NY 11217 | **Prospect Heights**

Photo courtesy of the venue

Sleek is the first word that comes to mind upon entering the Hungry Ghost Coffee Bar & Café. With its cool gray undertones and comfortable seating, it is the perfect spot to relax with a cold brew and one of their much sought after scones. Conversation and community is encouraged within the space, as laptop use is restricted to a select area. This emphasis on community, combined with the quality of product, makes Hungry Ghost a Prospect Heights destination for everyone from coffee connoisseurs to creative collaborators.

(718) 483-8666
www.hungryghostbrooklyn.com
Subway 2, 3 (Bergen St)

MON-SUN.   6:30am - 9:00pm

First opened 2012
Roaster Stumptown Coffee Roasters
Machine La Marzocco GB5
Grinder Mazzer Luigi Robur

Espresso	$2.75
Cappuccino	$3.25
Latte	$4.00

Sister locations Fort Greene / Greenwich Village / Prospect Heights

MAP REF. 139

 **COFFEE** 4.25 / 5

OVERALL 4.25 / 5

Little Zelda

728 Franklin Avenue, Brooklyn, NY 11238 | **Crown Heights**

Little Zelda is the quintessential neighborhood spot, a charming little space where coffee isn't just a beverage but something that brings people together. You'll find local writers and readers getting literary while sipping lattes at this delightfully vintage café with well-used and ever lovely Toby's Estate coffees. There's a community board where people looking for roommates or apartments may post to find a match. This cozy shop and its cheery staff make Little Zelda a lovely little home away from home.

(646) 320-7347
Subway S (Park Pl)

MON-FRI. 7:00am - 6:00pm
SAT-SUN. 8:00am - 6:00pm

First opened 2012
Roaster Toby's Estate Coffee
Machine La Marzocco Linea, 2 groups
Grinder Mazzer Luigi Major

Espresso $2.50
Cappuccino $3.50
Latte $4.00

MAP REF. 140

 **COFFEE** 4.00 / 5   **OVERALL** 4.00 / 5 ★★★★☆

Manhattanville Coffee

167 Rogers Avenue, Brooklyn, NY 11216 | **Crown Heights**

Manhattanville is a welcome sight on one of those long Crown Heights blocks that offer little in the way of refreshment. Order from the counter, staffed by friendly young people, then settle down with your friends or your laptop. There are also board games on hand if you need other entertainment, and families are particularly welcome. The walls are an attractive dark gray, the coffee is expertly made using Intelligentsia beans, and the food is fully kosher. Manhattanville is an unusual but delightful coffee spot.

(646) 781-9900
www.manhattanvillecoffee.com
Subway 2, 3, 4 (Nostrand Ave)

MON-FRI. 6:30am - 8:00pm
SAT-SUN. 7:30am - 8:00pm

First opened 2015
Roaster Intelligentsia Coffee
Machine La Marzocco GB5, 2 groups
Grinder Mahlkönig EK 43

Espresso $2.50
Cappuccino $3.50
Latte $4.00

Sister locations Harlem   MAP REF. 141

 COFFEE 4.00 / 5   **OVERALL** 4.25 / 5 ★★★★

Milk & Honey

1119 Newkirk Avenue, Brooklyn, NY 11230 | **Ditmas Park**

 NEW

Trendy, hip, and delicious - these are just a few words to describe Milk & Honey, a bustling café on Newkirk Avenue. Upon entering this unique café, there is a lush plant wall that creates a striking first impression. Order at the counter and then find a place to sit, we recommend choosing a spot on the outdoor patio if weather permits. More café than coffee shop, the food is truly superb and their coffee never disappoints either. Try the Crème Brulee French Toast at brunch; a local favorite.

(301) 477-2195
www.milkandhoneycafeny.com
Subway B, Q (Newkirk Plaza)

MON-SUN.   7:00am - 9:00pm

First opened 2013
Roaster Counter Culture Coffee
Machine La Marzocco, 3 groups
Grinder Mazzer Luigi

MAP REF. **142**

Milk Bar

620 Vanderbilt Avenue, Brooklyn, NY 11238 | **Prospect Heights**

Tiny, light-filled Milk Bar is run like a restaurant - a waiter acts as host, seating your party when you arrive. In other hands, this type of set-up could feel highly-strung, but the staff are so pleasant that having the attention of a waiter is a relaxed affair. Located in Prospect Heights, it's a quiet neighborhood shop, but is also good enough to go out of your way for. You can't go wrong with the drinks here - Counter Culture provides the beans - but honor the shop's Australian roots and go with the excellent, strong flat white.

(718) 230-0844
www.milkbarbrooklyn.com
Subway 2, 3, 4 (Grand Army Plaza) or B, Q (7th Ave)

MON-FRI.	7:30am - 5:00pm
SAT-SUN.	8:00am - 5:00pm

First opened 2009
Roaster Counter Culture Coffee
Machine La Marzocco Linea, 2 groups
Grinder Mazzer Luigi

Espresso	$3.50
Cappuccino	$4.00
Latte	$4.50

MAP REF. 143

COFFEE
4.25 / 5

OVERALL
4.25 / 5 ★★★★☆

Qathra

1112 Cortelyou Road, Brooklyn, NY 11218 | **Ditmas Park**

This Ditmas Park neighborhood shop has developed quite a following, and when you taste the coffee it's easy to see why. Despite its unassuming hand-painted decor (think 1990s Portland) Qathra is deadly serious about its coffee. Don't add milk to the excellent, robust Hario pour-overs. If you do happen to be in the mood for something milky, indulge in a frothy, sweet latte. Snag a spot in the delightful backyard and start wondering why you haven't already moved to Brooklyn.

(347) 305-3250
www.qathracafe.com
Subway Q (Cortelyou Rd)

MON–SUN. 7:00am – 9:00pm

First opened 2010
Roaster Café Integral
Machine La Marzocco Strada MP, 3 groups
Grinder Mazzer Luigi SRL,
Mahlkönig Guatemala

Espresso	$2.50
Cappuccino	$3.50
Latte	$4.00

MAP REF. **144**

COFFEE 4.25 / 5		OVERALL 4.25 / 5	★ ★ ★ ★ ☆

Roots Cafe

639a Fifth Avenue, Brooklyn, NY 11215 | **Park Slope**

In many ways, walking into Roots Café feels like walking into someone's home. Along the walls hang quirky paintings, musical instruments, and bookshelves filled with the classics. The 'hominess' is not merely aesthetic; it is a quality that extends to the service. Walk through to the counter in the back and interact with the engaging baristas who serve excellent espresso-based beverages alongside a variety of breakfast and lunch sandwiches. If you're craving something sweet, be sure to try the salted caramel latte or peppermint mocha.

(615) 419-7877
www.rootsbrooklyn.com
Subway D, N, R (Prospect Ave)

MON–FRI. 6:30am – 5:00pm
SAT–SUN. 8:00am – 5:00pm

First opened 2008
Roaster Forty Weight Coffee Roasters
Machine La Marzocco Linea
Grinder La Marzocco

Espresso	$2.50
Cappuccino	$3.50
Latte	$4.00

MAP REF. **145**

COFFEE 4.25 / 5		OVERALL 4.00 / 5	★ ★ ★ ★ ☆

Seven Point Espresso

637 Washington Avenue, Brooklyn, NY 11238 | **Prospect Heights**

This adorable Australian café truly has the perfect beverage for everyone - excellent Counter Culture coffee, delicious matcha by Chalait, and Prana Chai teas. The all-day menu is as satisfying as the beverages, full of beautifully presented and extremely Instagram-able Aussie staples like avocado toast and acai bowls. If you're looking for something a little more sweet and indulgent, we would recommend trying their tantalizing Tim Tam Waffin (waffle/muffin!). There is plenty of seating for visitors to enjoy the lovely ambiance, created by the low hanging lights and exposed brick wall. Seven Point is a quiet spot, perfect for working or catching up with a friend or two. With such delicious food options, it tends to fill up from around 11am on weekends, so make sure you get in early if you're planning on stopping for brunch!

MAP REF. 146

COFFEE	OVERALL
4.25 / 5	4.25 / 5

MON–FRI.   7:00am – 5:00pm
SAT–SUN.   8:00am – 6:00pm

First opened 2016
Roaster Counter Culture Coffee
Machine La Marzocco, 3 groups
Grinder Nuova Simonelli G60

Espresso $3.75
Cappuccino $4.00
Latte $4.50

(718) 230-0178
www.sevenpointespresso.com
Subway A, C (Clinton – Washington Aves)

Park Slope & Surrounding

Stonefruit Espresso + Kitchen

TOP 40

1058 Bedford Avenue, Brooklyn, NY 11205 | **Bed-Stuy**

A major spot for Bed-Stuy, Stonefruit is a little slice of Los Angeles, in the best sense possible. It's a coffee shop, it's a florist, it's a candle and used-book shop, it's a restaurant that serves wine. Comfortable rope-swing chairs hang from the ceiling in this beautifully designed, light-filled space. The baristas are perfectionists at handling milk. The single-origin pour-overs are delicious, but the flat white is even better. The matcha latte is just as good; it's hard to choose what to drink here because they get everything right.

(718) 230-4147
www.stonefruitespresso.com
Subway G (Classon Ave)

MON–FRI.   7:30am – 6:00pm
SAT–SUN.   8:30am – 6:00pm

First opened 2015
Roaster Counter Culture Coffee
Machine La Marzocco GB5, 2 groups
Grinder Mahlkönig EK 43,
Nuova Simonelli Mythos

Espresso	$3.00
Cappuccino	$3.75
Latte	$4.25

MAP REF. 147

COFFEE 4.50 / 5

OVERALL 4.50 / 5 ★★★★⯨

Tygershark

581 Vanderbilt Avenue, Brooklyn, NY 11238 | **Prospect Heights**

Photo courtesy of the venue

Tygershark proves once and for all that a chilled barista can also be a perfectionist barista. First and foremost an ultra-hip (and excellent) Korean restaurant and bar, with a coffee bar/surfshop in the front - yes, you can buy a surfboard should the urge strike you. The beautiful, Sydney-esque space features a lovely backyard. The atmosphere couldn't be more laid-back, and the espresso drinks couldn't be better.

(718) 576-6233
www.tygershark.nyc
Subway A,C (Clinton - Washington Aves)

MON.	Closed
TUE-FRI.	8:30am - 4:00pm
SAT-SUN.	9:00am - 5:30pm
	(5:30pm - 11:00pm for dinner)

First opened 2015
Roaster Concave
Machine La Marzocco Linea, 2 groups
Grinder Mazzer Luigi Kony,
Mahlkönig EK 43

Espresso	$3.00
Cappuccino	$4.00
Latte	$4.25

MAP REF. **148**

COFFEE
4.25 / 5

OVERALL
4.25 / 5 ★★★★☆

160

With The Brooklyn Academy of Music in Fort Greene, the beautiful and historic Promenade along the water in Brooklyn Heights and all the fashionable shops and restaurants in Carroll Gardens and Cobble Hill, it's easy to wander a day away in Downtown Brooklyn. These largely residential areas are filled with beautiful tree-lined streets and quiet parks, and are known for being home to many of New York's greatest artists, writers and musicians.

Downtown Brooklyn

Bluestone Lane Dumbo

55 Prospect Street, Brooklyn, NY 11201 | **Dumbo**

Part of the new Dumbo Heights campus, Bluestone Lane goes all-out in its impressive first foray into Brooklyn. Upon entering this sophisticated café, it feels so similar yet so different from other Bluestone Lane locations all at once. Similar: the seafoam green tiles and light wood aesthetic that forms Bluestone Lane's brand identity - and of course the superb Aussie-inspired coffee. Different: a white marble bar and polished concrete flooring. Like its Manhattan cafés, the all-day menu focuses on seasonal offerings, and the avocado smash is their signature.

(347) 202-0352
www.bluestonelaneny.com
Subway F (York St)

Sister locations Multiple locations

MON-SUN. 8:00am - 7:00pm

First opened 2016
Roaster Bluestone Lane Coffee
Machine La Marzocco Strada AV
Grinder Mazzer Robur

Espresso	$3.00
Cappuccino	$4.00
Latte	$4.00

MAP REF. **149**

COFFEE 4.50 / 5	OVERALL 4.75 / 5

Brewklyn Grind

557 Myrtle Avenue, Brooklyn, NY 11205 | **Clinton Hill**

Photo courtesy of the venue

In 2006, the three Farrelly brothers from Bay Ridge Brooklyn - an engineer, a banker and a high school drop-out - opened a roastery in Red Hook. Before long, they were serving high profile clients like Facebook, and opening this quiet, unassuming neighborhood shop. An impressive 40% of their beans come from farmers they have a direct relationship with. Go for a single origin pour over, or the ultra-strong but somehow still sweet and silky cold brew. Brewklyn Grind features a lovely backyard which fills up with students from the nearby Pratt Institute.

(347) 452-8866
www.bkgcoffee.com
Subway G (Classon Ave)

MON-SUN.   8:00am - 6:00pm

First opened 2014
Roaster Brewklyn Grind Coffee Roasters
Machine Faema E61
Grinder Mazzer Luigi

Espresso	$2.75
Cappuccino	$3.75
Latte	$4.50

MAP REF.

COFFEE 4.25 / 5	OVERALL 4.25 / 5
🫘🫘🫘🫘◗	★★★★⯪

Brooklyn Roasting Company Dumbo

25 Jay Street, Brooklyn, NY 11201 | **Dumbo**

Brooklyn's flagship Navy Yard branch is a big, bustling operation that packs in customers of just about every age. Hipsters abound, but so do toddlers. This is one thing that makes the place so lively. Brooklyn Roasting Company offers a large and varied food menu and a good selection of non-caffeinated drinks such as fresh juices, and smoothies. But the coffee is the real star here, whether well-made milky drinks or daily brewed coffees (a changing selection) from excellent single-origin beans. Sit back and watch live roasting in operation at one end of this enormous café.

(718) 514-2874
www.brooklynroasting.com
Subway F (York St)

Sister locations Multiple locations

MON–SUN. 7:00am – 7:00pm

First opened 2010
Roaster Brooklyn Roasting Company
Machine La Marzocco Linea GB5, 2 groups
Grinder Nuova Simonelli Mythos

Espresso	$2.50
Cappuccino	$3.75
Latte	$4.50

MAP REF. **151**

COFFEE
4.50 / 5

OVERALL
4.50 / 5
★★★★⯪

165

East One Coffee Roasters

384 Court Street, Brooklyn, NY 11231 | **Carroll Gardens**

Coffee connoisseurs will fall in love with East One Coffee Roasters (E1), a hip new venue in Carroll Gardens. Located on a lovely corner spot, this venue is striking in both the atmosphere and the quality of the roast. In addition to the spacious café up front, there is a large restaurant with a full-service menu - and trust us you do not want to skip it! The food is absolutely delicious, their beans are well roasted, and there is plenty of space to enjoy yourself with family and friends.

(347) 987-4919
www.eastonecoffee.com
Subway F, G (Carroll St)

MON-THU.	7:00am - 9:00pm
FRI.	7:00am - 10:00pm
SAT.	9:00am - 10:00pm
SUN.	9:00am - 9:00pm

First opened 2017
Roaster East One Coffee Roasters
Machine Slayer, 3 groups
Grinder Mazzer Luigi

Espresso	$3.00
Cappuccino	$4.00
Latte	$4.50

MAP REF. **152**

Extraction Lab by Alpha Dominche

51 35th Street, Brooklyn, NY 11232 | **Park Slope**

Coffee connoisseurs looking for a truly unique experience, look no further than this hip showroom in the heart of Industry City. The Alpha Dominche Extraction Lab is a showroom, first and foremost, featuring Alpha Dominche's advanced coffee and tea brewing machines, the STEAMPUNK and SIGHT. Best described as a cross between a siphon and a French press, the single-serving machine brews the perfect pour-over every time. They offer a tantalizing array of Nordic pastries, perfectly complementing the delicious brews. The minimalist space suits its Industry City setting perfectly, with wooden tables, potted plants and an open-air feel,

to create a perfectly Zen atmosphere. Extraction Lab sources single-origin beans from over fifty world class roasters - and their offerings rotate weekly, so there is always something new to try!

MAP REF. **153**

| COFFEE 4.50 / 5 | | OVERALL 4.75 / 5 | |

Downtown Brooklyn

MON-FRI.	8:00am - 4:00pm
SAT-SUN.	Closed

First opened 2017
Roaster Rotating menu of over 50 roasters
Machine STEAMPUNK, SIGHT
Grinder Mazzer Luigi

Espresso	Varies by roaster
Cappuccino	Varies by roaster
Latte	Varies by roaster

(718) 704-0840
www.adextractionlab.com
Subway D, N, Q, R, W (36th Street)

Smith Canteen

343 Smith Street, Brooklyn, NY 11231 | **Carroll Gardens**

Photo courtesy of the venue

Smith Canteen is bright and welcoming, a true gem in Brooklyn's Carroll Park area. It is not surprising for the line to be out the door, but the wait is always worth it. From coffee brewed to perfection, to their variety of organic pastries, the café is committed to serving quality products. Being environmentally conscious is important to the café; they serve Counter Culture beans, a roaster that prides itself on sustainability. Even during peak hours, baristas engage in personalized conversation with customers.

(718) 422-0444
www.smithcanteen.com
Subway F, G (Carroll St)

MON–SUN.   7:00am – 5:00pm

First opened 2011
Roaster Counter Culture Coffee
Machine La Marzocco Linea
Grinder Mazzer Luigi

Espresso	$2.50
Cappuccino	$4.00
Latte	$4.50

MAP REF. **154**

COFFEE 4.25 / 5	OVERALL 4.25 / 5
🫘🫘🫘🫘◗	★★★★☆

DRINK REAL TEA

teapigs.

teapigs teas are the very best quality you'll find. Trained tea taster, Louise, selects only real whole leaf teas, whole berries, flowers, herbs and spices - not the dusty stull you'll find in regular teabags.

Their teas come in biodegradable tea "temples" - so you can enjoy quality loose tea without the fuss.

Discover our range of 32 teas online, in all shapes and sizes.

15% OFF first online order

H-Cellat

Featuring the Northern part of Brooklyn, Bushwick is fast becoming one of the most sought after neighborhoods. Spilling over from trendy Williamsburg, cafes, restaurants and boutiques are all finding new spots to feature their expanding retail offerings. With neighboring Bedford-Stuyvesant expanding from Bushwick this area now has a lot to be desired.

Bushwick & Surrounding

AP Café

420 Troutman Street, Brooklyn, NY 11237 | **Bushwick**

AP Café is a beautifully minimalist café that lets its fine coffee and food take focus within its vast, white-washed walls. The shop is bright, fresh, and the perfect spot to grab a drink and partake in its extensive menu of food offerings, ranging from quinoa bowls to freshly prepared seasonal juices. The coffee comes from Toby's Estate, and the menu features specialty drinks like Vietnamese iced coffee.

(347) 404-6147
www.apcafenyc.com
Subway L (Jefferson St)

MON.-THU.	8:00am - 5:00pm
FRI.	8:00am - 7:00pm
SAT.-SUN.	9:00am - 7:00pm

First opened 2013
Roaster Toby's Estate Coffee
Machine Faema E61 Legend
Grinder BUNN

Espresso	$2.50
Cappuccino	$4.00
Latte	$4.00

MAP REF. 155

COFFEE 4.25 / 5		OVERALL 4.25 / 5	★★★★⯪

Baby Skips

1158 Myrtle Avenue, Brooklyn, NY 11221 | **Bushwick**

NEW

Baby Skips, the adorable younger sibling of Little Skips, is an oasis in Bushwick. Yes, it is smaller than Little Skips (hence the name), but what it lacks in size it makes up for in atmosphere - and you can always find a seat. Friendly baristas serve Counter Culture coffee with great enthusiasm - stop by a handful of times and they will almost certainly remember your order. Pair your morning latte with one of their delicious pastries, which are as fresh as you can get. We love you Baby Skips!

(929) 210-8101
www.littleskips.nyc
Subway M, J, Z (Myrtle Ave)

Sister locations Bushwick

MON.	7:00pm - 12:00am
TUE-FRI.	12:00pm - 6:00pm | 7:00pm - 12:00am
SAT.	Closed
SUN.	8:00am - 6:00pm

First opened 2017
Roaster Counter Culture Coffee
Machine La Marzocco Linea
Grinder Mazzer Robur E

Espresso	$2.75
Cappuccino	$3.75
Latte	$4.00 / $4.50

MAP REF. 156

COFFEE 4.25 / 5		OVERALL 4.25 / 5	★★★★⯪

Caffe Vita Bushwick

576 Johnson Avenue, Brooklyn, NY 11237 | **Bushwick**

Right in the still-industrial heart of old Bushwick, Caffe Vita's roaster/café has plenty of seating and a bird's eye view of the roaster in action. The Vita folks buy beans direct from producers, something they championed at an early stage in third-wave coffee history, and they put the product to great use. In addition to expertly-made pour-over and espresso-based drinks, you shouldn't miss out on their sweetened take on nitro-brewed cold brew, as well as their unconventional rolls.

(929) 295-9328
www.caffevita.com
Subway L (Jefferson St)

Sister locations Lower East Side

MON-FRI.	8:00am – 6:00pm
SAT-SUN.	9:00am – 4:00pm

First opened 2015
Roaster Caffe Vita
Machine Kees van der Westen Spirit, 3 groups
Grinder Mazzer Luigi Robur E

Espresso	$3.25
Cappuccino	$4.65
Latte	$4.65 / $4.95 / $5.25

MAP REF. **157**

COFFEE 4.50 / 5   OVERALL 4.25 / 5 ★★★★☆

City of Saints Bushwick

299 Meserole Street, Brooklyn, NY 11206 | **Bushwick**

The industrial part of Bushwick is full of warehouses, many of which are being converted into trendy businesses and fancy apartments. Refreshingly, City of Saints still feels very much like a warehouse, with its corrugated metal pull-down door entrance and a beautiful graffiti mural decorating one of its walls. This is where City of Saints roast their beans - in full view, if you're curious to watch - with a few café tables in front. Their excellent coffee bar always has a constantly rotating selection to tempt you, but for an ultimate palate experience, the cold brew is the one to try.

(929) 900-5282
www.cityofsaintscoffee.com
Subway L (Montrose Ave)

MON-FRI.	7:00am - 6:00pm
SAT-SUN.	10:00am - 5:00pm

First opened 2015
Roaster City of Saints Coffee Roaster
Machine Victoria Arduino Black Eagle
Grinder Nuova Simonelli Mythos One

Espresso	$3.00
Cappuccino	$3.50
Latte	$4.00

Sister locations East Village

MAP REF. **158**

COFFEE 4.25 / 5   OVERALL 4.50 / 5 ★★★★☆

Little Skips is a total neighborhood haunt, with a clientele of young artists and intellectuals who sit and work for hours. Come join in and sip on a nice espresso while finishing your latest book. Or just sit back and enjoy their quality coffees from Counter Culture in this laid-back shop. Little Skips also offers freshly prepared sandwiches, great vegan treats and cool tunes.

(718) 484-0980
www.littleskips.com
Subway M (Central Ave)

Sister locations Bushwick

MON-FRI.	7:00am - 9:00pm
SAT-SUN.	8:00am - 9:00pm

First opened 2010
Roaster Counter Culture Coffee
Machine La Marzocco Linea
Grinder Mazzer Luigi Robur E

Espresso	$2.75
Cappuccino	$3.75
Latte	$4.00 / $4.50

MAP REF.

COFFEE 4.25 / 5   **OVERALL** 4.00 / 5 ★★★★☆

Milk & Pull Bushwick

181 Irving Avenue, Brooklyn, NY 11237 | **Bushwick**

Photo courtesy of the venue

Milk & Pull couldn't be a more unassuming local, nestled in a quiet block in Bushwick with just a few seats outside and a modest frontage. But it's a wonderful place, with a long, narrow, brightly-painted interior and a tempting array of baked goodies to ogle while waiting for your coffee, which is exceptionally well made. Stumptown beans are treated royally on the La Marzocco and there is great latte art even on a macchiato. Milk & Pull has a solid core of regulars; you'll see why they keep on coming back.

(347) 627-8511
www.milkandpull.com
Subway L (DeKalb Ave)

Sister locations Ridgewood

MON–FRI.	7:00am – 6:00pm	
SAT.	8:00am – 6:00pm	
SUN.	8:00am – 5:00pm	

First opened 2013
Roaster Stumptown Coffee Roasters
Machine La Marzocco Linea, 2 groups
Grinder Mazzer Luigi Robur E

Espresso	$3.00
Cappuccino	$3.50
Latte	$4.00

MAP REF. **160**

COFFEE
4.25 / 5

OVERALL
4.25 / 5

Milk & Pull Ridgewood

778 Seneca Avenue, Queens, NY 11385 | **Ridgewood**

Photo courtesy of the venue

This Ridgewood outpost of Milk & Pull brings well-made coffee to this burgeoning neighborhood. The menu features coffee from Portland star roaster Stumptown with espressos and cold brew, a standard for serious cafés today. They prepare fresh sandwiches and bagels and offer a nice variety of local baked goods. Exposed brick and natural wood make up the bright, airy place that features large tables spread leisurely apart, allowing for plenty of space to sit and relax.

(718) 821-1155
www.milkandpull.com
Subway M (Seneca Ave)

Sister locations Bushwick

MON–FRI.	7:00am – 7:00pm
SAT.	8:00am – 7:00pm
SUN.	8:00am – 6:00pm

First opened 2015
Roaster Stumptown Coffee Roasters
Machine La Marzocco GB5
Grinder Mazzer Luigi Super Jolly

Espresso	$3.00
Cappuccino	$3.50
Latte	$4.00

MAP REF. **161**

COFFEE 4.25 / 5

OVERALL 4.00 / 5 ★★★★☆

Supercrown Coffee Roasters

8 Wilson Avenue, Brooklyn, NY 11237 | **Bushwick**

Darleen Scherer founded Gorilla Coffee before setting up Supercrown, and her experience in high-end quality shows in every aspect of this impressive café/ roastery in light-industrial Bushwick. It used to be an automotive glass shop, and you can imagine SUVs in the space where their vintage Probat now turns out fragrant beans behind a big window - a spectator sport for those drinking on the premises. Pour-over and espresso-based drinks are equally good, but you owe it to yourself to try their coffee lemonade - an exquisite drink by any measure.

(347) 295-3161
www.supercrown.coffee
Subway L (Morgan Ave)

MON-FRI.	7:00am - 7:00pm
SAT.	8:00am - 6:00pm
SUN.	7:00am - 7:00pm

First opened 2016
Roaster Supercrown Coffee Roaster
Machine La Marzocco Strada, 3 groups
Grinder Nuova Simonelli Mythos Clima Pro, Mahlkönig EK 43

Espresso	$3.00
Cappuccino	$4.00
Latte	$4.25 / $4.50

MAP REF.

Variety Coffee Roasters Bushwick

146 Wyckoff Avenue, Brooklyn, NY 11237 | **Bushwick**

Any place where you can play Ms Pac Man on a real arcade table has got to be legendary, and this big Variety flagship boasts exactly that. But it's not all fun and games here, as plenty of people sit and work. The décor is dominated by white paint, dark wood and exposed brick. The coffee offering is Variety's usual high-class stuff, brewed by experts using beans roasted at the back of the room. Service is swift and friendly, and you can get plenty of sound advice about what to drink.

(718) 497-2326
www.varietycoffeeroasters.com
Subway L (DeKalb Ave)

Sister locations Greenpoint / Williamsburg / Chelsea

MON-SUN. 7:00am - 9:00pm

First opened 2014
Roaster Variety Coffee Roasters
Machine La Marzocco Linea, 3 groups
Grinder Mazzer Luigi Robur E

Espresso	$2.50
Cappuccino	$3.50
Latte	$4.00

MAP REF. 163

COFFEE 4.75 / 5

OVERALL 4.50 / 5 ★★★★⯪

Walter's Coffee Roastery

65 Irving Avenue, Brooklyn, NY 11237 | **Bushwick**

Photo courtesy of the venue

A relative newcomer to the New York coffee scene, Walter's Coffee was founded in Istanbul and is now expanding with this Bushwick store and a venue in Dubai. In the words of Walter's, "we respect coffee and its chemistry. We have coffee down to a science." Owner Deniz has over 10 years of experience in the industry and has used his knowledge to create something amazing. From their signature yellow suits to their magnificent coffee, Walter's Coffee is one to watch.

(646) 642-3267
www.walterscoffeeroastery.com
Subway L (Jefferson St)

MON-THU.	7:00am - 10:00pm
FRI-SAT.	7:00am - 12:00am
SUN.	9:00am - 10:00pm

First opened 2016
Roaster Walter's Coffee Roasters
Machine Mavam UCME, 2 groups
Grinder Mahlkönig K30

Espresso	$3.00
Cappuccino	$3.75
Latte	$4.25

MAP REF. **164**

COFFEE VENUES KEY

Williamsburg

165 Black Brick p183 *
166 Charter Coffee p185
167 Devoción p186 ◊
168 Gimme! Coffee (Williamsburg) p187
169 JANE Motorcycles p188 *
170 Oslo Coffee Roasters (Williamsburg) p189
171 Starbucks Reserve p190
172 Sweatshop p191
173 Tar Pit p192
174 Toby's Estate (Williamsburg) p193 ◊
175 True North Brooklyn p194 *
176 Upstate Stock p194

* NEW
◊ TOP 40

Williamsburg is a popular, trendy neighborhood with a lively, youthful feel. This area is a mecca for foodies, featuring lots of coffee roasteries housed in its converted warehouses, the Smorgasburg food market on the waterfront in the summertime and plenty of exciting restaurants. It's also home to a range of vintage shops, art galleries, music venues and McCarren Park on its northern edge.

Williamsburg

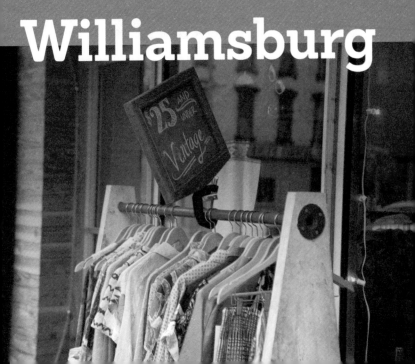

Black Brick

300 Bedford Avenue, Brooklyn, NY 11211 | **Williamsburg**

Relaxed, cozy, dark, exposed brick, hipster - these are a few words that describe Black Brick. Conveniently located in the center of South Williamsburg, this café is known for its laid-back atmosphere, country vintage aesthetic, and perfect Stumptown brew. Seriously, the coffee is as smooth as the customers who consume it. There is ample seating to work or just to hang out - anything goes at Black Brick. In the summer months, be sure to take your Stumptown brew and Doughnut Factory donut outside and sit in the beautiful private patio which is a computer-free zone, designed to encourage conversation.

A great place to socialize with friends or kick back with a good book, and the unique tea selection is served in the most wonderful tea pots.

MAP REF. **165**

COFFEE
4.25 / 5

OVERALL
4.25 / 5
★ ★ ★ ★

| MON–FRI. | 7:00am – 8:00pm |
| SAT–SUN. | 8:00am – 8:00pm |

First opened 2016
Roaster Stumptown Coffee Roasters
Machine La Marzocco, 2 groups
Grinder Mazzer Luigi

Espresso	$2.50
Cappuccino	$3.50
Latte	$3.75 / $4.25 / $4.75

(718) 384-0075
www.blackbrickcoffee.com
Subway L (Bedford Ave)

Williamsburg

Charter Coffee

309 Graham Avenue, Brooklyn, NY 11211 | **Williamsburg**

Photo courtesy of the venue

Serving up expertly brewed coffee, Charter Coffee is a cozy, compact 20-seater café in the heart of Williamsburg. Raw and reused wood make for a quirky, laid back edge. The owners, Scott Cameron & Chrissy Tsang, have set out not only to deliver fantastic coffee, but also to support the people behind that beans by donating 5% of all profits to help the development of the coffee farming communities. And as if all of that wasn't reason enough to visit, Chrissy has a background in hair-cutting, and she practices her art out back. Sip and snip anyone?

(347) 721-3735
www.chartercoffee.com
Subway L (Graham Ave)

MON-FRI. 7:00am - 7:00pm
SAT-SUN. 8:00am - 7:00pm

First opened 2016
Roaster Ceremony Coffee Roasters, MiddleState
Machine La Marzocco Linea, 2 groups
Grinder Nuova Simonelli Mythos, Mahlkönig EK 43

Espresso	$3.00
Cappuccino	$4.00
Latte	$4.50

MAP REF.

COFFEE
4.25 / 5

OVERALL
4.25 / 5 ★★★★⯪

Devoción

69 Grand Street, Brooklyn, NY 11249 | **Williamsburg**

Photo courtesy of the venue

You can enjoy the world's finest artisan Colombian coffees here at this sprawling café, as Devoción sources and purchases all their coffee from Colombia. The shop reflects this focus with its spectacular space, outfitted with its roastery in the front where you can see the roasters hard at work. The main room is an impressive chamber, bursting with sun from a center skylight. The space is huge, with plenty of tables and deliciously sunken-in couches, accented by an incredible living wall, with impressive plants all native to Colombia.

(718) 285-6180
devocion.com
Subway J, Z (Marcy Ave) or L (Bedford Ave) or G (Metropolitan Ave)

MON–FRI.	7:00am – 7:00pm
SAT–SUN.	8:00am – 7:00pm

First opened 2014
Roaster Devoción
Machine Kees Van der Westen Mirage, 3 groups, Slayer Steam, 2 groups
Grinder Ceado E92

Espresso	$3.25
Cappuccino	$4.25
Latte	$4.75

MAP REF.

COFFEE
4.75 / 5

OVERALL
4.75 / 5 ★★★★⯪

Gimme! Coffee Williamsburg

495 Lorimer Street, Brooklyn, NY 11211 | **Williamsburg**

Gimme! Coffee's unassuming design might fool you into thinking that this is just another nice neighborhood coffee joint. In reality it's a decade-and-a-half old branch of an Ithica based roaster that's as serious about the expertise of its baristas as it is the ethics by which they procure their beans. While they meticulously prepare your delicately-flavored pour-over, an amiable barista might tell you about new equipment the farmers purchased with funding provided by Gimme. The maple latte might sound like it's for teenagers, but they use just a touch of syrup, so the sweetness never overpowers the rich flavor of the espresso, insanely delicious.

(718) 388-7771
buy.gimmecoffee.com
Subway L (Lorimer St) or G (Metropolitan Ave)

MON–SUN. 7:00am - 7:00pm

First opened 2003
Roaster Gimme! Coffee
Machine La Marzocco GB5, 3 groups
Grinder Mazzer Luigi

Espresso $3.00
Cappuccino $3.75
Latte $4.00 / $4.50

Sister locations Nolita / Williamsburg

MAP REF. 168

COFFEE 4.25 / 5

OVERALL 4.25 / 5 ★★★★⯪

JANE Motorcycles

396 Wythe Avenue, Brooklyn, NY 11249 | **Williamsburg**

NEW

JANE Motorcycles is the one-stop-shop for all of your bike (and coffee!) needs. Serving up Counter Culture Coffee, a staple Brooklyn roaster, and all the motorcycle related attire one could hope for, JANE Motorcycles is truly a gem in the Williamsburg coffee scene. Grab your cup of joe in the front before browsing the gear. The well-designed shop is bright, airy, and easy on the eye. Whether you're a biker or not, ride on in for the coffee alone; it's well worth the visit.

(347) 844-9075
www.janemotorcycles.com
Subway J, M, Z (Marcy Ave)

MON-FRI.	7:00am - 7:00pm
SAT.	8:00am - 7:00pm
SUN.	9:00am - 7:00pm

First opened 2015
Roaster Counter Culture
Machine La Marzocco, 2 groups
Grinder Mazzer Luigi

Espresso	$3.00
Cappuccino	$4.00
Latte	$4.50

MAP REF. **169**

Oslo Coffee Roasters Williamsburg

133b Roebling Street, Brooklyn, NY 11211 | **Williamsburg**

Away from the hub of Williamsburg's eat/drink/shop district, but close enough for easy access, this branch of Oslo is a fantastic place to while away the hours. You'll look through big windows fronting the high-ceilinged corner room, with fellow drinkers ranging from solitary workers to lively family groups. The coffee is roasted nearby, from beans bought through direct trade and sold as three house blends. Lovingly brewed into some of New York City's best cups, this Oslo outpost a destination in its own right.

(718) 782-0332
www.oslocoffee.com
Subway L (Bedford Ave)

Sister locations Upper East Side / Williamsburg (Bedford Ave)

MON-FRI.	7:00am - 7:00pm
SAT-SUN.	8:00am - 7:00pm
	(6:00pm in winter)

First opened 2003
Roaster Oslo Coffee Roasters
Machine Synesso Cyncra, 2 groups
Grinder Mazzer Luigi

Espresso	$3.00
Cappuccino	$3.75
Latte	$3.75

MAP REF.

COFFEE 4.25 / 5

OVERALL 4.50 / 5 ★★★★⯪

Starbucks Reserve

154 North 7th Street, Brooklyn, NY 11211 | **Williamsburg**

For polish and breadth of offering, few places in Williamsburg can match Starbucks. This is their flagship store, one of the locations offering the chain's 'Reserve' range, lots of rare and exquisite single-origin beans. It's also a place where you can think well outside the espresso box, with an exceptionally wide range of alternative brewing methods. You're just as likely to stand in line behind moms pushing strollers as college students on their iPhones. Starbucks may be a global brand, but Starbucks Williamsburg is a genuine local hangout.

www.starbucks.com
Subway L (Bedford Ave)

Sister locations Multiple locations

| MON-THU. | 5:30am - 9:00pm |
| FRI-SUN. | 5:30am - 10:00pm |

First opened 2014
Roaster Starbucks Corporation
Machine Victoria Arduino Black Eagle, 2 groups
Grinder Nuova Simonelli Mythos x2, Ditting

Espresso	$3.00
Cappuccino	$4.50
Latte	$4.50

MAP REF. **171**

Sweatshop

232 Metropolitan Avenue, Brooklyn, NY 11211 | **Williamsburg**

TOP
40

Australian-owned Sweatshop is full of things that'll make you smile, from the big neon Sweatshop sign to the 'Death Before Decaf' tote bags, to the hand-painted stool-tops. Smiles continue when you start sipping brews from the sleek La Marzocco espresso machine. The single-origin espresso from Counter Culture Coffee changes every one or two weeks, and latte and macchiato boast exquisite latte art. Food is simple but well executed, with healthy Aussie-style breakfasts giving way at lunch to 'jaffles'(toasted sandwiches). In the words of co-owner Luke, 'We do what we do back home and hope that people dig it.' Full seats both indoors and out suggest they do.

(917) 960-7232
www.sweatshop.nyc
Subway L (Bedford Ave)

MON–FRI.	7:00am – 6:00pm
SAT–SUN.	8:00am – 6:00pm

First opened 2014
Roaster Counter Culture Coffee
Machine La Marzocco FB80, 2 groups
Grinder Mahlkönig Peak

Espresso	$3.00
Cappuccino	$4.00
Latte	$4.00

MAP REF. **172**

COFFEE 4.50 / 5

OVERALL 4.50 / 5 ★★★★½

Tar Pit

135 Woodpoint Road, Brooklyn, NY 11211 | **Williamsburg**

Photo courtesy of the venue

Tucked away on a residential block in Williamsburg, this best-kept-secret might be the most tranquil, cozy coffee experience in the city. Everything about Tar Pit feels handcrafted - the copper and wood-bric-a-brac-strewn space was designed by the owner, a motorcycle mechanic. The coffee is excellent, from the espresso to the two kinds of cold-brew, to the pour overs (the drip, from Plowshares, is also single-origin). But treat yourself to a cortado - the milk, from Battenkill Creamery, is of such high quality and handled so delicately it's sweeter and smoother than most lattes you'll ever have.

(917) 705-8031
www.tarpitcafe.com
Subway L (Graham Ave)

| MON-FRI. | 7:00am - 7:00pm |
| SAT-SUN. | 8:00am - 7:00pm |

First opened 2011
Roaster Plowshares Coffee Roasters
Machine La Marzocco Linea Paddle
Grinder Mazzer Luigi Major

Espresso	$2.50
Cappuccino	$3.75
Latte	$4.00

MAP REF. **173**

| COFFEE 4.25 / 5 | 🫘🫘🫘🫘🫘 | OVERALL 4.25 / 5 | ★★★★⯨ |

Toby's Estate Williamsburg

125 North 6th Street, Brooklyn, NY 11249 | **Williamsburg**

Williamsburg

Williamsburg wasn't complete until Toby's came to town. Everything on the menu (both beverage and food) is worth making the trip for, but go for the bright, single-origin espresso, straight up. Trust us, there really is a difference between this and the house blend espresso, especially fresh as the beans are roasted in front of you. Toby's near-flawlessness extends to the friendly, efficient service and the stylish, comfortable, loft-reminiscent design - which is often mobbed with laptops. Before you go, you also have to try the signature flat white, so smooth and rich it takes you to another world.

(347) 457-6160
www.tobysestate.com
Subway L (Bedford Ave)

MON-FRI.	7:00am - 7:00pm
SAT-SUN.	8:00am - 7:00pm

First opened 2012
Roaster Toby's Estate Coffee
Machine Spirit Triplette
Grinder Mahlkönig Guatemala Lab

Espresso	$3.00
Cappuccino	$3.75
Latte	$4.50

Sister locations Long Island City / Flatiron / West Village / Midtown East

MAP REF. **174**

 COFFEE 4.75 / 5   **OVERALL** 4.75 / 5 ★★★★

True North Brooklyn

561 Lorimer Street, Brooklyn, NY 11211 | **Williamsburg**

Enthusiasm and passion is the lifeblood of True North Brooklyn, a lovely spot just moments away from the Lorimer Street L train. Founded by two individuals who fell head over heels for the culture of coffee, True North is a must visit destination in the Brooklyn coffee scene. Its interior is gorgeous, with soothing green walls and earthy tones providing a calm and tranquil space. As a "working café," the back serves as a communal workspace, fully equipped with outlets and free WiFi; a perfect spot for Brooklyn creatives to sip their lattes and flex their imaginations.

(646) 284-0268
www.truenorthbrooklyn.com
Subway L (Lorimer St)

MON-SUN. 7:00am - 7:00pm

First opened 2017
Roaster Plowshares Coffee Roasters
Machine La Marzocco Linea, 3 groups
Grinder Mazzer Luigi

Espresso $3.25
Cappuccino $4.00
Latte $4.25

MAP REF. **175**

COFFEE 4.25 / 5	OVERALL 4.25 / 5

Upstate Stock

2 Berry Street, Brooklyn, NY 11249 | **Williamsburg**

Almost too-Brooklyn-to-be-true, in the best possible sense, Upstate Stock is a store that sells a selection of home & beauty products, which happens to have a great coffee bar in the front with plenty of seating (a generous touch). This is the only place in America you can get beans from Toronto-based Cut, who tend to roast their beans light, bucking the prevailing trend to dark-roast. The resulting espresso, pulled by a barista who knows what he's doing, is nicely bright. The campfire latte might sound gimmicky but it's essential - touched with delicious smoked maple syrup and sea salt, it truly smells and tastes like summer camp.

www.upstatestock.com
Subway G (Nassau Ave)

MON-SUN. 8:00am - 6:30pm

First opened 2016
Roaster Cut Coffee
Machine Astoria Gloria
Grinder Mazzer Luigi

Espresso $2.50
Cappuccino $3.50
Latte $4.00

MAP REF. **176**

COFFEE 4.00 / 5	OVERALL 4.00 / 5

Two Hands

Growing in popularity, the neighborhoods of Astoria, Long Island City and Greenpoint are hubs of culture, history and lots of good food. Greenpoint adjoins Williamsburg on the other side of McCarren Park and, although quiet, is full of innovative eateries and shops. Walk over Pulaski Bridge to Long Island City and explore a burgeoning part of Queens where lots of new restaurants, MoMA's contemporary art affiliate PS1 and a thriving creative community can be found. Astoria boasts a diverse cultural mix that includes Italian, Jewish and Greek communities.

Greenpoint & Queens

Greenpoint Avenue

60 Beans

36-02 Ditmars Boulevard, Queens, NY 11105 | **Astoria**

60 Beans positively bursts with charm. This lovely neighborhood shop takes care of its customers with a real old-school kind of charm and attention. Their beautiful marble-topped bars are equipped with built-in outlets for those diligently working, while their large front windows open fully to let in the breeze when the weather is fine. They use Café Grumpy blends and serve their espressos traditionally, with sparkling water on the side. There's also a beautiful back area with comfy couches and ample sidewalk seating outside too.

(347) 987-3994
www.60beanskitchen.com
Subway N, W (Astoria - Ditmars Blvd)

MON.	7:00am - 6:00pm
TUE-FRI.	7:00am - 7:00pm
SAT.	8:00am - 7:00pm
SUN.	8:00am - 7:00pm

First opened 2014
Roaster Café Grumpy Coffee
Machine Kees van der Westen Spirit
Grinder Nuova Simonelli

Espresso	$2.50
Cappuccino	$3.75
Latte	$4.25

MAP REF. **177**

COFFEE 4.25 / 5	OVERALL 4.50 / 5 ★★★★⯪

Astoria Coffee

30-04 30th Street, Queens, NY 11102 | **Astoria**

Astoria Coffee brings a special love for the glorious bean at this neighborhood shop, hosting a variety of different coffees here. They source from multiple American roasters, and have the beans available to purchase. They keep at least two different types of roasts on the bar for espresso drinks. Don't hesitate to ask questions because the baristas are more than happy to walk you through the tasting notes to get you just what you're looking for.

(347) 410-7399
www.astoriacoffeeny.com
Subway N, W (30th Ave)

MON-FRI.	7:00am - 8:00pm
SAT-SUN.	8:00am - 8:00pm

First opened 2014
Roaster Multi-Roaster
Machine Synesso Hydra
Grinder Mahlkönig EK 43, Mahlkönig K 30

Espresso	$3.00
Cappuccino	$4.00
Latte	$4.00

MAP REF. **178**

COFFEE 4.50 / 5	OVERALL 4.25 / 5 ★★★★⯪

Birch Coffee Long Island City

40-37 23rd Street, Long Island City, NY 11101 | **Long Island City**

You can't actually walk around the beautiful roastery here, but the views, scent, and sounds of it behind glass are exciting enough to bring out every coffee geek's inner child. You can't get beans any fresher than this, and you can taste it in every drink. The espresso is so intense that even the latte has a strong flavor. It's been said that what separates a good barista from a great barista is that a great barista throws out a lot of shots, and on a recent visit, a barista threw out three shots before he felt it was worthy of being served, a testament to Birch's commitment to quality.

(212) 686-1444
www.birchcoffee.com
Subway F (21 St - Queensbridge)

Sister locations Multiple locations

MON-FRI.	8:00am - 5:00pm
SAT-SUN.	Closed

First opened 2015
Roaster Birch Coffee Roasters
Machine La Marzocco Linea
Grinder Mahlkönig K 30 Twin

Espresso	$3.00
Cappuccino	$4.00
Latte	$4.00

MAP REF. **179**

COFFEE
4.25 / 5

OVERALL
4.25 / 5
★★★★⯪

198

Búðin

114 Greenpoint Avenue, Brooklyn, NY 11222 | **Greenpoint**

Photo: Ivor Ip

Búðin is a shop specializing in Nordic coffee, culture, and aesthetic, featuring roasts from Iceland and Norway, as well as home-goods and handmade clothes from Scandinavian purveyors. Coffee beans are all available to buy, should you like to brew some Nordic beans in your own home. The sleek, minimalist space is expansive with plenty of seating and gets beautiful sunlight during the day. In the evenings, Búðin offers a variety of Nordic-related beers too. In the summertime, head out to the backyard for a peaceful paradise.

(347) 844-9639
www.budin-nyc.com
Subway G (Greenpoint Ave)

MON–THU.	7:00am – 11:00pm
FRI.	7:00am – 12:00am
SAT.	8:00am – 12:00am
SUN.	8:00am – 11:00pm

First opened 2014
Roaster Lofted Coffee, Tim Wendelboe, Koppi, Drop, Good Life, other Nordic Roasters
Machine ModBar
Grinder Mahlkönig EK 43

Espresso	$3.00
Cappuccino	$4.00
Latte	$4.50

MAP REF. **180**

  COFFEE 4.50 / 5 OVERALL 4.25 / 5 ★★★★☆

199

Café Grumpy Greenpoint

193 Meserole Avenue, Brooklyn, NY 11222 | **Greenpoint**

Café Grumpy's original location, in the quiet residential edge of Greenpoint, is so large and the clientele exude such laid-back artsiness that you get the sense you could bring in an easel and start painting a portrait, and no one would raise an eyebrow. Anyone can appreciate the frothy light texture of their latte, but Grumpy, who roast their own beans in the back, cater to coffee nerds. In addition to reliably delicate, rich pour overs (which really do get more flavorful as they cool down), they offer a single-origin espresso in addition to a house blend.

(718) 349-7623
www.cafegrumpy.com
Subway G (Nassau Ave)

Sister locations Multiple locations

| MON-FRI. | 7:00am - 7:30pm |
| SAT-SUN. | 7:30am - 7:30pm |

First opened 2005
Roaster Café Grumpy Coffee
Machine Synesso, 2 groups
Grinder Nuova Simonelli Mythos, Mazzer Luigi Robur E, Mahlkönig Guatemala

Espresso $3.25
Cappuccino $4.00
Latte $4.50   MAP REF. **181**

| COFFEE 4.50 / 5 | OVERALL 4.50 / 5 | ★★★★⯪ |

Champion Coffee

142 Nassau Avenue, Brooklyn, NY 11222 | **Greenpoint**

A small but powerful coffee bar at the far end of Greenpoint's Manhattan Avenue, this place makes for a particularly lovely visit when the weather is nice and the garden is open in the back. Champion is a quiet little gem over in this neck of the woods, they use their own blend making it that little bit more special.

(718) 383-3251
www.championcoffee.net
Subway G (Nassau Ave)

| MON-SUN. | 7:00am - 8:00pm |

First opened 2006
Roaster Champion Coffee
Machine La Marzocco, 3 groups
Grinder Mahlkönig

Espresso $3.00
Cappuccino $4.00
Latte $4.50

MAP REF. **182**

| COFFEE 4.25 / 5 | OVERALL 4.25 / 5 | ★★★★⯪ |

COFFEED Long Island City

37-18 Northern Boulevard, Queens, NY 11101 | **Long Island City**

COFFEED cares about bringing not just great coffee but a sense of community to all its locations. That's why it pairs each café with a local charity and makes an effort to use locally sourced ingredients. Here at the roastery in Long Island City, COFFEED use produce from their rooftop farm as they churn out their fresh roasts constantly throughout the day. They offer four different batch-brewed coffees in house, all fair or direct trade single origins, and in the evenings share refreshing local beers on tap too.

(718) 606-1299
www.coffeednyc.com
Subway E, M, R (36th Street)

MON-FRI.	7:00am - 4:00pm
SAT-SUN.	9:00am - 4:00pm

First opened 2012
Roaster COFFEED
Machine La Marzocco Linea
Grinder Mazzer Luigi

Espresso	$2.25
Cappuccino	$3.50
Latte	$3.50

Sister locations Long Island City (Hunters Point South Park) / Long Island city (47th Ave) / Chelsea

MAP REF. **183**

COFFEE 4.00 / 5		OVERALL 4.00 / 5	★★★★☆

Gossip Coffee

3704 30th Avenue, Queens, NY 11103 | **Astoria**

With its pristine, 1950's-inspired interior, and beautiful outdoor seating area, Gossip stands out in this neighborhood. Their quality beans are roasted in Queens, just a few miles away. Gossip often offers several types of cold brew, including a "New Orleans style," with vanilla extract and half-and-half, as well as excellent single origin cold brews, which have delicate, fruity, tea-esque flavors. Try them without milk to fully experience their nuance.

(718) 440-8792
www.gossipcoffee.com
Subway N, W (30th St)

MON-FRI.	7:00am - 9:00pm
SAT-SUN.	8:00am - 9:00pm

First opened 2015
Roaster Gossip Coffee
Machine La Marzocco Strada
Grinder Mazzer Luigi Major

Espresso	$3.00 / $3.50
Cappuccino	$4.00
Latte	$4.50

MAP REF. **184**

COFFEE 4.00 / 5		OVERALL 4.00 / 5	★★★★☆

Homecoming

107 Franklin Street, Brooklyn, NY 11222 | **Greenpoint**

Photo courtesy of the venue

Homecoming is a beautiful flower shop on this busy little stretch of Franklin Street that couples fresh fantastic coffees with their floral arrangements. They serve Verve coffee, as well as fine teas, made by charming baristas at this loveable shop. They have a carefully curated selection of home goods here as well, with handmade notebooks, soaps and pots for your plants. It's easy to imagine building your perfect home here, right down to the coffee on the table.

(347) 457-5385
www.home-coming.com
Subway G (Greenpoint Ave)

| MON-FRI. | 7:30am - 7:00pm |
| SAT-SUN. | 8:30am - 7:00pm |

First opened 2013
Roaster Verve Coffee
Machine La Marzocco Linea, 2 groups
Grinder Mazzer Luigi Major E

Espresso	$3.00
Cappuccino	$4.25
Latte	$4.50

MAP REF. **185**

 COFFEE 4.00 / 5   **OVERALL** 4.00 / 5 ★★★★☆

Kinship Coffee Cooperative

30-5 Steinway Street, Queens, NY 11103 | **Astoria**

Stumptown Coffee is served at this charming Astoria shop, but they also keep a rotating menu of seasonal single and dual-origins from a variety of roasters. It's got fresh pastries from not one, not two, but three of the very best bakeries in the city, as well as specialty chocolates for good measure. Though the space is small, the shop is bright and has just enough leg room to be a local favorite.

(646) 468-7149
Subway N, W (30th Ave)

MON-FRI.	7:00am - 9:00pm
SAT-SUN.	Closed

First opened 2014
Roaster Stumptown, Heart, Parlor, Sweet Bloom, Supersonic, Tandem, Ceremony
Machine Synesso Cyncra, 2 groups
Grinder Compak K10, Mahlkönig EK 43

Espresso	$3.25
Cappuccino	$4.00
Latte	$4.50

MAP REF.

COFFEE 4.50 / 5	OVERALL 4.25 / 5

New York City Bagel and Coffee House

40-05 Broadway, Queens, NY 11103 | **Astoria**

You know how some places feel like they've been around forever? Little more than two year's old in Astoria, NYC Bagel and Coffee House is one of them. People seem to feel at home here. They come for bagels, sure: outstanding specimens in two sizes (the "mini" is plenty) with loads of interesting fillings. But also for the coffee and baked sweet goods including enticing donuts. Note: though there are no loyalty cards, but "familiar faces get a 'loyalty bonus.'" No wonder 50 per cent of customers are regulars.

(718) 728-9511
www.nycbch.com
Subway M, R (46th St)

MON-SAT.	6:00am – 10:00pm
SUN.	7:00am – 10:00pm

First opened 2015
Roaster Stone Street
Machine La Marzocco FB80, 3 groups
Grinder Mazzer Luigi Super Jolly

Espresso	$1.75 / $2.25
Cappuccino	$3.25 / $4.00 / $4.50
Latte	$3.25 / $4.00 / $4.50

Sister locations Long Island City

MAP REF. 187

COFFEE 4.00 / 5

OVERALL 4.25 / 5 ★★★★✫

204

Odd Fox Coffee

984 Manhattan Avenue, Brooklyn, NY 11222 | **Greenpoint**

Odd Fox doesn't deny that its name is a bit strange, but that's all part of the fun. Serving first rate products, including Propeller coffee and Ovenly pastries, Odd Fox has established itself as a strong player in the Greenpoint coffee scene. Its low-key ambiance, soft lighting, and gentle music make it a great place to come with a book or your laptop (there are outlets next to every table!). The quick service makes it a great option for a grab and go coffee if you're in a rush to catch a train, or feel free to sit in and take it easy - the friendly baristas won't mind! If you're in the mood for something a little adventurous, why not try one of their other delicious drinks such as their hot cider. Coffee connoisseurs, take the opportunity to chat with the friendly and knowledgeable baristas as they pull flavorful espressos.

MAP REF. **188**

COFFEE
4.25 / 5

OVERALL
4.25 / 5

★★★★⯪

MON-FRI. 7:00am - 7:00pm
SAT-SUN. 8:00am - 8:00pm

First opened 2016
Roaster Parlor Coffee
Machine La Marzocco Linea, 2 groups
Grinder Mazzer Luigi Robur E

Espresso $3.00
Cappuccino $4.00 / $4.50 / $5.00
Latte $4.00 / $4.50 / $5.00

www.oddfoxcoffee.com
Subway G (Nassau Ave)

The Queens Kickshaw

40-17 Broadway, Queens, NY 11103 | **Astoria**

Photo courtesy of the venue

There's really no reason to ever leave The Queens Kickshaw. This spacious, rough-hewn-wood-filled café starts out in the morning as a coffee bar, serves gourmet grilled cheese, salads and desserts from 10am, and turns into a beer-and-wine bar at night. The baristas really know what they're doing-the espresso drinks are excellent, as are the single-origin pour-overs. It definitely feels like a neighborhood spot, but at the same time is worth going out of your way to experience.

(718) 777-0913
www.thequeenskickshaw.com
Subway E, M, R (Steinway St)

MON-THU.	7:30am - 12:00am
FRI.	7:30am - 1:00am
SAT.	9:00am - 1:00am
SUN.	9:00am - 12:00am

First opened 2011
Roaster Counter Culture Coffee
Machine La Marzocco Strada MP, 3 groups
Grinder La Marzocco Vulcano

Espresso	$3.00
Cappuccino	$4.00
Latte	$4.50

MAP REF. 189

COFFEE
4.25 / 5

OVERALL
4.25 / 5 ★★★★⯪

Sweetleaf Center Boulevard

4615 Center Boulevard, Queens, NY 11101 | **Long Island City**

Long Island City is a neighborhood full of very-recently-constructed buildings, but this outpost of Sweetleaf feels like it's been here for decades. At night it turns into a bar serving cocktails and American beers, but during the day it's perfect for parents with babies and freelancers tapping at laptops. True to its name, the espresso at Sweetleaf tastes ever so slightly of honey, and goes down smoothly. Order it straight up or in a macchiato to fully appreciate it.

(347) 527-1038
www.sweetleafcoffee.com
Subway E, M (Court Square - 23rd St)

Sister locations Greenpoint /
Long Island City

MON-THU.	7:00am - 12:00am
FRI.	7:00am - 2:00am
SAT.	8:00am - 2:00am
SUN.	8:00am - 12:00am

First opened 2012
Roaster Sweetleaf Coffee Roasters
Machine La Marzocco GB5, 2 groups
Grinder Mazzer Luigi Robur E

Espresso	$3.00
Cappuccino	$3.75
Latte	$4.00

MAP REF. **190**

Greenpoint & Queens

COFFEE 4.25 / 5	OVERALL 4.25 / 5

208

Sweetleaf Greenpoint

159 Freeman Street, Brooklyn, NY 11222 | **Greenpoint**

TOP
40

Photo: Shawn Brackbill

You can't miss Sweetleaf's flagship roastery/café, which has the company name stencilled in huge lettering on the exterior. A converted warehouse makes an exceptionally attractive space, wood-beamed and high-ceilinged, and there's plenty of antique seating in both the larger front room and the smaller space in the back, not to mention outside on the benches. Sweetleaf's signature brews are made to a high standard, with lip-smacking cold drinks given equal prominence to the hot stuff. In addition to selling beans, they offer a large range of brewing equipment and coffee making paraphernalia.

(347) 987-3732
www.sweetleafcoffee.com
Subway G (Greenpoint Ave)

MON-FRI.	7:00am - 7:00pm
SAT-SUN.	8:00am - 7:00pm

First opened 2015
Roaster Sweetleaf Coffee Roasters
Machine La Marzocco Strada, 2 groups
Grinder Mazzer Luigi Robur E

Espresso	$3.00
Cappuccino	$3.75
Latte	$4.00

Sister locations Williamsburg / Long Island City

MAP REF. **191**

COFFEE
4.50 / 5

OVERALL
4.75 / 5 ★★★★⯪

Sweetleaf Jackson Avenue

10-93 Jackson Avenue, Queens, NY 11101 | **Long Island City**

The prevailing aesthetic in Long Island City is glass and steel, making the cozy design of Sweetleaf all the more welcome. From couches and a table in the front, you can see through big windows into the bakery where excellent cinnamon donuts and other goodies are made. In the back is a room with a record player where guests are encouraged to pick something out from the collection or bring their records to play (no laptops allowed in there). Go for an espresso drink - Sweetleaf roast their own beans nearby.

(917) 832-6726
www.sweetleafcoffee.com
Subway G (21st St)

Sister locations Greenpoint / Long Island City

MON-FRI.	7:00am - 7:00pm
SAT-SUN.	8:00am - 7:00pm

First opened 2008
Roaster Sweetleaf Coffee Roasters
Machine La Marzocco Strada, 2 groups
Grinder Mazzer Luigi Robur E

Espresso	$3.00
Cappuccino	$3.75
Latte	$4.00

MAP REF. **192**

COFFEE 4.50 / 5	OVERALL 4.50 / 5

210

Toby's Estate Long Island City

26-25 Jackson Avenue, Queens, NY 11101 | **Long Island City**

This area of Long Island City is sprouting a forest of high-rise hotels and apartment buildings, and their future residents have a treat awaiting them at Toby's. This latest branch is also one of the best, with the company's usual top-quality beans brewed beautifully whichever method you go for. Lovers of cold brew should check out their 'Black + White', milky, slightly sweetened, totally addictive. The only thing that can make the coffee better is the space; an early 20th-century building that served as an art gallery in one of its earlier incarnations. The whole building has been hollowed out so the room goes right up into the roof, with massive steel and wooden beams and gorgeous lighting including contemporary-style chandeliers over the counter and main seating area. It's a little like being in a coffee cathedral. As if that weren't enough, there's a garden out back where you can pretty much forget you're in booming LIC. Toby has really hit it out of the park with this one. Long Island City is truly lucky!

MAP REF. 193

COFFEE 4.50 / 5

OVERALL 4.75 / 5 ★★★★½

MON-FRI. 6.30am – 6:00pm
SAT-SUN. 8:00am – 6:00pm

First opened 2017
Roaster Toby's Estate Coffee
Machine La Marzocco Strada, 3 groups
Grinder Mazzer Luigi Robur E, Nuova
Simonelli Mythos One, Mazzer Luigi Super
Jolly E, Mahlkönig Tanzania

Espresso $3.00
Cappuccino $3.75
Latte $4.50

(347) 531-0477
www.tobysestate.com
Subway E, M, R (Queens Plaza)

Sister locations Williamsburg / Flatiron /
West Village / Midtown East

Greenpoint & Queens

Upright Coffee

860 Manhattan Avenue, Brooklyn, NY 11222 | **Greenpoint**

A gem hidden in Greenpoint, Upright balances seriousness with neighborhood amiability. Using their own Upright blend they pour drinks to impress. The space is streamlined and there are only a few stools, hence the shop's name. Though the compact size of the shop might not give you cause to linger, the care and friendliness of the baristas will. Greenpointers are surely lucky to have it.

(718) 215-9910
www.uprightcoffee.com
Subway G (Nassau Ave)

Sister locations West Village

MON-FRI.	7:00am - 7:00pm
SAT.	8:00am - 7:00pm
SUN.	8:00am - 6:00pm

First opened 2011
Roaster Upright Roasting
Machine La Marzocco Linea
Grinder Mazzer Luigi

Espresso	$2.50
Cappuccino	$3.50
Latte	$3.75

MAP REF. **194**

| COFFEE 4.25 / 5 | | OVERALL 4.00 / 5 | ★★★★☆ |

Variety Coffee Roasters Greenpoint

145 Driggs Avenue, Brooklyn, NY 11222 | **Greenpoint**

Variety's Greenpoint outlet is almost as small as a café can get, it has seating for just eight. But it's really attractive, with its turquoise wainscoting and bare wood floor, and has a great vibe. The barista describes it as 'intimate and welcoming, but cool,' and that nails it almost perfectly. Milky drinks are expertly handled, but the changing roster of single-origin coffees is a special source of delight.

(718) 383-2326
www.varietycoffeeroasters.com
Subway G (Nassau Ave)

Sister locations Bushwick / Williamsburg / Chelsea

| MON-SUN. | 8:00am - 4:00pm |

First opened 2009
Roaster Variety Coffee Roasters
Machine La Marzocco Linea, 2 groups
Grinder Mazzer Luigi Robur E

Espresso	$2.50
Cappuccino	$3.50
Latte	$4.00

MAP REF. **195**

| COFFEE 4.50 / 5 | OVERALL 4.25 / 5 | ★★★★☆ |

The New York Coffee Festival

PROUDLY

OCTOBER 2018

New York's Flagship Coffee Event

 @NYCoffeeFest   The New York Coffee Festival   @newyorkcoffeefestival

SUPPORTING

PROJECT WATER FALL

BRINGING CLEAN WATER
TO COFFEE GROWING COMMUNITIES

50% OF TICKET SALES FROM THE NEW YORK COFFEE FESTIVAL WILL SUPPORT PROJECT WATERFALL, BRINGING CLEAN DRINKING WATER TO COFFEE GROWING COMMUNITIES AROUND THE WORLD.

projectwaterfall.org

 @projectwaterf   Project Waterfall   @project_waterfall

Behind every cup of coffee is a unique story. On its journey from coffee tree to cup, coffee passes through the hands of a number of skilled individuals. Over the following pages, expert contributors share their specialist knowledge. As you will see, the coffee we enjoy is the result of a rich and complex process, and there is always something new to learn.

Coffee
Knowledge

Gorilla Coffee

Coffee at Origin

by **Mike Riley**, Falcon Speciality Green Coffee Importers

If you go into New York's vibrant coffee community today and ask any good barista what makes a perfect cup of coffee, they will always tell you that it starts with the bean. Beyond the roasting technique, the perfect grind, and exact temperatures and precision pressure of a modern espresso machine, we must look to the dedicated coffee farmer who toils away in the tropical lands of Africa, Asia and Latin America. They are the first heroes of our trade.

Approximately 25 million people in over 50 countries are involved in producing coffee. The bean, or seed to be exact, is extracted from cherries that most commonly ripen red but sometimes orange or yellow. The cherries are usually hand-picked then processed by various means. Sometimes they are dried in the fruit under tropical sunshine until they resemble raisins - a process known as 'natural'. The 'honey process' involves pulping the fresh cherries to extract the beans which are then sundried, still coated in their sticky mucilage. Alternatively, in the 'washed process', the freshly pulped beans are left to stand in tanks of water for several hours where enzyme activity breaks down the mucilage, before they are sundried on concrete patios or raised beds. Each method has a profound impact on the ultimate flavor of the coffee.

The term 'speciality coffee' is used to differentiate the world's best from the rest. This means it has to be Arabica, the species of coffee that is often bestowed with incredible flavors - unlike its hardy cousin Robusta which is usually reserved for commercial products and many instant blends. But being Arabica alone is by no means enough for a coffee to achieve the speciality tag, since the best beans are usually those grown at higher altitude on rich and fertile soils. As well as country and region of origin, the variety is important too; Bourbon, Typica, Caturra, Catuai, Pacamara and Geisha to name but a few. Just as Shiraz and Chardonnay grapes have their own complex flavors, the same is true of coffee's varieties. Some of the world's most amazing coffees are the result of the farmer's innovative approach to experimentation with growing and production techniques, meaning that today's speciality roaster is able to source coffees of incredible complexity and variation.

A good coffee establishment will showcase coffees when they are at their best - freshly harvested and seasonal, just like good fruit and vegetables. Seasonal espresso blends change throughout the year to reflect this.

As speciality coffee importers we source stand-out coffees by regularly travelling to origin countries. Direct trade with farmers is always our aim. Above all, we pay sustainable prices and encourage them to treat their land, and those who work it, with respect. Such an approach is increasingly demanded by New York's speciality coffee community in order to safeguard the industry's future.

Small Batch Roasting

by **Jonathan Withers**, Green Coffee Buyer, Toby's Estate Brooklyn

Coffee roasted in small batches is a pillar of the specialty coffee industry. It's an essential part of how we elevate our product above the classic American perception of coffee as a simple common commodity. At Toby's Estate, we and our customers celebrate a small batch methodology. It is an artisanal, hand-crafted approach that facilitates and advances deep connections between tradesperson and material, removed from the industrial construct of mass production prioritized above quality; fostering instead a relationship with the client centered on a product made-to-order, carefully and skillfully.

Successfully delivering quality with this approach relies on the implementation of systems which are focused towards consistently achieving a high standard - batch to batch and day to day. From the perspective of the customer, quality is only as high as our ability to fulfill every time. Among the artisanal aspects of small batch roasting, experienced craftspeople have the tools at hand to achieve these high degrees of quality; it's only a matter of applying them towards the goal of consistency.

The operation of small batch equipment allows for the manipulation of multiple controls towards the progress and outcome of a roast: heat via gas burners, airflow via fan speed,damper position, drum speed, and chosen batch size. These variables all independently influence the roast and are essential avenues for exploration in obtaining the sweet-spot. That is the reference profile of how to best roast that coffee in production. Too many variables moving at once however, will diminish the roaster's control over the batch. Once this ideal roasting of a coffee is established, reducing the complexity of variables is key. In most production machines, this is commonly achieved by setting all variables other than gas pressure. Then the batch is controlled solely by manipulating the heat applied to the roaster.

Having limited the variables to simplify and improve repeatability, we need points of feedback with which to monitor and react to controls and results during the roast. Temperature readings at multiple points in the roasting system are essential. These are done with a probe that measures the air exiting the drum and a probe placed awash in the beans to measure the temperature of coffee mass. Gauges on the gas supply and roaster exhaust air allow for hard measurements of the values of heat being applied (burners) and removed (airflow). Associating a reference profile to a static batch size allows these values to serve as a meaningful reference. Therefore, we can replicate the precise conditions and adjustments in future production batches. For recording, collating, and parsing all this data, many options exist to digitally log roasting data and display the information as a referable curve. By drawing the current curve over that of the reference, batches can be skillfully manipulated to be precisely replicated.

After the batch is dropped and cooled, other points to control consistency exist to ensure perfect uniformity. Measuring the weight of the roasted coffee against that of the initial green shows the moisture mass lost during roasting. This number will change as the green coffee ages throughout its lifespan, but from day to day it provides a simple metric as to how similarly the coffee was roasted. More precisely, color analyzers exist which optically meter roasted, ground coffee to give a numeric value indicating the degree to which the coffee has roasted. Cupping your roasted product is of course the most direct connection with the success of the final consistency.

Multiple batches appearing together on the same table are incredibly meaningful as they can be directly compared against one another. Carefully recording and collating this sensory data allows a full picture of success as well as areas for focused improvements.

Successfully delivering quality from small batch roasting relies on the skills, talent, and experience of the operator. Yet to ensure that this artistry is maintained and guaranteed with every batch over long days and weeks, a rigorous system of variable control, monitoring metrics and tight quality control is paramount. When they catch problems, you're glad the mistakes weren't able to slip through the cracks.

Coffee Grinding

by **Jeremy Challender**, Co-owner and Director of Training, Prufrock Coffee and the

Grinder technology is about to change radically. Machine design, techniques behind the bar and hand brewing methodology have improved rapidly over recent years. Manufacturers are starting to address this by seeking feedback from users as well as lab testing. Home users can benefit from these changes too. New designs entering the market have drawn directly from the experiences of barista champions. Grinder designers are seeking professional and consumer feedback on taste, flavor and ergonomics through direct collaboration and field testing. Manufacturers are aware that we need development to continue and, now more than ever, baristas have a voice in this process. To be a barista in this time of grinder development is very exciting.

With all brew methods the challenge is replicating flavor and strength. Once we've got a precise brew recipe for a coffee we stand a better chance of extracting our coffee consistently. Commercially, the easiest way to navigate from this baseline towards the optimum extraction level is with micro-adjustments in the exposed surface area of the grinds - so the grinder is key to managing flavor in the cup.

The challenge grinder designers face is how to create consistency of grind size and shape. If you get out the microscope, and a set of test sieves, you start to realize all your grinds aren't the same size, nor are they all the same shape. If they were all the same size and shape, brewing would be much easier to control. In espresso you will have seen tiny granules in your cup that are smaller than the holes in the filter basket. We call these fines. These small particles have very high surface area and extract very quickly. As a home brewer, you could consider following the example of many championship baristas; invest in laboratory test sieves to remove a portion of particles under a certain size to reduce over-extracted flavors.

There is a portion of particles that fit side-on between the burrs and are planed rather than ground. We call these larger particles boulders. They have a much lower surface area relative to their size and in a 30 second espresso extraction will under-extract. Wobbly hand grinders are real offenders in the production of boulders. These too can be sieved out.

Sharp burrs are considered to reduce fines production. Ceramic burrs, which many hand grinders are fitted with, are very durable but are often not very sharp to start with. The material of choice at the moment is titanium-coated steel. Large burr diameter is linked to lower production of fines and boulders (more 'modal' distribution) so enormous bag grinders are being examined for application in espresso making. Cutting systems like spice grinders produce a very high proportion of fines and boulders, so are not recommended.

Keeping the coffee cool during grinding is a challenge. Burrs get hot in use because of friction, and some of the most exciting developments recently have focused on temperature stability of the burrs and burr casing with the addition of heating elements and fans. A warm grinder behaves differently to a cold or a hot one, so the particle shape and size are dependent on both grind setting and temperature.

Modern grinder design is very focused on ease of access for regular cleaning. Arabica coffee has up to 17% fat content. We only extract a small percentage of this into a beverage but even after a day of commercial use, a grinder will have a slick of fats and tiny fine particles built up around the burr casing and the barrel and throat of the grinder. Oils oxidise, so grinders must be opened up and thoroughly swept out on a regular basis. Burrs can be washed in soapy water or coffee cleaner, or abrasive oil absorbing grinder cleaning granules can be used. Home baristas have an advantage here by being able to clean after a few shots rather than after a full day's usage.

The final hurdle to overcome is grind retention: many grinders on the market have large barrels and throats that can store as much as 40g of grinds that must be squeezed out before fresh grinds appear. At Prufrock, we are moving away from grinders with a high retention of grinds as we are looking to optimize freshness. When grind changes are required we want the benefit of micro-adjustment to be immediate. Here, home baristas are also well placed, as hand grinders have zero retention of grinds and some very high quality espresso hand grinders are now available on the market.

Over the last decade we have felt that machine technology has been in advance of grinders. We often comment that a barista's top priority should be the choice of grinder. Find a great grinding solution and great coffee will follow.

Photo: Jacob Thue

Water – The Enigma

by **Maxwell Colonna-Dashwood**, Co-owner, Colonna and Small's, UK Barista Champion 2012 & 2014

This vital ingredient is the foundation of every cup of coffee you have ever tasted, apart from the bean itself of course.

It's not just coffee that relies so dramatically on this everyday and seemingly straightforward substance. The worlds of craft beer and whiskey are suitable comparisons, with breweries and distilleries proudly signifying the provenance of their water as being a vital part of their product.

A roaster, though, sells coffee, the water bit comes post sale. The water will be different and unique based on the locality of brewing, and this is on top of all of the other variables that define coffee brewing such as grinding, temperature and brew ratios. The reality is that the impact of water is rarely directly witnessed, with the other variables often being seen as the cause for dramatic flavor changes. You may be wondering right now, how big an impact can it really have?

I'm yet to present the same coffee brewed with different waters to drinkers and not have them exclaim "I can't believe how different they are, they taste like different coffees'. These aren't "coffee people" either, but customers who contested prior to the tasting that "you may be able to taste the difference but I doubt I can tell."

It may make you question whether the coffee that you tried and weren't particularly keen on, was a representative version of what the bean actually tastes like, or at the least what it is capable of tasting of like.

So, why the big difference, what is in the water?

Nearly all water that trickles out of a tap or sits in a bottle is not just water. As well as the H2O there are other bits and bobs in the water. Minerals mainly. These have a big impact not only on what we extract from the coffee but also how that flavor sits in the cup of coffee.

It's fair to say that currently the way the coffee industry discusses water is through the use of a measurement called Total Dissolved Solids (TDS).

TDS has become the measurement which is relied upon to distinguish and inform us about how water will affect our coffee. It gives us a total of everything in the water. The problem though, is that TDS doesn't tell us everything we need to know about the water; it doesn't tell us about what those solids are. On top of this, TDS meters don't measure some non-solids that have a huge impact on flavor.

In the water, we need the minerals calcium and magnesium to help pull out a lot of the desirable flavor in the coffee, but we also need the right amount of buffering ability in the water to balance the acids. This buffering ability can be noted as the bicarbonate content of the water.

So for example an "empty" soft water with no minerals will lack flavor complexity and the lack of buffer will mean a more vinegary acidity.

However the coffee shops in this guide will most likely have a trick up their sleeve. The industry filtration systems that have been developed primarily to stop scale build up in the striking and valuable espresso machines, also produce water compositions that are more often than not preferable for coffee brewing. Speciality coffee shops require all manner of specifics to be obsessed over and carefully executed. That cup of coffee that hits you and stops you in your step with intense, balanced and complex flavor will owe its brilliance to careful brewing, a knowledgeable brewer and superb equipment. However, it also owes a significant part of its beautiful character and flavor to the water it is brewed with.

Brewing Coffee at Home

by **Christian Baker, David Robson, Sam Mason & The New York Coffee Guide**

Y ou may be surprised to know that coffee brewed at home can rival that of your favorite coffee shop. All you need is good quality ingredients and some inexpensive equipment. Keep in mind that small variations in grind coarseness, coffee/water ratio and brew time will make a significant difference to flavor, and that trial and error is the key to unlocking perfection.

Whole Beans: Whole bean coffee is superior to pre-ground. Coffee rapidly deteriorates once ground, so buy your coffee in whole bean form and store it in an air-tight container at room temperature. It should be consumed between three and thirty days after roast and ground only moments before brewing.

Water: Water is important because it makes up over 98% of the finished drink. Only use bottled water, preferably with a dry residue between 80-150mg/l. It will inhibit your ability to extract flavor and reveal only a fraction of a coffee's potential.

Digital scales: Get a set of scales accurate to 1g and large enough to hold your coffee brewer. Coffee is commonly measured in 'scoops' or 'tablespoons', but coffee and water are best measured by weight for greater accuracy and to ensure repeatability. Small changes in the ratio of coffee to water can have a significant impact on flavor. A good starting point is 60-70g of coffee per litre of water. Apply this ratio to meet the size of your brewer.

Grinder

A burr grinder is essential. Burr grinders are superior to blade grinders because they allow the grind coarseness to be set and produce a more consistent size of coffee fragment (critical for an even extraction). As a general rule, the coarser the grind the longer the brew time required, and vice versa. For example, an espresso needs a very fine grind whereas a French Press works with a coarser grind.

French Press

Preheat the French Press with hot water, and discard. Add 34g of coarsely ground coffee and pour in 500g of water just below boiling point (201-203°F). Steep for 4 to 5 minutes then gently plunge to the bottom. Decant the coffee straight away to avoid over-brewing (known as over-extraction).

AeroPress

The AeroPress is wonderfully versatile. It can be used with finely ground coffee and a short steep time, or with a coarser grind and a longer steep time. The latter is our preferred method for its flavor and repeatability. Preheat the AeroPress using hot water, and discard. Rinse the paper filter before securing, and place the AeroPress over a sturdy cup or jug. Add 16g of coffee and pour in 240g of water at 203°F. Secure the plunger on top, creating a seal. Steep for 3 minutes then plunge over 20 seconds.

Pour Over

We recommend using a pouring kettle for better pouring control. Place a filter paper in the cone and rinse through with hot water. Add 15g of coffee and slowly pour 30g of 203°F water to pre-soak the coffee grounds. This creates the 'bloom'. After 30 seconds add 250g of water, pouring steadily in a circular motion over the center. It should take 1 minute and 45 seconds to pour and between 30-45 seconds to drain through. The key is to keep the flow of water steady. If the water drains too quickly/slowly, adjust the coarseness of the grind to compensate.

Stovetop

A stovetop will not make an espresso, it will, however, make a strong coffee. Pour hot water in to the base to the fill-line or just below the pressure release valve. Fill the basket with ground coffee of medium coarseness (between Pour Over and French Press). Traditional wisdom suggests a fine grind in pursuit of espresso, but stovetops extract differently to espresso machines and grinding fine is a recipe for bitter, over-extracted coffee. Screw the base to the top and place on the heat. When you hear bubbling, remove immediately and decant to ensure the brewing has stopped.

Illustrations: Zoë Barker

Traditional Pump Espresso Machine

Traditional pump espresso machines are ideal for that barista experience to create espresso-based coffee at home. Coffee should be freshly and finely ground and dosed into single or double shot filter baskets. It is then tamped to extract full flavor aroma and coffee crema. The machine controls temperature for a more consistent cup. To enjoy milk drinks such as flat whites and cappuccinos simply froth fresh milk using the steam wand (stay below 158°F) and top up your espresso.

Bean to Cup Machine

Bean to Cup provides the perfect 'coffee shop' fix and fast. It gives you all the versatility of choice and personalization of a traditional pump machine. At the touch of a button, it burr-grinds fresh beans and froths milk (some machines even have a built in carafe), creating a fresh taste for your cup. You can personalize the strength, length, temperature, and even the froth setting. One-touch drink options make your personalized coffee time and again, without mess or fuss.

Latte Art

by **Jai Lott**, Coffee Director for Bluestone Lane

Latte art is the barista's signature in a milk based espresso drink.

Over the years latte art has shifted from being 'etched' chocolate sauce designs and foamy 'hand spooned' structures, to a fragile and carefully constructed pattern where the slightest movement of the hand can make or break a masterpiece.

There are 3 major components to world-class latte art: espresso, milk and execution.

1 Espresso

Perfect espresso is your canvas. Well-executed fresh extraction with a thick stable crema sets the foundation for your latte art. A double shot or around 40 grams of yield and medium roast is a great starting point. This helps create contrast in the cup. Espresso and milk preparation should happen simultaneously to ensure crema does not have time to dissipate.

2 Milk

The colder your milk, the better. This gives it more chances at rotation in the pitcher before reaching temperature, which in turn increases your milk's texture. Once the steam wand is in position slightly below the surface of the milk and sits slightly off center, engage the wand and slowly lower the jug adding small amounts of air while simultaneously keeping the milk spinning solid. All air should be added prior to the milk reaching room temperature for great results. Turn off the steam when you reach your desired temperature.

Ideal learning tools:

- A steaming pitcher that has perfect spout symmetry. Using the same jug every time is vital to getting comfortable with latte art.

- A wide ceramic cup of around 8oz is great to start with. This gives you plenty of breathing space.

- An environment where you can concentrate and not be bumped!

3 Execution

If everything worked out (and trust me it takes practice even getting to this point) you should have beautiful espresso and a hot pitcher with milk resembling freshly applied paint. Its time to pour!

Tilting the cup at 45 degrees, pour into the center of the espresso at a height of 2-3 inches. Imagine a diving board and a diver trying to pierce the espresso without disrupting the surface. Keep an even flow for the entire pour.

Once the cup gets to the low edge of the cup, two things need to happen:

Firstly, flatten out the cup while simultaneously bringing the pitcher all the way down to almost full contact with the espresso. This will increase the amount of microfoam allowed from behind the pitchers spout and a white dot will begin to appear (remember keep the same flow the whole time!)

Secondly, in the final moment of the pour, exit the cup by lifting the jug and cutting through the center of your white dot. Imagine the milk from the spout is an airplane taking off.

Perfect love heart!

Once you master our love hearts, move on to a two-stack tulip.

The big secret - stick to one design for days, weeks if needed. Get each design mastered before progressing to the next. This is the way to get good fast and an understanding of what each movement will result in.

Spill milk, make a mess and most importantly have fun! That's what coffee should be all about. Just don't forget that latte art certainly makes coffee look great, but great espresso and milk are more important!

What Does 'Local' Coffee Mean?

by **Teresa von Fuchs**, Sales Director at Volcafe Specialty

When the Eastman Egg Company in Chicago revamped their coffee program, they didn't partner with a company from Chicago. Even though there are great roasters in the area, they found that the partnership that met all of their goals and matched their values was New York. This got them thinking about ways to quickly explain this choice to their customers and what 'local' means in coffee.

Local coffee isn't as straightforward as local eggs, local arugula or even local bread (which may or may not contain locally grown and milled grain!). By necessity, coffee must travel hundreds and thousands of miles. Most people who drink coffee every day in the U.S. have never seen a coffee tree in person - they might not even know that coffee starts as a fruit. Given the distance from the source, it's challenging for most people to truly grasp the vast amount of work that must happen before coffee ends up in your cup. Yet it's this connection and understanding to where something comes from and how it's made that people seek when they look for 'local' products.

In the journal "Renewable Agriculture and Food Systems" CJ Peters writes, "Most researchers accept that eating locally means minimizing the distance between production and consumption." When the Food Marketing Institute conducted a study asking Americans across the country why they buy local; knowing where a product came from was in the top three responses. Supporting the local economy came in second. While it's logistically not possible to actually shorten the distance between where coffee is grown and all the places it's consumed, there are ways to bring producers and consumers closer together. For coffee, 'local' is about relationships and knowledge, not 'locale.'

For the team at Eastman, it was the connection their new roasting partner helped forge with the farms and people growing and processing their coffee that helped them answer the questions about why their roaster wasn't 'local.' It wasn't about where the roastery was located. It was about developing a connection to the process from seed to cup that made their coffee more local.

What I love about this lens is that it can extend everyone's experience of coffee, not just café owners looking for a roaster. When you go to your local café, the staff know you. They remember what you drink, your name, what days or times you usually come in, snippets of conversations you've shared. It's your café. And that café is your opportunity for local coffee. Whether your want to know the exact altitude of the farm where the coffee was grown or not, you can still participate in minimizing the distance between the production of coffee and drinking it. Get to know your barista. What do they drink? Why do they work there? What do they like about coffee?

If you buy beans from a store to brew at home, find out about the roaster. Where do they get the beans from? How did they start roasting coffee? What do they love about it?

The longer I work in coffee, the more expanded my idea of "local" and "community" becomes. When I taste coffee, I think about the places and the people that grow the coffee, all the hands that pick and process and pack and ship that coffee. I think about how far it travels to where it will be roasted. I think about who roasted it. When I go to a café for coffee, I think about all that, as well as the care and time someone took to craft it into a cup. When I sip, I feel connected to that whole world.

Espresso

by **Bill McAllister**, Director of the Service Department, Irving Farm Coffee Roasters

The definition of espresso is a method of brewing coffee according to the Specialty Coffee Association of America, a trade group that represents and undoubtedly has some direct connection to every person and place in this book. Yet the difference between a coffee made using a Chemex versus a vacuum pot or any other coffee maker is negligible compared to what an espresso machine produces. The root cause is pressure. Espresso machines take water that would normally be poured or sprinkled onto coffee and forces it through the pressure of the atmosphere. But who came up with that? How did they know it could make coffee so much more delicious than normal?

The etymology of espresso reveals a lot about the intention of this technology. If we Anglicize the word into "expresso", it is easy to see that the drink needs to be made quickly, but also that it needs to be made expressly for a consumer. Back in Italian, it's just as easily interpreted as "to press out", bringing pressure back into the picture. Put it all together, and you have a device that makes coffee quickly, one at a time, using pressure. All of this is according to Andrea Illy (yes, that Illy) as written in Espresso Coffee, one of the few textbooks on coffee.

It paints a somewhat primitive picture of Italy in the 1880s, where the first patents for espresso machines are traced. The technology at the time was coarse and rugged. It relied on huge boilers heated by fire that used a head of steam to push water through the ground coffee. A barista would be hard-pressed to make anything that wasn't quite bitter. This was espresso for decades. But then, manufacturers introduced a lever and piston as an alternative method of generating pressure. This change allowed the machines to be much smaller, brew at pressures that have become today's standard, and use water that isn't super-heated. All of a sudden espresso carts became a reality, bringing the means of caffeination to even more people. But the most important part of the change in the machines is that it is no longer impossible for a shot to be pulled that is more than something used as a dose of energy.

The espresso of today and its potential to be mind-blowingly delicious has a culture surrounding it that elevates it above the rest of coffee. Cafes have moved far beyond just dishing out shots to give workers a boost mid-afternoon. A coffee shop that wants to be the talk of the town these days draws customers in by talking about the specific farms their coffee is from, the agronomy of the plant from which the coffee is harvested, and a level of precision that requires scales that wouldn't be out of place in a display on St Marks Place.

How we went from pre-industrial caffeine machines relying on levers and pistons to today's models doesn't contain any big eureka moments, but is mostly a steady stream of smart revisions. Baristas realized early on that their ability to reliably make the most delicious espresso they've tasted required having a machine they could count on to work the same way every time. To this end, springs and levers were replaced by electric pumps and gas burners were replaced by heating elements controlled by computers. Yet with all of these, advances were driven by the trial and error of passionate baristas, because despite the long history of espresso, there is not a lot of scientific writing about the process with which it is made. When a handful of videos featuring clear plastic portafilters started trickling out in the last few years, coffee pros everywhere were astounded - the first real evidence in over a century as to what's happening when making espresso!

Explanations of how and why espresso works may be lacking, but we can still gather a few lessons as consumers. A properly prepared shot looks elegant as it pours into a cup, flowing thick but steady, like warm honey, a promise of flavor that delivers on the intoxicating smell characteristic of coffee shops everywhere. At its best, a coffee brewed as espresso sees its flavors held under a magnifying glass. The experience is intense, but often divisive: fruity Ethiopian coffees taste like someone plopped jam in the bottom of your demitasse, so lush with fruit flavor and sweetness it seems impossible that the only ingredient is coffee. The second you sip a good espresso, all thoughts of history are fleeting memories; you thoughts are now on the delicious beverage in your hands.

Coffee History in New York City

by **Erin Meister**, Coffee Professional, Journalist & Author of a forthcoming book about NYC's coffee

What makes New York a coffee town, exactly? Is it the reputation as the "city that never sleeps," or the fact that caffeine is necessary to get anything done in a New York minute? Do residents of the city drink an estimated 25 percent more coffee than anyone else in the country because the stuff can be bought on every street corner? Or could it be the other way around - that the sheer ubiquity of the stuff is what makes it practically a way of life for locals? Does it mean something that the average cup costs less than a copy of the daily paper?

No matter the reason, facts are facts: New York and coffee are made for each other.

Of course it's true that the regular Joes here simply love their "regular" joe (which usually means a cup of drip with milk and sugar, in deli shorthand). But there's actually more coffee flowing in the veins of the city than even gets poured on its surface. So much of what happens with coffee here is behind-the-scenes that most New Yorkers don't even know quite how caffeinated they really are. Even the history of the city and the beverage go all the way back - further, actually, than the name "New York." The coffee habit actually got brewed up when the city was still New Amsterdam, under Dutch control.

From the green-coffee contracts to the containers they come in, to the roasting machines that turn them from hard little seeds into semi-precious brown beans, New York has had a tremendous influence on every step in the journey of billions of bags, brews, and cups.

The city's position as an East Coast hub has allowed for its unique junction of caffeine and culture, not only just among its fellow American metro centers, but also worldwide. The coffee history here has influenced global market structures, supply and demand trends, shipping routes and intercontinental trade, roasting and preparation technology and innovation, marketing strategy, and even cafe life. The first truly successful commercial coffee-roasting machine was patented by a New Yorker, Jabez Burns, whose company would go on to become one of the most enduring and consistently innovative in the industry for over 130 years. The Green Coffee Association of New York was founded as the first significant overseeing body to ensure, and insure, the integrity and fulfillment of contracts. Depending on whom you ask, the first espresso machine in the country was imported and installed either uptown at Barbetta Restaurant in 1911 or downtown at Caffè Reggio, which opened in 1927.

The combination of a crush of people from all types and all walks, overwhelming sparking creative energy, and the fearlessness of failure is certainly in part to thank, but coffee itself contributes something to the dynamic and living nature of New York - it keeps the gears turning.

There is also a special something about New York City that not just allows for rebirth and reinvention, but actually thrives on it. Perhaps the most classic "only in New York" moments in the timeline of coffee's history here is the fact that one of the very men who was responsible for the first tremendous "coffee collapse" in 1880 - a failed attempted corner on the coffee market by a syndicate of large brokerage houses, the result of which was widespread bankruptcy and at least one alleged coffee suicide - was elected just two years later to serve as the first president of the Coffee Exchange, which his misadventure had inspired the coffee men to create.

That's only one of hundreds of "only in New York" stories, of course. Here's another in 1907, a woman named Alice Foote MacDougall used her last $38 to establish herself as the only female coffee broker in the waterfront Coffee District. Within two decades she was signing a $1 million lease on her fifth hugely successful coffee shop - the modern equivalent of nearly $14 million. Just like the city itself, MacDougall was a beautiful mess of contradictions. Though she was a successful business owner herself, she regularly advised women to stay at home and out of the commercial and corporate worlds, and was an ardent anti-suffragist.

From coffeehouse counter-culture in the late 1950s and 1960s, to the Central Perk-inspired, overstuffed, mismatched café of the 90s, to the minimal and coffee-quality-obsessed espresso and slow-pour bars of the early 2000s; NYC coffee shops have always managed to define their era. They have been capturing and capitalizing on the shifting moods and cravings of 8 million people, even if only for a finite period. The coffee lovers of today in Brooklyn, Manhattan, and Queens (the Bronx and Staten Island will catch up eventually) go about their daily rituals, drinking their morning cups or evening espresso, knowing full well that there's no telling what will be on the next generation of menus, in the next wave of shops.

Beyond the bars, there are the beans. Millions and millions of bags of them that travel through New York every year, on their way to roasters and consumers around the country and world. Despite the fact that New Jersey actually claims the country's first fully containerized shipping port, this transformed the intercontinental transit of loads of green coffee and knocked a few pegs out of NYC's dominance in that arena.

Even the world's most famous mermaid has a Brooklyn connection: Starbucks chairman and CEO Howard Schultz grew up in the Canarsie section of the borough - a neighborhood that perhaps ironically remains a good-coffee desert today, but even that will surely change with time.

Gotham's inexhaustible need to create, destroy, and re-create might make it difficult to keep up with the trends (or "waves," if we must). But at least we can all be assured that the revolutions will be caffeinated. "There is something in the New York air that makes sleep useless," wrote Simone de Beauvoir in 1947, and it's as true today as it was then, only the answer is obvious. It must simply be the coffee.

Coffee Glossary

Acidity: the pleasant tartness of a coffee. Examples of acidity descriptors include lively and flat. One of the principal attributes evaluated by professional tasters when determining the quality of a coffee.

AeroPress: a hand-powered coffee brewer marketed by Aerobie Inc., and launched in 2005. Consists of two cylinders, one sliding within the other, somewhat resembling a large syringe. Water is forced through ground coffee held in place by a paper filter, creating a concentrated filter brew.

Affogato: one or more scoops of vanilla ice cream topped with a shot of espresso, served as a dessert.

Americano, Caffè Americano: a long coffee consisting of espresso with hot water added on top. Originates from the style of coffee favored by American GIs stationed in Europe during WWII.

Arabica, Coffea arabica: the earliest cultivated species of coffee tree and the most widely grown, Arabica accounts for approximately 70% of the world's coffee. Superior in quality to Robusta, it is more delicate and is generally grown at higher altitudes.

Aroma: the fragrance produced by brewed coffee. Examples of aroma descriptors include earthy, spicy and floral. One of the principal attributes evaluated by professional tasters when determining the quality of a coffee.

Barista: a professional person skilled in making coffee, particularly one working at an espresso bar.

Blend: a combination of coffees from different countries or regions. Mixed together, they achieve a balanced flavor profile no single coffee can offer alone.

Body: describes the heaviness, thickness or relative weight of coffee on the tongue. One of the principal attributes evaluated by professional tasters when determining the quality of a coffee.

Bottomless portafilter, naked portafilter: a portafilter without spouts, allowing espresso to flow directly from the bottom of the filter basket into the cup. Allows the extraction to be monitored visually.

Brew group: the assembly protruding from the front of an espresso machine consisting of the grouphead, portafilter and basket. The brew group must be heated to a sufficient temperature to produce a good espresso.

Brew pressure: pressure of 9 bar is required for espresso extraction.

Brew temperature: the water temperature at the point of contact with coffee. Optimum brew temperature varies by extraction method. Espresso brew temperature is typically 194-203°F. A stable brew temperature is crucial for good espresso.

Brew time, extraction time: the contact time between water and coffee. Espresso brew time is typically 25-30 seconds. Brew times are dictated by a variety of factors including the grind coarseness and degree of roast.

Burr set: an integral part of a coffee grinder. Consists of a pair of rotating steel discs between which coffee beans are ground. Burrs are either flat or conical in shape.

Café con leche: a traditional Spanish coffee consisting of espresso topped with scalded milk.

Caffeine: an odorless, slightly bitter

alkaloid responsible for the stimulating effect of coffee.

Cappuccino: a classic Italian coffee comprising espresso, steamed milk and topped with a layer of foam. Traditionally served in a 6oz cup and sometimes topped with powdered chocolate or cinnamon.

Capsule: a self-contained, pre-ground, pre-pressed portion of coffee, individually sealed inside a plastic capsule. Capsule brewing systems are commonly found in domestic coffee machines. Often compatible only with certain equipment brands.

Chemex: A type of pour over coffee brewer with a distinctive hourglass-shaped vessel. Invented in 1941, the Chemex has become regarded as a design classic and is on permanent display at the Museum of Modern Art in New York City.

Cherry: the fruit of the coffee plant. Each cherry contains two coffee seeds (beans).

Cold brew: Cold brew refers to the process of steeping coffee grounds in room temperature or cold water for an extended period. Cold brew coffee is not to be confused with iced coffee.

Cortado: a traditional short Spanish coffee consisting of espresso cut with a small quantity of steamed milk. Similar to an Italian piccolo.

Crema: the dense caramel-colored layer that forms on the surface of an espresso. Consists of emulsified oils created by the dispersion of gases in liquid at high pressure. The presence of crema is commonly equated with a good espresso.

Cupping: a method by which professional tasters perform sensory evaluation of coffee. Hot water is poured over ground coffee and left to extract. The taster first samples the aroma, then tastes the coffee by slurping it from a spoon.

Decaffeinated: coffee with approximately 97% or more of its naturally occurring caffeine removed is classified as decaffeinated.

Dispersion screen, shower screen: a component of the grouphead that ensures even distribution of brewing water over the coffee bed in the filter basket.

Dosage: the mass of ground coffee used for a given brewing method. Espresso dosage is typically 7-10g of ground coffee (14-20g for a double).

Double espresso, doppio: typically 30-50ml extracted from 14-20g of ground coffee. The majority of coffee venues in this guide serve double shots as standard.

Drip method: a brewing method that allows brew water to seep through a bed of ground coffee by gravity, not pressure.

Espresso: the short, strong shot of coffee that forms the basis for many other coffee beverages. Made by forcing hot water at high pressure through a compressed bed of finely ground coffee.

Espresso machine: in a typical configuration, a pump delivers hot water from a boiler to the brew group, where it is forced under pressure through ground coffee held in the portafilter. A separate boiler delivers steam for milk steaming.

Extraction: the process of infusing coffee with hot water to release flavor, accomplished either by allowing ground coffee to sit in hot water for a period of time or by forcing hot water through ground coffee under pressure.

Coffee Glossary contd.

Filter method: any brewing method in which water filters through a bed of ground coffee. Most commonly used to describe drip method brewers that use a paper filter to separate grounds from brewed coffee.

Flat white: an espresso-based beverage first made popular in Australia and New Zealand. Made with a double shot of espresso with finely steamed milk and a thin layer of microfoam. Typically served as a 5-6oz drink with latte art.

Flavor: the way a coffee tastes. Flavor descriptors include nutty and earthy. One of the principal attributes evaluated by professional tasters when determining the quality of a coffee.

French press, plunger pot, cafetiere: a brewing method that separates grounds from brewed coffee by pressing them to the bottom of the brewing receptacle with a mesh filter attached to a plunger.

Froth, foam: created when milk is heated and aerated, usually with hot steam from an espresso machine's steam wand. Used to create a traditional cappuccino.

Green coffee, green beans: unroasted coffee. The dried seeds from the coffee cherry.

Grind: the degree of coarseness to which coffee beans are ground. A crucial factor in determining the nature of a coffee brew. Grind coarseness should be varied in accordance with the brewing method. Methods involving longer brew times call for a coarse grind. A fine grind is required for brew methods with a short extraction time such as espresso.

Grinder: a vital piece of equipment for making coffee. Coffee beans must be ground evenly for a good extraction. Most commonly motorised, but occasionally manual. Burr grinders are the best choice for an even grind.

Group: see Brew Group

Grouphead: a component of the brew group containing the locking connector for the portafilter and the dispersion screen.

Honey process, pulped natural, semi-washed: a method of processing coffee where the cherry is removed (pulped), but the beans are sun-dried with mucilage intact. Typically results in a sweet flavor profile with a balanced acidity.

Latte, caffè latte: an Italian beverage made with espresso combined with steamed milk, traditionally topped with foamed milk and served in a glass. Typically at least 8oz in volume, usually larger.

Latte art: the pattern or design created by pouring steamed milk on top of espresso. Only finely steamed milk is suitable for creating latte art. Popular patterns include the rosetta and heart.

Lever espresso machine: lever machines use manual force to drive a piston that generates the pressure required for espresso extraction. Common in the first half of the 20th century, but now largely superseded by electric pump-driven machines. Lever machines retain a small but passionate group of proponents.

Long black: a coffee beverage made by adding an espresso on top of hot water. Similar to an Americano, but usually shorter and the crema is preserved.

Macchiato: a coffee beverage consisting of espresso 'stained' with a dash of steamed milk (espresso macchiato) or a tall glass of steamed milk 'stained' with espresso (latte macchiato).

Macrofoam: stiff foam containing large bubbles used to make a traditional cappuccino. Achieved by incorporating a greater quantity of air during the milk steaming process.

Matcha: Finely ground powder of specially grown and processed green tea. The matcha plants are shade-grown for three weeks before harvest.

Microfoam: the preferred texture of finely-steamed milk for espresso-based coffee drinks. Essential for pouring latte art. Achieved by incorporating a lesser quantity of air during the milk steaming process.

Micro-lot coffee: coffee originating from a small, discrete area within a farm, typically benefiting from conditions favorable to the development of a particular set of characteristics. Micro-lot coffees tend to fetch higher prices due to their unique nature.

Mocha, caffè mocha: similar to a caffè latte, but with added chocolate syrup or powder.

Natural process: a simple method of processing coffee where whole cherries (with the bean inside) are dried on raised beds under the sun. Typically results in a lower acidity coffee with a heavier body and exotic flavors.

Over extracted: describes coffee with a bitter or burnt taste, resulting from ground coffee exposed to hot water for too long.

Peaberry: a small, round coffee bean formed when only one seed, rather than the usual two, develops in a coffee cherry. Peaberry beans produce a different flavor profile,

typically lighter-bodied with higher acidy.

Piccolo: a short Italian coffee beverage made with espresso topped with an equal quantity of steamed milk. Traditionally served in a glass.

Pod: a self-contained, pre-ground, pre-pressed puck of coffee, individually wrapped inside a perforated paper filter. Mostly found in domestic espresso machines. Often compatible only with certain equipment brands.

Pour over: a type of drip filter method in which a thin, steady stream of water is poured slowly over a bed of ground coffee contained within a filter cone.

Pouring kettle: a kettle with a narrow swan-neck spout specifically designed to deliver a steady, thin stream of water.

Portafilter: consists of a handle (usually plastic) attached to a metal cradle that holds the filter basket. Inserted into the group head and locked in place in preparation for making an espresso. Usually features a single or double spout on the underside to direct the flow of coffee into a cup.

Portafilter basket: a flat bottomed, bowl-shaped metal insert that sits in the portafilter and holds a bed of ground coffee. The basket has an array of tiny holes in the base allowing extracted coffee to seep through and pour into a cup.

Puck: immediately after an espresso extraction, the bed of spent coffee grounds forms compressed waste matter resembling a small hockey puck.

Pull: the act of pouring an espresso. The term originates from the first half of the 20th century when manual machines were the norm, and baristas pulled a lever to

Coffee Glossary contd.

create an espresso.

Ristretto: a shorter 'restricted' shot of espresso. Made using the same dose and brew time as for a regular espresso, but with less water. The result is a richer and more intense beverage.

Roast: the process by which green coffee is heated in order to produce coffee beans ready for consumption. Caramelization occurs as intense heat converts starches in the bean to simple sugars, imbuing the bean with flavor and transforming its color to a golden brown.

Robusta, Coffea canephora: the second most widely cultivated coffee species after arabica, robusta accounts for approximately 30% of the world's coffee. Robusta is hardier and grown at lower altitudes than arabica. It has a much higher caffeine content than arabica, and a less refined flavor. Commonly used in instant coffee blends.

Shot: a single unit of brewed espresso.

Single origin, single estate: coffee from one particular region or farm.

Siphon brewer, vacuum brewer: an unusual brewing method that relies on the action of a vacuum to draw hot water through coffee from one glass chamber to another. The resulting brew is remarkably clean.

Small batch: refers to roasting beans in small quantities, typically between 4-24kg, but sometimes larger.

Speciality coffee: a premium quality coffee scoring 80 points or above (from a total of 100) in the SCAA grading scale.

Steam wand: the protruding pipe found on an espresso machine that supplies hot steam used to froth and steam milk.

Stovetop, moka pot: a brewing method that makes strong coffee (but not espresso). Placed directly on a heat source, hot water is forced by steam pressure from the lower chamber to the upper chamber, passing through a bed of coffee.

Tamp: the process of distributing and pressing ground coffee into a compact bed within the portafilter basket in preparation for brewing espresso. The degree of pressure applied during tamping is a key variable in espresso extraction. Too light and the brew water will percolate rapidly (tending to under extract), too firm and the water flow will be impeded (tending to over extract).

Tamper: the small pestle-like tool used to distribute and compact ground coffee in the filter basket.

Third wave coffee: the movement that treats coffee as an artisanal foodstuff rather than a commodity product. Quality coffee reflects its terroir, in a similar manner to wine.

Under extracted: describes coffee that has not been exposed to brew water for long enough. The resulting brew is often sour and thin-bodied.

V60: a popular type of pour over coffee brewer marketed by Hario. The product takes its name from the 60° angle of the V-shaped cone. Typically used to brew one or two cups only.

Washed process: one of the most common methods of processing coffee cherries. Involves fermentation in tanks of water to remove mucilage. Typically results in a clean and bright flavor profile with higher acidity.

Whole bean: coffee that has been roasted but not ground.

A-Z List of Coffee Venues

60 Beans p197

Abraço p19

AP Café p173

Astoria Coffee p197

Baby Skips p173

Banter p65

Birch Coffee (Flatiron District) p93

Birch Coffee (Long Island City) p198

Birch Coffee (Soho) p45

Black Brick p183

Black Fox Coffee Co. p5

Blue Bottle (Chelsea) p81

Blue Bottle (Clinton Street) p20

Blue Bottle (Park Slope) p143

Bluestone Lane (Astor Place) p21

Bluestone Lane (Dumbo) p163

Bluestone Lane (Financial District) p6

Bluestone Lane (Greenwich Village) p67

Bluestone Lane (Upper East Side) p123

Bluestone Lane (West Village) p68

Box Kite (Upper West Side) p124

Breukelen Coffee House p145

Brewklyn Grind p164

Brooklyn Roasting Company (Dumbo) p165

Brooklyn Roasting Company (Flatiron District) p94

Búðin p199

Café Grumpy (Financial District) p6

Café Grumpy (Grand Central Terminal) p94

Café Grumpy (Greenpoint) p200

Café Grumpy (Lower East Side) p23

Café Grumpy (Nolita) p47

Café Henrie p23

Café Integral p48

Café Jax p125

Café Regular du Nord p146

Caffe Vita (Bushwick) p174

Caffe Vita (Lower East Side) p24

Chalait (Hudson Square) p49

Chalait (Nomad) p95

Champion Coffee p200

Charter Coffee p185

Chipped Cup, The p126

City of Saints (Bushwick) p174

City of Saints (East Village) p24

Clever Blend p147

Coffee Mob p148

COFFEED p201

Commons Chelsea, The p82

Culture 36 p96

Culture Espresso p96

Darling Coffee p126

Dean Street Café p148

Dear Mama p127

Devoción p186

Double Dutch Espresso p129

Dr Smood p97

East One Coffee Roasters p166

El Rey p25

Everyman Espresso (East Village) p26

Everyman Espresso (Park Slope) p149

Extraction Lab by Alpha Dominche p167

Fair Folks & a Goat p68

FIKA Tower & Bakery p99

Filtered Coffee p130

Frisson Espresso p100

Gasoline Alley (Flatiron District) p101

A-Z List of Coffee Venues contd.

Gasoline Alley Coffee (Noho) p27

Gasoline Alley Coffee (Nolita) p49

Gimme! Coffee (Nolita) p50

Gimme! Coffee (Williamsburg) p187

Gorilla Coffee p151

Gossip Coffee p201

Gotan p7

Greecologies p51

Gregorys Coffee (Gramercy) p102

Gregorys Coffee (Upper East Side) p130

Ground Central Coffee Co. (2nd Avenue) p102

Ground Central Coffee Co. (52nd Street) p103

Ground Support Cafe p52

Happy Bones p53

Hi-Collar p28

Hole in the Wall p104

Homecoming p202

Housing Works Bookstore Cafe p54

Hungry Ghost p152

Intelligentsia Coffee p83

Irving Farm Coffee Roasters (Gramercy) p105

Irving Farm Coffee Roasters (Lower Manhattan) p8

Irving Farm Coffee Roasters (Midtown East) p106

Irving Farm Coffee Roasters (Upper East Side) p131

Jack's Stir Brew Coffee p69

JANE Motorcycles p188

Joe & The Juice (Midtown East) p106

Joe & The Juice (Soho) p55

Joe Coffee (Upper East Side) p133

Joe Coffee (World Trade Center) p9

Joe Coffee Pro Shop + HQ p84

Kaffe 1668 p10

Kahve p107

Kava Cafe p69

Kinship Coffee Cooperative p203

Kobrick Coffee Co. p70

Kuro Kuma Espresso & Coffee p134

La Colombe (Chelsea) p84

La Colombe (Financial District) p11

La Colombe Torrefaction p29

Laughing Man p12

Lazy Llama, The p30

Le Café Coffee p108

Little Canal p31

Little Collins p109

Little Skips p175

Little Zelda p153

Ludlow Coffee Supply p33

Manhattanville Coffee p153

MatchaBar (Chelsea) p85

McNally Jackson Café p55

Merriweather p71

Milk & Honey p154

Milk & Pull (Bushwick) p176

Milk & Pull (Ridgewood) p177

Milk Bar p155

Monkey Cup, The p134

Moss Café p135

New York City Bagel and Coffee House p204

Ninth Street Espresso (East Village) p33

Ninth Street Espresso (Midtown East) p110

Nobletree p13

Odd Fox Coffee p205

Oren's Daily Roast (Greenwich Village) p73

Oren's Daily Roast (Midtown West) p110

Oslo Coffee Roasters (Upper East Side) p136

A-Z List of Coffee Venues contd.

Oslo Coffee Roasters (Williamsburg) p189

Ost Cafe p34

Perk Kafé p111

Petite Shell p137

Plowshares p138

Porto Rico Importing Company p73

Prodigy Coffee p74

Pushcart Coffee p112

Qathra p156

Queens Kickshaw, The p207

R & R Coffee p15

Ramini Espresso Bar and Café p113

Rebel Coffee p74

REX p114

River Coyote p35

Roost, The p36

Roots Café p156

Round K p37

Ruby's Café (Murray Hill) p115

Ruby's Café (Soho) p56

Saturdays Surf NYC p57

Seven Grams Caffè (Chelsea) p86

Seven Grams Caffè (Soho) p58

Seven Point Espresso p157

Simon Sips p115

Smith Canteen p169

Spreadhouse p38

Starbucks Reserve p190

Stonefruit Espresso + Kitchen p159

Stumptown (Ace Hotel) p116

Stumptown (Greenwich Village) p75

Supercrown Coffee Roasters p178

Sweatshop p191

Sweetleaf (Center Boulevard) p208

Sweetleaf (Greenpoint) p209

Sweetleaf (Jackson Avenue) p210

Tar Pit p192

Taylor St. Baristas p117

Think Coffee (Chelsea) p87

Think Coffee (Gramercy) p118

Third Rail Coffee p76

Three Seat Espresso & Barber p39

Toby's Estate (Long Island City) p211

Toby's Estate (West Village) p77

Toby's Estate (Williamsburg) p193

TOMS Roasting Co. p59

Trademark p118

True North Brooklyn p194

Two Hands (Soho) p61

Two Hands (Tribeca) p15

Tygershark p160

Underline Coffee p88

Upright Coffee p213

Upstate Stock p194

Uptown Roasters p138

Variety Coffee Roasters (Bushwick) p179

Variety Coffee Roasters (Chelsea) p89

Variety Coffee Roasters (Greenpoint) p213

Voyager Espresso p16

Walter's Coffee Roastery p180

Whynot p41

Wooly Daily, The p16

Zibetto Espresso Bar p119

THE NEW YORK COFFEE MAP

Notes, sketches, phone numbers etc.